INTERNATIONA
ROBYN YOUNG'S B

D0642400

"Combining rich historical detail, clever plotting and engaging characters, Young has crafted a historical thriller that will have readers turning pages and envisioning the sequel." —*Publishers Weekly*

"Young writes with remarkable accuracy, action-packed efficiency and gut-wrenching violence." —*The Times* (London)

"One of the best historical debuts in recent memory. Exciting and enthralling; it gripped me from the first page and left me waiting anxiously for the next instalment." —John Connolly, author of *Every Dead Thing*

"Exhilarating. . . . Evokes the atmosphere of the times brilliantly." —*Birmingham Post*

"A sweeping historical adventure as well as a cracking sequel." —*Financial Times*

"Satisfyingly complex." —*Sunday Telegraph*

"Richly worked and captivating. . . . An epic story of war, intrigue and heroism." —*The Good Book Guide*

"El Cid meets *The Da Vinci Code*! Exciting, page-turning fiction." —Boyd Hilton (Simon Mayo's book panel)

"A sweeping historical adventure with strong characters and serious verve." —*The Baltimore Sun*

"In a word: Gripping." —*The Weekend Gold Coast Bulletin*

"Young combines historical detail, lively characterisation and strong narrative drive." —*The Canberra Times*

Also by Robyn Young

Brethren
Crusade
Requiem

ROBYN YOUNG

INSURRECTION

HarperCollins*Publishers*Ltd

Published by HarperCollins Publishers Ltd

Originally published in Great Britain in 2010 by Hodder & Stoughton
An Hachette UK company

First Canadian edition

HarperCollins books may be purchased for educational, business,
or sales promotional use through our Special Markets Department.

HarperCollins Publishers Ltd
2 Bloor Street East, 20th Floor
Toronto, Ontario, Canada
M4W 1A8

www.harpercollins.ca

Library and Archives Canada Cataloguing in Publication
information is available upon request

ISBN 978-1-44340-805-9

Map © Sandra Oakins. All rights reserved.

Printed in the United States of America
RRD 9 8 7 6 5 4 3 2 1

ACKNOWLEDGEMENTS

Writing a novel is a prolonged, unwieldy task, seldom accomplished in its entirety by one single person. This was no exception and I'd like to thank the following people for their help along the way. First, the guides and curators I met across Scotland and Wales, who spoke with such knowledge and passion about the history of the many castles, abbeys and battlegrounds I visited, with added thanks to Clair for the incredible ride through Glen Trool. My gratitude goes to Jane Spooner at the Tower of London for taking the time to show me round and offering invaluable insights into the history of the place. Thank you to John Dudency for not letting his horses kill me and for the terrifying, but rewarding year in the paddock . . . I have so much more respect for the skill of my knights now. A sincere thank you to Ken Hames for talking to me so frankly and incisively about his combat experiences, which gave me a deeper glimpse into the psyche of war. I owe a great deal to historian Marc Morris, author of *A Great and Terrible King*, for reading so thoroughly and for the weight of knowledge he brought to bear on the manuscript. Without scholars of his calibre, many of whose works I plundered for treasures, this novel would not exist. Thanks also to Richard Foreman for the valuable introductions. My gratitude to the writers' group for editorial gems and the pleasure of shared words, with special thanks to Niall Christie for the reading and to dear friend and fellow writer C.J. Sansom for an ear in the dark days. To the rest of my friends and family, but most especially to Lee – thank you, your support and love mean more than you know.

Much appreciation goes as ever to my fantastic agent, Rupert Heath, also to Dan Conaway at Writers House, the team at the Marsh Agency and indeed all the publishers who work on the international editions. Last, but certainly not least, my gratitude to all at Hodder & Stoughton, whose great commitment to the books continues to overwhelm me. Extra special thanks are due to my wonderful editor, Nick Sayers, to Anne, Laura, Emma, and the fabulous sales and marketing teams and often unsung heroes: copy-editor, proof reader and the art and production teams.

CONTENTS

BRITAIN 1286AD

ORKNEY

SCOTLAND

BUCHAN

BADENOCH MAR • Aberdeen

ATHOLL ANGUS
LENNOX MENTIETH • Dundee
Stirling Perth • St.Andrews
Falkirk Kinghorn
Glasgow Edinburgh DUNBAR
Irvine Peebles • Berwick
Ayr Lanark • Roxburgh
ISLAY The Forest
ARRAN • Turnberry • Lochmaben NORTHUMBERLAND
CARRICK ANNANDALE • Newcastle
ANTRIM GALLOWAY

THE NORTH SEA

ULSTER • Carlisle • Durham

ENGLAND

• Lancaster
YORKSHIRE • York

IRELAND

ANGLESEY LINCOLN

• Conwy
Caernarfon Snowdon
Nefyn GWYNEDD • Leicester NORFOLK

POWYS

WALES WARWICK • Cambridge
HEREFORD ESSEX
PEMBROKE • GLOUCESTER • Oxford
GWENT London •
Canterbury •
• Dover
Salisbury • Lewes •
Portsmouth

CORNWALL ENGLISH CHANNEL

Ah God! how often Merlin said the truth
In his prophecies, if you read them!
Now are the two waters united in one
Which have been separated by great mountains;
And one realm made of two different kingdoms
Which used to be governed by two kings.
Now are the islanders all joined together
And Albany reunited to the regalities
Of which king Edward is proclaimed lord.
Cornwall and Wales are in his power
And Ireland the great at his will.
There is neither king nor prince of all the countries
Except king Edward, who has thus united them . . .

Peter Langtoft (English chronicler d. c.1307)

PROLOGUE
1262 AD

King Arthur himself was mortally wounded; and being carried thence to the isle of Avallon to be cured of his wounds, he gave up the crown of Britain to his kinsman Constantine, the son of Cador, duke of Cornwall, in the five hundred and forty-second year of our Lord's incarnation.

The History of the Kings of Britain, *Geoffrey of Monmouth*

Gascony, France

1262 AD

*T*he horses were screaming. Blades carved the air, chopping down into shields, battering helms. Men spat threats and panted curses through visors, their arms and shoulders singing with the raw pain of every swing and strike. Dust from the dry soil had been kicked into clouds by their press, turning the air above the vineyard yellow. The smell of grapes, swollen in the heat, was sour in their parched throats and sweat dripped its salt sting into their eyes, blinding them.

In the thick of battle a man in a red and gold surcoat raised his shield to block another blow. His horse wheeled beneath him. Bringing the beast back round with a prick of his spur, he lunged in retaliation, ramming his sword into his enemy's side, piercing linen and padding to crunch into the mail shirt beneath. Alongside him a huge man, clad in a blue and white striped cloak, swung his weapon viciously into a knight's back, snarling spit into his ventail with the effort. The man it struck fell forward, losing grip on his sword. As his horse stumbled, the knight was bucked from the saddle. He hit the ground, black with the juice of burst grapes, and rolled, trying to avoid the hooves of the destriers, punching down around him. One caught him on the side of the head, crushing his helm and leaving his body to be trampled as the men battled on above.

The man in red and gold thrust his sword into the air with a fierce cry, swiftly taken up by others.

'Arthur!' they yelled. 'Arthur!'

New strength surged in limbs and new breath in lungs. They fought on, ruthless now, giving no quarter. As more opponents were knocked or pulled from horses a banner was hoisted above the mêlée, rippling in the searing wind. It was blood scarlet with a dragon rearing, fire-wreathed, in its centre.

'Arthur! Arthur!'

The man in the blue and white striped cloak had lost his blade, but he battled on in the crush using his shield as a weapon. Bringing the top edge cracking up under one man's jaw, he turned to slam it into the visor of another. Frustrated by one knight, who refused to yield, he grabbed the man around the neck and dragged him from the saddle. As his opponent slid down between the horses, flailing for purchase and roaring in fury, there came three long blasts on a horn.

Those still mounted lowered their swords, one by one, at the sound. Fighting for breath, they struggled to rein in their agitated chargers. Those on the ground were stumbling to their feet, trying to push their way through the mob. They were surrounded by waiting foot soldiers, who wielded falchions. One man, scrabbling free through the vines, was hauled back and kicked into submission. Squires began to round up the stray horses that had scattered during the fight.

The man in red and gold tugged off his helm, surmounted by silver dragon wings, to reveal a young, sharp-boned face set with intense grey eyes, one of which drooped a little at the lid, giving him a rather sly expression. Sucking in lungfuls of gritty air, Edward surveyed the defeated men, the last of whom were having their weapons taken. Several had been wounded in the battle, two seriously. One swayed in the grip of his comrades, groaning through gums, his front teeth shattered. Triumph beat a song inside Edward, in the hot pulse of blood in his veins.

'Another victory, nephew.'

The gruff statement came from the man in the blue and white striped cloak, embroidered here and there with tiny red birds. William de Valence had taken off his helm and released his mail ventail from his jaw, which hung down over the iron collar that kept the helm in place. His broad face was running with sweat.

Before Edward could respond, one of the squires called out.

'There's one dead here, my lord.'

Edward turned to see the squire bent over a body. The dead man's surcoat was covered with dust and there was a dent in the side of his helm. Blood had burst up out of one of the eye holes. Other men were looking over, their gazes on the corpse as they wiped the sweat from their faces.

'Take his armour and sword,' Edward told the squire, after a pause.

'Lord Edward!' protested one of the men, who had been rounded up and disarmed. He stepped forward, but was blocked from going any further by the surrounding foot soldiers. 'I demand the rights to my comrade's body!'

'You will have the body for burial after your ransoms have been agreed and paid, I give you my word. But his gear is mine.' With that, Edward passed his dragon-winged helm and shield to a squire and, taking up the reins, urged his horse away between the vines.

'Bring the prisoners,' William de Valence ordered the foot soldiers.

The rest of Edward's men fell in behind, the dragon banner raised like a red fist over their heads, dark against the encroaching dusk. Leaving squires to gather broken weapons and injured horses, the company moved out, ignoring the workers who came running, shouting at the sight of the destroyed vineyard. The tournament ground, established last night, had been set between two towns as usual, but the inclusion of crop fields, grazing lands, even villages, was inevitable.

As he rode his horse at a walk across the fields, Edward pulled off his gauntlets. The skin on the ridges of his palms was blistered, despite the leather padding. Behind him he could hear murmurs coming from some of his men. He guessed they were speaking of the death and his harsh reaction to it — this was, after all, just a game and their opponents mock enemies. But tournaments wouldn't last for ever. Soon, the battleground and the foes upon it would be real enough. He needed them to be ready.

Flexing his aching hands, Edward glanced at Valence, riding beside him. The man was sitting at ease, his massive frame resting against the high back of the saddle, the interlinked rings of his hauberk clinking against the wood. Unlike the younger knights, he showed no regret for the accident at all, running a scrap of cloth down the length of his sword, which was notched with use. The blade appeared much keener than the dulled weapons Edward and the rest of the men had used.

Catching Edward's look, Valence gave a knowing smile. 'Needs must when the devil drives, nephew. Needs must.'

Edward said nothing, but he nodded as he turned back to the road. He wasn't going to argue about tournament rules, not when his half-uncle had helped him win most of the tourneys his company had entered this season. This had brought him enough horses, weapons and armour to equip an army, not to mention the scores of young bachelors who had been drawn by his growing reputation. At a victory feast, several months earlier, one of them had called him a new Arthur and the name had stuck, more and more flocking to join the company under the dragon banner. Valence might be a truculent man, whose reputation for viciousness had travelled far beyond the borders of the French town of his birth, but his brutal skill on the tournament field, along with the fact that he was one of the few members of Edward's family who hadn't deserted him, made him invaluable, and so Edward gave his uncle free rein, ignoring his violent outbursts and many indiscretions.

As a couple of the older knights struck up a ribald victory song that the others soon joined in with, Edward looked behind him to see rows of grinning, sweat-streaked faces. Most were in their early twenties like him, many of them younger sons of French nobility, drawn by the promise of plunder and glory. After months on the tournament circuit, Edward knew them well. All of them would fight for him now, without question. Just a few more weeks of training and they would be ready. Then, he would return to England at the head of the company, to regain his honour and his lands.

It was nine months since his father, the king, had sent him into exile. Even his mother had been silent at the judgement: the revoking of his lands in Wales and England that he had been given, aged fifteen, as part of his marriage agreement. King Henry had been grim and silent as his son had ridden out from Westminster Palace, bound for Portsmouth and the ship that would carry him to the only lands left to him in Gascony. Edward recalled looking back, just once, to see that his father had already turned away and was heading through the palace gates. His jaw tightening, he forced out the memory and concentrated on the sight of the elated knights following him on their weary mounts, all chanting the name of Arthur. His father would be forced to apologise when he saw the warrior his son had become, named by his men after the greatest king who ever lived.

The blush of evening was fading, the first stars pricking the sky as the company rode into the courtyard of the timber-beamed hunting lodge, surrounded by outbuildings and shrouded by trees. Edward dismounted. Handing his horse to a groom and telling William de Valence to hold the prisoners when they arrived, he headed for the main house, wanting to wash the dust from his face and quench his thirst before the other commanders appeared and the ransoms could be agreed. Forced to duck his long body under the lintel, he entered the lodge and made his way past servants to the upper rooms and his private chamber.

He stepped inside the room, his mail coat and spurs jingling as he moved across the wooden floor. Unfastening his belt, from which his broadsword hung, he tossed the weapon on the bed, feeling the pressure around his waist drop away. The room was in shadow, apart from the shimmer of a single candle on a table by the window. Behind was a looking-glass. As he came closer, entering the pool of candlelight, Edward saw himself appear in the depths. There was a jug of water, basin and cloth set out for him. Pushing away the stool in front of the table, he poured water into the basin and leaned over, cupping his hands. It was like ice against his hot face. He cupped more, felt it running freezing lines down his skin, washing away dirt and blood. When he was done, he reached for the cloth and wiped the water from his eyes. As he lowered it, Edward saw his wife standing before him. Her thick hair fell in waves, flowing over the contours of her shoulders to her waist. So often it was piled up and hidden beneath veils and headdresses. He loved to see it loose, the only man who was allowed.

Eleanor of Castile's almond eyes narrowed as she smiled. 'You won.'

'How do you know?' he asked, drawing her to him.

'I heard your men singing a mile distant. But even if I hadn't, I would see it in your face.' She stroked his stubble-rough cheek.

Edward reached out, taking her face in his hands and bringing her to kiss him. He smelled honey and herbs from the soap she used, brought from the Holy Land.

Eleanor pulled back, laughing. 'You're wet!'

Edward grinned and kissed his young wife again, pulling her to him despite her protests, covering her spotless shift in filth from his surcoat and mail. Finally, he let her go, looking around for wine. On tiptoes to grasp his shoulders, Eleanor pushed him down to the stool by the table, bidding him to sit.

Sitting, rigid in his armour, but too weary to go about the business of removing it, Edward watched Eleanor in the looking-glass, pouring wine from a glazed jug, decorated with peacock feathers. As she set down the jug, running a finger quickly under the rim to catch a stray drop that she licked away, he felt a stab of affection. It was the kind of sharp love that comes with the realisation of the potential for loss. Other than his uncle, she was the only one who had followed him into exile. She could have stayed in London, in the comfort and safety of Windsor or Westminster, for the judgement didn't extend to her. But not once had she suggested it.

When he had boarded the ship at Portsmouth, Edward had sat alone in the hold. There, his head in his hands, he had wept, the first time he'd done so since he was a boy, watching his father sail out from those same docks, bound for France without him. As he swiped at the tears of humiliation and, he admitted it, fear, for he had lost almost everything, Eleanor had come to him. Kneeling before him, taking his hands, she told him they didn't need the king or the queen, didn't need his conniving godfather, Simon de Montfort: the cause of his banishment. They needed no one. She had been fierce, her voice stronger, more determined than he'd heard before. Later, they made love in the sour-smelling hold below deck. Married for seven years, their unions until that moment had been mostly gentle, almost polite. Now they were hungry and tearing, pouring their rage and fear into one another until both were consumed, as the timbers creaked around them and the sea carried them from England's shores.

Their child, the first to come to term, perhaps the product of that savage lovemaking, was swelling in her stomach, distended in the mirror, beneath the voluminous shift.

Eleanor moved in behind him, passing the cup into his hand. Edward took a draught, the wine stinging his dry throat. As he put down the cup, his eyes alighted on a book placed on the edge of the table, just outside the sphere of candlelight, where he had left it that morning.

'I'll have the servants bring you some food.'

At her murmur and the squeeze of her hand on his shoulder, Edward caught sight of his face in the mirror, all at once furrowed and pensive. He touched her fingers, grateful she knew him well enough to understand he wanted to be left alone. As she turned away, draping a mantle around her, Edward watched her recede in the mirror, her black hair fading into shadows. When the door closed, he looked at the book, drawing it to him across the pitted wood. It was old now, for he'd had it since boyhood, the boards coming apart, the pages stained. The words on the cover, scored into the leather, were mostly worn away, but he could still see their outline.

The Prophecies of Merlin
By Geoffrey of Monmouth

It was one of the few personal possessions he had brought with him from England. He had read it many times over the years, along with Monmouth's other works: The Life of Merlin and The History of the Kings of Britain, of which it was rumoured there were now more copies than of the Bible. Edward knew by heart the deeds of Brutus, the warrior from Troy, who after the Trojan War had sailed north and founded Britain, knew the story of King Lear and the coming of Caesar. But it was the tales of King Arthur that had appealed to him most, from the first prophecy Merlin told to Utherpendragon that he would be king and that his son, in turn, would rule all of Britain, to Arthur's terrible defeat at Camblam, where-upon he had passed his crown to his cousin, Constantine, before sailing to Avalon to be healed. When Edward watched his first tournament at Smithfield in London, he had been in awe of the knights dressed as men from Arthur's court, with one of them the legendary king himself.

As Edward picked up the book, its ancient pages flapped open at a page where a piece of parchment had been inserted. He stared at the scribe's writing, hearing in his mind the words being dictated in the king's pompous tones. He had read this letter many times since he received it, the first contact he'd had with his father since leaving London. The anger he had felt initially was gone. What remained was burning anticipation.

The letter spoke of castles razed and towns looted, crops and pastures laid waste, the earth left scorched, corpses littering streets and fields, the stink clouding the air. Men under the command of the warlord, Llywelyn ap Gruffudd, had raided down from their mountain strongholds in the ancient Welsh kingdom of Gwynedd. On his marriage to Eleanor, Edward had been given a great deal of land by his father, including a swathe of territory along the north coast of Wales, from the border at Chester to the shores of the River Conwy. It was these lands that were now burning, according to the letter. But it wasn't the first time.

Six years ago, when Edward was seventeen, Llywelyn led the men of Gwynedd in an uprising against English occupation of this territory. The raid proved brutally effec-tive and within days the region was in Llywelyn's control, English castles left burning, garrisons forced to flee. Edward, short of funds, had gone to his father as soon as the first reports had filtered through. The king denied him aid, saying this was his chance to prove himself as a warrior and a commander of men. The reality, Edward knew, was that Henry was too preoccupied trying to get his youngest son, Edmund, crowned King of Sicily, to spare the funds or support. In the end, obtaining a loan from one of his uncles, he had gone alone with his men to save his lands in Wales. Llywelyn had annihilated him. Forced to retreat after just one battle, his army and his reputation in tatters, Edward still remembered the taunting songs he had heard sung of him, the jubilant Welshmen revelling in his defeat.

Henry, meanwhile, had made himself increasingly unpopular in court with the absurd Sicilian endeavour and by his favouritism towards his half-brothers, the notorious Valences, who had recently arrived in England. The leader of the protests against the king was Edward's godfather, Simon de Montfort, Earl of Leicester. Montfort had drawn many supporters to his challenge of Henry, which culminated in a parliament at Oxford, at which the king lost most of his authority to the barons. Angered by Henry's foolish actions and by his own defeat at the hands of Llywelyn, Edward had taken the side of his godfather, who persuaded him to enter into a pact against his father. The king, upon learning of the treachery, had revoked his inheritance and sent him into exile.

Edward read the letter once last time, lingering over the final passages. What made this uprising different was that Llywelyn ap Gruffudd had done the unthinkable and united all of Wales beneath him. Until now, north and south had been divided by more than just the mountain barrier of Snowdonia. For centuries the warlord rulers of the three ancient kingdoms of Wales had vied for supremacy, constantly fighting with one another and with the English lords who bordered them to the south and east. It was ever a country in turmoil. Now, Llywelyn had drawn these dissident, warring people together and, turning their spears and bows from one another, had fixed them east towards England. Henry had written that Llywelyn had donned a golden crown and was styling himself Prince of Wales. The crown wasn't just any crown. It was the Crown of Arthur.

Edward stared at the parchment for a moment longer, then held it over the candle. The skin smouldered, the flame flickering madly around his father's promise that if he returned and defeated Llywelyn all his lands would be restored to him. He was ready. Ready to go home with the men who had flocked to his banner, take his place in England again and accept his parents' apology, ready to deal with Llywelyn. The Welsh might stand united for the first time, but therein lay their vulnerability, exposed to Edward in the lines of that letter. He had seen first-hand the power in taking on the mantle of a legend. Llywelyn clearly understood that himself, for he could not have chosen a more effective symbol with which to unify the people of Wales. Arthur was more than just a champion to them, he was the last great British king, before the Saxons, before the Normans. But if something so potent could unite a people in common identity, did it not follow that it could also destroy them?

As the parchment shrivelled into black cinders there came a rap at the door. It opened to reveal the hulking form of William de Valence.

'The commanders have arrived to discuss the ransom of their men.'

Edward rose, leaving the remains of the letter to turn to ash on the table. He left the book lying open, the words on the pages dark in the shifting candle flame.

PART 1

1286 AD

It was night and the horns of the bright moon were shining . . . From the top of a lofty mountain the prophet was regarding the courses of the stars, speaking to himself out in the open air. 'What does this ray of Mars mean? Does its fresh redness mean that one king is dead and that there shall be another?'

The Life of Merlin, *Geoffrey of Monmouth*

I

It was the voice of God. And God was furious.

The king's butler, weaving between the trestles and benches, winced as the sky cracked open in another ugly roar that bellowed into the distance. Across the crowded hall one of the younger servants bowed his head in what the old butler took to be prayer. The storm was on top of them, bearing down on the towers and battlements, smothering the bruised afternoon light and plunging the castle into early midnight. The sense of dread, stirred several months earlier with the rumours, had now reached such a height that even Guthred — having scoffed at all the talk — couldn't fail to feel it.

At the next lightning strike he glanced up into the riddle of beams far above the feverish torchlight, wondering what would happen if it struck the roof. He saw a biblical scene: white fire raining down, charred bodies strewn across the floor, knives and goblets still gripped in their fists. Would they rise the way they fell? He looked at the jug in his liver-spotted hands. Would he? Half closing his eyes, Guthred formed the beginnings of a supplication, then stopped short. It was nonsense. It was these terrible March storms that had caused the old wives to fret and the clerics to proclaim. But, as he continued his journey between the tables, it was hard to ignore the voice that murmured a reminder that the rumours had begun long before the north had opened its maw and howled down snow and gale and thunder upon Scotland.

Gripping the jug firmly lest he spill a drop of the precious liquid inside, the butler climbed the wooden stairs of the dais that straddled one end of the great hall. With each step he rose above the heads of the lords, royal officials, servants, dogs and hangers-on that jostled for space and attention below. Guthred had already seen the ushers, on the steward's command, remove several youths who had managed to steal uninvited into the hall. Feast days were always chaotic: the stables became overcrowded, a lord's lodgings weren't readied, messages went awry, servants became clumsy in their haste and their masters hot-tempered. Still, despite these difficulties and the afternoon's turbulent weather, the king seemed in good humour. He was laughing at something the Bishop of Glasgow had just said as Guthred approached. The king's face was flushed with drink and the fierce heat that buffeted from the hall's hearths, and he had spilled something on his robe. Around the table that spanned the dais, the straw, fresh that morning, was sticky underfoot with crumbs of honey cake, drops of wine and globs of bloody gravy. Guthred eyed the panoply of silver platters and vessels, able to tell, with a discreet incline of his head, whose goblet needed filling. The voices of the eight men who sat to either side of the king were loud, in competition with the storm and each other, and the old butler had to lean in close to make himself heard.

'More wine, my lord?'

Without interrupting his conversation, King Alexander offered up his goblet, larger than the others and encrusted with gems. 'I thought we had laid this matter to rest already,' he said, addressing the man to his left. After the butler finished pouring the crimson wine, the king took a draught.

'Forgive me, my lord,' replied the man, placing a hand over his own goblet when the butler went to fill it, 'but the request for—'

'Thank you, Guthred,' said the king, as the butler moved on to the Bishop of Glasgow, who had his cup out ready.

The man's jaw tightened. 'My lord, the request for the release of the prisoner comes directly from my brother-in-law and as both his kinsman and Justiciar of Galloway it would be remiss of me not to afford his plea the attention it deserves.'

King Alexander frowned as John Comyn's dark eyes continued to scrutinise him. The Lord of Badenoch's long face was waxy in the torchlight, his expression as sober as his clothes: a black woollen cloak, trimmed all around the shoulders with the grizzled pelt of a wolf that matched his hair so exactly it was hard to tell where he ended and wolf began. The device on the surcoat he wore beneath was just visible: a red shield embroidered with three white sheaves of wheat. The king was struck by how like his father the Red Comyn was – the same cold demeanour and joyless expression. Were all Comyn men like this? Was it something in their blood? Alexander's gaze roved along the table to the Earl of Buchan, head of the Black Comyns,

named, as the Red Comyn was, by the colour of his arms: a black shield
decorated with the three wheat sheaves. Alexander was rewarded with
long, pinched features and a guarded stare. If they weren't such able officials, he might have excluded all of them from his court years ago. Truth be
told, the Comyns made him uneasy. 'As I said, I will think on it. Thomas of
Galloway was imprisoned over fifty years ago. No doubt he will be able to
bear another few weeks in his cell.'

'Even a day must seem an eternity to an innocent man.' John Comyn
spoke lightly, but the challenge was unmistakable.

'Innocent?' Alexander's blue eyes narrowed. He set down his goblet, his
humour spent. 'The man rebelled against my father.'

'The man was but a boy, my lord. It was the people of Galloway who
chose him as their leader.'

'And my father saw that they paid for it in blood.' Alexander's tone
was vehement, the drink running hot in him, mottling his face. 'Thomas
of Galloway was a bastard. He had no right to be lord and the people
knew it.'

'They were faced with an unpalatable choice – to be ruled by a bastard,
or else see their land divided between three daughters. Surely you can
understand their plight, Lord King?'

Alexander caught something sly in Comyn's tone. Was the Lord of
Badenoch trying to insinuate that his own situation was in any way compa
rable to what had happened in Galloway over half a century ago? Before he
could decide, a cool voice sounded from further along the table.

'You are keeping our gracious host from his meal with your talk, Sir
John. The council is over.'

John Comyn's eyes flicked to the speaker. As he met the calm gaze of
James Stewart, the high steward, his poised veneer slipped momentarily,
unmasking a glint of hostility, but before he could respond, the forceful
voice of Robert Wishart, the Bishop of Glasgow, rang out.

'Well spoken, Sir James. Our mouths now are for the eating and for
praising the Good Lord for His bounteous gifts.' Wishart raised his goblet.
'This wine is remarkable, my lord. From Gascony, is it?'

The king's response was lost in an almighty clap of thunder that set the
dogs off and caused the Bishop of St Andrews to spill his drink.

Wishart grinned fiercely. 'If this is indeed the Day of Judgement then
we shall arise with our bellies full!' He took a deep drink that stained the
corners of his mouth. The Bishop of St Andrews, as thin and grave as Wishart
was stout and animated, began to protest at these words, but Wishart spoke

over him. 'You know as well as I, your grace, if every day proclaimed to be the Day of Judgement had been we would have risen a dozen times over by now!'

The king went to speak, but stopped, seeing a familiar face moving through the crowd below. It was one of the squires from the queen's household, a capable Frenchman named Adam. His travelling cloak glistened in the torchlight and his hair was plastered dark against his head with rain. As Adam passed one of the hearths, the king could see the cold curling off him as mist. The squire hastened up the dais steps.

'My lord.' Adam paused before the king to bow and catch his breath. 'I bring a message from Kinghorn.'

'In this tempest?' questioned Wishart, as the squire leaned in and began to speak quietly to the king.

As Adam finished, a smile played at the corners of Alexander's mouth and the flush of wine on his cheeks spread down his throat. 'Adam, go and fetch Tom from his lodgings. Tell him to bring my cloak and have my horse saddled. We leave for Kinghorn at once.'

'As you wish, my lord.'

'Has something happened?' enquired the Bishop of St Andrews, as the squire hastened across the dais. 'The queen, she is . . .?'

'The queen is well,' said Alexander, smiling fully now. 'She requests my company.' He got to his feet. There was a loud scraping of benches and shuffling of feet as all the occupants of the hall rose with him, some nudging drink-addled neighbours to follow suit. The king raised his hands and voice to address them. 'Please, be seated. I must take my leave. But stay, all of you, enjoy the festivities.' He gestured to his harper, who at once began to play, the metallic notes climbing over the roar of the wind.

As the king stepped from the table, James Stewart moved in front of him. 'My lord, wait until morning,' he murmured. 'It is a foul day for travel, especially on that road.'

The king paused at the concern in the steward's face. Glancing back, he saw the same worry in the eyes of the other men at his table, with the exception of John Comyn who had leaned over to talk quietly with his kinsman, the Earl of Buchan. For a moment the king hesitated, on the brink of returning to his seat and calling Guthred back with more wine. But something stronger compelled him. That last thing Comyn had said remained with him like a bitter aftertaste. *Surely you can understand their plight?* Alexander could, all too well, for the matter of succession had plagued

him for two long years, ever since the day when the heir in whom all his
hopes had been placed had followed his wife, his daughter and his youngest
son to the grave with devastating finality. With the death of his eldest boy,
Alexander's line had been cut short, like a song halted before the chorus.
It continued now only as a faint echo across the North Sea, in the form of
his three-year-old granddaughter, Margaret, child of his dead daughter and
the King of Norway. Yes, Alexander understood very clearly the unpalatable
choice that had faced the people of Galloway fifty years ago, when their lord
had died without male issue.

'I must go, James.' The king's voice was quiet, but firm. 'It is almost
six months since my wedding night and still Yolande is without child, not
for want of trying. If she takes my seed tonight, God willing, I could have
an heir by this time next year. I can chance a storm for that.' Removing
the gold circlet he had been wearing through the council and the feast,
Alexander handed it to the steward. He pushed a hand through his hair,
flattened where the band had lain. 'I will return soon.' He paused, his eyes
on John Comyn. 'In the meantime, you can tell the Lord of Badenoch I will
grant his brother-in-law's request.' Alexander's eyes glinted. 'But wait until
tomorrow.'

James's mouth twitched in the beginnings of a smile. 'My lord.'

Alexander strode across the dais, following in the squire's muddy footsteps, the gold on his scarlet robe glittering. As the doorward bowed and
pushed open the hall's double doors, the king swept through, the notes of
the harp fading behind him.

Once outside, the force of the storm struck the king like a fist. Icy
rain stung his face, half blinding him as he made his way down the steps
to the courtyard. He flinched as lightning ripped through the sullen sky.
The clouds were so low they seemed to skim the rooftops of the buildings that stretched before him to the inner walls, below which the ground
fell sharply away to the outer defences. From his high vantage point, the
king could look right over the line of the outer walls to the royal town of
Edinburgh that tumbled eastwards down the spine of the great rock on
which the castle perched.

In the distance, at the foot of the hill, he made out the pale silhouette of
Holyrood Abbey, behind which black slabs of rock reared into windswept
cliffs that disappeared in cloud. To the north, the land levelled out into
grazing pastures and crop fields, then marshes that slipped into the vast
expanse of the Firth of Forth, which the English called the Scottish Sea.
Over that stretch of water, illuminated by muted after-flickers of lightning,

were the wooded hills of Fife and the track he must take. Kinghorn, twenty miles away, seemed further than it ever had before. Thinking of the Bishop of St Andrews doom-laden words that when the Day of Judgement came this would certainly be its temperament, Alexander faltered on the bottom step, the rain pelting him. But, then, seeing Adam sprinting towards him, he forced his feet down into the mud, holding in his mind a vision of his young bride waiting for him in a warm bed. There would be spiced wine and firelight.

'My lord, Tom has taken ill,' called Adam, raising his voice above the gale. He was carrying the king's travelling cloak.

'Ill?' Alexander's brow furrowed as the squire draped the fur-lined garment around his shoulders. Tom, who had served him for over thirty years, always travelled with him. Adam might be capable, but he was the queen's favourite, having come to Scotland in her retinue last autumn. 'Tom was well this afternoon. Has the physician seen him?'

'He says there is no need,' answered Adam, guiding the king across the waterlogged ground. 'Watch your step here, Sire.'

There were lanterns burning ahead, the flames inside like caged birds, fluttering and beating at the glass. The whinnies of horses and the calls of men hung on the wind.

'Who will escort me?'

'Tom sent Master Brice in his place.'

Alexander's frown deepened as Adam led the way into the stables. The pungent odour of straw and dung clogged his nostrils.

'My lord king,' greeted the stable-master. He was leading a handsome grey courser. 'I saddled Winter for you myself, although I could hardly believe it when Master Brice told me you were leaving in this weather.'

Alexander's gaze moved to Brice, a taciturn, rather slow-witted man who had been in his service for less than a month, hired to help out Tom who had been stretched looking after the king with a new bride. Alexander had been meaning to ask the steward to find him someone better, but what with the preparations for today's council he hadn't found the time. Brice bowed, but said nothing. Grunting his displeasure and feeling suddenly all too sober, Alexander pulled on the riding gloves the stable-master handed to him. As he climbed on to the block and swung into the saddle, his robe hitched up around his hose, already hemmed black with mud. He would have changed had he not been worried about losing what was left of the day. While the stable-master tightened the girth with a firm tug that caused Winter to stamp impatiently, the two squires mounted the horses that had been led out of the stalls for them. Both were palfreys, smaller and lighter than the king's beast. Adam was on a fresh horse, his own having been spent on the ride to Edinburgh.

The stable-master's voice followed them out into the rain. 'God speed, my lord.'

Adam led the way through the castle courtyard, the horses sure on the well-worn ground. It was not yet evening, but already there were torches burning in the windows of the gatehouse, the rough dark pushing against the light. The guards hauled open the gates and the three men made their way down the steep track beyond. The gatehouse was soon looming sheer above them on the black rocks, the torchlight turning the windows into amber eyes. As they passed through a second gate in the lower walls, the guards greeted the king with surprise.

The main street that led through the town was running with rainwater, but empty of people or carts and the king and his squires quickened their pace. The wild wind tore at their cloaks and hair, and by the time they reached the town limits they were soaked and frozen. From here they sped out across the miles of open country towards the Firth of Forth, leaving Edinburgh far behind them.

At Dalmeny, buffeted by the gusts coming off the estuary, they dismounted outside the ferry-master's lodgings. It was fully dark now. While Adam banged on the door, the king stared out across the two-mile stretch of swollen, inky water. Lightning pulsed above the distant hills and thunder came rolling like a wave towards him. The storm was moving north over Fife.

The ferry-master opened the door, holding a lantern. 'Yes?' he said in gruff Scots. 'Ah, it's you again.' Peering past Adam, the ferry-master looked taken aback when he saw the king's face in the glow from his light. 'My lord!' He pulled the door wider. 'I beg your pardon. Please, come in from the rain.'

'I'm headed for Kinghorn,' said Alexander, switching briskly from the French he had been speaking all day in council into the blunt Scots-English dialect.

'In this gale?' The ferry-master looked worriedly down the slip of sand beyond his house to where the broad shadow of the ferry rocked in the black. 'I wouldn't say that would be wise.'

'Your king has given you a command,' responded Adam sharply. 'He doesn't need to know what you think of it.'

Pulling up his hood against the rain, the ferry-master moved past Adam to the king. 'My lord, I implore you, wait until morning. I can provide lodgings here for you and your men. It won't be well fit, but it will be dry.'

'You were happy enough to row my man across earlier.'

'That was long before this storm blew in proper. Now – well, my lord, it is simply too perilous.'

Alexander's impatience erupted. At every step he seemed to be thwarted in his attempts to reach his wife. 'If you are afraid then I will have my squires take the oars. But either way, I will cross tonight!'

The ferry-master bowed his head in consternation. 'Yes, my lord.' He went to head into his lodgings, then turned back. 'Our Lord God knows I could not die better than in the company of your father's son.'

Alexander clenched his jaw as the ferry-master disappeared inside.

He returned shortly with six men, all of them monks from Dunfermline Abbey that had owned the right to run the ferry from the distant days of St Margaret. Their woollen habits and sandals must have afforded little protection from the biting wind, but they didn't complain as they guided the king down to the water's edge. Behind came Brice and Adam, who had looped the iron stirrups of the horses through the leather straps to keep them from swinging against the animals on the voyage.

The crossing was long and uncomfortable, the men bowed beneath the ceaseless pounding of the rain on their hoods, the horses disturbed by the vessel's erratic motion. Spray skimmed off the choppy surface and coated their lips with salt as the ferry rose and fell. Alexander sat hunched at the stern, wrapped in a sodden fur which the ferry-master had offered to keep him warm. The thunder had faded to distant growls, but the wind showed no sign of decreasing and the monks' mournful song as they rowed through the darkness was barely audible above its moans. Despite the ferry-master's concern, however, the vessel made safe landfall at the royal burgh of Inverkeithing.

'We'll take the path along the shore,' said Alexander, as Adam led Winter off the ferry and up the wet sand. There was firelight in some of the houses beyond the beach, winking invitingly. 'It will be more sheltered.'

'Not tonight, my lord,' warned the ferry-master, taking the wet fur the king handed to him. 'The spring tides are washing the water right to the cliffs in places. You could find yourself cut off.'

'We'll take the high track, Sire,' called Adam, tugging down the king's stirrups. 'It will be quicker.'

Their course set, the king and his squires rode their horses along the track that led up the wooded slopes beyond Inverkeithing to the cliff path. The going was slow in the rushing blackness beneath the canopy of trees, but at least the branches afforded some shelter. Once out of the woods, they were again at the mercy of the gale, which battled constantly against them as they followed the path's winding ascent through the cliffs, which continued above and below them. The ground was boggy, the horses' hooves sinking deep into the mud, forcing them to a torturous walk. Adam went in front, bidding Brice to ride behind him and shout warnings of the more treacherous places to the king. Alexander was an extremely experienced rider, but his horse, several hands larger than the squires' palfreys, found the climb through the sticky mud increasingly difficult and, soon, the king was left behind. He could hear the calls of his men on the wind, but couldn't see them in the howling dark. Gritting his teeth and berating himself for not heeding the advice of the steward, he forced Winter on, kicking him harder and harder, now swearing, now cursing, until the horse was snorting in agitation. In his mind, the king still cradled the image of his young bride in their warm bed, but now the vision had a sense of salvation about it.

Alexander struggled with his horse on the incline, the beast thrashing its head against his fierce twists on the reins. This was madness. He should have listened to James, waited until morning. He went to call to his squires, thinking to turn back. They could seek shelter in Inverkeithing until the storm had passed. Then, as lightning seared the night, the king saw the cliffs ahead rising sharply above the path. Beyond that swoop of headland lay Kinghorn. It wasn't far, only a mile or so. Bearing forward in the saddle, the king struck at Winter's sides, urging the exhausted animal on. The way became even steeper and Alexander caught the cries of gulls, wheeling in the teeth of the storm. He could no longer hear his men. The path narrowed, bare rocks to his left and a precipitous drop to the right, the yawning black of which opened sickeningly beside him. He knew it wasn't much more than a hundred feet down to the shore, but it might as well have stretched into hell for all he could see. As his horse slipped, he pulled it up sharply. His hands ached with the effort. 'On!' he roared, as the courser slipped again, neighed in fear and tried to turn. '*On!*'

A black shape loomed before him. 'Sire!'

Relief flooded Alexander. 'Take my reins,' he shouted to Adam, over the gale. 'I'm going to have to dismount. Winter cannot carry me up here.'

'Wait, my lord, and I'll come alongside you. The ground is firmer further on. I can lead you.'

'Careful, I'm at the edge here,' warned the king, feeling the rain trickling inside his cloak, threading an icy line down his back. 'Where's Brice?'

'I sent him on ahead.' Adam manoeuvred his palfrey between the king and the rocks that rose beside the path. A snap of lightning lit his face, revealing an intent expression as he reached across and grasped hold of the king's reins, steadying his own horse with his knees.

'Right, man,' said Alexander, readying himself. 'One last push.'

'One last push, my lord,' echoed Adam, thrusting towards him.

The first thing Alexander felt was a jolt as his horse lurched. He guessed in an instant that the beast had been lamed and its sharp cry confirmed it. His own shout vanished in a winded grunt as he fell forward, his stomach striking the wooden pommel. He grabbed at the beast's neck for purchase and felt another pain, this time in his leg as something crashed into him from the side. He had time to realise that it was Adam's horse and time to realise that the squire had let go of his reins. Then, he and Winter were falling into darkness.

Adam strove to get his panicked horse under control as the king's cry vanished. After a moment, he managed to calm it enough to dismount. Holding the reins in one hand, he bent to clean the blood from the dagger he gripped in the other, wiping it in the wet grass that sprouted from the path. When he was done, he lifted his short hose and pushed the blade inside the leather sheath strapped around his calf. Moving cautiously to the cliff edge, he waited, sniffing rainwater from the end of his nose. After several minutes lightning struck again. Adam's sharp eyes picked out a large, grey shape on the shore below. He waited. There was supposed to have been a moon tonight, but the storm had obscured it. Still, the wind and rain would have masked the king's scream from Brice's ears, although the fool should have been far enough ahead not to have heard it. The lightning came again in three flashes. The horse remained where it had fallen and this time Adam caught sight of a smaller shape lying close by. The king's scarlet robe was as bright as a flag. Satisfied, the squire dug his foot into his stirrup and swung into the saddle. Even if the king had survived the fall, he would die from the cold before anyone found him, for Adam would make sure to send the search party in the wrong direction. Digging in his spurs, he continued up the cliff path towards Kinghorn, rehearsing the lies he planned to tell the young queen.

Down on the shore, the dying horse turned its head. Blood pumped from the deep cut in its foreleg, which had severed the tendons and taken its balance, indistinguishable now from the injuries caused by the fall. A few feet away lay its royal charge, arms splayed, neck twisted at an impossible angle. The ragged wind coming off the Forth lifted a corner of the king's cloak, making it flap against the sand, but other than that there was no movement.

The dead would not be rising today.

2

The boy's breaths came hard and fast as the beast thundered across the beach, kicking up sand in wet clods and taking him further from the shouts that echoed behind him. One hand gripping the reins, the boy leaned far back in the saddle, almost standing in the stirrups, striving to bring the horse to a stop, until his muscles were throbbing with the effort. The raw wind whipped his hair into his eyes, blinding him, and the lance, couched in his right hand, bounced wildly. Without warning, the horse jerked forward, pulling the reins painfully fast through the boy's clenched fist. As the animal veered towards the crashing surf in a furious gallop, the boy lost his hold on the lance, which thumped to the sand to be splintered beneath one of the beast's hooves. Faint in the distance, he heard his name being yelled.

'*Robert!*'

Snatching up the reins with both hands now, the boy fought against the animal, shouting in frustration and fear as it continued its crazed path towards the seething water. The sea, dazzling white in the sunlight, was coming up fast, filling his world with its rush and tumble. The roar of it was in his ears. All at once, he felt a violent jolt beneath him. The sky rolled over in his vision and, for a second, he saw clouds and a gull wheeling. Then he was hurtling headlong into the waves.

The cold slammed him, making him gulp a lungful of salt water as he disappeared beneath the churning surf. He was tossed over, then sucked under, any sense of up or down driven from him by the icy shock and his rising panic. His chest was constricting, closing in on itself. He couldn't breathe. Suddenly, his foot struck the bottom. He pushed himself up, breaking the surface with a shuddering gasp. The next wave struck him in the back, but although he was brought to his knees and propelled along by it, he managed to keep his head above the water. Eyes fixed on the shore, he struggled out of the breakers, his tunic clinging to him. As he waded on to the sand, coughing up seawater, he realised his shoes had been torn off by the force of the waves. The grit of broken shells on the shoreline stung his bare feet as he bent over, letting water trickle from his nose and ears.

'Robert!'

The boy straightened at the shout to see a figure striding down the beach towards him. His heart sank as he saw the broken lance, a smaller version of the great lances of men, in his instructor's hand.

'Why didn't you shorten your reins?' The man came to a halt before the soaking boy, brandishing the splintered lance. 'Ruined! All because you couldn't follow a basic instruction!'

Robert, shivering in the wind, met his instructor's livid gaze. The squat bull of a man was red in the face and sweating from the race to catch him up. That, at least, gave him some measure of satisfaction. 'I tried, Master Yothre,' he said tightly, glancing up the beach to where the beast had come to a halt, reins dangling free. It tossed its head and snorted as if laughing. Anger rose in Robert as he recalled being led to the stables four weeks ago, his excitement at his new phase of instruction draining when he saw the only animal saddled in his father's stables was the massive warhorse. He had learned to ride on a sweet-natured hobby and, more recently, had mastered a spirited young palfrey. The black beast was nothing like either of them. It was like riding the devil. Robert's gaze switched back to Yothre. 'My father has more than thirty horses in his stables. Why did you choose Ironfoot? Even the grooms won't go near him. He's too strong.'

'It isn't your lack of strength that's the trouble,' grunted Yothre, 'it's your lack of skill. The horse will respond if you follow my instructions. Anyway,' he added, his tone losing a little of its acidity, 'I didn't choose him for you. Your father did.'

Robert fell silent. The sunlight glistened on his wet cheeks as he looked out to sea. His face, pale under his fringe of dark hair, was taut. Beyond the crashing breakers, the waters were a deep, lucid green. Further out, by the hump of Ailsa Craig, the Fairy Rock, they darkened to slate grey and, further still, towards the distant Isle of Arran, they turned black. Here on the Carrick coast it was a bright, windy spring day, but over the Arran hills a bank of clouds had built up through the morning trailing veils of rain, a remnant of the violent storms that had ravaged Scotland since the start of the year. Robert's eyes picked out the smudge on the southern horizon that marked the northern tip of Ireland. Catching sight of that faint line, so often shrouded in mist or haze, he felt a pang of loss.

His brother was still somewhere on that strip of land in the care of the Irish lord, a vassal of their father's, to whom they had both been fostered. No doubt Edward would have already finished his training and schooling for the day. He would probably be racing the small wooden boats they had carved down the river outside the manor house in Antrim with their foster-brothers, laughing and chasing through the shallows. Tonight they would eat salmon and, by firelight, drink sweet beer in the lord's hall and listen to his tales of Irish heroes, thundering battles and quests for treasure. The twelve months Robert had spent in Antrim had been some of the best of his life, his foster-father teaching him all he should know as the eldest son of one of the most powerful families in Scotland. Robert had thought he would return home to take his proper place at his father's side, no longer a boy, but a youth on the path to knighthood. The reality had been a crushing disappointment.

'Come, we will start again,' Yothre was saying, gesturing for Robert to follow as he headed up the beach towards Ironfoot. 'And this time, if you do as I say, we can avoid any further—' His words were cut off by a high-pitched shout.

A small boy was racing across the dunes towards them. Behind him Turnberry Castle perched on its promontory of rock over the surging sea, its battlements crowned by the circling silhouettes of cormorants and gulls.

Robert smiled as the boy ran faster, his short legs puffing sand into a cloud around him. 'Niall!'

His youngest brother came to a breathless halt before him, blithely ignoring Yothre who looked infuriated.

'Men have come, and' – Niall sucked in a breath – 'and Grandfather!'

Robert's face broke into a wide grin of surprise. At once, he set off across the sand with Niall, his tunic flapping wetly around his legs.

'Master Robert,' barked Yothre behind him, 'your lesson isn't over.' As the boys turned, the man thrust the broken lance towards Ironfoot. 'You'll ride him again before we're finished.'

'I'll ride him tomorrow.'

'Your father will be told of your disobedience.'

Robert's storm-blue eyes narrowed. 'Tell him then,' he said, sprinting after his brother.

Once over the dunes, the two boys passed the little cluster of houses, fishermen's boats and farmsteads that made up Turnberry village and raced on to the sandy track that led to the castle. Here, Robert picked up speed, his long legs punching into the ground as he left Niall far behind him. The earth beneath his feet was pocked with the fresh prints of many horses. His lungs burned, the exertion driving out the ice in his limbs, driving out too Yothre's threat.

As he approached the gates, which had been thrown wide open, one of the guards called to him.

'Master Robert!' The guard grinned. 'What did that devil do to you today?'

Ignoring him, Robert slowed as he entered the castle courtyard. There were many men and horses here being directed by the stable-master. In between the slow-moving animals, Robert caught sight of his family, all of whom had come out to greet the unexpected arrivals. He glanced impatiently over his two brothers, his mother and three sisters, one of whom was bawling in the arms of her wet nurse. His eyes lingered for a moment on his father, the Earl of Carrick, dressed in a crimson cloak trimmed with gold braid, then moved to take in the newcomers. He recognised, with some surprise, James Stewart. The High Steward of Scotland, one of the chief officials in the kingdom whose powerful family had held the stewardship for generations, was standing with a great earl from the east. There were others too, but all of them faded away as Robert's gaze came to rest on the leonine man in their centre, with that great mane of silver hair and that hard, ancient face. Robert Bruce, Lord of Annandale. The man whose name both he and his father shared.

Hearing Niall come gasping up behind him, Robert moved towards his grandfather, who was clad in a dust-stained surcoat and mantle, emblazoned with the arms of Annandale. His smile froze on his lips as he saw the old man's grave expression. It was reflected, he realised, in the faces of the other adults. His mother looked shocked, his father was shaking his head. Then, Robert heard the words. They sounded impossible, but the look of the adults proved their truth. He spoke loudly, without thinking, repeating those words in a question. 'The king is dead?'

They turned to look at him, standing there sopping wet, seaweed in his hair and a graze of sand on his cheek. He saw his mother's concern and his father's disapproval, before his grandfather's voice filled the silence.

'Come here and let me see you, boy.'

And those eyes, dark and fierce as a hawk's, were on him.

3

With the unforeseen arrival of the great lords, the castle's servants were kept busy late into the day, lighting fires in empty chambers, finding fresh linen for beds and clearing space in the stables. Nowhere was more frenetic than the kitchen, the cooks faced with turning a meal for the earl's already sizeable household into a grand feast for seven noblemen and their army of retainers. This number swelled, late in the afternoon, when another six men rode in through the castle gates. To Robert, watching from the window of the room he shared with his brothers, the day had the feeling of something portentous about it; something hushed and expectant that went beyond the news of the king's death. He wondered what this meant and what would now happen as down in the courtyard the guards pulled the gates shut behind the six riders. Somewhere in the castle a bell clanged. The last of the light was fading in the west, where lightning danced silently over the hills of Arran.

As the men entered the castle's hall, servants slipped in among them, pouring ruby-red wine into rows of pewter goblets. Outside, the sea's muffled boom was ever present, the salty tang mingling with the smells of food and wood-smoke. Three extra trestles and boards had been put out to seat everyone and the hall was crowded, the air stuffy with the heat from the fire in the cavernous hearth. On the wall behind the head table hung the earl's banner, emblazoned with the arms of Carrick: a red chevron on white. On another was strung a grand tapestry capturing, in twists of vivid silk, the moment Malcolm Canmore killed his hated rival, Macbeth, in battle and took the throne, beginning the illustrious dynasty of which the Bruce family were distant descendants. Robert had always thought the figure of the victorious king looked remarkably like his father.

He shifted impatiently outside the hall's doors as the guests filed through, the magnates settling into their places at the head table, their knights and retainers filling the benches around the other trestles. With Robert were his younger brothers, Alexander, Thomas and Niall, and his older sister, Isabel. When the last of the men, a youth with startlingly blue eyes, one of which winked at the waiting children, entered, Robert went to step through, determined to find a seat as close to his grandfather as possible. He was brought up short by his mother's voice.

'You'll be eating in your room this evening.'

Robert turned, thunderstruck by the announcement. The formidably tall figure of his mother, the Countess of Carrick, through whom his father had become earl of the wild county on their marriage, moved out of the shadows of the passage. Her abundant black hair was coiled on her head in a complex arrangement of braids, held in place by silver wire. Her white linen gown stretched smoothly over her stomach, swollen with her tenth child.

Her gaze fixed on Robert as she came towards him, holding the hand of a toddling girl. 'Do you hear me?'

'Mother . . .' began Isabel.

'Bid your father and grandfather good night, then upstairs with you.' This she said in Gaelic, which the children knew meant the conversation was over. She only spoke Gaelic when she was angry or addressing the servants. 'Go on now,' she said, switching back into French, her husband's preferred tongue.

Entering the hall, which was full of the low murmur of conversation, Robert approached his father, seated at the head table. He tried to catch his gaze, searching for signs of the anger he knew must come had his father been told he had shunned his day's training. The earl was deep in conversation with a bear of a man, draped in black furs. Robert recognised him as one of the men who had arrived late in the day. 'Good night, Father,' he murmured.

The earl glanced at him, but continued his intent conversation. Wondering, with a burgeoning sense of relief, if the day's extraordinary events meant Yothre hadn't told his father after all, Robert moved swiftly towards his grandfather, seated at the table's other end. The Lord of Annandale had picked up his little sister Christian, who had toddled in with their mother.

'What have you been feeding her, Lady Marjorie?' the old Bruce was saying as he set the child down with a grunt.

The countess smiled warmly at the old man. 'Come on now,' she chided, ushering her dallying children towards the door, where their nurse was waiting to lead them upstairs.

As Robert loitered hopefully, his father's harsh tones struck out.

'You heard your mother. Out!'

The Lord of Annandale glanced over at Robert, then focused on the earl. 'After you, son, the boy is head of this household. He should stay for this.' The old man nodded to Marjorie. 'With your permission, my lady.'

Before the countess could answer, Robert's father spoke again. 'Head of the household?' His voice was a whip. 'At eleven and unable to stay in the saddle with a lance? I wonder why I sent him to Antrim at all if that is the fruit of my labour.'

Heat prickled in Robert's cheeks and he lowered his head, thinking all the men in the hall could see his shame.

In truth, none of them was looking at him; their attention was divided between the two men at either end of the head table, whose eyes were locked in a silent war, one set black and fierce, filled with steel and arrogance, the other glacial blue, narrowed in contempt.

'I do not mind if Robert stays.' The countess moved to her husband and placed two calm hands on his shoulders.

The earl muttered something as his wife eased herself on to the cushioned chair set out for her, but Robert wasn't listening. He bit his lip to hide his grin as his grandfather gestured to the bench closest to him. The three men seated upon it, one of whom was the high steward himself, moved along to make room. Robert caught a jealous look from his brother, Alexander, which made the victory even sweeter, and then the rest of the children were led away. Glancing round as he sat, Robert realised he was next to the blue-eyed youth who had winked at him. He inclined his head somewhere between a nod and a bow, unsure whether the young man deserved simple politeness or deep respect. The youth smiled in return.

'Lord Steward,' began Robert's grandfather, his voice curt with authority, silencing the men around him, 'would you open our council by sharing with my son and the Lord of Islay the news from the royal court that we now know.' He nodded to the bear-like man in the furs, who had been in conversation with the earl. 'My summons informed you, Angus, of the black tidings that are the cause of our gathering this evening, but there are other details I could not risk revealing in a message and—'

'I believe, Father,' the earl cut across him, 'that some introductions are in order before we begin. Our comrades here may know one another by name, but not all by sight.' He didn't wait for an answer, but rose, his crimson robe settling around him as he extended a hand to a broad-shouldered man with black, oily hair, seated along the head table. 'Sir Patrick, Earl of Dunbar.'

Robert tore his gaze from his grandfather's rigid expression as his father continued.

'Sir Walter Stewart, Earl of Menteith, and his sons, Alexander and John.' The earl moved his hand to three men who shared the same red hair and ruddy, freckled skin. He then gestured to the aged Lord of Islay seated to his right, wrapped in the furs. 'Sir Angus Mór MacDonald.' He nodded down the table to a stocky man with a frank expression and the blue-eyed youth beside Robert. 'His sons Alexander and Angus Og.' At last, the earl motioned to the steward. 'And, of course, Sir James Stewart and his brother, John.' He seated himself beside the countess, his arms spread expansively. 'The Lady Marjorie and I are honoured to welcome you to our hall, despite the circumstances.' He inclined his head to James as the servants entered, bearing tureens of steaming venison stew, laced with fragrant thyme. 'Now, Lord Steward, do begin. I am anxious to hear your tidings in full.'

Robert stared around the table, putting names and histories to the faces before him. He knew he was in the company of some of the most powerful men in the kingdom, which was thrilling enough to take the sting out of the fact that his father had ignored him in the introductions.

The steward rose. 'You all now know the devastating truth that our noble king and lord, Alexander, died last month while riding to visit his queen at Kinghorn. He was separated from his escort in a storm. It appears his horse lost its footing and took him over the cliff. His neck was broken by the fall.'

Only the scrape of ladles against the tureens accompanied the steward's grave words, the servants waiting on the head table first. Robert's nose filled with the smell of meat as a servant spooned the thick stew on to the trencher in front of him. The slab of bread had a hollow in the centre to catch the juices. Glancing at his father, Robert saw he was sitting forward, listening intently. As he felt for a spoon, he realised he hadn't been given one. The servant had passed on down the line of men and Robert didn't dare call out. He hadn't eaten since that morning and his stomach wrenched.

'No sooner was his body discovered than the Comyns sought to take control.' A note of anger entered the steward's poised tone. 'Fortunately, many of the king's officials had been in Edinburgh for a council and we were able to halt their ambitions.' He nodded to the Earl of Dunbar. 'Sir Patrick and I, with the support of the Bishop of Glasgow, forced the election of a council of six guardians. They will rule until the throne is filled.'

'Who are the six?' asked the Lord of Islay, his rumbling voice filling the chamber. His French was blunt and awkward, Gaelic his native tongue.

'Myself,' answered the steward, 'the bishops of Glasgow and St Andrews, the Earl of Fife, and the heads of the Red and the Black Comyns.'

'A balance of power,' muttered the Earl of Carrick, digging his spoon into the stew. 'It is a pity you could not swing the scales more firmly in your favour, Lord Steward.'

'The Comyns hold some of the most powerful offices in our kingdom. They could not well be kept out.'

Robert was studying his dinner, wondering if he could eat with his hands, when a spoon slid into view from his right. Angus Og MacDonald took a small knife from a sheath on his belt, sliced a wedge out of his trencher and stuffed it in his mouth, his blue eyes glittering in the torchlight. Robert nodded his thanks to the Lord of Islay's son then thrust the spoon into the stew.

'We are all well aware of the Comyns' endeavours to control the throne,' continued James. 'They have always done so, even by force, as some of us well remember.' The steward's eyes moved to the Lord of Annandale, who nodded but said nothing. 'But there is something more worrying than their rush to power.' He returned to addressing the rest of the men. 'At court, I have learned that it pays to watch those closest to the king. For a time now, my men have kept an eye on dealings in the royal household. In the wake of the king's death, one of my spies overheard Sir John Comyn directing one of his knights to take a message to Galloway. Comyn spoke of Alexander's death and that the king had granted the release of a prisoner, petitioned for during the council. But there was one thing in particular that caught my man's attention. Comyn said, tell my brother-in-law that I will meet him soon, for the time is at hand when the white lion will blush.'

Several of the men spoke up at once.

The Earl of Carrick stared at the steward, his brow furrowing. 'Balliol?' he said sharply.

'We believe,' said James, nodding at the earl's expression, 'that the Red Comyn intends to put the Lord of Galloway on the throne.'

Robert's spoon halted mid-way to his mouth. He looked around the table at the men's grim faces, but none of them revealed how this startling conclusion had been reached. He put down his spoon as the men began to talk over one another. All at once, he got the connection. The lion on the banner of Galloway was white. The lion on the royal banner of Scotland was red. When the white lion will blush.

The Lord of Islay's deep voice sounded over the others. 'That is a grave charge to lay upon men who have taken the oath of fealty.' Angus Mór MacDonald leaned forward, his furs shifting on his huge frame. 'It is only two years since the lords of Scotland swore to recognise Alexander's grand-daughter as his heir. Margaret now holds the right to the throne. All of us made that pledge. I have no love for the Comyn men, but to accuse them and John Balliol of Galloway of breaking that oath . . .?'

'Who among us imagined we would have to fulfil it, especially after the king's marriage to Yolande?' countered Patrick of Dunbar, running a hand through his oily hair. 'The recognition of the king's granddaughter in Norway as his heir was a sensible precaution, not a reality any of us wanted to face. The fealty we swore on that day sits heavily upon all of our shoulders. How many will now sit back, content to be governed from afar by an infant queen in a foreign court?' He nodded to the steward. 'I have no doubt that Balliol, led by the ambitions of the Comyns, aims for the throne.'

'We must move swiftly,' said the Earl of Carrick. 'We cannot let the Comyns put their kinsman on the Stone of Destiny.' He banged his fist on the table, rattling dishes and goblets. 'We cannot let them take what is ours!' He stopped, glancing at the Lord of Annandale. 'What is yours, Father,' he corrected. 'If any man in this kingdom should take the throne it is you. Your claim is greater than Balliol's.'

'Not by primogeniture,' said the Earl of Menteith quietly, his eyes on the lord of Annandale, who had remained silent. 'By the law of first blood, Balliol's claim wins.'

'It isn't simply through blood that my father can claim the throne. He was designated heir presumptive by the father of the king!'

As the men began speaking at once, Robert stared at his grandfather. The old lord had spoken to him of this once, several years ago. Robert remembered well the look of pride in his grandfather's face as he had recalled in vivid detail the day King Alexander II had named him as his successor. They had been on a hunt and the king had fallen from his horse. He wasn't badly hurt, but the event clearly touched a concern, for he made all the lords with him get down on their knees in the dust of that forest track. There, he bade them recognise Sir Robert Bruce, whose veins ran with royal blood, as his heir should he die without issue. His grandfather had been eighteen at the time. Two years later, the king had a son and the royal line was secured, but the promise made remained embedded in the Bruce through all the years after. It had seemed, to Robert, just an incredible story in the telling; true, but relevant only to the distant past, like the stories of the Irish hero Fionn mac Cumhaill his foster-father had told him in Antrim. Now, sitting here in his father's hall with these great men, the story took on a reality that sent shivers through him.

His grandfather could be king.

As the conversation among the men grew louder, threatening to swell into argument, the Lord of Annandale rose, the firelight casting a red glow across his craggy face. 'Enough.' His voice cut through their words, silencing them to a man. 'I loved Alexander not only as a subject loves his king, but as a father loves a son.'

Robert saw a flush rise in his own father's cheeks at this.

'I promised to serve him with my last breath,' continued the lord, staring at each of them in turn. 'And that means fulfilling the oath that I, that all of us swore — to recognise his granddaughter as our queen. We must keep John Balliol from the throne. We must protect it. But for her. A man who breaks his oath isn't worth his breath,' he finished harshly, sitting back down.

'I agree,' said James Stewart in the quiet that followed. 'But how do we protect the throne? If the Comyns intend for Balliol to become king they will not listen to anyone's protests. I fear they wield enough power in the realm to make it come to pass, with or without the support of the guardians.'

'Councils and guardians are not the answer,' replied the Lord of Annandale. 'I thought about this long on our journey here. There is only one thing Comyn men understand and that is force.' He looked at the others. 'We must put a ring of steel around Galloway. With a series of attacks we will seize key strongholds held by the justiciar, John Comyn, and by the Balliols. With one stroke we can nullify Comyn presence in Galloway and discredit Balliol as a weak man who cannot even defend his own borders, let alone be king.'

Robert knew his grandfather's hatred of the Comyn men, who controlled vast areas of Scotland and had been influential in royal circles for generations. When the first Comyns crossed the English Sea with William the Conqueror they had done so not as lords of rich estates in Normandy, as Robert's ancestors had been, but as humble clerks. It was in this role that they thrived in England under the succession of kings that followed the Conquest, later coming north to Scotland. Through patronage and cunning their fortunes reached such magnitude that it was a Comyn, not a Bruce, who became the first Norman earl in Scotland and even secured a minor claim to the throne through marriage. The sons of clerks had no place in the nobility, Robert's grandfather had always maintained. Yet, still, the old man's hatred had always seemed to run far deeper than mere disdain. Robert had never fully understood it and, until now, had never thought to ask.

'We should contact Richard de Burgh,' said Robert's father. 'The Earl of Ulster will be only too willing to provide arms and soldiers. The men of Galloway have long been a thorn in his side with their attacks on Ireland. Also, we should inform King Edward. As Alexander's brother-in-law he will want to be involved in the succession as soon as he learns of his death.'

'The King of England was the first to be informed outside Scotland,' responded the steward. 'The Bishop of St Andrews sent a message to Edward in France the day Alexander's body was discovered.'

'All the more reason we should contact him ourselves,' said the earl, fixing on his father. 'If Margaret is brought here to rule she will need a regent to govern in her stead until she comes of age and an heir presumptive will have to be chosen. By seizing Comyn strongholds we prove our worthiness to be named in such a capacity. We also prove our strength. And strength,' he added firmly, 'is something King Edward appreciates.'

'We will petition Sir Richard de Burgh should the need arise,' agreed the Lord of Annandale. 'But there is no need to involve the king in our affairs.'

'I disagree,' countered the earl. 'With Edward's support we will be best placed to establish ourselves at the head of the new government.'

'King Edward is a good friend and ally, and our family owes much of our fortune to him, but he is his own man and will do what is in the best interests of his kingdom, and none other.' The old man's tone was implacable.

The earl continued to stare at his father for a moment longer, then nodded. 'I will raise the men of Carrick.'

'I too can spare some men,' said the Lord of Islay.

'We cannot all support you openly,' said James Stewart, 'not with arms. This kingdom has been divided enough over the years. I cannot let a blood feud become a civil war.' He paused. 'But I agree. The throne must go to Margaret.'

The Lord of Annandale sat back and took up his goblet. 'Then God grant us strength.'

4

Robert sank to his knees in the grass, gasping for air. Sweat trickled down his cheeks as he hung there, the blood thumping in his head. As the black spots in his vision cleared, he collapsed on to his back. He could hear breathless voices getting closer, muffled footsteps pounding the earth. Propping himself up on his elbows, he squinted into the sunlight and watched his three brothers come panting up the hill towards him.

Thomas came first, head down, concentrating on making the ascent. Niall was behind, scrabbling hand over foot, desperate to beat Thomas, despite being two years younger. Alexander was last by some distance, making his way up deliberately slow. Thomas won, slumping on the warm grass beside Robert, drawing breaths through his teeth. His tunic was drenched.

Some moments later, Niall joined them. 'How are you so fast?'

Robert grinned at his youngest brother and lay back, letting the pain fade from his muscles.

It was several minutes before Alexander reached them. His shadow fell across Robert. 'We would have been quicker taking the track home,' he said, clearly trying to stifle his breaths.

'We haven't been this way in years. Besides' – Robert's grin widened – 'I wanted to see if I could still do it.'

'You'll always beat us. You're the oldest,' murmured Thomas, sitting up. His hair, wet with sweat, had flopped into his eyes. It was curly and blond like their little sister Christian's. The rest of the children were dark like their mother, except for their fair half-sister, Margaret, married now and gone.

'Alexander's older than you and Niall,' replied Robert, 'and you both beat him.'

'I didn't try,' responded Alexander tautly. 'Now that you've won, let's go back.'

Robert sat up with a sigh. He was restless after weeks without training or schooling. The castle had been frantic with preparations for the attack, the adults tense and preoccupied. Each day, more knights arrived from towns and manors across Carrick, all vassals of their father. Robert knew most of them, for all, at one time, had paid homage to the earl, kneeling before him to take the sacred vow, their hands in his as they swore their undying loyalty in return for a grant of land. Just as their father held his lands by right of the king and was expected to serve in war, pay rents and perform duties such as the guarding of castles, the men of Carrick, by their act of homage, were required to fight for the earl. They brought with them their own squires and foot soldiers, each man armed, ready for the assault on Galloway.

The chaotic coming and going had put their father in a foul temper and earlier, Robert and his brothers had slipped out of the gates, alone. The freedom away from the oppressive atmosphere and the earl's harsh tones was a relief and the golden late afternoon was one of the most glorious since Robert had returned from Ireland. He wasn't inclined to waste it. 'Let's stay a while longer.'

'Someone will miss us. We've been gone almost an hour.'

'Who will notice? Everyone is busy.'

'Are you saying you won't come?'

Robert stared at his brother, standing above him, hands tight at his sides. Alexander had always been serious, even as a boy of Niall's age, but lately he had become as sombre as a monk. He wondered at the change, so noticeable since his return from Antrim. He'd thought it might have something to do with their father; perhaps the earl had been hard on his brother in his absence? But their father still seemed to be most pleased with Alexander and Thomas, respectively the most obedient and quiet of the five brothers. An answer struck him. With him and Edward in fosterage in Ireland, Alexander had effectively become the oldest son in the household. Now he was back, perhaps his brother felt robbed of that place? Robert couldn't feel sorry for him. Alexander had no idea how fortunate he was not to be the one on whom all the future hopes of their family were pinned. Especially, Robert mused darkly, when their father seemed determined to make it impossible for him to prove himself worthy of that great responsibility. 'Go if you want,' he said, lying back and closing his eyes. 'I'm staying.'

'You should both come,' said Alexander, addressing Thomas and Niall. 'Unless you want to feel Father's belt.'

Robert opened one eye a crack as Thomas pushed himself to his feet. He felt a knot of anger tighten in him as the two boys walked away down the hillside together. There was a time when Thomas, like Niall, would have done anything he said. He put his head back on the grass, listening to the thrum of bees in the heather and wishing Edward was here. But his brother, who was a year younger than him, had six months of his own fosterage left. Edward was a dervish with a practice sword, could climb trees higher than anyone, knew how to lie effectively and would dare any challenge. Things were dull without him.

Niall scrabbled over. 'What shall we do?'

After a pause, Robert jumped up, determined not to let Alexander ruin his afternoon. 'I'll teach you how to fight.' Sprinting to a clump of wind-blown trees, he snatched at a thin branch and pulled hard until it snapped. Breaking it in two, Robert stripped the leaves and handed the longer stick to his eager-eyed brother. 'We'll practise over here.' He motioned to a flat expanse of grass. In the distance, the tall hills of Carrick marched east. The lower slopes were clad with trees, but the crowns were bare. Robert used to think of them as bald old men, standing in a guarding ring around Turnberry. 'Like this,' he said, planting his legs apart and grasping the stick two-handed.

Niall, his face serious, imitated his brother. The knees of his hose were grass-stained.

Robert swung the stick slowly through the air, curving down towards the boy's neck. 'Now you block my blade.'

Niall swiped at Robert's stick.

'Too quick. You have to start slow. Like this.' Robert brandished the stick again, keeping it central to his body, then swept it round in a slow motion, first one side, then the other, now up and over his head. 'Then faster,' he said, the stick picking up speed in his hands, whistling as it carved the air. 'Pretend you're fighting someone,' he shouted over his shoulder.

'Who?' Niall called, running after him.

'An enemy. A Comyn man!'

Niall whipped his stick at the grass. 'Look, Robert! I got two!'

'Two?' Robert pointed his stick down the hillside. 'There's a whole army down there!' He let out a yell and charged down the steep slope, the stick high above his head. 'Death to all Comyns!'

Niall came behind him, his shouts exploding into laughter as Robert tripped and went sprawling. Robert grunted as his brother landed on top of him with a cry of victory. Together, the two of them rolled down the hillside, their makeshift weapons abandoned in the grass behind them. They came to a winded stop near the bottom, oblivious to the figure standing there watching them.

'What are you doing?'

At the unfamiliar voice, Robert's eyes opened. He realised he was staring at a girl, upside down. Pushing his brother off him, he faced her. The girl was whip-thin, with long black hair that twisted lankly around her bony shoulders like rat's tails. She wore a threadbare dress that had perhaps once been white, but was now grey with dirt and in her grubby hand she clutched a small sack. A heady smell of earth and flowers clung to her, but Robert was drawn mostly to her eyes, for they seemed the largest thing about her, overwhelming in her lean face. 'What business is it of yours?' he answered in Gaelic, her intense stare making him uncomfortable.

The girl cocked her head to one side. 'Who are you?'

'He's the heir of the Earl of Carrick, lord of these lands.'

Robert shot Niall a look to silence him, but the girl didn't seem to notice. Her probing gaze moved from his sweat-soaked tunic to his dirty face. Her lips twitched as her eyes came to rest on his hair. Raising his hand unconsciously, Robert found a sprig of heather lodged in his fringe. It crumbled in his fingers as the girl shrugged her shoulders.

'You do not look like an earl,' she said, turning and walking away across the grass.

Robert, watching her go, realised she wasn't wearing any shoes, not even the wooden clogs that the peasants who worked the fields wore. He knew the faces of everyone in Turnberry and many thereabouts: the retainers and vassals of his father, farmers and fishermen, and their wives and children, even merchants and officials from Ayr and other nearby towns. So why didn't he know this brazen girl, out walking in the wild on her own?

'How dare she talk like that,' muttered Niall.

Robert wasn't listening. 'Come on,' he murmured, moving through the grass towards the trees that clad the lower slopes of the hill.

'We're going the wrong way,' said Niall, glancing down the valley towards the sea, visible as a flat sheet of blue in the distance. He ran to keep up with his brother's long-legged stride. 'Robert!'

'Quiet,' said Robert sharply, as they entered the tree line. The girl was strolling unhurriedly along a stony track that followed the curves of a shallow river. Faint on the warm wind, above the burbling water he could hear her singing. At a crossing of stones, she lifted the skirts of her grey dress and skipped across, then threaded her way up the bracken-covered hill on the other side. Robert studied the ground, thinking of a hunt his grandfather had taken him on in the woods of Annandale. The old man had drilled him on the importance of adequate cover to conceal the hunter from his quarry. There was a copse of rowan trees, a small hillock and several boulders between him and the water's edge.

'We should go home, Robert,' whispered Niall, at his side. 'Alexander's right. Someone will miss us.'

Robert paused, his eyes on the girl. His mind conjured Alexander's prim expression and he felt a stab of irritation, imagining himself and Niall trailing obediently in through the castle gates. 'Do as I do,' he instructed, setting off at a run towards the trees, as the girl continued her ascent.

It was a game, but as serious as any hunt, the two boys darting from tree to hillock, from rock to bush, as they pursued the girl across the river, over the spine of the hill and down into the next valley, more densely wooded than the first. Now and then the girl would pause and look round, and the boys would throw themselves into the tangled undergrowth. She seemed to be leading them a winding course, over streams and under the curved arches of fallen trees. After a while, she climbed another steep bank.

As she disappeared over the ridge, Robert set after her. He looked back when Niall didn't follow. 'Come on!'

'I know where we are,' whispered Niall. His face, half shadowed by the swaying branches, was troubled.

Robert nodded impatiently. 'We're not far from Turnberry, I know. We'll see where she's going, then we'll go home.'

'Robert, wait!'

Not heeding his brother, Robert clambered up the bank. At the top, he caught a glimpse of grey in the woods below and slithered down, grasping at snaking roots for purchase. As he reached the bottom, he caught the tang of wood-smoke. He wondered if it was coming from the village, but Turnberry was two miles to the west. Ahead, the trees thinned out. Robert halted. The girl was heading into a green valley, overshadowed by a hulk of a hill that reared up, dotted with rocks and brown gorse. The crown was flushed pink in the sunset, but in the valley all was in shadow. Crouched at the foot of the hill was a small house of mud and timber. Smoke twisted from an opening in the roof. Beside the house, in a pen of bound stakes, two ponderous pigs rooted in the dirt. Robert looked round as his brother moved up behind him. 'It's her house,' he murmured, glancing back at the squat dwelling.

'That's what I was saying,' whispered Niall, looking at once vindicated and fearful.

The girl was almost at the door, passing under the shadow of a large oak. Through the thicket of leaves, Robert glimpsed several webbed shapes hanging from the branches. He had been in this valley a few times before and had seen that tree, but even Edward had never dared get close enough to find out what those strange webs were.

'Let's go,' pleaded Niall, taking hold of his arm.

Robert hesitated, his eyes on the house. The old woman who lived there was well known, for she was a witch. She had two dogs that Edward called Wolves of Hell. Alexander had once been chased and bitten by one. Robert had watched from the door to his parents' bedchamber as the physician had stitched the gash. He expected to witness his father's furious retribution – men sent to the old woman's house to kill the savage beast, but his father had merely gripped Alexander's shoulders until the boy winced. *Never go near her house again*, the earl had murmured fiercely. *Never*.

Robert was halfway to letting Niall pull him away when the girl stopped at the door. Turning, she raised her hand in their direction and waved. Robert's eyes widened. As she pushed open the door and disappeared inside, he heard the bark of a dog, then silence. Shrugging from Niall's grip, he made his way purposefully down the hillside. He was the heir of an earl, second only to a king in the ranks of the nobility. He would one day inherit land in Ireland and England, the rich domains of Annandale and the ancient county of Carrick, and the men who now came at his father's summons would one day kneel before him. He would go wherever he damn well pleased.

There was a loud splintering sound as he stepped on a rotten branch. Robert looked back, hoping Niall hadn't seen him start. He grinned boldly, then whipped round hearing a mad barking. From around the side of the house streaked two huge shadows. Robert caught yellow teeth and matted black hair, and then he was sprinting for the trees, Niall ahead of him, crying out in terror.

5

A grey dawn was breaking over the hills of Galloway. Mist gathered in the fields and cattle made strange shapes within the white. It would be a hot day, but without sun, the sky in the east promising only humid blankness. Gulls made slow circles over the brown waters of the River Urr as they searched the mud-banks. The water was low, sinking with the tide on the Solway Firth.

On the west bank, rising from a wide mound of earth, was a castle, protected by the river on one side and on the landward by a deep fosse. The bottom of the trench was layered with sticky, red clay and the only way across was by drawbridge, raised for the night. A double line of timber piers rose from the depths like a row of pallbearers at a funeral waiting to take their burden. At the foot of the piers, shrouded in gloom, invisible to the castle guards that walked the battlements far above, were seven men. The clay caked their hands and the arms and chests of their padded gambesons. It smudged their faces, shadowed by woollen hoods, and daubed their hose and boots. For over an hour they had been there, up to their knees in the sludge, their feet turning to stone with the cold. None spoke. Only the listless cries of the gulls and the muted conversation of the guards drifted down to them. Occasionally they caught one another's eyes; pools of shifting brightness, but they would look away soon enough, each cocooned in his own silent world, waiting for the morning bell, wondering if it would come before the mist concealing them lifted, or the sky lightened to a whiter shade of ash.

The minutes crawled by until, from the belly of the castle, a clanging arose. The men in the fosse stiffened at the noise. A few cautiously flexed their hands and shifted their weight in the oozing mud. The guards' murmurs became brusque shouts as they embarked on the daily task of lowering the drawbridge. It shuddered down on thick twists of rope and the men in the trench raised their heads to watch as the darkness bore down on them, the mists disturbed by its approach. The bridge landed on the tops of the piers with a thud. It was followed by the sound of bolts on the castle gates being drawn back and the footfalls of guards on the boards above.

One of the guards strolled to the edge of the drawbridge. Yawning loudly, he parted the front of his gambeson and opened up his drawers.

'Use the piss chute, Boli.'

The guard looked over his shoulder. 'His lordship's gone. No one's here to see.'

'Except us,' said another. 'And even your wife doesn't want to see your shrivelled cock.'

Boli grunted something obscene at his sniggering comrades and continued to piss into the fosse.

The yellow stream trickled down one of the piers, pooled briefly in the notched surface of the wood, then continued into the trench to run hotly over the hands of one of the men pressed against the timber. He turned his head.

As Boli was stuffing himself back into his drawers, there came a faint rumbling. Turning in the direction of the dirt track that led off from the drawbridge into woods, the guard saw two figures coming out of the mist. His comrades had seen them too. All had quietened and had their hands near their swords. Boli squinted into the murk as the rumbling grew louder. After a moment, he realised it was two men rolling a barrel. 'Halt,' he called, straightening his gambeson and going to meet them. He nodded to the barrel. 'What are you peddling?'

'The finest mead this side of the Solway,' replied one of the men, coming to a stop at the edge of the drawbridge. 'Our master has come for the market in Buittle, but he sent us with this gift for Lord John Balliol. Perhaps, if his lordship finds it to his liking, our master can provide more, at a reasonable price.'

'Sir John isn't here.' Boli walked around the barrel, inspecting it.

'What is it?' called one of the other guards, heading down the drawbridge, his hand around the pommel of his sword.

'Mead for Sir John.'

'None for us then?'

Boli grinned at the merchants. 'Well, I'll have a taste, just to see if it's worthy.' He unhooked a stained clay cup from his belt, where it sat beside a sheathed broadsword. 'And make it a lord's measure.'

The merchant took the cup while the other upended the barrel. Bending down, the man fiddled with the stopper. Out along the drawbridge, a red-daubed hand curled over the edge of the boards. All at once, the merchant straightened. With one brutal movement, he thrust his fist, with the cup still in it, into the guard's face.

The vessel smashed against Boli's jaw, shattering on impact and driving a shard of clay into his cheek. He was knocked to one side, blood flying from his shredded cheek and lips. As the other guard shouted and broke into a run, the second merchant raised his foot, revealing the glint of mail beneath his tunic. He kicked hard at the barrel. The wood split under his boot and he plunged his hands into the splintered opening, revealing cloud-like tufts of lamb's wool from which he yanked two short swords. He tossed one to his companion, just as Boli was recovering and drawing his own blade with a howl of anguished rage. As the men went at one another, more shouts sounded. The rest of the guards had seen the figures hauling themselves over the sides of the drawbridge.

The first man over had a knife clenched between his teeth. As a guard came at him, he hit the boards and rolled, grabbing the knife. The guard stabbed down. Throwing himself sideways, the man lunged up to shove the blade into the back of the guard's leg, between the straps of his greaves. As the guard collapsed with a cry, his attacker withdrew the knife and rammed it into his eye. The guard crumpled, his body convulsing. The attacker looked past the others, heaving themselves on to the bridge, to where the two with the barrel were still battling. He didn't have time to go for the weapons as another guard was charging at him. He ducked the first swing of the guard's sword, but the second caught him in the stomach. The padding in his gambeson absorbed some of the thrust, but it drove him backwards, hard. His foot came down into nothing and he plummeted into the trench.

Boli, blood pumping from his cheek where the shard of clay was still embedded, rammed his sword at the man who had wounded him, snarling in pain and fury. The attacker blocked the blow, then slammed his hand into Boli's cheek, pushing the shard in further. Boli yelled and tried to pull back, but his attacker rocked forward, using his weight against him. Shoving him in the chest with his free hand, the attacker toppled the bleeding guard into the fosse.

While his comrade battled on, the man dropped down beside the broken barrel and pulled more short swords from the lamb's wool inside. He sprinted along the drawbridge towards the others, unarmed except for their knives, which offered scant defence against the guards' broadswords.

Two had already been killed. But now, as the remaining attackers fell back to take the weapons from him, the odds evened.

As the attackers regrouped and stepped up their assault, a bell began to sound. The commotion had roused the rest of the castle guards. Arrows stabbed down from the battlements. One punched into the ground behind the man who had delivered the weapons to his comrades and was now running fast along the drawbridge. Vaulting a dead guard, he reached the gates, just as a defender raced out to meet him. The guard's momentum drove him on to the point of the attacker's sword. The blade pierced cloth and padding to puncture him in the soft flesh of his stomach. The attacker wedged his weight into the blade, driving it further in, then withdrew it with a rough twist. Leaving the guard to sink to his knees, clutching at the wound that blossomed red on his surcoat, upon which was stitched a white lion, the attacker ducked past him to the drawbridge winch inside the gates. He hacked at the rope, fronds of it unravelling beneath his blows. As it snapped and slackened, the man pulled a horn from inside his tunic. Setting it to his lips, he blew one single, solid sound.

The noise that followed the call of the horn began as a muffled pounding from within the woods bordering the castle. It increased to a drumming din as, from out of the fringes of the trees, came sixty or so men, twenty on horseback, the rest on foot, running hard along the track in the wake of the riders. As they neared the drawbridge, one rider broke from the pack and hurtled across, the iron-shod hooves of his white mare crashing against the wood. He had a broadsword in one hand and a shield strapped to his other arm, which bore a red chevron on white. Under his white cloak, emblazoned with the same device, he wore a mail coat and hose which tapered to points at his feet, and a great helm covered his face. The rider spurred his horse towards the gates. Scattering the remaining guards, who had been struggling to close them, he plunged into the courtyard.

Ignoring the fleeing guards, the rider pulled his mare to a stop outside a large hall. Hearing shouts and cries erupt behind him as more mounted men galloped in, he thrust his free hand against the doors and pushed. They creaked open enough for him to manoeuvre his horse inside, ducking his head under the lintel. Only a few torches were burning in the hall beyond, but there was enough light for him to see that the place was deserted. By the bowls scattered on a table, an overturned basket of laundry on the floor and the lighter patch on one wall where a tapestry had clearly hung, the place looked as though it had been abandoned in haste. The rider compelled the horse further in, her hooves on the flagstones echoing, hollow. Behind a table on a dais, an enormous blue banner decorated with a rearing white lion hung on the wall. Its one visible eye glared. Sheathing his sword, the rider pulled off his helm to reveal a hard-boned face and steel-blue eyes. Robert Bruce, Earl of Carrick, met the lion's gaze. 'Balliol,' he murmured.

The earl could hear fighting outside, but the castle was only defended by a small garrison. It was clear its chief occupant was no longer here, despite rumours to the contrary. Leaning over, he placed his helm on one of the trestles and boards, and removed his shield from his arm. His mare was champing at the bit, her mouth frothy. Kicking his feet from the stirrups, Bruce dismounted, his mail settling with a shiver of metal. Moving to one of the low-burning torches, he swiped it from its bracket and strode to the dais. Jaw set, he climbed the steps, the flames excited by the air. He paused, his eyes on the white lion, then thrust the torch to the bottom of the banner. The frail silk caught instantly and the earl stepped back, a small smile, malicious and childlike, playing about his mouth.

He was standing there, watching the flames spread greedily across the banner, when he felt something punch into his back. The earl jolted, dropping the torch, which went rolling across the dais, the flames gusting. He staggered round to see a man, eyes wide, holding a kitchen knife. Realising his armour had done its job and turned the blade, Bruce moved in with a snarl, swinging a mailed fist into the man's face. The man reeled back off the dais and crashed into a table, which shattered beneath him, sending silver bowls ringing across the floor. The earl stamped down the dais steps, drawing his broadsword. Kicking aside a stool, he loomed over the man, who lay on his back among the wreckage of wood.

'Please!' groaned the man, holding up his hands. 'Please, I—'

The earl stabbed down, forcing the tip of his broadsword into the man's throat. The man uttered a strangled gurgling sound that ended in a dark eruption of blood. It spewed from his stretched mouth and the wound as the earl ground the blade in until it struck stone and would go no further. The man's body thrashed for a few moments, then shuddered to still. As the earl bent to wipe his blade on the man's tunic, the doors opened and a company of men entered.

At the head was Bruce's father. The old Lord of Annandale had his helm clasped under one arm, his silver hair almost translucent in the light seeping through the doors. His surcoat bore a blue lion, the ancient arms of the Bruce family from the time of King David I, who granted them the lordship of Annandale. Pinned over his heart was a dried brown leaf: a piece of palm frond from the Holy Land, a pious reminder of their time on crusade. For the earl it sparked a memory of an ochre vista stretching beyond the walls of the crusaders' capital at Acre beneath a vermilion sky, calls to prayer echoing from minarets to be drowned by church bells. They had fought against the Saracens under Lord Edward's banner and he had rewarded them for their loyal service, elevating their already considerable status in England. The earl felt suddenly determined that those glorious days would not be confined to a dried and brittle keepsake, pinned to his father's chest.

The lord took in Balliol's banner, curling into flames behind his blood-stained son. 'The garrison has surrendered. Buittle is ours.'

A sharp cry rose over his words. It came from a young man, one of several being held by the knights with the lord. He wrenched from his captors, taking them by surprise, and ran to the man sprawled in the ruins of the table. Dropping down, he thrust the cracked boards aside and cradled the man's head in his hands. The pool of blood seeped into his clothes. His eyes moved to Bruce, whose sword still had a wide smear of red on it. 'Bastard,' he breathed, rising. '*Bastard!*'

The earl's eyes narrowed. 'Kill this whelp,' he said, gesturing to two of his vassals, both knights from Carrick.

The knights started forward, but the Lord of Annandale's voice cut across them. 'I said it is over. The garrison are free to leave.'

The knights looked from the earl to the lord, their weapons lowering.

'You can go,' said the Lord of Annandale to the youth, oblivious to the fury in his son's face. 'No harm will come to you.'

'Not without my father,' said the young man, forcing the words through his teeth. 'He was Sir John Balliol's steward. He deserves proper burial.'

After a pause, the lord nodded to two of his men. 'Help him.'

Bearing his father's bloody body, aided by two knights from Annandale, the young man passed the Earl of Carrick. 'The curse of St Malachy for ever upon you!' he hissed.

Bruce gave a bark of scornful laughter. 'Malachy? Save your threats for someone who believes in such things,' he rasped, stepping forward.

The lord stopped him. 'Leave him.' It was spoken forcefully.

But as he watched the young man carry the corpse into the ashen morning, the Lord of Annandale's face was full of fear.

6

'Please, his lordship is in prayer. If you will wait in the parlour I can—'

Ignoring the monk's protestations, John Comyn pushed open the doors of the Church of St Mary. The nave stretched before him into dusky shadows perfumed with incense. Letting his eyes become accustomed to the gloom, he noticed a figure halfway down, kneeling in front of an altar alight with candles. As Comyn started forward, the monk moved in front of him.

'Sir, I beg you. He asked not to be disturbed.'

'He'll make an exception,' said Comyn, heading purposefully towards the kneeling figure.

The figure raised his head abruptly as Comyn approached. The anger in his face vanished, replaced by relief. 'Brother,' he called, rising and holding out his hands in greeting. 'Thank the Lord, you received my message.' He waved away the monk who was lingering uncertainly, then turned his gaze back to Comyn, appraising the bulk of armour beneath the man's cloak, which was emblazoned with the arms of the Red Comyns: three white sheaves of wheat on red. 'You are a tonic for a troubled mind.'

As he met John Balliol's eager eyes, Comyn felt a stab of resentment. It was hard to suppress, even as he accepted his brother-in-law's embrace. Comyn's attention moved over Balliol's shoulder, caught by the altar. Surrounded by a ring of candlelight, beneath a slender statue of the Virgin, was an ivory casket. As Comyn saw it his resentment flared into anger. Galloway – which Balliol would assume full lordship over when his mother died – was being invaded by enemies and here the man was on his knees in this isolated monastery, praying before his dead father's heart. If Comyn set his finger upon his own family's pedigree and followed the creeping lines of Latin back, he too could claim descent from the royal house of Canmore, just not as directly as Balliol could. How slippery a thing blood was; how arbitrarily it chose who would rise to power. He quashed the thought. The Red Comyns had always done well behind the throne. The king was but an instrument, as his father used to say. They were the musicians.

Balliol followed his brother-in-law's gaze to the ivory casket. He nodded soberly, mistaking Comyn's preoccupied expression for compassion. 'It was the first thing my mother took from Buittle when we left. She still sets a place for it at dinner every night.' Raising his hands to encompass the thick-set pillars that formed arches down both sides of the nave, Balliol turned in a half-circle. 'It is incredible, isn't it, what love can inspire? My mother built this abbey in my father's memory. I told her to bury his heart here when the high altar was finished, but she refuses to be parted from that casket, not until her own passing when she has ordered that it be buried with her. I wonder at her strength, a woman widowed in the winter of her life, to complete such a creation as this.' Balliol's faraway stare fixed on Comyn, coming back into sharp focus. 'Do you think they could destroy it?'

'Destroy what?' questioned Comyn, still thinking of the casket with the former Lord of Galloway's heart trapped inside.

'This place.' Balliol was pacing now. 'Will those sons of whores come for me here?'

Comyn watched Balliol thrust a hand through his hair, chestnut like his sister's, who Comyn had married eleven years earlier. The similarity ended there. Balliol was possessed of neither his sister's passion nor her shrewd mind. Comyn had always thought the women of the Balliol family had been endowed with the men's share of mettle. 'Do you have word on their position?'

'Yes, I have word,' responded Balliol bitterly. 'The Bruces have taken Buittle.'

Comyn digested the bad news slowly. The Bruces' attacks on the castles at Wigtown and Dumfries had struck at the roots of Comyn power in south-west Scotland, but although the capture of the two strongholds had wounded the family's pride, it had done little damage to the Comyns' long-term plans. Buittle, Balliol's chief stronghold, was another matter. 'How do you know the castle has fallen? In your message you said you were leaving for Sweetheart Abbey as a precaution, when the Bruce men entered Galloway.'

'The son of my steward informed me. I left his father at Buittle to safeguard the possessions I could not carry, along with a garrison. My steward was killed in the attack by that bastard the Earl of Carrick.' Balliol spat the name. 'Along with eight of my men. Eight!'

'When did this happen?' pressed Comyn.

'A fortnight ago.'

'And you have heard nothing of the Bruces' movements since?'

'From what we can gather they have paused at Buittle.'

Comyn frowned thoughtfully. 'Your steward's son, is he still here?'

'Yes. I recruited him for the army of Galloway. His hatred of the Bruces will make him an able fighter in the reckoning that will come.'

'I want to speak to him.'

Balliol followed as Comyn headed down the nave. 'Of course, but first let us make arrangements for your men. There is a field beyond the abbey precinct where they can make camp. I will have one of the monks show you.'

'That will not be necessary. I have only my squires with me.'

Balliol halted. 'Squires? Then where is your army?'

Comyn turned to face him. 'There is no army. I came alone.'

'But in my message I told you I needed men and swords to stop the Bruces' advance. My vassals are scattered, I have had no chance to muster a resistance. How can I fight alone?' Balliol's voice rose in pitch and temper. 'I was relying on you, both as my brother and as Justiciar of Galloway.' He threw up his hands. 'Why in God's name are you even here?'

'Let me speak to this man and I will tell you.'

Balliol went to argue, but seeing Comyn's obdurate expression, he motioned to the church doors. 'Come then,' he said tightly, 'Dungal will be at his father's grave. He has hardly left it.'

Blinking in the light, harsh after the gloom of the church, Balliol led the way through the monastery. The midday sun was unkind on his face, high-lighting the shadows around his eyes, accentuating the downward curve of his mouth and the pockmarks of a childhood disease that scarred his cheeks. At thirty-seven he was five years younger than Comyn, but he looked older, wearing the years heavily in his blemished skin and thinning hair. 'Are the other guardians even aware of what is happening in Galloway?' Balliol sounded sour. 'Do they not care?'

'Reports coming to Edinburgh have been confused, but everyone at court now knows of the Bruces' assault.'

'Well, they have made no attempt to hide it,' responded Balliol. 'I have heard they have been marching through the countryside, banners flying.' He balled his hands into fists as he strode through the cloisters. Two of the lay brothers who helped the monks run the monastery were picking herbs in the garden, which was parched by the July sun. 'Indeed, it seems they want the whole of Scotland to know what they are doing.'

'They want to discredit you,' said Comyn, after a pause. 'I believe that is the motive behind their attacks. I feared the Bruces must have discovered our plan when the first reports came in. Now, with the fall of Buittle, I am certain of it. That meddler James Stewart has eyes and ears everywhere.'

'You should have been more careful!'

'Our intention to set you on the throne could not have remained secret for long.' Comyn scowled. 'Although admittedly we would have been better prepared to resist those who would compete with us if its discovery had been later.'

'The Lord of Annandale isn't competing for the throne. He has declared himself to be fighting in the name of the Maid of Norway.'

'Maid of Norway?'

'It is what they are calling Alexander's granddaughter, Margaret.' Balliol stared fiercely at his brother-in-law. 'All will soon see him as some kind of saviour and me at best a brigand and at worst a treasonous wretch who has broken his oath and intends to steal the throne from a child! I might have lost everything, John!'

'This isn't finished yet, brother, and I wouldn't worry about your reputation. The Lord of Annandale is doing far greater damage to his own. By their aggressions on Galloway the Bruces threaten to undermine the entire realm. I am making sure the growing resentment towards them is being used to our advantage.'

Balliol didn't respond, but fell into a tense silence as they passed out of the cloisters beneath a covered walkway that led to a gate in the precinct wall. Beyond, yellow fields rippled away, distorted by heat. The air was thick with insects that swarmed around the two men as they made their way across to the graveyard at the back of the towering church, the red brick walls of which cast a shadow across rows of wooden crosses. As they drew nearer, Comyn saw a young man crouched beside a mound of freshly turned earth.

The youth got to his feet at their approach. 'My lord,' he said, bowing to Balliol and glancing apprehensively at Comyn. 'I have done my chores. I swear my prayers for my father aren't interfering with my duties.'

'I'm not here to punish you,' replied Balliol. 'This man is my brother-in-law, Sir John Comyn, Justiciar of Galloway and Lord of Badenoch. He wishes to speak to you.'

As the young man glanced at him again, Comyn saw how sunken his eyes were. He looked as though he hadn't slept in days. Comyn guessed he was in late adolescence. He gestured for the young man to follow him, away from the grave. 'Dungal, is it?'

'Yes, sir, Dungal MacDouall.'

'Tell me about the attack on Buittle, Dungal.'

Comyn listened as the young man spoke. His voice, at first tentative, soon became clearer and stronger, until, as he described the murder of his father at the hands of the Earl of Carrick, it was rough with fury.

'And you came here to tell Sir John what had befallen Buittle?' said Comyn, when Dungal had finished.

'Not at once,' responded Dungal. 'The rest of the men who were freed made for Sweetheart Abbey to inform Sir John and Lady Dervorguilla. I put my father's body in their care and volunteered to keep watch on the castle to see where the Bruces were headed next.'

'How long did you stay?'

'Ten days.'

'And in that time the Bruces made no move to leave?' Comyn turned to Balliol. 'When they seized Wigtown and Dumfries the Bruces established a garrison in both and then moved on, staying no more than a few days in either. Clearly, something detained them at Buittle.'

'A rider came,' said Dungal slowly, staring at Comyn. 'I think on the fourth morning after they had taken the castle. I got a good view of him from my hiding place in the woods. He was let in at once.' Dungal lowered his head to Balliol. 'I am sorry, I had forgotten this.' His eyes drifted to his father's grave.

'Did the rider wear any devices?'

'His shield was gold, with a blue and white chequered band.'

'The arms of the Stewarts,' said Balliol at once.

Comyn forced back his rising ire at the proof the high steward was somehow involved. 'The time fits,' he said tightly. 'My guess is the Bruces learned from this rider what the rest of us in court now know and that is why they paused.' He pushed from the wall, motioning for Balliol to follow. 'I believe the battle is over,' he said quietly, as they walked the uneven ground between the graves. 'For now.' Comyn stopped, some distance from Dungal and faced Balliol. 'It isn't public knowledge yet, but it soon will be. It is why I came. I wanted to tell you in person.'

'Tell me what?'

'The queen is pregnant, John.'

Balliol looked as though he had been struck.

Comyn continued. 'She must have conceived just weeks before Alexander's death. The midwife who examined her proclaimed her to be five months into her term. She had apparently shown symptoms before, but it had been presumed she was suffering with grief after the king's passing.'

'Then it was all for nothing? All the risk. All for nothing?' Balliol stared at Comyn, his face contorting. 'I have lost my home, my men. My respect!'

'It isn't over,' said Comyn sharply.

'Of course it is. This isn't some babe in a foreign court. This child will be the king's true heir!'

'Yes, but this child, boy or girl, will have to be governed by a regency council until they come of age.' Comyn followed Balliol's eyes with his own, forcing his brother-in-law to look at him. 'We still have time.'

7

Tightening his grip on the reins, Robert pulled Ironfoot's great head back as the horse fought against his hold. He swore at the animal through gritted teeth, using a word one of his foster-brothers in Ireland had taught him, then eased the lance into position.

'Shorten your reins!' barked Yothre.

Murmuring the word again for his instructor, but keeping his eyes fixed on the target, Robert jabbed his heels into the charger's muscular sides. Ironfoot set off across the beach, moving swiftly into a gallop. The boy crouched forward to match the furious rhythm. Ahead, the shield fixed to one side of the quintain's pivoting beam was coming up rapidly. The sand-bag that hung from the beam's other side bulged expectantly. With a thrust of his arm, Robert lunged. Pain shot through his fingers and, at the last second, his aim went wide. He swept on past the quintain, the lance striking the air above the shield.

Robert jerked on the reins as Ironfoot plunged on, swerving towards the sea, today a serene turquoise. Yothre was shouting instructions. Planting his feet in the stirrups, Robert heaved backwards, bringing the horse to an abrupt and ungainly halt that almost pitched him from the saddle.

'Poor,' shouted Yothre. 'Again.'

Robert held the horse steady, recovering his balance. He was breathing hard and the pain in his fingers was biting. Two of them were bound in a splint, making his grip on the lance that much weaker. During a training session the week before he had struck the quintain at a bad angle and with such force that his fingers had been bent back against the shaft, so hard the bones had snapped. He paused there, ignoring for a moment Yothre's shouts for him to turn, thankful for the cool, salty wind. It was September, but the heat was as fierce as July. The long summer had been burned into his skin and the day he turned twelve had come and gone without word from his father or grandfather. They had been away for three months. He wished he were with them, serving his family, but he knew he wasn't ready. Not yet. Easing the lance into position, Robert turned the horse and lined up with the target. Determined.

'Concentrate!' called Yothre.

Robert kicked the warhorse's sides. Turnberry Castle filled his vision, but he saw it only as a hulking shadow crowned by a wedge of sky, all his attention focusing in on that small shield, coming up fast. He lunged with a shout and rammed the point home, every part of him and the horse moving in unison, for one graceful moment fluent with one another. The lance struck the centre of the shield with a *thock* and the target was knocked aside. The pivoting beam spun round fast. Robert ducked, expecting the sandbag to come swinging into the back of his skull, but he was past. He grinned broadly, exhilaration shooting through him.

'Good, Master Robert. Again.'

Without letting Ironfoot break canter, Robert steered in a wide circle, itching for another shot, determined to do it just like the last. The warhorse was moving well, obeying every flick of the reins, every nudge of his knees. It was like riding his palfrey again, only faster and more thrilling. The shield had swung round almost to its starting position. Robert spurred the horse into a gallop, rose up. Aimed. Out over the water came a shriek and a mad whirl of wings as two gulls spiralled from the waves, fighting over a fish. Ironfoot's head tossed up at the piercing sound. Veering away, he bolted up the beach.

Across the sand they went, away from Yothre's running form, up over the dunes and across the boggy fields that surrounded the castle. Robert, bouncing wildly in the saddle and realising Ironfoot wasn't going to be halted so easily, threw the lance aside. The horse vaulted a narrow stream without warning. As he was flung forward, both of Robert's feet came out of the stirrups. He lost his grip on the reins and grabbed hold of the high pommel on the front of the saddle. The horse ploughed on, heading for the woods that led into the hills beyond Turnberry. Robert clung on, trying to match the warhorse's rhythm, his legs flapping uselessly at the animal's sides, struggling for purchase in the swinging stirrups. The trees were looming. All at once they were in, under the canopy, branches whipping past.

The horse continued his crazed path, further and deeper in. A branch snapped across Robert's face, stinging his cheek. He ducked, closing his eyes to avoid being blinded by another. Lunging forward, he grabbed at the reins. His fingers brushed them, but couldn't get purchase. Robert rocked sideways with a shout as Ironfoot swung left to avoid a tree. His shout became a yell as his knee clipped the trunk on the way past. All his attention diverted by the bolt of pain, he didn't see the branch rushing up in front of him. As it struck him, he was thrown back over the saddle. He landed hard, sending up a cloud of dust and leaves. Ironfoot continued on, crashing through the trees, leaving Robert on the forest floor, motionless.

Light danced behind his eyes. He struggled to open them and flinched at the brightness. Turning his head to one side he saw a broken line of bracken, behind which rose trees. Fungus had bubbled up out of the trunks, fleshy and poisonous. Something was on his face. He could feel it creeping down his cheek. As he tried to push himself up his head pounded so hard he thought he would vomit. Collapsing back, Robert lay still, letting his vision settle. Far above him the trees made webs of light. Lifting his hand to his face, he touched his forehead. His fingers came away red. As the hammering in his head dulled to a monotonous thudding he felt other pains erupting. His knee was a flare of agony. Planting his hands in the soil, Robert raised himself up, gasping with the effort. His broken fingers throbbed. The knee of his hose was ripped open, the edges dark with blood. He could see the skin beneath, raw and wet. He looked away, trying to get his bearings. Trees hemmed him in on all sides, stretching into green shadows. It had been late afternoon on the beach, but day had since become coppery dusk. He realised that the woods around him were silent. He could hear the creaking of branches and the wind in the leaves, but there was no birdsong, no sounds of small animals in the undergrowth. Then he heard it – a low growl.

Looking to his left, Robert saw the bracken moving. His head jerked round at a snarl, this time from the right. Propping himself up on his hands, fighting off waves of pain, he tried to stand, then froze as the bracken parted and a large, black head emerged. For a second he thought it was a wolf, but the angular jaw and square head were those of a hound. Its lips curled back, revealing liver-coloured gums ribbed over bared teeth. Its shoulder muscles flexed as it stalked towards him, head thrust forward. Out of the bushes to his right came another, with bloodshot eyes that held a wild look. Robert shouted fiercely at them, but it only made their growls deeper. His fingers scrabbled through the leaves, searching for a rock, a stick, anything. There was a harsh call somewhere off through the trees. Both dogs flopped down on their bellies at the sound. The wild-eyed one whined.

An old woman appeared, forcing her way through the undergrowth, a gnarled stick in one hand, a leather pouch in the other. She wore a brown cloak, the bottom of which was covered in briers and caked with mud. Her hair fell thick down her back, dark beneath, but streaked white at the roots. Twigs and leaves were tangled in it. Her face was brutal. Sharp cheekbones made ridges over a humourless mouth, before sweeping up to a prominent brow, creased with furrowed lines of sweat and dirt. Robert had seen her before in these woods and once, long ago, in the village. She was the witch from the house in the valley and the hounds, looking lovingly at her, were the dogs that had chased him and Niall.

The woman halted as she saw him, her brow knotting in study. She made a hissed sound through her teeth that made Robert's stomach spasm, but it wasn't directed at him. At the noise the dogs rose and loped to her side. As she came towards him, Robert saw something moving inside the pouch, limbs or scales sliding against the leather. Planting her stick against a tree, she bent over him, holding out a withered hand. Robert recoiled, repelled by the smell of her, but, more than that, afraid to let her touch him. The woman's eyes narrowed to slits.

'Stay there then,' she spat, 'and let the wolves take you.'

Her Gaelic was broad and pure, as if she had never spoken anything else. It was richer than his, whose mouth had been forming itself around French, Scots, Latin and Gaelic since he learned to speak. Snatching up her stick, she headed through the bushes, the dogs following. As Robert tried to push himself up his knee was lanced with pain. 'Wait!'

The woman kept on walking. She was almost out of sight, the branches falling into place behind her.

'Please!'

There was silence, then the undergrowth shifted as she returned. Robert held out his hand. Without a word, the woman grasped it. The strength in her grip surprised him. He came up quickly, too quickly, biting back a cry as the weight came down on his knee.

'Here,' she said roughly, handing him the stick.

Robert took it, thinking of an image he had once seen in a book of a sorcerer tracing a circle in the ground with a staff, a black demon rising out of fire and smoke in its centre. He half expected the stick not to feel like wood at all, but it did. The shaft was warm where she had been gripping it.

Together, the woman holding his arm on one side, him digging the staff into the ground on the other, they made their way slowly through the woods, the dogs roaming ahead. After a time the trees thinned out and the ground sloped into a sheltered valley. As he saw the house under the hill, Robert realised Ironfoot had taken him further into the woods than he'd reckoned. Wincing with every step, he looked up as they approached the oak that towered over the dwelling. This close he had a clear view of the webbed shapes hanging from the branches. The webs were twigs, stripped of leaves and bark, their thin limbs, bone-white, bound together to make crude cages. Hanging in the centre of each like misshapen spiders, from lengths of braided twine, were objects. Robert saw a scrap of yellow cloth, a tiny silver dagger, its blade tarnished, a weathered roll of parchment, then the woman was pushing open the door of the house and they were moving inside.

A fire crackled and spat in the centre of the room, throwing a pool of amber light into cramped shadows beyond. The dogs lay down beside the flames, panting. As his eyes grew used to the shifting light, Robert saw that the chamber was crowded with things. Pots and pans clustered from the beams above, skimming the woman's head in places. In between were bundles of herbs and flowers. Robert felt as though he were deep under-ground, looking up at the roots of plants growing down. The earthy smell made his head swim. There was a pallet against the far wall, heaped with furs. Skulls and bones were scattered on the floor in front of it, animal, he realised after a pause. There were smooth pebbles from the beach, tools made of wood and stone, and a brace of birds, their dead eyes like tiny beads. Most surprising of all, stacked in one corner by a bundle of skins, was a pile of books. Some were clearly very old, the boards coming away. Robert glanced at the woman, who had set her squirming pouch on a shelf beside a row of clay pots and several wicked-looking knives. He edged towards the books, intrigued. He and his brothers and sisters had been taught to read and write, but these were skills usually reserved for the clergy, the nobility and some merchants and wealthy tradesmen. This woman didn't fit any of those groups. But neither did she fit any other; a woman of property and possessions, living on her own in the wilderness.

The woman returned from the shadows holding a stool, which she placed before the fire. 'Brigid!'

Robert started as the heap of furs on the pallet moved and a figure unravelled from within. It was the girl he had followed here months ago. She yawned deeply and rose from the bed, her grey dress falling crumpled around her. Her large eyes fixed on him and filled with curious surprise.

'Sit,' said the old woman to Robert, taking the stick, 'and fetch me water,' she said in the same breath to the girl.

As Robert sat, the girl headed out and the woman busied herself at a shelf, grinding fistfuls of herbs with a pestle. A bitter smell rose. The girl returned carrying a bucket, her thin arms taut with the weight. She set it down by the fire then crossed to the old woman. The two of them murmured something Robert couldn't hear. He watched apprehensively as the girl came towards him, holding a wad of linen. Crouching beside the bucket, she dipped the cloth inside. Her dress hung off her gaunt frame and he could see down the front of it to the bones that splayed across her chest. She rose and moved to him, the linen bunched and dripping between her fingers.

Robert drew back as she stretched out her hand. 'I can do it.'

Letting him take the cloth, Brigid hunkered down beside the fire, wrapping her arms around her bony knees. One of the dogs raised its head and whined at her. Ignoring it, she watched as Robert wiped the blood from his face. 'Perhaps he was attacked?' she ventured, addressing the old woman.

'I came off my horse,' answered Robert.

'He is an earl, you know.'

'The son of an earl,' responded Robert shortly, discomforted by the way the girl was speaking as if he couldn't hear.

'I know who he is,' said the old woman, coming out of the shadows with a bowl of dark matter. 'I delivered him.'

Robert went still, the cloth pausing against his cheek. When he spoke his voice sounded loud in his ears. 'No. That's not true. My mother had the same midwife for all her children.' He shook his head, angered by the woman's unchanging expression. 'She wouldn't have let a . . .' He trailed off.

The old woman didn't respond, but scooped out a handful of the herb mixture. Parting the shredded cloth of his hose she slapped it thickly on his skinned knee, making him wince, then handed him the stick. 'Take him to the woods, Brigid. He knows his way home.' Her eyes bored into his. 'Don't come here again,' she said fiercely. 'You, or any of your family.'

Robert let himself be led by the girl out into the dusk. The air was fresh after the oppressive heat inside and he shivered as he passed beneath the oak, adorned with its slow-turning webs. His head felt clearer and the cold of the herbs had numbed his knee, although every step still felt like a needle in his bone. He glanced at the girl, walking in silence beside him as he limped up the hill. 'Is she your mother?'

'My mother's dead. I came to live with Affraig in the winter. She's my aunt.'

'Is she a witch?'

Brigid lifted her shoulders in answer.

Robert was about to ask if she thought her aunt had been lying about what she had said, when he heard shouts in the distance. He caught his name in the calls. 'That's my instructor,' he told the girl.

'Why do you need an instructor?'

'He's teaching me to ride. For war.'

The girl's lips split in a grin. 'You should find a better one,' she said, skipping away across the grass.

Robert watched her go, then headed into the woods, answering the calls with a shout of his own.

With Yothre in the search party were several servants from the castle and Robert's brothers. Niall saw him first. He gave a cry of relief and ran towards him, then came to an abrupt halt, looking shocked. Yothre came striding in behind, thrusting branches out of his way.

'Where's Ironfoot?' Robert asked, as his instructor put a thick arm around his waist to support him. He kept hold of the stick.

'We found him wandering loose near the village,' said Thomas breathlessly, coming over with Alexander and the servants. 'We've been searching for hours. What happened?'

'I fell.'

'But where have you been?'

'Come on,' said Yothre brusquely, 'let's get him home. No doubt his mother will want the physician to look at him.'

All the way back to the castle, Robert's head was filled with the old woman's revelation. He was certain it was a lie, although he didn't see what purpose it would serve her to speak false, except perhaps to be cruel. But wasn't that what witches did? Toyed with men's emotions and preyed on their weaknesses? Robert's speculations were cut short as they neared Turnberry and saw a company trailing in through the castle gates.

The men had returned from war.

Robert, trying to walk faster, grimaced in pain and frustration as his brothers ran away ahead of him, calling out in joy. Some of the men looked round at the boys' shouts, their faces weary and sunburned. There were two carts drawn by oxen behind them. Robert let out a breath of relief as he caught sight of his grandfather in the midst of the host. Some way ahead of the Lord of Annandale rode the Earl of Carrick on his white mare. Robert felt a confusion of emotions as he saw his father, then was distracted by one of the carts that was trundling past. He and Yothre stopped, seeing ten or more men on the back.

Robert's eyes moved over their soiled clothes and bandaged limbs. One had a wad of cloth bound over his right eye, his cheek below crusted with blood. Another had a stump where his left hand used to be, the bulb of his wrist swaddled in linen, his face waxy white. Most were sitting hunched against the sides of the cart, lolling listlessly with the motion. Three were laid out in the middle, one of whom was covered over with a blanket, only his bare feet, livid and swollen, visible. Huddled there, decorated with their ugly wounds, they had a strange blankness about them, as if, like their bodies, their souls were no longer whole. Robert couldn't take his eyes off them, even as Yothre led him away and the cart rumbled on, taking the injured men towards the castle. He had seen mutilated bodies once before: outlaws strung up in cages outside a castle on the way to Annandale, their flesh eaten by birds. But there had been something unreal about them. They weren't people he knew.

8

Robert limped across the room, careful not to disturb the sleeping forms of his brothers. Alexander was curled on his side, his face in the nightlight's glow tense with some inner concern. Thomas was on his back, one arm flung over the edge of his bed, the blanket tangled around his legs. Passing Niall, Robert saw his brother's eyes were open, watching him. Putting a finger to his lips, he slipped out of the door.

He headed down the gloomy passageway, using the wall for support, the boom of the sea masking his footsteps. He passed the room his sisters shared. Further down, an urgent crying was coming from the small chamber adjacent to his parents' room. The door was ajar and candlelight spilled out. Robert edged closer, his knee beneath the tight wrap of linen throbbing. He glimpsed the back of the wet nurse as she turned in a slow circle, cradling his sister Matilda, the source of the wails. Then he was moving on, heading for his parents' room.

He paused outside, dreading to hear his father's voice. Perhaps the council was finished already? But, no, it was still early and he hadn't heard his father's footsteps on the stairs. There was silence beyond. Robert pushed open the door, causing the flames of the candles in the room to flicker.

'Is that you, Robert?'

His mother's voice came from the bed, surrounded at the head by wine-red drapes.

'No,' murmured Robert, knowing she meant his father.

The covers shifted as she sat up. She parted the drapes, her hair tumbling around her shoulders. The room's shadows were caught in her face, bruising her eyes and filling the hollows of her cheeks. The birth of Matilda the month before had not been easy and his mother had hardly left her bed since.

'Are you in pain?' Concern filtered through her tired voice.

Robert's knee was aching, so too was the gash on his head that the physician had stitched, but he didn't want this to get in the way of what he had come here for. 'No,' he said, limping closer to the bed, unable to imagine the old woman from the cramped house in the valley ever setting foot in this fine room, adorned with its drapes, rugs and carved furniture. 'Tell me about my birth.'

His mother's face filled with surprise, then she looked away. Something seized Robert inside. There had been guilt in that look.

'Why such a question?'

'I . . .' He faltered. The cry of his baby sister filled his silence. 'Matilda,' he said suddenly. 'It made me wonder what my birth was like. Was it difficult like hers?'

His mother stared at him, then sighed. 'We thought for some time that you would never come into this world.' She reached out and touched his cheek. 'But you did.'

Robert pulled away at her touch, impatient for answers. He decided to be blunt. 'I lied today.' He saw her frown and he looked down, picking at a fingernail, torn in the fall. 'I wasn't on my own in the woods. Someone found me. Helped me.'

His mother had drawn back from him.

'The old woman with the dogs.'

Her hand tightened around the bedcovers.

'She said something.' Robert met his mother's gaze. 'She said she delivered me.'

'Yes,' murmured the countess.

Robert shook his head, not wanting to believe it. 'But she's a witch! How could you let her . . .?' He couldn't finish. The thought of the old woman's filthy hands being the first thing on his naked body made him feel sick. He didn't stop to think that she would have been younger then. In his mind she had always been a withered crone.

'Some might call her a witch,' said his mother quietly, 'others a healer.'

'I thought Ede delivered me. You told me she delivered all your children, even Margaret.' Robert noticed her face grow taut at the careless reference to his half-sister. His mother's first husband had been a knight who died on crusade when she was pregnant. The knight's comrade-in-arms, Sir Robert Bruce, had returned from the Holy Land to tell the widowed countess what had happened and the two had grown close. Within a few short months they married in haste, without securing the permission of King Alexander, who in his anger removed them both of their lands. It was only through the intervention of the Lord of Annandale that the dispute was smoothed over and Robert's father was allowed to acquire Carrick by right of his new wife.

'Ede did deliver you, or at least she tried. You were dying inside me, Robert.' Her eyes had grown bright in the candlelight. 'The labour was going on too long. Affraig lived in the village then. She was well known for her skills as a healer. She saved your life. And mine.'

Robert knew there was more to the story. Other questions crowded in. Why had his parents never mentioned this, even after Alexander had been bitten by one of her dogs? And why had the woman seemed so angry? *Don't come here again*, she had said. *You, or any of your family.* Robert glanced round, hearing footsteps along the passage. His mother didn't seem to have noticed. 'Why did she leave the village?' he asked quickly. 'Why did she go into the hills?'

'She was banished,' answered his mother hesitantly. 'Your father—' She stopped abruptly, hearing the footfalls. Her cheeks stained. 'Back to bed with you, Robert,' she ordered, her voice unnaturally loud.

Hearing the door open behind him, Robert turned to see his father's pensive face.

The earl scowled and pulled the door wider. 'Leave.'

Robert went to go, then felt his mother's cool hand on his.

She leaned forward, laying a soft kiss by the wound on his brow. 'No more talk of it now,' she breathed into his ear, while her husband shrugged off his fur-lined robe and hung it on a clothes perch.

Robert headed from the room, glancing at his father, who had sat on a stool to remove his boot. The earl's face was wan in the candlelight. Robert wondered what had happened in Galloway. He longed to go and see his grandfather and find out, but it was late, his wounds were tormenting him and he had too many other questions to fit more answers in his head.

Marjorie watched her son limp from the chamber. Her husband, rubbing at his foot, chafed by his boot, didn't look up. He could be so loving. Couldn't he show just a little of that to the boy? He had always told her he didn't want his heir growing up soft and that was why he was hard on him, but Marjorie knew that wasn't the real truth of it.

'What is it?'

Realising she had been caught staring at him, she forced a smile. 'I am just tired.' She frowned as he eased his boot back on with a wince. 'Aren't you coming to bed?'

'In a moment,' he said, crossing to her.

Marjorie rested her head against the pillow. She closed her eyes as he kissed her. She wasn't tired, she was exhausted. The labour had drained what felt like the last of her youth. Ten children was a lot for any woman to bear.

'Get some rest.'

She felt the bed shift as his hand left it, heard him moving about the room, pouring a goblet of wine, opening a chest. She began to drift towards sleep, the familiar sounds of her husband soothing after so many months alone. A little while later, she heard a rap at the door. Marjorie came awake, worried Robert had returned with more questions. The boy had no idea how angry his father would be if he knew he had been in Affraig's house. But it wasn't her son. It was one of her husband's retainers. She watched the earl give the man a purse. In his other hand, her husband held a rolled piece of parchment.

'There is enough here to buy you passage to France and back. Be careful.'

'Do not fear, my lord,' said the man, taking the purse and stuffing it inside a pouch fixed to his belt beside his broadsword. 'I'll get it safe to Gascony.'

'Deliver it directly to King Edward. I do not want some servant reading it.'

The man bowed and left, taking the roll of parchment. As her husband shut the door, the countess closed her eyes. After a moment, she felt the familiar shift as his weight came down beside her. It was less comforting now.

9

Robert hastened through the woods, holding up his hood as the rain splattered between the branches. The rushing trees drowned the distant roar of waves on Turnberry beach. The first autumn storms had come early this year. Only last week the men of Carrick had been toiling under blue skies to bring in the last of the harvest. Days later and the crops of oats and barley would have been drowning in the fields. Now, the cattle were being driven down from the higher pastures. Those that could not be fed through the winter months would be slaughtered for the meat. It was a busy time, when all hands were called to help work the land. The men the Bruce family had lost during the assault on Galloway had been sorely missed.

Robert thumped the gnarled stick into the ground, every stride propelling him deeper into the woods. He felt foolish, using the stick as his excuse, but it was the only one he had been able to think of. And think on it he had, all through the turbulence of the past few weeks.

The victories won in the capture of the castles of Wigtown, Dumfries and Buittle had been all but swept aside by the queen's pregnancy, tidings of which had spread swiftly through the kingdom. Robert hadn't been invited to attend any of the councils that had followed the men's return, but from snatches of conversation gleaned he knew his grandfather had decided to withdraw from Galloway, leaving a small garrison in each castle until the queen gave birth and the ambition of Comyn and Balliol was ended. His father had clearly been angered by the decision to leave and when the old Bruce departed a fortnight ago, returning with his knights to Annandale, the two had been silent and tense. Despite the unrest within his family, Robert had been preoccupied with his own thoughts, but today had been the first day since the harvest had begun that he'd been able to slip away unnoticed.

As the trees thinned, he could see the house under the hill. Great puddles lay around the base of the oak, the leaves of which were russet and gold. The last glory of a dying summer. The pigs were huddled in the corner of their pen, close under the eaves. Three fine red heifers had joined them. Wondering how the old woman had the money to buy the animals, Robert made his way down the muddy hillside, using the staff for balance.

As he approached the door, a ferocious baying sounded. From around the side of the house came the black dogs, barking and snarling. Resisting the urge to run, Robert stood his ground. The hounds slowed, slinking low to the ground, shoulders hunched. Robert opened his free hand, palm up, towards the beasts, as he used to do with his grandfather's hunting dogs. Rain dripped steadily from his nose. The larger of the two came closer, growling. Raising its head, it thrust its nose towards his outstretched hand. Robert laughed in relief as its tongue uncurled pink and wet into his palm. The door banged open, revealing the old woman framed in the doorway. The dogs slunk away through the puddles towards her.

'I told you not to come here.' Her voice, raised above the torrent, was hard.

Robert went towards her, holding out the staff. 'I wanted to return this.' As soon as he said it, he realised how feeble it sounded, how like a lie. He could see it reflected in the old woman's face in a sneer of contempt. When she moved to close the door, he called out, 'And to see Brigid.'

The woman paused, her expression caught between humour and irritation. Both were derisive. 'She's gone, boy.'

'Gone?'

'To Ayrshire. A farrier took a fancy to her.' Affraig nodded to the stick. 'Leave it outside,' she said, shutting the door.

Robert stared at the pitted wood, barring his way. He felt a surge of anger, fuelled by humiliation and disappointment. Until that moment he hadn't realised that the last part of his excuse had been true: he had wanted to see the strange girl again. Making a fist, he banged on the door. It opened. 'Why did you let her go?'

Cruel humour broke full across the woman's face. 'If I'd known the heir of an earl would have been interested I would have waited. Perhaps the girl would have fetched more than three cows!'

Robert felt repugnance as her lips cracked open to reveal yellow teeth in a laughing mouth. Tossing the stick down in the mud, he made to leave. Then, finding sudden power, he turned back. 'When I am earl I'll make sure your banishment continues. You'll never enter Turnberry again.'

Her scornful laughter faded. 'How like your father you are,' she murmured. 'I wouldn't have believed two runts could be born of the great Lord of Annandale, but here you are, proof of the failure of that mighty line.' Her voice lowered further. 'Shame it is. Shame.'

Robert's cheeks flamed. 'How dare you! You don't even *know* my grandfather!'

The old woman pointed a bony finger at the higher branches of the oak. Turning, Robert saw one of the webs swinging in the wind. He hadn't noticed this one when he was here before and the tree was full and green. This web looked older than the others. The cage of sticks was weathered and brittle-looking. Inside was a thin rope, dark with rain. It was knotted like a noose.

'What is it?' he wanted to know, looking back. But the old woman had disappeared inside the house. The door, however, was open. Robert hesitated, but his curiosity was greater than his anger and so he stepped forward, over the threshold. 'What does it have to do with my grandfather?'

Affraig was stoking the fire. Sparks flared around her. She didn't answer.

'What is the tree?' he pressed.

'An oak,' she replied curtly.

'I meant what are the—'

'I know what you were meaning.' Affraig straightened and faced him. She studied him in the half-light, the rain drumming on the roof. 'Close the door. You'll let the warm out.'

Robert did so. Pushing back his sodden hood, he realised his cloak and boots had made puddles on the floor. The old woman didn't seem to have noticed. She had set herself on a stool and was hunched in front of the fire, her eyes fixed on some bright point within. Her hair had fallen over her shoulder and hung down like a knotted curtain. The hounds were flopped at her feet, their heads resting on their huge paws, bodies rising and falling in the ruddy glow.

'Destinies.'

Robert shook his head after she said the word, not understanding her meaning. He waited for her to continue.

'When men and women have something they desire they come to me. I weave those desires into their destinies. Use the power of the oak to make them come to pass.'

'They should go to church and pray. Ask God for His blessings,' responded Robert, intrigued by her candour, yet also uneasy. He knew a word for what she was implying, a word even stronger than sorcery. Heresy. Only God could make the future come to pass, decide a man's fate.

Her eyes flicked to him. 'There are some prayers that will not be answered. Not by this God.'

Robert felt a thrill of fear, but he took a step closer to the fire, his wet clothes forgotten. 'There isn't any other.'

'What do you know of the land beneath your feet?' Her voice was abrasive again, commanding. 'Of the wild past?'

Robert was reminded of a tutor who had made him write the names of Scotland's kings over and over, from Kenneth mac Alpin, through Malcolm Canmore, down to Alexander, until he got them right. 'My mother inherited the earldom from her father, Niall of Carrick and from her mother our lands in Antrim. When my father returned from the Holy Land he—'

'You think history starts with your family?' she cut across him. 'No, boy. What do you know of these islands?' She spread her hands wide. 'Scotland, England, Ireland, the old kingdoms of Wales?'

Faint, disparate images filled Robert's mind and he heard again his tutor's voice, describing the coming of the Romans; great men of the ancient world who had marched across Britain with their vast armies, dealing death to the pagans who stood against them. The Saxons, fur-clad and fair-haired, pushing the Britons back into the wild hills of Wales and Cornwall, carving out the land that would become known as England. Then the Normans under the banner of the Conqueror. His tutor's tone had always changed at this point, becoming softer, more gracious. It was only after hearing different stories in Ireland that it dawned on Robert that the man had perhaps tempered the tale of the coming of the Conqueror to suit his pupil: a descendant of a Norman lord, Adam de Brus. His tutor's voice faded, replaced by his grandfather's gruff tones speaking of the battle against the Norsemen in their dragon-prowed ships at Largs, not much more than twenty years ago. Then there were the saints of course, Columba and Ninian, Andrew and Margaret. The images and names were too many for Robert to know where to start. In the end he lifted his shoulders in answer.

Affraig made a sharp sound through her teeth that caused one of the dogs to raise its head and bark. She kicked out and it hushed with a whimper.

'The Romans then,' Robert said with a rough sigh, 'the Saxons, the Normans. I know of them.'

Affraig looked at him. 'Was it the Christian God the Romans worshipped in their temples with their sacrifices?'

'They were pagans,' admitted Robert, 'until Constantine.'

'And the men from the east? What of their deities? What of Woden and Frigg?'

'The Saxons became Christians too,' retorted Robert.

'And your Irish ancestors on your mother's side, what of their gods? What of the gods of Britain? What of Lugh of the bright spear and the Dagda? Rhiannon and Bel?' She continued before Robert could answer. 'There are your other gods, boy.'

'But they are false gods of the old world. No one worships them now.'

'No? Who is it women call upon to ease the pains of labour? You must have heard your mother's prayers before.'

'St Bride,' said Robert at once. 'A Christian saint.'

'Once she was Brigantia, goddess of childbirth and spring.' Affraig bent forward and picked up another log, which she thrust into the fire. 'The priests pretend to forget that.'

As the flames brightened her face, Robert realised she wasn't as ancient as he had first thought, maybe only a few years older than his mother. Beneath the sweat and grime he glimpsed something striking in her face, some echo of the girl, Brigid, but all stone and bone and iron hardness. He wondered how she knew so much, then remembered the books that had surprised him before. Robert glanced at the pile of them, just visible beyond the firelight, then asked the question that was still unanswered. 'Why did you point at that – that web in the tree when I asked about my grandfather?'

'You must know of St Malachy.' Affraig laughed again when Robert crossed himself, but this time respectfully. 'Yes, it was a powerful curse the Irish saint laid upon your family. Powerful enough to cause the river to rise at Annan and wash away the castle there. Powerful enough to remain as a shadow upon the Bruce family, over one hundred years after Malachy uttered it.'

Robert nodded, silent. He had known of the curse for as long as he could remember, long before his tutor had taught him of Scotland's history. In the last century, Malachy, an Archbishop of Armagh, had been travelling through Annandale on a journey to Rome. While staying at the Castle of Annan, which belonged to one of Robert's ancestors, the archbishop discovered that a man accused by the Bruce family of robbery was due to be hanged. Malachy begged that the robber be spared, a request the lord had granted. But the next day, the archbishop saw the accused man hanging from a gallows. Malachy's vengeful curse upon the Bruce family had been blamed for the subsequent destruction of their stronghold and all their woes thereafter. Robert had seen the ruins of his ancestor's castle at Annan and knew well the terrible story of the river's rising. He understood now why the rope inside the woven web was knotted like a hangman's noose.

Affraig was speaking again.

'On his journey home from the Holy Land your grandfather burned candles at the saint's shrine. But some years ago he came to me. Believing his prayers had not been answered, he asked me to lift the curse. He wanted his line finally to be free of it.'

Robert saw an odd look come over her face, fondness perhaps, but it was gone from his thoughts in an instant, forced away by the startling revelation that his grandfather had asked a witch to work a spell for him. Yet, still, he remained intrigued. 'When will it be lifted?'

Affraig shook her head. 'That I cannot say. The oak must do its work. When it is done, the web will fall.'

Robert wondered whether it could be cut down, if falling was all it took, but he guessed she would say this would not work. There was still one thing he didn't understand. The day Alexander was bitten by the dog his father had told his brother never to go near the old woman's house again. Robert had assumed this was due to the threat from the dogs, rather than the woman herself, for the earl had always been scornful of any superstition. But since his mother had intimated that Affraig's exile was the earl's doing, he'd found himself wondering if there was more to his father's order. 'Why were you banished from Turnberry?'

All at once her face closed in on itself and she drew back. 'You should go,' she said, standing and moving to the shelf where she had made the compress for his knee.

Robert had come too close to the answers he wanted to be so easily brushed aside. 'Tell me. I want to know.'

'I said leave.' She grabbed a clump of roots and took up a knife, her back to him.

'I can ask my father.'

She jerked round, the blade glinting in her fist. Robert took several steps back at the fury in her eyes. He thought for a second that she was going to attack him. But then her face changed, the harsh lines softening into creases of age. Slowly she lowered the knife, her hand trembling. 'I wove your father his destiny once.'

Robert stared at her. The revelation about his grandfather had been a shock, but he simply couldn't imagine his father asking the fierce crone to make a spell for his future. The idea was so preposterous it was laughable. Robert recalled his father sneering at his grandfather's fervent vigil at the shrine of St Malachy in an effort to break the curse, his ridicule of the local farmers for their talk of demons in the forests. He would even scowl and demand quiet whenever Robert spoke of Fionn mac Cumhaill and the other Irish heroes he had learned about in fosterage.

'I hung it in an oak for him,' murmured Affraig, 'but something happened. One of his men . . .' Her brow knotted and she looked at the knife in her hand. 'I asked for his aid in the matter, for justice. He refused me.' Her head rose defiantly and she met Robert's gaze. 'And so I tore down his destiny and left it in pieces outside the castle walls.'

Despite his incredulity, a shudder went through Robert at that statement.

Affraig moved away and set the knife back on the shelf. 'After that he banished me from the village. I know he wanted to banish me from Carrick, but your mother stopped him because I had saved the life of her first-born son. You,' she finished, without turning.

A log slipped and burst in the fire, but Robert didn't take his eyes off the old woman. 'What was my father's destiny?'

After a pause, Affraig answered. 'To be King of Scotland.'

The six men crowded the stuffy chamber, breathing one another's sweat. The servants had banked the fire in the hearth high so that the whole palace would be kept warm, even though the bedchamber, with its precious occupant, was some distance down the passage. It wasn't far enough away, however, that the men couldn't hear the screams. Between the tortured sounds, female voices came to them, raised and urgent. Now and then, the cries would fade to whimpers and the women's voices would drop away to become indistinguishable. The men, hardly speaking as it was, would hush at these moments, straining to hear the next scream. It had been like this for hours, the tension swelling with the heat.

James Stewart leaned against the wall close to the door, the cold of the stone a relief against his back. Thick drapes covered the windows, beyond which came the faint patter of rain. He wondered what the hour was, but resisted the urge to cross the chamber and part the curtains. It had to be almost dawn. James shifted, trying to relieve the aching in his feet. There were only two stools in the room and these had been commandeered by the Black Comyn, Earl of Buchan, and the obese Earl of Fife, whose hereditary right it was to crown a new king. The steward glanced at the Bishop of St Andrews praying by the fire. He wondered how the frail old man had the stamina to remain on his knees all this time. The thickset form of Robert Wishart broke his view. As the Bishop of Glasgow paced by, James locked eyes with John Comyn, standing by the window.

The Lord of Badenoch stared back, his dark eyes filled with challenge.

James met his stare, sensing the deep hostility coming off the other man. The two of them had never trusted one another, their dealings at court only occurring with necessity, but since the Bruces' assault on Galloway the Red Comyn's antagonism towards him had swelled. James had the distinct impression that the Lord of Badenoch knew of his involvement in the invasion. Well, it did not matter now. Within the next few hours, the Comyn's attempts to set his brother-in-law upon the empty throne would be at an end.

Another ragged scream tore through the quiet, this one longer and louder than the others, more a howl of anguish than a cry of pain. It was followed by a lengthy silence. As the sound of hurried footsteps echoed in the passage, James's gaze shifted from Comyn. The Bishop of Glasgow stopped his pacing and the Bishop of St Andrews looked up from his clasped hands. The Earl of Buchan rose from the stool. Only the Earl of Fife, who had fallen asleep with his chins on his chest, didn't stir as the door opened.

The woman who appeared paused for a moment, surveying the expectant men. Her white apron was covered with blood. James could smell the sour tang of it. Her gaze came to rest on him.

'A boy, Lord Steward,' she declared.

'Praise be,' said Wishart.

James, however, didn't take his eyes off the woman's grave face. After a moment, she answered his forming question.

'He was dead in the womb, sir. I could do nothing for him.'

Wishart cursed loudly.

James turned away, thrusting a hand through his hair. As he did so, he caught sight of John Comyn's keen expression.

Bordeaux was awakening, the bell-tower of the cathedral pouring a cascade of clanging chimes across the labyrinth of streets. Birds flew up from the rooftops, their wings a flurry of white in the crisp blue sky. Shutters opened and banged against shop-fronts, buckets of night soil were emptied into gutters, and cobblers and mercers, smiths and farriers called to one another as they began their day's work, harsh stutters of words that echoed in the narrow streets.

Adam rode his palfrey through the waking city, the din of the cathedral bells filling his ears. It felt strange to be back in the place of his birth after so long in a foreign land. The city seemed oddly new and filled with promise, rather than somewhere that was as familiar as his own skin. Yet he knew each twist and turn of these alleyways and recognised the smells that greeted him at every corner, from the bloody stink of the slaughterhouses by the city gates, to the pungency of the cattle market and salty sourness of the Garonne River. The air was mild, the winter wind less cruel, and the weight of secrecy had fallen from his shoulders, allowing him to experience every sound that greeted him, every smell that assaulted him, every conversation overheard or altercation witnessed, without assessing either its danger or its merit.

As the cathedral bells fell silent, Adam urged his horse up the street towards the imposing walls of the castle that overlooked the city. Banners and flags flapped from the turrets, making gaudy statements in the sky. One scarlet banner, larger than the others and adorned with three golden lions, held Adam's gaze as he headed towards the gates, then the guards in their well-fitted gambesons and colourful hose were asking his business and his attention was diverted. Dismounting, Adam took a roll of parchment from the bag strapped to his saddle, the leather soiled from the journey through France. One guard inspected the seal attached to the document, while the other questioned him. His answers being to their satisfaction, they moved aside, allowing him to pass beneath the iron teeth of the portcullis.

Although it was early, the courtyard was bustling with servants and royal officials. The pale elegance of the buildings and the rich dress of the men and women Adam passed breathed sweetness into him after the long winter in Edinburgh, shipwrecked on that coarse black mountain, where the howling wind haunted the halls, along with so many white-faced Scotsmen. Seeing men unfurling lengths of coloured flags and tying them to the sides of the buildings, he realised with surprise that it must be approaching the Christ Mass. The mildness of the air, which had increased the further south he had travelled, had fooled him into believing spring had come. A girl with spice-brown hair passed him, escorting three plump geese. Adam allowed himself a moment to appreciate the supple swing of her young hips, before heading to the stables. After leaving his palfrey with a groom, he made his way to the tower in the west corner of the compound, from which flew the scarlet banner with the three lions.

There were more guards at the tower's entrance and more questions, but eventually he was led up a spiral of stairs to a small chamber where a smell of incense barely masked the caustic odour of fresh paint He waited as the page who had escorted him rapped on a door. When it opened, Adam caught sight of another servant as his escort slipped inside. Moving to the chamber's single window, he peered through the criss-cross panes of glass, which distorted his view of the city, spread out below. The door opened and he turned expectantly, but the page headed off down the stairs without further word or instruction. Adam leaned against the wall, for there was no furniture, just a tapestry showing a group of young knights all bearing scarlet shields, adorned with a symbol that was as familiar to Adam as his own family crest: a rearing golden dragon, wreathed in fire.

After a time the door opened again and a man beyond motioned Adam to enter. The solar was bright with morning sunlight that flooded in through arched windows. After the gloom, it took Adam a moment to become accustomed to the light. As he did so he saw a man standing behind a table that was laid out with neat stacks of parchment. At well over six feet, the man was still one of the tallest Adam had ever known. His shoulder-length hair, streaked with white, was curled at the ends as was the fashion, but his linen robe, dyed a solemn blue, was simple in design, unlike the flamboyant stripes and silks of his courtiers. It was perfectly tailored around his athletic frame and pulled in by a belt of leather, embossed with silver. His face was austere, an ash-coloured beard clipped close and neat around an unsmiling mouth. Only his intense grey eyes revealed anything of his thoughts, filled as they were with an alert impatience. One of his eyelids drooped a little, the one blemish in an otherwise orderly face. It was more prominent these days, Adam noted, than it had been when they had first met twenty-four years ago, when the man before him had been a fierce young lord in exile. Now, at almost fifty, he was King of England, Duke of Gascony, Lord of Ireland and conqueror of Wales.

'My lord,' greeted Adam, bowing low.

The king's pale eyes moved to the page by the door. 'Leave me.'

As the page left the chamber, Adam saw a painted scene on the far wall. It hadn't been here when he was last in this room. It too showed the knights with the dragon shields, but this time they were crowded around a man seated on a stone throne, wearing a gold circlet. In one hand the man held a sword, the blade of which was broken, in the other a slender gold staff. There was an ornately carved lectern positioned below the fresco. Adam noticed a large, leather-bound book lying on it at an angle. He could see words written in gold leaf on the cover. He hadn't seen the book before, but he knew what it was.

'I was expecting you sooner, Sir Adam.'

Adam looked back as Edward's voice broke his thoughts. 'The queen's labour came later than anticipated, my lord.'

'I take it you completed your business?'

Edward's tone, usually so poised, was sharp with agitation. Even more unusual was the concern in the king's gaze. He had leaned forward, planting his veined hands on the table.

'God did the work for us. The child was dead in the womb.'

Edward straightened. 'Good,' he said, after a moment. 'This is good.' He seated himself in a high-backed chair, his gaze at once hard, accusatory. 'This business should have been finished months ago, before the queen even fell pregnant.'

Anger swelled in Adam, although he was careful not to show it. He deserved Edward's praise, not his admonishment. True, the queen's pregnancy had been an unexpected hindrance, but killing the king had been no easy task. Had it been murder at a distance, a crossbow bolt through the throat, then Adam could have accomplished it long before the queen conceived. But Edward had insisted that the death be made to seem like an accident and so Adam had been appointed to travel north to Scotland in the retinue of Alexander's new bride, one faceless servant among many.

Poison, his first thought, had been ruled out instantly; he couldn't get near the kitchens without notice and, besides, the king had tasters. Each role in a royal household was fulfilled by specific servants and each man and woman guarded their duties zealously. It was some weeks before Adam reached a decision, after travelling the treacherous coastal path between Edinburgh and Kinghorn. Even with the location chosen it had taken time to plan the deed itself; ingratiating himself into the queen's trust and waiting for the right opportunity, which finally presented itself in the form of the feast. The king would have been drinking and easier to overpower if it came to it, and the spring tides meant the cliff path would be the only viable route. The only things he'd had to do were persuade the young queen to have him summon the king to her bedchamber, unwittingly sealing her husband's fate with a honey trap, and make sure the king's most competent manservant would be unable to escort him, leaving only that fool, Brice, to contend with. The storm had been a boon Adam couldn't have predicted, although the poetic symmetry of the proclaimed Day of Judgement had been mostly lost on him.

'Still,' said Edward, releasing Adam from his stare, 'it is done.'

As the king sifted through the documents on the table and pulled one from the pile, Adam saw a large seal fixed to the bottom. He had seen it before. It was from the papal curia in Rome.

'I have the permission of His Holiness,' said Edward, flattening the letter with a stroke of his palm. 'I will finalise the matter when I return to England. For now, I have more pressing concerns. King Philippe has been at pains to exercise his control over my dealings here in Gascony. It does not please my young cousin that I wield more power in the duchy than he does. I believe it makes him nervous.' There was satisfaction in Edward's eyes as he said this.

'Can you afford to wait that long, my lord? There has been great unrest in Scotland since the king's death. The Bruce family took up arms against the Balliols, accusing the Lord of Galloway of plotting to take the crown.'

'The Bruces do not concern me. The Earl of Carrick has already sent me a message, pledging his support for any decision I make on the future of the kingdom. He will do as I say. As for the rest of Scotland's magnates, I will send out missives, ordering them all to abide by the rule of their council of guardians, until such time as the child can be brought from Norway.'

'Do you think the magnates will obey?'

'None of them would risk their lands in England by defying me.'

Adam knew what this man had done in England, Wales and the Holy Land; knew what he had accomplished over the years and how. He nodded, respectful of the flat certainty in Edward's eyes. 'What do you wish me to do now, my lord?'

'You may return to your command.' Picking up the document with the pope's seal attached, Edward rose and crossed to an iron door embedded in the solar's inner wall. Adam saw a keyhole on one side. Edward opened it and placed the parchment inside. He pulled out a leather purse, tied with a drawstring. 'Here,' he said, offering it to Adam. 'Your final payment. I apologise for the dust it has gathered.'

'Thank you, my lord,' murmured Adam. He paused, then asked something he had wondered about since the king first charged him with the dangerous task. 'Have you told anyone else in the order of my involvement in this matter?'

Edward's eyes bored into his. 'King Alexander's death was an accident. It stays that way.'

'Yes, my lord,' said Adam, stowing the bulging purse in his belt-pouch. 'An accident.'

The door opened behind them and a soft, musical voice drifted in.

'I am sorry. I did not know you had a visitor.'

Adam turned to see a tall woman, with olive skin and delicate features. Her hair was hidden beneath a headdress that trailed gossamer silks and her floor-sweeping gown was richly embroidered. Adam hadn't seen her in some years and the lines that creased the queen's face surprised him.

'I will leave you.'

'There is no need, Eleanor,' said Edward, moving to her. 'It is only tidings from England.'

Eleanor's face filled with concern. 'The children?'

'Are fine,' said Edward, his hard face softening into a rare and surprisingly tender smile. 'It is politics, nothing more.' Putting a hand on his wife's slim shoulder and guiding her into the chamber, Edward glanced at Adam, his smile vanishing. 'Sir Adam was just leaving.'

As Adam headed for the door, he glanced at the fresco and the lectern beneath it. The elaborate gold writing on the front of the large book glinted in the light, spelling out words.

The Last Prophecy of Merlin

PART 2
1290–1292 AD

They do not wish to wait to get possession of the kingdom lawfully, but seize the crown.

The Life of Merlin, *Geoffrey of Monmouth*

I I

All around the horns were sounding, their strident calls echoing over the baying of the hounds. The pack was running hard, the scent thickening in their throats. For hours they had pursued their quarry, from the cold reaches of dawn to the early morning, the dense mists lightening to a diaphanous haze. Now, death was near and they plunged headlong to meet it, compelled by the horns.

Robert urged his horse on after the dogs, the woods flashing past. The trees were scattered with young green buds and the verdant smell of new growth filled his lungs as he fought to keep the pace, the courser obeying every twist of the reins in his gloved hands. Ahead was a fallen tree, a victim of the winter storms. He kicked hard at the horse's sides and rose to meet it. The courser vaulted the rotten trunk and thundered on, kicking up a shower of leaves. The dogs had disappeared over a steep ridge. Robert could hear their howls, louder than the horns, which echoed some distance behind him. Anticipation fierce within him, he drove the horse up the incline. At the top, the ground fell away into a bowl-like clearing, which ended at a high bank of earth, riddled with tree roots. Within this bank was a wide opening. The hounds were gathered outside, baying into the dark.

Realising the quarry had evaded the trap, Robert dismounted with a curse and made his way down to the dogs. The mists were thicker here, so too the dank odours of moss and earth. He reached for the horn that hung from his belt. As his fingers brushed it, he heard a noise from within the cave. It sounded like low thunder. Robert's fingers moved past the horn to grasp the hilt of his sword. The older hounds were snarling, ears pressed flat against their heads, hackles high. Some of the younger ones whined, hinds quivering with exertion and fear. With any other quarry, even fully grown harts and ferocious boar, they would not be so apprehensive. Robert

drew his sword and went forward through their guarding line, determination forcing back his nerves. He heard his name being called, somewhere
distant, off in the fog, but he ignored it.

As he moved closer, breathing hard, he saw the opening wasn't deep,
really just a hollow overhung with roots. He could see a hunched shape
within, darker than the shadows. It was larger than he had expected,
although not as large as some of the reports had stated. The face was long
and lean, the jaw thrust forward, lips peeled back to reveal hooked incisors.
Its fur was thick and black, its winter pelt not yet fully shed. The stink of
it was horrendous, a caustic animal reek that was like nothing Robert had
ever smelled before. But it was the eyes that were the most startling thing
about it, twin pools of molten gold. How many things, he wondered, had
died while staring into that burning gaze? He had seen the bloody destruction in the pastures outside the town over the course of the winter, sheep
ripped apart, cattle pulled down and gutted. The wolf, his grandfather
taught him, killed not just for food, but for the pleasure. His was a hunger
that could not be satisfied by blood alone. There was darkness in his heart
and poison in his bite.

The horns had silenced now. Robert could hear the shouts of men and
the drum of hooves as the rest of the hunting party converged on the
clearing. Gripping his sword, the hilt slick with sweat, he steeled himself
to lunge at the shadow in the cave. The wolf was faster. Out it sprang,
eyes blazing. Robert jabbed with his blade, but only managed to rake its
side as it passed him. The wolf gnashed at one of the dogs, then, finding
itself cornered, turned and leapt at Robert. He ducked away, but his foot
caught on a coiled tree root and he hit the ground, yelling as the wolf's
jaws clamped down around his ankle. Grabbing his fallen sword, Robert
twisted round and stabbed out, striking the creature in the neck. The
keen blade punctured the bushy pelt and entered thick tissue beneath.
The wolf relinquished its hold, went to spring again, then howled as three
hounds fell on it from behind, teeth punching into its hind legs and rump.
Rolling away from the thrashing limbs, Robert scrabbled upright as two
more dogs leapt in, pinning the animal. As they tore at its flesh it cried in
rage and pain. Blood splattered the dusty ground. Moving in, both hands
around the hilt, Robert stabbed down into the wolf's side. Blood erupted,
spraying his tunic and face, the hot stink of it catching in his throat. He
turned his head, trying not to gag, as the din of men and horses entered
the clearing.

The huntsmen came first, running down the bank, forked sticks in their hands, ready to pin down the quarry. They slowed as they saw Robert hunched over the wolf between the dogs. Two of them unhooked whips from their belts, ready to force the hounds away. Others drew leashes. Robert heard them calling to him, but he was watching the gold fire drain from the wolf's eyes. Its head had lolled back and it was panting shallowly. Finally, it shuddered to still. Robert pushed himself to his feet and withdrew his sword with a tug. As the huntsmen closed in, whipping away the hounds, he turned to see his grandfather. Behind came his father and his brother, Edward, along with ten local men, summoned to join the hunt. Robert met his grandfather's steel gaze. Feeling pride swell in him, he went to grin, but the old man strode past to where the huntsmen were rounding up the dogs. The wolf was lying prone in the dust, blood pooling around it. Two hounds had been injured in the fight. The old lord bent down beside one of them, inspecting the gash in the animal's side. It was Scáthach, his favourite bitch. Robert glanced queasily at the bite-marks in his boot.

The old lord straightened, turning to him. 'Why didn't you use your horn?'

Robert licked his dry lips. 'There wasn't time,' he lied, feeling victory slipping away.

His grandfather's scowl deepened. He motioned to the huntsmen. 'Make sure those cuts are well cleaned.'

'How badly is she wounded?' asked Robert's father grimly, heading over to inspect the dogs, not even glancing at his son.

Robert watched as the men crowded around the injured hounds, the excitement of the hunt gone, dead like the wolf, forgotten in their midst. Turning, he headed off through the trees, pushing branches out of his way. Finding a rotten tree stump, he threw his bloodstained sword down and sat. His fingers were shaking as he tugged off his boot. Slowly, he pulled up his hose. There were two livid red lines encircling the white skin of his ankle.

'Did it draw blood?'

Robert jerked round to see Edward heading towards him. He looked back at the marks. 'No,' he told his brother. 'The skin isn't broken.'

'You're lucky. I've heard the only cure for a wolf-bite is to bathe naked in the sea nine times.'

Robert said nothing, but busied himself pulling on his boot. Edward came and leaned against a tree in front of him, unavoidably filling his view. Robert glanced at him, suddenly aware of how tall his brother seemed, lounging nonchalantly against the trunk. His green tunic and brown hose made him one with the woods, and his dark sweep of hair was hidden beneath a feathered cap. At fourteen, his face was full and boyish, still marked with creases in his cheeks when he smiled. It no longer fitted his lengthening body. Although a year apart in age they had always looked alike, everyone said, and Robert wondered now at the changes that must have occurred in him in the two summers since he came to Annandale to serve as his grandfather's squire. He hadn't seen his brother, who had barely returned from Ireland before he left, in over a year.

'That thing was a *brute*,' Edward continued with relish. 'If I'd killed it I'd have it stuffed and hung in my hall, although the reek would drive out my guests.' His face wrinkled. 'It smelled like Father's boots!'

Robert chewed his lip, but couldn't stop the smile.

Edward was laughing, shaking his head. 'You must have got the fire of Mars in you, tackling it when it was cornered like that.'

Robert's smile vanished. He snatched up his sword, grabbed a handful of leaves and swiped at the blood on the blade. 'We've been after him for months. We took the rest of the pack, but he always evaded us.' He rose and faced his brother. He wanted to shout that Edward hadn't seen the bloody fields after the wolves had come, hadn't been out in midwinter with the men of Annan and Lochmaben, setting snares, working long into the raw dark, fingers needled with cold, breath steaming as they passed around the wine skins. The day of Robert's first hunt, when he helped run a wolf into the nets, his grandfather daubed a red line of the animal's blood across his brow, telling him he had become a man now. He turned away, the words stopping in his throat. They weren't meant for his brother. They were meant for his father.

After the crushing disappointment on his return from Ireland – his continued tutelage under the earl a gruelling, thankless experience – Robert had at last begun to thrive in his grandfather's household. At the old lord's side, he had taken his first steps on the path to manhood, moving with certainty and rising confidence towards the noble lord he was destined to become. He remembered well his first night in Lochmaben Castle, his grandfather sitting him down in the hall, his voice solemn with gravity as he impressed upon him the importance of the heritage into which he had been born.

'Think of our line as a mighty tree,' the old lord had said, 'with roots stretching back through the ages to the time of the Conqueror and the reign of Malcolm Canmore, then back further still, on your mother's side, to the ancient kings of Ireland. The roots go deep, nourishing the branches that spring from them, entwined by marriage, through the royal house of Scotland and the noble houses of England down to my father and to me. You, Robert, are a new shoot, sprung from the great boughs beneath you.'

Now, those same words rang hollow in his memory. The earl had arrived at Lochmaben only two days ago and already Robert felt as though he were twelve again, rather than fifteen – as if these past years and all his achievements had been erased. He could hunt and kill a vicious beast, but he was still powerless in the face of his father's cold disapproval.

'We thought there might be wolves in the woods outside Turnberry last winter,' said Edward, watching as Robert crouched and continued cleaning his blade. 'Some lambs were taken. Father reckoned it was the old woman's dogs.'

'Affraig?' said Robert, sitting back on his heels. He hadn't thought about the old woman with her tree of webs in a long while.

'I still can't believe what you told me before you left.' Edward paused. 'Did you ever ask Grandfather about it?'

Robert nodded, scraping the fistful of leaves along the flat of the sword.

'Well?' Edward urged.

'He wouldn't speak of it, or her.'

'He didn't deny it?'

'No. But he didn't admit it.' Robert stood, sheathing the sword in the scabbard that hung from his belt. He would clean it properly later. 'I take it you never spoke to Father?'

'I wouldn't have wanted the whipping. Father has been quick to anger lately. He took to Niall with his belt the other week. He had a fever a few months back and Mother blames his temper on that.' Edward gave a snort. 'But I heard him shouting about Salisbury enough times to know the physician could use a hundred leeches on him and it wouldn't put his humour right.'

'What was he saying?' asked Robert, his interest snared.

'That it wasn't right he wasn't involved in the negotiations with King Edward. That he should have been at Salisbury with Grandfather.'

Robert felt a stab of satisfaction. True, he hadn't been present at the council during which the Treaty of Salisbury had been sealed, but he had travelled to the town in his grandfather's retinue and had seen the stately party from Westminster arriving for the negotiations.

After the queen gave birth to a stillborn son tensions had threatened to rise, but, soon after, missives arrived from France in the name of King Edward, requesting that the men of the realm abide by their council of guardians until the infant Margaret could be enthroned. Robert's grandfather, pleased by the decision, had withdrawn the rest of his men from Galloway and, for the good of the kingdom, returned the captured castles to Balliol and the Comyns. After this, the air calmed, many agreeing with Edward's orders and those who didn't nonetheless unwilling to risk their estates in England by refusing the king. By the time Robert had been taken into his grandfather's household, the kingdom was again at peace.

Last autumn, King Edward returned after three years in Gascony and contacted the guardians to discuss the conveyance of young Margaret, now almost seven years old, from Norway to Scotland. Lord John Comyn contrived to head the Scottish delegation that would travel to England for the talks, but with the help of James Stewart, the Lord of Annandale had been elected into this party. Robert had journeyed south with his grandfather to one of the most important councils in decades, at which it had been agreed Margaret would come to Scotland by the end of the year. Now there were just the details to finalise, which would be done soon at the assembly to be held in the town of Birgham.

Robert wished his father hadn't been summoned to attend the final talks, but as one of the thirteen earls he couldn't have been omitted. He was determined, however, not to let him disregard the status he'd attained in his grandfather's household. The hunt had not been the success he'd hoped for. In his attempt to prove himself he had become reckless, but now he knew of his father's own frustrations he didn't feel quite so impotent. 'Come on,' he said to his brother, 'let's watch the unmaking.'

The two brothers walked through the trees to the rest of the party where the huntsmen had already set about disembowelling the wolf. Its stomach removed, the cavity would be washed out and filled with a mixture of mutton and oats. The hounds would then be released and allowed to have their fill, this sweet *curée* their reward for a successful hunt. The men were passing around skins of wine, their mood now jovial.

Robert headed to his grandfather, keeping his head high as he passed his father. 'Will Scáthach be all right?' he asked, looking at the bitch, who was licking her wounds.

'She's a tough girl,' responded his grandfather, after a pause.

Robert looked up at him. 'I'm sorry, Grandfather,' he said quietly. 'I should have waited for you.'

The old lord grunted.

Chastised, Robert nodded and moved off to tend to his horse, which was cropping the bushes close by. His grandfather's voice sounded behind him.

'But I'll wager the shepherds of Annandale will sleep easier tonight.'

As he took up the reins of his courser, a grin spread across Robert's face.

Robert rose up in his stirrups as they plodded along the track towards the small Borders town of Birgham, trying to catch a glimpse of the gathering crowds. His grandfather was riding at the head of their company, along with Earl Patrick of Dunbar, the powerful magnate who had been at the talks in Turnberry four years ago and at whose manor they had been staying for the past three nights. Robert's father rode behind with six knights from Carrick, and he and his brother brought up the rear with the squires and the other retainers. Ahead, in a field by a church, hundreds of tents had been erected. Smoke fanned from cooking pots and men stood talking, while squires tended to their horses. The whole place exuded an atmosphere of festivity. There was even a group of minstrels playing.

'Can you see the English?' asked Edward, following Robert's gaze and craning his neck. 'Are they here yet?'

'We're too far away,' replied Robert impatiently, as their grandfather continued the slow, steady pace, the horses' hooves squelching in the churned earth.

Gradually, the sounds of voices and music became louder and the odours of horse dung and wood-smoke stronger, until finally they were moving through into the field, behind another group of travellers. Robert looked around at the men they passed, quite a few of whom seemed to give his family a lot of attention. Not all their stares were friendly.

'Robert.'

At his grandfather's call, Robert slipped down from his saddle and led his horse over to the lord, who had halted near the row of tents. He took the reins of his grandfather's piebald courser, while the old man dismounted with a wince. Hearing orders being shouted, Robert turned to see men lugging benches over the church wall.

'The assembly was planned to take place inside the church,' explained his grandfather, watching as the benches were conveyed to the centre of the field, where a platform had been erected beneath the shading arms of an oak. 'But the roof was struck by lightning.'

Squinting into the sunlight, Robert saw a blackened hole in the side of the roof, where part of it had caved in.

'Maybe it's an omen,' murmured Edward, moving up behind, holding the reins of their father's white mare.

Their grandfather didn't seem to have heard. He had turned away, hailed by a frail, red-haired man with a ruddy complexion, limping across with two younger men.

Robert recognised them. 'That's Sir Walter, the Earl of Menteith and his sons,' he told his brother. 'They were at Turnberry when Grandfather planned the assault on Galloway.' As he said this his gaze was caught by a group heading across the field in front of them. Robert stared at the long, lean face of John Comyn, whom he had first seen in Salisbury. The lord's cloak, trimmed with wolf pelt, was emblazoned with three wheat sheaves on red. His hair hung loose around his shoulders. 'Look. It's the devil himself.'

Edward frowned. 'Who?'

Robert lowered his voice as the men crossed their path. 'That's the Lord of Badenoch, head of the Red Comyns.' There was a pale youth of about his own age with lank dark hair walking behind the lord. He looked too like Comyn not to be related. A son, Robert guessed.

'I thought he'd be taller,' said Edward. 'Who's that with him?'

Robert followed his brother's nod to the man with thin chestnut hair, pockmarked skin and a tense expression, walking at Comyn's side. 'I think that's the Lord of Galloway, John Balliol.'

Balliol looked round and, for a second, Robert thought he'd heard him, but he was well out of earshot and, besides, the lord's attention had fixed first on his father and grandfather. Balliol's faltering stride made the others with him look round. For a moment, both companies paused, the Bruce men halting their conversation with the earls of Menteith and Dunbar. Robert noticed a young man in Balliol's party wearing a leather aketon and carrying a pike. But it wasn't the armour or the weapon that had attracted his attention, rather the depth of hatred in the man's face. He was looking straight at his father.

'My lords. Welcome.'

The voice of James Stewart broke the moment. The high steward was striding across the grass towards the Lord of Annandale and the Earl of

Carrick. With him was a broad man with a tonsured head and a flushed, sweaty face. It was Robert Wishart, the Bishop of Glasgow. Robert had met him once, briefly, and had been a little in awe of the forceful clergyman.

As Balliol and Comyn continued towards the platform, Robert saw the young man with the pike spit in the grass, before drawing his hate-filled gaze from the Earl of Carrick and falling into step behind the Lord of Galloway.

James Stewart and the Lord of Annandale greeted one another with an embrace. The high steward, Robert noted, acknowledged his father more cordially.

'Your grace,' said the old Bruce, bending to kiss the hand of the Bishop of Glasgow. 'It is good to see you.'

'And on such a welcome occasion,' agreed the bishop. 'At last, after the great tragedy that befell our realm, the throne of our kingdom will once again be occupied. It augurs well that our new queen shares her name with one of our dearest saints. God speed young Margaret to our shores.'

Robert saw his father's face tighten at this. It dawned on him what this day meant. The destiny his father had dreamed of was about to be ended. Soon, Margaret would take the throne of Scotland and from her would spring a new line, a line that would branch away from the Bruce family and their claim. He realised, in the same moment, that this was a loss for him also. An image of Affraig tearing the web she had woven for his father into pieces flashed in his mind and he wondered if the witch had somehow made this come to pass. But then he heard the sound of trumpets ringing and he was turning with the others to see a stately procession making its way across the field, banners flying in swirls of colour above their mounted ranks. The English had come.

At their head was John de Warenne, Earl of Surrey and grandson of the legendary William Marshal, one of the greatest knights England had ever raised. Warenne was himself no stranger to battle and, at sixty years old, was a veteran of numerous campaigns under Henry III and his son, Edward. The earl had fought during the rebellion of Simon de Montfort and in Edward's bloody wars in Wales, and had risen to become one of the king's foremost commanders. His eminence preceded him and Robert felt no small amount of respect, staring at the thickset, flint-haired earl, riding in imperiously on a massive, sable-coloured destrier. He was clad in a sumptuously brocaded blue and gold mantle, drawn back over one shoulder to reveal the glitter of mail beneath his surcoat and a broadsword with a pommel of gold.

Behind the earl came a burly man in a violet robe who, despite being two decades younger, had almost as formidable a reputation. Anthony Bek, the

Bishop of Durham, had begun his illustrious career in the clergy after graduating from the University of Oxford. Returning with King Edward from the Holy Land he was made Constable of the Tower of London and then Bishop of Durham, the diocese of which formed the northernmost defence of England. The power granted to him in this office made him virtual king in his bishopric. Indeed, Bishop Bek looked to Robert less like a man of the cloth and more like a warrior prince as he rode in on his warhorse, with thirty knights in his train.

Robert had seen both of these men at the talks in Salisbury, but here in this sunlit field with the fanfare of trumpets they seemed even more impressive. Perhaps it was just the grandeur of the occasion, or maybe it was the contrast with the men in the field waiting for them. Many of the Scottish magnates had jewelled brooches or silver chains holding their fur-trimmed cloaks in place, feathers in their caps and well-made swords and dirks in decorated scabbards. But their clothes, of dyed wools and linens, were plainer than those worn by the English, and few of them wore mail. They hadn't come here to fight. No one, it seemed, had told the English that. All of them, from the earl and the bishop down through the knights and squires, wore armour of some kind, if only padded gambesons, and many were on barded horses. Their clothes were fine and gaudy: embroidered silks and patterned velvets in vivid hues that made Robert think of a flight of oversized butterflies sweeping in across the grass.

Dismounting, John de Warenne went first to Balliol and Comyn, who had crossed to meet him. This was no surprise, for Balliol was married to Warenne's daughter, but it was clearly a source of tension for Robert's father, who observed their greeting with a scowl. As the other magnates began making their way towards the dais and settling into the benches in front of the platform, James Stewart motioned for the Lord of Annandale and the rest of the party to follow. Robert went forward, but his grandfather turned to him.

'Stay here.'

Robert went to protest, but the lord was already walking away.

'I thought we were going to the assembly?' objected Edward, at his side.

The brothers watched as the men crossed to the growing crowd of earls and barons, bishops and abbots who spoke for the realm, leaving a horde of knights and squires, pages and grooms on the fringes of the field, holding horses, or tending campfires. The minstrels had stopped playing and were lounging in the grass, lutes and lyres replaced by cups of beer.

The excitement Robert had felt on the journey had evaporated in a simmering anger. His gaze lingered on the earl's back as he wondered if he would have been so excluded if his father wasn't here. He shaded his eyes from the sun as the men seated themselves. Bishop Bek was ascending the dais and the Earl of Surrey was greeting their grandfather, who had manoeuvred himself in beside John Balliol. 'Perhaps we'll hear them from here?' he murmured, but he could see that the men were speaking and, apart from the odd raised voice, their conversation was inaudible at this distance.

Edward shifted from one foot to the other, then headed to one of the younger knights from Carrick, leading his horse and their father's white mare. 'Sir Duncan, will you hold the horses?'

'That's your task, Master Edward,' chided the knight.

John de Warenne had ascended the platform beside Bishop Bek and was addressing the assembly. There were more men than benches and those who hadn't found a place had crowded in behind. Robert could no longer see his father and grandfather. He glanced round as Edward spoke again.

'Please, Duncan.'

'Why?'

Edward paused. 'If you do, I won't tell my father you once tried to kiss Isabel.'

The knight laughed. 'Your sister? I've never even spoken to her.'

'My father doesn't know that.'

'You're jesting,' said the knight, but his smile had disappeared.

Edward didn't respond.

The young knight's face tightened, but he held out his hand to take the reins. 'Wherever you're going, you had better be back here before the earl.'

Edward gestured to Robert, who, grinning, led his horse and his grandfather's courser to the indignant knight. The two youths made their way quickly across the field, ignoring the curious glances of the other squires. John de Warenne was speaking as they moved surreptitiously in behind the crowd.

'For one hundred years our kingdoms have enjoyed peace. Scotland and England have become true neighbours, flourishing through trade and the gifts of land and offices, and through the blessed union of marriage. King Alexander, God rest his soul, understood the benefits of joining our strength, through the marriage to his first wife, daughter of King Henry and sister to the gracious King Edward.'

Robert and Edward squeezed in behind a group of priors, whose tonsured heads gleamed in the sun.

'And while his death was a tragedy shared by us all, out of his sad passing a new hope now springs that may bring our kingdoms even closer in alliance. That hope exists in the form of his granddaughter, Margaret of Norway. As confirmed by the Treaty of Salisbury, the child will forthwith be transported to Scotland, where she will be enthroned as your queen.'

Appreciative murmurs followed his words. Robert stood on his toes to try to see over the heads of the priors. He could just make out the bulky form of Bishop Bek in between their shoulders, the violet of his robe garish. The bishop had something gripped in his fist. It was a thick roll of parchment.

'Two years before his death, Alexander wrote to King Edward, speaking of the possibility of a marriage between the royal houses of England and Scotland.'

As the earl spoke, Robert saw Bishop Bek unfurling the roll. It had a large seal attached to the bottom that hung down from the document.

'Now, the wish of both kings can at last be fulfilled. We have here a dispensation from His Holiness in Rome, granting the marriage of Margaret with Edward of Caernarfon, the king's son and heir.'

For a moment, after the Earl of Surrey uttered these words, there was silence. Then, the crowd erupted in a storm of stunned shouts of astonishment and protest.

13

'Did you know of this, Lord Steward?'
The Earl of Menteith's enquiry broke across the raised voices. One by one, the men seated around the table turned to look at James Stewart, the target of the question.

The high steward met the elderly earl's searching gaze. 'No, Walter. It was as much of a surprise to me as it was to you.'

'And you, Sir Robert?' Menteith moved his attention to the Lord of Annandale. 'You were in Salisbury for the signing of the treaty. Did the Earl of Surrey or Bishop Bek not mention anything of this proposal to you? Or you, your grace?' he asked of the Bishop of Glasgow, who was looking pensive, his chin thrust forward, resting on his clasped hands.

'No one knew of it,' said James firmly.

'Does anyone here believe Lord Alexander made any such proposition to Edward?' asked a young man with curly black hair and an intense expression. 'Because I cannot imagine he would have suggested a royal marriage without discussing it with his court.'

'Are you saying the English are lying, John?'

The younger man sat back with a defiant shrug. 'Perhaps.'

Several voices broke out in answer, but Robert, sitting with his brother on the edge of the hall's dais, kept his gaze on the curly-haired man who had spoken. He had met Sir John the year before, shortly after the young man had succeeded to the earldom of Atholl. The earl, who was also Sheriff of Aberdeen, had a reputation for being a firebrand, but Robert had found his frank outspokenness a pleasant change from the guarded manner of other lords he had met. John was married to a daughter of one of his grandfather's closest comrades, Donald, the stalwart Earl of Mar.

It was Donald who now turned to his son-in-law, his voice rising over the others. 'Be wary, John, of making such bold accusations without proof.

Lord Alexander was troubled, naturally so, by the death of his last son. Even after he made the men of the realm swear fealty to Margaret he was absorbed by the prospect of finding a more suitable heir, hence his search for a bride. We cannot know what he may have promised, or to whom in his time of uncertainty.'

Robert felt Edward lean in close and whisper in his ear.

'It seems the kings of Scotland promise many things.'

Robert guessed his brother was referring to the pledge made by Alexander's father, when he named their grandfather heir presumptive. His eyes moved to the old lord, who looked deep in thought. Robert took a drink of beer from the cup he had been given by one of Sir Patrick's servants. They had been ushered into the earl's hall with the rest of the men on their return from Birgham. There hadn't been enough room on the benches around the table, so the brothers had seated themselves on the dais. Robert had been waiting for his father to order them to leave, but the earl and the others seemed too occupied to notice their presence and so they had sat in silence, listening, as the men argued through the humid afternoon.

'Whatever Lord Alexander promised, it doesn't excuse the fact that Edward consulted the pope on the matter of this marriage behind our backs.' John of Atholl's voice was forceful. 'It is yet another example of the King of England's will to expand his borders. Do not forget what he did in Wales. The war there ended only seven years ago with the enslavement of its people and the death of Prince Llywelyn. Perhaps he means to do the same here, only with bonds of marriage rather than iron.'

'You speak of things you know little about,' the Earl of Carrick cut across him roughly.

Robert looked over at his father, who had served in Edward's army during the king's conquest of Wales. Robert had been eight when the earl had left with his men, only two of whom had come home. He recalled the change in his father on his return to Carrick: his sleeplessness, the way he drank more, his rough temper. The earl had been involved in some of the heaviest fighting of the campaign, one of many in the struggle that had been waged on and off for decades between the princes of Wales and the kings of England.

'With respect, Sir Robert,' continued John of Atholl, 'I believe your loyal service to King Edward colours your opinion in this matter.'

The Earl of Carrick's eyes narrowed. 'I would hope my service to any man to whom I had paid homage would be loyal.'

'Faithfulness as a vassal is one thing,' responded John, raising his voice

over James Stewart, who tried to enter the debate, 'but your intimacy with
the King of England is well known. You even named your second son after
him.' He gestured at Edward, sitting beside Robert on the dais. 'It was only
your third who was given the name Alexander.'

Robert glanced at his brother, who had sat up at the attention.

'I didn't realise there was a rule on naming one's children,' growled the
earl.

'This is getting us nowhere,' said James Stewart, his voice taut. 'John de
Warenne and Bishop Bek are expecting our answer in two days. We need to
make a decision.'

'You do not speak for all the guardians, Lord Steward,' cautioned Earl
Donald of Mar. 'Whatever decision we make here, it will need to be agreed
upon by Comyn and the others.'

'Let Bishop Wishart and I worry about that, Donald,' replied James. 'For
now, let us cease our arguments in favour of a conclusion.' He turned to the
Lord of Annandale, who was bowed and silent. 'You have been quiet, my
friend. I would know your thoughts.'

Some of the others nodded.

Silence descended. John of Atholl shifted on his seat as the hush dragged
on. Robert didn't think his grandfather was going to answer.

Finally, the old lord raised his leonine head. 'To my mind there are two
questions that must be answered before a conclusion can be reached. The
first is what do we stand to gain by accepting the proposal? The second
is what might we lose by rejecting it? The second question can be fairly
surmised in terms of what most of us have been granted by King Edward.
There are few among us here who do not own lands in England. My family
has benefited greatly from the patronage of its kings over the years. I think
it likely these gifts would be withdrawn if we reject the marriage. I have
always been on good terms with King Edward, but I know well he can be
swift to punish.'

Robert's father was nodding in unusual agreement with the lord. His
hard face was bullish as he scanned the others, defying any of them to argue.
No one did.

'But there is something that worries me even more than the loss of my
own fortune,' continued the lord, after a pause. 'And that is the cost to
our realm. Margaret is young. She has lived her short years in a foreign
court and she will be the first woman ever to be seated upon the Stone of
Destiny. She will require a regent or council to rule in her name for many
years. I remember well when Alexander took the throne at the age of eight.

I was witness to the power-mongering of the Comyns and their aggressive attempts to control him, even seizing him against his will and holding him captive. Alexander spent his youth as a pawn, used and fought over. It was only when he became a man that he was able to assert his will over those who sought to dominate him. Margaret will never be able to do this. It will only be through marriage that her position will be secured. One day, God willing, she will bear a son and through him our strength will return.'

'Then let her marry a Scot,' said John of Atholl. 'If Margaret marries Edward's son he will become king by right of her and our kingdom will lose its liberties. When Edward of Caernarfon takes the throne from his father Scotland will become just another limb on the swelling body of England, with him as its head. Sir James,' petitioned John, turning to the steward, 'do you want your great office taken over by an Englishman? And you, your grace' – he motioned to Wishart, who was frowning – 'do you want the Scottish Church to be subject to the sees of York and Canterbury? And what of the rest of you? Do you want to be taxed to the point of starvation like the Welsh?'

'I understand your fear, John,' said the Lord of Annandale, catching the younger man's impassioned gaze with his forceful stare. 'But this isn't comparable with what happened in Wales. The English are here to negotiate, not to make war. We can decide what terms the marriage will be subject to.' The old Bruce sat forward. Planting his large hands on the table, he surveyed the rest of them. 'We can determine our future.'

John Comyn rode into the camp as the sun was setting behind a towering bank of purple clouds. A westerly wind had picked up through the afternoon and the tents in the clearing were flapping wildly against their pegs and ropes. The great trees of Selkirk Forest swayed all around, their ancient branches creaking. A storm was coming.

Leaving his squires to tend to his horse, the Lord of Badenoch strode through the windswept dusk towards the largest tent, sprays of pine cones crunching under his boots. Sweeping aside the flaps, he entered.

John Balliol rose quickly from the low, fur-draped couch he'd been perched on the edge of. As he studied Comyn, his expression shifted. 'Leave me,' he told his pages. Before the servants had exited the tent, Balliol was crossing to Comyn. 'They did it, didn't they? I can see it in your face.' Even as he said it, hope rose in his tone, as if he might have read his brother-in-law wrong.

Comyn dashed it with a nod. 'I was outvoted.'

Balliol slumped on the couch.

Comyn spoke on. 'The others met with the English this afternoon to give their consent to the marriage.'

Balliol looked up numbly. 'I cannot believe the Lord of Annandale would agree to this.'

'Why not? This way he gets what he has petitioned for all along – the Maid of Norway will take the throne, as was Alexander's intention.'

'But by this marriage the Bruce and the others have signed away our sovereignty!'

'The guardians have agreed the marriage only if strict terms are met.' Comyn intoned the terms flatly. 'The liberties and customs of Scotland are to be maintained. Royal offices are to be held only by Scotsmen. Taxes shall be levied for the requirements of our kingdom alone. No Scot shall find himself subject to law beyond our borders and no other parliament shall deal with our affairs. Our kingdoms, although joined in marriage, will remain independent, ruled separately by queen and by king.' When Comyn finished, silence descended, broken only by the wind beating against the tent's sides.

'I have been sitting here for many hours fearing the worst,' Balliol said finally. 'But one glimmer of hope has shone upon me in that time.' He rose. 'Let us go to my father-in-law. Let us petition Sir John de Warenne to speak to King Edward, have the earl try to turn the king from this proposal.'

'Did you not see the papal Bull Bishop Bek produced? It was dated four years ago. Edward has been planning this since he learned of Alexander's death. Nothing will turn him from this course.'

Anger flared in Balliol. 'That is it?' he demanded, meeting his brother-in-law's dark eyes. 'You will not even try?'

'There is no use. These things are set in motion.'

Balliol took a step towards him, his hands reaching out as if to clutch around Comyn's throat. 'I gave up everything for this chance! A chance you persuaded me to take! In doing so I left myself open to attack by my enemies and marred my good name among the nobles of this kingdom. My mother went to her grave after the attack on Buittle. I am certain she would have lived longer had it not transpired. Now you expect me to retire to a life of – of –' Balliol wheeled away, groping for the words, then turned and spat them at Comyn. 'Of *obscurity*! Neither a king nor a respected lord at court.' His pockmarked cheeks were stained a feverish red. 'Well, you can be sure, *brother*, that whatever terms the guardians have agreed upon with the English, your family's long tenure behind the throne is at an end.' His face clenched in on itself, filling with rancour. 'I might be ruined, but I shall not be alone in the darkness, for I share my downfall with the mighty Comyns!'

Comyn maintained his cool in the face of Balliol's fury. 'I do not believe either of our families has to be ruined.'

'What could you possibly do to ensure that?' seethed Balliol. 'What? Will you seize the young queen as your family once did Alexander? Ransom her until your terms are met?' He shook his head. 'That abduction did not go well for the Red Comyns in the end. The Bruce saw to that. I doubt you will get the chance to take such action now.'

'If a fight for the throne began tomorrow our position would be different than it was four years ago. Our strongholds have been returned to us and greatly strengthened. I have not been idle in the interregnum and neither have the Black Comyns nor the Comyns of Kilbride. All of us have been making alliances, fortifying our positions and our territories.'

Balliol let out a frustrated sound. 'Why are you still speaking of fighting? The maid sets sail for Scotland to be betrothed to the heir of England. It is over, I tell you!'

Comyn glanced round as the tent flaps snapped and billowed. He could hear the sounds of the camp outside. Turning back, he met Balliol's gaze. 'Not if the girl never reaches our shore.'

Balliol went to speak, to blast Comyn with more of his wrath. He stopped, his face changing as what had just been said unfurled with sharp clarity in mind. 'I hope,' he murmured, 'that you do not mean what I think.'

'It is the only way this kingdom will survive, no matter what the guardians say, no matter what terms they impose on this marriage. Edward of Caernarfon is six years old, by God! He will have nothing to do with the rule of this realm for years to come and by the time he does his father will have tied us in legal knots so tight we will never cut ourselves free. Make no mistake, King Edward plans to take control of Scotland through his son.' Comyn's expression was grim. 'It is what I would do.'

Balliol went to him. 'You are speaking of infanticide, no – *regicide*! I will have no part in such evil.'

'Is it evil to safeguard our kingdom and its liberties? For that is what I am doing here. The girl will be a casualty of war. A necessary sacrifice. One life for the future of our realm. It is a small price to pay.'

'Small price? Is that what it costs to enter hell?'

'The guardians have arranged for an escort of Scottish knights to sail to Norway and travel back with the child. I can make sure one of our men goes in that escort.'

'Listen to your madness!' Balliol pushed past Comyn, heading for the tent flaps.

'No, you listen, John,' said Comyn, his voice turning to iron at Balliol's back. 'If that child sets foot on Scotland's shore, you will never sit on the Stone of Destiny. Tell me, are you willing to give up your only chance of becoming king?'

Balliol gripped the tent flaps, his head bowed between his outstretched arms, silhouetted in the ruddy glow of the campfires.

14

The longship carved a course through the deep, its dragon-head rear-ing over the waves, forty oars rising and falling along its sides like wings. The late afternoon sun picked out the gilt in the beast's painted scales, the gold reflected in the surface of the water in a rippling mirror image that flew beneath them as they ploughed westward through the North Sea.

Bishop Navre of Bergen sat hunched at the stern, sweating in his furs. It was mild for September, even out on the open water, although when the sun set and he was forced to bed down with the rest of the crew under the sail, he knew he would be glad of the skins. Four and a half days out from the coast of Norway and still he felt unsettled, the endless surge and swell of blue making his head swim and turning his legs to water. Gazing down the length of the vessel, past the oarsmen who lined the benches, Navre tried to catch a glimpse of the captain, keen to know when the man thought they might arrive at Orkney. He had been told by King Eric that the journey to the Norwegian islands shouldn't take longer than five days with a fair wind, but the breeze had hardly filled the sail since they left Bergen and they had been forced to rely for the most part on the oarsmen.

The bishop reclined, unable to see the captain past the white swoop of sail that filled his view at mid-ship and unwilling to make the precarious journey to the prow, over the ribs of timbers and the limbs and shields of so many men. The longship, called *Ormen Lange* in the tongue of his people, *Great Serpent*, was crowded, not only with crewmen, but with Scottish and English knights who had arrived at the Norwegian court some weeks apart, both parties insisting on escorting their precious cargo. The bishop had derived some satisfaction from King Eric's blunt dismissal of a galley sent by Edward of England, filled with gifts for the girl. The Scots might be gaining a queen and the English a wife for their future king, but she would be delivered to them in a Norwegian vessel in honour of her father and the kingdom into which she had been born. It was only twenty-seven years since Norse defeat at the Battle of Largs and twenty-four since the signing of the Treaty of Perth, by which the Western Isles and Man had been ceded to the Scots. For a people who had been masters of the northern seas for centuries this journey in the fearsome dragon-stemmed ship signalled the ending of an age and a last, proud act of defiance.

Hearing a girl's laughter coming from the wooden structure built against the stern, Navre looked round. The structure wasn't much more than a hut, with room enough for a child and one adult inside, but it had been beautifully fashioned from yew, with a little arched door and a slanting roof. The longship had no decks for shelter and the king had wanted his daughter to travel in comfort. The door opened and Margaret bobbed out with a fistful of gingerbread. There were crumbs around her mouth. She smiled at the bishop, then climbed on to a bench to peer over the gunwales at the water. He went to rise, anxious that the child was leaning so far out, but her maid was already ducking out of the shelter and cautioning her down. He sat back as Margaret pointed out a fish with an excited laugh. He was glad to see her joy, for she had wept bitterly as they had taken her away from her father and escorted her on to the ship. Navre's smile faded as he thought again of what this child, whom he had known since birth, was travelling towards. Right now, the lords of Scotland would be gathering at Scone, site of the ancient place of enthronement. Seven years old and the hopes of a kingdom were on her shoulders.

As the child crossed to the port side to look out over the water, the bishop caught a strong whiff of gingerbread. His stomach churned. 'You shouldn't let her have any more,' he told the maid. 'She'll make herself ill.'

'His lordship said—'

'I know what her father said,' Navre cut across the woman. 'He would have said anything to make her happy. But a chest full of sweetmeats isn't going to do that.' The bishop watched queasily as the girl pushed the last of the gingerbread into her mouth. Although King Eric had sent away the English ship he had accepted the gifts the Scots had brought the child in honour of her dead mother, daughter of the late King Alexander.

'When will we get to Orkney?' asked Margaret, sitting beside him and wiping the crumbs from her dress.

'Soon, child.'

As Margaret hummed a tune they had heard the oarsmen singing, the bishop put his head back and closed his eyes, the last of the sun warming his face.

Navre came awake, feeling someone's hand on his arm. Opening his eyes groggily, the bishop saw the maid staring down at him. Behind her, the sky was a softly undulating sheet of white. He realised, after a second, that the sail had been drawn down over the vessel for the evening and the longship was now rocking at anchor in a blue twilight. 'What is it?' he said, sitting up with a groan. His neck ached from the awkward position he had slept in.

'Please come, your grace.'

Navre rose unsteadily and followed the maid to the shelter. He ducked and forced his bulky frame through the narrow entrance. The smell of sickness struck him first, bitter in his throat. Margaret was curled on her fur-lined pallet, her face sallow in the glow of the single lantern. She was clutching her stomach. He bent down beside her and touched her head. It was clammy and her hair was damp. There were brown streaks of vomit on her chin and on her dress. Navre turned to the maid, lingering nervously in the doorway. 'I told you not to let her have any more sweets,' he murmured angrily.

'I didn't, your grace,' whispered the maid.

Navre reached out and picked up a bowl off the floor. There was a half-eaten portion of thick broth crusting the sides. He sniffed at it.

'Her meal was fresh,' said the maid, a note of indignation in her tone. 'I made it for her myself. It must be the foreigners' food. Or a fever.'

The girl whimpered and stretched back her head, her face screwing up in agony. Blue veins stood out on her skin. Her eyes had narrowed to slits. The bishop put down the bowl and pushed past the maid.

Bent almost double beneath the sail he made his way down the length of the ship, as the boat heaved in the water. He stumbled on a shield, continued on. Cracking his shin against a timber, he straightened with a wince of pain, his head thumping into the taut sail above. On he went, tripping over legs, his hands brushing heads. The boat pitched over a wave. Someone grabbed his arm as he toppled sideways.

'*Careful.*'

Navre muttered his thanks into the crowded shadows. Finally he reached the prow, where he found a group of men sharing a cup of mead and laughing over a story the captain was telling.

Seeing the bishop, the captain stopped short. 'Your grace?'

'How far from land are we?'

'If we set sail at dawn we'll be at Orkney by midday.'

'We must get there sooner.' Navre lowered his voice. 'The princess is ill.'

The captain frowned, then nodded. 'I'll wake the men. We'll row through the night.' He gestured to one of his crew. 'Svein is a healer. He will look at the child.'

As the bishop and the healer made their way back a bell began to clang and the captain shouted for the crew to hoist the sail. A whisper went down the boat. *The princess is sick.*

One of the English knights, roused by the commotion, stopped the bishop on the way to the stern. 'What is wrong?' he asked in Latin, a tongue common to them both. 'They're saying the girl is ill. Can we do anything?'

'You can pray,' answered Navre, ducking into the shelter.

The men heaved and pulled on the oars, propelling the ship through the dark, the dragon-head glowing in the starlight. In the shelter, the girl tossed and sweated in the furs, sometimes crying out for her father, but mostly quiet in her suffering, her ashen face strained in the lantern light. The healer tried to give her salt water to make her sick again and drain her body of any putrefaction in the food she had eaten, despite the maid's insistence that it was fresh. But she was too weak to take it. In the end, he settled for laying a wet cloth on her head to try to cool the fever. Navre knelt beside her. He had taken his crucifix from the chest of his belongings and now held it over her head to ward off any demons that might be circling, while he prayed for the child's soul.

Some hours later, a line of darkness appeared in the west. The sky, dusted with stars, was lightening, slowly. The oarsmen, exhausted and sweat-drenched, found new strength at the sight of land and, after a time, the longship drew towards a deserted strip of sand on one of Orkney's cluster of islands.

The crew vaulted over the gunwales and splashed down into the water, grabbing hold of the ropes. With the wash of the waves, they hauled the broad vessel on to the sand. Navre stooped to gather Margaret in his arms. Her breathing was faint now and she hadn't cried for some time. Fearful of the nearness of death, he had asked her the seven questions and administered the last rites. Her skin was as white as marble, a sign that she was in the shadow realm. He carried her out into the dawn where the cold wind lifted her hair. Svein and the maid moved in to help, but the bishop refused to relinquish his hold on the girl as he made his way carefully down the gangplank.

The men fell into a hush as the Bishop of Bergen waded into the shallows, the sea dragging at his cloak. The English and Scottish knights crowded in behind him, their faces tense. As the bishop laid the girl on the dry sand, her head fell back against his arm. He gazed down at her. Margaret's eyes were open, staring into the pale sky.

15

'I beg you, Sir Robert!' called the monk, hastening to keep up. 'Do not go armed into the house of God!'

The Lord of Annandale paid no heed, continuing in his determined stride as he headed for the church, his cloak, emblazoned with a blue lion, whipping around him in the breeze. Behind him came the Earl of Carrick with ten knights, all armed. The earl had his hand around the hilt of his sword and a coat of mail glinted beneath his surcoat and mantle. The church, rising ahead, was tinged with a bloody hue in the dying light. The doors were closed, but the arched windows were filled with shimmering torchlight.

Robert glanced round as he and Edward walked quickly in the wake of their father and grandfather. The brothers had swords sheathed at their sides and both wore leather gambesons, steeped in oil and wax to stiffen them. Beyond the abbey buildings, Robert picked out the slope of the Moot Hill rising into the red dusk. The tops of the circle of trees that surrounded the ancient place of enthronement flamed copper in the last of the light. His attention was distracted from the hill by one of his father's knights.

'Stay behind us,' warned the man, turning to the brothers as the company approached the church.

Ignoring the pleas of the monk, the Lord of Annandale pushed open the doors. A tumult of voices washed out with the feverish glow of torches. The voices broke off abruptly as the doors banged back against the walls.

Robert, moving in behind the knights, saw twenty or so men turn to look at them. Most he knew from the assembly at Birgham five months earlier: the bishops of Glasgow and St Andrews, Earl Patrick of Dunbar, Earl Walter of Menteith and others. The rest were Augustinian monks from the abbey, dressed in their habits. Beyond the crowd the nave stretched away, flanked by angels and saints, their stone faces turned towards the altar.

'Is it true?' demanded the Bruce, his voice blistering. His face was flushed and his mane of hair, blown by the ride to Scone Abbey, was wild about his head.

Robert had never seen his grandfather so wrathful. It surprised him, for until now the old man had seemed relatively calm, despite the disastrous events of the past month.

The Bruce family had been on their way to Scone to await the arrival of the maid, when news of the child's death had swept south to reach them. Rumour spoke of the longship that had conveyed the girl to Orkney turning around and sailing back across the North Sea, taking her body home, the marriage vessel now a funeral ship. The Bruces had parted company at once, the lord riding hard to Annandale to ensure his strongholds of Annan and Lochmaben were strengthened, and Robert's father returning to Carrick to fortify Turnberry and alert his vassals. The atmosphere of optimism that had pervaded Scotland during the summer, as people prepared for the inauguration and the betrothal, was at an end. The succession to the throne had been thrown wide open.

Robert had been with his grandfather at Lochmaben, when darker tidings had come, this time from Galloway. Even then, his grandfather remained calm, waiting for the return of his son before the company, strengthened by their knights, had gone with all speed to Scone, where the rest of the magnates were gathering.

Now, the lord's poise vanished.

'Tell me, is it true?' he growled again, his eyes raking the silent crowd. 'Has John Balliol declared himself king?'

'Yes,' said a voice.

Robert recognised it immediately and moved out from behind the knights to see James Stewart emerging from the throng.

'But it has not been endorsed by us all.'

'Endorsed?' came the harsh voice of John Comyn. 'You speak, Lord Steward, as if the succession to our throne can be decided upon by committee. It is a blood right!'

'There are others besides the Lord of Galloway who have a blood right,' replied James sternly. 'How else, other than by vote, will it be decided upon which of them has the greater claim?'

'Lord John Balliol has the greater claim,' responded Comyn. 'And all of us here know it. Primogeniture—'

'Our kingdom observes laws older than primogeniture,' the Earl of Carrick cut across him. 'By those ancient customs it is my father's right to take the throne.' He addressed the men, his voice ringing imperiously through the lofty nave. 'With Alexander's stock exhausted, the line of succession reverts to his great-great-grandfather, King David, the youngest son of Malcolm Canmore. David's next surviving progeny was the Earl of Huntingdon. As the son of one of the Earl of Huntingdon's three daughters my father is nearest in blood to the royal line that sprang from the House of Canmore.'

'But he is a son of the *second*-born daughter,' challenged Comyn. 'As grandson of Huntingdon's *first*-born, John Balliol should be king. By primogeniture, the elder line is the dominant line.'

'We have been one of the most influential families in this kingdom for almost two centuries. My father was designated heir to the throne by King Alexander II, for the sake of Christ!'

The Abbot of Scone winced at the earl's last words and tried to protest. John Comyn didn't give him the chance.

'That claim is as antiquated as your family's power in this realm,' spat the Comyn. 'The act was performed when the former king had no heirs. When his son was born it became meaningless. Who has held sway in the royal court these past decades?' he demanded, turning in a circle to confront the men. 'The Comyns. If power and influence should be called upon to determine the next king, then it is my family who stand at the fore.'

The earl's face flushed with fury, but as he went to argue the Lord of Annandale stepped in. 'We are in a dark and difficult time.' His voice echoed in the church. 'We lost a king and now we have lost the hope of a queen. What this kingdom needs is strength and unity. Choose Balliol and you will get nothing but a weak-willed man who is led by others.'

'And if they choose you?' demanded Comyn. He turned again to the magnates. 'Do not forget that this man who comes armed into a place of worship was the same man who, in our time of crisis, invaded Galloway. He speaks now of unity? King Alexander's body was not cold in the ground before the Bruce attacked his neighbour! Would you have a tyrant for a king?'

Robert, watching the exchange, stepped forward at this, clutching the hilt of his sword. The bands of leather around the grip were hot beneath his fingers. A few of his grandfather's knights also moved in, their faces tightening with anger at the insult to their lord. Some of the magnates retreated uneasily, but Comyn stood his ground, levelling the Lord of Annandale with a belligerent stare. Robert pulled his sword a little way out of its scabbard at the threat in Comyn's dark eyes.

'Please, my lords!' called the abbot, looking to the other nobles for support. 'This is not the place for such conflict!'

'I have a right to be heard,' the Lord of Annandale demanded, pushing past James Stewart, who stepped in front of him. 'My claim cannot be ignored!'

'Cease, my friend,' James was saying.

'You have no claim, Bruce,' responded Comyn. 'It is over.'

'By God is it not!' fumed the Earl of Carrick, forcing his way through the throng and striding down the aisle, eyes alight.

Robert saw his father was headed for the altar, upon which was a large block of stone. It was creamy-coloured with some sort of crystalline sand within that glittered in the torchlight. Two iron rings were fixed to either end and it was placed on a cloth of gold silk, upon which he made out the creased paws and head of a red lion. Robert knew at once that this was the Stone of Destiny, the ancient seat that would be carried up the Moot Hill for the inauguration of a new king. It had been brought to Scone more than four hundred years ago by the first King of Scots, Kenneth mac Alpin, but its origins were lost in the depths of time. It was the seat Macbeth had sat upon before being overthrown by Malcolm Canmore.

'I will take what belongs to my family by force!'

The Lord of Annandale shouted as his son went for the stone. Other nobles cried out in protest In the confusion, Comyn stepped towards the lord.

Robert saw Comyn reach for the food knife that hung from his belt beside a money-pouch. At once something fired in his blood. Pulling his blade free from its scabbard he lunged. There was a rasp of metal on leather and a flash of steel. The men all turned to the storm-eyed youth, standing between the Lord of Annandale and the Lord of Badenoch, his sword pointed at Comyn's throat. The Earl of Carrick had halted in the aisle between the rows of stone angels and was staring in disbelief at his son.

Robert, his heart hammering in his chest, met Comyn's gaze, his sword tip wavering inches from the lord's neck. He wanted to tell the men that the lord had no right to challenge his grandfather, who had fought justly against Comyn's secret scheme to put Balliol on the throne in defiance of King Alexander's wishes. He wanted to shout that his grandfather was a better and wiser man than any of them and they would be honoured to have him as their king. But before he could, he felt a hand come down upon his shoulder.

'Lower your sword, Robert,' said his grandfather, his voice low and implacably stern.

Slowly, Robert obeyed, realising the attention of every man in the church was now on him. He noticed his brother staring at him in astonishment from out of the line of Carrick knights.

'Nothing can be determined here tonight,' said James Stewart, surveying the hushed crowd. 'This decision must be made by the men of the realm. I suggest we convene again when cooler heads prevail and when all are present to make their voices heard.'

'I agree,' said Robert Wishart. His assent was joined by others.

The gathering began to move, murmuring agitatedly. The Earl of Carrick made his way back down the aisle, his face like thunder. As the Lord of Annandale turned to go, John Comyn grabbed his arm and leaned in close. Robert, caught between them, smelled a bitter odour coming from the wolf pelt that trimmed Comyn's cloak. He heard him breathe words.

'My father should have killed you in that cell in Lewes when he had the chance.'

The Lord of Annandale jerked from Comyn's grip. Propelling Robert in front of him, he headed for the church doors, past the Bishop of St Andrews who was speaking urgently with Wishart.

'There will be blood,' the bishop was saying. 'Unless this matter is settled quickly.'

16

As he stepped into the evening, Robert heard his father call his name harshly. He didn't look back, but fought to match his grandfather's stride. 'What did Comyn mean? About Lewes?' His brow knotted. 'Grandfather!'

The lord halted abruptly. 'Do not raise your voice to me, boy.' He took hold of Robert's chin roughly. 'And you should not have drawn your sword against him like that. Do you hear? It is time to make our case with words, not violence.'

'I thought Comyn was going to attack you,' said Robert, pulling from his grandfather's grip. 'And why would you care that I drew my sword against him, when you attacked his castles? You hate him!'

'Yes!' barked the old lord. 'And that hatred has the power to rip this kingdom apart!' He stopped, seeing the earl striding towards them. Turning from Robert, he headed for their horses.

Robert followed doggedly, his need for answers greater than his awe of this lion of a man. 'You've taught me to ride and to hunt, trained me to fight. You took me to Salisbury and Birgham, introduced me to the most powerful men in the kingdom. You tell me how important I am for the future of this family. Yet you've told me almost nothing about your hatred of the Comyns, despite all the times I've asked. I want the truth, Grandfather!'

'You're too young for it.'

Robert halted. 'If you become king, I will be an heir to the throne. That right is not determined by age. Why should the truth be?'

The Lord of Annandale turned, his craggy face changing, anger fading into surprise. After a moment, the lord crossed to him and grasped him by the shoulder. 'Come.' He glanced round as Robert's father approached with his knights and Edward. 'Get the horses. We'll follow.' Before the earl could respond, the lord steered Robert away across the courtyard.

As they came out from between the buildings, Robert realised his grandfather was leading him to the Moot Hill. Together, they climbed the slope to
the bare crown. The sun had set and the shadows were gathering. From the
royal burgh of Scone, beyond the abbey grounds, smoke drifted on the chill.
It would soon be All Souls. Their breath misted the air as they reached the
top. There was a stone plinth rising from the earth in the centre of the circle
of trees. As Robert saw it, he knew at once that it was where the Stone of
Destiny would be set for the inaugurations. He stared at it, struck by the
gravity of this place.

Even with all that had happened since the maid's death, he realised he
had still been seeing his grandfather's claim as something distant and unreal.
Now, in this hallowed setting, where since time immemorial Scotland's
kings had been made, he felt the profound weight of this truth settle inside
him: it wasn't just words, claims and counterclaims — it was something as
real and solid as the stone itself. He thought of the tree his grandfather had
spoken so seriously of when he first arrived at Lochmaben; the tree with
roots stretching back into the past. Men whose blood flowed in his veins
had ascended this hill to this very spot. He was standing on the echoes of
the footsteps of his ancestors. All around him now, in the dusky shadows,
Robert could feel them: the ghosts of his history. The kings of old.

In the dying light, his grandfather turned to him.

Lewes, England

1264 AD

The council of war had ended and letters of defiance had been exchanged. There were to be no more words. Now, only swords would make statements, expressing themselves in the flesh of the enemy.

One by one, the three divisions of the royal army left the safety of the town walls, riding behind their commanders. White clouds chased one another across the morning sky, sweeping vast shadows over the Downs that surrounded the town of Lewes. May blossom fell on the heads of the cavalry and their horses, and on the foot soldiers that followed in their wake. Sunlight flashed in and out, glinting on lance tips and glittering across mail. Riding up on to the higher ground, banners flying, they left the town below them. The castle keep was still visible for a time, jutting from its grassy motte, beyond which the land tumbled into the valley cut by the river. Ahead, nearer now, were the men they had come to meet.

The enemy was arrayed on the hillside in three contingents half a mile long. They had the advantage of the high ground, the terrain studded with trees at their backs. In the front and centre of one company a banner was raised, one half white, the other red. It was parted down the centre, a fitting image for the division in the kingdom that had led these men, once allies and comrades, to these cloud-crowned English hills. The knights of the royal army, who had ridden out of Lewes, were fixed on that banner like archers to a target, all their focus channelled into that distant, undulating cloth, the mark of so much hatred and the reason for their being here: the arms of Simon de Montfort, Earl of Leicester.

Sir Robert Bruce, Lord of Annandale, Sheriff of Cumberland and Governor of Carlisle, watched as the motionless enemy lines grew closer with every stride of his horse. His men rode around him, eleven lances in all, with a banneret to bear his standard. The ring of their bridles was loud in his ears, above the thunderous din of the three-thousand-strong company he moved within, led by the King of England. Beyond the circle of his knights were his countrymen, who, like himself, had crossed the border at King Henry's summons to do service for their English lands. Among them were John Balliol, Lord of Barnard Castle, and John Comyn of Badenoch. Both lords were in their fifties, ten years his senior and grey-haired and soft-bellied with it, but they were set for battle, their men formed up around them. The division between the two armies extended even into families, for while John Comyn was here to serve the king, another branch of the family, the Comyns of Kilbride, were with the rebels. Fighting for Simon de Montfort, they were no doubt hoping for a slice of the glory already attained by the more influential branches of the Red and the Black.

This was the closest Bruce had been to Comyn since his arrival in England. Until now, the two men had kept apart, their animosity seething, invisible between them. It was only seven years since the Comyns had kidnapped King Alexander in an attempt to gain control of Scotland. Despite the fact that Alexander had since been restored to his throne and peace bargains struck, it wasn't long enough for Bruce to forgive the treachery against the young king, whom he looked upon as a son. Neither was it long enough for the Red Comyns to forget that Bruce supported their enemies during the crisis and had been instrumental in Alexander's restoration, an act which almost destroyed their family.

It was thus with watchful unease that the Lord of Annandale rode his horse on to the Downs, aware that the enemy beside him might be more dangerous than the one arrayed on the hilltop. A stray blade in his back. A misdirected arrow. Such a thing would go against every code of chivalry, for nobles did not intentionally kill nobles, even in battle. But the Comyns had little true noble blood in them, despite their high position.

Hearing a horn, Bruce looked ahead to where King Henry's banner marked his position in the vanguard of the royal army's left flank. The front lines of the king's company were slowing. Bruce reined in his horse, his men gathering around him. Through the forest of lances he could see two more contingents stretching away across the hillside. The centre was commanded by Henry's brother, the Earl of Cornwall, the right flank by the king's son. Edward was visible even at this distance, unmistakable in scarlet and gold. He had returned from France the year before at the head of a large company of French nobles, intending to liberate his lands in Wales from Llywelyn ap Gruffudd. Instead, he had been plunged into the conflict between his father and godfather that had escalated into the unthinkable. Civil war.

For six months, Edward had pursued Montfort and his supporters across the realm and into Wales, challenged by the mountains and shadowed by the menace of Llywelyn. Bruce, who had been in the king's service since the start of the year, aiding in a victory over Montfort's forces at Northampton, had heard much of Edward's exploits. Despite reservations about the young man's impetuous and aggressive temperament, Bruce had been impressed. He had never seen a man so confident before battle. King Henry had ordered one of his barons to lead the left flank in the charge and the Earl of

Cornwall had chosen his eldest son to direct the centre's attack. But Edward would lead his own men. The Earl of Leicester might have the advantage of the high ground, but that was all. The royal army, ten thousand strong, outnumbered his rebel forces by more than two to one. Montfort was in his middle years and had never fought a pitched battle. Edward was twenty-five, filled with determination and a youthful sense of immortality, blooded all last summer on French tournament grounds.

On both sides shield straps were tightened, helms drawn down over padded coifs, stirrups adjusted, girths checked. Knights took their lances from their squires, gripping the ash shafts. There were no coronels to spread the force of impact, no dulled tips. These were lances of war. Behind the front lines of the royal cavalry the smaller contingents, Bruce's among them, readied themselves, but didn't yet pull on their helms. They would form part of a second wave. Behind them the foot soldiers covered the slopes in a thicket of spears and swords. Their part too was yet to come. First, the knights.

The horn blew again from Henry's ranks, followed by a deeper, answering call from the enemy lines; two beasts roaring at one another across the green hills. The knights of the royal army set out. They started at a walk, riding knee to knee. On the hillside, Montfort's forces remained motionless, keeping tight control over their horses. These men wore the white crosses of crusaders; a sign that theirs was a holy cause, as proclaimed by their leader. The royalists leaned forward in their saddles to aid their destriers on the slope. The walk turned into a trot, bells on caparisons ringing. As they neared the enemy the breaks between the three companies became more apparent, Henry's left flank driving towards Montfort's right, centre towards centre. Still, Montfort's forces waited. Battle cries sounded from the royalists, tearing from throats; feral sounds made by men who knew this charge could be their last. Now, trot turned to canter and the earth began to shudder. At the last moment, so as to preserve as much energy for the fight as possible, Montfort unleashed his cavalry. His knights spurred their chargers and plunged hard down the hill to meet the incoming force. Horses struck white wounds in the grass as hooves scuffed the chalk beneath. Lances swung down to level at the enemy as hundreds of tonnes of steel and muscle raced towards one another.

As the armies clashed, the Lord of Annandale, watching with the remainder of the king's flank, knew the awe of an English heavy cavalry charge. Lances shattered, horses reared, men tumbled from saddles. Blood flew, flesh opening beneath edges and points of iron that punctured padding and mail. The unhorsing, wounding and capture of the enemy was sought, for corpses fetched little ransom, but in the blind chaos of the charge, death was a whore who did not care who she drew into her darkness, veteran knight or callow bachelor.

Edward's company punched through the enemy's left flank like a fist through *parchment, tearing great holes in their lines. Lances, spent or smashed, were thrown aside as the ranks closed in, drawing swords and hacking at one another. The crack of steel on shields and screams of men and horses rose in a mad clamour. More knights fell, those unhorsed pulling at those still mounted, dragging them down into the crush beneath. Down here, swords were knocked from hands and daggers were drawn, the battle close and grim. All notions of chivalry were swept aside in the rough press. Weapons jabbed and slashed, seeking openings in defences. Arms and fingers were broken under hooves, spines cracked, groins gashed.*

The reek of blood swelled in the stew of the mêlée as Edward's company pushed against the rebels, half his men locking the left flank into the vicious brawl, while the others circled to outflank them. Montfort's men fought on bitterly, but were soon surrounded. Those still in their saddles found their horses attacked, the beasts toppled by the slash of blades across hind legs. Edward's men sounded his battle cry; a cry that had called so many ambitious bachelors to his banner, from the tournament grounds of France to the wars in Wales. Slowly, but surely, the enemy's lines began to break apart under the determined onslaught of Edward's forces. Horns rang out in encouragement as the young lord and his knights surged deep into the ragged left flank of Montfort's army.

The two other contingents of the royal forces were engaged in more sober, rooted battles against Montfort's right and centre. The rebels had used less energy in the initial charge, allowing the high ground to do its work in tiring the royal forces on the upward assault. Montfort himself, along with his seasoned knights, was concentrated in the centre, against the Earl of Cornwall. Cornwall's son had led a rather loose charge, his men splitting at the crucial point of impact. Montfort, by contrast, had kept his ranks tight, forming an indomitable barrier against which Cornwall's knights had dashed themselves, like waves upon rocks. The battle for the centre had since spread out across the hillside. Several times Cornwall's forces tried to outflank the rebels, but Montfort's horns had called his bowmen to repel the knights with a rain of arrows that blinded and disorientated them.

King Henry and his barons, at the head of the left flank, fought a slower, more entrenched campaign. Having called up the smaller contingents, they were making some progress against Montfort's right wing, but unlike Edward's ferocious attack which had smashed through the enemy lines, they were only able to chip away at the determined rebels, who refused to give quarter.

Across the hillside, above the chaos of Montfort's left flank, a scarlet banner was raised by Edward's men, the dragon at its centre a terror wreathed in golden flames, a sign that there was to be no mercy. The noblemen who survived the battle would be taken prisoner and ransomed, but no such chivalry awaited the foot soldiers beyond. Mostly made up of labourers from London, they would fetch no payment. They were nothing but an opportunity for the slaking of blood lust, nothing but fodder for worms. Edward's knights, bypassing the straggling remains of the cavalry, crashed straight through them. As the infantry, unable to withstand such brute force, turned and raced for the safety of the woods at their back, Edward's men followed. Rushing up the hillside, they thundered away down the other side to vanish from view.

Ahead was a mass of moving spears as Montfort's right flank pushed doggedly against King Henry's company. The Lord of Annandale gripped his lance, holding it steady as his horse was knocked and jostled. His helm channelled his vision into two slits of chaos and his knee was being crushed, wedged between his saddle and another man's destrier. The sweltering heat inside his helm and the stink of his own sweat were suffocating. Every now and then, when an opening appeared, Bruce roared at his men, still pressed tight around him and, together, they urged their horses forward to block it, jabbing and thrusting at any who attempted to push through. Edward's company was long gone, as were the foot soldiers they had been pursuing. Only Montfort's centre and right flank remained, but although their numbers were inferior, their resolve was anything but. Edward's disappearance had left Cornwall's company open to attack from the side and Montfort was using that advantage to full effect, leading his veteran knights to outflank the earl's forces.

The mob ahead of Bruce parted again and another of Montfort's men broke through. He was blood-spattered, his shield buckled and splintered in the centre. He came straight at Bruce, faceless in steel, only the arms on his surcoat and ailettes offering any clue to his identity. Both were unknown to Bruce as he lunged with his lance. It collided with the side of the man's helm. Iron tip screeched along metal cheek, then punched on past. The man reeled with the blow and lashed out with his sword, striking Bruce in the head. The Lord of Annandale felt the blow like a hammer on his brain. His head thudding with the concussion, he snarled against the pain and struck out, but the knight was already gone, pulled from his charger by one of Bruce's men to be trampled into the sludge of mud and blood welling up beneath the hooves. Bruce could hear cries all around him, punctuated by the squeals of horses. More of Montfort's men were pushing through, spearing holes in Henry's lines.

A horse reared up beside Bruce, sending its rider tumbling into him, clouting his lance out of his grip. Hauling on the reins as his mount panicked, refusing to let it turn, Bruce recovered his balance and wrenched his sword from his scabbard as another rebel came at him. Despite the fact that his horse was bucking beneath him, he caught the man in the neck with a crushing blow, the man's mail snapping with the force. The blade stuck in flesh, before the lord wrenched it free with a mist of blood. Somewhere, a horn was blaring.

The Earl of Cornwall had been outflanked by Montfort's forces. Finding himself *caught in a sea of enemy soldiers, his knights unable to reach him, the king's brother fought his way free in desperation. Spurring his horse out of the mêlée, he fled across the fields. As his household troops followed, their horns ringing a retreat, the battle for the centre disintegrated. The rest of Cornwall's forces, leaderless and panic-stricken, began to scatter, the rebels roaring in elation as they gave chase. The centre, breaking apart across the hillside, left the king's flank wide open to attack. Seeing the royal forces in disarray encouraged Montfort's men to an ever more determined assault and all along the front lines of King Henry's company gaps appeared as his knights were beaten back. Simon de Montfort had proclaimed this a holy war against the king. Now, it appeared, God was on his side.*

A cry went up. Retreat! Retreat!

King Henry and his royal knights led the flight, the king's banner trailing red behind him as he urged his destrier down from the high ground, back towards Lewes. Retreat turned into stampede. The Lord of Annandale found himself swept up and carried from the hillside in the blind tumult. One man went down in front of him, his horse smashing to the ground in a cloud of dust. Bruce kicked his charger and vaulted up and over, iron-shod hooves striking the chalk as it came down hard on the other side. His banneret was to the side of him. Some of his men were close behind. He could just glimpse them through the slits of his helm. All else was confusion, the king's infantry scattering across the hillside before the knights.

All around the town of Lewes, torches were burning. The flames billowed in the evening, giving off a haze of acrid smoke that drifted over the rooftops. Around one building, some distance from the castle and set in its own grounds, the torches formed a dense constellation in the gathering shadows.

In a cell in Lewes Priory, four men were waiting. One sat on the room's single pallet, his head in his hands, another leaned against the wall by the door, eyes closed, and one was on the floor, knees drawn up to his chest. The fourth stood by the window, staring out across the dark silhouettes of the priory's outbuildings to the flickering points of fire that lit a mass of men.

On the air, Bruce could hear screams as horses, too badly injured in the battle to be saved, were despatched. Above the pitiful noises rose the sound of raucous laughter and song. Montfort's men had not been slow to celebrate their victory. Bruce could see them through the cobweb-strung window of the cell. He glanced round, hearing a sniff. John Comyn, over by the door, still had his eyes closed and Balliol his head in his hands. Bruce guessed the sound had come from the third figure, huddled on the floor. The squire couldn't have been more than eighteen; not much younger than his eldest son, back in Scotland. His eyes were pools in the gloom. Bruce grunted, glancing at Balliol, the squire's master, who hadn't looked up. After a moment, he turned back to the window, unwilling to offer words of reassurance to someone else's man. Besides, he had none to offer, for what comfort was there in the face of capture and defeat?

Hours earlier, after the battle on the Downs turned into a rout, King Henry's forces had fled to the safety of the monks' precinct, which had formed the king's camp since his arrival in Lewes. Other cavalry made it into the town, but had holed up elsewhere. The infantry wouldn't have been so fortunate. Unable to match the swift retreat of the knights, they would have been easy targets for Montfort's pursuing forces. Their passing, although brutal, would at least have been quick. The humiliation of imprisonment, waiting for another man to decide his future, seemed, to Bruce, a worse fate. In battle a man had choices, in how he fought and how he died. He was still free. Here, all choice was suspended. He hated the death of his own control, fearing it more than the death of the flesh.

It wasn't long after the king and his men barricaded themselves in the priory that Montfort's forces stormed the town. The priory was surrounded and Montfort paraded some of the captives from the battlefield, including the Earl of Cornwall, outside. Montfort clearly took pleasure in shouting to Henry that his cowardly brother had fled the battle and hidden in a windmill. He then threatened to execute the earl in front of the priory, if the king refused to agree to his terms of surrender. Such a threat seemed impossible, for no earl had been executed in England for almost two centuries and it went against every code of war. But Montfort wasn't engaged in any normal battle: he was waging war on his king and trying to take control of the realm. Henry, Montfort demanded, would deliver himself into his mercy and agree to allow a council of barons to rule in his stead. He would remain king in name alone, almost all of his authority stripped from him and handed to this council.

Bruce had been in the refectory with his knights when five figures had burst in. One was grievously injured and was being held up by two comrades. All were coated in blood and filth, the reek that followed them appalling. At their head was Lord Edward. Bruce listened with the others as the young man recounted to one of the king's barons how he had destroyed Montfort's fleeing infantry, pursuing them for miles, but had returned only to find the battle was over. His company had been attacked trying to enter the town. He managed to escape and, guessing his father had retreated to the priory, crawled through a drainage ditch out of sight of Montfort's forces.

Shortly after, the king entered, pushing through the crowded hall. The concern and relief that flooded Henry's face quickly turned to anger, his cheeks mottling as he harangued his son, demanding to know why he had abandoned the battlefield. Edward stood his ground, towering over the king. He said, his voice imperious, that he thought his father would be able to defend his own flank. Silence followed, Henry seeming to slump, his fury draining along with his resolve as he told his son they had no choice but to surrender. Edward argued against this, saying they had supplies, they could hold Montfort off for weeks. But now it was the king's turn to stand firm. Montfort had threatened to execute his brother. It was over.

'You sealed our fate when you left the field of battle,' Henry finished. 'You will bear the bitterness of surrender.' He had turned to the silent crowd of men. 'All of you. I have made my decision.'

Negotiations between the royal forces and the rebels outside continued, but only formalities remained. The men inside the priory were split up on Montfort's orders, according to rank and region, their arms relinquished. The priory, their sanctuary, became their prison, where they would wait until Montfort decided their fates. Edward was to become a hostage, while Henry would be returned to London, where he would be allowed no more freedom of action than his captive son.

Bruce's jaw tightened as another sniff came from the squire. Arguably, out of the four of them in the cell, the young man was the most likely to come out of this unscathed. He wasn't a lowly foot soldier and so unless Montfort really was willing to execute the nobility he wouldn't be killed and any payment for his freedom would be negligible. To the Lord of Annandale, the prospect of ransom was an ugly apparition. He was a high official under King Henry and a powerful lord in Scotland. Montfort would not let him go lightly. This could ruin his family for generations. He closed his eyes, the wrath of St Malachy burning down the decades towards him, blackening his line, from his forefathers to his sons.

The rattle of a latch made all four look up. Balliol struggled to his feet with a wince, his old face furrowing with dogged determination. The door opened and a man appeared, holding a torch. Bruce recognised him. He had seen him before in Edinburgh. It was William Comyn, head of the Comyns of Kilbride.

John Comyn broke the silence. 'It appears you chose the right side for once, cousin.'

William Comyn smiled grimly. 'The Red Comyns have had their time in power, ruling our family with an iron fist. Now, perhaps, it is our turn.'

'If you have come here to gloat you can save your breath,' growled John. 'Whatever Montfort does to me, the Red Comyns will continue. My son and heir will make certain of that.' There was a threat veiled behind the words.

William Comyn's smile faded. 'On the contrary, cousin, I have come to release you.'

Balliol scoffed at this, although his squire had risen hopefully. 'I didn't realise the Earl of Leicester was taking orders from a Scot.'

'Sir Simon rewards those loyal to him. I petitioned for the release of my kinsman and he granted me three prisoners in return for my service.'

'Why would you do this?' murmured John.

'We may not always see eye to eye, cousin, but we are all Comyns beneath the shroud of our personal ambitions. It would not serve me, or the Comyns of Kilbride, to see you ruined by a ransom fee. What I want in return for your release is a greater share of the influence wielded by our family. A position in the royal court.'

Still, John seemed unconvinced. 'My fee alone would make Montfort a rich man. Why would he release three men?'

'Montfort has enough noble prisoners, including Lord Edward, to fill his treasury four times over and, besides, money isn't his motivation. He understands you were just doing your duty by the king. He would prefer you free, as cooperative allies,' added William, looking at Bruce and Balliol, 'rather than prisoners.'

Balliol nodded. 'Well, he can be assured of that. As can the Comyns of Kilbride. The Balliol family stands in your debt, Sir William.'

'Sir?' questioned the young squire fearfully, as Balliol went towards the open door.

Balliol glanced back at him. 'Your ransom will be met,' he said dismissively.

'Sir, I beg you,' implored the squire.

'Come,' said William Comyn, impatiently to the Lord of Annandale.

As Bruce went forward, John Comyn moved in front of the doorway. 'Not him,' he said, meeting the Lord of Annandale's eyes, his own dark and glittery in the torch flames.

'Cousin?'

John Comyn didn't take his gaze off Bruce. 'The Bruce stays.'

'Sir Simon de Montfort granted me the release of three men.'

'Did he stipulate which three?'

'No, but—'

'Then he is the third,' said John, gesturing to the squire, whose face flooded with relief.

'A squire's ransom will be next to nothing, cousin. It isn't worth it.'

'It is to me,' replied John Comyn. The corner of his mouth curled, puckering his face, but the smile was anything but humorous. 'Do you recall, Sir Robert, when my family came to you, asking for your support against our enemies when Alexander succeeded the throne so young? You must, of course, for it was a desperate time and none felt it more keenly than my family, the fortune and influence we had achieved through decades of hard work and loyal service to the crown threatening to slip through our fingers. You were the one man who could have aided us, who could have kept the balance of power during the king's minority, negating the need for the action we were later forced to take in our bid for survival.'

'Bid for survival?' spat Bruce, stepping forward. 'You held our king against his will!'

'But do you also recall your response?' John Comyn cut across him. 'That you would sooner serve the devil than the lowborn sons of clerks? I told you then that one day I would repay you for the ruin my family faced following your decision. This is that day.'

As William Comyn stepped aside and Balliol and the squire followed him out, John Comyn closed the cell door. The last thing the Lord of Annandale saw was Comyn's face, shining in the torchlight.

17

The city of Lincoln was drowned in rain. Clouds clotted the sky, seeping an endless deluge on the heads of the throng gathered outside the cathedral. Mothers and infants, guildsmen and farmers, innkeepers and paupers, the pious and the curious all huddled together in the downpour, waiting to catch another glimpse of the royal procession that had filed into the arched darkness of the cathedral an hour earlier. Above, the bell continued to toll, the sound reverberating over the heads of the silent multitude, across the waterlogged market square, out into the empty streets beyond.

In the cathedral's cavernous interior a sombre congregation stood bowed in prayer, filling the aisles to the Angel Choir. Lords and ladies, barons and knights, maids and royal officials, all were clad in black, their faces covered with hoods and veils. The knights bore shields shrouded with cloth that hid colours and devices, rendering the men anonymous, uniform in grief. The cathedral too was dressed for mourning with lengths of gossamer black silk draped from the arches. A wan light bled through the trefoils and quatrefoils on the middle storey, illuminating ghostly swirls of incense and wisps of candle smoke. Rain smeared the great eastern window and beat a tattoo on the stained glass that could be heard between the slow tolls of the bell.

To Edward, standing in front of the high altar, baleful in ink-black velvet, that bell was a hollow heartbeat. Behind him was the rood screen, beyond which the thickly moulded arches stretched away, curving over and over down the nave in a grotesque suggestion of a ribcage, the Purbeck marble veined and sinewy. Before the king, placed on a hearse and surrounded by a halo of candlelight, was a coffin. It had been covered with a pall of Venetian silk, embroidered with hundreds of tiny gold flowers, so that only its shape was visible: a black, angular outline, the size of a human. Inside that coffin was his wife.

Edward had been left stunned by how quickly his life had been shattered by the fist of death. Barely days after he had learned the devastating tidings that Margaret of Norway, his son's bride-to-be, had died on the way to Scotland, Eleanor had fallen ill. She had suffered with a sickness in Gascony that left her weak and the physician suspected that this had led to the fever that had taken hold so swiftly and so voraciously. Edward had Eleanor moved to Lincoln to be close to the shrine of St Hugh of Avalon, but nothing, not prayer, medicine or miracle had been able to save her.

Eleanor, his Spanish queen, had been with him for thirty-six years. On the day of their marriage in the kingdom of Castile he had been fifteen, Eleanor just twelve. In all that time she had rarely left his side, joining him on crusade in the Holy Land, supporting him through the campaigns in Wales and the bloody rebellion of Simon de Montfort. She had been with him in illness and defeat, in exile and in triumph, through the births of sixteen children and the deaths of eleven. She had been his reason and reflection, his compassion and his wisdom. Now, she was a corpse in a wooden box, her organs removed for enshrinement in Lincoln, her body to be conveyed to London with all the ceremony of state Edward could marshal. He had already paid for bedesmen to be sent out across the kingdom to proclaim the obit and, soon, all the towns of England would sound with the clang of the mourning bell, from Winchester and Exeter, to Warwick and York.

As the bishop intoned a psalm from the Breviary, the king heard weeping behind him. He glanced round to see his son, Edward of Caernarfon, standing with his four older sisters. The little boy was crying into his hands, his shoulders shaking. The king turned back without a word. His own grief was knitted inside him, woven into his muscles and sinews, bound up in his gut and chest. To release it would be to fall apart, to come undone. He had no intention of doing any such thing. He might have lost his love. But he had not lost his purpose.

When the last words of the Requiem Mass were uttered by the bishop the congregation began to shift. As the acolytes sprinkled the coffin with holy water dripped from sprigs of hyssop, the lords and bishops in the choir surged forward, intent on paying their respects to his dead wife and to him. Edward did not want their sympathy or their pity, which, from some, would be nothing more than show. Several of his more recalcitrant barons had been unhappy with his long absence in France and had made their frustrations known earlier in the month at parliament. To Edward, their sad expressions were nothing more than masks and he could no more stand to look upon their wooden visages than he could that shapeless coffin.

Motioning curtly to John de Warenne in the front row, the king strode to a
door in the north transept and entered the passage that led to the cloisters.
The Earl of Surrey followed a moment later.

Edward reached the cloisters, where rain was dripping steadily on to the
square of grass in the centre of the arched walkways. He closed his eyes,
drawing a breath of frigid November air that revived him after the cloying
smell of incense. He looked round as John de Warenne came to stand beside
him. The aged earl, who was several inches shorter than him, had recently
gained a paunch. The slabs of muscle, developed over years of training and
fighting, were softening to fat and swelling the earl's already bulky frame.
The king was struck by the change in his ablest commander's physique and
wondered if it was somehow a metaphor for his reign. Was he, too, softening? Becoming flaccid? Was this why his plans had gone so awry? His jaw
tightened at the thought. 'Tell me again what the Bishop of St Andrews said
in his message.'

John de Warenne paused, seeming to consider his answer.

'Well?' said Edward.

The earl cleared his throat. 'Forgive me, my lord, but is this the time for
such a discussion? Would you not rather wait and—'

'On the contrary,' said Edward coldly, 'I want to begin planning my next
move before the Scots close ranks and we are shut out. Answer my question.'

'The bishop said Sir John Balliol declared himself king in the wake of
Margaret's death, but that Sir Robert Bruce of Annandale has since countered the claim. The men of the realm are divided between the two and
the bishop fears this division will erupt into war. He implores you to come
north and help restore the peace. He believes the magnates of Scotland will
listen to you. He wants you to be involved in choosing the successor.'

Edward stared out over the sodden lawn, watching the rain cascade from
the arches. 'Is this not the same situation as that faced by my father when
Alexander first took the throne?'

John de Warenne grunted. 'There are similarities, but I wouldn't say it
was the same, my lord.'

'But the Scots requested my father's intervention after Alexander
succeeded to the throne as a child,' said Edward impatiently. 'And through
this intervention my father was able to arrange the marriage of my sister to
the king.'

The earl nodded. 'Yes, although the marriage gave your father little in the
way of control over the throne of Scotland. His grip on the realm remained
tenuous at best.'

'My father never knew how to turn a situation to his advantage,' responded Edward. 'What of Balliol and Bruce? What would each be like as a king, do you believe?'

'Well, as the man is wedded to my daughter, I know Sir John better than I do the Bruce.' Warenne shifted his broad shoulders. 'Balliol is a malleable man, I would say. Not a natural leader. More comfortable receiving orders than giving them. The Bruce on the other hand is shrewd and strong-willed, although he has always been a loyal ally of yours and the lands he holds in England make him as subject to you as he ever was to Alexander.'

The lines that marked Edward's brow deepened. 'I believed, when Alexander spoke of the possibility of marriage between our houses that I had found a way of accomplishing my aim without any need for great expenditure, or loss of men. You know how the wars in Wales crippled me. I cannot afford such a costly military campaign. Not now, when the barons are festering over my long absence.' Edward turned to Warenne. 'But neither will I let what I have worked so hard to achieve be in vain. My father may have been blind to the opportunity presented by the Scots' appeal for intervention. I am not. As soon as my wife's body has been laid to rest I will go north, finish what I started six years ago. I believe the prophecy can yet be fulfilled without war.'

Affraig pulled her cloak tight around her as she stepped into the late December evening. The wind bit into her skin and dragged tears from her eyes. The sky was ashen and the hill stood brown and bleak. Just a few leaves clung to the bare limbs of the oak and the ground around it was strewn with twigs and a papery carpet of russet. Affraig saw that two more destinies had fallen in the night, tossed from the branches by the gale that had danced like the devil through the valley to beat its fists against her walls. She would bring them in later, burn the twigs and the rope that bound them, then bury the objects, delivering them to the earth.

Crouching, Affraig set down the pestle and mortar she was carrying and ran her fingers across the ground. It was as hard as stone. Taking the pestle in both hands, she drove it into the earth, working the black soil loose. The effort warmed her body as she laboured, pausing to push her hair from her eyes. A dank smell filled the air as, slowly, the earth about her feet was broken into clods. Setting the pestle in the mortar, she drew a pouch from her belt. Already she could see a fat worm pushing its way out of one of the clods, seeking and blind. She grasped it, drawing its pink length out of the mud. It twisted in her pinching fingers as she stowed it in the pouch. Her hands turned the clods, searching for more. In this way, she collected seven earthworms. Holding the pouch closed, she picked up her pestle and rose.

The dogs looked up expectantly as she entered the house. Ignoring them, she went to her work area, where she set down the mortar and sack. The woman would be here soon. Shaking a handful of musty-smelling barley into the mortar, Affraig drew out the earthworms, one by one, and laid them on top of the grains. The worms squirmed against one another, their corded bodies glistening in the glow of a single candle. Affraig laid her palm over the top of the bowl, leaving enough room to wedge the pestle between the splay of her thumb and forefinger, then plunged the rounded end of the stone instrument into the mortar. It slipped and slid for a few moments, until the bodies burst and she found purchase, grinding the pestle in brisk movements. She closed her eyes and murmured a series of words before taking out the pestle and banging it on the side of the mortar. Inside was a raw, slippery mess, thickened by the barley. She wondered about sprinkling some dried lavender heads into it, but decided against it. The woman wasn't paying her enough for that.

Affraig was cleaning out the mortar when the dogs leapt up and began to bark. She hissed at them as she crossed the cluttered chamber and they quietened at once. Opening the door, she saw two women making their way down the hillside, their woollen cloaks tossed by the wind. She heard a peal of laughter come from the larger of the two. The sound nettled Affraig. There was a time when people came to her in reverent silence, their eyes filled with fear and awe. Now, the women laughed and teased one another as they filed to her door for their love spells and charms. In some senses, she doubted they even truly believed, despite the coins they gave her. It was something they did just in case, a spare chance if God didn't hear their prayers. They had forgotten the ancient days when warrior women called curses from the sky like lightning against their enemies; the days when Druids walked the land of Britain and all would cast down their eyes, forbidden to look upon the holy men. The old magic was fading. It had been for a long time.

The two women stepped into the house, close together, eyeing the dogs. Affraig went to the counter and picked up a linen pouch, tied with twine, into which she had spooned the mixture of worms and barley. She crossed to the larger woman. 'It is done.'

'What must I do?' asked the woman, taking the pouch eagerly in her stubby fingers.

'Put it into his food on the next night when the moon is full. You must make certain that he eats it all. When he has, he will be induced to love.'

The woman licked her lips as she stared at the pouch. 'And he'll ask me to marry him?'

'He will yearn for you, that much I can say.'

'How will you get it into his meal?' questioned the other woman, over her companion's plump shoulder.

'I'll make sure I'm in the kitchen before supper is served in the guardroom.'

'You'd better make sure he doesn't get the wrong portion,' sniggered the companion. 'You could end up being wooed by that old goat Yothre!'

The woman glared at her friend, then looked anxiously back at Affraig. 'What if he doesn't eat it by the next full moon?'

'Then it will not work. The spell will decay.'

The large woman frowned at her companion. 'He's in Annandale serving Sir Robert. Will he be back in time?'

'They're due any day now, so Lady Marjorie said.'

'The Earl of Carrick is in Annandale?' Affraig cut across them.

'Yes,' responded the plump woman, her eyes brightening, eager for gossip. 'Haven't you heard? Now poor Maid Margaret is dead a great council is to be held. Lady Marjorie says the King of England will come north in the spring to help choose our new king. Earl Robert will soon return to Turnberry to prepare his claim.'

'His claim?' Affraig's voice was taut. 'It is not the earl's right, but the right of his father, the Lord of Annandale, to take the throne of our kingdom.'

The large woman looked unconvinced. 'The lord is as ancient as these hills. He'll not wear the crown for long. The earl will succeed him.' She gave a self-satisfied smile. 'And his knights will benefit greatly by his elevation.'

'And so will you, if you marry one of them,' murmured her companion, pinching her arm and making her giggle.

The large woman held out her free hand to Affraig. 'Here's your payment.'

Affraig felt the hot pennies drop into her palm. Resisting an urge to throw them into the woman's pasty face, she clamped her cold fingers over the sticky metal and went to the door. She opened it without a word, her face grim.

The two women bustled past, out into the cutting wind. Affraig watched them head up the hill, the plump woman holding the pouch aloft and singing words in a girlish voice, while the other cackled. Affraig's eyes moved to the oak tree that towered above her, its branches like antlers against the white sky. Her gaze travelled up to the weathered web that hung from one of the higher boughs, the slender noose swinging inside. In her mind she saw herself weaving it while she chanted words against Malachy's wrathful curse. She remembered the lord's hand settling on her shoulder, the hiss of the fire, his breath on her neck and, outside, stars falling like fiery rain. Her gaze moved west towards Turnberry. Her memory clouded with thoughts of the earl, but as she thought of his son her mind cleared. The stars had been falling too on the night he was born. She remembered seeing Mars, full and red, a bloody eye winking in the black.

The River Tweed curved a broad course through meadows and crop fields. The southern banks marked the end of the kingdom of England while across the wind-ruffled water, on the northern bank, the kingdom of Scotland began.

At a large, lazy loop in the river on the English side was the small settlement of Norham. The town, slumbering in the treacle-thick heat of a midsummer afternoon, was dominated by a stone castle, one of the chief strongholds of Anthony Bek, the Bishop of Durham. The sheer whitewashed walls, reflected in the river's glassy surface, were gashed with arrow slits, all facing the reed-fringed northern bank. Hanging from the tallest turret was a scarlet banner, adorned with three golden lions.

Inside the castle's hall, a host of men was gathered. Beams criss-crossed the vertiginous space above their heads and the painted walls were bedecked with tapestries. On one half of the hall the hangings displayed scenes of salvation. The other side was dominated by judgement. At the end of the chamber a stained-glass window showed the archangel Michael weighing the souls of men, his grim face made up of hundreds of shards of ruby-red glass. Below the window, in the centre of a dais, was a throne. Seated upon it was the King of England. Around Edward stood his chief officials, the Earl of Surrey and Bishop Bek among them. They were joined on the platform by thirteen men.

Robert, standing beside his brother in the crowd of Scottish magnates, watched with the rest of the assembly as, one by one, the thirteen crossed the dais to kneel before the king. The hall was eerily silent. This was supposed to have been a momentous occasion and, indeed, it was, but just not in any way the Scots had envisaged. Robert noted that the only men in the gathering who appeared satisfied with this ceremony were the English. As well they might, for their king was now overlord of Scotland.

Only last month the Scots had been awaiting Edward's arrival with keen expectance. True, there had been wariness among some and the Bishop of Glasgow in particular had voiced his concerns over foreign intervention, but for the most part the atmosphere had been charged with hope. After five turbulent years, the matter of who would succeed Alexander would at last be determined. The guardians and the realm had remained divided between Balliol and the Bruce, despite fraught councils at Scone, and so King Edward was coming to act as arbiter between the two.

Late in April, the magnates began to gather at the royal burgh of Berwick on the north bank of the Tweed to await the king. But when Edward finally arrived he came not with the visage of a brother or friend, but with the face of a would-be conqueror, escorted by an army of lawyers and advisers, shadowed on the coast by a fleet of warships and on land by six hundred crossbowmen and five hundred knights. Here, in Norham Castle, Edward had told them he would indeed choose their king, but first they must recognise him as their overlord. He said he brought evidence, in the form of extensive documents wielded by his clerks, that proved his ancient right to this position. The guardians led by Bishop Wishart protested vigorously against the demand, but the king remained coldly defiant through the heated councils that ensued, and all the while his army kept an ominous presence on the banks of the Tweed.

In the end, despite their protests, the Scottish magnates were forced to yield, desperate for a conclusion that would end the uncertainty within the kingdom. The constables handed over control of the royal castles and the guardians were compelled to resign their authority, whereupon Edward reappointed them with the addition of an English official. There was, however, one condition to these terms which the guardians had refused to concede on. The condition was that Scotland's future independence be secured by Edward's agreement that he would act as overlord only until a new king was appointed. Within two months of the inauguration, he was to return control of the royal castles, resign his authority to the King of Scotland and, thereafter, would demand nothing more. Edward agreed, setting his seal to the arrangement, before announcing to the silent magnates that he was a fair man and that this would be a fair hearing, which meant all potential claimants should be allowed to make a case for the throne.

Robert looked on as a flamboyantly dressed man, who had arrived in Berwick with a large entourage the week before, crossed the dais to kneel before the English king.

Bishop Bek's voice boomed again through Norham's hall. 'Will you, Sir

Florence, Count of Holland, accept the judgement of the illustrious King Edward of England, Duke of Gascony, Lord of Ireland, conqueror of Wales and overlord of Scotland? And do you agree, before all present, that he has the legal right to try your case for the throne of this kingdom?'

The colourful count bent low before the throne and, as the nine men before him had, answered in the affirmative. There were only three men waiting now on the left-hand side of the dais.

Next, it was John Comyn's turn to walk the platform to the throne. When the Lord of Badenoch knelt, Robert noticed he did not incline his head as much as the others. Indeed, the lord's rigid body hardly seemed to bend at all. Robert felt a nudge and glanced at his brother. Edward nodded along the row of men beside them, past their father, to where a pale youth with lank black hair was standing. It was John Comyn's eldest son and heir, who shared the lord's name. Robert had seen him several times since the assembly at Birgham the year before, although they had never spoken. The youth's gaze was transfixed by his father's kneeling form and a flush mottled his wan cheeks. His expression was one of pride.

'Does he really think his father has a hope of being chosen?' muttered Edward.

'He must know he doesn't,' Robert murmured back. 'Comyn isn't even pressing his claim. He wants Balliol to be king. Grandfather reckons he just wanted his claim put on record, a formality.'

Young John glanced round, his look of pride shifting to one of hostile dislike as he met the gaze of the Bruce brothers.

Robert's attention moved to the men gathered on the king's right, now joined by the Count of Holland and John Comyn. Most, like Comyn, didn't seem truly to believe their claims were strong enough to gain them the throne. Despite the king's assertion of a fair hearing everyone knew that in reality there were only two men in this competition. Those two were the last to step forward and submit to the king's authority. First came John Balliol, eager and smiling.

'If he bows any lower he'll snap,' whispered Edward.

Next came the Lord of Annandale and it was Robert's turn to feel pride swell within him. His grandfather knelt slowly, with a pained expression, his huge frame protesting at the awkward position into which it was forced. But even as he bowed the lord lost not one inch of his authority.

Robert studied the English king while his grandfather was addressed by Bishop Bek. He could discern very little emotion in those grey eyes, except perhaps a distant sadness, but maybe he just thought he saw that, for tidings of Queen Eleanor's death had preceded the king. They had all heard how Edward had ordered masons to erect monumental crosses, marking the places where his wife's body had rested during its procession from Lincoln to London. Robert had imagined these stony pillars of grief dotted along England's countryside. He had heard a great deal about the king: his valour as a crusader, his skill and fearlessness as a warrior, his canniness as a statesman and his passion for hunting and the joust. He had been surprised by Edward's cold and threatening demeanour, for it seemed so at odds with the man his father had always spoken of with such admiration.

His grandfather rose, stoop-backed, to join the other claimants. As Bishop Bek addressed the assembled men, Robert felt a rush of impatience. Since the moment his grandfather had led him on to the Moot Hill, the old man's fight had entered his blood. If his grandfather was named king by Edward, he in turn would be heir to the throne, second in line only to his father. Still, Robert tried to force away his impatience, knowing the hearing would not be over for months, maybe longer. After today, once his grandfather's petition had been lodged, the Bruces would be returning to their homes like everyone else, to await the verdict of Scotland's new overlord.

19

'She's looking at you.'

Robert took a mouthful of plum-dark wine as Edward leaned in close, his voice filled with mirth. 'Oh?' Robert leaned nonchalantly against the wall, but his gaze darted furtively across the bobbing heads of the dancers to the other side of the hall.

His brother laughed, seeing the look. 'No, not really.'

'Cur,' muttered Robert. He scanned the crowd, his eyes searching for the scarlet veil that had been there only a few minutes ago. The hall was filled with music, the whine of bagpipes and the thud of drums rising over the footfalls of the men and women. The trestles and boards, on which the feast had been presented earlier, had been pushed aside to make room for dancing. A line of laughing women criss-crossed back to meet the men, obscuring Robert's view. He looked away and, as he did so, caught a flash of scarlet up on the dais. It was her.

Her name was Eva and she was a daughter of Earl Donald of Mar, one of his grandfather's staunchest allies. Robert had met her on several occasions over the past year, her father journeying to Annandale to support the lord through the hearing. She wasn't the first woman he had noticed: there were one or two girls in Lochmaben who had captured his attention during his residency, including the niece of one of his grandfather's vassals, who had made him a man in a cobweb-strung barn on the edge of the woods. But Eva was different. She was of his rank and, as a young lady of standing with education, was far more self-assured than the town girls. Robert feared she wouldn't be so easy to impress.

As he watched, Eva bent down beside her father, draping an arm companionably around the elderly earl's broad shoulders. The silk folds of her scarlet veil, held in place by a circlet of braid, slipped over her shoulder, framing her face. A few strands of honey-blonde hair floated around her cheeks, flushed with heat and wine. She smiled as the Lord of Annandale leaned over and said something to the earl. Robert pushed himself determinedly from the wall, ignoring his brother's grin, and made his way through the crowd. There was a rush of skirts and breathless laughter as a woman twirled in front of him and away again, back into the arms of a waiting man. Robert lifted his goblet to his lips and tipped the last of the wine into his mouth, then handed the vessel to a passing servant. He wasn't a squire tonight. Tonight, he was the grandson of the man who might be king.

It was a year since the thirteen men had knelt before King Edward in Norham Castle. A year since the English king had taken control of Scotland. The hearing had opened in the royal burgh of Berwick last summer with written petitions from each claimant lodged, along with rolls detailing their pedigrees. A court had been chosen, composed of one hundred and four men, eighty of whom had been selected by each of the two chief claimants: the Lord of Annandale and Balliol, and the rest by Edward himself. The pedigrees the king had sent to France, to be studied in detail by scholars from the Sorbonne. Now, it was almost over. The king was due to announce his verdict any day and the Lord of Annandale had arranged this evening's feast at Lochmaben to thank some of the magnates who had endorsed him. The old Bruce, now in his seventieth year, was confident, with good reason. The lord had a blood claim rivalled only by Balliol's, was a staunch vassal of the English king, serving under Edward in the Holy Land and fighting for Henry against Simon de Montfort. And, most crucially of all, he had garnered the support of seven of the thirteen earls of Scotland, who, by ancient law, could choose a king.

Robert was approaching the dais, his eyes on Eva, when he heard his name called. He turned to see his mother. Lady Marjorie's raven-black hair, streaked with silver, tumbled from beneath a padded mesh of blue silk that matched her gown. To Robert, she looked like a queen, erect and beautiful. It was only as he went towards her that he saw the shadows around her eyes and the skin stretched taut over her bones. Realising his grandfather wasn't the only one this hearing had weighed heavy on, he felt ashamed that he hadn't thought of her in these months. Robert glanced at his father, up on the dais. The earl had a drink in his fist and his face, dark in the plunging shadows thrown by the torchlight, was beetle-browed and glowering. He doubted the man had been easy to live with.

'My son,' said the countess, appraising the tall figure Robert cut in black hose and buttoned tunic. 'You look so handsome.'

Hearing a giggle, Robert saw one of his sisters peering out from behind the countess's skirts. It was the youngest, Matilda. Still giggling, she ran to where the rest of his sisters were sitting with their nurse. He couldn't believe how much they had changed since he had seen them last. Mary was an unruly seven-year-old, apparently always in trouble like Edward. At nine, Christian, with her curly fair hair, was serious and sensible, and Isabel was a proud young woman. He wished his other brothers had been able to attend the feast tonight, but Niall and Thomas were in fosterage in Antrim, following in his footsteps, and Alexander was due to enter the priesthood. There was talk of him going to Cambridge to study divinity.

'I haven't seen you dancing yet,' continued the countess, laying a cool hand on his hot cheek.

'It is still early,' said Robert, his gaze roving towards the dais.

Lady Marjorie gave him a knowing look. 'Ask her,' she murmured, before melting back into the crowd.

Discomforted by his mother's shrewdness, Robert made his way up on to the dais over the heads of the crowd. He walked down the table, scattered with the remnants of the feast, past his brooding father to his grandfather and the Earl of Mar. The Earl of Atholl, Sir John, was there with his wife, an older daughter of Earl Donald, dressed in red like her sister. Robert approached the men, trying to ignore the blush of scarlet that threatened to fill his view. He opened his mouth, hoping something appropriately courtly might emerge, but his grandfather beat him to it.

'Ah, Robert, we were just speaking about you.' The lord's face was blotchy and tiny purple veins webbed his nostrils.

'Indeed we were,' said John of Atholl. 'Your grandfather was telling us of your exploits on the hunt today.' The intense young earl leaned towards Robert with a keen smile, his hair curling around his brow. 'I hear yours was the killing strike. I'm sorry I missed it.'

'A hart of sixteen tines,' said the Lord of Annandale, sitting back with a satisfied grunt, grasping his goblet. 'The best and last of the season.'

Robert couldn't resist any longer. His eyes flicked to the patch of scarlet crowding his periphery. He locked eyes with Eva. She too was smiling, but it was a cooler, more appraising smile than the men's, as if she were still judging him and was yet to be impressed. Her eyes were a paler shade of blue than his own. The colour of a spring sky, he decided.

'Eva.'

She turned as one of her younger sisters, a thin girl, whose hair was more mouse-brown than honey-gold, came tentatively up the steps.

'Yes, Isobel?'

'Will you dance with me?'

With a squeeze of her father's shoulders, Eva stepped lightly down from the dais, taking her sister by the hand. She threw a brief, backward glance at Robert, before disappearing in the throng, leaving a wisp of scarlet to trail in his vision.

The Earl of Atholl rose, taking his pretty wife's arm. 'I think we will join them.' John grinned broadly. 'Beware, Robert. All the best daughters will soon be taken.'

The young man winked at the Earl of Mar and the Lord of Annandale, who both chuckled in a way that made Robert suspect they had been talking about more than his hunting skills. He was eighteen; no doubt the question of marriage wasn't far from any of their minds these days, especially given the circumstances. A suitable bride, of high standing and dowry to match, would soon be chosen. If indeed, he thought, taking in the men's knowing smiles, she hadn't been already. Keen to change the subject, he fixed on the dried palm leaf pinned to his grandfather's mantle. 'Do you think King Edward will answer the pope's call to crusade?'

As the men's expressions sobered Robert wished he had thought of a less bleak conversation. It was six months now since tidings had reached them of the fall of Acre, the crusaders' last stronghold in the Holy Land. Rumour spoke of men and women jumping into the sea to escape the Saracens' blades, chaos and fire, streets running with blood and ships filled to the gunwales with tattered refugees limping into harbours across Christendom. The pope had since been calling for a new crusade, but nothing had been set.

'Perhaps, when our throne is filled, we might all answer that call,' replied his grandfather in a low voice. He drained his goblet.

Earl Donald was nodding. 'What we need is new blood for the holy war.' He inclined his head to Robert. 'If a young and powerful lord were to take the Cross, others would follow.'

There was a hiss from along the table. They turned to see the Earl of Carrick glaring at them, his eyes hooded and bloodshot. 'Powerful lord!' He staggered to his feet, his chair screeching back behind him. He flung an arm towards Robert, his goblet still gripped in his fist. Wine splattered the table. 'If that is your hope for the Holy Land then God help us!'

His words were slurred, but clear enough to ring like a bell in Robert's ears.

'Enough,' growled the Lord of Annandale.

'I speak the truth. He hasn't fought in a war. He knows only how to kill *beasts*, not men. New blood?' The earl grimaced. 'The blood runs thin in all our sons. Thin as watered wine. How will we make crusaders out of such diluted stock?' The earl continued his poisoned stream, but Robert didn't wait to hear any more.

Turning, he strode down the steps into the crowd. Ignoring the protests of people he pushed roughly past, he made it to the doors and out into the night, leaving the music and voices to fade behind him, swallowed by darkness. Out across the bailey he went, past chapel and kitchens, stables and kennels, the buildings silhouetted in the pallid light of a half-moon. Before him, over the rooftops, rose the humped blackness of the motte, its steep sides carapaced in clay. Atop the reinforced mound a round tower pointed a blunt finger towards the distant stars. Instead of climbing the motte to the keep, where he shared lodgings with his grandfather, Robert headed to the palisade that encircled the castle compound. He was almost at the gate, when he heard his name. He turned to see Eva hastening towards him, her scarlet veil black in the moonlight.

'You're leaving the feast?'

'I needed air.' Not wanting to remain inside the castle another moment, even for her, Robert continued towards the palisade.

Eva fell into step beside him, the skirts of her dress rustling over the icy ground. It was late autumn and the trees were splayed naked against the sky. The guards at the palisade greeted Robert as he approached. One opened the gate with a lingering look at Eva.

'Careful how you go, Master Robert,' he called, a smirk lacing his voice. 'It's wet down by the loch tonight.'

Robert led the way through the trees along the dark path to Kirk Loch. Neither of them spoke. Robert's mind was oddly still now, frozen between rage and rising anticipation. After a moment, the trees fell away and the small body of water opened before them, glittering in the moonlight, edged all around with reeds. His grandfather's castle, seat of the family for over a century, had been built strategically close to water, but unlike the stronghold of his ancestors at nearby Annan the motte and bailey were a safe distance from the loch-side, the Bruce family having learned the price of Malachy's curse.

Robert came to a stop, staring out across the water.

Beside him, Eva shivered in the glacial air and moved closer, wrapping her arms about her.

Robert knew what he should do, knew even what she wanted him to do, but his father's twisted face was breaking through into his thoughts, those words dripping like venom from his mouth. After a moment, he felt something brush against his hand and realised it was her fingers. They threaded through his. Somewhere in the woods an owl screeched. Robert's heart quickened, his breath coming in clouds. The image of his father was fading, pushed aside by the solidity of her hand in his. He could feel her pulse, rapid as his own. He turned to her, keen to banish the rest of his thoughts, and sought her mouth with his. She tensed, seemingly surprised by his eagerness, then softened against him. She tasted of wine.

Hearing a distant drumming, Robert assumed it was the blood pounding in his head, until the sound grew louder and he realised it was hoof-beats. Three, maybe four sets. He drew back from Eva.

'More guests?' she murmured. Her lips were glistening wetly in the moonlight.

The look of them made him spasm uncomfortably and when he spoke his voice came out strained. 'No.' He cleared his throat. 'Everyone's here.' Robert hesitated. He wanted to stay out here with her, but those hoof-beats had distracted him. It was late for travel. 'Come.' He took her hand and led the way back into the woods, leaving the loch hushed and unruffled behind them.

As they approached the palisade, Robert realised he could no longer hear the bagpipes. Passing through the gate, he caught raised voices coming from the hall. He quickened his pace, Eva almost running beside him, her skirts gathered in her free hand. There were horses in the bailey and the smell of fresh dung. Robert made for the hall, the doors of which had been flung wide open. He could see people milling, a mass of faces. Edward emerged from the crowd. As his gaze alighted on Robert, he came forward. Robert had never seen his younger brother look so grim. 'What is it?'

'It's been announced. John Balliol will be king.'

20

Robert walked the gloomy track through the woods, head down, thumbs stuffed into his belt. The wind rattled the bare boughs of the trees and sent the dead leaves scattering about his feet. His pup, Uathach, one of Scáthach's last brood, chased them in mad circles, her jaws snapping at the swirling carpet. Usually, the young bitch's antics amused him, but he hardly noticed today. Robert's mind, clouded with thoughts, was turned inward, his mood as dark as the November afternoon.

It was a week since the feast and the atmosphere in Lochmaben couldn't have been more different than before the announcement had come. Many who had supported his grandfather during the hearing had since made their excuses and left, distancing themselves, as if the family had contracted some malady that might be contagious. Robert knew such thoughts were perhaps unjust, for the earls of Mar, Atholl and Dunbar had clearly been stunned and angered by the English king's decision. But the castle had been unusually quiet for the past seven days and there was no denying that, as enemies of Scotland's new king, the Bruces' standing in the realm was now very much in question.

Robert's father and mother had remained at Lochmaben, although the earl's wrathful presence had done little to ease the tension. The old lord spent much of the week in his chambers alone, only leaving to pray in the chapel. Two nights ago, Robert had found his grandfather slumped on his knees before a blaze of candles on the altar, saying a fervent prayer over and over, wine sour on his breath. *The curse*, he had groaned, as Robert helped him to his feet. *We must make amends.*

Robert had kept apart, spending his days walking in the woods, avoiding even his brother. The country around Lochmaben was quiet now the hunting season was over. The autumn rains had erased the tracks made by horses and men, the forest reclaiming its territory. In the past twelve months, his life had taken on a thrilling momentum. His apprenticeship in Antrim, the training at Turnberry, the path to knighthood he had set out upon in his grandfather's household, all had finally converged, leading to a grand destination — far grander than he could have imagined. The throne of Scotland. Now he knew what lay ahead was nothing more than a mirage, something glittering and deceptive; the road before him had ended in darkness and uncertainty. He might still be heir to his family's fortunes, but what would become of those fortunes with an enemy on the throne and the Comyns promoted to even higher offices? Would Annandale and Carrick be safe, or would Balliol enact his revenge on the men who had invaded his lands six years ago? They had heard the lord had recently made Dungal MacDouall captain of the army of Galloway. MacDouall's father, Robert knew, had been killed by his father during the attack on Buittle and no doubt a desire for vengeance was something these Galloway men had been sitting with for a long time. True, his family owned rich estates in England if it came to it, but that was cold comfort given King Edward's decision. Perhaps they could retire to their lands in Ireland? That felt too much like defeat, however, and Robert dismissed it from his thoughts as he emerged from the trees.

Lochmaben Castle dominated the landscape before him, the keep rising from the motte over the bailey and the town. Standing strategically between two lochs, it formed the gateway to the west of Scotland. Smoke hung in tattered banners, snatched from rooftops by the grasping wind. It was late in the day and the smells of food coming from the town made Robert's stomach cramp. With a whistle at Uathach, who was chasing a flock of cawing crows, he made for the south gate, set in the town's earthen ramparts. It was quicker to go through the settlement than around it. The guards greeted him, but with none of their usual jokes or conversation. Robert felt their stares, worried and full of questions, on his back as he walked away.

He was approaching the square, busy with traders after the market, when he caught sight of a familiar figure by the church steps. It was his grandfather. His mane of silver hair was trapped beneath a felt cap and he looked painfully stooped, his shoulders seeming too heavy for his frame. The lord was talking to someone and it was this second figure that gripped Robert's attention. It was an old woman in a soiled brown cloak, leaning on a gnarled staff. She was some distance from him, but he could clearly see her face.

Affraig.

It was a shock to see her, as if part of his childhood had manifested itself in a corner of his adult life, filling him with memories and feelings long forgotten. Robert was too far away to hear what they were saying, but their expressions were tense. It looked as though they were arguing. The wind snatched back Affraig's hood, revealing her hair, now more white than black. Robert moved through the groups of traders packing away their wares, past horses and carts. He saw his grandfather tip back his head and stare at the sky. Then, the old man nodded. Affraig raised her hand to his face and touched his cheek in a familiar and affectionate gesture that surprised and disturbed Robert, then she moved off, leaning on the staff. After a moment, she disappeared behind the church. Robert set off towards his grandfather. The old man was heading for the gate that led to the castle. Before Robert could reach him someone stepped into his path. It was one of his grandfather's vassals, a knight of a nearby estate.

'Master Robert,' greeted the man. 'I have been meaning to seek an audience with the lord for several days now. I wish to offer my condolences that he wasn't chosen as our king. I pray Sir Robert doesn't reproach my tardiness, but with the recent storms I have had my hands full dealing with a flood and all manner of—'

'I'll pass on your condolences,' Robert cut across him, moving past. On the other side of the square he paused, realising his grandfather had disappeared, then he sprinted to the church. Ducking down the side of the building, he entered the little warren of streets, looking for Affraig. But after a few minutes' fruitless searching, he turned and headed back the way he had come, towards the castle.

Robert was crossing the bailey when he heard raised voices coming from the upper floor of the guest lodgings. Recognising his grandfather's growl, then the rough-barked response of his father, he went to the door. It opened as he reached it and two serving girls came out, carrying baskets of laundry. They stepped aside, heads bobbing politely. Robert smelled something sour and saw what looked to be a watery bloodstain on one of the sheets, then he was inside and making his way up the stairs to the second storey. He paused in the passage outside the room his parents had been lodged in. The voices of his father and grandfather came clearly through the door.

'I cannot believe you listened to that crone! You're a damned *fool*!' The earl's voice was contorted with rage. 'A relic of the past, still believing in curses and magic like some old wife who knows no better! It is no wonder King Edward picked that whoreson John Balliol over you!'

'You once believed, as I recall.'

'I was drunk when I sought out that hag,' hissed the earl. 'Drunk on the blood I'd seen spilled in those Welsh hills, drunk on the deaths of my men. I was not in my own mind.'

The voice of Robert's grandfather cracked with sudden emotion. 'Did you send your man after her because you were ashamed? Did you want to punish her for doing as you asked?'

'I had nothing to do with that,' muttered the earl in response.

'But neither did you give her the justice she deserved.'

'Justice?' There was a rush of cruel laughter. 'A woman living alone who deceives men with her trickery for money will sooner or later get what she deserves.'

For a long moment there was silence. When the old lord spoke again his voice was as cold as marble. 'The only thing that matters now is that our claim is preserved.'

'We have no claim, damn you!'

Robert's grandfather continued, as if the earl hadn't spoken. 'I will resign my claim to you today, but tomorrow you will resign it to him.'

Robert took a step back, his brow knotting.

'I will have no part in your madness!'

Footsteps sounded, coming straight for the door.

'You will heed me!' the Lord of Annandale's voice blasted out. 'Or by God I will see you stripped of everything!'

The footsteps stopped dead.

'I know you deceived me and informed King Edward of our attack on Galloway. I know you have been in contact with the king ever since, keeping him advised of our plans.'

Robert's shock was caught between the revelation and by the molten rage in his grandfather's voice.

'There are men in Carrick who are loyal to me,' the lord went on. 'It sickens me that I have been forced to spy on my own son, but you have never given me reason to trust you. I said nothing about your betrayal. I let it pass, just as I did your many misdeeds, but it proved to me at last that if there is any hope left for this family it does not lie with you.'

'With you then? You will wear a shroud before you wear a crown! I am the one who secured real power for this family when I married Marjorie.'

'How quick you are to forget that by marrying Marjorie without King Alexander's consent you brought the king's wrath down upon you both. You almost lost everything! It was only by my influence that the king forgave you and restored Carrick to your wife.'

'And you have always hated me for that. I will not now give up what is mine by right!'

'If you do not then you will not inherit Annandale. Neither will you have my lands in England, nor my fortune. When I die, you will get nothing.'

'You wouldn't do that. I saved you from that cell in Lewes. I paid your ransom. If not for me, you wouldn't have an inheritance to give!'

'Agree, son, and I promise you will live out the end of your days in comfort. Refuse and I swear by God I will see you reduced to nothing.'

There was a creak on the stairs. Robert jerked round to see his mother. She was holding a candle, her face sallow in its gleam.

'What are you doing, Robert?'

The voices on the other side of the door silenced at her sharp question. Footfalls were followed by the snap of a latch. The door opened and Robert met his grandfather's gaze.

The old lord opened the door wider. 'In, boy.'

Robert glanced at his mother, then entered. His grandfather hadn't called him boy in years. It made him feel young and nervous. His father was standing in the centre of the chamber, his face white with fury. Beyond him, a bed dominated the room. It had been stripped of sheets. Robert thought of the bloodstains in the laundry basket, then heard his grandfather's voice at his back.

'Your father has something to say to you.'

The earl strode to the door. Moving past Robert without a word, he halted, facing his father. 'I wish to God I had left you to rot in Lewes,' he murmured, before heading from the room.

The lord's jaw pulsed. As he went to speak, his shoulders sagged and he crossed instead to the stripped bed, where he sat slumped. Robert stared at his grandfather in silence. He looked so terribly frail. His hands, clasped on his knees, were gnarled and shaking, and his skin was as thin as parchment. The creases of age had become furrows, puckering his eyes and mouth. Robert had heard a poet once proclaim that it was better for men to die young and glorious in battle, than to let their strength and youth be plundered by the great thief, Time. He glanced at his own hands, the skin of which was supple, lined only with strong, blue veins.

'I don't know how much you heard,' said the old lord, 'but you should know that I am going to resign my claim to the throne to your father. It is a blood right of our family and cannot be ignored, whatever King Edward or anyone else decrees. I want it kept alive by one who is worthy of the honour.' He rose slowly and crossed to Robert. 'In turn, your father will resign that claim to you and with it the earldom of Carrick.' The Lord of Annandale grasped Robert's shoulders. 'Tomorrow, you will be knighted and dubbed as one of the thirteen earls of Scotland.' The lord's hawk-like eyes bored into Robert's. 'Promise me you will respect our family's claim and uphold it with dignity for all the years to come, no matter the pretenders who sit upon that throne in defiance of our right.'

'I swear it, sir,' murmured Robert. His voice sounded strange, as if someone else were speaking for him. His mind was reeling.

His grandfather's eyes filled with concern. 'I am sorry, Robert, for this burden. Just know I would not pass it to you if I did not believe you capable of bearing it.'

'It is no burden, Grandfather. It is an honour.'

His grandfather said nothing, but gripped his shoulders tighter.

The procession filed slowly up the Moot Hill in the winter rain, ladies holding their skirts out of the mud, lords and knights cautious on the waterlogged ground. The trees swayed, lashing great drops on to the crowd that gathered on the crown of the hill beside the abbey. From out of their ranks came two men, holding a stout iron pole, from which a large block of creamy stone hung from iron rings. The men's faces were red and straining as they heaved the stone between them across the muddy ground to the plinth that stood in the centre of the circle of trees. The monks of Scone Abbey watched anxiously as the stone was lowered on to the wide plinth, then covered with a golden cloth, embroidered with a red lion. The rest of the assembly was focused on the lean man dressed in sodden robes of scarlet, girded with a naked sword, who now emerged and walked towards the stone.

James Stewart, the Bishop of St Andrews and the Abbot of Scone followed. John Balliol hardly waited for them to halt before he sat himself upon the Stone of Destiny and faced the masses, his thinning hair plastered to his scalp with rain, which ran in streams down his pockmarked cheeks. The steward came forward, a jewel-encrusted sceptre in his hands. In silence, he handed the symbol of authority to Balliol, whose face twitched in a smile. Next the frail Bishop of St Andrews draped a mantle around Balliol's shoulders, over which the abbot placed a stole of snow-white ermine. The three men stepped back to stand behind the throne as John Balliol's pedigree was read out solemnly to the rain-drenched throng.

Standing to the right of the plinth, under a canopy held aloft by his pages, King Edward watched as the cleric intoned the names of kings past. The wind lifted a flap of the embroidered cloth on which Balliol was sitting, revealing a pale corner of stone.

John de Warenne leaned in close at Edward's side. 'When do you plan to act, my lord?'

'Soon,' replied Edward, not taking his eyes off Balliol.

PART 3

1293–1295 AD

. . . there appeared a star of wonderful magnitude and brightness, darting forth a ray, at the end of which was a globe of fire in form of a dragon.

From this time, therefore, he was called Uther Pendragon, which in the British tongue signifies the dragon's head; the occasion of this appellation being Merlin's predicting, from the appearance of a dragon, that he should be king.

The History of the Kings of Britain, *Geoffrey of Monmouth*

The weeks that followed Robert's rise to knighthood were dark for the Bruce family, shunned by allies and threatened by enemies. Not since the days of Malachy were their fortunes so beset by disaster and the old lord spent many nights on his knees in Lochmaben's chapel, begging the saint to remove the hateful curse. Robert joined him at times, worried by his grandfather's erratic moods and plagued by thoughts of Affraig and her tree of destinies. Had the web containing the noose ever fallen, or was it still hanging there weathered by time, obstinate as the saint who had cursed their line? Torn between heading home to Carrick, now his earldom, and staying in Lochmaben with the old man, the decision had been taken from him that frozen December by the cold hand of death.

Soon after the enthronement of John Balliol, when their supporters were edging away, unwilling or scared to defend the sworn enemies of Scotland's new king, Lady Marjorie had taken ill. The countess had been frail for some time, never seeming to recover from the birth of Matilda, but gradually she worsened, the bouts of fever and sickness becoming more frequent until one bitter night she slipped away. When word of her passing came to Lochmaben, Robert had gone to Carrick, to stand at her graveside and face his father's frigid silence. Her death shattered them. It was as if she had been the rope that bound the family together and when she was gone they could only fall apart.

Barely weeks later, Robert's father had taken his eldest daughter, Isabel, and sailed to Norway, where they remained as guests of King Eric. After his departure, Robert, left alone to deal with his mother's death and the complexities of the earldom, was grateful to receive a message from his grandfather in March of the new year, asking him to come to Lochmaben. Leaving Carrick in the hands of one of his vassals, a capable knight called Andrew Boyd, Robert and Edward returned to their grandfather's castle.

On the brothers' arrival, the old Bruce had called Robert to his solar in the keep. Despite being only a matter of months since he had seen him last, Robert had been shocked by the change in the lord, as the page ushered him into the chamber. A well-built man, whose muscular physique had always belied his age, his grandfather was shrunken and stooped, huddled in a chair by the hearth, his mane of hair as white as frost.

He rose stiffly as Robert crossed the room, the page closing the door behind.

Robert embraced the old man, feeling bones beneath his hands. 'It is good to see you, Grandfather.'

'And you, my boy,' rasped the lord, gesturing him to the other stool set by the fire. 'Sit, sit.'

Robert glanced around as he sat, noting the familiar tapestry that hung from one wall near the large bed, showing a group of knights on black coursers, pursuing a white stag. It reminded him of the hunts his grandfather had taken him on in Annandale's woods and he felt a pang for what had passed. He'd been forced to step quickly into his new role as earl, his adolescence smothered by the duties of adulthood. The joys of youth seemed a hazy memory.

'How are matters in Carrick?' the old man questioned, studying him.

'I am finding my feet,' Robert replied slowly, after a pause. 'Sir Andrew Boyd has been a great help. I've left him in charge of the garrison at Turnberry.'

'And your vassals?'

'I've accepted the homage of those who live closest to Turnberry. But what with the bad weather and the lambing season just begun I haven't been able to summon them all yet.'

'It is early days,' said the old lord, nodding. 'There will be time for you to come to know your people.' His black eyes glimmered in the firelight. 'Fortune has not favoured our family this past year, Robert, but we must not let these adversities erase two hundred years of influence in this realm. I meant what I said the day I saw you dubbed – that I want you to uphold and preserve our claim.' He exhaled, looking down at his wrinkled hands. 'I am tired. Tired in my bones and in my heart. Your father is abroad, trying to build alliances in Norway, and I have no idea when he will return. It is your time now to take on the mantle we wore for so long.' He paused, fixing Robert with his stare. 'But I do not believe it can be done in Scotland. The memory of our defeat and Balliol's victory is still too fresh in the minds of people here. I do not want you tainted with my failure.'

Robert went to protest at the admission, but the old lord held up a hand.

'I have thought long about this and I feel that the fortunes of our family will best be served elsewhere, for the present. Which is why I want you to go to England. You will spend the next year at our manors in Yorkshire and Essex, acting as de facto lord in the absence of your father. These estates form part of your inheritance and it is important that you take the time to understand their value and meet the men who will one day swear homage to you. After this, you will pay your respects to King Edward in London.'

'He chose our enemy to take the throne.' Robert's voice hardened. 'Why should I pay my respects at his court?'

'Because, despite the king's decision, we are still his vassals. We cannot afford to allow resentment to prejudice our standing in his realm. Indeed, I believe we must cultivate that standing.'

Robert shook his head. He would have expected such a proposition from his father, but not the lord, who had always been careful to maintain a respectful distance from the English king.

The old Bruce, however, was adamant. 'Our place in Scotland is gravely weakened. We must strengthen it elsewhere if our family is to regain its former authority. You will take your brother,' continued the lord, reaching for a goblet of wine on the table beside him. 'And a small group of men I have chosen for you. I am afraid the entourage will not quite befit a man of your position, but with your father abroad and an enemy on the throne I need all the men I have here.' He raised the goblet and pointed it at his silent grandson. 'I am counting on you, Robert.'

The warhorse tossed its massive head, eyes rolling wide and white through the slits in the black caparison that covered its bulk. As the knight in the saddle leaned out to take the lance from his squire, his surcoat flapped aside to reveal the fish-scale shimmer of mail. Steadying the spirited destrier he drew back the reins in his left hand, behind the shield strapped to his arm. The shield, flat at the top and tapering to a point at his knee, was black, with a red harp in the centre. The wooden ailettes on his shoulders also bore the device, his only identifying feature outside the encumbering armour and steel helm.

The cheers of the crowd that thronged Smithfield tournament ground built to a crescendo as down the field a second knight reached for his lance. This man was clad in blue with a white stripe slashed diagonally across his surcoat between six gold lions. His shield bore a striking design. Painted a deep, blood scarlet, its centre was embossed with a golden dragon.

There was a burst on a horn. The knights dug in their spurs and the horses lurched forward from opposite ends of the field, thrusting into a gallop through the mud and splintered remains of lances. The knight with the dragon shield almost lost control of his horse and it threatened to veer off the line, but with a twist of the reins he brought it back in time to level his lance. All along the field the crowds jostled to see the clash. Iron tip smashed into wooden shield, the lance shaft exploding into shards. The impact was brutal. The knight with the red harp on his shield was slammed backwards, his own lance swinging wide, the strike sending him plunging over the high saddle as the horse continued on. He hit the ground with a crunch of metal and a spray of muddy water. The crowd roared.

The knight with the dragon shield slowed his destrier to a canter as he approached the far end of the field, onlookers scrabbling to get out of the path of the armoured beast. Wheeling around at the last moment, he unsheathed his broadsword and urged the horse back down the field to where his opponent lay prone. He came to a stop, prepared to dismount and fight on foot. The knight on the ground remained motionless. A horn sounded and three squires bearing the mark of the red harp sprinted on to the field, one running to take the reins of the horse, the others tending their fallen master. The knight with the dragon shield waited, his destrier stomping its hooves. The crowds had quietened to an expectant hush. Was the man just unconscious, or had they witnessed death here on this breezy May morning in London? It was a common enough sight in the tourney, even though these days lances were tipped with three-pronged coronels to spread the force of the blow and swords were made of whalebone.

There was movement from the floor, glimpsed through the legs of the squires, a raised arm, fingers uncurling. The squires moved back as the knight struggled to his feet, his battered shield hanging off his arm by a strap, his lance on the ground, unbroken. Swaying upright, he tugged off the great helm, signalling he would not continue the fight. The knight with the dragon shield jabbed his sword into the air and spurred his horse down the field in a rush of blue silk, amid wild cheers.

Robert, seated with his brother in the royal stand, clapped his approval as the wounded knight was led off and two more opponents trotted their destriers on. It was only the third joust of the day and already he'd seen more skill and power on this field than he'd ever witnessed before. He had been to a few tournaments in Scotland, but nothing like this lavish display. Everything here was grander; the horses bigger, the garb of the knights finer, from the silk pennons on their lance shafts to the crests and feathers that adorned their helms. The crowds too were greater. Robert could still see people filing into the enclosure between rows of striped tents, the knights of the royal household checking them for weapons, forbidden on tournament grounds. This was a relatively old law, passed after one too many tourneys had turned into riots with dozens killed. Jousting had since become more popular than the dust-choked violence of the mêlée and tournaments were refined occasions with judges, prizes and only knights of pedigree allowed to enter, each paying a princely sum. Even so, the royal knights seemed to be amassing a tidy hoard of daggers and knives.

As Robert turned his attention back to the field his gaze fell on the tournament's host. King Edward, several rows in front, was erect in a cushioned throne, his surcoat embroidered front and back with three golden lions, his ash-white hair neatly curled at the ends. Around him the royal box was filled to the boards with prominent barons and lords from all over England, along with ladies in jewel-dappled gowns and precarious headdresses, the silks of which flew like flags in the brisk wind. Pages in turquoise tunics hovered on the edges like kingfishers, waiting to dart in and attend to any command.

Robert's gaze lingered on the king. Shortly before the Christ Mass, obeying his grandfather's command, he had written to Edward from the Essex estate, explaining he was representing his family's interests in England and wished to pay his respects at court. In the new year of 1294 a message came bearing the royal seal, inviting him to the spring parliament, called to discuss the king's plans for a new crusade. Robert hadn't yet been offered an audience by the king, even though he'd arrived in London a week ago, something his brother had already commented on darkly. He had found some measure of relief in the king's reticence, however, for he still harboured resentment towards him and knew it wouldn't do to make this apparent. Not here in London's seething grandeur, where the court seemed full of wolves.

Robert's attention fixed on the two new opponents trotting down the field, followed by their squires holding lances. He felt a twinge of envy, wishing it was him out there on the best horse money could buy, adored and admired. The difficulties of dealing with the English estates – listening to tenants' complaints and resolving petty squabbles – had weighed on him this past year. But the thrill of the tournament and the drama of London had reawakened him to possibilities beyond the burdens of responsibility. This grand display epitomised the knighthood he had longed for as a boy: the exhilaration, the glory. The rewards.

He applauded with the rest of the crowds as the knights did a circuit of the field, punching their fists into the air to elicit ever more fervent support. One was emblazoned with a silver lion, while the other was dressed in yellow silk adorned with a green eagle. Robert faltered in his applause as he saw that the knight with the green eagle bore a blood-scarlet shield with a golden dragon in the centre. He leaned over to his brother. 'Do you see his shield?' he said, raising his voice above the din. 'It's the same as the last winner's.'

'Perhaps they are from the same household?' suggested Edward, as the knight spurred his horse past the royal box with a bow towards the king.

'Why the different devices on their surcoats?'

Edward shook his head, not knowing. As the knights cantered to their places at either end of the field he pointed to the lists, where other men were waiting with their squires. 'Look. There're more of them over here.'

Robert saw thirteen knights, all distinguished by their own coats of arms, yet all carrying the same shield, decorated with the dragon. He had never seen anything like it. Usually, a knight's shield would be painted with the arms of his house. He glanced around, thinking to ask one of the lords in the stands, but they were all now rising to watch the joust. Not wanting to miss the action, Robert rose with them, as the knights levelled their lances in a storm of mud and thunder.

The royal procession wound its way along the dusty road, the drums announcing their progress. At the head rode King Edward with his chief officials, among them the Earl of Surrey, Sir John de Warenne, and Anthony Bek, the Bishop of Durham. Behind came the knights from the tournament, most of whom had changed helms and mail for linen shirts and embroidered mantles. They were flushed and triumphant astride their chargers. Several still bore the favours from ladies that they had carried into the joust, scraps from veils and sleeves, gossamer as butterfly wings. Their good mood was a pleasant change after a subdued few days, the court preoccupied by rising tensions in France, where King Edward's younger brother, Edmund, was engaged in fraught negotiations, following a sea battle the summer before between English merchant ships and the French fleet.

Squires followed in the wake of the knights, bearing the detritus of the tourney: broken lances and swords, shattered shields, and one man, dazed and bloody, on a litter. Pack-horses carried the rest of the equipment. For a time, in the muddy streets beyond Smithfield, grey-faced children had run alongside them, calling for pennies. Now, the procession was entering the Outer Liberties, passing through quiet, breezy orchards, where white blossom fell from the trees like snow.

Robert, riding with his brother and their squires, glanced down at the muddy slush of petals, trampled by so many feet and hooves. He and his men were far back in the procession, with other foreign lords and those perhaps once close to the king who had found themselves out of favour. It was what they had grown up with, these systems of rank and favouritism, where the top table in a hall and the prime lodgings in a castle were used like bait to reel in recalcitrant vassals, or else reward faithful followers. But here in London, so clogged with nobility, from the most powerful earls in the realm down to the most rapacious knights, hungry for scraps of land and wealth, these symbols of status existed in a bewildering maze of etiquette that Robert wasn't sure he would ever understand. In Scotland he had just been finding his feet as one of the elite. By comparison, he felt decidedly out of his depth here. In his mind, his grandfather's rough voice reminded him of his illustrious heritage, sprung from kings and lords. He sat a little straighter at the thought.

A cheer sounded as one man rode out from the column of knights, clad in blue with a bold white stripe slashed across the back. It was the winner of the tournament, who had unhorsed his first opponent and had gone on to break fourteen lances. He wielded aloft his prize, a beautifully fashioned dagger, as another cheer rose. Robert had been surprised when, at the end of the joust, the man had taken off his helm and stood before the royal box to accept his trophy, for the fresh-faced knight couldn't have been any older than him. There was a flash of red from the ruby embedded in the dagger's hilt, then the victorious young knight was gone from view, sucked back into the ranks. As the procession emerged from the cover of the orchard trees the Tower of London appeared to the left. The massive walls of King Edward's citadel stretched to the sky and fell sheer to the moat below. Built by the Conqueror, the Tower had been added to over the centuries by a succession of kings, but none, Robert had been told, had done as much as Edward, during the twenty years of his reign.

The head of the company had already reached the stone causeway at the edge of the moat and soon, Robert and Edward were riding through the first defences that guarded each step of the way into the king's fortress. Once over the causeway they entered a semicircular barbican, surrounded by water and guarded by soldiers. Next came the first of two gatehouses, reached by drawbridges, over which iron portcullises hung suspended and murder holes opened into blackness. Below, the green waters were filled with the shifting shadows of fish. Beyond the royal docks that enclosed the moat the Thames flowed sluggishly along the south walls where the king's apartments, cornered by flute-like towers, were built out into the river.

After the second gatehouse they were moving through the outer ward between a double line of walls. The procession slowed to funnel through an arched opening, the noise of the drums echoing off the towers. Making their way with the rest of the company, through one archway and then another, Robert and Edward passed the water gate, where the royal barge was docked beneath the king's quarters. Here they were in the shadow of another colossal gatehouse, the last and most impressive before they entered the inner ward. As they moved through the long dark, then out into sunlight on the other side, the White Tower rose before them. The radiant gem in the heart of Edward's crown.

A wide avenue, flanked by walls, led them to the immense tower, where they found themselves dwarfed by its God-like scale. Robert thought of his grandfather's motte and bailey at Lochmaben, a toy castle by comparison. One more gatehouse, this one strung with banners, and they were in the inmost ward, where a giant stone staircase marched up to the tower's entrance. As the knights and lords dismounted, grooms escorted the horses to the stable blocks, while attendants ushered the nobility towards the tower.

Robert handed the reins of his horse to his squire, Nes. Out of the small entourage of six squires, two servants, a steward and a cook that had accompanied him and Edward from Scotland, he had formed the closest bond with the quiet, young Nes, son of a knight from Annandale, one of his grandfather's vassals. As the squires led the horses away, the brothers headed up the grand stairs. The din of the drums had faded and the sweeter sounds of pipes and lyres drifted to them. As they approached the oversized doors, they heard people ahead of them murmuring in surprise. Together, they entered a huge hall. Rows of marble pillars flanked the cavernous space, the walls of which were covered with tapestries, but it wasn't the architecture that transfixed the brothers, rather the scores of plants and trees that filled the place with such abundant greenery it was as if a forest had sprung up inside. Dark trails of ivy snaked around pillars and the scent from the carpet of petals that covered the tiled floor perfumed the air. Edward let an appreciative breath through his teeth as a string of girls dressed in ethereal gowns wove in front of them between the trees. They were being chased by cavorting men who wore grotesque masks.

The music was louder. A timber staircase ahead led out of the enchanted forest and up to the next storey. So intent on what lay above was he that

Robert didn't see what guarded the foot of the stairs until Edward gripped his arm and pointed. There, restrained by three pages, was a massive beast with a shaggy black mane. Thick chains were fixed to the collar of iron around the creature's neck, but even so the pages were clearly struggling to hold it as it shifted and snarled at the passing crowds. Muscles rippled beneath its ochre skin, scarred with pale, bald lines, made by whips. Robert had only ever seen images of these creatures on shields and surcoats. The lion was far more menacing than he had imagined. Its growls were thunderous, echoing in his chest and gut, the bestial reek of it setting all his nerves on edge. Up the stairs, Robert looking back over his shoulder as the beast roared, they entered the great hall.

22

As King Edward and his officials made their way up to the hall's dais, ushers showed the guests to their places. Those seats nearest to the platform were reserved for knights from the tournament. Robert and his brother were in the middle of the hall, a polite yet aloof distance from the king's table.

The boards were laden with glazed jugs and goblets, and silver basins filled with water and rose petals for the guests to wash their hands in. As lords and ladies sat, servants entered bearing roasted swans, the flesh crackling with heat. There was pickled salmon from Ireland garnished with sweet lemons from Spain, bowls of yellow butter, sour-smelling cheese from Brie and wrinkle-skinned figs. After everyone was seated, Bishop Bek led them in saying grace. The king's pantler tested the dishes on the top table in case of poison and servants began to pour the wine.

'You are Sir Robert Bruce?'

Robert glanced up as a thin, well-dressed man spoke across the table over the clatter of knives. He inclined his head.

The man, leaning to cut a wedge of cheese from the block between them, didn't offer his own name, but addressed a fleshy woman beside him, who wore a too-tight gown, the ribboned sides of which were bulging. 'From Scotland.'

'Truly, sir?' The woman stared at Robert. 'I hear it is a wild place.' She shuddered. 'Poor, desolate lands, blighted by cold and endless rain.'

Before Robert could answer, Edward nodded soberly. 'It is, madam. So cold, in fact, that we can only bathe for three days in June, when the ice that covers the lochs melts just long enough.'

The thin man frowned sceptically as he cut the cheese into neat slivers.

The woman was shaking her head. 'How you must relish being in England.'

Edward grinned. 'Well, I no longer stink like a pig.'

The woman tittered nervously and focused on a slab of beef that was running blood across her plate. The man looked away, his mouth pursing.

Robert leaned in to his brother as the couple struck up a conversation with someone else. 'You'll not make many friends if you keep doing that.'

Edward's grin faded. 'You've heard how they talk about our kingdom. The only good thing is we're seen as *civilised*, rather than barbarians like the Welsh and Irish.'

'Can you blame them for thinking anything less than this is inferior?' Robert picked up his goblet and gestured at the crowded opulence of the great hall. 'You cannot tell me you're not impressed.'

'Impressed I may be, but that doesn't mean I like being treated like a churl.' Edward's eyes narrowed in challenge. 'The king hasn't even greeted you yet, brother. We've been here a week. You should be welcomed as an honoured guest.'

'I doubt the king has had the chance to speak to many here,' responded Robert, nettled by the truth in the words. He might be glad he hadn't had to face the king immediately, but the lengthening wait was passing out of respite and heading towards insult. He couldn't well do what his grandfather expected and raise the Bruce family's standing in England if the king wouldn't even bid him welcome. 'I imagine the matter of France has taken up his time.'

'France?'

At the gruff voice, Robert glanced round to see an elderly man in a brocaded mantle, fastened at his wrinkled throat by a jewelled clasp.

'So, even our distant Scottish neighbours know of our troubles?'

Robert had heard of the battle that started the conflict soon after it occurred the summer before. The French fleet had attacked several merchant ships crewed by English and Gascon sailors off the coast of Brittany, apparently without provocation, but in the skirmish that followed it was the English who were victorious, capturing three ships and putting the rest to flight. Before he could explain that he had been in England for the past year the old noble continued.

'Mark my words,' rasped the man, gesturing with his knife, a slice of meat slipping off the end on to the table, 'tournaments and feasts will only buoy up the barons for so long. Their high spirits will sink as swiftly as a stone ship come the parliament.'

Robert's interest was snared by the mention of the parliament. Despite his reservations, he had been looking forward to hearing the king's plans for a new crusade and the opportunity therein, for one way he would be certain to further his family's standing would be to take the Cross under Edward's banner. He could still hear his father's bitter words the night they learned Balliol would be king, clear as the moment they were uttered.

The blood runs thin in all our sons. Thin as watered wine. How will we make crusaders out of such diluted stock?

He had suffered those words for a long time, the last of any feeling his father had said to him before leaving for Norway. Part of him had fought against them – they had come from one of his father's drunken rages and were of no substance, just sour bile like all the rest. Another, more persistent part had told him this was true. He couldn't live up to the crusaders who had gone before him; he who had been raised in years of peace with only a quintain on a deserted beach to tilt at. This, perhaps, was his chance to prove the man wrong. Robert had been envisioning the prospect of heading home to Annandale with grants of land, bags of bright Saracen gold and a reputation as formidable as his grandfather's to present the old lord with a new palm frond for his mantle, taken from Jerusalem itself.

The elderly noble's attention, however, was far from crusading. 'The king is in for a difficult session,' he told Robert, nodding enthusiastically. 'Yes indeed.'

The thin, well-dressed man across from Robert cleared his throat meaningfully, his stare full of warning.

'You know I'm right,' the old man growled at him. 'King Edward never should have sent his brother to treat with Philippe on his behalf. If he'd gone himself he wouldn't now be facing the loss of English rule in Gascony.'

'From what I've heard,' said Robert, looking between the two men, 'the surrender of the king's lands in Gascony is only temporary, until a peace agreement is sealed with King Philippe. It was meant as a gesture of good faith.'

'That is correct,' said the thin man emphatically. 'King Edward was to return the captured ships and cede the duchy. When he goes to France to make peace with Philippe, Gascony will be restored to him. Those are the terms Earl Edmund has agreed in Paris.'

'Bah!' spat the old noble. 'Did you not wonder how a couple of merchant cogs managed to defeat the French fleet in the first place?'

The thin man frowned. 'What are you saying?'

'I'm saying it was a trap and our king walked right into it! Philippe made it clear from the start of his reign that he didn't want an English king to rule in any part of France. He told the captains of those ships to let themselves be captured and give him a reason to demand the surrender of Gascony.'

'Preposterous,' scoffed the thin man. But his tone held a note of discomfort.

'And I know too why King Edward agreed so readily to Philippe's terms,' said the old man, pointing his knife towards the dais, where the king was seated with his officials. He arched his shaggy eyebrows. 'It was the promise of young flesh.'

Robert leaned forward expectantly. He had heard rumour of the marriage agreement that had been part of the French negotiations for the ceding of Gascony, but it hadn't been confirmed.

'King Philippe's sister, Princess Marguerite,' murmured the old man with relish, nodding at Robert. 'Not a day over thirteen. Mark my words.' He dug his knife into a bloody piece of beef and sucked it from the blade. 'Our king traded his wide French lands for a tight French hole.' With that, he licked his knife clean and pushed away his food. Ignoring the stares of those who had overheard his diatribe, he shuffled from the table and disappeared in the noisy crowd.

The thin man began muttering to someone next to him.

Robert looked at his brother. 'As I said,' he murmured, 'the king has been busy.'

Edward leaned back, picking something from his teeth. 'I still think he should have welcomed you properly, no matter how preoccupied he is. You are an earl, brother. And it wasn't so long ago that our grandfather was competing for the throne.'

Robert tucked into his meal in taut silence.

At first, his anger over the loss of the throne had been dampened by grief following his mother's death, but over the past year it had risen again to plague him. The only cold comfort had come in the knowledge that the reign of Scotland's new king was anything but content.

After his enthronement, John Balliol had been forced by English lawyers meekly to accept that as King of Scotland he was subject to Edward's superior authority. The promise Edward had made, assuring the Scots that his overlordship would be only temporary, had been revoked – Edward compelling Balliol to issue documents declaring this guarantee null and void. The English king then set about demonstrating his clear superiority by interfering in Scottish affairs. Lawsuits that ought to have been settled in Scotland were soon being reviewed in Westminster. When the Scots, led by John Comyn, protested, Balliol was summoned to present himself before Edward's judges. In mourning following the recent death of his wife and queen, a subdued Balliol was treated to a humiliating dressing-down from the king himself and sentenced to lose three royal towns and castles for his contempt.

Robert's brother had reflected it was a poisoned chalice Balliol had supped from and that they were better off without it, but Robert couldn't help but think their grandfather would have been able to stand up to the English king better. These thoughts had since grown into the darkening suspicion that this was the prime reason why his grandfather had not been chosen. More than once in the past few months, Robert had recalled the words of Bishop Wishart of Glasgow and the fiery Earl John of Atholl: that King Edward was only interested in expanding his own borders, at the expense of his neighbours. His grandfather had charged him with upholding the Bruce claim to the throne of Scotland, no matter who sat upon it in defiance of their right. But it seemed as though a fight for control of that throne was already well under way and he wasn't even in the running.

Robert drained his wine and pushed away his plate as the servants began to clear the tables. The minstrels struck up a spirited tune and a line of men and women thronged into the centre of the hall to dance. People clapped as they laced between one another. Edward was talking to the fat woman again, telling her about monstrous beasts that roamed the Scottish hills and snatched children from villages.

'Sir, are you the Earl of Carrick?'

At the question, Robert's jaw tightened. He looked round, no longer in the mood for conversation, to see a man dressed in a blue cloak with a bold white stripe. Up close, the knight looked even younger than he had on the tournament ground. He had brown hair that had flopped in his eyes, a striking shade of green set in a broad, open face. Robert's irritation vanished. 'I am. You're Sir Humphrey de Bohun, Earl of Hereford and Essex?'

Humphrey smiled, a cleft appearing in his cheek. 'Not quite. My father is the earl. But as I am his heir I suppose the title isn't far wrong.'

'Let me introduce . . .' Robert went to motion to Edward, but his brother had risen and was leading the tittering fat woman into the centre of the hall, as the dancers beckoned guests to join them. Robert turned back. 'Congratulations on your win today. It was well deserved.' He wanted to go further and tell Humphrey he hadn't seen a display like it, but he stopped himself, not wanting the knight to think him unsophisticated.

'It is I who should be congratulating you, Sir Robert. The way in which you resolved that dispute between our fathers' tenants in Essex was admirable.'

Robert shook his head, embarrassed by the gratitude. 'It was the least I could do. Our men were clearly in the wrong. They should never have been hunting in your father's park in the first place. I hope the reparations I had them make to the earl were satisfactory?'

'More than. My father wanted me to extend his thanks. He asked after your family.'

'Well, my brother Alexander is at Cambridge studying divinity and my sister Christian is due to be married to the heir of the Earl of Mar.' Robert thought about Mary and Matilda in Lochmaben, and Niall and Thomas in Antrim training for knighthood, but he guessed the knight was just being polite. 'And I believe my father is well,' he finished, his tone cooling. 'He is in Norway at the court of King Eric.'

'Ah, yes, your new brother-in-law.'

Robert was taken aback. Some months ago he'd received a message with the unexpected announcement that his sister was to marry the Norwegian king. The letter had been brief, perfunctory, with no word of greeting from his father. Robert had sent a gift of a silver brooch in the shape of a rose to Isabel, hoping it was a fitting present for a woman who was to become a queen, but he had heard nothing more from over the sea. He hadn't expected the engagement to be common knowledge yet.

Humphrey laughed at his expression. 'You shouldn't be surprised, Sir Robert. Your family's noble name is well known here and you'll soon discover that your business is everyone else's in court.'

'I'm a little behind in the game.'

'You'll catch up. Just keep your eyes open and watch your back.' Humphrey's amiable grin seemed out of odds with the warning. 'Enjoy the celebrations.'

Robert rose. 'Perhaps we can speak more later? I'm keen to know how I might enter the lists.'

'Is that so?' Humphrey looked interested, but then shook his head regretfully. 'Another time. I'm afraid there is a gathering I must attend this evening.'

'Of course,' said Robert, trying to conceal his disappointment. Humphrey's easy manner was refreshing after the guarded arrogance of most of the other nobles he had met so far. Sitting back down as the knight walked away, he toyed with his goblet, watching his brother spin the fat woman in breathless circles. Perhaps if he wasn't the one on whom all the family's hopes were pinned he too could be that carefree. As eldest son, Robert had known this day would come, but at nineteen it had come far sooner than he'd expected. He couldn't well use youth as an excuse, however, for by this age his grandfather had been designated heir to the throne and had married the daughter of an English earl, obtaining enough property south of the border to rival his Scottish lands.

Robert's gaze was caught by the sight of Humphrey de Bohun returning.

The young knight looked hesitant, but he smiled. 'Do you want to join me?'

Robert stood after a pause, sensing that silent acceptance was more valuable than gratitude in the face of the cautious offer. As he followed Humphrey across the crowded hall, he tried to catch his brother's eye, but Edward was too engrossed in the dance to notice and now they were moving through the press of bodies and out of a door into a narrow passage.

Humphrey led him past watchful guards on to a walkway that spanned the walls of the inmost ward. Day had turned to evening and banks of clouds had drawn in from the east. A chill wind blew their cloaks about them as they made their way along the parapet and down stone steps towards a huge, round tower.

'These are King Henry's former apartments,' said Humphrey, as they passed more guards outside the tower's entrance. 'King Edward lets us use them sometimes.'

Wondering who the *us* were, Robert nodded, but said nothing. He felt anticipation bubble up through him. Ascending spiralled stairs inside the tower behind Humphrey, he could hear voices and laughter drifting down. Humphrey opened the arched door at the top and Robert followed him into a spacious chamber with a high, vaulted ceiling, the walls of which were painted dark green, scattered with yellow stars. Couches draped with silks had been placed either side of a grand hearth. There were ten men in the chamber, several of whom Robert recognised from the tournament. Before he could attempt to put any names to the young men's faces, his attention was caught by a large banner that hung down from supports on one wall. The material was worn and it had been patched in places, but the colour, while faded, was unmistakably scarlet and the embroidered threads, though frayed, showed a golden dragon, shrouded in fire. Robert wanted to ask Humphrey the significance of the symbol, the same emblem that decorated their shields, but the men in the chamber had fallen silent and were staring at him.

'What is this, Humphrey?' The man who had spoken was long-limbed and well-built, with black hair swept back from a hard, angular face. He gestured at Robert, a goblet grasped in his extended fist. 'Who is he?'

'Did you leave your manners in the lists?' asked Humphrey, his tone, although jocular, holding a note of caution. 'This is a guest.'

The black-haired knight kept his gaze on Robert. '*This* is a private gathering.'

Ignoring him, Humphrey addressed the others. 'May I present Sir Robert Bruce, the Earl of Carrick.'

'Of course,' said one knight, nodding to Robert from the couch where he was sprawled. He was stocky, with thick blond hair and a lazy smile that wasn't quite reflected in his eyes, a chilly shade of blue. 'Your family owns lands near mine in Yorkshire, Sir Robert. My father knows yours well. I'm Henry Percy, Lord of Alnwick.'

There was a natural haughtiness in the man's tone, which by now was quite familiar to Robert. He recognised the name and knew the young man was the grandson of Earl John de Warenne.

Another youth, barely out of adolescence and wearing a bold grin, raised a hand in greeting. 'Welcome, Sir Robert. I'm Thomas.'

Robert inclined his head. A few nodded in return, the rest striking up their conversations once more. Eventually, the black-haired knight turned his hostile gaze away.

'Don't pay Aymer any heed,' murmured Humphrey, leading Robert to where a servant was standing with a jug of wine. At Humphrey's gesture, the servant poured two goblets. 'He is just sore that I beat him today.'

'Aymer?'

Humphrey took a sip of wine. 'Aymer de Valence.' He motioned subtly to the black-haired knight. 'Son and heir of Sir William de Valence, the Earl of Pembroke. You must have heard of him.'

Robert had. His grandfather had fought alongside William de Valence at the Battle of Lewes and his father had been on campaign with him in Wales. A half-brother of Henry, born and raised in Poitou, Valence had come to England as a young man and had been one of the main causes of the war between the king and Simon de Montfort. If Aymer was William's son that made him King Edward's cousin. 'I know the Valences by reputation,' he said carefully.

Humphrey chuckled, seeming to get his meaning, then pointed to the youth who had introduced himself as Thomas. 'That's Thomas of Lancaster, son of Earl Edmund, the king's brother.'

'I don't think I saw him in the joust today.'

'You wouldn't have. He's only sixteen.' Humphrey pursed his lips appreciatively. 'But he'll be in the lists the day he's dubbed. I've never seen anyone so good so young.' Polishing off his wine and handing the goblet to the servant for refilling, Humphrey gestured, one by one, to the other men in the chamber.

Robert listened as he drank the potent wine, impressed by the list of titles. These men, despite their youth, were lords of England's greatest estates, or else were due to inherit them. As an earl, not in waiting but in name, he outranked them all, but there was no denying the blatant power held by these young men, relaxing in a former king's apartments. The setting seemed worlds away from the sea-stained walls of Turnberry.

Before Humphrey could finish the private introductions, the door burst open and a boy darted in. Slamming it shut behind him, he dived behind one of the couches.

Some moments later, the door opened again and an elderly man appeared. 'My lords,' he wheezed, staring around at the group. 'Have you seen the young master?'

'He came and then he went,' said Thomas of Lancaster, motioning to a door on the other side of the chamber.

'Thank you, Master Thomas,' breathed the man, heading on through. 'Good evening to you, my lords.'

When the old man had disappeared, his footsteps fading, the boy vaulted over the couch and wedged himself between a grinning Thomas and Henry Percy. He was rather lanky, with feathery fair hair and a very familiar face. Robert realised he was staring when Humphrey leaned in.

'He looks a lot like his father, doesn't he?'

Robert knew at once where the familiarity came from. It was with the king himself. The boy must be his son, Edward of Caernarfon, heir to the throne of England. Robert recalled the meeting years ago, after Birgham, at which so many men had argued over the future of this boy and his marriage to Scotland's queen. It seemed strange now to be standing in his presence.

Thomas of Lancaster snapped his fingers at the servant, who poured out a goblet of wine. 'If you tell your father, I'll deny it,' he warned when the servant handed the goblet to Edward. 'Wine is not for the young and silly,' he intoned, as if reciting something an adult had once said. 'It is for men.'

The boy's pale brow creased as he took the goblet and drank, the wine staining his mouth. 'My father doesn't care what I do, so long as it is out of his sight.' He shrugged. 'Not since Mother died.' As he caught sight of Robert, his frown deepened. 'Who is he?'

Humphrey went to answer for Robert, then paused at the sound of more hurried footsteps outside. He raised an eyebrow. 'How many governors are chasing you tonight, my lord?'

The door opened and a man appeared, clad in a yellow mantle

embroidered with a green eagle. Robert recognised the coat of arms from the joust.

The man glanced quickly around the room. Seeing Humphrey he crossed to him.

Humphrey's smile of greeting faded at the man's grim expression. 'What is it, Ralph?'

'Earl Edmund has returned from France.'

Thomas of Lancaster stood at the mention of his father.

'King Philippe has gone back on his word and confiscated Gascony. He has withdrawn the invitation to King Edward to seal the peace agreement and has poured an army into the duchy.' The knight glanced around at the silent men in the chamber. 'It is a declaration of war.'

23

Gone were the dancers and the music, the silver platters piled with delicacies and the jugs of wine. Gone too was the gaiety. All that remained of the feast was a lingering smell of burned meat and a few crushed rose petals, missed by the servants' brooms. The great hall was filled with men, their voices raised not in song or laughter, but in anger. The spring parliament the king had summoned to discuss his hopes for the liberation of the Holy Land had been taken over by the matter of France. King Philippe himself had recently pledged his support for a new crusade and had built a fleet of ships for the move east. Now, it seemed, those ships were turned towards England.

King Edward was on the dais above the assembly of nobles, his hands curled around the arms of his throne. He wore his fifty-five years heavily this morning, the pallid light filtering through the hall's high windows turning his hair to coarse silver and highlighting the droop of his eye, the defect inherited from his father. John de Warenne and Anthony Bek had joined the king on the platform along with several black-robed clerks. The rest of the company were packed in on benches that faced the throne, their heads turned towards the Seneschal of Gascony, who was speaking.

'After the order came from England that we were to surrender the towns temporarily, we waited for King Philippe's men to arrive and take our posts.' The seneschal looked up at Edward. 'But it wasn't just officials who came, my lord. It was an army.' His voice strengthened with feeling. 'They told us that Philippe had declared the duchy forfeit and he was now its ruler. The knights that poured into Bordeaux and the Agenais, Bayonne and Blaye told our men the same thing. They said Gascony was no longer English territory and that if we ever returned the soil would run with English blood.'

'How could this have happened?' said the Earl of Arundel, rising as the seneschal finished speaking. 'My lord,' he said, facing Edward, 'none here could have known that King Philippe had no intention of returning Gascony to you after its surrender, or that the peace agreement and marriage settlement were nothing but ruses intended to force you to yield the duchy without a struggle. But what I cannot comprehend is how his lies were so readily believed?' He looked around the hall. 'And why none of us was consulted on the terms Earl Edmund delivered from Paris? I think I speak for many when I say we would have strongly urged the sealing of the peace agreement before the duchy was ceded.'

Robert, some distance back, craned his head to look at the Earl of Lancaster, seated in silence on one of the benches. He had initially been surprised to see the king's brother on the floor with the barons and knights, rather than on the dais, but it seemed this was perhaps punishment for Earl Edmund's handling of the negotiations in Paris, which had ended in this disaster. If it had been Edward's intention to make an example of his younger brother, however, it didn't seem to have worked, for few of the noblemen present were blaming the withdrawn Earl of Lancaster, all their anger instead directed to the throne.

'The king did consult,' responded John de Warenne roughly, 'with his officials.'

Warenne, his flint grey hair cropped brutally close to his head and his stare bellicose, seemed more aggressive than Robert remembered. He wondered if the change in the earl's character might be due to the recent death of his daughter, John Balliol's wife.

The Earl of Gloucester, a beefy man with thinning auburn hair, got to his feet. On the bench beside the earl, Robert saw the elderly nobleman who had criticised the king at the feast the evening before.

'He may have consulted them,' said Gloucester, his strident voice echoing, 'but from what I heard, our lord dismissed the advice of those closest to him in favour of his own counsel. The chancellor advised him to reject the terms from Paris, as the rest of us would have done if presented with them.' He turned his belligerent gaze on the king. 'My question, Lord King, would be why. If I did not already know the answer.'

As the Earl of Gloucester's words rang accusingly, Robert's gaze remained on the king. He had never imagined the man on that throne, above all others except for God, so privileged, so powerful, could appear vulnerable, but Edward did – vulnerable and alone – a rigid mast thrust above a sea of accusatory faces. Recognising something occasionally glimpsed in his father and grandfather, Robert realised he was looking at the isolation that came with power. Perhaps the Comyns had the right idea: to be close enough to the throne to control it, but not so close as to become the object of men's discontent.

'Earl Gilbert,' warned John de Warenne, 'you would be advised to keep a civil tongue.'

'Why?' demanded Gloucester. 'When it is my sword that will be required to win back the duchy? My men who will have to be raised for the fight? Had all of us here been equally betrayed by France then we would stand with our king united in anger and defiance. But we were not given the choice of rejecting Philippe's terms. Neither did any of us have the hand of a French virgin dangled before us on a hook. We were not the ones reeled in. Why should we be served up on Philippe's platter?'

As a host of voices, some incensed, others concurring, broke across the hall, Robert looked over at the aged Earl of Gloucester, whose long history of antagonism towards the king was well known. Gloucester had recently been married to one of the king's daughters, a surprise considering his reputation, but then by bringing the powerful earl into the royal family and keeping him close, Edward had no doubt hoped to avoid just this kind of altercation. Recalling his grandfather's talk of the war between Simon de Montfort and King Henry, Robert guessed Edward must have learned well at the feet of his father how an unhappy baron could be a dangerous one.

More earls were rising, some adding their agreement to Gloucester's accusations. Others were coming to the king's defence. Robert saw that one man, who now stood to harangue the Earl of Gloucester, had been sitting beside Humphrey de Bohun. Gone was the young knight's amiable manner as he looked up solemnly at the man speaking, whose broad face was so alike his own that Robert guessed he must be his father, the Earl of Hereford and Essex, and Constable of England. Hereford wasn't the only one defending Edward. The voice of Anthony Bek boomed out, demanding Gloucester be held in contempt for his lack of respect for his king, who had been deceived not by lust for a new bride, but by the cunning of his iniquitous cousin, who, like a wolf garbed in the wool of a lamb, had offered peace and delivered wickedness. France, not their king, deserved their wrath, he fulminated, raising his fist to the gathering as if he were on a pulpit.

Edward rose from his throne. 'Enough!'

At the harsh command all fell silent, those on their feet sitting back down, one by one. For a long moment, the king said nothing, but stood there in his black robe, a dark tower of rage. Then, all at once, the fury seemed to drain from him and he hung his head. 'Earl Gilbert is right.'

Men glanced at one another. Many looked over at Gloucester, who was staring at Edward, his face filled with uneasy mistrust.

Edward raised his eyes. 'I was a fool to trust Philippe.'

For a moment, Robert thought he saw anger still struggling within the king's face, then it was gone and his expression was one of remorse.

'I admit the marriage agreement seemed a blessing to me. Most of my children are dead. I have only one male heir and one is hardly enough.'

Robert found himself nodding, thinking of King Alexander.

'It was not lust, but duty to this realm and to my subjects that spurred me to act as I did. Rash though it may have been, imprudent though it was.'

The barons were hushed to a man. Gloucester looked uncomfortable, no longer able to meet the king's gaze.

Edward walked from his throne, down the steps of the dais. He paused for a moment before them all, then knelt on the floor in front of the benches. Robert sat up to get a better view of the kneeling monarch. His hair steely in the morning light, his robes settling around him in a black pool, Edward looked more regal in that moment than he ever had before.

'I beg your forgiveness.' The king's voice carried through the hall. 'Not as your king, rather as a man, fallible as any born of Adam's line.' He lifted his head. 'And just as I beg your forgiveness for my folly, made for the sake of the realm, I beg for your aid to help me take back what has been stolen from us all. Stand with me, men of England, and I will not fail you again.'

The Earl of Hereford rose. 'I will follow you, my lord. In life and death.'

Humphrey de Bohun got to his feet beside his father, head held high, his face filled with pride.

Slowly others followed, rising and pledging themselves to Edward.

'Knights of the realm, mount your warhorses,' Anthony Bek's voice rumbled from the dais. 'Take up your lances! We go to win back the lands of our king!'

Robert looked around him as the earls of Norfolk and Arundel and others who had challenged the king began to stand, either genuinely moved by Edward's astonishing speech, or else too discomforted to be in the minority still seated. He sat there for a moment longer, then rose with the rest. It might not be a crusade, but there was no denying the opportunities presented by a war in France: seized estates, possible prisoners for ransom and a king's gratitude. As the Earl of Gloucester got to his feet, grim, but defeated, Robert, standing among the barons of England, felt a jolt of anticipation. This was what he had trained for, all those months in Ireland and the years in Carrick and Annandale. This was his chance to win his spurs, serving in one of the most formidable armies in the world.

24

The mountains were shrouded in blue twilight. Stars crowned the vault of sky above the mass of rock and scree-covered slopes of Snowdon. In the shadows of the higher peaks a swift stream flowed down the spine of a ridge, its banks clustered with thorny trees and bushes. Along this stream ran two men, scrabbling over boulders and splashing down into sharp shingle, the rush of water loud in their ears. The stream was icy, even now in late August when the fields of Gwynedd, far below, were burned gold by the sun. The echo of a night bird's cry made one of the men look up. He took a moment to catch his breath, the freezing water washing over his legs, then, as his companion glanced back, he continued on, digging his spear into the stream to aid him.

At a worn stone marker that jutted from the tumbling waters, the men climbed the bank into a web of trees, thick with night. Smells of earth and wild herbs rose around them and moths batted softly against their faces. After some time one of them stopped suddenly, holding out a hand to halt the other. With barely a rustle of undergrowth, several figures emerged from the hazy darkness.

'Who's there?'

'Rhys and Hywel from Caernarfon,' answered one of the men. 'We must see Madog.'

After a pause, the shadowy figures parted and the two passed through their midst.

The trees thinned out and the ground rose steeply to a grassy plateau, beneath the hulk of Snowdon. In the milky starlight the fortress that thrust from a rocky mound appeared silvery and smooth. Rhys and Hywel knew that by day its scars would not be so concealed, the fire stains and gashes in the stonework a testimony to its violent past. For eight years after its fall the castle had stood as a ruin, inhabited only by industrious spiders and peregrines that hunted from the heights. Its restoration had been a painstaking process, scaffolding still balanced precariously on the rocks around its western façade, the mossy stones being gathered from the crumbled piles they had been left to moulder in and slowly reassembled.

Making their way quickly up the track that wound around the rocks, the two approached the castle gate. Torches billowed on the parapets, where the outlines of men were moving. After being questioned they hastened through the courtyard, noisy with the bleating of goats and sheep. Men in woollen cloaks and hukes shared cups of beer around. Huts lined the walls, fashioned from turf and timber, and the smell of food mixed uneasily with the greasy stench of a latrine. Up the outer steps of the castle's keep, passing more guards, the two men entered a dull-lit hall, where the floor and walls were green with lichen. A fire spat from a pit in the centre, smoke rising to the ceiling, which was riddled with holes. The tendrils swirled through the gaps to the floor above, then up to the roof, part of which opened into the star-strewn sky. There were several men seated on logs around the fire. They looked round as Rhys and Hywel entered.

One, the youngest, who had keen eyes beneath a fringe of soot-black hair, rose. 'You weren't to leave your post for another two months.'

Hywel stepped forward. 'Where is Lord Madog, Dafydd?'

'Here.'

A broad-shouldered man was heading down a set of creaking wooden steps from the upper floor. His black hair was tousled from sleep, his chin rough with stubble. He descended the last few stairs and walked across the hall towards them, pulling his fur-trimmed cloak tighter about his muscular shoulders. He glanced at the young man by the fire. 'Be seated, brother,' he said, before turning his gaze on the two men. 'Why have you come?'

'The English are leaving, Madog,' said Hywel. His chest was heaving with the effort of the long climb, but his eyes were shining. He paused to clear his dry throat.

Madog gestured to one of the men by the fire. 'Give them something to drink.'

'It began over a week ago,' said Hywel, gratefully accepting the cup of beer that was passed to him. He gulped at it, before passing it to Rhys. 'Word came from England that the King of France had seized the duchy of Gascony and King Edward had declared war upon him. The garrison at Caernarfon was called to serve.'

'The same happened at Conwy and Rhuddlan, according to our men there,' Rhys cut in. 'Everywhere in Gwynedd – everywhere in Wales

— English soldiers are moving out. There are only a few who remain in the castles. It is our chance, Madog.'

'But the towns will still be full of English settlers,' said Dafydd, coming to stand beside his older brother.

'Without soldiers to protect them they are nothing but lambs in pens.' Madog's eyes moved to the fractured ceiling, intent in thought.

'There is more,' said Hywel. 'King Edward has issued writs that are being proclaimed by English officials throughout Gwynedd. The men of Wales are to fight. We have all been summoned to serve him in France.'

Madog's face hardened in the gloom. 'Gather the men,' he said, before turning to Dafydd. 'And bring me my cousin's chest.'

The men around the fire, his chiefs, had all risen.

Madog nodded at the unspoken question in their faces. 'It is time.'

Torches burned around the courtyard, sparks whirling into the black before winking into nothing. Madog stood on the steps of the keep wrapped in his fur-lined cloak, the scarred tower rising behind him. Beside him stood his chiefs, including his young brother, Dafydd, at whose feet was a wooden chest, engraved with silver words in the old British tongue. Below, the faces of his men were ruddy in the torch flames. Every one of them was silent, waiting. Madog stared at their upturned heads, seeing hope and fear, hunger and anticipation.

Some of them had been with him in the wilderness for years, ever since the death of Llywelyn ap Gruffudd. For a long time they had stayed hidden, licking the wounds inflicted by the English in the conquest over a decade ago, when their hopes for a liberated Wales had been shattered by the iron of the English cavalry. Other men, unwilling to live under the yoke of the English officials and their strange laws, followed him into the hills over the years, as the foreign settlers established new towns and filled them with their own people, forcing the Welsh to adapt to English customs and obey their rule.

Madog began to speak. 'Down in the walled towns and castles, in the well-stocked halls of foreign officials they call us outlaws. But this is not what we are, for no English law do we observe, only the laws of the kingdom of Gwynedd. Some of you think yourselves prisoners, locked away in our mountain fastness. I say we are neither outlaws nor prisoners. Up here, in freedom, we are kings!'

A few scattered calls of approval followed his words. One or two men laughed appreciatively.

Madog went on. 'For a long time we have waited for the chance to win back our lands. Now, that chance has come. Edward's towns have been left undefended, the soldiers called away for his war. We have been summoned to fight by this king whose officials have long taxed our people into misery. But we shall not lift our spears for him, this tyrant.'

The calls of his men grew louder.

'We shall lift them against him!'

A roar followed, men stamping spear butts on the ground.

Madog's voice rose above their thunder. 'We have allies in the mountains to the south and west, men who will rally to this cause. We have weapons. We have the will!'

The shouts continued, fierce now, all humour gone.

'For centuries our people have spoken of the *mab darogan*: the warrior who will lead us to victory against the foreign invaders, the man who will usher in a new age. The prophets say he will come with signs and portents.' Madog gestured to his brother. 'I say this is our sign! Our portent!'

Dafydd crouched beside the engraved wooden chest to open it. Carefully, reverently, he lifted out a slender gold circlet, the metal of which was dented and scratched. As he passed it to his brother, the men's shouts scattered away into silence.

Madog stood before them, his black hair whipping about his face in the night wind. 'This crown was once worn by a man whose blood I share. Before the mighty Llywelyn fell in battle he passed it to me. I hid it from King Edward when he came searching, desiring its power for himself.' Madog raised the crown, his heart hammering. His life, for more than a decade, had been leading to this point. 'Now, it is time for us to come down from the shelter of these hills, time to raise our spears against our enemies. And I shall lead you, not as Madog ap Llywelyn, but as your prince, for I hold in my hands the Crown of Arthur and whoever wears this band, by ancient prophecy, shall be the Prince of Wales.'

Caernarfon, Wales

1284 AD

*O*utside, the birds were crying, calling the dawn as if they were God's messengers, the first to hear His command to wake, as it descended from heaven. Gulls and geese, herons and ragged-winged cormorants, little dragons some of the English soldiers who had never seen the sea before had named them.

Edward lay in silence listening to their muffled cries as he stared at the wall through the gap in the bed drapes, where a patch of light had been growing for the past hour. Beneath his back the linen sheet was damp. He had slept maybe two hours of the night, but he wasn't tired. A new wail joined the birds' chorus, echoing down the passage and beneath the bedchamber door. Edward looked at his wife, lying warm beside him, her black hair veined with grey tumbling across the silk pillow. She didn't stir. After a moment, he sat up, the fur-lined cover slipping down to his waist. The floor beneath his feet was softened by a rug, one of many Eleanor had insisted be transported with their bed and the rest of the furniture. All across the shires of England this bed and these rugs had travelled, across the border, into Snowdonia's mountainous heart.

As Edward crossed the chamber the dawn air raised gooseflesh on his skin. He pulled on his braies and laced the thin cord around the top to keep them in place. As he reached for his shirt, he caught sight of himself in the looking-glass. A tall figure stood in the gloom, long legs slabbed with muscle, broad chest and arms sharply contoured in the shadows. The campaign had toughened him, honing his body to the tower of strength it had been in youth. It couldn't take the ash from his hair, however, or the lines from his brow, which had only increased. He had celebrated his forty-fifth birthday two months ago and those years were showing in his eyes and the roughness of his skin, burned brown and leather-like by sun and wind. Turning from the glass, Edward put on his shirt, then a robe pulled in at his waist with a belt and, lastly, a pair of hide boots, scuffed and dusty despite the vigorous clean his page had given them. Heading out of the chamber, he made his way down the passage.

The wailing was louder and had been joined by soft singing. Edward stopped by the closed door, his ears assaulted by the hungry cries that pierced through the wood into his mind. He heard the wet nurse's footsteps pacing the floor as the infant silenced to drag in a breath before opening his lungs again. Edward closed his eyes and placed a hand on the wood, letting that sound shudder over him. It was only a week since messengers had come from London to tell him his eldest son had died at Westminster, taken without warning, like so many of his children over the years.

His first had been dead in the womb, no chance at life. His second, sweet Katherine, delivered in Gascony, had died six months after the battle at Lewes, aged three. Joan only made it to eight months, John reached five years and Henry six. Ten of them gone, one by one, and now Alfonso, his beautiful boy, whom he had been so certain would live to wear the crown, had joined their silent ranks. The raging child beyond the door, his sixteenth, born in a war and named after himself, was now his only son and England's only heir. Those powerful screams were a comfort Edward lingered to listen to for some moments more, before moving on down the stairs of the royal apartments and out into the dawn.

The sky over the distant mountains was flooding with rose-gold light, while over the waters of the Menai Strait and out across the narrow hump of Anglesey it was stony blue, still lit by a milk-white moon. Birds swooped, circling the banks of the estuary that flowed past the castle's southern walls into the strait. Edward could smell the brine of the river over the sweeter odour of sawn timbers that came from the building he had left. The apartments had been built for him and his pregnant queen for their arrival in Caernarfon in the spring. Here, Eleanor had given birth to their son, as had been his wish; a testimony to a conquered nation that this land now belonged to him and to his heirs. The massive stone castle slowly taking shape around the timber apartments was still in its early stages, but already he could see the mighty structure it would become.

The moat had been dug and lined, the foundations for the great towers and walls laid by hundreds of diggers, the stone quarried from Anglesey and brought across the strait by boat. The walls of the castle and the town beyond were going up, block by block, every inch of the enormous site bristling with scaffolding, the air cloudy with dust. In places, the bases of the towers were visible, almost twenty feet thick. Doorways stood open on to nothing, postern gates made holes in unfinished walls, stairs spiralled to nowhere. Only one tower, the largest, that squatted before him and loomed out over the strait, had gone up to first-floor level. Edward had seen the plans his master mason, James of St George, had drawn up and could, with his mind, fill in the blank blue of the sky with a tower that soared three storeys high to be crowned by three angular turrets, topped at the heights with life-size stone eagles.

Built on the site where a thousand years earlier a Roman fort had glowered across the strait at the Druids' stronghold on the Isle of Anglesey, Caernarfon was to be the greatest castle in the iron ring he had created around the coast, his presence fixed in stone. The strength of Rome was crumbling and moss-covered beyond the new town walls, but Edward had not ignored the power in that history and his fortress, fashioned in likeness of the Roman walls of Constantinople, would resonate with imperial might, deep in the heart of conquered Wales.

As he walked towards the unfinished tower people moved about him in the dawn, grooms tending horses, servants carrying baskets of provisions and squires stoking campfires. A line of women, laundry baskets hefted on their shoulders, headed for the river gate. Some men bowed as he moved across the muddy ground, others carried on their business, unaware that their king was passing by, a solitary figure in the dawn-washed shadows, taller than most of them, his eyes haunted by lack of sleep. Walking between the rows of tents that belonged to his knights, the canvas sodden with dew, Edward noticed discarded barrels of beer and caught the sour odour of vomit. The celebrations he had organised at the village of Nefyn, forty miles south of Caernarfon, were clearly still continuing here. He couldn't begrudge them that, for it had been a hard campaign, his fourth in this unforgiving land, which had spawned so many rebellions against him and had caused him to delve so deeply into the purses of his subjects.

Seven years earlier, Edward had imagined he had dealt with Llywelyn ap Gruffudd once and for all. Having returned from the Holy Land to take up his father's crown, he had wasted little time in tearing the self-proclaimed Welsh prince down to size, driving giant armies into Wales, undoing Llywelyn's earlier conquests and confining him and his men to the fastness of Snowdonia. But events soon showed that Edward's campaign had not been decisive enough. Just two years ago, the prince had risen again and all of Wales had risen with him. In defiant letters, Llywelyn declared that Wales belonged purely to the Welsh and that he ruled it as the true descendant of Brutus, the founder of Britain. This appeal to the ancient history set down by Geoffrey of Monmouth had angered Edward deeply, almost as much as the celebrated crown the prince wore on his head. And so he invaded Wales once again, this time bent on outright conquest.

Here, in Gwynedd, Edward had suffered one of the worst disasters of his life. His best commanders, sent out on a reconnaissance mission, had led a rash assault against the northern coast, reckoning on a quick victory against the inferior forces of the Welsh. Taken unawares in the unfamiliar terrain, they were overwhelmed by Llywelyn's men and hundreds of English lives were lost. When Edward learned of the rebels' triumph echoes of those songs the Welsh had sung of him, when his army had been annihilated by Llywelyn decades earlier, had taunted him from down the years.

Grimly determined, his reputation once again threatened, he battled on through the Welsh winter, hampered by storms and the cunning of his adversary. While the Welsh evaded him in the hills, he employed hundreds of woodcutters to carve massive paths through the inhospitable forests, clearing the way for more troops and for the labourers who worked to raise up the massive stone fortresses that provided secure bases from which he could strike back at the Welsh.

Reaching the foot of the Eagle Tower, beneath a tight labyrinth of scaffold poles, past guards who saluted him, Edward entered the vestibule and climbed the steps that led up to the first floor. The grand, ten-sided chamber that opened before him was hazy with dust that lingered in the air in shifting layers. It was here that most of the royal belongings had been stored and the walls were lined with chests and furniture. In the centre was a round table, the bare wood creamy.

Edward went to it, his pale eyes following the Latin inscriptions around the edge, each skilful cut of the carpenter's tools carving a name in oak. Kay, Galahad, Gawain, Mordred, Bors, Perceval. Twenty-four names for twenty-four knights. He'd had it made for the celebrations at Nefyn, to mark the end of the war and the beginning of a new order, an order of men who had followed him into hell, their loyalty fused to him in the endless circle of the table. Beyond, fixed to the smooth stone wall, was the dragon banner he once carried into tournaments in Gascony over twenty years earlier. He had been Arthur then in name alone, a tournament guise to inspire fear in his opponents and respect from his followers. Now, he was Arthur in reputation, his lands expanded, his reign over Britain almost complete. After two tough years, he had accomplished what so many English kings had planned for and desired but never achieved: the conquest and subjugation of Wales.

Llywelyn, whose forces had entrenched themselves in the hills above the River Wye, from where they were continuing to conduct raids against the king's positions, had finally been pinned down, the prince's location betrayed by one of his own people. · Edward's forces had crept by the frosty dark of a winter dawn into the heights of the hills, led by the informant, whereupon they fell hard upon the prince and his men, who were taken by surprise. In the bloody fight that followed, Llywelyn had been cut down, run through by an English lance. With the death of their prince, Welsh resistance had finally died.

As the gold sunlight filtering through the unfinished tower's windows shone across the table and the dragon banner, Edward tasted the bitterness of that victory.

Llywelyn's severed head now adorned the battlements of the Tower in London. The rest of his line had been destroyed, his men captured or killed. The bards were singing songs of despair, begging God to cover their land in sea. New towns were being laid out and English settlers were pouring in, driving the Welsh to subsist on the margins. Statutes were being drawn up for the English sheriffs and bailiffs who would govern the region under a justiciar and more of Edward's fortresses were going up, block by block, around the coast. But, for him, one vital piece was still missing.

Going to one of the chests along the wall, Edward bent to retrieve something wrapped in black silk. Moving to the table, he placed it on the wood and unfolded the material to reveal a book. The writing on the cover caught the morning sun.

The Last Prophecy of Merlin

As he turned the soft pages, he could smell the ink, made from precious stones, powdered down and mixed with egg and wine. The colours were vivid, glorious. Around the words, fabulous beasts were entwined with flowers and birds. Edward had presented it to his knights at Nefyn, the place where the prophecies of Merlin had been found, which Geoffrey of Monmouth had translated for the world. On one page was an image of a man standing before a great fortress, behind which towered green mountains. In his hands, he held aloft a simple, gold coronet. It was this image Edward had seen for months — more so when he lay down to sleep, the distractions of the day fading in the silence. He had questioned those followers of Llywelyn he had caught, then tortured them, but either they had not known, or else refused even into death to reveal the whereabouts of the thing he had vowed to seize twenty years ago: the object that had united Wales against him. The Crown of Arthur.

25

The fire flared as the guard stoked the embers. He screwed up his eyes against the heat, took two logs from the basket and tossed them in. The flames trailed along the edges of the wood, while insects rushed from cracks in the grain. They burned brightly as they caught, vanishing in the conflagration.

'Hugh.'

The guard turned to see Simon holding out a cup of beer. The oldest, Ulf, was sitting back on one of the barrels, his leg, splinted from a fall, stretched out in front of him. His stick was propped against the wall and he had a cup wedged in his gnarled hands.

'One each?' questioned Hugh, rising with a wince and wiping soot on his gambeson. 'Aren't we sharing?'

'Why share?' Simon wanted to know, shaking the cup at him. 'There're more rations now the others have gone.' He grinned, revealing brown stubs of teeth, as Hugh took it.

'Don't let the commander see,' warned Hugh, taking up his place on a stool by the hearth.

'Can he see from half a mile away?' asked Simon, gulping back the beer that left a white scum on his lip.

Hugh sipped the malt-sweet liquid slowly in the fire's glow. There were perhaps some benefits to being the ones left behind.

Simon sat forward with a wet belch, resting his arms on his thighs. 'Do you think we would have got better pay in France?' he mused, frowning at Hugh.

Ulf grunted from the shadows before Hugh could answer. 'At our age? King Edward wanted destriers, not nags.'

'I'm ten years younger than you,' growled Simon.

Ignoring their banter, Hugh drained the dregs of the drink. 'I'd better have a last look.'

'Bed soon,' muttered Ulf, resting his head on the wall. 'I swear by God these watches get longer every night.'

'It's the autumn dark,' said Hugh, heading past a neat row of swords, bows and shields placed against the wall and ducking through the arch that led up to the top of the gatehouse tower.

The air blowing down the curving stone stairway was frigid and Hugh shuddered as the warmth of the fire was leached from his face and hands. As he neared the top, dust scattered into his eyes and he was forced to duck his head. It was several years since the twin-towered gatehouse and the town walls from which it jutted had been completed, yet grit still filled the air. For a long time, Hugh had been able to smell the vinegar that had been soaked into the lime to make the grey mortar. One of the masons' apprentices had told him it was to protect the walls from fiery missiles thrown by siege engines, but Hugh hadn't known whether this was right.

Coming out on the windy tower top, he pulled his felt cap firmly around his ears. His breath foggy, he looked out over the town of Caernarfon. The night sky was obscured by slow-moving clouds, but in the tattered breaks between faint glimmers of blue revealed the dawn. Just another hour and he could sleep. His gaze moved over silent streets and dark orchards to the patchwork of market gardens, mostly stripped of produce preserved for the coming winter. There were shimmering points of light where people were waking and stoking fires or lighting candles, but these were few. The town had been quiet for the past month, after most of the garrison and many of the younger townsmen had left, summoned to Gascony.

Hugh's gaze moved to the south-western walls that marched alongside the waters of the Menai Strait, the fires in the guard towers at long intervals, the garrison stretched thinly around the walls of the town and the castle, which loomed as a great, angular shadow in the distance. The towers on the castle's seaward side were complete, but scaffold still shrouded the town-side walls, which in places were only twelve feet high. The ditch and wooden barricade that had protected the building for the ten years since work had begun remained, but were mostly redundant since the completion of the town walls. Soon it would be All Souls and work on the castle would finish until spring, many of the labourers returning to their homes. Hugh thought briefly of his own home, far away in Sussex, as he stared at the castle, wondering what it would be like to have something so monumental built at your word. There was something God-like about the process, yet King Edward, its creator, hadn't seen Caernarfon since the early stages of building.

Hearing the bleating of sheep, Hugh crossed the tower top to gaze out over the moat that encircled the town to the gloomy landscape of huddled trees and mist-shrouded fields that gradually rose into far-off mountains. The ragged calls of the sheep echoed, louder now. Hugh frowned, squinting into the darkness, wondering what had disturbed them. It was too early in the year for wolves. It could be thieves, but the shepherds and their dogs usually saw them off. He could see them, a large flock scattering across a wide field. His eye was caught by more movement, away from where the sheep were fleeing. Dark shapes were moving quickly along the tree line. Hugh's eyes darted, picking out more shadows, on the other side of the trees, hundreds of them. They were all running in the same direction: towards the moat, towards the town. Hugh's skin tightened in shock. Pushing himself from the battlements, he plunged down the spiral of stairs, shouting as he went.

'Raise the drawbridge!'

He stumbled in the dizzy descent and just managed to stop himself tumbling headlong down the steep steps, his fingers scraping dust from the walls. Recovering his balance, he continued on, still shouting. He collided with Simon near the bottom, who was sprinting up. '*Raise the drawbridge!*' Hugh shouted in his face, pushing the man ahead of him.

In the guardroom, Ulf was on his feet, bleary-eyed and confused. 'We're under attack?'

'Here,' said Hugh, grabbing two swords and thrusting one at him.

Simon had gone pale, but took a shield and sword from the neat stack of weapons. 'How many?'

'Hundreds,' snapped Hugh, 'maybe more.'

'Dear God,' breathed Ulf, his eyes clearing as he followed Hugh and Simon to the archway that led down a tight twist of steps to the ground floor of the tower, where a small chamber, built into the thickness of the wall, contained the winch for the drawbridge, which adjoined the end of a long wooden bridge that spanned the moat.

In the early days of building, soon after the war, when the town walls and towers were slowly going up, the drawbridge had always been raised at night. But for the past few years, with the labourers coming and going so often, they relied instead on the portcullis to bar entry to thieves and beggars.

As Hugh reached the bottom, he shouted behind him to Ulf, who was limping awkwardly down on his injured leg. 'Raise the alarm. We'll work the winch.'

Faint sounds came from across the water, the dull thud of many feet pounding the frost-packed earth.

Hugh and Simon entered the winch chamber as Ulf stumbled down the last few steps, out into the arched vault between the towers, spanned by the portcullis. A torch burned from a bracket on the wall. Ulf halted in its glow, staring through the iron bars of the portcullis, across the bridge to the opposite banks of the moat. There was a tide of men flooding from the woods, visible in the growing light. Ulf's eyes widened. He could see ladders being carried by lines of men and the weapons in their raised fists weren't swords or spears, but axes, hammers and picks, as if they were a mad horde of labourers rushing in to start a day's work. As the drawbridge ropes snapped taut and the boards wobbled, Ulf heard Hugh and Simon grunting with effort, the winch shrieking in protest, unused for so long. The first wave of attackers funnelled along the bridge.

Ulf, frozen in the glow of the torch, didn't see one man on the bank tug an arrow from the quiver at his belt, didn't see him fix it to the bow in his hands, aim and pull back. The missile shot through the darkness, invisible until the last second, when Ulf, who was turning towards the tower where the bell was stored, caught its blur. Too late. The old guard was thrown back as the arrow punched into him, piercing his gambeson. He didn't have time to make a sound as the awful force wrenched through him, snatching away his breath. Beyond the portcullis the drawbridge was inching up, but the first attackers were leaping on to the boards, their weight forcing it back down.

'Ulf! For the sake of Christ!' Hugh shouted, as he struggled with the winch. 'The bell!' Hearing nothing but drumming footsteps, he left Simon heaving on the handle and ran out. Hugh threw himself back in as an arrow came flying past. Ulf was on the ground, a few feet away. Hugh breathed a curse and crouched, glancing round the edge of the opening. There were lots of men beyond, murmuring breathlessly. The Welsh only came into Caernarfon to trade during the day. Most of them had been banished when King Edward established the site for his new seat of government, their houses pulled down to make way for the town's foundations, the timber used for building works. Hugh didn't understand their language. Here in this English town in the heart of Wales he hadn't needed to.

More men were vaulting on to the drawbridge. A ladder had been let down the side to the boggy bank that stretched around the curtain walls. Hugh heard splashing as men disappeared over the side, descending into the shallow mud. Simon was straining at the winch, shouting for help. It was no use. They could never raise it now. Their only hope lay in alerting the rest of the garrison to the attack. Hugh pushed himself back inside. 'Leave it,' he told Simon. 'There're too many. Ulf's dead.'

Simon held on to the winch for a moment longer, then let go, the rope coiling back round sharply. He watched as Hugh hefted his shield. 'What are you doing?'

'I need to get to the bell.'

Hugh paused in the doorway, staring across the small stretch of torch-lit ground towards the arched opening that led into the opposite tower. Bending down, holding his shield up to cover his left side and head, he sucked in a breath, refusing to let his eyes look at the prone form of Ulf, his splinted leg splayed beside him. Hugh breathed a prayer, then launched himself into the open space between the towers. There was a shout above the breathless murmurs beyond the portcullis, followed a moment later by a sharp concussion in his left arm as something thumped into the shield. Hugh stumbled with the impact, then felt another strike, this time in his calf, followed by ferocious pain. He fell with a cry, the shield crashing down on top of him. Another arrow plunged into his thigh as he lay screaming. Under the rim of the shield, through eyes slitted with agony, he saw many men jumping down from the bridge on to the banks. His gaze flickered dimly over one in their midst, broad-shouldered and black-haired, wearing a fur-lined cloak. He was carrying a massive hammer in both hands and on his head was a band of scratched and dented gold. He looked like some warrior king, stepping out of the dark and distant past. Hugh felt someone grab him under the arms and twisted round to see Simon's clenched face. Arrows lanced past as the guard hauled him back into the safety of the tower.

Hugh gritted his teeth and put his head back on the stone floor of the winch room, feeling sweat breaking out all over his body. He was freezing, except for the two bolts of fiery pain in his calf and thigh. 'Upstairs,' he hissed through his teeth. 'Alert – the castle.'

Simon hesitated, staring at him, then disappeared up the tower stairs. Hugh lay gasping, hearing his footsteps fade. Nearer, were the dull thuds of hammers against stone. It sounded as though the tools had been muffled.

Reaching the guardroom, Simon halted, looking wildly around. Alert the castle how? He could shout, but it was unlikely anyone would hear him. His gaze fell on the fire. He went to it, gazing hopelessly at the bright flames, then caught sight of Ulf's stick, still propped against the wall. Unfastening his belt with shaking hands, he hauled off his gambeson, which was padded with straw, and wrenched his undershirt over his head. Grabbing Ulf's stick, he bundled the shirt around the top of it, then ripped open the gambeson. Crouching beside the basket of logs, his bare chest prickling in the heat, he stuffed straw and shards of kindling into the folds of the shirt. As he thrust the end of the stick into the flames, it caught, flaring yellow. Simon rose and raced up the steps to the tower top, cursing as the wind fanned the flames towards him, threatening to blow them out. He reached the top and crouched, swinging the beacon back and forth, as the twigs and straw went up and the material burned, showering his bare chest with cinders.

26

In the Tower's inner ward, on a patch of ground by the orchards, a group of young men had gathered with their horses. Their winter cloaks were wrapped tight around them, long riding boots caked with mud, faces mottled by the cold. A few bore tethered birds of prey on their gloved hands. The knights carried speckled sakers from the Holy Land, the squires smoke-coloured lanners. Moving among the men were several girls, the hems of their gowns sodden. The wind snatched at their mantles and sent flurries of rust-coloured leaves scattering from piles that the servants in the orchards were trying vainly to sweep up. The sky over London was low and leaden, threatening more rain.

Autumn had arrived from out of tranquil September skies, the winds howling in ahead of a week-long deluge that drowned the shires of England. The Thames burst its banks, flooding a row of slaughterhouses and polluting the streets with a bloody sludge. The labourers of the Tower were kept busy mending a leak in the king's bedchamber, where rainwater ruined a rug that had belonged to Eleanor. The damaged carpet had been the least of the king's concerns, for the storms had struck the south coast just as the first half of his fleet set sail for Gascony. The treacherous wind blew half the departing ships back to Portsmouth and forced the rest to shelter down the coast at Plymouth. Nor was the inclement weather the only thing that had hampered Edward's move towards France and his warmongering cousin. Following the spring parliament, the king turned to the Church to fund his campaign, but found the clergy unwilling to open their coffers for his cause. When Edward threatened to outlaw them, the Dean of St Paul's crumbled in the face of his furious demands, but there was little doubt that the delay had enabled Philippe to gain a firmer hold over Gascony.

Robert glanced round from checking his stirrup lengths, hearing a peal of laughter. Two girls were behind him watching a servant chase the scurrying leaves with a broom. One, barely out of childhood, wore a dove-grey gown under a mantle lined with miniver that wisped about her pale neck. Elizabeth, the king's youngest daughter, had inherited her father's long limbs and her mother's dark hair, strands of which had floated free from beneath her cowl and switched about her face. As Robert watched, she tugged one impatiently behind her ear and leaned over to whisper something to the older girl beside her, Helena, who had springy auburn hair and milky skin that was chapped a provocative red at her cheeks and lips. On her gloved hand was a merlin, its wings ruffled by the wind. The flame-haired girl, a daughter of the Earl of Warwick, was promised to a high-ranking knight of the king's household, but for some weeks now Robert had been unable to take his eyes off her, despite quiet warnings from Humphrey. Out of the corner of his eye, he noticed a young man staring at him. The rangy, red-haired knight with a grim expression was Helena's brother, Guy de Beauchamp, Warwick's heir. Robert turned back to his horse, shortening the stirrup with a forceful wrench.

'Are you ready, Sir Robert?' Humphrey called, heading across. The tall knight had a skin of wine in one hand. He gestured at the expanse of muddy ground, where two posts had been erected. A thin rope was suspended between them from which dangled a small iron ring, invisible at this distance. 'You have two chances, remember.'

Robert returned the knight's goading grin. 'That would be one less than you then, Sir Humphrey.'

Humphrey, who failed to lance the ring on his two tries, narrowed his eyes at the provocation as a few of the other knights laughed.

Edward, standing with their squires, clapped Robert on the back as he dug his foot into the stirrup. 'Show these southerners what Scots are made of, brother,' he murmured.

Robert swung up into the saddle and grasped the reins as Nes came forward to tighten the girth. The horse, a handsome roan charger called Hunter, was one of the swiftest, most responsive animals Robert had ever owned, a true joy to ride. But that good temperament had cost him, for horses of Hunter's breeding did not come cheap and the sixty marcs he'd handed to the trader had seemed a huge sum. Convincing himself of the necessity of a suitable horse that would carry him into war in France, he had ignored his brother's intimations that it was more to do with the fact that the sturdy-legged coursers and gentle palfreys they had brought from their grandfather's stables had seemed lowly in comparison to the power-ful French and Spanish-bred destriers of the English knights. Afterwards, Robert had dug deeper into his purse to buy new clothes for himself and his brother, more in accordance with the London fashion. Soon after the spring parliament, he had been granted his first audience by the king, who had welcomed his pledge to serve him in war, as his father and grandfather before him. Following this, Robert found himself invited to many subsequent royal councils and feasts. Moving within the higher circles of the king's court, the effort to blend in with the other barons had seemed fitting.

Nes passed Robert his lance, which he took in his gloved hand. The soft leather was still smooth from lack of wear and he had to grip all the harder to keep the shaft in place.

'Wait, Sir Robert!' came a girlish voice from the crowd.

Robert looked round to see Princess Elizabeth, whom he'd heard affectionately referred to as Bess, wielding a fistful of white silk. It looked as though it had once been part of a veil. As he watched, the young princess stuffed the rumpled cloth into Helena's hand with a furtive grin. Helena's cheeks flushed a deeper shade of red and she shot the princess a furious glance, but stepped reluctantly out of the crowd. Robert felt his chest tighten as she held up the cloth and met his gaze. The merlin on her hand raised its wings in expectation of flight as Robert bent down to take the favour and Bess clapped laughingly. His fingers brushed against Helena's when he grasped the silk and he wished to God he wasn't wearing the gloves. She moved quickly back into the crowd, her head bowed, while he wrapped the fluttering length of silk around his lance shaft, ignoring the glare he knew Guy de Beauchamp was giving him. Steadying himself, Robert turned towards the distant posts and kicked hard at Hunter's sides.

The servants in the orchard stopped sweeping to watch as Robert plunged down the field, lance raised into the canter, before being levelled for the gallop. Mud sprayed, splattering his new boots. The iron ring came up quickly, his focus narrowing on it. Robert's fingers tightened around the shaft, the pad of his glove slipping against the wood as he rushed towards the posts, the silk favour billowing ahead of him. His mind filled with the image of Helena, arm raised, her sleeve slipping down to reveal more skin. She flashed through his thoughts only briefly, but it was enough to distract him. He lunged, a second too early. The tip of the lance grazed the iron circle, but didn't enter it. Leaving the small ring swinging madly in his wake, Robert shot on past the posts, cursing. Slowing Hunter, he turned in a wide circle back down the mud-churned field towards the company.

Humphrey raised the wine skin. 'One left!' he called, laughing as Robert approached.

'I'll wager he makes the second,' said Edward, turning to the knight, his eyes glinting with challenge.

Humphrey chuckled good-naturedly and shook his head, but Henry Percy, the Earl of Surrey's grandson, nodded to Edward.

'I'll accept that wager,' said the stocky, blond lord with his lazy smile. On his wrist was a handsome buzzard, its talons hooked over a thick glove. Henry motioned to Robert, who had pulled Hunter to a halt. 'Ten pounds he doesn't take the ring.'

Robert looked over at his brother and shook his head discreetly at the sum. Acting as lord of their English estates in the absence of his father, he had summoned three knights and five squires from Essex to serve him, along with his brother and their Scottish entourage, in the war in France. It was Robert's duty to provide for them all on campaign and unwise wagers were the last thing he needed.

Edward, however, ignored his look. 'Done,' he told Henry Percy.

Some of the other knights clapped approvingly, eager for the sport. They had been training for months, all through the delay, and the spice added to their usual practice session was appreciated.

Unable to back down now the wager had been set, Robert turned his horse and moved into position, gritting his teeth and hefting the lance. Forcing all else from his mind, he waited for that single, perfect moment when everything, the horse beneath him, the lance in his hand, his gaze on that distant ring were aligned. When it came it felt like a push. He dug in his spurs and Hunter set off, racing down the centre of the field towards the posts. The wind stung his cheeks, but Robert didn't take his gaze off the ring. He crouched forward, lance swinging down. Suddenly, a flash of white darted across his path. Hunter's head jerked round at the motion. The horse missed the next step and came down hard, front hoof slipping in the mud. As the destrier smashed into the ground at furious speed, Robert was flung from the saddle. Tumbling over and over, Hunter's scream of pain echoing behind him, he came to a shuddering stop.

After a few moments, Robert swayed up on to his hands, spitting blood and mud from his mouth. He could see his horse struggling to stand. His squires were running towards him, Nes heading straight for Hunter. Edward was sprinting with them, his face filled not with concern, but fury, fixed on two men and a woman who had appeared on the edge of the field. One was taller than the others, his sleek black hair swept back from his angular face. On Aymer de Valence's wrist, swallowing down a piece of meat, was a white saker. Robert realised the flash of white that had spooked Hunter had been the rush of a bird's wings.

'What were you thinking, Aymer?' demanded Humphrey, heading over as Robert swiped blood from his split lip.

'I thought we were flying our birds today.' Aymer's tone was smooth, but he was looking at Robert as he spoke, his eyes bright with amusement. 'I apologise, Sir Robert. I didn't mean to distract you.'

Beside him, his sister, Joan de Valence, wore a delicate smirk, half hidden by her gloved hand. Robert's gaze moved from Joan to the young man next to her with pallid skin and lank black hair, her new husband, John Comyn. He hadn't even bothered to hide his mirth. It was plastered across his lean face.

The son of the Lord of Badenoch had arrived in London two months earlier with his father and other Scottish magnates, summoned by King Edward to do service in France for their English lands. It was said that Comyn, backed by his fellow Scots, told the king that none of them would serve in a foreign war unless he adhered to the provisions agreed at Birgham and left Balliol to rule his kingdom without English interference. Robert and the other knights didn't know whether the king had accepted these terms. What they did know was that soon after, a hasty wedding had taken place at the Tower, between Comyn's eighteen-year-old heir and Edward's cousin, Joan, the daughter of the Earl of Pembroke. The growing closeness between the new brothers-in-law had turned the air between Robert and Aymer, who hadn't warmed to him at all, even colder. He sensed the knight was resentful of his burgeoning friendship with Humphrey, but until now Aymer had vaunted his disapproval with nothing more than snide comments and snubs, all of which had been easy to ignore.

Edward stepped towards the three, wrathful at the cheap trick, which had wounded his brother and lost him the wager. 'You cast that bird on purpose, Valence. Anyone can see that.' His eyes flicked to John. 'Take that smile off your face, Comyn.'

John Comyn scowled, but before he could respond Henry Percy moved in, stroking the dappled chest of his buzzard.

'I say all's fair.' Henry looked from Aymer to Robert. 'We're training for war. Do you not think there will be distractions on the field?'

Some of the other men nodded in agreement, but Humphrey shook his head adamantly. 'This isn't the field of war. There are rules.'

Robert took the wine skin one of his squires handed to him and swilled the liquid round his bloody mouth. He glanced round as Nes called to him. The squire had hold of Hunter's reins and was trying to help the distressed animal.

'I think he's lamed, sir.'

Robert stared at Nes's troubled face, his thoughts filling with the money he'd paid for the beautiful animal, his best weapon for the coming fight. As he turned back to Aymer, fury flooded him. He went for his sword, meaning to challenge the French knight, determined to recover his loss and his pride, but before he could act there came a shout.

Thomas of Lancaster was sprinting across the grass towards them. 'There's rebellion in Wales!' he panted, as he reached the group. 'Messengers arrived an hour ago. The king is gathering the magnates for an emergency council.'

'A rebellion?' questioned Humphrey sharply. 'Led by whom?'

'A man called Madog. My father says he's a cousin of Llywelyn ap Gruffudd.'

'All of Llywelyn's line were captured in the last war,' said Henry Percy. 'King Edward made certain of it.'

Thomas shrugged this away, breathing hard. 'Well, whoever he is, it is serious. Caernarfon has fallen and other castles are under attack. The king is to take immediate action.' He paused to catch his breath, excitement in his eyes as he met Humphrey's gaze. 'The rebels have the Crown of Arthur.'

27

Taking a swig from the skin, Robert savoured the warmth of the wine that flooded his throat. It was colder this far north and west, winter closing in. The sky beyond the broken screen of trees was a frost-tinged blue. He was reminded of Carrick by the clarity of the air, so different to London, clogged with the stink of its seething multitude.

Returning the skin to his pack, Robert leaned back in the saddle, letting Hunter find his own path along the furrowed track. The branches of oak and silver-white birch were almost bare, the ground dense with rotting leaves. Around him men, horses and carts moved through the trees, following the deep ruts in the soil, made by many who had gone before.

Six days out from Chester and he was surprised by the peaceful region through which they travelled. From his father's talk of wild mountains and scarred plains of rock, gale-swept hills and rain-dashed coastline, he had imagined something quite different to the green, rolling land that opened slowly before them. There were no desolate peaks, no plunging waterfalls, just hills like knucklebones protruding from the soft haze of distant wood-lands. He wasn't complaining, for although Hunter had mended well from the injury and was stronger than he'd dared hope, he was still cautious of pushing the animal too hard. His anger towards Aymer de Valence for the malicious trick played on the practice field hadn't diminished, despite Hunter's recovery, but there had been no chance to vent it, the shock that greeted the Welsh revolt consuming the court.

The intensity with which the king had fixed on Wales was visible in the fact that many of the commanders, infantry and supplies at Portsmouth that had been destined for France had at once been redirected. Leaving the Seneschal of Gascony to lead a diminished fleet to France to mount a hold-ing operation, the king chose his bases for the advance, one at Cardiff, the others at Brecon and Chester; a three-pronged attack designed to strike

at the rebels from all sides. According to reports that were soon flooding
in, each more desperate than the last, English castles were being besieged,
towns burned and officials murdered all across Wales, the uprising begun by
Madog ap Llywelyn in the north setting flame to the whole country, from
Conwy and Caernarfon to Gwent and Glamorgan.

Robert, undeterred by the sudden change of enemy, had been placed
in the king's division with the three knights and five squires he had raised
from the Essex estate, and his Scottish entourage. To his satisfaction, neither
Aymer de Valence nor John Comyn was present. William de Valence, veteran
of many of Edward's campaigns, was heading the division from Cardiff and
his son had gone with him. John Comyn meanwhile had been ordered to
serve in France, along with a number of Scottish nobles. On the journey
from Westminster, Robert's brother had gleefully imagined various fates
the young knight might meet on hostile, foreign fields.

At Chester, the king's company, made up of more than six hundred lances,
had been augmented by throngs of milling foot soldiers from Shropshire
and Gloucestershire. They were followed by seventy skilled crossbowmen
and a mass of infantry from Lancashire, led by a pompous, grossly fat royal
clerk named Hugh de Cressingham, who had been forced to change horses
three times already, each tiring under his weight. From here, the head of
this force, several thousand strong, had crossed the border into Wales, the
mass of men channelled into a long line that crept, slow and dark as a slick
of oil, through the landscape.

The company was split into smaller contingents, who all moved at different paces and had since spread out along the route. Robert and his men
had been placed under the joint command of John de Warenne and the Earl
of Lincoln, who saw the first action of the campaign when the Welsh in
his district at Denbigh had risen, forcing him to flee into England. Henry
Percy was also in this company, along with Humphrey de Bohun. Robert
had been surprised by this since Humphrey's father was in the south leading
the advance from Brecon, but on the march Humphrey had confided that
his father and the king wanted him to prove himself on this campaign.

Hearing the haughty tones of Henry Percy ahead, Robert saw the lord
manoeuvring his horse in beside Humphrey.

'My grandfather is going to order a rest. The terrain gets harder further
on.'

Pulling up Hunter's head, Robert nudged the horse into a faster walk,
leaving his brother frowning after him. The knights looked round from their
conversation as he came up alongside.

'We're stopping at the top of this hill,' Humphrey told him, nodding to the path through the trees that climbed steadily upwards.

'Did you say the way gets harder?'

'According to my grandfather,' answered Henry.

Humphrey gestured to Hunter. 'How is he faring?'

'I think he's good for a couple of hours.' As Robert rubbed the horse's neck, he noticed Henry look away, his chilly blue eyes showing a lack of interest. Doubtless he cared nothing for the horse now he'd been paid the ten pounds Edward had owed him for the wager. Robert was still annoyed with his brother for that. Edward's audacity had amused him when they were children, but here it just felt reckless and unnecessary.

The ground ascended, their horses pushing into the climb. Gnarled oaks gave way to birch and ash.

'At this rate we'll reach Conwy by the Christ Mass,' said Humphrey, settling back into his saddle and sniffing at the wintry air.

'And, God willing, be back in Westminster with the crown by Easter,' added Henry with a hostile smile.

Humphrey gave him a look, but the lord didn't seem to notice.

'King Edward hopes to find this crown in the possession of the rebels?' Robert asked, keeping his voice light to disguise his interest. 'Is it valuable?'

Ahead, men's voices lifted as the vanguard reached the crest of the hill.

'Time for a rest,' said Humphrey.

Robert bit back the urge to press his friend further. On the journey through the endless woods there had been much opportunity for talk and on several occasions he'd heard the Crown of Arthur mentioned. He had asked Humphrey about this crown, but the knight had guided the conversation, politely yet firmly, in other directions. It had made Robert think back to that private gathering in King Henry's former apartments the night of the feast, months ago. He'd had a sense then of some bond between these men, beyond their status and wealth, something he guessed not all the young nobles in Edward's court were privy to – something to do with those dragon shields, which he hadn't seen since the tournament. The crown had lingered in his mind, hinting at a greater meaning behind the hasty December campaign. His father had spoken in slurred, broken sentences of his service in Wales in winter: the blizzards and the brutal cold that could kill a man at night, wolves gathering after a battle, slinking in before the victors had gone, teeth tearing at warm flesh before it froze. This seemed to be more than just a rebellion to be put down, rather something personal to the king and his knights that would make them risk such conditions.

Something that had rendered the older men silent and pensive, and their sons restless and eager.

Hearing murmurs of surprise from up ahead, Robert turned from Humphrey to see the cause. Before them the hill dropped away, plunging into a valley where the trees became an impenetrable cloud of cover, bare boughs of ash and willow interspersed with thick yew, holly and towering pines. It looked to Robert like the Forest of Selkirk, the dark vastness of which stretched from the Scottish Borders to Carrick in the west and Edinburgh in the east. To either side of the valley hills rose in waves, the tree-cover marching almost to the top, where it gave way to ridges of slate. The sight of the dense forest fading into green haze was breathtaking enough, but even more striking was the wide path that had been hacked right through it. It was a dead, grey scar that slashed across the vista, following the contours of the land, its desolation starkly at odds with the verdant woods that bordered it on both sides. Robert had heard his father mention the enormous number of woodcutters and carters the king had employed during the conquest of Wales to clear paths through the impassable forest that covered most of the kingdom of Gwynedd. Here, stretching before him into the far distance, was the evidence of that great labour.

'Perhaps not by Easter,' muttered Henry, his eyes narrowing at the horizon.

The men dismounted, spreading out among the trees on the hilltop to give those behind room to arrive. Servants unpacked food and drink for the knights, while grooms saw to horses, tightening girths and adjusting saddle-cloths. Leaving Hunter in Nes's care and his steward to divide the rations among his men, Robert stretched his legs and downed a cup of beer. Close by, he saw John de Warenne and the Earl of Lincoln talking intently with two men, whose gambesons were partitioned in yellow and red. As Robert noticed a line of gold crosses embroidered on their chests, his interest was piqued. The men were wearing the colours of the Earl of Warwick, whose company had set out from Chester ahead of Warenne's. In that company were Warwick's wife and sons, and his daughter, Helena.

It was not unheard of for the most high-ranking to bring family with them, no one knowing how long a campaign might last. The magnates only owed Edward forty days' service, but new contracts were usually drawn up after that period and no baron would abandon his king lightly in the middle of a war, whatever his rights. The women and children would be barracked in Conwy with the cooks, tailors, physicians and priests. Other camp

followers, uninvited by anyone yet welcomed by many, included pardon-
ers, minstrels and whores, to whom the army was a moving train of money.

John de Warenne paused in his discussion and looked round. Seeing his
grandson, he beckoned him over, along with Robert and Humphrey.

'What is it, sir?' Henry asked, as the three approached.

'Warwick's rearguard saw smoke in the woods ahead. Their company was
too far ahead to turn back and investigate, so his scouts waited for us. I want
you to take a look, Henry.' Warenne nodded to Humphrey and Robert. 'Go
with him. It's probably just poachers or brigands. But we aren't many miles
from Denbigh, where Lincoln was attacked.'

The Earl of Lincoln nodded soberly. 'I lost many men to the rebels. They
were a large force, mostly armed with spears, but some had use of the short
bow.'

'We should be grateful for that mercy at least,' muttered Warenne.
'Pembroke is facing the men of Gwent and their longbows. Christ knows
there is no weapon more deadly.' He turned back to his grandson. 'Report
back to me what you find, Henry. If the enemy is here we will engage them.
We do not want our way home barred.'

After listening to Warwick's scouts describing where they had seen the
smoke the three headed back to their men. Edward grumbled as Robert
explained the mission, but he swallowed his drink and swung up into his
saddle with the three knights and eleven squires that formed Robert's fighting force. Nes unfurled Robert's banner as the parties, made up of forty-eight
men, walked their horses through the groups of soldiers to join the woodcutters' path that cut a grey swathe down into the tree-tangled valley.

28

The winter sun was stark in their eyes as they made their way down the cleared route, three banners snapping in the breeze. Henry Percy's blue lion on gold was at the front, followed by Humphrey's blue flag slashed with white between six gold lions, then Robert's red chevron on white. Robert kept Hunter's reins long, allowing the horse to check for stumps and roots, but the way was relatively easy to negotiate, the path recently flattened by hundreds of feet and hooves. Even though he was tired from the morning's ride, he felt a sense of relief in the change of pace, the smaller group able to move more swiftly alone than in the train, weighed down by carts and infantry. Glancing at Humphrey, who grinned back, he saw the same lift in the others' spirits. Until now, he hadn't realised how listless they had all become in the drudgery of the march.

After a couple of miles, where the ground levelled out along the valley floor, the company came to a track leading off between the trees to either side of the cleared path. There was a scrap of red and yellow cloth fluttering from a branch, left there by Warwick's scouts to mark the way.

'This is it.' Humphrey craned his head to stare up at the rising tree line. 'They said they saw the smoke beyond this hill.'

'It must lead to a hamlet,' said Henry, peering at the track. 'It looks old.'

'But not well used,' added Robert, eyeing the carpet of brown bracken. The track was wide enough for only one horse and branches overhung it, treacherously low.

Henry gestured to two of his knights. 'Take the van.'

The men left the cleared path and rode single file into the gloom, ducking branches, cobwebs trailing against their faces. The ground rose sharply and birds chattered in the press of trees, angry at the intrusion. The men were disturbed by constant movement, from the rustle of a bush to flickers of red glimpsed faint and far off as deer flitted away through the trees. The branches crowded in, obscuring the sky and turning day to green twilight. If there was anyone in these trees it was doubtful they would be able to see them in the crush of foliage. They were disoriented, no longer knowing in which direction they were headed, only that the hill was still climbing torturously before them and they were desperate for sky and light. They soon got their wish. As they reached the top the trees gradually thinned out and the track widened, giving the knights room to ride two abreast at a steady trot, the mossy ground deadening the hoof-beats.

Robert was near the front with Humphrey when one of Henry's men hissed a warning. Bringing his horse to a halt, Robert saw the knight pointing through the trees to where two large shapes were strung from the branches of an oak. They were deer, their long necks hanging limp. Their stomach cavities were empty, lips of liver-coloured flesh ribbed with yellow fat sagging open to either side. There was a rancid odour of blood on the air.

'Perhaps we should continue on foot?' said Robert. His relief at the freedom offered by the ride had vanished with the sight of the deer. He could feel the shift in the others, some of whom had their hands on the hilts of their swords, their faces tense.

'No,' Henry said. 'Those kills could be anyone's. I don't want to waste time trudging through this forest over a couple of poachers. We'll continue for another mile then make our way back. The smoke couldn't have been coming from much further, not for the scouts to have seen it.' Without waiting for them to respond, Henry urged his horse on, followed by his men.

They had been going for only a short while when they smelled it: the subtle tang of wood-smoke. In the distance between the maze of trees the woods opened out on to a bare slope of hillside, amber in the late afternoon sun. In the centre of the cleared area were the remains of a settlement. Crumbled piles of stone and splintered timbers, some still retaining the vague shape of a wall or doorway, protruded from the ground. Dry fronds of bracken half hid other structures, covering the evidence of human occupation in a papery shroud of orange and brown. It would have seemed that no one had lived here for decades, if not for the obvious signs of life. In the centre of the dilapidated buildings a fire snapped and spat in a large pit, a plume of grey smoke drifting into the sky. Temporary shelters made of twigs and grass leaned up against the tumbled shells of the buildings, dark bolt-holes with room enough for several men in each. Some way beyond the settlement, the woods closed in again, disappearing into another dense valley of leaves and shadows.

The knights formed up in silence, many fixed on the camp through the trees, others glancing warily into the sun-dappled shade around them.

'I can't see anyone,' Humphrey murmured.

'Neither can I, but that fire has only recently been stoked. They can't have gone far.' Henry lifted his reins as if to impel his horse forward, but Humphrey stopped him.

'What are you doing?'

'We need to get a closer look.'

'Most likely, from the size of that camp, this is the company that attacked the Earl of Lincoln. We need to let Sir John know, before we're seen.'

'Why waste another hour when we can deal with these churls now? It'll be dark before we can get any more men up here and if we leave it until morning they might have gone.'

'It looks like they've been here for some while,' said Robert, moving in alongside Humphrey. 'I doubt they'll be going anywhere.'

Henry glanced at him irritably. 'You don't know that.' He focused on Humphrey, speaking intently. 'You wanted to prove yourself on this campaign. Well, this is your chance. *Our* chance. Our fathers and grandfathers won glory under King Edward. We need to show them we are worthy to take their places. That we are able successors.' His tone intensified. 'You know what it is he aims for, Humphrey. Don't you want a place at the king's table when the prophecy is fulfilled? Don't you want a part of his new kingdom?'

'Careful,' murmured Humphrey, his eyes flicking to the others.

As the knight caught his gaze, Robert's brow knotted in question, but Humphrey didn't speak.

Henry continued, adamant. 'You're wasting a chance, perhaps the only one either of us will get on this campaign.'

'The Earl of Lincoln said the group that attacked him was a hundred strong at least. If this is that force they outnumber us two to one.'

'Lincoln let himself get caught by surprise. We have the advantage here.'

Humphrey looked away, seeming to wrestle with the options. Finally, his eyes narrowed and he drew his sword.

Henry smiled, his blue eyes glinting in the sunlight. 'Let's deal with these vermin,' he growled, urging his horse forward.

'Humphrey,' called Robert, as the knight moved to follow. He stared at his comrade. 'These weren't our orders.'

Humphrey's face tightened. 'We go in,' he said, digging his spurs into his destrier's sides.

Robert looked behind him to his waiting men. Edward was frowning in question. The younger squires, including Nes, appeared nervous, their swords already drawn. How would it look if he refused to lead them into this: if Henry and Humphrey returned to Warenne triumphant, having dealt with the rebels, while he cowered in the trees? If this was a chance for them to prove their worth to their king, then for him it was an opportunity to prove himself to them. So far these young men, heirs to the earldoms of England, had kept him at a distance, even Humphrey, but he had seen the power and influence they wielded and he desired it for himself. His father and grandfather had served English kings in war and had been rewarded with lands. He had come to England to recover the authority they had lost upon Balliol's enthronement, but, so far, rather than advance his family's ailing fortunes he'd done little more than spend them.

Nodding for his brother and his men to follow, Robert kicked at Hunter's sides.

Henry hadn't paused at the tree line, but had ridden brazenly out on to the sunlit hillside, cantering towards the settlement. Any element of surprise they might have had was gone and the others followed, drawing swords. Henry rode in through the rows of shelters and heaps of stones, Humphrey and Robert behind him. The large fire glowed in the centre of the camp, throwing out waves of heat. The knights spread out around the settlement to the crackle of the flames. The ground was covered with piles of dry bracken that had been hacked from the hillside and strewn around the camp. There were a few logs placed by the fire pit, perhaps for seats, and charred animal bones littered the ring of ashes. A couple of spears had been dug into the mud a short distance beyond the shelters and some barrels and battered-looking crates were stacked up close by. Other than that, the place seemed abandoned.

Henry steered his horse to one of the shelters and slashed through the flimsy roof of woven twigs with his sword. It buckled in a shower of bracken and leaves. Inside, a shabby deer skin carpeted the bare earth. Bending down, he poked his sword tip into a filthy, ragged cloak bundled on the skin and raised it to dangle on the blade, before flicking it free with a scowl.

Humphrey dismounted and went to the fire. There were a couple of wooden bowls littering the grass and a huge iron pot on a tree stump. Crouching, he picked up one of the bowls and sniffed at it. He tossed it aside with a grimace. 'They must have heard us coming,' he said, rising and looking at Henry. 'Robert was right. We should have continued on foot when we saw the deer.'

Robert had remained in the saddle and was staring around the settlement. If it wasn't for the well-stoked fire he would have said no one had been here for some time. 'It doesn't look like much of a camp.'

Humphrey glanced round as he spoke, but one of his knights caught his attention.

'Sir, we could follow them into the woods? Try to track them?'

Some of Henry's men had dismounted and were kicking over shelters to check for anything valuable.

Humphrey shook his head, studying the trees that hemmed them in. 'We could search for days and never find them.'

Robert urged Hunter over to the spears thrust into the mud beyond the shelters. The shafts were notched with use, the wood worn smooth and shiny in places where men had gripped them. He grasped one and tugged it from the ground, wondering why its owner had left it. There were holes where other spears had been ripped out and footprints indented the mud, but the ground, for the most part, was hidden by the heaps of bracken. As Robert's gaze moved over the dead foliage he noticed that the fronds were gleaming. He peered closer and saw some sort of substance covering the brittle leaves. There were smears of it clinging to the undergrowth, grey and viscous. Robert dug the spear tip into some, then swung the shaft over in his hand to get a closer look. He took some in his thumb and forefinger. It was sticky and smelled like animal fat. He turned away, guessing the bracken had been used to scrape grease from a cooking pot, then realised that other men, still rifling through the camp, were muttering in disgust. Robert saw one knight sniffing at his fingers. Another was wiping his hands on his gambeson. A squire was holding up a cloak, on which more of the grease glistened in the sunlight. Robert felt a chill. Memories of the hunts he had gone on with his grandfather flashed in his mind: setting snares and traps, leaving trails of blood and stringing carcasses of sheep from trees to lure the wolves.

Still grasping the grease-tipped spear, Robert wheeled Hunter around. 'Humphrey!'

The knight jerked round at the shout, but even as it left Robert's mouth the sky filled with glowing stars that shot up from the woods around them. They continued their upward trajectory for a moment, curled almost lazily over then came rushing towards the camp. The men had time to realise they were flaming arrows before the missiles were thumping down all around them. Knights and squires raised shields over their heads or threw themselves behind shelters, but the arrows weren't aimed at them. As the barbed tips stuck in the piles of papery bracken the burning tows fixed behind the arrowheads flickered for a few seconds, then flared. Wherever they struck the grease-smeared ground they caught quickly, fire bursting up in brilliant trails that swept along the ground. Horses reared as smoke fanned and heat pulsed, thick and sudden. Several animals turned and bolted.

More arrows shot down, the knights yelling in alarm, those who had dismounted running to their panicked mounts. Edward Bruce hoisted his shield as an arrow hurtled towards him. It stuck fast in the wood, the fire licking around the painted centre. Humphrey's destrier cried in terror as smoke billowed up and, vaulting a low line of fire, it galloped away towards the woods. Humphrey yelled after it, but was forced to duck as another hail came in. One of Henry's squires leapt back out of the path of the missiles, only to stagger into the fire pit. The flames caught his cloak, which went up quickly. He reeled away, tearing at the clasp, but the fire enfolded him in a blistering embrace.

One of Humphrey's knights was struggling to mount his horse when an arrow caught him in the back. The tip didn't pierce his gambeson, but stuck fast in the cloth. His hands scrabbled behind him as the flaming brand seared his neck. As his hair caught and went up like a torch, his horse fled, with his foot still in the saddle. The knight fell, the impact as he struck the ground thrusting the arrowhead through the material and into his lung. He convulsed, blood retching from his mouth, as the horse dragged him away.

Robert struggled to keep Hunter under control, scanning the sky for arrows. He shouted at his brother and men, trying to keep them near. Edward and his squires were close by. There was a splintered hole in Edward's shield, blackened around the edges, where he had pulled out an arrow. The men from Essex had been scattered around the camp when the attack began, but they were riding towards him now, urging their horses around the flames, seeking a path through. Hearing a roar, Robert saw hundreds of figures rushing up the hillside towards them, spears in their hands. Henry shouted as he saw them, calling his knights to him, but few were able to heed his command, their horses too panicked to obey.

Robert fought with Hunter as the horse reared. For a moment, he was suspended in the chaos, torn between the decision to fight or flee. The spear he had tugged from the ground was still in his hands and he felt a drive to kick the horse down the hillside at the incoming hordes. But even as the urge came upon him, he knew the futility of it. They were in no state to regroup and charge, the fires dividing them. Several of their number had fled to the woods, either of their own volition, or their horses' will. Casting the spear aside, Robert spurred Hunter away, leaping a smouldering heap of bracken that scattered burning embers in his wake. 'Back!' he yelled, flinging a hand towards the trees.

Henry, his face red with heat and fury, caught the shout. His lips peeled back in a snarl of frustration, but he turned his horse and led his men after Robert. One by one they sped away as behind them the rebels poured into the fringes of the camp, flinging their spears through the flames. One squire was thrown to the ground, a spear embedded in his side. Another shaft pierced the rump of a horse, causing the animal to buck violently and toss its rider from the saddle. The knight landed on the roof of a burning shelter in a burst of fire.

Robert was almost at the tree line, his brother and his men ahead, when he heard a shout, louder than the indistinct cries of the rebels. He twisted round to see Humphrey sprinting across the grass, flames lighting the hillside behind him. The knight was running for his life, a mob of men following, whooping in murderous jubilation. Robert pulled Hunter around. He heard his brother cry a warning, but didn't heed it. Kicking fiercely at the horse's sides, he galloped towards the knight, bringing Hunter to a brutal stop. As Humphrey grabbed for the back of the saddle, the horse stumbled under the extra weight. Robert grasped the back of Humphrey's gambeson, straining to help him. Clutching at his waist, Humphrey kicked himself up until he was sideways in the saddle behind him. Robert went to spur Hunter on, then saw another figure racing towards them. It was one of the squires from the Essex estate. Behind him came the rebels. The young man cried out in desperation, his face stricken.

'Go!' Humphrey shouted.

For a moment, Robert paused. The squire's face filled with hope and he put on a burst of speed. Several of the rebels halted and drew back their arms. Robert yelled a warning as their spears shot through the air. The squire arched in mid-stride as one plunged into his back. His chest thrust out and his hands flung up as the barbed tip punched through his gambeson.

'*Robert!*' Humphrey yelled in his ear.

Robert struck at Hunter's sides as the squire collapsed behind him. More of the rebels paused to take aim, but their spears hit grass as the horse carried the two men towards the trees, leaving the settlement to burn.

29

Robert stood on the battlements, staring out over the moon-washed estuary. Across the channel a hump of headland rose above the distant sea like some hunched beast, silver-backed in the ghostly light. The waters of the estuary, riddled with long stretches of mud, glittered like cracked glass.

It was late, but the town of Conwy that bordered the castle was flushed with torchlight, the brands of fire moving through the streets as soldiers were shown to barracks and the camp followers settled into new homes. On the other side of the river that bordered the castle's north-eastern walls more pools of firelight, some close, others distant, showed where the companies who hadn't been able to make it to the boats before dark had bedded down. No doubt people would be filtering in for days.

Warenne's company had arrived on those banks several hours earlier as the sun was sinking. Silhouetted against the wine-dark sky on a high outcrop of rock, Conwy Castle had appeared to the weary soldiers like something in a dream, its lime-rendered walls, white as frost, sweeping down to the rocks over the river where it was mirrored in the inky depths, the columns of torchlight on the battlements shimmering on the surface like jewels. The king had arrived already and from four slender turrets on the north-eastern towers flew his red standard, emblazoned with three lions. Shields with the same device decorated the battlements and others, bearing different arms and colours, hung from some of the towers, showing where various earls and barons had been lodged. Beyond the castle and the walled town, ranked with twenty-one towers, the hills rose steeply, one behind the other, into the black heights of Snowdon, cloaked by clouds and the falling dark.

The sight of the castle had caused relief to sweep through Warenne's company, men smiling and talking for the first time in days. The hillside assault had proven that the sprawling forest shielded an enemy who not only knew the terrain well, but had the cunning to use it and the men had grown tense and wary. As the boats rowed them across the river to a wooden pier that led up to a stone ramp that curved between the rocks to a gateway, a few had even struck up a song.

Robert hadn't smiled, nor had he joined in the uplifted conversations. On the journey across the river he had found himself sitting opposite one of the knights from Essex – the father of the squire who died in the ambush. The knight had said nothing to him about the death of his son, going about his orders in grim silence. An image of the young squire running desperately across the grass, while behind him the rebels took aim, played in Robert's thoughts as he'd stared at the hard-faced older man on the voyage, wanting to say something but unable to find the words.

After fleeing the burning settlement, they had crashed down the overgrown track to the path, Humphrey clinging on behind Robert. For a time they heard sounds of pursuit, but the whoops of the rebels faded long before they joined the cleared path and met up with the rest of their company. There Humphrey, Henry and Robert were forced to explain the trap they had blundered into to a furious Earl Warenne. The next morning, Warenne and Lincoln led their veterans into the hills, while the three young men, rebuked and reprimanded, were made to stay behind. The day after, the men returned, blooded and satisfied, having tracked the rebels from the burned-out settlement the knights had been lured to, to their real base in the woods several miles north. Here, the Welsh were made to pay for their audacity with wholesale butchery. Warenne denied his men any victory, however, denouncing the three young commanders whose rashness lost them two knights, four squires and six horses. Humphrey had admitted that Robert had cautioned against entering the camp, but the earl showed little sympathy.

Pushing himself from the wall, Robert headed along the walkway that spanned the heights over the castle's inner ward, above lead roofs and chimneys that belched smoke. The cramped courtyard, lined with stone and timber-clad buildings, was chaotic. In the torchlight squires hefted packs on their shoulders as they followed their knight-masters to lodgings and servants hurried by, carrying armfuls of blankets. Making his way down a set of steps on the walkway, Robert was approaching the tower where he and his men had been billeted when he heard someone call his name. He turned to see Humphrey.

'I called you three times,' said the knight.

'I didn't hear.' Robert met the knight's gaze, then looked away across the busy courtyard. He hadn't spoken with Humphrey much since the attack, except to listen to the knight's quiet gratitude for saving his life. He had avoided Henry altogether. It hadn't been hard. All three had kept to themselves, the sense of accusation from others in their company palpable. 'Did you want something?'

'I need you to come with me.'

Robert frowned. There was something different about Humphrey tonight. His face was tense, not with apprehension, but a keen impatience. 'I should see to my men.'

Humphrey caught his arm. 'Please, Robert.'

'Go with you where?' Robert's voice was harder than he meant it to be.

Humphrey faltered, then fixed him with a dogged stare. 'Do you trust me?'

Robert didn't answer at once. He had trusted Humphrey, but the way the knight had entered the deserted settlement: his face closing in, obstinate determination forcing aside reason, had given him pause. He hadn't seen this side of his comrade before and it had surprised him. But he still liked the young man, that hadn't changed and, if truth be told, he had missed his company these past days. 'I trust you.'

'Then come.'

The knight led him along the walkway, past the north-eastern towers that loomed over walled gardens and orchards, below which the stone ramp coiled down to the wooden pier, where supplies were being offloaded from the last boats. Guards, hunkered down along the walkway against the wind, watched them pass. At length they came to a tower that looked out over the rooftops of the town to the moon-bathed hills. As Humphrey opened the door, Robert noticed the knight's blue banner hanging from a window above.

The round room beyond was like his own lodgings, mostly bare except for a grand hearth and a few faded cushions on the window seat that was framed by stone mullions. The window was of leaded glass, the small squares mirroring the fire in the hearth. Sacks and chests lined the walls, as yet unpacked. The one difference between Robert's chamber and Humphrey's was the large group of men that filled it.

Over by the window, his yellow surcoat decorated with a green eagle, was Ralph de Monthermer, a knight of the king's household. Seated on the cushions beside Ralph was young Thomas of Lancaster, who had joined the campaign as squire to Earl Edmund. By the fire was Henry Percy, his stocky frame lit by the red glow, his cold gaze on Robert. Next to him was the rangy figure of Guy de Beauchamp, brother of Helena. There was another royal knight, a quiet, courteous man named Robert Clifford, and three others. All were silent as Humphrey closed the door. Robert realised each had a shield on the floor by his feet. The scarlet was almost black in the shadows, but the liquid gold dragons blazed in the firelight, their shapes on the wood seeming to curl, alive. He noticed that one shield had been placed in the centre of the room on its own. At the sight of it a spear of excitement lanced through him.

'We want you to join us.'

Robert turned to Humphrey, whose broad face was sharpened by shadows. The knight gestured to the others, who picked up their shields and moved into a circle around the solitary one. At first, after the joust at Smithfield in the spring, Robert had assumed these shields were part of a tournament guise, something won through feats of daring in the lists. In the months that followed, seeing this tight group operating within the court, with Humphrey as some sort of fulcrum, he had begun to suspect that this band had a wider purpose. This suspicion had become certainty during the march into Wales, hearing the veiled talk of the Crown of Arthur and a prophecy. Robert had wanted in, not just out of curiosity, but because he had seen the esteem these young men were held in, by the court and by the king. For years the Bruces had stood among the highest stratums of power, favoured by kings and respected by their peers. No longer. It was King Edward who had caused their fall from grace with his choice of Balliol and Robert had resented him for that, but his resentment faded as he realised what was being offered in this fire-rouged chamber.

Without a word, he stepped into the centre of the knights and Humphrey closed the gap behind him.

'Pick up the shield,' Humphrey began. He held up a cautioning hand as Robert bent towards it. 'Only if you are willing to become one within the whole, one part of the circle that binds us in loyalty to our king and his cause.'

Robert straightened as Humphrey continued, sensing he must listen first.

'Ten years ago after defeating Llywelyn ap Gruffudd, King Edward created an order of knights to whom he entrusted the greatest knowledge of our time. Some months after Llywelyn's fall our king was at Nefyn, a village not far from where we now stand, where the prophecies of Merlin were discovered and translated by Geoffrey of Monmouth. There, in a former stronghold of Llywelyn's, King Edward found the last of those prophecies. One that had not been translated by Monmouth. One that had remained hidden for centuries, kept secret by the Welsh princes of Gwynedd.'

Robert knew of Monmouth and his writings. His brother, Alexander, had owned a copy of *The History of the Kings of Britain* that he had skimmed through once. He hadn't read the *Prophecies* though and had no idea that another had been discovered so recently.

'King Edward had the Last Prophecy translated by a Welshman who was loyal to him and presented it to his knights, who vowed to help him fulfil its instructions. As a symbol of their unified purpose the king had a Round Table fashioned in likeness of the one in Arthur's court. Those knights were our fathers, our grandfathers and brothers,' Humphrey continued, his eyes moving over the silent men around Robert. 'Now, we follow in their footsteps. Our aim is to prove ourselves worthy to serve our king as they have and one day take up our own places around his table, sharing in the glory of his reign.'

'We are the Knights of the Dragon,' said Henry Percy, his forceful voice sounding at Robert's back, 'named after the sign that appeared in Utherpendragon's dream, the sign by which Merlin prophesied that Uther would be king and his son, Arthur, would rule all of Britain.'

As Henry fell silent, Thomas of Lancaster took up the thread, his young voice clear. 'Geoffrey of Monmouth tells us of the ruin of Britain that followed Arthur's death, during the invasions of the Saxons. He says that in this time God sent an angelic voice to tell the Britons that they would no longer be the rulers of their kingdom. But one day in the future, at a time foreseen by Merlin, if the relics of Britain were gathered together it could once again be united, a kingdom in peace, overflowing with riches.'

'In the Last Prophecy,' said Ralph de Monthermer, 'found at Nefyn ten years ago, these relics are named as a throne, a sword, a staff and a crown. They are the regalia of Britain, first carried by the founder of our lands, Brutus of Troy. On his death the four relics and the kingdom were divided between his sons. This division was what began Britain's long decline into war, famine and poverty. The Last Prophecy tells us our lands will face their final destruction unless these four relics are gathered again under one ruler at the time God decreed.'

Humphrey spoke again. 'The crown in the prophecy is the diadem worn by Brutus himself and handed down to all British kings thereafter.

It is the crown worn by Arthur, who passed it to his cousin at Camblam, whereupon it slipped out of knowledge until Llywelyn ap Gruffudd united Wales beneath him with its power. It is this crown that we must now find. If you are willing to pledge yourself to this quest and to prove yourself worthy to be admitted into the Round Table one day, then pick up the shield.'

When Humphrey fell silent, Robert knew it was his turn. Thoughts of treasures and knightly quests filled his head. Faint in his memory, he heard his foster-father in Antrim speaking of Fionn mac Cumhaill and his band of warriors. He had listened then in awe, wondering if his own knighthood would yield such adventure, but the older he had grown the more he had seen that the coming of age was more about duty and politics than great journeys of discovery, tournaments and glory, and the more those stories had faded from his mind. It didn't seem real, what these men were saying, but their solemn faces hinted at truth and a gravity that made the skin on Robert's neck tighten as if cold, and made those distant tales at once vivid with possibility. He hesitated for a moment, aware that this was an oath he was making, as sacred as any vow of homage or fealty; an oath that bound him in loyalty to the king. Humphrey's words echoed in his mind . . . *take up our own places around his table, sharing in the glory of his reign.* Bending, Robert lifted the dragon shield.

The atmosphere lightened at once, the men nodding and smiling.

Humphrey moved to him. 'Welcome,' he said, embracing him.

Robert faltered, not wanting to diminish the solemnity of the moment, but he had to ask the question. 'Did everyone accept me?' He knew enough to know that Aymer de Valence was part of this order.

'The others will be told later.' Humphrey seemed to catch his meaning. 'They cannot refuse you though. The king permitted it.'

'King Edward knows?'

'I spoke to Sir John de Warenne, who petitioned the king personally for your admittance.'

Robert nodded, privately pleased at the evidence he had made a good impression on the king, despite the disaster on the march.

Ralph de Monthermer headed over with two goblets of wine that he handed to them.

Robert took one. 'If the Crown of Arthur is one relic, what are the other three?'

'It is believed one is Curtana,' said Ralph, before Humphrey could answer. 'Also known as the Sword of Mercy. The blade was once wielded by St Edward the Confessor, but its true origins were unknown, until the prophecy. The king keeps it at Westminster.'

'And the staff? The throne? Does he have these?'

'Not yet,' replied Humphrey, raising his goblet. 'Now, drink, brother!'

Robert lifted his vessel and drank, Humphrey's intense gaze fixed on him.

30

'Where were you last night?' Robert turned at the question. His brother Edward was crouched against the wall of the armoury that bordered the outer ward of Conwy Castle, hands clasped over his knees. The air was filled with a harsh grating sound as Nes rolled Robert's mail in a sand-filled barrel back and forth across the ground, to chafe the rust from the metal. Other men were there, mending links in mail and cleaning swords. Gusts of icy wind buffeted through the yard, scattering sand into their eyes. Last week, shortly after the Christ Mass, a breath of snow had arrived in the teeth of that wind, but it hadn't settled. By the threat in the slate-dark sky there would be more before long.

'Last night?' Robert looked away. 'I was with Humphrey.'

'I've hardly seen you these past ten days. What have you been doing?'

Robert shrugged off the enquiry. 'Training.'

This wasn't a complete lie. In the ten days since the king's army arrived at Conwy, there had been little to do but wait, while scouting parties were sent out to gather information on the enemy's location. So far, since the attack by the rebels in the forest, they had seen no signs of anyone but a few peasants out working in the fields, the lands eerily quiet. Training had kept them occupied. But it wasn't the sole cause of Robert's absences.

Edward rose, his face tightening. The scrape of the barrel sounded over his murmured words. 'I saw your new shield, brother.'

As he realised Edward had guessed at the wrong secret, Robert felt relief. On the back of it came guilt. Humphrey had impressed upon him the need to keep the matter of the prophecy within the order, but had told him he was free to call himself a Knight of the Dragon and bear the shield in tournaments and in war. Still, Robert had kept his induction private, reluctant to confide in Edward. He knew deep down that his brother would not approve of the oath he had taken before these men. He masked it with anger. 'You went through my belongings? You had no right!'

'I was in your room. I happened to see it.'

'It was under my bed. Wrapped in sacking.' As Nes glanced at them, Robert moved off, nodding for his brother to follow. When they were out of earshot, he turned. 'Not everything I do is your business.'

Edward's mouth flattened. 'I'm one of your men. Do you not have a duty to let me know your plans on this campaign?'

'As one of my men you should obey me without question,' said Robert sharply, 'like any other squire.' He averted his eyes from the offence in his brother's face. 'What I mean—'

'It's clear what you meant,' Edward cut across him. 'Am I beneath you now? Not worthy because I'm not a knight like your new comrades?'

Robert leaned back against the armoury wall with a rough sigh. He had known this had been coming for a while now.

He had first noticed the change in his brother soon after he was dubbed. On the journey through England, the two of them brought closer by the unfamiliarity of a foreign land, the resentment he had sensed from Edward seemed to diminish. But during the summer in London and his strengthening friendship with Humphrey, it had become apparent again. He had wondered if it was the cause of Edward's increasingly unruly behaviour: the way he stood up to the knights as if he were their equal, the disparaging manner in which he talked about some of the barons, the way he liked to challenge people, at the feast table in conversation or on the training field with a lance. Whatever the reason, Robert had found himself ever more annoyed by his brother's conduct and more reluctant to do what it was Edward wanted most.

'Why won't you dub me?'

There it was: the question Robert had known was coming. 'I said we would discuss it when we returned home.'

'That was before the war. We've been gone from Scotland eighteen months already and you don't know how long this campaign will last.' Edward stepped in front of Robert, forcing him to look at him. 'Brother, I'll be nineteen next year.'

'That's still young to be dubbed. Have patience.' Robert put his hands on Edward's shoulders. 'Let us finish what we came here to do and then, I promise, I will see you knighted.'

Edward paused, resistance struggling in his face. Finally, he nodded.

Robert broke his hold as a bell in the town began to clang, ringing the afternoon office. At the sound he felt a grip in his stomach, a tense thrill, like the one he got at that moment before he kicked a horse towards a target. 'I have to go,' he told his brother. He called to his squire. 'Check on Hunter for me, Nes, when you're done here.'

'Of course, sir.'

'Enjoy your training,' Edward called after him, sarcasm crisping his words.

Robert didn't look back, but headed across the busy outer ward, towards a set of steps that led on to the battlements. By the time he reached the top the bell had ceased its chimes, leaving the echo of its ring to ripple over the estuary. As he hastened along the walkway, intent on the north-eastern tower, a voice inside him challenged his double standards: only moments ago he had been berating his brother's carelessness and here he was, reckless as a child who swings himself off the high branch of a tree without a care for what lies beneath, or the height of the fall. Robert forced the voice aside as the thrill took hold, carrying him beyond the point where reason or caution could follow.

As he passed alongside the tower that loomed over the main gate, he saw a company, several hundred strong, heading towards the castle. Most were mounted, their banners garish in the stormy light. Men had been filtering in for the past fortnight from the divisions that had been sent south to relieve the castles besieged by the rebels. This was the largest company so far. Robert wondered if they brought with them tidings of the enemy's whereabouts. In many senses it would be a relief to leave the increasingly cramped confines of the castle. But there was one thing he would miss.

Robert came to a tower overlooking the wide estuary. There was a smell of sewage rising from where the latrine chutes opened on to the rocks. Gulls hopped across the gleaming boulders, squabbling over the pickings. Opening the tower door, Robert entered the darkness of a stairwell that spiralled down within the wall. On the floor below, he headed cautiously into a large round chamber, where the only light came through arrow loops cut into the walls. He paused in the gloom, seeing the vague outlines of footprints in the dusty floor leading to a stacked row of grain sacks. There were far fewer sacks now than there had been at the beginning of the week, when he'd first found this place. The floor around them was powdery with grain, in which more footprints could be seen. The shrieks of gulls echoed outside. Between their cries, he caught a whisper that held his name.

Robert went forward and squeezed himself through a gap in the bulging sacks, tighter since they had been disturbed. Pressing against the coarse material, he pushed his way in, the grain shifting beneath his touch, like muscles under skin. The musty smell reminded him of harvest time in Carrick. All at once he was through, a window seat with two stone benches opposite one another before him. The seats ended at a narrowing shaft cut by an arrow loop. Standing between them, silhouetted in the slit of light, was Helena de Beauchamp, her hair, piled on her head, a fire-tinged halo.

The girls back in Lochmaben had been sweet and willing, but ultimately unsatisfying, like tilting at a quintain from a standstill, with none of the fury of the ride. Eva, whom he'd kissed by the loch the night his family lost the throne, had been different and had lingered in his memory to tantalise him, the chase cut short by the events that followed. Helena, an English earl's daughter, sixteen and promised to another man, was an even more reckless target, but that had only made Robert desire her more. She had presented herself to him. What could he do but tilt?

Helena wore a navy gown that was pulled in tight at her waist by a plaited belt, before falling in abundant folds to the ground. In that dark robe, with her lean figure, she looked almost boyish, but Robert knew the malleable softness beneath those clothes was anything but masculine. She smiled, but didn't speak. Their meetings so far hadn't been about words. Robert was comfortable with that. Here in this musty bolt-hole, behind the grain sacks, there was only one goal. A goal he had so far been thwarted in, which he aimed for more ardently each afternoon.

As they came together, Robert clasped Helena's face, his palms tingling against the marble of her cheeks as he moved his mouth over hers. He smelled the now familiar scent of olive oil, she had told him from the soap she used, shipped from Spain. Her lips were warm, her breath hot, mingling with his as they exhaled into one another with every changing circle of their lips. Her hands pushed tentatively up to his neck, fingers coiling in his dark hair, while his left her face and slid over her shoulders, down her spine. As his hands travelled lower, edging over that supple curve where her taut body became so surprisingly soft and full, Helena pulled back with an intake of breath. Robert tensed, frustration struggling within him, threatening to overpower his sense of decorum. This was it. The point when the challenge began. They would be here for a while now, him moving his hands back to the base of her spine, her yielding again, the passion building, his hands shifting once more, perhaps trailing a little further before she pulled away and the whole contest began again.

Robert had just found his place, some time later, his hands confidently positioned, when the door of the chamber opened. At the sound of voices and footsteps, Robert and Helena jerked from one another. Catching glimpses of movement through the gap in the sacks, Robert drew her back. She stared past him large-eyed, her cheeks aflame. His heart was thudding and he fancied he could feel hers, echoed in that rapid pulse of blood. Beyond the sacks, two men were speaking.

'This should do for your men, sir. You can take the chamber above. I'm afraid we're a little unprepared. The king wasn't expecting you for a while. We'll have the rest of those sacks moved immediately.'

'See that you do. My knights are weary.'

Robert frowned, hearing that rasping voice with its sharp accent. The recognition struck him. It was the old Earl of Pembroke, William de Valence.

'Certainly, sir.'

The footsteps receded and the door banged shut. Robert waited for a moment, listening to the fading voices, then turned to Helena. 'We'll leave separately. I'll go first and make sure it's clear.'

As he went to move, Helena gripped his arm. 'Where will we meet now, Sir Robert?' she whispered.

'I'll find us somewhere.' Robert bent to kiss her, tenderly now, before pushing through the sacks, Helena following behind. He listened at the door, shoulder pressed against the wood. Hearing nothing, he opened it a crack. The stairwell beyond was empty. Turning to smile reassuringly at Helena, he headed out, leaving the door ajar for her. He was making his way up the stairs, thanking God for those sheltering sacks, when he heard two sets of footsteps coming down. He went to turn back, but there was no time and he had to give Helena a chance to leave. If she heard voices, she would know to head down rather than up.

The first figure's boots appeared, grey with dust. A blue and white striped surcoat, stained with mud and decorated with tiny red birds, flapped over them as they descended. For a moment, as he caught sight of the arms, Robert thought it was Pembroke himself, then, as the hard, angular face appeared, he realised it was his son.

Aymer de Valence halted at the sight of him. His jaw was dark with stubble and there was a jagged wound on his cheek that had been recently stitched. Behind him was a squire, a sack bag slung over his shoulder and a bundle of clothes in his arms, stained with blood. There was more of it on Aymer's surcoat, great smears of it obscuring the red birds. 'I was told these were our lodgings,' Aymer said harshly, looking back at his squire.

'That is right, sir,' answered the man, staring uncertainly at Robert.

There was a recess a few steps up, where an arrow slit looked out over the estuary. Robert made his way to it and stood aside. 'Go ahead,' he said, not taking his eyes off the knight.

Aymer paused a moment longer, then carried on down the steps, the sour smell of blood following him, along with the squire. Robert continued, not looking back, until he was pushing through the door and out into the wind that stung his hot face.

Back in his room, Robert washed his hands in the basin by the window. He bent to splash his face, then planted his palms on the wooden stand, staring out across the battlements.

It was almost dark, low clouds skimming the castle turrets. The chamber, with its straw-filled mattress, was in shadow apart from the single stub of a candle. Below, Robert could hear the voices of his brother and the rest of his men as they shared a meal. Firelight glowed in the gaps in the floorboards. Edward was telling some story, his voice lifting above the others' laughter. Robert usually joined them, but he didn't feel like company now.

There was a knock at the door. Crossing the chamber, Robert opened it to see Humphrey before him, his face half lit by the pallid glow of the candle. He was unsmiling.

'What is it?' Robert asked, thinking by his comrade's grave face that word had come from the scouts on the enemy's location.

'Get your sword.'

The instruction seemed to confirm Robert's guess, but there was something about Humphrey's grim manner that gave him pause for doubt. Still, he went for his broadsword. 'Has the enemy been sighted?' he asked, looping the belt the scabbard was attached to around his waist. 'Are we under attack?'

As Robert reached for his gambeson, Humphrey motioned to him. 'Not that,' he said flatly, 'just your sword.' He moved into the passage as if expecting Robert to follow.

Robert did after a moment. 'What's wrong, Humphrey?'

Humphrey didn't respond, but led the way up several steps to a door that opened on to the battlements.

Robert grimaced as he headed into the perishing air. He was only wearing his black hose and a white linen shirt, open at the neck. A mist of rain in the frozen wind dampened his face. As Humphrey led the way towards the north-eastern towers, Robert searched for signs of imminent attack, but the castle was quiet, torches flickering down in the courtyards, illuminating groups of guards. Beyond the walls, the streets of Conwy were in darkness. After a few moments, Humphrey marching ahead in silence, he'd had enough.

Humphrey turned as Robert halted. 'Come on.'

'Not until you tell me where we're going. You don't even have a sword yourself.'

Humphrey's rigid face flooded with anger. He strode to Robert, coming right up in his face. 'Why did you do it? I warned you not to!'

'Do what?' Robert demanded, his own anger building with the confusion.

'Helena.'

Robert went silent, the shock of the name hanging between them. 'How did you know?' His voice had thickened.

'Aymer,' said Humphrey caustically. 'He saw her leaving the tower.'

'She told him?' murmured Robert disbelievingly. Helena stood to be in almost as much trouble as him if caught.

'Aymer guessed something having seen you both. He made her confirm it for him.'

'Made her?' Robert said sharply.

'He threatened to go to her father if she didn't tell him the truth. Was it some reckless game, Robert, like the ones your brother plays? Is this how things are done in your family? In Scotland?'

Robert stared at him. In all the months he had known Humphrey he had never caught anything in his tone that disparaged his homeland, unlike some of the others. It pricked him through the shock.

Humphrey seemed to realise he had gone too far, for his voice lost some of its vehemence. 'Didn't you think you might get caught?'

'Did Aymer tell her father?' Now the initial blow had faded, reality was settling coldly in Robert. The Earl of Warwick had the king's ear. He might well have jeopardised his place here, having only just secured it through his induction into the order. The concern wasn't new; he'd had it since the first feverish moment with Helena, but after his initiation he had been feeling somewhat invincible and had convinced himself no one would discover his secret. It was true then, what poets and priests said: a woman could destroy a man better than any blade. He thought of Eve with her apple and he thought of his father, marrying his mother without the king's permission — passion had almost lost him his lands.

'No,' answered Humphrey, quietly now. 'He told her brother.'

With the sword's solid weight against his leg, Robert realised what Humphrey was leading him to.

'I couldn't stop it,' said Humphrey, reading his changing face. 'I tried, but the others . . .' He drew a breath. 'Guy has been a part of our circle for four years and his father is a member of the Round Table. He demanded justice that wouldn't ruin his sister in the process. It was agreed it should be served.'

Robert felt a tightening sensation in his chest, but he wrapped his hand around the hilt of his sword, determination lengthening his stride. This was his doing, yes. But he wouldn't pay for it with his life. Not willingly.

Humphrey led the way down through the corner tower and out into the gardens that were set on a terrace between the castle's inner and outer walls, the latter rising above the rocks over the river. Passing four guards, one of whom nodded discreetly to Humphrey, they headed out through the gate on to the stone ramp that curved around the rocks to the wooden pier. For a moment, Robert thought Humphrey meant for them to board a boat, but as they turned a pillar of rock he saw torchlight on the pier illuminating a group of men. One, in their centre, was swinging a sword back and forth. Robert glanced over his shoulder, realising that apart from the four guards at the gatehouse and a small section of the walkway far above, the pier was hidden from view. This wasn't the way duels were usually fought, without arbiter, without judgement.

The wind chased white peaks across the surface of the river. Robert blew into his hands, trying to breathe warmth into his rigid fingers. Guy would have had time to loosen up already, but his own muscles were stiff. Humphrey led the way on to the pier, the sound of his boots moving from stone to wood loud on the expectant quiet, broken only by the water sloshing around the rocks. At the end an empty boat swung to and fro, grating against the boards. The men turned to look at them. Guy stopped swinging his sword and stood still, his hair, red like his sister's, burnished by the light of the torches that lit the pier. The knight's gaze was hooded, his anger pent up, ready to be released in the fight. Thomas and Henry were there, along with Ralph and the others. Robert's eyes came to rest on Aymer de Valence. Loathing flooded him at the sight of the knight's hard face. Aymer looked eager, as if he were hungry for this.

Humphrey moved in front, breaking his view. 'Sir Guy, are you ready?'

Guy nodded once, his gaze not leaving Robert's. He was dressed in a black shirt that came down to his thighs, beneath which he wore woollen hose and hide boots criss-crossed with thongs of leather to hold the soft material in place. His sword belt, studded with silver, was double-looped around his waist and he wore leather gloves.

Humphrey looked between the two men. 'You will fight until first blood.' He spoke loudly, so all the group could hear. 'The victor will then decide the terms of his opponent's surrender.' Pulling off his gloves, he lowered his voice. 'Here,' he said, handing them to Robert, 'these should help.'

The royal knight Robert Clifford came forward, bearing two bucklers as Robert drew on the gloves, warm from Humphrey's hands, the leather wrinkled. He took one of the small shields Clifford passed to him, grasping the handle in the centre of the disc, the front of which was bowl-shaped. Robert hadn't used a buckler since his training days with Yothre. In comparison to the large, tapering shield he bore when mounted it felt incredibly small, leaving most of his body exposed to a strike. He remembered Yothre barking at him on Turnberry beach after he'd been knocked flat on his back, the buckler on the sand beside him and the pugnacious man shouting that one of his sisters would hold the shield better. How many times had his instructor punched in through his defences? Robert forced away the thought as he faced Guy. The mist of rain had grown heavier, darkening their clothes. Drops of water sputtered and hissed as they hit the torch flames.

Robert drew his broadsword. The blade's length was balanced by a ball-shaped pommel of bronze, stained turquoise with use, and the grip, of bound leather wrapped around bone, was worn. The weapon had been presented to him at his knighting by his grandfather, who had carried it into battle in the Holy Land. The steel was from Damascus, the strongest in the world and the sword, his grandfather told him, had been christened with the blood of Saracens. Guy's sword looked newer, the blade longer, the teardrop pommel larger to compensate. His grip was bound in red and yellow cord, the colours of the Beauchamp arms. The weapon looked comfortable in his right hand, the buckler covering his left. Robert gave his sword a few turns, using his thumb as a lever, spinning it first this way then that, keeping his wrist loose. He lunged a couple of times, finding his footing on the pier boards and stretching the taut muscles in his thighs. Then he moved back and was still, his eyes fixed on Guy.

Humphrey's voice sounded. 'The duel may begin.'

Guy didn't wait, but came straight in, swinging his sword in a fierce arc directed at Robert's neck. Robert brought his blade up quickly to block and the weapons crashed in a concussion of steel. He shoved forward, forcing Guy's sword away to regain his space. The knight was pushed back a few paces, but retaliated immediately, giving Robert little chance to recover. Their weapons collided again as Guy struck at Robert's side.

In this way, they went at one another for several minutes, Guy attacking, furious and rapid, Robert defending strongly. The torches glowed in the faces of the watching men, Aymer's teeth flashing white as he grinned, enjoying Guy's rage-fuelled assault. Neither Robert nor Guy saw them, all their attention focused on one another, as they hammered and hacked and blocked, the rain now dashing their faces. Humphrey had said until first blood only, but Guy's brutal strokes, if any struck, would do far worse.

Robert tossed back his fringe that was dripping rainwater into his eyes, the pier's boards becoming slippery underfoot. Guy lunged at his chest. Robert smashed the blade away with his shield, the crack harsh on the air. As he did so, he felt a hot rush that burned away any lingering sense of compunction, along with his intent to follow Humphrey's instruction. He had felt it before, in training: a burst of something ferocious that crackled inside him – a desire to win. His pride was at stake here, his reputation and perhaps even his life. Guy was angry, that was what fuelled him, but anger made a man rash. A man could only use anger for so long in a fight like this. It would make him tire quickly, each blow expending more energy than necessary. If Robert used that against him, he could beat him. He could win.

Recovering well, he pressed in with his own attack, forcing Guy to counter. The red-haired knight snarled through clenched teeth as he fought him off. Robert's lips peeled back in a grin than only goaded the knight more, until he was spitting curses as they clashed, sparks shooting from the blades in tiny slivers of metal, heated red-hot by the vicious impact. Robert heard Humphrey shouting at them, but he ignored the knight's sharp reminder of the rules. Exhilaration and determination pulsed through him, making him crave that win, even if he had to kill the man in front of him to achieve it.

As he feinted left, Guy swung to follow, then Robert switched back fast and pressed in. His foot stamped down as he lunged, but his boot slipped on the wet boards, unbalancing him in mid-strike. Guy brought his sword slashing back towards him, seeing the opening. The blades met in a screech of metal. Guy pushed in, using his body's weight to jam Robert's sword down with his blade, while he punched up with his buckler. Robert had time to see the circle of steel sailing towards his face, then he ducked to one side and brought his own shield up to crack away Guy's hand. The rim of the buckler caught Guy's wrist, flinging his arm wide and making him shout in pain. He wheeled away, causing some of the watching men to fall back. Gathering shield and sword to his centre again, he barrelled in, intent on battering Robert to the ground.

Robert raised his sword against an overhead chop to his head, the blades making a cross in mid-air. Guy growled as he shoved down with all his might. Robert dodged suddenly. Pivoting under Guy's now sharp falling thrust, he slammed his buckler into the knight's stomach. Guy doubled up over the punch. The breath rushing from him, he collapsed to his knees in the wet, dropping his sword. He flung up his buckler, expectant of a blow to the head, but Robert didn't strike. Instead, he stepped back, licking salt from his lips and pushing his wet hair from his eyes. The watching men were hushed. Humphrey stepped in, clearly ready to end it, but Henry Percy caught his arm. After a moment, Guy snatched up his sword and staggered to his feet, grimacing with the effort. Both men were drenched, lines of water and sweat streaking their faces.

Silent now, except for his wheezing breaths, Guy moved in. He struck again, three fierce, rapid blows, designed to hammer through Robert's defences. But Robert was ready. With all those beatings and taunts on the sands of Turnberry, Yothre had trained him well, as had his grandfather. He could see the defeat in his opponent's eyes, the awful tiredness, the crushing pain in his arm and shoulder, from the weight of the sword. Robert felt those things too, but he had not used as much energy in that first burst of attacks as Guy had. Slower, more reasoned strokes had left him with just enough to finish it. On the fourth strike, he caught Guy's sword between his blade and his buckler, then wrenched to one side, pulling Guy with him. Kicking out as they were both hunched over, he caught the knight above the knee. Guy's leg buckled and gave way, sending him crashing to the boards. This time, Robert stamped down on the sword, crushing Guy's fingers beneath it. He flicked his blade to Guy's throat, where it wavered, rain dripping from it. Guy stared up its length from his knees, meeting Robert's storm-blue eyes. He closed his in defeat.

Robert stepped back and raised his head to the sky, taking in lungfuls of air.

'It is done,' said Humphrey. His voice was tight, but the respect in his eyes was unmistakable as he met Robert's gaze. 'Sir Robert is the victor. You must now decide the terms of Sir Guy's surrender.'

Robert shook his head, struggling through his breaths. 'I don't want anything from him.'

Some of the knights frowned, surprised. Guy was breathing through his teeth, his gaze fixed on Robert as if he wanted nothing more than to continue the fight even though he could barely stand.

'You won the duel, Robert,' said Humphrey. 'You have the right.'

'He owes me nothing. But this is over,' Robert added to Guy. He meant the dispute, as well as the trysts with Helena.

Guy stared at him. After a moment, he nodded, seeming to understand. Aymer de Valence crossed to him, his face tight, but Guy pushed him away angrily and rose, handing his buckler to Clifford. As Aymer looked over at him, Robert realised the duel had been his idea. Meeting the knight's vicious gaze, he smiled coldly in triumph.

32

The train of men wound slowly through bare hills. To the right the brittle grass stretched into brown fields that sloped towards the sea, while to the left the ground rose steeply into tree-tangled summits.

Near the front of the train rode King Edward, his destrier sure-footed on the frost-bitten ground. Bayard, his favourite, was a huge, muscular warhorse, a necessity considering his burden. A quilted caparison covered the animal from head to tail, hiding a skirt of mail that swayed stiff about his legs. On top of the trapper, which took two grooms to haul over the beast's back, was the wooden saddle in which the king sat at ease, the horse taking the weight of his armour: a long-sleeved mail hauberk, over which he wore a coat of plates, buckled at his back. Leather gauntlets, covered with more steel plates, protected his hands and mail chausses his legs. The upper ranks of Edward's army, with him in the vanguard, were similarly dressed, whereas the infantry made do with tunics of boiled leather or gambesons stuffed with straw. But all, high or low, wore armour of some kind, for they were deep in hostile lands, Madog and his men lurking somewhere in these frozen hills.

Four days earlier, Edward's scouts brought him the news he had been impatient for. The enemy had been sighted south of Caernarfon, not far from the village of Nefyn. Gathering his knights around his table, he had announced his decision to move out. A few of them had cautioned against this, fearing the weather could turn any day and the snow, threatening for weeks, would finally fall. More were keen to wait for the other companies to meet up with them from the south so that they might strike out in strength. The Earl of Pembroke, fresh from a successful attack on a group of rebels who had laid siege to an English-held castle near Cardiff, had bolstered their number, but there were several more divisions yet to join them.

Edward had poured scorn on the implication that his army, mostly made up of heavy cavalry, couldn't stand against an inferior force of insurgents, armed with spears and short bows. He was angered by their reticence, for he had spoken of his fears ten years earlier around the very same table, the wood newly carved with the names of Arthur's knights. He had told them then of the necessity of securing the crown that had united Wales. Now, his fears had been proven right. The Crown of Arthur had risen on the head of another, as predicted, and the country was aflame with rebellion. Madog must be put down, yes. But, more importantly, the crown must be seized.

The next day the king's company left Conwy, heading down the thin coastal strip between Snowdonia and the sea. The first town they came to was Caernarfon.

Edward knew his greatest fortress had been attacked: all the reports had told him so. He had steeled himself, expecting to be greeted with damage, but he had not been prepared for the scene of total devastation that met him. The town was visible for several miles before the English army reached it, the destruction slowly unfolding before their eyes, the men becoming hushed with disbelief. Caernarfon's walls were battered into rubble in places, gashes torn through the fortified line as if slashed open by the claws of some giant. The town beyond was unrecognisable. Houses were blackened ruins, the trees in the orchards charred stumps. The sour smell of smoke still haunted the air.

Edward had ridden through the ruins, his eyes on his castle; the birthplace of his son and heir. There were scores of bodies in the ditch below the walls, the flesh mutilated by scavengers. Crows circled the battlements, death's shadows in the winter sky. Two skeletal forms, wearing the tattered remains of surcoats recognisable as belonging to the constable and local sheriff, were strung from one of the towers. Cawing birds hopped on the parapet close by, wary of the men moving below, yet keen for the last scraps of their meal.

Inside the castle the ground was thick with debris: crumbled masonry, spent arrows, more corpses, of men and horses. There were heaps of timbers where roofs of buildings had collapsed in flames. To Edward it had seemed another life when he had stood here last. Back then he had ridden in to the din of drums and trumpets, a victory song in the mouths of his men. The land had been golden with summer and his wife had been at his side, her perfume sweetening the air. Wales had been in his control, his enemies dead or captured. His boy, Alfonso, had been alive in London and his thoughts had teemed with the future, the carpenter already carving the wood for his table. Standing there in the midst of the smoking devastation, the fallen castle felt like the ruin of his reign. He had stayed less than an hour in the wreckage, before turning his back on the sight and heading south towards Nefyn, murder in his mind.

The sound of laughter distracted the king from the brooding memory. Turning to seek its cause, Edward saw Humphrey de Bohun and Henry Percy close behind him at the head of a group of young knights. Humphrey was speaking, a grin on his face. Seeing their youthful high spirits, despite the grave circumstances, Edward felt a sharp nostalgia. The day was fading for him and his men, cold twilight approaching. Bold midday was for the young bloods, these knights who would soon take the place of their fathers around his table, or the table of his son. In their faces, unlined with age or grief, Edward saw the future and the past: his past, their future. They were stalwart men, loyal and keen, but as yet untested in battle, like molten metal in a sword mould, all fire and heat, but no structure, not yet cooled and tempered to steel.

Edward's calculating gaze moved over Robert Bruce who rode at Humphrey's side. The earl seemed inseparable from Hereford's son of late. The king had pondered the decision to allow his induction into the order when John de Warenne proposed it, for Bruce had seemed reticent in London. But the young man's father had always been pliable and Scottish allies would no doubt prove important in the months to come. After all the difficulties that followed King Alexander's death — Yolande's pregnancy, the loss of Margaret and the protracted hearing to find a successor — matters were finally progressing in the north. Comyn seemed to have been placated by his son's marriage to Pembroke's daughter and Balliol was weakening rapidly in the face of his lawyers. Edward had forced Scotland's king to relinquish so many rights and liberties to him that his authority as overlord was becoming impossible to dispute. Soon Balliol would lose the last of his failing credibility. When that happened, Edward would take full control of his kingdom.

'My lord.'

Edward looked round as John de Warenne steered his horse in beside him.

'We should reach Nefyn before dark, but the supply wagons are some miles behind.' Warenne nodded to three hills that jutted ahead. 'The climb to the village will slow them further. Should we find somewhere closer to camp tonight?'

The baggage train contained not only Edward's personal belongings, but also tents, hay and the barrels of beer and sacks of grain that supplied his men. There was scarce opportunity to find food in the winter wilderness and almost everything had been taken out from Conwy to sustain them on the campaign. It would be a hungry night if the wagons were late into Nefyn, but the king's impatience was greater than his appetite. Nefyn was the nearest settlement and would provide a good base while he sent scouts to search for the enemy. 'We're too exposed out here. We keep going.'

The long line of men continued, the land ascending slowly with every mile. There was a smell of snow in the air, the clouds pressing down. Soon, the sea was lost from view as they skirted the lower slopes of the hills. Behind, distant Snowdon glowered beneath a green sky, full of menace. The climb into the hills was slow going for the bulk of Edward's army, slower still for the baggage train, the carters' whips cracking ceaselessly to goad the weary carthorses over the rough ground. The vanguard pushed on into the encroaching dark through a series of narrow gorges, hemmed in by ridges of rock. Then, all at once, the sea swelled ahead in a vast bay filled with great white breakers that roared inland.

Dismounting in the village of Nefyn, Robert stared around, trying to imagine the forlorn settlement as the cradle of prophecy. A few dilapidated homes huddled around a church in a cleft of land between wooded slopes to the east and south. Back the way they had come, over steep cliffs and the booming sea, a fading line of torchlight marked the rest of the king's company still making its way in, like a necklace of fire draped around the hills.

The men of the vanguard were spreading out, some heading to search the deserted homes, others looking for fresh water for the horses, more moving down on to the shore to find driftwood for fires. In the blue wash of evening, several boats were visible, beached on the expanse of sand, left by those who had abandoned their homes at the start of the war and headed into the forests, driving their livestock before them to keep them from the advancing English. They had left behind a land of echoes, in the frozen silence of winter. The knights were subdued, numb fingers plucking at bridle buckles and packs, breath fogging the air, muscles tortured by the march.

'Where should we bed down?'

Robert looked round at his brother's voice. Edward wore a heavy cloak over his mail and surcoat, but his face was tinged blue and his lips were chapped. The air was pure ice. 'By those trees will do.' Robert nodded to a copse of hoary oaks by a tumbled-down house. 'Have the squires get a fire going.'

Half an hour later, he was leaning against the trunk of an oak, the undersides of the branches flushed by firelight. His body thawed slowly in the burgeoning heat as he rested, half listening to murmured conversations, punctuated by the whinnies of horses. Men busied themselves digging pits for fires and collecting brittle branches. Nes and some of the other squires had gone to collect more fuel, and his servants and steward were preparing the evening meal, such as it was. Watching the knights sharing dregs from skins and breaking stale bread that was swallowed down with difficulty, Robert felt his stomach ache. It would be at least a few hours until the wagons arrived with more supplies. Humphrey was nearby, as were some of the others who had travelled in the vanguard.

Since the fight, Robert had kept himself at a distance, partly not wanting the animosity that lingered with Guy to be noted by anyone outside their circle, partly stung that the ending of his affair with Helena had been down to them, the choice taken from him. The duel with Guy didn't seem to have damaged his standing in the order; if anything Humphrey, Thomas and Ralph respected him more, but the divisions that already existed had been made clearer, the lines drawn, immutable. The enmity between himself and Aymer, which before had been little more than juvenile aggression, had formed into something solid, something adult and dangerous.

'Do you trust him?'

Robert glanced over at his brother's question, realising he had been caught staring at Humphrey. Edward was sitting opposite, the fire writhing between them, illuminating his face. They were alone for a moment, the knights from Essex seeing to the horses, the servants searching through the packs for more food to dole out. When Robert didn't respond, Edward continued, his voice barely audible over the crackle of the flames.

'I know you won't speak of this order, or whatever it is you have been accepted into, but I wonder if you've stopped to think about what it is you now belong to.' Edward picked up a twig that had jumped from the fire and was smouldering on the grass. He tossed it back into the flames, his face taut in the amber glow. 'These knights serve a man who robbed our family of the throne. Do not forget that.'

'I haven't,' said Robert sharply, meeting his brother's gaze. 'Our grandfather sent me here to raise our standing. He knew I could do nothing to further our position in Scotland, not with Balliol on the throne, but he believed I could recover some of our losses here. That is what I am trying to do.'

Edward leaned forward. 'Is it?' he asked intently. 'Because from where I stand this has nothing to do with strengthening our family and everything to do with you. I think you've been seduced, brother, just as our father was, by King Edward's dazzling promises. These men – and all their talk of King Arthur – have turned your head to the truth. By joining their ranks, by making whatever oaths you made, you have forsaken the very thing our grandfather charged you with. How, by furthering the ambitions of a king who denied our right to the throne, are you helping our family?' Edward shook his head, his expression bullish. 'Next you'll be bowing to St George, St Andrew forgotten.'

Robert kept his voice low with effort. 'If anyone is endangering our family's standing here it is you. You say you don't like being treated like a churl. Stop acting like one.' He glanced past Edward, seeing Nes and the others approaching, carrying bundles of firewood. Robert looked back at his brother, his tone hard. 'You aren't the one on whom our future depends, Edward. If you were, maybe you would not be so quick to judge me.'

He fell silent as the others settled in around the fire. Edward accepted a wine skin one of the servants handed to him, his gaze lingering on Robert, who leaned back against the tree trunk and closed his eyes.

Some time later, Robert woke from the fog of a disturbing dream to the sound of raised voices. He sat up groggily, his neck stiff. His brother and the Essex knights were on their feet, staring into the darkness beyond their pool of firelight. As Robert stood, he saw men hastening past, their faces agitated in the glow of the campfires. The raised voices grew louder, more urgent. He caught sight of the broad figure of John de Warenne heading for the church, in which the king had bedded down. Robert moved in behind his men. 'What is it?'

'Look,' murmured Edward.

Following his gaze, back into the hills they had come from, Robert saw a faint orange glow beyond one ridge. It was a large fire, some miles away. He was distracted by two figures, emerging from the blackness ahead. Between them they were hauling a third man, whose hand was clamped around a wad of cloth at his neck. As they passed, Robert saw the cloth was sodden with blood.

'Wake the others,' Robert ordered his knights, bending to grasp his mail coat. He was pulling on his arming cap when Humphrey met him, dressed and armoured. The shield on his arm didn't bear his coat of arms, but rather the golden dragon. 'What's happening?' Robert asked him.

'The baggage train has been attacked. We're riding out.'

'Nes, saddle Hunter for me,' Robert called to his squire, who nodded and disappeared. 'Madog's force?' he questioned, looking back at Humphrey.

'We don't know. It happened quickly.' Humphrey watched as Robert hefted his sword from the pile of his belongings. 'Get your shield. Just you, Robert,' he added, glancing at Edward and the Essex knights. 'We need the bulk of our troops to stay, in case the attack was a diversion for a larger assault. The Earl of Warwick will be in command here.'

As Humphrey moved into the commotion of the waking camp, Robert crouched down beside the sack that contained the shield. He paused for a moment, then pulled it out, feeling a tightening in his chest as the blood scarlet bloomed in the firelight. As he rose, he met Edward's gaze.

Nes's voice called out. 'Hunter's ready, sir.'

Swinging his cloak around his shoulders, Robert moved to follow the squire.

'Brother,' said Edward, grasping his arm.

'Warwick will tell you what to do,' Robert said, heading past him, into the black.

King Edward was already mounted on Bayard, a large group gathered around him. Torches held by several knights blazed, reflected in the dragons on their shields. The king's face was filled with anger, a righteous, burning anger, which would only be sated by bloodshed. The enemy had attacked without warning, not man against man on an open field, but in the dark, exploiting their weakness.

As the king dug his spurs into Bayard's sides, the company, several hundred strong, followed him determinedly out of Nefyn. Robert, riding beside Humphrey, glimpsed his brother by the fire pulling on his sword belt, alone. Gripping his shield, he kicked Hunter on, moving in the midst of the knights, their differences for the moment put aside, any enmity gathered together and turned outwards, towards the invisible enemy on the hillside. For the first time on the long campaign, Robert felt a sense of exhilaration. He was part of the king's company now, chosen and trusted. His brother didn't understand.

Up over the cliffs they went, the crashing waves loud beneath them. Robert could see the white peaks tumbling all along the shore, faint in the grey light seeping from the east. Another hour or so and it would be dawn. Feeling something soft against his face, he realised it was snow.

After a couple of miles, the glow on the horizon growing steadily brighter, they rounded a steep slope and saw flames gusting in a rocky valley between two hills. The snow was falling thickly now. The company slowed, the men staring into the shadowy heights to either side, wary of attack. The devastation became apparent in the feverish flames as they rode in through the wreckage of the baggage train. Bodies were strewn on the ground, scattered with a dusting of snow. Some had arrows protruding from them, while others had clearly been involved in closer combat, their enemies armed with brutal weapons: axe and spear in the main, the telltale wounds in their flesh deep and jagged. Necks were torn open, faces split, heads cleaved to the brain, limbs hacked from bodies. Most of the dead were carters or squires, their armour no match for the forces that had attacked them.

The knights of the king's company dismounted, kicking over the bodies of a few Welshmen, whose drab woollen garments were bright with blood. The thick stench of death was muted by the smoke swirling from the crackling fire that had been set in a large group of carts. Dead carthorses made bulky shapes between the men. One, wounded, squealed piteously as the knights moved in. It staggered upright, entrails hanging from the gash in its stomach. At the approach of the men, the beast stumbled a few steps, ropes of intestines sliding from it with the movement, until it collapsed on to its knees.

King Edward surveyed the destruction in silence from the saddle of his destrier. Several knights had split off on the orders of John de Warenne to search the hillside for any signs of the enemy, but it was clear they had gone, melting back into the darkness that had been their cover. There were a few scattered barrels littering the valley and some visible as hazy shapes within the flames, but it was obvious that most of their supplies, if not ruined or burned, had been taken.

'Bastards,' murmured Humphrey.

In the ashen light, Robert could see snow settling on the knight's shoulders.

'There's one alive here, Sire!'

The king turned sharply as two of his men hauled a figure upright from between two smashed beer barrels. The man was dressed in a brown woollen cloak. He groaned bitterly as the men dragged him towards the king. His side was washed with blood.

Edward spoke in English, his voice cutting the smoke-tinged air. 'Where is Madog?'

When the man didn't respond, one of the knights punched him in the side. 'Answer your king,' he said roughly, his fist coming back red.

The man sagged between the knights, sweat and snow glistening on his face. He licked his lips and met Edward's gaze. Grimacing, he hissed words through his teeth in Welsh, before averting his eyes.

Edward stared at him for a pause. 'Throw him on the fire.'

As the knights who had hold of him pulled him towards the burning carts, the man yelled and struggled in their grip, blood pumping from his wound. 'No! I speak! *I speak!*' The English was thick in his mouth.

Edward held up his hand. 'Where is Madog?' he repeated, as the knights halted.

'Snowdon,' gasped the rebel, jerking his head towards the jagged darkness of the distant skyline. 'Mountain.'

'Where on Snowdon?' demanded one of the knights.

'I know not where. *Dinas tomen* . . .' The man shook his head wildly and rushed into a stream of Welsh. 'I know not!' he finished.

'He said something about a fortress,' said one of the knights, frowning. 'A ruined fortress on a hill under Snowdon. I don't think he's been there.'

'There are several fortresses beneath Snowdon, but only two that are in ruins.' As he switched back into French, Edward's tone was poised.

The man peeled back his lips in a pained half-smile. 'Mercy, King,' he said tentatively.

Edward's gaze didn't leave his. 'Burn the wretch.'

The knights picked up the man, one grabbing his ankles, the other his wrists. Some of the watching men cheered harshly as they carried him to the fire. The man screamed, throwing back his head and twisting in their grasp, but, wounded, he was no match for them. The knights began to swing him, to and fro, the curves his body made in the air getting wider.

Robert, watching with the others, was reminded of a game he had played with his brothers when they were younger. They had taken it in turns to fling one another into the sea one summer in Turnberry. That same action played out here in the wreckage of carts and corpses, the man in the centre screaming blood from his mouth, was obscene.

Finally, the knights let go and the man was flung into the centre of the bonfire. He flailed and shrieked for a moment, a writhing thing in the heart of the flames, before his hair and clothes went up and his skin shrivelled and blistered away.

'I want Madog found,' said Edward over the dying man's insane screaming, as he turned to John de Warenne.

'As do we all, my lord,' said Warenne. The earl blinked into the snow swirling around them. 'But we cannot last out here in this weather without supplies.'

As the king's men made their way back to Nefyn to gather the rest of the army, the snow began to fall in earnest, covering the bodies of the dead and smothering the fire.

33

The waters of the Menai Strait were clogged with boats, filling the narrow channel where the water churned in the fast-flowing tide. Men strained at the oars as the vessels pitched. The air was crowded with drums. Ahead, a long wedge of land rose from the strait, above which the sky was a watery mess of blues and greys. The blizzards that had covered the north of Wales in a shroud since January were over, but the higher ground was still stubbled with snow, soil peppered dark amid the white. On a ridge that sloped up from Anglesey's shoreline, beacons burned weakly, warning those in the fields beyond what was coming.

Robert grasped the gunwales as the boat rocked over a wave. April's chill had tightened the skin on his face, but the rest of him, encased in armour, was protected from the cold. It made him awkward, bulky in the confined space of the deck. Mail chausses covered his hose, tied to a belt, over which he wore a tunic, gambeson, hauberk and surcoat. The gambeson was stained red with rust. He could smell the metal of it. Around him his men were hunched between the oarsmen with the other knights. The squires were ranked precariously at the back, holding the horses. Lying along the deck of one vessel was a tree trunk, bristling with spikes and looped with chains. Foot soldiers were hunkered down around its length, binding cloth around their hands. All were fixed on the island looming ahead. Robert knew fewer faces now. Many men had joined them last month from the south when the passes through the mountain barriers of Cader Idris and Snowdon had cleared, rivers thawing to rush in torrents from the peaks. Others, those he had known since the start of the war, were barely recognisable after the weakness that had blighted them through the winter. Faces once full and hale were gaunt, skin loose, eyes hollow.

After the attack on the baggage train, King Edward had wanted to strike back, but the Welsh, faster on foot in the rocky terrain, had disappeared, the snow obscuring any trace. Wrathful, humiliated, the king was forced to lead his army back to Conwy. With no supplies on the march they weakened quickly. By the second day they were drinking melted snow. By the third the first deaths occurred, men not sleeping close enough to the fires. Horses lost their footing in the deepening drifts and the knights were forced to abandon the few carts that survived the assault. Conwy, appearing late on the fourth day, its walls almost invisible in the surrounding white, had been an answered prayer. It was comfort short-lived, the king's steward counting the few grain sacks left in the castle's stores in uneasy silence. The next day the wind stiffened, howling in from the sea where waves rolled into the mouth of the estuary. The sky, sickly green, swarmed with snow, blinding those on the battlements, who searched the horizon for the ships from the Cinque Ports and Ireland that were due to supply them. The winds raged, the sea swelled and the ships didn't come.

The new year of 1295 came with bitter hunger. The trees in Conwy's orchards were hacked down for fuel. The last sheep were slaughtered. The wine and beer went quickly and soon everyone, the king included, was forced to drink water mixed with honey. It was only late in February when the blizzards died away to leave a land wreathed in white that the seas calmed and through breaks in the clouds the snowy caps of the mountains became visible. One leaden afternoon, soon after, the first ships were sighted in the estuary. Men cheered on the battlements, their lips cracking as they grinned. After the supplies, came men from the south, including Humphrey's father, who had annihilated the insurgents he had been arrayed against in Brecon. Nonetheless the king was not appeased, for the nearness of Madog's force, somewhere in the peaks above Conwy, had taunted him all through the storms.

As the snowstorms receded, a large force was sent out under the command of the earls of Hereford and Warwick. Acting on the confession of the Welshman at Nefyn they headed into the mountains to seek out Madog's stronghold. Their men disguised in white cloaks to hide them in the snow, the earls led their force unnoticed all the way up to the walls of the ruined fortress in the shadow of Snowdon. There, as morning was breaking, vengeance was served. Hundreds of Welsh insurgents perished in the brutal assault, the English overrunning the rubble-strewn compound where many of the king's belongings, stolen from the baggage train, were seized. It was only after the bloody battle ended that Hereford's men saw trails in the snow leading into the woods and realised some insurgents had fled.

As they searched through the dead and roughly questioned the survivors, they discovered Madog had been among them. Days later, scouts brought word of the rebel's location. Madog and his commanders had gone by boat to Anglesey. They had him on the run, the net closing around his scattered forces. Less than a month after it seemed the king and his army might waste away inside the snow-locked walls of Conwy, the tide had turned.

As the drummers increased their rhythm, Robert saw men on the beach ahead turning to run, courage failing them in the face of the incoming fleet. Beyond, behind a ditch and earth ramparts crowned with a wooden palisade, was the town of Llanfaes. The men were running towards the gates of the town, where a stream of people and animals were flooding in across a bridge of banked mud. Some of the soldiers in the boats jeered, but there was little humour in the sound. As men began to pull on helms, Robert sensed their tension. He felt as taut as a bowstring. Like many here he had seen no real action in this campaign, unlike Pembroke, Hereford and Warwick's forces, already blooded, their mettle tested. Now was the chance the rest had been waiting for to prove their worth to their king.

The first boats ground into the shore's shingle. Men stowed the oars and jumped into the icy waters, hauling the vessels through the foaming waves. Archers leapt down behind, lining up on the sand while the knights and horses disembarked. Destriers stamped in agitation as gangplanks were thrown down and the beasts were led on to the beach, their hooves sinking in the mud. The knights mounted first, snapping down visors and drawing swords. More boats were grinding ashore in the gaps between. The spiked tree trunk was lifted off by sixteen men, heaving on the chains to lug its length up the beach. The king mounted Bayard and, amid the shouts of his commanders, he and his men began to ride, the archers moving to make way, then falling in behind. The sixteen men with the ram came in their wake, muscles straining. The foot soldiers were last, wielding pikes, hammers and falchions.

Robert rode beneath the banner of Carrick, the dragon shield on his left arm. He wore it proudly now in common cause; this symbol of Arthur, the warrior king. As he caught sight of Humphrey, the knight raised his fist in a defiant gesture that Robert returned. Today, God willing, they would finish this campaign. He wanted to return home blooded, to be able to tell his grandfather that he too had won his spurs in the king's war. Nerves and anticipation battled within him, his breaths coming hard and fast in the tight encasement of his helm.

The vanguard approached the gates of Llanfaes. At a signal from John de Warenne the knights and squires slowed, keeping their distance from the earthen ramparts, while the men with the ram came in. Archers were ordered into a line, ready to fire volleys over the palisade. A few missiles shot down from beyond the barricade as the sixteen soldiers hefted the ram across the bank of mud that formed a bridge to the gates. One caught a man in the back of the neck. As he dropped, two more soldiers were sent in, ducking down and throwing wary glances at the palisade. One dragged the wounded man out of the way while the other took his place, grasping the chain. Together, the sixteen stumbled forth, charging the ram's weight towards the gates. The barriers shuddered with the impact, but didn't break. The men hauled it back and ran in again, wincing with the effort. The knights watched, their horses stamping in agitation. More arrows plunged down. After them came bundles of burning straw that scattered on the men at the ram, causing them to break their stride, several forced to swat away the flaming debris. The English archers were given a signal and they let loose over the gates. A few cries, some of warning, some of pain, sounded beyond.

The ram's head smashed against the barrier, again and again, the gates now showing signs of buckling with every impact. At last, there was a cracking sound as the head punched its way through. To frantic shouts behind the gates it was dragged free, the spikes ripping at the timbers. As the men carried the ram back across the mud bridge, soldiers raced in with hammers and pikes to smash apart the remains of the gates. The wood splintered to reveal figures scattering beyond. Trumpets bellowed and the first knights spurred their destriers across, hooves kicking up mud and smouldering embers of straw. King Edward himself rode in the van, sword raised, Bayard fearless in the charge. Arrows shot towards them from defensive positions in the streets. Barbed tips stuck in caparisons and shields. One horse reared as it was hit, its hooves slipping to send it toppling into the ditch, crushing its rider beneath its weight.

There was a press at the gates. Robert found himself in the thick of it, men yelling, horses gnashing, then he was through into a storm of noise and motion, his vision channelled by his helm. Something glanced off his head, an arrow perhaps, before he was swept off down the street ahead, mud and timber houses flashing past. The rebels and townsmen who had been defending the gates fled before the incoming tide of cavalry. The knights in front of Robert swung down their blades at the running figures, few of whom wore armour. One man fell, bounced between two horses. He disappeared beneath the iron-shod hooves of those who came behind. Robert felt Hunter plunge down into something soft, before being caught up in the wake of Sir John de Warenne and his men, drawn along by the momentum of their horses. His brother and the Essex knights and squires had been close behind him through the gates, but there was no way of telling if they were still there, the fury of the charge making it impossible to do anything but fix his gaze forward and make sure he didn't collide with those in front.

As they rode down a muddy thoroughfare into an orchard where the ground was grey with melted snow, Robert glimpsed knights breaking away to fling torches on to the thatch roofs of buildings. The Welsh broke up among the trees, trying desperately to outrun the charge. One man threw himself at a low branch and hauled himself up. A knight spurred his horse towards him, swinging his sword brutally into the man's back. The blade scythed through flesh and muscle, opening a wide gash in the man's torso with a burst of blood and organs. The man, almost severed in two, slid from the branch and crumpled in the slush as the knight galloped on. Another man, his back against a tree, lifted his hands and shouted for mercy. A knight stabbed down as he thundered past, the tip of his sword punching fast through the Welshman's neck then out again, leaving the man to collapse, coughing red down his chest. Others were hacked apart in brief shocks of blood.

More knights were pouring into the streets behind as Robert followed Warenne. He saw them splitting off, leading troops down side streets in pursuit of the townsfolk, among whom were the remains of Madog's forces. He caught pale faces in the windows of houses, heard screams as smoke sharpened the air. Commanders roared through the iron teeth of their helms and men shrieked like devils as they killed, or were killed. Horror opened up down every street in every thrust of sword, every swing of hammer and pike. Flesh, life, soul: these things of men were reduced to targets, to be destroyed without remorse.

Robert held back in the press, letting others go after the rebels fleeing before the charge. Their orders were to slaughter anyone found in the streets to provoke a quick surrender, after which mercy would be granted to those left alive. He had seen death throughout his life, but the duel he'd had with Guy was the closest he'd come to ending someone's life and even then there had been rules imposed. There were no such boundaries here. The freedom to kill was a dizzying, precipitous feeling. But the veteran knights were pushing in behind him, forcing the issue. With a snarl of frustration at his own hesitation, Robert fixed on one man darting away down an alley and spurred his horse out of the crush in pursuit.

Sunlight flashed in puddles that burst in sprays as his horse plunged through them. In the gaps between the buildings he glimpsed other men scurrying like rats through the rubbish and mud. Infantry were pouring into the alleys and battering through doorways to hunt down the rebels. Smoke billowed up with screams. The Welshman he'd fixed upon was just ahead, arms and legs pumping frantically. Robert raised his sword, a mad pounding in his head. Suddenly, the man ducked down another street and Robert went crashing on past. With a curse, he brought Hunter to a halt. Turning the animal with a pull on the left rein and a rough kick of his right spur, he pursued.

The man was some distance away now. Robert saw him try to push into one of the houses, but the door was barred. In desperation he sprinted on. Robert rode quickly up behind, closing the gap, tensing for the kill, as he had done a hundred times with wolf and stag and boar. Swinging his broadsword up and round, he brought the blade slamming down into the curve between the man's shoulder and neck. The impact of the strike was a shock, not just in Robert's arm and shoulder, but in his gut and chest. It was nothing like striking at an animal. Wrenching his sword free, he cantered on down the alley. The blade in his hand gleamed with blood, shocking red in the winter sunlight.

In the streets beyond, the fighting had centred near Llanfaes's market square. Madog ap Llywelyn and the last of the rebels had barricaded themselves along a street that led off the square, using abandoned wagons and furniture ripped from houses. A few score townsmen were with them, wielding kitchen knives and hunting bows, but many more had given up the struggle, fleeing in terror before the knights and infantry who were overrunning the town and racing to their homes to protect their families.

Under Madog's shouted orders they had so far withstood two charges Edward had sent into their ranks, their spears bristling out along the barrier to turn the knights' attacks. Some of the townsmen had cheered seeing the knights falling back, frustrated by the wall of spears. The rebels and Madog, who wore the Crown of Arthur over a coif of mail, remained grim and soon the last of the cheering died away as the king lined up his crossbowmen in front of the barricades.

For decades the men of Gascony had been adept in the use of this weapon, outlawed in some parts of Christendom, condemned by popes and considered by most to be the tool of mercenaries. Flames fanned from nearby rooftops gusting clouds of smoke across the space between the crossbowmen and the Welsh blockade. The people of Gwynedd had little to fear from English archers, who like themselves used the short bow. It was only the men of south Wales who were adept at the powerful, lethal long-bow. Arrows shot from a short bow could blind and disorient the enemy, but unless they struck exposed flesh they rarely killed a man, clattering harmlessly off mail or sticking in the padding of gambesons. Longbows and crossbows were a different matter: one well-shot arrow or bolt could pierce a knight's mail chausses, his leg, the saddle and the horse beneath. To a Welsh warrior, clad in little more than a stiffened leather tunic, they augured instant, brutal death.

With swift, practised moves, each crossbowman dug his foot into the stirrup attached to the bow and pulled back, fixing the cord over the trig-ger. Taking a quarrel from a basket attached to his belt, each fitted it in the slot, raised the bow, aimed and loosed. The bolts shot through the barricade, punching through gaps in wagon wheels and benches. Men fell, the missiles piercing shoulders, throats, faces, stomachs. Madog, who had crouched behind a stack of grain sacks, yelled orders over the chaos, the bolts coming so rapidly they darkened the air.

The rebels threw themselves down, some using the bodies of dying and wounded comrades as shields. The townsfolk, maddened by the vicious onslaught, began to flee. Many fell, quarrels plunging into their backs. In the confusion and panic, King Edward ordered his knights to charge. As the last bolt was shot, the cavalry plunged towards the barricade. Madog and the rebels, many wounded, the rest hunched down for cover, had no chance to turn their spears on the enemy. As knights urged their horses over or around the barrier, the fight for Anglesey resumed at close quarters. It was brief and bloody. Madog went down roaring as John de Warenne cut the spear from out of his hand.

34

As Robert pulled off his helm the freezing air was like a slap on his sweat-drenched cheeks. He tasted salt and steel. Leaning back against the mud wall of a house, he tugged the stopper from his wine skin with his teeth. He spat out the cork, and drank until it was empty. There were bodies in the street all around him and bloodstains daubed the walls of houses with garish sprays. The scalp of one man, lying close by, was splintered, pink-grey matter oozing from the wide gash between his matted hair. Perhaps a horse had trodden on him, or perhaps it was an axe wound. Robert didn't think he had been responsible, but it was hard to tell. Memories of the moments spent in this killing ground were already hazy and unfamiliar.

Other knights and squires were nearby, gulping down drink and recovering their breath, the mercy order having come moments ago. Some were already revelling in the victory, but their laughter sounded high and forced. Others were silent, their eyes averted from the bloody scene spread out before them. Robert had seen several men stagger away, rip off their helms and vomit. Pushing himself from the wall he moved to where he had left Hunter, tethered to an abandoned cart on the back of which he'd placed his sword.

Hefting his shield higher on his arm with a wince at the painful spasm in his muscles, Robert stowed his wine skin in the saddlebag and took up his broadsword. The weapon was sticky with blood, the smell of it like old pennies held too long in the hand. His jaw tight, he wedged his helm on top of the saddlebag. He had lost track of his brother and his men in the assault. He felt disorientated, the smoke that filled the sky obscuring any sense of the day. It could have been minutes since he entered the town, or hours. Infantry were trudging through the street ahead, despatching the dying and ordering survivors from houses as the thatched roofs continued to burn. More knights were arriving, the air filling with the clatter of hooves. Among them were the colours of Pembroke, the red birds on blue and white stripes catching in Robert's vision. Turning away as the company approached, he took up Hunter's reins and set off down an adjacent alley, deciding to retrace his steps in search of his brother.

He had not gone far when the alley behind him filled with hoof-beats. Robert turned to see a knight riding towards him. He had time to see a rush of blue and white stripes, time to see a sword swinging in the fist and time to realise the knight wasn't slowing. The blood still pumping hot in him from battle, he reacted quickly. Cuffing Hunter's hind and sending the horse galloping down the alley, Robert slammed himself against the wall of a building, out of the path of the warhorse and the swing of the sword. Knight and charger went thundering on past, before coming to a skidding stop some distance down the muddy passage. The knight turned the horse with a wrench of reins. Snatching at his helm, which had fallen from the saddlebag when Hunter bolted, Robert saw the knight snap up his visor. Behind the metal guard, Aymer de Valence's eyes, glittering with hate, were wild. The man was blood-drunk. His surcoat was awash with gore, as was the trapper of his horse. As he kicked at the sides of his destrier and came at Robert again, his intention was clear.

Robert threw himself at the door of a ramshackle dwelling opposite. He barrelled through it just as Aymer came charging towards him, the ring of iron-shod hooves harsh in the alley. The door banged open, splintering with the force, as Robert went crashing into the dark beyond. Staggering to a stop, he found himself in a musty kitchen, dominated by a trestle and boards littered with the remains of a meal. Cracks of light slanted through shuttered windows to either side of the splintered door. A few stools were scattered about the room and there was a dull glow coming from a hearth, but no sign of any occupants. Outside, Robert heard a horse's heavy snort and the jangle of spurs striking the ground. Dropping his helm, he pulled his shield into place, gripping the straps with his left hand, while in the right he brandished his bloodstained sword.

Aymer's frame appeared in the doorway, blocking the light. He had his blade ready in his hand and he too bore the dragon shield against his left side. The knight stepped into the room, his hate-filled eyes fixed on Robert, who stood waiting, his chest rising and falling beneath his surcoat.

'Another churl hiding in a hovel, waiting to be cut down.' Aymer's voice was acerbic, his French full of malice. 'By the time they find your corpse, I'll be long gone.'

Robert licked his lips uneasily. 'A fine notion,' he said, hefting his sword, 'being that it works both ways.'

Aymer gave a bark of laughter. 'I am not Guy. I will not be beaten down so easily.' His eyes alighted on the shield on Robert's arm, the dragon shining dully in the glow from the hearth. 'You think you're worthy because Humphrey chose you?' he spat suddenly. 'You're a convenience. Someone with power and lands who can help him advance his position. In truth you're a foreigner to my brothers. An outsider.'

'That eats at you, doesn't it? The fact they chose me so soon and yet you had to wait three years before being invited to join the order. Yes,' said Robert, enjoying the look on Aymer's face, 'your so-called *brothers* told me that.' He took a step towards the knight, loathing firing his blood-lust. 'Foreigner I may be, but they trusted me far quicker than they trusted you. Humphrey had your measure, Valence, the moment he met you.'

All at once Aymer was rushing at him, his sword carving the air. The knight came in hard, forcing Robert to block swiftly. The clash of sword on shield was deafening in the cramped chamber. Robert felt the shock of it shoot through his arm, but he reacted at once, knocking away Aymer's blade fiercely with his shield. The knight stumbled back with the strength behind Robert's thrust, his leg catching one of the stools, which skittered away behind him. It distracted him, only for a second, but enough for Robert to lunge and slam his shield into Aymer's face. Aymer's helm took the brunt of it, but he was rocked back so hard he lost his balance. As he crashed to the floor the impact jolted the sword from his hand. Aymer scrabbled to his feet as Robert came in again. He ducked under a mighty swing of Robert's sword and was forced to wheel away before he could retrieve his fallen weapon. He raised his shield to deflect a second blow, aimed at his head. Robert's sword smashed into the painted wood, scoring a deep line across the dragon. Aymer hissed through his teeth at the power of the strike, then shoved furiously with his shield, forcing Robert's blade away. As the weapon went wide, Aymer barrelled into him.

Taken unawares by the knight's brute strength, Robert found himself propelled into the trestle and boards, which screeched across the flagstones. He toppled back, until he was half on the table top, Aymer pinning him down under the shield, teeth bared. He lifted his sword with a grunt of effort, bringing it round into Aymer's side as the breath was squeezed out of him. The blow wasn't hard and the knight's mail absorbed it, but he was thrown off balance, giving Robert the opening he needed to push him away and recover his stance. He rushed Aymer, not allowing the knight to go for his sword. Aymer crouched and grabbed Robert's helm, on the floor where he'd dropped it. Swinging it up, the knight smacked it into his groin. With a sharp exhalation of breath, Robert collapsed. On his knees, he saw Aymer scrabble past, heard a clang and a scrape as the knight abandoned the helm and picked up the fallen blade. Through the sickening pain, he heard the clink of his spurs on the stone floor. The expectation of Aymer's blade slicing its steel through his scalp jolted enough fear through him to make him stagger to his feet and turn to defend himself.

With a blade in his hand, Aymer was fast and furious. Robert had never seen him fight on foot before. The knight's muscular frame and broad shoulders lent great power to his strokes. He seemed to have little fear, for he showed no hesitation in coming in again and again, hacking like a woodcutter with his sword, punching like a wrestler with his shield. The ache in Robert's groin had almost receded, but he felt himself tiring quickly. He mistimed a blow, allowing Aymer to stamp in sideways and punch the pommel of his sword into his face. Robert felt a snap as his nose broke and his throat flooded with blood. Blinded and choking, he staggered away. Through watery eyes he saw Aymer grinning. Frustration made him want to throw himself forward, but he stumbled back around the table giving himself time to recover as he spat blood through his teeth.

'Coward!' Aymer seethed, his grin contorting. 'You don't deserve that shield, you cur.'

As Robert focused on the knight's twisted face he felt a surge of fury. He pitched forward, propelling the table into Aymer and knocking him flying. The knight landed on a stool, which broke beneath his back, sending him crashing to the floor among the shards. His sword fell from his fingers and his helm clanged back against the stone floor, the strap snapping with the impact. Before the knight could move, Robert charged round the table and dropped down on top of him, straddling his stomach. Tossing his sword aside, he pulled the knight's helm from his head. Aymer, momentarily winded by the fall, started to struggle, but Robert punched him in the face, his mailed fist mashing Aymer's lips and snapping two of his teeth. He punched in again, and again, tearing the skin around Aymer's eye, breaking his nose, then his jaw.

As Robert, drenched in sweat and panting, pulled his fist back for a fifth strike, he heard hoof-beats and shouts outside. He faltered, recognising his name in the voices. It was his men. At the sound of his brother's voice, Robert lowered his bloodied fist. 'In here!' he shouted hoarsely, pushing himself off Aymer. As he bent to pick up his sword, his head pounding,

Robert paused, staring down at Aymer, who was groaning faintly through bloody teeth. The blade hovered in his grip, wavering over the knight's form. 'Next time, I will kill you.'

Leaving Aymer senseless on the kitchen floor, Robert staggered out into the smoke-tinged daylight.

On the snow-dappled hillside above Llanfaes, the English had set up camp. Fires still burned unchecked in the ruins below, the flames garish in the early evening. The last survivors were being led in by knights. It was a miserable group they had been herded into, children weeping, men and women pale and shocked, some wounded.

Robert stood alone, his muscles aching, his broken nose throbbing. The older knights were jovial, pleased with the quick work they had made of the town and the rebels. The younger men were subdued, many left silent by their first taste of blood, a taste they had been so eager for. Aymer, his face swollen beyond recognition and missing two teeth, was among their number. Earlier, Robert had heard the knight telling Humphrey he had been set upon by three rebels. Robert doubted Aymer would ever tell a soul the truth.

As Robert watched, Madog ap Llywelyn was brought out, wounded but alive, in front of the waiting knights and survivors. His hands had been bound behind his back, but he walked upright between the two knights who held him, his head raised defiantly. The golden circlet he had worn into battle remained on his head, the dented metal sticky with blood. He was brought before Edward, who stood tall against the sombre sky, his scarlet surcoat snapping in the wind. Behind the king, two flags were raised, one, his standard bearing the royal arms of England, the other, the faded dragon banner. At a nod from the king, a black-robed cleric moved forward to remove the crown from Madog's head. The Welsh rebel spat fierce words, but the knights held him firmly and Madog was powerless to stop the cleric taking the Crown of Arthur and conveying it to the English king.

Edward stared at the blood-crusted circle of gold that had brought a nation together against him. Then, seemingly satisfied, he waved it away. 'We will have it cleaned and made good.' As the cleric took it, the king's gaze alighted on Madog. 'You have incited rebellion, committed murder and trespass, assault and robbery. You have destroyed property, fomented unrest and disturbed your king's peace.'

Madog didn't flinch, but kept his eyes on Edward.

Robert, watching with the others, wondered if Madog or any of the survivors even understood what the king had said.

'For your crimes you will be taken to the Tower where you will spend the remainder of your days.' The king paused, the wind rippling in the dragon banner. 'Ten years is a long time. The people of Wales have forgotten the price of rebellion.' Edward looked behind him, to where John de Warenne and the English earls were gathered. 'They need another reminder.'

Robert heard a cry and, as the group parted, he saw a figure dragged out. It was a young man with soot-black hair.

Madog shouted and tried to break free.

'Your brother, Dafydd, so we were told,' said Edward.

Dafydd's bruised face was terrified, but he spat on the ground as the knights hauled him past Edward to where two horses were waiting, held by the king's squires. One of the knights drew back a fist to cuff him, but the king shook his head. Madog fought against his captors, shouting incoherent streams of Welsh at the king and at his brother, whose white face had fixed on the horses, both of which had thick ropes attached to the pommels of their saddles, the free ends held by soldiers.

Dafydd's arms were pulled apart by the knights. The soldiers holding the ropes came forward and bound them around his wrists, checking each knot to make sure they were secure. The horses snorted as the squires led them into position on either side of Dafydd, whose chest was heaving in and out. The ropes attached to Dafydd's wrists and the saddle pommels uncurled from their loops on the ground, but still hung slack. Knights ushered the watching men back, out of the paths of the horses. Some of the survivors had turned away, women pressing children's faces into their skirts, men closing their eyes. More watched in muted silence. Edward stood with his officials, his face impassive.

A couple of soldiers jostled in beside Robert, looking at Dafydd, who stood alone, his hands clenched by his sides.

One of the soldiers grinned at the other. 'I once saw a man's arms ripped clean away.'

Robert let the two men move in front of him as the king gestured to his squires, who raised their whips and cracked at the horses' sides. The beasts plunged in opposite directions, the ropes leaping up to snap taut, pulling Dafydd's arms up into the air and apart. Madog's howl of anguish rose to join his brother's scream.

When Dafydd's dislocated arms were untied, the butchery continued, his limp body hauled to a trestle and boards where he was brusquely eviscerated with cruel wrenches of the executioner's knife. Finally, he was quartered and the bloody pieces of him packed in barrels to be sent around the re-conquered kingdom, evidence of the price of rebellion. The crown, worn by Brutus and by Arthur himself, would be conveyed to Westminster, the final nail in the coffin of Welsh liberty.

Leaving Madog's tortured cries to fade behind him, Robert walked away down the hillside.

Near the town walls the king's engineers and master masons were in animated discussion, surveying the terrain, measuring and marking out areas with lengths of rope. The king was already intending for another of his fortresses to be built in place of the ruined town. Soldiers were carting the dead down to the beach. Bodies were being tossed into the waters, the waves rushing in to cover them. Already, Robert could see the humps of backs and heads, swirling out into the channel, food for fish and birds. Sensing someone move up behind him, he turned to see Humphrey. The knight bore the dragon shield, his sword sheathed at his side. There was blood on his face and a spray of it up his surcoat.

'It is done.' Letting out a breath, Humphrey stared across the water, slowly filling with corpses. 'Soon we can go home.' When Robert remained silent, he continued. 'Rest assured, my friend, you will be rewarded when the Crown of Arthur is displayed beside Curtana in Westminster Abbey. Now, we only have two relics left to find.'

Robert saw a fervent determination in Humphrey's face. The man seemed so certain, so assured that he was on the right path and that when the instructions in the prophecy were fulfilled everything would be made good in the realm. There had been little time to question the ultimate intentions of the order, or the others' belief in the visions of Merlin, the dangers of war and winter more immediate, but now, with the dead washing out into the channel before them, Robert wondered. He had been so ready to believe on the night of his initiation; boyhood tales of warriors filling his head with golden prospects. Those stories had portrayed battle as something glorious, the words of the poets raising the heroes above the bloody reality. Robert thought of his father; of how the war here had changed him. For the first time, he had a fleeting sense of understanding. No wonder his father did not believe in things beyond the grim truth of the temporal world, no wonder he had ridiculed men who did. The words of his brother the night the baggage train was attacked in Nefyn came back to him. *Do you trust him?* 'You still haven't told me what King Edward will do when he has all four relics,' Robert said, fixing Humphrey with his gaze.

'We aren't privy to all his plans, Robert, as I've told you. Only the men of the Round Table know his full intentions. We have to prove ourselves worthy to be trusted as they are.'

'Do you not ever wonder?'

Humphrey paused. 'I just know my king will do what is best for my kingdom.'

Robert said nothing. He thought of his own kingdom, beleaguered by Edward's interference, and a ghost of a threat drifted in his mind. But even as it appeared, he pushed it away. Scotland was its own kingdom, with its own king. It wasn't Wales or Ireland, fractured and isolated. However much Edward had desired the Crown of Arthur he had come here, first and foremost, to put down a rebellion.

Yet still, on this bleak shore with Humphrey beside him, Robert felt a sense of standing at a crossroads with many paths leading away before him. In his mind they all led into darkness.

35

Candlelight bathed their ranks in a hallowed glow, shining in the eyes of the men and in the gilt-work on the tombs that surrounded them. Dominating the sanctuary at the heart of Westminster Abbey was a shrine, the stone base of which contained steps rising into recesses. The shrine, built by King Henry for the bones of St Edward the Confessor, along with the soaring abbey that enclosed it, had been erected only twenty-six years ago, but already the steps had been worn smooth by the knees of pilgrims. Atop the base a gold feretory contained the saint's remains, above which was a canopy, decorated with holy scenes. Beyond, shadows slipped into the epic darkness of the vault.

Beneath the gazes of painted saints, King Edward knelt, his scarlet robes pooling around him on the steps of the shrine. His head was bowed. Behind him, his men stood in rows, radiating out from him, their faces fading into soft gloom beyond the candle flames. At the front were those closest to the king's confidence, the men of his Round Table: John de Warenne and Bishop Bek, the earls of Lincoln and Warwick, Arundel, Pembroke, Hereford and the king's brother, Edmund of Lancaster, among others. Behind, stood the Knights of the Dragon, their shields held stiffly before them.

Robert, standing between Humphrey de Bohun and Ralph de Monthermer, sensed someone's gaze on him. He glanced down the line of men to meet the eyes of Aymer de Valence. The knight's bruises had faded after Anglesey, but he had a scar on his cheek where he had been injured on the campaign. Robert had seen that his two teeth, broken in the fight, had since been replaced by others. Nestled snugly in the gaps, they had been bound to his own teeth with thin silver wires, giving him a strange, glimmering smile. He had wondered where the knight had got the new ones from. Aymer held him in his stare, then turned away, his gaze fixing on the king. It had been months since Robert had seen him. With the fall of

Anglesey many nobles had been released from the king's service to return to their estates and Aymer had gone with his father to Pembroke. By the malice in his eyes it was clear none of his hatred had been dulled by time. Robert didn't feel any regret for the beating he'd given the knight, or for the reckoning he guessed might one day come. Even now, he felt a vicious joy when he recalled punching his fists into Aymer's face; a face that had grinned at his misfortunes and been eager for his pain and humiliation. The bastard had deserved it. He would do it again in a heartbeat.

When King Edward left the island, with the work on his new castle, named Beaumaris, already under way, Robert had remained in his diminished company. He had been with the king as they travelled first to Caernarfon to oversee the plans for its reconstruction, then south, making a royal progress through forlorn coastal towns and sea-battered ports, past his formidable castles at Cricieth and Harlech. Madog ap Llywelyn had been conveyed in chains to the Tower, sentenced to life imprisonment. With the bloody execution of his brother, the Welsh rebel's spirit had been broken and he had seemed, in his despair, to embody the very essence of the land of which he had been prince for such a short time.

In each settlement Edward obtained formal surrenders from the Welsh and accepted their vows of homage. Everywhere he went, through the blossoming months of May and June, the Crown of Arthur went with him, a symbol of his supreme authority. The people, bereft of a prince and mourning the loss of so many men, were subdued and frightened. But Edward, who, weeks earlier, had torn apart Madog's young brother in a brutal display, was lenient, establishing a body of lawyers to conduct hearings into grievances the Welsh had against his overbearing officials, grievances that ultimately led to the rebellion. He even let many rebels return to their families without penalty. Robert, surprised by his show of forgiveness, had soon come to see the sense in it. Edward needed the Welsh content with his rule if their obligations to pay his taxes and serve in his wars were to be enforced and further rebellion prevented.

Despite the king's success in Wales, he wasn't free of woe throughout the summer. With the receding snows and the arrival of spring, reports had begun to trickle through from England. Initial news that Edward's men in Gascony had captured three key towns from the French had been welcome, but when the reports revealed there had been no movement since, the king had become pensive. The two wars along with the enormous costs involved in the building of Beaumaris and the reconstruction of Caernarfon had bled his coffers dangerously dry. Robert had overheard many uneasy conversations during their return to London, the barons wondering when he would start looking to them for more money.

But today in Westminster those troubled voices were quiet, all the men's attention on the king and the altar before the shrine of the Confessor.

On the altar, which was draped with red and gold cloth, were three objects. One was a sword. *Curtana*, Humphrey had whispered as it was brought into the chapel. Rather than tapering to a point, the blade, once wielded by the saint whose bones lay within the gold tomb, was flat at the tip. It had been carried in every coronation since 1066 when the Conqueror was crowned King of England. Humphrey had murmured a line from the Last Prophecy as he and Robert had watched it carried in by a priest.

The blade of a saint, borne by kings, broken in mercy.

Next to the sword was a plain black box, gleaming in the candles' glow. When asked what it was, Humphrey told Robert it contained the original prophecy King Edward had found in Nefyn after his first conquest of Wales. From that book of Merlin's visions, so ancient it could not be removed from the box again lest it crumble into nothing, the king had his translation made, the words of which spurred him to seek the four relics, divided between Brutus's sons, to prevent the foreseen ruin of Britain. To these was now added the Crown of Arthur, restored by the king's goldsmiths. Taking it from the silk cushion at the foot of the shrine, Edward rose.

Robert saw some crane their heads to watch as the king placed the crown on the altar. A few bowed in prayer. Humphrey's eyes were shining, although other men appeared less humbled by the occasion. Robert felt caught somewhere between. Part of him wanted to throw himself headlong into this quest with Humphrey and the others, still believing his loyalty to the king could serve his family. Another part of him hung back, doubting the course he had taken. His brother's accusations at Nefyn had pushed an uneasy truth to the surface, reminding him that he had made a pledge to his grandfather on the day he was dubbed: a pledge to uphold their claim to the throne. However uncertain that route seemed in comparison to this one that glittered with treasures, he could not deny he had sworn to that, or that he was now following a very different path. With the reminder came words his grandfather had so often said.

A man who breaks his oath isn't worth his breath.

As King Edward turned from the shrine of the saint, the ceremony was concluded. At a signal from Sir John de Warenne, the earls, barons and clergy filed through a doorway in the painted screen that divided the sanctuary from the rest of the church, eager for the feast the king had organised in the palace and the chance to mutter about the conflict in Gascony. The king didn't join them, but headed slowly to one of the tombs that stood near the Confessor's shrine. It had a bronze effigy of a woman on top of it. The inscription on the side read:

Here lies Eleanor, on whose soul God in His pity have mercy.

As men moved in front of Robert, blocking the view of the king kneeling alone, he followed Humphrey out of the abbey's heart and into its cavernous belly. The windows that marched down the aisles were of ruby and sapphire glass, decorated with shields, and the walls between the moulded marble pillars were gold and vermilion.

Robert was halfway down the choir when he glimpsed a man, a royal messenger by his distinctive striped tunic, speaking with Ralph de Monthermer. Ralph turned, his gaze searching. Fixing on Robert, he pointed. As the messenger approached, Robert halted, Humphrey pausing quizzically beside him.

'Sir Robert of Carrick.' The messenger held out a rolled letter. 'A message from Scotland, sir. It arrived some time ago, but we were unable to deliver it to you.'

Robert hefted his shield higher on his arm to take the message, guessing it was from his grandfather. He had sent word to Scotland before he left for Wales, telling the lord that he had been summoned to serve the king. He smiled as he saw his grandfather's seal, then opened it and began to read, men brushing past him through the choir. His smile faded the further he read.

'What is it?' Humphrey asked, watching his expression change.

Robert didn't answer, but reread the letter. When Humphrey repeated the question, he looked up numbly, meeting his friend's questioning gaze. 'I am to return home.' He paused to clear the thickness in his throat. 'To be married.'

'Married?'

'To a daughter of Sir Donald, the Earl of Mar.' Robert faltered, glancing numbly at the shield on his arm, scarred from battle. 'I must take my leave of the king as soon as possible.' He paused, then held the dragon shield out to Humphrey. 'I should return this to you. I don't know how long I will be gone.'

Humphrey didn't move to take the shield. 'Once a Knight of the Dragon, always so. It is yours to keep, Robert.' He let out a whistle through his teeth that ended in a laugh. 'Well, we will have to make tonight's feast one to remember if this is to be your last with us as a bachelor. Married?' He shook his head and laughed again. 'I suppose it is a burden we will all bear soon enough.'

Ralph joined them along with Thomas of Lancaster, wanting to know what tidings the messenger had delivered. Humphrey told them. Ralph clapped Robert's back solemnly and told him he was sorry.

'Have you met her?' Thomas asked.

Robert's mind filled with an image of a midnight lake, the air misting with his breath as he moved towards Eva, her hair silver in the moonlight. He recalled his grandfather and the Earl of Mar's conversation from that night. He had sensed then that they were planning such an alliance.

'Is she beautiful?' Ralph pressed.

'As Holy Mary and all her angels,' said Robert finally, a shaky grin spreading across his face.

Their laughter echoed up past the marble faces of saints and kings, up into the dark reaches of the abbey's vault.

36

John Balliol stood on the walls of Stirling Castle, the sun setting in his eyes. In the marshy plains below the castle rock, distant pools of water reflected the light. The crimson sky was filled with flocks of birds. Their spiralling formations hinted at meaning, at some language of flight unknown to man. The air was fragrant with the smell of herbs from the garden where servants worked in the dusk collecting plants for the kitchens. The king could see other people moving through the castle grounds and the grassy stockade below the walls, where the rocks formed a plateau, before falling sheer to flower-speckled meadows that sloped down to the banks of the Forth. The great river flowed east from the distant mountains towards Edinburgh, where the royal castle perched like Stirling's twin on its own spur of rock. There, the water-way that almost carved Scotland in two widened to become the sea. In the twilight, Balliol could just make out the wooden bridge over the inky waters below, the clasp that pinched the two halves of his realm together. For years, Stirling Castle had been called the key to the north, for whosoever controlled the castle that guarded the bridge controlled the only viable route into the Highlands.

It was a tranquil evening, drowsy with summer, but the approaching darkness seeping from the east behind the bald Ochil Hills seemed to Balliol to herald so much more than falling night. He didn't want to let this land from his sight, to see it slip into that black. He wanted to reach out and scoop the sun from the horizon, hold it to his chest to blaze in the face of his enemies. But the air was cooling on his pockmarked cheeks and the first stars were pricking the eastern sky.

'My lord.'

Balliol turned at the voice. On the walkway, heading towards him, was John Comyn, his face bronze in the last of the light. The Lord of Badenoch had aged little in the three years since Balliol was enthroned at Scone and the king resented his brother-in-law's hale appearance. He knew those same years weighed heavily on him, he who, since gaining a throne, had lost his wife and almost all of his authority. The sense of time passing made him think of both their fathers fighting at Lewes under King Henry: the moment when the bonds of their families' alliance had been cemented. Balliol wondered if William Comyn hadn't offered his father freedom from that priory cell in Lewes would he be standing here today, facing such loss? Would the tides of fortune have run different if the Balliols had gone their own way at that moment rather than allow themselves to fall into the Comyns' debt? The thought and the memory of his father fired his blood.

'Are you ready, my lord? The men are gathered in the hall.'

'I cannot believe this is our only option,' said Balliol, turning back to the dimming view, knowing his brother-in-law would be furious at the suggestion.

When he spoke, Comyn sounded rigid. 'You agreed, Sire. We all agreed.'

'No, you agreed. This was your plan, not mine.'

'Did I have any choice?' demanded Comyn, anger roughening his voice. 'When you let King Edward bully and manipulate you? When you allowed him to remain as overlord of Scotland, despite the agreements sealed? He judged you to forfeit three towns in that mockery of a trial he conducted last year. When did we give such liberties to a foreign king?'

'Perhaps you should have asked him that yourself when you were in London marrying your son to the daughter of one of his allies.'

Comyn didn't back down at the cutting accusation. 'I have a duty to choose a worthy bride for my heir. Just as you have duties as our king. You were supposed to preserve our rights. Instead, you surrendered them to Edward.'

'There has to be another way. Twelve men to rule in place of one?'

'They are not to replace you, merely to advise you.' Comyn's face tightened. 'The men of the realm have come here tonight for this purpose. Four earls, four bishops, four barons. You cannot refuse us.'

'And if I do? What then, brother?' In the fading red light, Balliol's face was tortured. 'Will you have me killed as you did my predecessor's granddaughter?'

Comyn looked around as Balliol's words echoed in the evening. 'Beware, my lord,' he murmured. 'I was not the only man in that conspiracy.' His voice changed, becoming softer. 'In the days that must come you cannot be our sole voice.' As the king looked away, Comyn stepped in front of him.

'You will still be king, John, but you must be guided by the council. Let them deal with King Edward. When Scotland's safety is assured, it may be that such guidance is no longer necessary.'

'When will that be?' Balliol knew he had lost; his own voice, tired and feeble, told him so.

Comyn planted his hands on the stone wall and looked out over the marshy plains that stretched from the castle rock, around which the royal burgh of Stirling clustered. 'It will depend on Edward's move, when he finds out we have made an alliance of swords with his enemy. He may back down then and return our liberties to us. The wars in Wales and Gascony will have cost him dearly. Another campaign would be the last thing he would want.'

'And if he doesn't back down?'

Comyn was silent for a while, but his tone when he spoke was resolute. 'Then it will be longer.'

'Will King Philippe support us militarily?'

'I believe so, based on our initial discussions.'

The king watched the rays of sun disappear behind the mountains. When the light had gone, Balliol turned to his brother-in-law. 'Come then, and let this be done with.'

The day was drawing to a close as Robert and Edward, accompanied by their retinue, made their way across the border. Having been granted the king's permission to leave Westminster it had taken Robert longer than anticipated to set his affairs in order and after almost a fortnight on the road this, the last stretch of their journey, had felt the longest. For some hours now, after skirting the walled city of Carlisle, England's last town, he had ridden in restless silence, fixed on his destination, tauntingly close beyond the lonely marshes of the Solway Firth.

To Robert it felt strange returning to his homeland after so many months away, not least because it didn't seem to have changed at all, yet he felt as though he were coming home a different person, in body and mind. He had left a youth of nineteen, but returned a man of twenty-one, blooded in war. He was in the king's favour and had made influential friends in England. Mingled with this sense of homecoming was a desire to speak to his grandfather about all that had happened in the two years he had been away. He had already decided to confide in the old man about his induction into the Knights of the Dragon and his allegiance to King Edward, certain his grandfather would tell him whether the decisions made had been the right ones.

Through these thoughts, Robert felt his nerves rising at the prospect of the marriage that had summoned him home. This would constitute another change, one he hoped he was ready for. Eva was beautiful, certainly, but would she be a good wife? A suitable mother for his children? The thought made him feel more discomforted and he pushed it out of his mind as they followed the familiar road that circled the gentle hills of Annandale, towards Lochmaben.

In the rosy evening, they reached the outskirts of the town. At the sight of the blunt stone keep rising from the motte, Robert felt his heart leap. He turned to grin at his brother and saw the same excitement reflected there. Pressing their weary horses into a trot, they and their squires headed through the town, towards the gates in the castle's palisade. Smoke was rising from chimneys beyond. Robert wondered if any of his brothers or sisters would be here. The closer he had come to Scotland he had found himself thinking of Niall's joyous laughter and Thomas's sturdy silence, Christian's shy sweetness, Mary's wildness, even Alexander's bookishness. He had missed them all, but none more so than his grandfather.

Robert didn't recognise the dour-faced men on the gates, but the guards let them in at once when he gave his name. The bailey beyond was quiet, a few torches flickering in the balmy air. Robert dismounted and handed the reins of his horse to Nes, wondering why no one had come out come to greet them.

'Perhaps Grandfather isn't here?' said Edward, staring around the deserted yard.

Robert's gaze moved to the motte that rose above the bailey. The keep stood solid against the sky. 'No banner,' he murmured.

'What?'

'Grandfather's banner isn't raised on the keep. You're right. He can't be here.' Robert felt disappointment slump through him. On receiving his grandfather's letter in Westminster he had sent one of his squires on ahead to inform the old man that they would be returning home within the month. He now wondered if something had delayed the squire and his message, for surely his grandfather wouldn't have left knowing they were due to arrive? Robert turned, hearing a door open in one of the buildings. As a young woman came out carrying a bucket, he hailed her. 'Where is the Lord of Annandale?'

The maid halted, looking at the group of weary men. 'Is he expecting you, sir?'

'No, but he'll see me.'

The maid clutched the bucket nervously. 'He told us no more visitors, sir.'

Robert felt his irritation rise. He was exhausted from the long journey and impatient to see his grandfather. The hush of the courtyard and the unfamiliarity of the staff were disconcerting. Had something happened in his absence? 'I am Sir Robert Bruce, the Earl of Carrick. His grandson,' he told the woman. 'As I said, he will see me.'

Her eyes widened, but if anything she looked even more hesitant. 'Sir . . .' she began.

'Just tell me where the lord is.'

'He is dead.'

At the cold voice, which slid like a knife through him, Robert jerked round.

Standing in the doorway of the main lodging was his father. His broad frame, swathed in a black, fur-trimmed cloak, filled the opening. His hard face was older, marked with deep lines of age and resentment. His hair was coarse and streaked with grey. As the shock of him wore off the words his father had uttered filled Robert's mind. 'Dead?' he murmured, the word slipping between his lips.

'Your grandfather died in March. I returned from Norway to take over the estates.' The Bruce's glacial blue eyes flicked from Robert to Edward, then to their attendants and horses. His gaze lingered on Hunter, his brow knotting.

Robert felt the pain of his father's indifference only dimly, a mere pin-prick in the midst of the agony he felt for his grandfather's death. His mind conjured that creased, leonine face, that silver mane of hair, those hawk-like eyes. Beside him, he faintly heard Edward greeting their father, his voice hoarse. Robert couldn't speak. The words dammed in his throat. Clogged with sorrow, they turned into swollen, incoherent sounds. He could feel them struggling to break free. With effort, he managed to mumble, 'I need to wash.' Then turned to leave, determined not to show his grief in front of his father. He would not bear the salt of his disdain rubbed into this opening wound.

'There will be time for that later,' said his father sharply. 'First, there is someone for you to meet. When I received word of your return I sent a message to Earl Donald. He arrived last week to finalise the arrangements that were made with your grandfather. The marriage will go ahead as soon as possible now you are here.'

The Bruce turned to the main building and Robert saw another figure lingering in the doorway. As his father beckoned, she stepped out into the torchlight, which bruised her thin features. She was gangly in a plain green gown, her arms wrapping nervously around her as she approached. Her mouse-brown hair had been plaited and fixed tightly to her head with pins, making her face look even more pinched and hungry. It wasn't Eva. It was her younger sister. Robert couldn't remember her name. He stared numbly at her.

'This is Isobel,' said his father. 'Your bride.'

PART 4

1296 AD

. . . the Britons, by merit of their faith, should again recover the island, when the time decreed for it was come. But this would not be accomplished before they should be possessed of his reliques . . .

The History of the Kings of Britain, *Geoffrey of Monmouth*

37

Black skies filled with storm and the beating of war drums ushered in the autumn of 1295. Doom-laden omens abounded, from a child born with two heads to a fisherman who claimed to have seen the ghost of King Alexander haunting the cliffs near Kinghorn, his spectral hand raised towards Edinburgh.

In towns and villages across Scotland word spread quickly that John Balliol had been replaced by the new Council of Twelve. Men conversed in worried tones, wondering what would happen. A few were pleased by the change, blaming the king's weakness for the loss of Scotland's liberties at King Edward's hands and believing the establishment of the council would restore their rights. Many more were troubled, in light of Edward's bloody conquest of Wales. As rumours flew, saying the twelve had sent a delegation to the King of France seeking a pact of strength with England's enemy, all awaited the approach of the new year with bated breath.

Robert, whose return to Scotland had been greeted by the toll of a wedding bell, had been preoccupied through these portentous days, mourning the loss of his grandfather and coming to terms with the arrival of his father. But even he hadn't failed to hear the growing beat of conflict. The feast of All Souls came with gales that battered the east coast and caused a new wall of St Andrews Cathedral to collapse, killing five masons. The day after word went up that the Scottish delegation had sealed an alliance of swords with King Philippe against Edward. War, men said, must surely come soon. Robert, whose young wife had fallen pregnant, had expected the English king to come to some agreement with the Council of Twelve. He knew how much the victory in Wales had cost Edward and doubted the king or his barons had the stomach for another conflict, especially when English soldiers remained entrenched in Gascony. Edward's response had surprised him.

On learning of the alliance the king demanded the surrender of three castles in Scotland and banned any Frenchman from entering Scottish territory. Where Balliol would have crumbled the council stood firm and, led by the Comyns, denied the surrender of the castles. In retaliation, Edward confiscated the English lands and property of these men, and ordered his sheriffs to arrest any Scot found in his realm. These, it was soon clear, were final acts before the inevitable. Rising through the bottleneck of the negotiations, the tension could only erupt.

Before the Christ Mass orders arrived at Lochmaben bearing the seal of King John, but witnessed by John Comyn on behalf of the twelve. The message demanded that the Lord of Annandale and his son be ready for a weapons' inspection in the new year. It was a stark choice: either fight for a king they hated and lose their English estates, or betray their kingdom and lose their Scottish lands. Robert had felt torn in two, his Scottish heritage and his oath to the Knights of the Dragon and King Edward pulling him in opposite directions. For his father, however, the choice seemed clear. He had been scathing, telling the king's messengers that he would rather lose his lands and his life than lift his sword for the pretender on the throne. Robert, disturbed by his father's rebelliousness, hadn't known that the lord had already been in contact with his ally of old, King Edward. Soon after, the Bruce led his family and his men out of Annandale. Bearing as much as they could carry, Robert's wife Isobel now five months into her term, they had made their way across the border to Carlisle, where his father was made governor of the city, in the name of the English king.

Scattered reports had come to them in the weeks that followed, but none so clear as a message from King John himself telling Robert and his father that their lands of Carrick and Annandale were forfeit and had been placed in the custody of John Comyn's cousin, the Earl of Buchan, head of the Black Comyns. The Bruces weren't the only Scottish nobles to face such losses. Their old comrade and member of the alliance at Turnberry, Earl Patrick of Dunbar, also declined to fight for Balliol as did the Earl of Angus and both, in choosing to remain loyal to Edward, were summarily disinherited. But this didn't make the loss of Robert's lands in Carrick, the place of his birth and the right of which had been bestowed upon him by his grandfather, any less unbearable.

As the snows of February receded and the ice on the ground turned to slush in the March rains, carts of grain and beer began to move north through England, shadowed along the coast by ships loaded with stones and timber for siege engines. They were followed by companies of knights and squadrons of infantry, all marching to converge on Newcastle, the staging ground for the campaign.

War was upon them.

Robert rode through the dark streets of Carlisle, Hunter's hooves skidding in the wet. In the distance, the castle squatted on its low hill, its red walls bloody in the light of torches. Clouds raced across a bloated, yellow moon, the spectral glow of which filled the puddles on the ground. Across the city, a bell continued to clang.

With Robert rode his brother Edward, knighted at the beginning of the year in a hasty ceremony. They were joined by two knights from Carrick and two of their father's vassals. Fires burned, illuminating huddled groups beneath the overhangs of buildings, where water dripped steadily. The faces of men and women showed fear and uncertainty, the children sleepy confusion. Many had handcarts piled with sacks and blankets, tools, pots and the odd silver plate or candlestick, not a necessity perhaps, but something they couldn't bear to be parted from in their race to the protection of the city's stone walls. Inns, churches and stables were crammed with these refugees from the outlying areas, the last people in forced to sleep in the streets.

'Make way!' shouted Edward, as they cantered down the fire lit thoroughfare towards the market cross, 'Make way for the Earl of Carrick! Make way for the governor's men!'

At the market, teeming with penned livestock, they turned on to the street that led to the north-eastern walls, where a gate-tower loomed over the road to Scotland. The bell was louder now, its disjointed clanging coming from the tower ahead. As they approached, Robert saw men offloading baskets of arrows and sacks of sand from a wagon. Bringing Hunter to a stop, he dismounted, leaving the horse with his knights. The square tower straddled a passageway between two arched openings. The gates at the end of the passage were closed and more men were there, hammering timbers across the wood. The bangs echoed in the confined space as Robert entered, followed by his brother. They hastened past a frenetic guardroom on the ground level, then up uneven steps to the second storey, where an opening led out on to the city walls.

Three men were on the walkway, their clothes whipping in the wind. They turned as Robert and Edward emerged. Smoke swirled from a torch that lit their troubled faces.

'Thank Christ,' greeted one, the captain, going to Robert. He wore mail beneath his cloak and had a helm under one arm. His broad English sounded much like that of the men of Annandale, which lay less than ten miles away, beyond the crumbling Roman wall and the treacherous mud-flats of the Solway Firth. The captain had to raise his voice over the monotonous chime of the bell. 'I was about to send one of my men to the castle.'

'We heard the alarm from the English Gate,' said Robert. 'What is it?'

'Tom here saw it first,' said the captain, nodding to one of his guards, whose face beneath the rim of his kettle hat was grim.

Tom pointed through an arrow slit. 'Out there, sir. See for yourself.'

Robert crossed the walkway and stood beside the man to peer out. He could smell boiled meat on the guard's breath. Far below, the moat that encircled the city reflected the torchlight on the walls. Beyond, the land disappeared into murk. Robert discerned the ghostly River Eden and the outlines of distant hills, but little else. 'I can't see anything.'

'Over north aways,' insisted the guard, frowning up at the scurrying clouds obscuring the moon.

Robert felt grit from the wall prickling his eyes as he stared north. Above him, the bell continued its hollow clanging. For a long moment he saw nothing, then the moon sailed into view. As its sallow light bled across the land, Robert picked out what appeared to be a long, narrow river glinting in the distance, except he knew there was no river where his eyes were fixed. It wasn't moonlight shining on water, but on metal: spear tips and helms, shields and mail. Robert felt a spasm in his gut. The small part of him that all through the troubled autumn and winter, and even into the turbulence of these past months, had hoped that this could yet be resolved died with the sight of the advancing army. 'Come,' he said tightly to Edward. 'We must tell Father.'

'What are the governor's orders?' the English captain called after him.

'You'll be told with the rest of us,' responded Robert, hastening along the walkway.

'This cannot be happening,' said Edward, catching Robert's arm as they exited the tower and headed for their horses. 'Earl Donald? And Atholl?'

'You've just seen the truth of it for yourself,' Robert said flatly.

'Your father-in-law is coming to raze this city to the ground.' Edward flung his hand towards the castle, a red block in the distance. 'His daughter is carrying your child! How did it come to this?'

'You know how. The Comyns.'

'These men aren't just our countrymen. They are kin. We should be fighting alongside them!'

Robert met his brother's gaze. He knew how Edward felt; that sensation

of being pulled apart. But they had made their decision on the eve of this
war, unbearable though it had been, and now they must face it head-on.
'You've heard the same reports as me,' he told his brother harshly. 'Those
men out there, my father-in-law and John of Atholl included, have burned
our lands to ash. They aren't comrades and kin any more. They are enemies.
Would you stand with them now?'

Edward didn't answer. He turned his eyes skyward, where clouds raced
through the dark. 'Our grandfather wouldn't have let this come to pass. He
would have found another way. A way that didn't mean we had to betray
our country.'

'Our grandfather is dead. And we've made a pledge to defend this city.'
Pushing past his brother, Robert strode to his father's knights, waiting with
the horses.

Edward shouted after him, but as Robert mounted he could only follow.

As they rode, more bells joined the toll from the north-east tower. The
cacophony echoed through the city, causing citizens to throw open shutters and stumble sleep-dazed and frightened from doorways. A few people
hailed the six knights as they cantered down Castle Street, but none of them
answered the worried calls. Riding swiftly, they made for the bridge across
the city ditch, which led through orchards to a second crossing over a moat
below the castle's walls.

After passing through two heavily manned gatehouses, where guard
captains were shouting orders, the brothers entered the inner bailey,
which was crammed with men. Some wore the red chevron of Carrick
on their surcoats and gambesons, and were under Robert's command,
but most wore the colours of their father. There was no sign of the blue
lion, the ancient symbol of the lordship of Annandale favoured by their
grandfather. These knights all wore the device preferred by their new
lord: a red cross, banded at the top and set against a yellow background.
Some were hauling sacks of grain off carts into the stores. More were
handing out weapons. Robert dismounted in the chaos. He guessed his
father must be aware of the danger now, but he still needed to be given
his own orders.

After questioning one of the knights, who told him the governor was with
his commanders in the castle's hall, Robert was making his way through the
mass of men when he saw a young woman struggling through the press
towards him. It was his wife's maid, Katherine. Her face was agitated, a high
flush of colour on her cheeks.

'Sir Robert!' Her voice carried over the rough din of the soldiers.

Robert went to her, filling with concern. 'Is something wrong? Where is Isobel?' He looked past Katherine up to the window of the room he had moved his wife to last week, when scouts had seen the smoke across the border. Torchlight glared behind the drapes.

'She's in her labour, sir. She begged me to find you.'

'The child isn't due for another month, at least.'

'The midwife thinks her fretting about her father caused it to come early.'

'Brother,' said Edward, moving up behind him.

Robert turned distractedly as his brother nodded to the doors of the hall, out of which had come their father with three commanders.

The Lord of Annandale, imperious in a gleaming coat of mail given to him by his new son-in-law, the King of Norway, stood on the steps of the hall, looking down on the crowded bailey. His surcoat, partitioned in red and yellow with the cross over his heart, was pulled in tight at his thick waist by a belt, from which hung a broadsword. He began to speak, his voice sounding over the soldiers below, who quietened to listen, the men who had been emptying the supply wagon setting down their sacks of grain.

'All of us here have paid a high price for our honour. I, more than most, am aware of the great sacrifice made in the service of loyalty these past months.'

Robert felt his chest tighten at his father's words. *Great sacrifice?* he thought bitterly. His father still owned his rich lands in Essex and Yorkshire through his continued loyalty to King Edward. He himself had been left with nothing.

'My scouts inform me that the Comyns' host has laid waste to my lands. All of us here have lost things dear to us. All of us here have reason to hate the men who now come for us in the dark, like the cowardly sons of whores they are!'

Some of the soldiers in the yard shouted in vehement agreement.

'Annandale is burning and the Black Comyns and their kin will build upon the ashes. If we let them. But I say we defy them! I say we stand against these seven earls and their false king! I say we show them what the men of Annandale and Carrick, and Carlisle are made of!'

The men roared their approval, the din reverberating around the bailey.

'King Edward waits to our east in Newcastle with the English host. We are the bait and while the bastards dangle on our hook, he will attack where they have left themselves vulnerable. Stand with me and you will see your homes returned to you. Stand with me and you will be rewarded!' The Lord of Annandale drew his sword and raised it.

The soldiers unsheathed their own blades and began to beat the flats of them against their shields.

Robert turned to Katherine. The maid had pressed her hands over her ears. 'See that my wife has everything she needs,' he shouted, as the clattering of swords beat the air. 'I will come when I can.'

38

O ver Carlisle, the last city in England, dawn was breaking. A veil of smoke hung in the air above the hordes beyond the walls. In the cold light, fire pits flamed, from which foot soldiers lit torches that were carried across the moat to the north-east gate where a mass of men held shields above their heads to form a screen. It was under this protective canopy that the foot soldiers bore these flaming brands. More men followed, carrying bundles of hay.

On the walls, defenders crowded the narrow walkway, wary of the arrows darting up from the banks of the moat. To them, the upturned shields were a confusion of colour, shifting like an uneasy sea with the tide of men beneath. Their faces pressed to arrow loops, the men of Carlisle watched as the soldiers with the torches continued to disappear beneath. Smoke filtered through the gaps between the shields, all the way up to the gates at the foot of the tower.

Robert was shouting orders, his voice hoarse and the siege barely begun. What started as a steady deployment of his troops along the walkway had descended into chaos, the enemy's horns blaring and arrows flying up to clatter against the walls or arc into the streets below. His father had posted him in command of the north-east gate with his brother and soldiers of Carrick. Bolstered by men from Carlisle, they formed a company of twenty-five knights, with more than twice as many squires and foot soldiers. Having been in charge of only a small number of men in Wales, Robert swiftly discovered how hard it was to remain in control of a large division. It was harder still since the men of Carrick had been his father's liegemen for so long. He had spent only a few months in his earldom before leaving for England and many remembered him more as a boy in Turnberry than their lord. As Robert had gathered these scarred veterans in the dawn, he felt they listened to his orders out of duty, rather than respect. There had been no time to dwell on this, however, with the enemy advancing, the fields filling with their mass.

Robert had watched their approach in silence, his eyes on the banners of Mar, Ross, Lennox, Strathearn, Atholl and Menteith that followed behind a black standard bearing three white sheaves of wheat, the arms of the Black Comyn, who had taken his family's lands. Menteith, once their ally, had been succeeded by his red-haired son. Robert remembered Menteith's son from the gathering in Turnberry, sitting opposite him at his father's table. Who would have thought he would be facing him across the walls of an English city, or the fiery Earl John of Atholl – his own brother-in-law? Of them all, though, it was the banner of Mar that was the hardest for Robert to behold. Earl Donald had been one of his grandfather's closest comrades and it was the earl's sword that dubbed him on the day of his knighthood. He was wed to Mar's daughter and his sister, Christian, was married to the earl's son and heir. It seemed inconceivable that this elderly man, whom he'd always thought of with great fondness, was now seeking his destruction. But the truth of it was there in that standard, lit by the glare of the fires. His grandfather would be twisting in his grave.

As the enemy spread out, marching to other gates around the city, Robert had been confronted by around seven hundred men, under the banners of Buchan, Mar and Ross. Within those ranks was spied the arms of the Red Comyns, borne by the Lord of Badenoch's son, so recently wed to Aymer de Valence's sister. John the Younger, who survived the war in Gascony, had deserted King Edward to fight with his father against England. Despite the torment of seeing so many countrymen arrayed against him, it had seemed to Robert that the Scottish host would be able to do little, for they had no siege engines with which to batter the walls. Then, the soldiers had come with their shield screen and fire, and the calm of his troops had turned to alarm.

The smoke was thickest in front of the gates, where the soldiers had set light to the bundles of hay they had carried across the bridge. Yelling for his archers to keep shooting, Robert watched as the arrows stabbed down, cursing as most of them stuck uselessly in the shields, which already bristled with spent missiles. He saw one shield buckle as the man holding it was caught in the shoulder, but the gap he made was quickly tightened by those around him. Robert swallowed thickly as smoke scratched his throat. Water was sloshing down from the tower top, as he'd ordered, but much of the liquid simply sprayed off the tops of the shields. They needed to smash through that screen if they were to get at the men and the fire they were starting beneath.

Amidst the turmoil, Robert scanned the streets below. He saw his brother by a cart, overseeing the unloading of the sacks of sand he had hoped would help put out the blaze. Edward was grim-faced and drenched in sweat, but his reservations seemed to have vanished in the chaos of the siege and he had thrown himself into the defence of Carlisle with as much vigour as any man in the city garrison. It was hard to feel compunction towards men who were trying to kill you. Robert's gaze moved on, over the lines of women bringing water to the men and the priests who had come at dawn with Bibles and prayers. His eyes stopped, caught by a pile of rubble heaped against the wall adjacent to the tower. When they feared the Scottish host would be coming for them his father had ordered repairs on the defences, with particular attention paid to areas near the gates. Old crumbling masonry had been hacked away by the city's labourers and patched in with new stone and mortar.

'With me,' Robert shouted, calling several knights to follow as he hastened from the walls. Out in the street, he sprinted to the cart where his brother was. Grabbing one of the sacks, he dragged it off. 'We need to empty these,' he told his knights, flipping the bag over with a rush of sand. 'Fill them with stones.'

'Brother?' Edward shouted after him in confusion.

But Robert had raced to the pile of masonry and was tossing the crumbled blocks inside the sack. He kept shouting orders as the knights crowded in around him. Sweat dripped from his nose as he worked, his mail weighing on his limbs. He was used to a horse taking the burden and his broadsword was awkward at his side. Straightening, he searched for Nes, somewhere on the crowded walls above. Unable to see him, Robert looked around, his gaze alighting on a lanky youth with fair hair, clambering in over the rubble to help. The squire was the son of a Yorkshire knight, one of his father's vassals. 'Christopher, isn't it?' Robert called, unbuckling his sword belt.

'Yes, sir,' answered the fair-haired youth, scrabbling over, 'Christopher Seton.'

'Hold this for me.'

Christopher took the broadsword as Robert handed it to him.

'What do you plan to do with this, sir?' asked one of the knights, breathing hard as he lobbed great handfuls of stone into the sack another was holding open.

'We're going to empty it on the bastards.' Taking an arrow basket one
of the Carlisle men had carried over, Robert continued heaping masonry
inside. Edward, seeing the plan, had pitched in to help, calling more men
to carry the sacks and baskets of rubble up on to the walls. Christopher
stood close by, grasping Robert's sword. When the basket was filled,
Robert strained to lift it, but it was too heavy for one and the others
were already loaded down. Cursing, he went to remove some of the
rocks, when a pair of hands appeared and took hold of the other side.
He glanced up to grunt his thanks and saw a woman. She was short and
stocky, the sleeves of her dress rolled to the elbow. Robert was about to
tell her to fetch a man, when he saw the determination in her face and
realised she was more than capable. Other women and girls who had
been fetching water were joining them, helping stack the stones inside
baskets. Some were even piling them into their skirts. It was an odd
sight, these women in wool, moving among the armoured knights. As
the matron hefted her side of the basket, Robert lifted his and between
them they carried the load into the tower. Christopher followed, bearing
Robert's blade.

On the battlements, Robert ordered the sacks split up across the walls
to either side of the tower and on the tower top itself. The smoke was
dense and choking now, although the water being tossed over the side was
hampering the efforts of the soldiers below. Robert shouted for the archers to hold, but to stay ready, then, telling Edward to relay his plan along
the walls, he headed swiftly to the top of the tower. Here, he had a dizzying
view across the walls to the Scots beyond the moat, who were sending in
more men with hay and other combustibles to burn down the gates. Robert
could see behind him too, out over the city. Somewhere in the streets near
the castle a huge fire was raging, a dark tower of smoke billowing into the
sky. He wondered if the enemy had punched their way through somewhere,
but had no time to worry.

As Robert yelled the order, the knights and townsmen hefted up baskets
and sacks of stone, balancing them on knees or against the parapet. When
they were ready, he threw back his head and roared. Together, the men
emptied the rubble over the walls. Women were among them, flinging
rocks with their bare hands. Christopher Seton, who had fastened Robert's
broadsword around his waist, moved to help as Robert grasped one of the
sacks. Between them they lifted it on to the parapet. Catching Robert's eye,
the English squire nodded and together they dumped it over.

Below, horns sounded. Too late. Before the men beneath the shields

knew what was happening, the sky was falling in on them in a thundering rain of rubble, timbers and grit. Men cried out, their shields buckling.
Some soldiers, those hit by the heavier pieces, collapsed, more just stumbled with the shock of it, but it was the opening Robert needed and, with
his second command, the archers slipped in between the knights and began
shooting into the confusion, their arrows striking exposed shoulders, necks
and backs. The men were foot soldiers and few wore armour. Some arrows
snagged in gambesons, but many more found openings into flesh. Screams
of pain and panic erupted. The men near the front, who had been working
at fanning the smouldering piles of hay, were toppled by falling comrades
into the burning stacks, sending up smoke and embers. Burned or choking,
they scrabbled back, causing alarm to spread through the ranks and creating
more openings for the archers. Men fell, dropping into the path of others,
who stumbled over them only to be shot themselves. Horns bellowed from
the Scottish host, the commanders across the moat shouting for their own
archers to retaliate.

As missiles flew up, cries rose along the city walls. The woman who had
helped Robert carry up the basket of rubble caught one in the face and went
spinning from the walkway. She crashed on to a wagon in the street below,
startling the horses. They bolted, the wagon veering off. Christopher was
hauling another sack on to the wall as a hail of arrows shot towards the tower
top. Robert, seeing them coming, yelled a warning. Grabbing the squire,
he pulled him down. Christopher dropped the sack as he was forced below
the wall, sending lumps of rock skittering away. A soldier from Carlisle,
standing next to them, wasn't so fortunate. He got an arrow in the throat
and collapsed, choking and writhing. Christopher, hunkered down beside
Robert, stared at the dying man, his chest heaving.

Despite these losses, the archers of Carlisle kept firing and Robert's men
continued to sling rocks down, and soon the confusion below turned into
a rout as the enemy soldiers fell back across the moat. As they ran they
exposed the piles of smouldering straw heaped against the gates and now
Robert was yelling again for water. The burning piles hissed as the buckets
were emptied on top of them. In among the piles of masonry, the mud was
strewn with arrows, shields and bodies. Some of the wounded were dragging themselves towards the bridge. Others moved in to help, but were
repelled by arrows, which the defenders continued to shoot over the walls.
As the horns blew, the last of the infantry retreated, leaving the dead and
dying behind them. On the walls, the morning glowed golden in the sweat-
soaked faces of the triumphant defenders.

39

It was midday when the Scots at the north-east gate pulled back. They made three more attempts to get through to the gates and finish the fire they had started, but, the ground thick with corpses and rubble, they couldn't make the same steady advance they had made the first time. The heaps of sodden straw were stubborn against the torch flames and the defenders ever more determined after their success. Finally, the infantry were withdrawn with heavy losses and the host retreated into the fields, the cheers of the people of Carlisle following them. The host remained there for several hours, men tending to wounded comrades as more companies joined them from around the city.

Robert and his forces rested warily, sharing wine and warm loaves of bread, brought by townsfolk. The priests helped the wounded, administering the last rites where necessary. Bodies of men and women were laid out, as reports filtered in slowly from other parts of the city. The gates and walls had held, the Scots unable to break through. The large fire near the castle, which had engulfed several buildings including a vintner's, was still burning fiercely. It had been started by a Comyn spy, who had apparently come into the city with the flood of refugees and had been hiding out, waiting for the attack. He had been captured by knights of Annandale and hanged from the castle walls.

At last, the Scottish host moved out, defeated by their lack of siege engines and the city's staunch defence. After an hour, they had become a haze in the distance, crows circling over their slow-moving lines, eager for the worms disturbed by their trudging feet.

Robert sat on the edge of the walkway. Draining the last of the wine from his skin, he closed his eyes against the afternoon sun. His throat burned from the smoke and dust in the air, and he had a cut on the side of his head that hadn't stopped bleeding. He couldn't remember getting it. The others were celebrating around him, their voices sharp with relief, but he couldn't muster the will to join them. Today was only the first battle. Carlisle was now an island in a sea of enemy soldiers. North, south: neither was safe. His father was confident King Edward would win this war and return their lands to them, but the thought of that victory made Robert uneasy. Several days earlier he had overheard his father saying to one of his knights that the king planned to depose the treacherous Balliol. The lord had spoken, in a tone of keen expectation, of the throne that would need to be filled, not once mentioning Robert – the one to whom that right had been passed.

'Sir.'

Robert glanced round as Christopher Seton crouched beside him. The fair-haired squire, whose face was smudged with grime, held out Robert's broadsword, which he had kept during the siege. 'Here, sir.'

As Robert took the blade an image came vividly to mind of his grand-father watching while the Earl of Mar girded him with it the day he was knighted. Pride had gleamed in the old lord's black eyes. The memory filled Robert with a profound sense of loss, not just for the man himself, but for a time when things had been clear and his own path certain. Now, everywhere he turned, the way seemed shadowed and obscure. He felt his brother had spoken true that morning in saying their grandfather would not have fought against Scotland, but what the old man would have done if faced with this dire predicament seemed impossible to guess at.

'I wanted to thank you, Sir Robert,' said Christopher, in his blunt, north-ern English dialect. 'If you hadn't pulled me down I . . .' The squire frowned at his hands, bruised and bleeding from heaving the sacks over the walls. 'I owe you my life,' he finished.

As Robert went to dismiss this, not wanting the burden of the young man's earnest pledge, he heard his brother shout his name. Scanning the street below, he saw Edward. With him was Katherine. At the sight of the maid, Robert stood. Concern for his wife had been kept at bay through the turmoil of the siege, now it flooded him. Leaving Christopher on the walkway, he hastened down through the tower. 'How is she?' he called, going straight to Katherine. 'How is my wife? Has the baby come?'

Katherine was breathing hard, but she managed to answer. 'A girl, Sir Robert. Lady Isobel had a girl.'

A smile broke across Robert's face at the words and he laughed, joy mixing headily with exhaustion. Edward was grinning too. But Katherine's flushed face remained tight. She was shaking her head at his laughter, her eyes fearful. Robert's mirth drained. 'What is it?'

'You need to go to her, sir.'

Robert stared at her grave face, then turned to his brother.

'Go,' Edward told him. 'I'll man the gates.'

Needing no further encouragement, Robert raced to where Hunter was tethered. Mounting, he galloped away, heading for the castle on the hill, its walls red in the afternoon sun.

Up through the streets he cantered, past groups of people cheering, past a slow-moving cart piled with the dead, past lines of men tossing water into the burning buildings near the castle. The flames that had engulfed the vintner's were curling into the black sky.

The castle courtyard was relatively quiet, most of the men still down on the walls. Slinging his leg over the saddle, Robert jumped down, shouting at a passing foot soldier to take his horse. He jogged up the steps and into the gloomy interior of the keep, his armour feeling like lead. As he pounded the stairs to the rooms he and his wife had been given, he could hear a wailing cry.

Robert entered the chamber, struck by heat and a rank smell of blood. On the bed, surrounded by stained sheets, lay Isobel. A priest was crouched beside her, his cross in his hand. By the window the midwife clutched a bundle of cloth. It was the bundle that was making the cries. Robert went to his wife, throwing a hostile look at the priest, who rose and stepped back.

Isobel's face was greasy. Sweat glistened in the hollow of her throat and between the bones of her chest. She had stayed thin through the pregnancy, only her stomach swelling. There was a wad of cloth balled between her legs, red at the centre, the stain spreading. Blood had covered her shift and her palms were sticky with it. Kneeling stiffly in his armour, Robert tugged off his mail gloves and took one of her bloody hands in his.

Isobel's eyes fluttered open. The pupils drifted back and forth, before her gaze found his. She groaned his name.

'I'm here,' he murmured.

'My father?' Her eyes drifted, then came back to him.

'They've gone,' he said, touching her brow, which burned against his palm. 'It is over.'

She licked the sweat from her lips. When she spoke again, her words were little more than breath. 'I know you wanted my sister.'

Robert felt this as a blow. He shook his head to deny it, but she continued.

'It doesn't matter. You were a kind husband.' As Robert kissed her palm, Isobel's eyes narrowed, tears leaking from them.

Her breathing was shallow now. The red stain had covered most of the white cloth. Robert felt her fingers slacken in his. As the priest moved in, his murmuring prayers filling the silence, Robert bowed over the bed, his forehead touching his wife's chest.

After a long moment, he pushed himself up weakly and went to the midwife. As he held out his arms, she silently handed his daughter to him. Robert cradled her tiny form close against the cold of his armour, her cries piercing the air. Standing in the window of the hot room, the sky outside bruised with smoke, a memory of his mother holding one of his sisters entered his mind. 'Marjorie,' Robert whispered. 'I'll name you Marjorie.'

40

A mile from the River Tweed, beyond the splintered remnants of Berwick's gates, the rotten wood of which had proved of no consequence to the English army, a group of labourers was waiting to begin a day's work. Below the town's earth ramparts was a narrow fosse, littered with shards from the shattered palisade above. Men lined the banks of this trench, grasping picks and leaning on shovels, coughing and sniffing in the damp air. They were eager to begin, to work the chill from their muscles, but first there was a ceremony to be observed.

Between their rows moved King Edward, his cloak stiff with gold brocade. Taller than most of the watching labourers, he towered over the squat figure of Hugh de Cressingham, who was struggling to match his stride. Gluttony had trebled the royal clerk's chins and his round face was as pale and shiny as melting tallow. The smell coming off him was like rancid meat and Edward lengthened his walk as the fat clerk waddled and puffed beside him. He had already decided that when he returned to England Cressingham would remain behind as his treasurer in Scotland. The man was an able official, but his presence was far from pleasing.

'Here, my lord,' panted Cressingham, ushering the king towards a barrow, placed just beyond the edge of the fosse. It was filled with a neat heap of dark soil. 'Here we are.'

The air felt wet in Edward's lungs and he marched quickly to the barrow, keen to return to his planning in the comfort of the castle, one of the few buildings left unscathed by the attack. Even now, smoke sharpened the air over the ruins of Berwick, the fires brightening the nights, visible for miles, until the April rains turned the blazes into columns of smoke that covered the town in choking clouds.

After the English host swept through the town's defences, the slaughter had continued for two days. It was only after more than seven thousand inhabitants had perished that Edward ordered his men to cease the killing. Just a handful of prisoners were taken after the town's capitulation, including the garrison's commander, a fierce bull of a man named Sir William Douglas, who had raged and ranted at the massacre of Berwick's citizens, damning Edward and his knights to hell even as he was dragged to the castle's dungeon. Mass graves had been dug for the dead, but the deep pits hadn't been enough to contain them. The rest had been carted down to the river and dumped. The surviving women and children had been allowed to leave with their lives. Nothing more. Lines of them had trailed through the broken gates, white-faced and silent. Watching from the castle battlements, Edward had felt little pity. The inhabitants of Berwick, who had taunted him and his knights from behind their rot-riddled palisade, had helped teach the rest of Scotland a valuable lesson. The Scots' resolve would be that much weaker now they knew the price of rebellion. He would beat them down that much quicker. And, more than anything, Edward wanted a swift end to this campaign.

After the war in Wales, he had returned to England to find the Scots in alliance against him with King Philippe. Edward sent William de Valence and his brother, Edmund of Lancaster, with a contingent of knights to reinforce his presence in Gascony, then issued a military summons to his vassals. Despite their misgivings over another war, the barons, knights and infantry heeded his call to arms and more than twenty thousand met him at Newcastle, including longbowmen from conquered Wales. While the Scottish host advanced on Carlisle, leaving the eastern approach to their kingdom wide open, Edward forded the Tweed at the village of Coldstream and moved north, reaching Berwick before Easter. He was followed along the coast by forty-four galleys that sailed up from East Anglia, carrying supplies and stones for the siege engines. As Edward's knights attacked the town's ramparts, the galleys moved into the estuary to strike from the water. Despite some losses, including three ships that ran aground and were set alight by Douglas's men, the English forced their way through.

Edward had few funds for this campaign, but what he lacked in coin he made up for in determination. In a way the Scots' rebellion, coming so close on the heels of the Welsh insurgency, had proved an advantage. His war machine was well oiled and ready to move, and the victory in Wales and the taking of the Crown of Arthur had won him the renewed support of his men. Edward had never expected to subdue Scotland by force, unlike Wales or Ireland. Since he first set his sights on the kingdom, he had always hoped for an open door through which to reach his target. The first door:

the marriage of his son to the infant Margaret had been slammed in his face with the girl's untimely death; the second: his mastery over King John, had been closed by the Comyns when he wasn't looking. Now, by sword and fire, he would break it down.

Beyond Berwick, in tantalising reach, lay the kingdom's beating heart. Edward just needed to stretch out his hand and grasp it. He had no doubt that once the Scots were beaten and the symbol of their sovereignty was in his possession all resistance would end, as it had in Wales. Then, his hopes for a Britain united beneath his rule would be one step away from fulfilment and he would set his clerics to work revealing the Last Prophecy to the rest of his subjects so that they would know the scale of his greatness. The Scots weren't the Welsh, hardened by decades of bitter fighting and struggle. One good push and this war would be over. Berwick was just the first foundation of Edward's new kingdom north of the border, a foundation that would now be laid for all to see.

Edward approached the barrow of earth, the labourers and the knights of his army watching. Eventually, the town's earthworks would be supplanted by stone walls and watchtowers; a bastion of imperial might to rival his fortresses in Wales. Until then, he had ordered the existing fosse to be enlarged to eighty feet wide and forty feet deep.

The handles of the barrow, Edward noticed, had been carefully brushed clean of soil. As he reached for them, he wondered whether the statement he had wanted to make would be rendered meaningless by the sterility of the demonstration, a mere sham visible to every man here. The thought caused him to falter. He had made the effort to leave his planning in the castle to make this spectacle. It should be worth while.

Glancing around, the king's gaze fixed on a labourer close by, leaning on a spade. He crossed to the man, leaving Cressingham calling uncertainly after him. The labourer straightened immediately and looked about worriedly, clearly wondering what he had done wrong. As Edward came towards him, the man lowered his head, his hands on the spade turning white with his grip. To the curious stares of the other workers, the king took the spade from the speechless man and stalked to the edge of the fosse. He thrust the tool into the wet soil, pushing it down through the loam, deep into the clay. The gold hem of his cloak trailed in the mud as he worked. Gripping the shaft, worn smooth by the labourer's hands, he dug up a clod of earth. Hefting the load, Edward headed back to the barrow and, under awe-filled stares, tossed it on top of the neat pile of mud placed inside by someone else. If today marked the establishment of his new northern territory then it seemed important that it was his hands, rather than any other's, that were the first marked with the soil of this labour. Pleased by the gesture, Edward returned to dig another square of earth from the fosse. The king was so engrossed in the task that he didn't see the group of riders approaching the town gates from the north road.

After three more spadefuls, his officials watching in astonishment, Edward wedged the spade into the soil and took up the handles of the barrow. Cressingham smiled and nodded encouragingly, pleased that the king was now doing what was expected. Edward wheeled the barrow past the lines of men and upended it in the arranged place, the smell of soil rising rich around him. The labourers applauded heartily.

Cressingham crossed to the king, puffing. 'Well, that should fire their limbs, my lord,' he said decidedly, as the labourers began picking up their own barrows and spades, and moving down into the fosse to hack at the soil.

'My lord king.'

Edward looked up at the forceful voice to see John de Warenne heading towards him through the crowds of workers. With Warenne was the Scottish earl, Patrick of Dunbar, who had aided him in the sack of Berwick. The earl wore a travel-stained cloak and his face, framed by oily, dark hair, was troubled. Behind them, Edward saw a band of riders, who had dismounted and were speaking with Anthony Bek. Brushing the dirt from his hands, he met the two earls, closely followed by Cressingham.

'My lord king,' greeted Patrick of Dunbar, bowing.

'You have word on the whereabouts of my enemies?' Edward's voice was sharp. He had been impatient for news ever since reports that the Scottish army had stormed across the border into Northumberland, burning and raiding. He relied on loyal vassals such as Earl Patrick of Dunbar and the Bruces in Carlisle, who knew the lands well, to be his eyes and ears, but with no word since the fall of Berwick, he'd been growing restless.

'The Scottish host crossed the border back into Scotland five days ago, my lord. They are now some thirty miles from here, barring your way north. They are camped out in my lands.' Earl Patrick's face was grim. 'I returned to my castle after taking my leave of you to find it surrounded. Dunbar has fallen into the hands of the Black Comyn and his men.'

'How?' Edward demanded, angered by the unwelcome tidings. He had chosen his route north partly because Dunbar, under his ally's control, offered safe haven in the midst of enemy territory: a place of strength to retreat to if necessary. 'You told me it was well defended.'

Sir Patrick didn't answer immediately. Emotions struggled in his face. 'My wife let them in, Sire.' His voice came out strained. 'She betrayed me.'

Edward held him in his stare for a long moment. 'And Balliol?'

'The king is with the main army.'

Edward was silent, thinking. Days after the fall of Berwick he had received a formal renouncement of homage from King John. The tone, defiant and determined, had been at stark odds with the weak man he knew. John Comyn, Edward guessed, had been the voice behind it. The Lord of Badenoch was shrewder than he'd estimated. The king had hoped the marriage of his son to William de Valence's daughter would placate the man. Clearly, Comyn needed a more definite demonstration of his power. They all did.

Edward switched his attention to John de Warenne. 'I want you to lead a company north to deal with these churls. Capture the castle and the brigands that hold it. I do not want anything to stand in my way north. Take the young bloods with you,' he added, glancing over at Humphrey de Bohun and the Knights of the Dragon.

'Yes, my lord.'

Edward moved to head off, then paused, his eyes flicking back to Earl Patrick. 'You should have kept your wife on a shorter leash, Dunbar.'

41

Sir John de Warenne left his tent and headed into the fog, pulling his mantle around his shoulders and sniffing vigorously. Almost May and the early mornings were still wintry. He hated the bleakness of this north-eastern coastline, with its bitter sea and rust-coloured cliffs. In truth, he despised all of Scotland. No proper roads, dense tracts of forest and scarred mountains to bar the way, the snows in winter, the humid air that swarmed with biting insects in the summer. He longed to be back in the mild woodlands of his English estates. Soon, the hunting season would begin. God willing, the war would be over before then.

Ahead, between rows of tents, outlines of men moved in the fog. Warenne and his knights had arrived in Dunbar the day before, scouts having informed the earl that although the castle was occupied by a company of enemy soldiers, the Scottish army was nowhere to be seen. Entering the deserted town, Warenne's men had made camp a safe distance from the castle, which was perched precariously on a rocky cliff overlooking a harbour.

Stepping over guy ropes, the earl strode past horses being given their morning feed by grooms. Campfires stirred smoke into the gloom, the sour smell of burning wood mixing with sweeter, richer odours of oats and herbs. The cooks had been up for an hour already. In front of Warenne four angular structures loomed in the soupy air. He approached, pleased to see the engineers hard at work, getting the contraptions ready. The siege engines were perriers, much slighter than the giant trebuchets Warenne had seen employed in other campaigns during his long career. A slim, movable beam with a sling attached to one end and four ropes hanging from the other, was pivoted over a tall, wooden frame. Trebuchets worked on a counterweight principle, whereas the perrier was manpowered, the four ropes being pulled by men, who swung their end of the beam down causing the other to fly up and project a missile, usually a specially hewn rock, from the sling. The perriers were easier to transport and construct, being smaller and lighter, but they weren't quite as effective as the trebuchets, which could fling stones of up to three hundred pounds over four hundred yards.

One of the engineers, hammering a nail in place on the timber frame, glanced round as Warenne emerged from the fog. 'Sir,' he greeted, straightening. 'The engines should be ready within the hour.'

Warenne grunted as he looked to the castle. The ground sloped up towards the walls, barely visible within the murk. He could smell the sea and hear the echoing cries of gulls, but he could see almost nothing. 'If this fog doesn't clear, we won't be shooting anything.'

Two hours later, the rising sun had burned away the mists and, by midmorning, just a few tendrils were left, drifting raggedly over the walls of Dunbar Castle.

Birds scattered into the sky as the first stone struck. There was an earsplitting crack on impact and a cloud of dust exploded. The rock fell to earth in a shower of grit and rolled down the grassy bank beneath the walls. It was followed, moments later, by three more. Shards of stone and clumps of mortar broke from the curtain wall with each strike.

John de Warenne watched as the engineers methodically loaded and loosed the perriers, the men hauling on the ropes like bell-ringers in a church. The beams swung up, one after the other, to sling their missiles at the fortress on the cliff. In retaliation, arrows shot down from the battlements, but the engineers had erected a palisade from behind which they worked their machines in safety. As the stones continued to smash into the walls, shouts echoed along the ramparts. Warenne caught glimpses of movement through the arrow loops, but unless they were willing to sally forth from the gates, there was little the Scots could do to stop the siege. They did, however, have one thing on their side. Time.

Some of the English knights had cheered at the first few strikes, but the explosions of dust and grit looked more impressive than they actually were. In truth, Warenne knew, it could take a long while for a siege engine, even a trebuchet, to break down enough of the walls for the attackers to enter. King Edward wanted Dunbar captured swiftly, but Warenne wasn't sure how easily this could be accomplished. The quickest way to take a castle was to have cooperation from someone on the inside, but that was unlikely to happen, while the castle was held by soldiers of the Black Comyn, a staunch supporter of Balliol.

John de Warenne's gaze moved to the broad figure of Patrick of Dunbar, standing close by. The earl was watching his castle being bombarded in stony-faced silence. No doubt his treacherous wife was somewhere inside. Warenne felt a measure of pity for the man, thinking of the conflict he must feel watching his home being battered by the engines. Three years ago, Warenne's daughter had died. She had been queen for only a matter of months, but John Balliol's wife for ten years and had given him a son and heir. The only comfort Warenne had found in her passing was that she had not lived through this war. He wondered if there was part of the Earl of Dunbar that hoped the siege would fail. If it succeeded his wife would have to be dealt with, along with the rest of the rebels. Warenne wondered if the earl would have the stomach for it. Would he?

Another stone struck the curtain wall, exploding on impact. A group of infantry dragged a handcart filled with stones over to the engines, where the piles were already diminishing. They had transported two cartloads of the rounded rocks that had been brought to Berwick by ship, but these would run out before too long and they would need to search for more. The beach below the cliffs should provide a good supply, if Warenne could get masons down there to quarry more.

Hearing someone come up behind him, he looked round to see Humphrey de Bohun. The young knight was breathing hard, but his face was calm, despite the constant crashing of the rocks, which was making some of the other soldiers wince.

'Did you find a suitable tree?' Warenne shouted over the din.

'Yes, sir. The men are cutting it down now. I've left six knights to escort it here as soon as it's felled.'

Warenne nodded. After the debacle with the ambush on the road to Wales, Hereford's heir was proving himself an able commander. He and the others had won their spurs at Berwick. All had been blooded and were becoming hardened to the trials of war. Humphrey, in particular, was showing great potential. The king, Warenne knew, had high hopes for him. 'We'll use the ram on the gates,' he told the knight, 'when it's been stripped and reinforced.'

At the sound of hoof-beats, they both turned to see four men riding swiftly into the camp. Warenne frowned in expectation, seeing it was one of the scouting parties he had deployed the day before. Leaving the engineers to continue battering the castle walls, he crossed to meet them, followed by Humphrey. One of the scouts hailed him.

'Sir!' The scout dismounted and hastened towards the earl. 'The Scots are approaching from the west.'

'Led by whom?' Warenne questioned quickly. 'How many?'

'All of them, sir, the whole Scottish army, led by the Comyns and King John. They should be visible any moment.' The scout turned and pointed west to where the land ascended into long, sloping moors, studded with trees. 'On the brow of that hill.'

Warenne stared at the hill, feeling a pulse of excitement in his chest. The thought of open warfare was far more pleasing to the aged earl than the tedious prospect of a drawn-out siege, his men demoralised by the wait and subject to the many dangers facing a besieging army: diminishing supplies, surprise raids from the castle or attacks by the main body of the enemy, their retreat routes blocked. All the years fighting on tournament grounds and on campaign had trained them well. Warenne was confident that these men, a mixture of toughened veterans and eager young knights, could crush the Scots in one bold move.

Moments later, he saw a dark line growing on the distant hill, formed by many men on horseback. Flashes of colour brightened the ranks from banners held aloft. A shout went up on the walls of Dunbar Castle. The Scots there had seen the army coming to relieve them.

Warenne turned to Humphrey, raising his voice over the cheers of the defenders. 'Hold the camp,' he ordered. 'Comyn's men mustn't be allowed to leave the castle and outflank me.'

'Sir,' said Humphrey, bowing at the honour.

Leaving the knight to gather the rest of the young bloods, Warenne hastened through the camp, calling his commanders to him. The captains of the cavalry and infantry moved into action, rounding up their troops. Squires and grooms went to horses, hoisting up saddles, their fingers working at buckles on girths and bridles. Most of the knights wore some armour in readiness of possible attack, but they now pulled on the more awkward pieces: mail or plate gauntlets, helms and shields. Infantry adjusted sword belts and hefted hammers and pikes, forming up in their companies. The siege engines still pounded the castle walls, but the thud of stones was soon drowned by shouts and the neighing of horses as the knights mounted up.

As they rode out of the camp, heading west towards the Scottish host on the distant hill, the defiant cries of the defenders faded behind them. Blue patches of sky appeared between the white banners of cloud that flew fast overhead. Sunlight lanced through the breaks, warming the faces of the knights and the infantry who marched behind. John de Warenne led the vanguard, his eyes on the distant army. The Scots had the high ground, but that did not trouble the grandson of the legendary William Marshal. His men rode with him in confident columns, pennons fluttering on lance shafts, helm crests waving. The foot soldiers brought up the rear, striding across the muddy ground that sloped steadily upwards.

The colours of the enemy's flags grew clearer. Among them was the royal banner of Scotland, the red lion rampant on gold. The Scots shouted as the English came, their cries carrying on the wind to meet the advancing men. Contained in those faint sounds, Warenne guessed there would be cries for vengeance. He doubted there was a man left in Scotland who hadn't learned of the slaughter at Berwick. Such thirst for revenge was good. It would make the Scots rash. In contrast his men remained silent, intent on closing the gap between themselves and the enemy, marshalling their strength for the fight.

As the English knights reached the top of the first incline, Warenne raised his hand to call a halt. His commanders moved in around him, while he surveyed the terrain. Ahead, the ground fell sharply into a valley, clustered with trees and bushes that grew thicker in the defile, partially concealing a glistening burn. Beyond the narrow stream, the trees thinned out again as the ground rose in a long, ridged slope, all the way up to the Scottish host on the crest. Giving orders to his commanders, who spread out to relay them to the men, Warenne led the English down the steep hillside. The knights leaned back in their saddles, allowing their destriers to find the best routes. Still, the fell voices of the Scots came to them from the distance. The infantry followed, using spear butts to aid them on the decline. The sun disappeared behind a cloud, a shadow sweeping in across the grass. Ahead, between the trees, the waters of the burn dulled from bronze to slate in the changing light.

The first knights reached the stream, Warenne among them. In places the banks were high and the men were forced to spread out to seek safe cross-ing. Their lines broke as they moved between the trees, some turning back to find better routes by which to urge their destriers across. Others rode carefully down shallower, sandy banks, into the cold running water. The mud on the stream-bed, churned by the hooves, turned the burn cloudy. Kicking hard at the sides of their horses, the men forced them up on to the other side, water dripping from the beasts' legs. A few chargers skidded and panicked, but the knights controlled them with sharp commands. Behind, more cavalry came, following comrades across.

Warenne formed up with his men in the trees on the other side. He turned, barking orders as the knights continued to spread out along the banks. Behind them soldiers crowded in, waiting to cross. Suddenly, from the hill above, Warenne heard the shrill ringing of many horns. It was followed by the unmistakable thunder of hooves. Spurring his horse forward to get a better view, the Earl of Surrey saw the Scottish army riding pell-mell down the ridged hillside towards the burn. For a moment, he was struck dumb by the sight, stunned by the unexpectedness of the charge. Then he heard the roared words in between the horns.

'*On them!*'

'*On them! The cowards are fleeing!*'

In a second, Warenne took in his men fanned out along the valley floor, some moving back through the trees to search for a place to cross. He realised that what was a breaking of ranks to cross the burn must, to the Scots, have looked like his forces were in disarray. Then, he was yelling commands, ordering his men across by any means. The last knights charged their horses at the stream. Most vaulted up and over, but a few fell, toppling on the banks, horses screaming and twisting as they crashed back. Behind, the infantry splashed down the slick banks in their hundreds, holding their weapons high as they waded through the water and crawled up the other side. Snapping down his visor and snatching his lance from his squire, Warenne spurred his horse out of the trees, followed by his men.

The Scots, plunging headlong down the hillside in a disorderly mass, saw a line of knights emerging through the trees ahead forming up as they came, ranks closing, shields rising. What they had thought was a host of men fleeing in fear, was suddenly a well-disciplined wall of steel, thundering up the slope to meet them. Some of the Scots at the front of the haphazard assault, those who saw the knights first, tried to rein in their mounts, tried to slow, or turn. But they were committed now, propelled by the masses coming behind them, straight into the English heavy cavalry, their thirst for blood drying in their mouths. Those Scots who had seen battle before roared the others on, trying their best to tighten the ranks, but it was too late. The English knights battered straight through them.

Men, tossed from saddles with the violent impact, were hurled into the ground. Some were knocked senseless, others went down beneath the trampling hooves, pummelled into the mud. As the English punched through the Scottish host, turning the disorderly mass into unbridled panic, the infantry poured in behind. Like locusts, they swarmed over fallen men and horses, surrounding earls and knights who were disarmed and taken prisoner. Some nobles went down, fighting vainly, as the infantry closed over the top of them, disabling them with blows from hammers or sword pommels.

Warenne, his lance spent, swung out with his great sword, hacking at a Scottish knight. As the man reeled with the strike, Warenne turned his horse with a jerk of the reins, causing the beast to barrel into the side of the Scot's charger, jolting the man from the saddle. He went down with a cry and a crunch of armour. As the Scot tried to push himself up, three English foot soldiers surrounded him. One swung a hammer into his stomach, causing him to double up, while the others beat and kicked him until he could be disarmed. Warenne pushed on, leading his soldiers deeper into the torn Scottish ranks, battling through to the foot soldiers behind, where the killing became indiscriminate. Warenne's knights slashed down at the men scattering across the hillside before them, gashing scalps, severing limbs and heads from bodies. The armoured warhorses clouted men aside like they were saplings, or else reared to stamp down with their hooves, bursting skulls and snapping spines beneath their massive weight, as they had been trained to do. The ground was soon awash with gore, infantry groaning as they dragged themselves along, unable to escape the English foot soldiers, who finished them with brutal thrusts of their falchions.

All across the field, the Scots were trying to struggle free, the battle for them now a desperate bid for survival. Warenne glimpsed the royal banner of Scotland disappearing up the slope, followed by the standard of the Red Comyns. The hillside between was clogged with dead and dying foot soldiers, making it impossible to give chase. Hissing a curse through his visor, Warenne fought on.

In less than an hour, the battle was over. The grassy slopes were littered with dead men and horses. Some Scottish nobles had perished, but that was nothing compared to the foot soldiers, who had fallen in the hundreds. In places, the dead were so many that their blood trickled into pools that dribbled down the hillside into the waters of the burn, turning them red. The English infantry moved between the piles, finishing off the wounded.

Warenne surveyed the battleground from the saddle of his blood-splattered destrier, the stink of death thick in his mouth and nose. It disappointed him that the King of Scotland wasn't among the defeated ranks of the Scottish nobles being rounded up by his knights, but nonetheless the battle was won. And won well. Many Scottish magnates, including a number of earls and barons, had been captured, most of whom had made up the leadership of the realm since Balliol's surrender of authority. It was a grim day for Scotland. In one charge, the Earl of Surrey had destroyed a large part of the kingdom's army and most of its leaders.

42

The midday sun blazed on the heads of the company. The verges to either side of the track droned with insects and the parched grass rustled in the hot wind that blew dust into the eyes of the travellers and carried on its currents the salt smell of the sea.

Robert, riding behind his father's men, felt the sun burning the skin between his arming cap and the collar of his hauberk. With him rode his brother and the knights of Carrick. They had been travelling for hours and the horses were tiring, hanging their heads as they plodded along the track. Their tails switched constantly to ward off the flies that had thickened into clouds the nearer they came to the sea, a dazzling metal sheet in the distance.

Behind the knights, on rouncies and hobbies, rode squires, grooms and servants. Among them was Isobel's maid, Katherine, riding the good-natured chestnut mare that once belonged to her mistress. Robert could have sold the animal, but the horse was one of the possessions Isobel had loved most and it was more practical, he had reasoned, to offer the mare up for the use of the maid who had become the prime guardian of his daughter. He had intended to find a more appropriate warden, a governess from a noble household, but there had been no time to think about such things since the death of his wife and the start of the war. Besides, Katherine had so far proven more than capable with the infant's care. Behind her, on a sturdy grey pony, was a skinny girl of fifteen, his daughter's wet nurse. Katherine had found Judith in Carlisle, shortly after Isobel died. The daughter of a knight of the city's garrison, Judith had given birth several weeks earlier, but the infant had been stillborn. Nobody mentioned anything about a husband and it had seemed a relief to her father to have her taken into the Bruce household. She was a sullen creature, but she had the milk his baby needed and so Robert tolerated her presence.

Bringing up the rear were two wagons, drawn by carthorses and filled with supplies: food for the men and their horses, tents, armour and equipment, all of which were necessary for the journey. There were few places for the Bruce family to stay in Scotland now, few friends to offer beds for the night. They were returning home victorious. And hated.

The defeat of the Scottish army at Dunbar had signalled the ending of the brief war with England. Most of their leaders captured and half their army destroyed, the Scots' resistance crumbled. Their alliance with King Philippe had proven of little use, none of the promised ships or soldiers from France coming to their aid. After Dunbar, Roxburgh, Dumbarton and Jedburgh castles had surrendered in rapid succession and Edinburgh fell after a week's siege. Stirling, the key to the north, was found abandoned. In Perth, at the end of June, Edward received word from King John, who had fled north with the Comyns. Scotland's king, with the agreement of his beleaguered Council of Twelve, had offered unconditional surrender.

It had been a mixed blessing for Robert, crossing the border back into Scotland at the end of the four-month war. King Edward had fulfilled his promise and restored the Bruce lands, taken by the Comyns on the eve of the conflict. On their return, the lord and the knights of Annandale and Carrick had been triumphant, but despite his relief at the restoration of his domains, Robert had found it hard to celebrate with his men as they entered Annandale. Crops lay ravaged, those not destroyed by the Scottish host left to wither in the fields with no hands to tend them. Towns and hamlets were quiet, many of the men and women of the region having fled when the Comyns' host had come with fire and sword. Lochmaben, at least, was still standing, the host content with burning and raiding the lands around the town. It was, however, a forlorn sight, the castle ransacked for anything valuable, tapestries ripped down, unwieldy items of furniture left broken or soiled, stores emptied of grain and wine. A smell of urine pervaded the place, which was littered with refuse, animal bones, discarded sacks, empty barrels, as if many men had stayed here for a brief time, before moving on.

There had been little time to set about clearing it, however, for word had soon come from King Edward, summoning the Lord of Annandale and Robert to the north-eastern town of Montrose, and his presence.

'Sir, should we rest a while?'

Robert looked up as one of the knights of Annandale addressed his father. He had been going to suggest the same thing himself. The midday heat was becoming unbearable and the horses were desperate for water. He was riding one of his palfreys, Hunter being led by Nes. Marjorie, swaddled in a cloth sling against Katherine's chest, was beginning to whimper.

'No, we're almost there.' The lord turned to the knight with a self-satisfied expression. 'I want to greet King Edward as soon as possible. I expect he has important tidings for me.'

Robert's gaze lingered on his father, whose yellow surcoat, adorned with a red banded cross, was garish in the sunlight, his mail hauberk polished to a glittery gleam. Despite the heat, he wore a mantle of fine Flemish cloth over his surcoat and mail, lined in red silk. He was sweating profusely, lines of perspiration dribbling down his face. Above him, the standard of Annandale was hoisted high. He had made his banner-bearer carry it through every town and village they had passed, from Lochmaben to the north-east coast, as if on some royal progress. Robert wore the arms of Carrick on his surcoat, but bore no standard, his banner curled around its shaft on the back of one of the wagons. As his father spoke these words, he sensed his brother trying to catch his eye, but knowing what Edward was trying to communicate with that look, he remained gazing straight ahead.

As they continued, advancing through midday into early afternoon, a large lagoon opened before them. Between this lagoon and the North Sea was the town of Montrose, rising from a strip of sand, the buildings overlooked by a squat castle. Beyond the castle walls, where scrubby fields edged into grey dunes, many tents had been erected in a colourful sea of canvas. In the midst of the tents was a large wooden platform, which looked like a stage.

In Montrose, the streets were packed with English knights and soldiers. Riding through the crowds, most of the men Robert heard speaking were English, their accents suggesting a multitude of localities from which they had travelled to converge on this Scottish port. A few spoke Irish, which gave him faint recollections of Antrim. Others spoke Welsh, provoking more recent memories. A fight erupted outside a ramshackle inn as the company passed, one soldier punching another, before being set upon. Some men moved to stop the brawl, more cheered it on. There was a sense of indolence among the soldiery who thronged these streets, gorging themselves on food and ale, yelling for songs from minstrels and fools. These weren't men exhausted by a hard campaign, celebrating a victory well won. They were revellers at a feast day. It was a very different scene from the one Robert had witnessed after the campaign in Wales. How had this happened so quickly? How had Scotland fallen so easily? It was shocking to think of it.

Winding their way through the streets they came at last to the castle, where a scarlet banner emblazoned with three golden lions flew from the tower. The gates were closed and four guards, dressed in the king's colours, stood outside, leaning on pikes. One came forward, crossing the bridge that spanned a ditch, as the Lord of Annandale approached.

'Good day,' he called, his eyes on the banner raised above the company. 'What is your business?'

As Robert's father gestured, one of his knights rode forward.

'Sir Robert Bruce, Lord of Annandale, has arrived. He wishes to speak with King Edward.'

'The lord king is in council,' answered the guard.

Robert noticed his father's face twitch with irritation.

The Bruce urged his white mare towards the guard. 'King Edward summoned me here to meet with him on an urgent matter. I am sure he will see me.'

'My orders were to allow entry only to those whose names I was given. Yours, sir, was not among them. I suggest you make camp with the other men the king has summoned here. No doubt he will send for you when he is ready.' With that, the guard headed back across the bridge.

As the lord wheeled his mare roughly around, Robert took in his humiliation with a stab of gratification. The Bruce blustered off the rebuke and led the way towards the encampment of tents, a grimace splitting his flushed face.

There wasn't much room left in the fields beyond the castle walls, the tents stretching all the way to the sand dunes, and they were forced to spread out on a patch of ground close to the stinking mud-banks of the lagoon, where the air was full of the shrieks of birds. As the knights dismounted, the servants set about removing tents and equipment from the wagons. Several headed off in search of water for the horses, while others dug pits for fires and latrines. Robert went to the back of one wagon as two servants carried off a large wooden cage. Inside was his hound, Uathach. On his return to Scotland the summer before, he had rekindled his affection for the young bitch, the pup of his grandfather's favourite. She reminded him of the old man and his old life. 'Fetch me her leash,' he told one of the servants.

The servant rifled through a hunting bag, while the other opened the cage. Uathach uncurled and moved, snake-like, through the cage door.

She was tall, almost up to his hip, lean-limbed and smoke-coloured like
her mother. She came straight to Robert, her tongue out, panting. He
took the leash from the servant and fixed it to her collar. Unlike his
father's dogs, that had silk leashes, Uathach's gear was of soft brown
leather. His grandfather had always been scornful of men who adorned
their hounds with pretty tethers, saying such frippery was for fools
with more money than wit. Binding the leash around his hand to keep
the bitch close, Robert moved off through the rows of tents, leaving
the servants to unpack and Katherine to place his wailing daughter in
Judith's outstretched hands for a feed. He hadn't gone far when Edward
came jogging up behind him.

'Where are you going, brother?'

'Uathach needs to relieve herself. As do I.' Without waiting for a response,
Robert carried on. He didn't want another argument.

'You're not going to speak to him, are you? You're going to keep on
avoiding him until it is too late and the choice is taken from you.'

Robert halted. Turning, he met his brother's challenging stare. 'Why
can't you leave it be?'

Edward shook his head, incredulous. 'Leave it be?' He strode up to
Robert. 'It is the future of our kingdom we are speaking about! You have a
chance to make right the wrongs of these past months. Why, in God's name,
will you not seize it?'

'We know nothing of King Edward's intentions. The summons was
unclear. How can I seize something that hasn't been made real? How can—?'

'Tomorrow,' Edward cut across him, 'John Balliol will be formally
deposed. Our father believes he is going to take his place as King of Scotland.
It is what he came here for. But the right to lay claim to the throne was
passed from our grandfather to you, the day you inherited Carrick. Why
haven't you confronted him?'

'Why does this even trouble you?' Robert demanded, the heat and his
tiredness fraying his temper. 'It is better for you if he does become king. If I
died first, you would be his heir.'

Edward shook his head and turned away. 'I want to see our realm at
peace again, brother. I don't want to fight my countrymen any more. It
has sickened me, this war. Our father . . .' He paused, his brow furrowing.
'He might have been born a Scot, but his veins run with English blood.
Already, our mother's tongue is disappearing from our lands and the ways
and customs of our ancestors, held dear by our grandfather, are fading. Our
father would quicken that passing. As king he would create a court in the

shadow of Westminster, subservient to King Edward. Our kingdom would have less independence than it did under Balliol.'

Robert stared at his brother. Rarely had he heard him speak so earnestly. 'What makes you believe I would be any different?'

'I still hope you might see through your mistakes.'

Robert knew his brother meant his association with the Knights of the Dragon. 'We don't know what the king is planning, or whether he will even offer the throne.' His voice hardened. 'I will not tear our family apart fighting for a fantasy, God damn it!'

This time, as he walked away, his brother made no move to follow. Robert kept going, past groups of soldiers lounging in the hot sun, drinking, sleeping. Others crowded around trestles erected under canopies, while servants brought them food. He saw a few banners he recognised, strung from the sides of tents and wondered who was here. The face of Aymer de Valence leered in his mind until he forced it away, striding purposefully over the sand dunes towards the sea, Uathach trotting at his side.

The sea was golden in the afternoon sun, waves whispering over the sand. The breeze coming off the water dried the sweat on Robert's face as he sat, letting Uathach off the leash. The bitch bounded down to the water, leaping like a deer into the waves. There were a few fishing boats pulled up on the sand. Some way past the boats servants were cleaning out pots and pans in a stream that ran down into the surf. Uathach raced excitedly in their direction, but Robert called her back to his side with a sharp whistle. As the bitch flopped obediently beside him, he leaned forward, resting his elbows on his knees. He stared out to sea, its blue serenity at odds with the turmoil in his mind.

Ever since their father had been awarded the governorship of Carlisle, he had been hinting at the prospect that if Edward won the war, he would make him king. Now, the English had won and tomorrow Balliol would be deposed. Robert was grateful their lands had been restored to them and satisfied by the fate of Balliol and the hated Comyns, but riding through the lands of his birth, seeing his countrymen subdued and humiliated, he had felt like an invader, as despised as King Edward and his soldiers. Did he want to be king of a people who loathed him? And what of the throne itself? He had seen for himself Edward's attempts to control it over the past six years, first with the proposed marriage of Margaret and his heir, then through his interference in Balliol's reign. Now that Edward had taken the kingdom by force any man he set up in Balliol's place would be nothing more than an obedient vassal on the end of a very tight cord. Was it not,

Robert reasoned, better to be a trusted warrior in the king's elite, than his puppet on a shackled throne?

As he sat there, his grandfather's voice sounded, harsh in his thoughts, asking if centuries of history would end with him: if Alexander and David, and Malcolm Canmore had fought and bled for their kingdom, only to have him yield it without a struggle? In his mind, Robert saw a vast tree standing on a hillside. It was withered and dying, its proud branches blackened with rot that was seeping down through the great trunk, into its roots. You caused this, his grandfather's voice told him. *You were the death of our heritage.*

'What do you want from me?' Robert shouted suddenly, pushing himself to his feet.

Uathach barked at the anger in his voice and the servants washing the pans looked over. Robert strode down to the water's edge, pushing his hands hard through his hair. In four short years, his family's place in the world had changed beyond recognition. They had lost the fight for the throne, their power in the realm and most of their former allies. He had lost his mother, his grandfather and his wife in rapid succession, then had suffered the trauma of fighting a war against his own people. With the victory, he could only taste the bitterness of their defeat. Somewhere up in the clouds of heaven, St Malachy was surely laughing.

'Sir Robert?'

He turned abruptly at the call to see a tall young man in a blue silk surcoat crossing the dunes towards him. Humphrey de Bohun's sun-browned face split in a wide grin. At the sight of his friend, Robert felt a great wash of relief. His grandfather's accusations and the image of the withered tree faded as he headed up the beach to meet him. They embraced, Humphrey laughing as Robert hugged him fiercely.

'I saw your standard going up in the camp,' he said, pulling back. 'Your brother told me you were here.' Humphrey glanced down as Uathach nosed him. 'Is this your hound? She's beautiful.'

'How long have you been in Montrose?' Robert had been hoping the knight would be here, for he had sorely missed the young man's friendship. Just seeing him felt like being back in London that summer, training on the practice ground, feasting in the Tower. As if the past year hadn't happened.

'Only a few days. We came up from Perth.'

'Were you at Berwick?'

Humphrey's grin faded. He looked out to sea, then turned back to

Robert with a forced smile. 'Let us not speak of battles now the war is over. Tell me of yourself. Everything! Where is your pretty wife? Is she here? I cannot wait to meet her.'

'Isobel died four months ago at Carlisle,' said Robert, after a pause, 'giving birth to our daughter.'

Humphrey's face fell. He clasped Robert's shoulder. 'My friend, I—'

Robert waved away the apology before it could be uttered. He felt undeserving of sympathy when he had grieved comparatively little. 'She was a good woman. A good wife. But we were together only for a year and what with the troubles and then the war we did not see one another often. In truth, I didn't know her very well. I . . .' Robert faltered. He hadn't spoken to anyone of this. 'I do miss her,' he admitted, 'but more for the sake of our child than for myself.'

Humphrey nodded.

They stood in silence, watching the waves crash into the sand, their faces sun-dark and rough with stubble. After a time, Robert went to speak, but the knight beat him to it.

'I am glad you're here, Robert,' Humphrey said, turning to him. 'For I would welcome your help.'

'Of course. With what?'

'There is something King Edward needs the Knights of the Dragon to accomplish. A special task. I want you to join us.'

'What is this task?'

They turned, hearing a call, to see Edward Bruce crossing the dunes towards them.

'We will speak later,' said Humphrey, looking back at Robert. He smiled and grasped his shoulder. 'It is good to see you, my friend.'

'And you.'

Robert lay in the tent, listening to his brother's breaths beside him. He was exhausted from the long journey. The atmosphere in their camp that evening, his father blistering over the fact the king hadn't welcomed him, had wearied him further. So had the momentous question still hanging unanswered, of what would happen tomorrow when King John was deposed. But despite his tiredness he couldn't sleep.

A sultry breeze lifted the tent flaps, revealing a fat, red-tinged moon, hanging low in the sky. Robert wondered if it was a bad omen. The thought took him wandering back through the soft haze of a Carrick summer to a house in the hills and a tree of webs. Was the old woman still there in that cramped dwelling, full of books and bones, weaving men's destinies? Affraig would be ancient now, or dead. The thought of Carrick made him long for careless childhood when his mother and grandfather were alive and their halls were filled with friends and laughter. He had spent so little time in his earldom since he had inherited it, his vassal, Andrew Boyd, collecting the annual rents and dealing with any problems, that it hardly felt as though it belonged to him. He should return now the war was over.

Hearing voices outside, Robert recognised the voice of one of his father's knights, set on watch to guard the camp, then Humphrey's quiet, insistent tones. Careful not to disturb his brother, Robert rose and ducked out of the tent. He went over, nodding to his father's man to return to his post.

As he greeted Humphrey, he realised the knight was wearing mail beneath a plain, dark riding cloak.

Humphrey's eyes glittered in the firelight. 'I need you to dress, quickly.'

'Where are we going?'

'To fulfil the prophecy.'

Humphrey continued to speak for some moments more, telling him what to bring and where to meet him. When the knight finished, Robert went to press him on the mission, but he stopped himself. The sense of belonging he had felt on seeing Humphrey was a relief in the face of the stark isolation he had experienced since his return to Scotland. He didn't want to diminish that by questioning the knight's motives and, in truth, the thought of leaving Montrose was a blessing. He was tired of being caught between choices, tired of not knowing which direction to take.

You're going to keep on avoiding him, until it's too late and the choice is taken from you.

His brother was right. And he cared not.

After Humphrey left, Robert woke Nes to saddle Hunter for him and returned to his tent to dress. As he was pulling his gambeson over his shirt, he heard the urgent cries of his daughter. They were followed by the sleepy whisper of a woman. Robert went out, carrying his sword, just as Katherine slipped out of the tent she shared with Judith and three of the women. The maid held Marjorie in her arms and was shushing her softly. She looked up, seeing Robert crossing the camp. Her brow creased as her eyes went to the sword in his hand. He didn't say anything, but continued to the wagon, where he dragged out the large chest that contained his armour. Behind him, Marjorie's cries continued. As Robert took out his hauberk, Katherine began to sing softly. She had a low, strong voice when she sang that sounded as though it belonged to someone else, someone older. It soothed the infant, her whimpering fading into shuddery breaths. Robert, realising he had paused to listen and the hauberk was growing heavy in his hands, struggled into the armour, then reached for his shield, which Humphrey had told him to bring. The dragon shield was wrapped in cloth to keep it from being damaged. Robert hadn't looked at it since he left England a year ago. In the light from the fire, he realised how scarred the wood was. He was pulling on a plain riding cloak, as Humphrey had instructed, when he heard a voice behind him.

'You're leaving, sir?'

He turned and looked down into Katherine's upturned face. The bridge of her nose was peppered with freckles and her dark hair was sleep-tangled, falling loose and long over her shoulders. Marjorie was held close to her chest. Robert smiled as he looked upon his sleeping daughter. Bending, he kissed her gently, then rose, meeting Katherine's eyes as he fastened his sword belt around his waist. 'I'll return soon.'

Picking up his shield, he spoke briefly to the knight on watch by the fire, then, taking Hunter's reins from Nes, Robert headed across the camp.

The wooden platform he had seen when they entered Montrose loomed ahead as he followed Humphrey's directions. In the red moonlight it looked less like a stage, more like a gallows. Some distance beyond the dais, he could see a group of mounted men lit by torchlight. With them was a wagon, drawn by carthorses and driven by two royal knights. As he approached, Robert saw Humphrey and a host of familiar faces.

There was Henry Percy, stockier than he remembered and Guy de Beauchamp, with no smile for him. Thomas of Lancaster was among them, older and taller, poised on the brink of manhood, mounted alongside Robert Clifford, who nodded courteously and Ralph de Monthermer, who smiled in greeting. Then, lastly, Robert looked over at Aymer de Valence. That hateful face slammed him back to Anglesey — to a musty kitchen, Aymer's black eyes filling with hatred as he rushed in for the kill.

As Robert mounted, Humphrey nodded to the others. 'Let's move. We have a three-day ride ahead of us.'

'Three days?' questioned Thomas. 'We'll miss the ceremony tomorrow.'

'You still haven't told us where we are going, or to what end, brother,' added Ralph.

Robert was pleased he wasn't the only one Humphrey was keeping in the dark. Again, a flicker of doubt passed across his mind, but he pushed it aside. Whatever their plan, it had to be preferable to staying here, faced with an impossible decision.

'I'll explain on the road,' answered Humphrey, his tone firm.

Kicking at his horse, the knight led the company from the camp, towards the road out of Montrose. The wagon trundled in their wake and the huge, blood-tinged moon lit the way before them.

43

The crowd of men looked on in silence as the solitary figure walked the aisle formed by their ranks, heading for the platform at the centre of the encampment. Tendrils of mist shrouded the waters of the lagoon, the early morning air humid with the promise of another sweltering day. The eastern sky was liquid gold, the burnished light glowing in the faces of the hundreds who thronged the area around the dais. In front of the platform a row of men had been lined up, under the eyes of the king's knights. They stood together, subdued and pale, dwarfed by the wooden structure that loomed behind them. Only a few of their number watched the lone man moving inexorably towards them.

Robert Bruce, Lord of Annandale, waited in the ranks of the English nobles, keeping his gaze on the figure of John Balliol, slowly approaching. The King of Scotland was gaunt, his eyes sunken. His face was grey, despite the heat, the gold surcoat that displayed the royal arms of Scotland the only thing of colour about him.

After Dunbar, Balliol had fled with the Comyns, but with Edward's unstoppable march north, castles and towns falling before him, there had been no safe haven for King John and the last of his men. The weeks spent on the road were visible in his wasted face and body. In June, he had written to Edward, renouncing the treaty made with Philippe of France and offering unconditional surrender. Now, hobbled by humiliation and crippled by despair, he bore all the wretchedness of a doomed man heading for the executioner's block.

As Balliol trudged past, Bruce craned his head, willing his enemy to look in his direction: to see him standing there, watching his final moments as king. But Balliol's eyes didn't stray from the dais ahead. Behind him, the crowds closed in.

Balliol reached the prisoners corralled before the platform and they were forced to part, allowing him to mount the steps. One man moved forward, as if to say something to the king, but he was compelled back by the swords of Edward's knights. Bruce, staring over the heads of those in front, realised it was John Comyn. The Lord of Badenoch moved back, but didn't take his eyes from his brother-in-law, now ascending the steps. With Comyn was his son and heir, the disgraced husband of Joan de Valence, along with the Black Comyn and the earls of Atholl, Menteith and Ross. Bruce's keen gaze moved over them all. Many of them had been comrades of his father. Like him, their days were over. The past belonged in the ground with the bones of the dead. It was time for a new era in Scotland.

Hearing his son, Edward, murmuring to one of his vassals, Bruce turned with a glare to silence him. At dawn, when told Robert had left in the night on business for the king, Bruce had been incensed. He had questioned Edward at length, but either his son was a better liar than he knew, or he truly did not know why his older brother had disappeared without explanation. Since then, his fury cooling to a rigid anger, the lord had felt a slow-rising relief.

Not once, since the start of the war and his alliance with the King of England, had he openly acknowledged the fact that his son held the right to lay claim to the throne, but the truth of it had burned in him. Haunted by the fear that Robert might assert that claim, he had distanced himself further from his already estranged son. Perhaps, he had speculated, Robert's absence on the eve of such a crucial moment in their family's campaign was a sign that he would yield without a struggle. Bruce hoped this was the case, for he himself would not. His father had passed him over to spite him. Now, he would right that wrong. How he hoped the bastard was twisting in his grave.

As the Lord of Annandale looked to the platform, he saw that Balliol had reached the top and was walking towards the centre, where his father-in-law, John de Warenne, waited, with a roll of parchment. Behind the Earl of Surrey crowded English clerks, lawyers and royal officials, Bishop Anthony Bek among them. They stood to either side of a throne upon which sat King Edward. The king was a little blurred at this distance, Bruce's eyesight not what it once was, but it seemed clear his focus was on Balliol. The Earl of Surrey's gruff tones sounded as he unrolled the document to read the charges against Balliol, whose treacherous acts as a vassal of the King of England had led to the confiscation of his fief. As agreed by his surrender, he would now resign his kingdom and his royal dignity to his overlord.

When he was finished reading, John de Warenne stepped back, his eyes fixed somewhere distant of his wretched son-in-law. For a moment, Balliol stood alone. He looked around uncertainly, then flinched as two royal knights moved towards him. Each held a dagger. Some of the Scottish magnates below began to protest, but bodily harm was not the intention of the king's men. Instead, they began picking at the threads on the rampant red lion that adorned Balliol's surcoat. Balliol's dumb, defeated expression as they worked showed he had known this was coming. When the head of the lion embroidered on the material was loose, one of the king's men gave his dagger to his comrade and took hold of the flap of cloth. With one mighty tug, he ripped downward, tearing the royal arms clean off the surcoat. There was a scatter of cheers and applause from the crowd that faded into silence. Balliol staggered forward, off-balanced, but the knight steadied him, holding him upright before the assembly, his gold surcoat trailing red threads.

King Edward had made John Balliol the King of Scotland. Now, he unmade him. Bruce couldn't be certain, but in the golden dawn he thought he could see tears glistening on Balliol's pockmarked face.

As Balliol was led away down the steps of the dais, to be escorted to the Tower in London, along with the rest of the Scottish nobles, King Edward rose. Seeing the king heading from the platform, surrounded by his officials, Bruce forced his way through the crowds determinedly. He still hadn't been granted an audience with the English king, who had summoned him to witness this moment. Impatience was a spur in his side.

'My lord king!'

Bruce ignored the complaints his forceful advance drew from those in his path, calling as he went, trying to attract the king's attention. He had almost caught up to Edward, who was making his way across the camp ground with John de Warenne and his chief officials, when two royal knights stepped into his path, barring his way. Seeing they meant business, Bruce called vainly at the king's retreating back.

'My lord, I beg you. I must speak to you!'

Edward turned, his gaze alighting on Bruce, standing between the two knights, red-faced from the struggle through the crowd. Edward's officials turned with him, looking to see who had dared accost the king.

'My lord,' said Bruce, pausing to recover his composure and bow. 'I wanted to talk to you about a matter of importance.' When Edward continued to stare at him, as if expecting him to state his business here and now, Bruce added, 'In private.'

King Edward's gaze didn't waver or lose its chill. 'My time here is limited. I will meet with all my vassals in Berwick next month, after my progress north is completed. There, I will accept the homage of the people of Scotland. You may speak to me then, Sir Robert of Annandale.' He moved to head off.

Seeing the thing he craved, the thing that was now so tantalisingly near, slipping away, the Lord of Annandale forgot himself. 'I insist, my lord!' he shouted at the king's back, his voice striking the air.

At the command, the royal officials looked stunned and the knights barring Bruce's way grasped the hilts of their swords, clearly intending to draw them should he make any move forward.

Edward turned slowly, the hard lines of his face sharpened by the sun's blaze. His grey eyes narrowed, all the strength and purpose behind them focusing in on Bruce, pinning him beneath that steel gaze.

Bruce backtracked hastily. 'What I mean to say, my lord, is that this matter cannot wait.' Ignoring the stares of the officials, he continued. 'Now King John has been removed of his title, the throne of Scotland lies empty. My father held the right to that claim after Balliol, as determined by your judicious hearing, but on his death last year that right passed to me. You yourself acknowledged this when I accepted the governorship of Carlisle.'

For a long moment Edward did not speak. When he did, his voice was acid. 'Do you think, Sir Robert, that I have nothing better to do than win kingdoms for you?'

As the king moved off with his officials, the knights turned and followed, leaving the Lord of Annandale standing there alone, stock-still, in the midst of the crowds.

44

The knights had ridden hard out of Montrose, only stopping to rest for a few hours at a time, when their horses could go no further. Now, as dusk fell on the third day and they descended a hill, Robert realised he could see the walled town of Perth on the banks of the mighty River Tay in the distance. Nearer, by a mile or so, was the royal burgh of Scone, where he and his grandfather had climbed the Moot Hill and the old man had spoken of the Battle of Lewes and the origin of his hatred of the Comyns.

As they approached the outskirts of the burgh, trotting their horses along a worn road, the wagon trundling behind, Humphrey gestured for them to slow. He veered right, leading them off the track into some sparse woods. The wagon's wheels bumped over the rough ground, twigs snapping and breaking. All around the trees whispered, their branches forming webs against the purple sky, where the first stars glittered. After a short distance, they came to a clearing. Humphrey looked around and, seemingly satisfied, called the others to halt.

'Are we making camp, Sir Humphrey?' questioned Robert Clifford, staring into the shadows of the trees.

'No,' said Humphrey, dismounting with a wince, the mail beneath his cloak clinking. 'Get the shields,' he said to the two royal knights who had driven the wagon.

The others swung down from their horses, frowning questioningly at one another and at Humphrey, who had looped the reins of his destrier over a branch and was waiting in the centre of the clearing. After a few moments they joined him, the only sounds the scrape of wood as the knights dragged the shields from the wagon.

Leaving Hunter to crop the bushes, Robert crossed to Humphrey. All through the long ride, Humphrey remaining tight-lipped and reserved, tension had been building inside Robert. The initial relief he felt upon leaving Montrose had faded in the face of his rising questions, which Humphrey had so far refused to answer. 'Enough secrecy,' he said, before anyone else could speak. 'What are we doing, Humphrey? We've been riding for three days with no idea of where we are headed, or to what end.'

'I am sorry for that,' said Humphrey, meeting Robert's gaze, 'but King Edward gave me that order. I was oath-bound to follow it.' He looked at the rest. 'You may have noticed that we have been retracing our steps. Beyond these trees lies the royal town of Scone, which we passed by on our way to Montrose. This is our destination.'

The two knights began handing out the dragon shields.

As the men took them, Robert felt his tension break in a shock of revelation. It flooded through him like ice water. 'The stone,' he said, staring into Humphrey's face. 'That's it, isn't it? You've come for the Stone of Destiny?'

Some of the others began speaking, their voices taut with excitement.

'The throne,' murmured Guy de Beauchamp. 'The third relic.'

Robert hardly heard.

Humphrey had nodded in answer. 'The stone is one of the four relics set down in Merlin's Last Prophecy.'

'Why didn't I know this?' Robert demanded, feeling betrayed and furious. 'Why didn't you tell me?'

Humphrey's voice sharpened. 'I didn't tell you because you went back to Scotland barely months after you were inducted into the order. There was no time to tell you, to explain.'

'Explain what? That you were planning to take my throne?'

'Your family lost the throne when Balliol took it,' responded Humphrey quietly. 'King Edward doesn't plan to promote anyone else, not now. It is over, Robert. Scotland will become part of England, as Wales and Ireland are. The stone is no longer needed here. No new king will be enthroned upon it.'

'Wales, Ireland – they are different.' Robert's voice rose in the clearing. 'Scotland is a sovereign kingdom with its own liberties. That cannot just be swept aside!'

Ralph de Monthermer stepped in, his tone reasoning. 'Our invasion has proven just how weak Scotland is alone. United with England it will be that much stronger. Both kingdoms will benefit from such a union. Together, now the treaty has been renounced, we can fight France and win back our king's lands. You must see the sense in this, Sir Robert. If you didn't believe in Edward's cause, you wouldn't have fought against your own countrymen for him.'

Before Robert could answer, Humphrey interjected. 'The prophecy states that unless the four relics of Brutus are brought together under one ruler, Britain will face ruin. That means Scotland would suffer as much as England. We have to take the stone to ensure that doesn't happen.'

'How do you know the prophecy is real?' Robert challenged, staring at them. 'Have any of you seen the book the king's translation came from? No. It is locked away, isn't it? Supposedly too fragile to be exposed.'

'I would be careful, Sir Robert,' cautioned Ralph, 'of making such suggestions.'

'Even if it is real,' Robert continued, turning to Humphrey, 'it doesn't mean it was written about this time. What if the danger the Last Prophecy foresaw was hundreds of years ago? Or what if it meant Britain would face ruin hundreds of years in the future? I read Monmouth's *History* when I was a boy and I read it again on my return to Scotland. Yes, he speaks of an appointed moment when certain relics should be gathered, but he doesn't say when that appointed moment is.'

'The Last Prophecy doesn't just clarify the relics Geoffrey of Monmouth mentions,' answered Humphrey. 'It also speaks of specific events that will herald Britain's descent into disaster. Signs to watch for.' He hesitated, as if considering, then went on. 'One of these signs was the death of King Alexander.'

Robert met this with silence. Until now, a large part of him had held back from believing in the prophecy. He knew other men, Aymer and Henry Percy among them, didn't truly believe, but rather saw, as he had, their adherence to the order as a way to curry favour with King Edward. Robert saw surprise in the faces around him. Humphrey, it appeared, knew more of the prophecy than the rest of them. 'It mentions the king by name?'

'*When the last King of Albany dies without issue,*' Humphrey intoned, '*the kingdom will be thrown into disarray. And the sons of Brutus will mourn that day the one of the great name.*'

'Alexander?' said Robert. 'Alexander the Great?'

'How could anyone but a seer have known that would happen?' responded Humphrey.

'Why weren't we told of this?' Aymer's voice cut the silence.

'It is something the men of the Round Table are aware of,' responded Humphrey. 'You would have all been told in time, if chosen to join.'

'Since when were you enlisted to the table?'

Humphrey ignored Aymer's caustic question. 'Robert, I need you to trust me and King Edward needs you to trust him, as you have this past

year. What we are doing is for the good of these islands.' His tone strengthened when Robert didn't respond. 'You swore an oath to the Knights of the
Dragon, to become one in the circle that binds us in loyalty to our king and
his cause. This, Robert, is his cause. One relic from each corner of the old
kingdom, England, Scotland, Ireland, Wales, must be gathered under him
to prevent the ruin of all. Unless you will now break your oath, this is your
cause too. The king has told me where the stone is kept. I can find it myself,
but it will be quicker if you lead the way. I had hoped to do this without
bloodshed,' he added. 'But if we are waylaid in our goal the death of inno-
cents may prove inevitable.'

Robert stared at Humphrey, whose face was resolute. He could break
his oath, refuse to aid him, and make an enemy of every man here and the
king, or he could do as Humphrey asked and help fulfil the prophecy. He
felt more torn than ever, his loyalty to his kingdom pulling at his loyalty to
these men. Rising through his confusion, one stream of thought came clear.
He couldn't refute what Ralph had said about how easily the English had
invaded Scotland. He himself had been left stunned by it. Things had not
been well in the kingdom, not since Alexander's death. *What if it is true?*
What if the prophecy is real? He needed time to think this through, to make
sense of it all. But they were looking at him, waiting for his answer. There
was no time.

Robert didn't speak, but he held out his hand to one of the knights who
had been giving out the shields.

As the knight crossed to Robert and passed him the last dragon shield,
Humphrey turned to the others. 'We must do this quickly. Sir Robert
Clifford and Sir Henry Percy will help me take the stone from the abbey
church. Once we have secured it in the wagon, we leave. Do not raise your
sword against anyone unless attacked,' he added. His eyes moved to Aymer
de Valence, who scowled and gripped the hilt of his blade.

Together, the knights mounted their horses. Making their way out of the
trees, they formed up on the road, heading for Scone Abbey. Robert rode
at the front with Humphrey, the shield heavy on his arm, his heart fierce in
his chest.

After turning on to a narrower road that crossed the river by a bridge,
they came upon the abbey, the buildings rising before them in the twilight.
Beyond the trees that surrounded the abbey grounds, smoke drifted from
roof vents over the royal burgh of Scone. The monks' precinct wasn't walled
and the knights rode straight in, through the grounds. The place was quiet.
Torchlight burned in the windows of a low hall, most likely the monks'

refectory. In the distance, Robert made out the circle of trees atop the ancient Moot Hill. He remembered his grandfather standing beside him in the dying evening light. He remembered the plinth where the stone would be placed and the gravity he felt.

Humphrey reined in his horse, the others slowing behind him. At the sound of his name, Robert realised the knight was calling him to direct them to the abbey church. It was years since he had been here, following his grandfather's stride through this courtyard, but he knew the way. Kicking at Hunter's sides, he led them past living quarters and gardens to where the church rose in the purple gloom. They passed a few figures, who started as they rode out of the dusk. One, dressed in a habit, shouted in alarm, wanting to know who they were, but the knights thundered past without answer. Humphrey overtook Robert, galloping towards the church. Behind him, Robert heard shouts and doors banging, as the monks heard the hoof-beats. Somewhere, dogs began to bark. They didn't have long.

The knights pulled up their horses outside the church doors, the wagon wheels skidding in the dust. They jumped down, some drawing swords as they hastened towards the church. A few stayed by the doors at Humphrey's command while he handed his shield to Ralph, then entered with Percy and Clifford. The church was filled with a smell of incense and molten wax. The glass in the windows shone dully in the candlelight. Robert followed, pulling up the hood of his cloak to hide his face. He was glad of the plain garment. Here, tonight, the red chevron of Carrick would have been like a brand.

Humphrey strode down the aisle, beneath the stern gazes of the angels that bowed from the pillars, heading for the altar, before which was placed a pale block of stone on a cloth of gold. Robert was struck by the memory of his father striding down this very aisle, the voices of the magnates of Scotland raised in protest behind him. He thought of his father's eagerness for this prize; this ancient stone upon which the man had set his life's ambitions. What dire fate had brought him, a Bruce, here at last, not to sit upon the throne, but to seize it for an invader?

Henry Percy and Robert Clifford had followed Humphrey. Together, the three of them hefted up the stone, Percy and Clifford grasping the iron rings to either side, Humphrey taking the weight from underneath. They stumbled down the aisle. Outside, Robert could hear shouts coming closer. The knights guarding the doors yelled for Humphrey to hurry. Robert drew his sword as Percy and Clifford approached. His gaze was on the sacred stone between them, the pale surface of which glittered in the candlelight. Beyond the doors a crowd was coming towards the abbey church, some holding torches. Most wore the habits of monks, but a few looked like labourers or servants. These men held knives and sticks. One had an axe.

The knights moved forward in a guarding ring, Humphrey and the others coming out behind them. Aymer de Valence was at the front. Robert joined them as Percy and Clifford staggered towards the wagon. Humphrey had let go of the stone and had grabbed his shield from Ralph. He moved to confront the approaching men.

The monks of Scone were led by a stooped, elderly man, no doubt the abbot by his fur-trimmed robes. His face had filled with shock at the sight of Percy and Clifford hauling the stone between them.

'In the name of God, what is the meaning of this?' he called hoarsely, coming to a halt before the ring of knights. 'Who are you?'

'We are the Knights of the Dragon,' answered Humphrey. 'We have come to take the Stone of Destiny on the orders of King Edward of England, Duke of Gascony, Lord of Ireland, conqueror of Wales and overlord of Scotland. Stand aside and you will not be harmed.'

'By God, I will not,' murmured the abbot, stepping forward, closely followed by the man with the axe. His voice trembled, but his wizened face was adamant in the torchlight. 'I will not stand aside!'

Percy and Clifford were struggling to lift the stone into the wagon. Ralph moved to aid them.

'None of us will,' the abbot went on, raising his voice. In answer, the monks clustered forward. Most of them looked terrified.

'Then you will die,' growled Aymer de Valence.

Humphrey called out, but Aymer ignored him and thrust towards the abbot, who staggered back in terror. Before Aymer could strike, Robert brought his own sword slicing round to Aymer's throat. He checked the blade at the last second, but it made contact with Aymer's skin, just above the collar of his mail. The knight stopped dead, head tilted back from the edge of steel pushed up against him.

'Lower your weapon,' Robert said through his teeth. 'Or I'll slit you.'

Aymer's black eyes flicked to Guy, standing behind Robert. 'Do it then!' he hissed, 'and I shall die watching as you're run through.'

Robert felt Guy's sword point as a pressure against his back.

The man with the axe had moved closer, his gaze darting between Aymer and Robert, his shoulders hunching, as if to strike. Some of the monks were closing in, clutching their sticks and knives. A bell began to ring somewhere and distant shouts echoed in the dusk, from the town. More help was coming.

Humphrey stepped in. 'Robert.' When Robert didn't move, the knight placed a mailed hand on his blade and pushed it firmly down.

Freed, Aymer stepped back. As he did so, the man with the axe made his move. Aymer turned, whip fast, and ran him through, spitting with effort as he twisted the sword in the man's gut. The man's eyes bulged and his mouth stretched. The axe fell from his fingers to clang in the dust. The abbot cried out as Aymer wrenched the blade free with a spray of blood and the man thudded to his knees, curling over the gaping wound, trying to hold his stomach together with his hands.

Shouts erupted from the company. Some men fell back in fear, others surged forward. As one of the monks went for Humphrey, brandishing his knife, the knight punched him in the face. There was a crunch of bone as the man's nose broke and he reeled away, blood flowing between his fingers. The other knights closed in, forming a wall to block the monks as Percy and Clifford finally hauled the stone into the wagon. The knights moved forward determinedly, their shields raised, Robert caught up among them. Aymer, his blade dripping blood, was at their head. Two of the monks grabbed the abbot and pulled him back from their advance.

'Let's go!' yelled Ralph.

Through the trees came the gleam of torchlight as people from the town hurried to see what the commotion at the abbey was. Mounting, Ralph led the way, the knights on the wagon cracking the whip, sending the horses into a canter.

'*Go!*' shouted Humphrey, racing for his horse.

The wagon bounced over the dusty ground, the horses pulling it straight towards the crowd of monks. They scattered. Two tried to grab hold as it rumbled past. One was sent spinning away, struck by a wheel. The other managed to cling on for a few moments, before being tossed off as the wagon jolted over a rock.

The knights mounted and spurred on their horses, leaving the body of the man Aymer had killed spilling blood across the ground outside the church. Robert's cowl had slipped down in the scuffle and, as he grasped the reins and hauled himself up, he met the gaze of the abbot. There was no recognition in the old man's face, just helpless rage.

Robert rode hard after the Knights of the Dragon. Ahead, the wedge of stone in the belly of the wagon shuddered with the ruts of the road. In his mind, Robert saw his grandfather, his black eyes blazing.

PART 5

1297 AD

Meanwhile Taliesin had come to see Merlin the prophet who had sent for him to find out what wind or rain storm was coming up, for both together were drawing near and the clouds were thickening.

The Life of Merlin, *Geoffrey of Monmouth*

45

The English Justiciar of Scotland, Sir William Ormesby, stood in the window of the hall looking out over the royal burgh of Scone. Smoke bled from roof vents to disappear in the white sky. The sun was up there somewhere, struggling to burn through the fug. Ormesby could feel sweat prickling in his armpits. His fur-trimmed robe felt like an encasement of armour and he longed to slough it off, but he still had many more appointments this morning. The next one, he had been informed, was waiting downstairs. Ormesby would make him wait a while longer. It was good to have them restless and agitated before they were brought to him. He found it made them less able to articulate their objections.

Down below, people went about their business, traipsing through the muddy thoroughfares. Ormesby watched a skinny swineherd corralling his pigs. Further down the street an elderly friar was shuffling along. He paused as a woman in a tatty shawl stooped out of a butcher's in front of him, a thin package clasped in her hands. Dotted among the townsfolk were soldiers, swords slung from their hips. They stood out from the drab people of Scone in their military garb, each man wearing a white band of cloth around his upper arm, decorated with the red cross of St George. The bands had been prescribed by King Edward so that the English soldiery would recognise their own. The red crosses moved in groups of two or three, or else lingered around the hall, the soldiers' hands resting on the pommels of their swords. There were more of them these days, reinforcements having been sent up from Berwick after reports of growing unrest had begun to circulate. Most of the trouble seemed confined to the Highlands, far north of Scone, and in the west, where the MacRuaries had captured, looted and burned three English ships on patrol in the Isles. The MacRuaries were a notorious family, mercenaries and cut-throats all, who would capture any ship that strayed into their territory, no matter the colours it was flying. The English offi-cials at Berwick, however, were taking no chances and had strengthened all major garrisons.

As Ormesby watched, two of the soldiers outside the hall peeled away and headed towards a huddle of beggars, who had emerged from a side street and were trailing after townsfolk, hands outstretched. They looked more like beasts than humans, tattered skins and hides swaddling their forms, their hair matted, faces daubed with filth. There were more of them these days too. Since Ormesby had taken up his post as justiciar, the sights of ragged mendicant friars or lepers with their clacker bowls had been supplanted by the uneasy vision of former freemen with homes and trades reduced to begging on the streets. Although better dressed, they showed clear signs of the destitution that would envelop them in its grey, anonymous shroud in the coming months. Ormesby found it disturbing how someone of standing, however humble, could fall so quickly from grace.

The soldiers were gesturing at the beggars, ordering them to move on. One of the soldiers shoved a man moving too slowly for his liking. Another drew his sword threateningly. Turning from the scene, Ormesby headed back to his table, which was covered in rolls of parchment. The spacious hall, cluttered with fine furniture and wall-hangings, was occupied by four clerks perched at writing desks and two royal officials, quietly conferring over a document. One of the clerks, seated close to Ormesby, glanced round. He wore a pair of thick, wood-rimmed spectacles balanced on his nose and gave Ormesby the impression of a large-eyed fish, blinking at him.

'Should I have the next sent in, sir?'

Ormesby took a breath that puffed out his chest. 'Do.' He seated himself behind his table as the clerk crossed the hall.

After a brief exchange with the soldiers outside, the clerk sat back down, a goose-feather quill poised in his grip over a fresh sheet of parchment. Moments later, a man was escorted in between two soldiers, clutching his cap in his hands.

As he was brought to stand before Ormesby, the justiciar noticed the felt hat looked crushed, as if the man had been grasping the thing for some time. Satisfied, he granted him an officious smile. 'Good day to you, Master Donald.'

'Sir,' murmured the man, glancing round warily as the soldiers left.

'I have been informed by the sheriff that you have refused to pay the taxes for your holding this season.'

'No, sir,' replied Donald firmly, 'not refused. I couldn't.'

'Is that not the same thing?'

Donald gave his head a curt shake, but said nothing. In the quiet, the clerk's quill scratched at the sheet, summarising their words.

Ormesby felt a stab of impatience. Clearly, these churls had no idea who they were dealing with. This was the fourth one this morning who had given him this response, almost verbatim. The man, he realised, was staring him straight in the eyes, despite the fact he was still wringing the cap in his hands. The air of nervous defiance ruffled Ormesby's calm. Was this some plot against him, devised by the local landholders? This would not do at all. Hugh de Cressingham in Berwick had been adamant that revenues due be paid on time. Lords such as Sir Henry Percy, who had been granted Galloway and Ayr on the occupation, hadn't yet been paid their wages and this was apparently a priority. It was rumoured even Sir John de Warenne hadn't received his dues. Ormesby wasn't particularly sorry for that. The earl had been made Lieutenant of Scotland last autumn, but barely weeks after King Edward crossed the border back into England Warenne had followed, preferring to spend his time on his Yorkshire estates. Cressingham, though, was a hard taskmaster and it would not do to anger the man, who in Warenne's absence had become virtual ruler of Scotland. Images of the beggars outside fresh in his thoughts, Ormesby rose stiffly. 'These monies are owed to us by law, Master Donald. By refusing to pay them you are in violation of that law. It is a punishable crime.'

Donald blinked, but shook his head again. 'Sir, I do not have the money. The rents are too high for me to pay.' He hesitated, then continued in a rush. 'They are too high for anyone. People are losing everything. Families are starving, children sickening. Animals are slaughtered needlessly because they cannot be fed. Our churches are falling into ruin, the clergy forced to hand over everything to the Treacherer.' He stopped abruptly, realising his mistake.

Treacherer. Ormesby had heard this name before, although not so openly. It was what the Scots were calling Cressingham. Privately he rather enjoyed it, for he disliked the obese royal treasurer, who dominated the kingdom's administrative centre at Berwick. But, personal feelings aside, he had a job to do here and he wasn't going to let the failings or insolence of a few sorry men interfere with it. Ormesby planted his hands on the crowded table, sending a few rolls of parchment skittering. 'It would be a fool, Master Donald, who put money above his freedom. For that is what is at stake here. Your freedom.'

The man flushed, but didn't take his eyes from Ormesby's. 'Freedom?' he said quietly. 'Is that what this is?'

From outside came sounds of shouting. Neither Ormesby nor Donald heard.

'I have the authority to imprison any who refuse to pay their dues on time. I *will* exercise that authority. Do not test me!'

The shouting was louder, joined now by screams and the thud of running feet. The clerk stopped scratching at the parchment and looked up, his spectacles flashing in the daylight. Ormesby faltered in his tirade, jerking round as a roar came from outside, swelling to fill the chamber with a ferocious torrent of sound. Beneath the incoherent noise came the rumble of hooves. The officials had dropped the document they had been consulting and the clerks had risen. Ormesby crossed to the window and stared out.

From the woods that surrounded the burgh came a mass of men. Some rode, others ran. All carried weapons, mainly axes or spears. A few wore mail shirts and cloaks, but most just leather aketons. Among them were a handful of men clad in the short tunics favoured by Highlanders. These men were bare from thigh to foot, an alarming sight to Ormesby, who had only heard rumour of these wild men of the north. As they came, they roared a multitude of battle cries. Ormesby caught one name in the din, issuing from a group of mailed riders who followed a burly man on a finely capari-soned horse.

'For Douglas!' they howled. '*For Douglas!*'

Below, the townsfolk were scattering. The English soldiers had formed a tight knot outside the hall, blades drawn, but even as Ormesby watched, the forlorn group of beggars he had seen threw off their ragged skins and furs, revealing thickly muscled warriors. They fell upon the soldiers with savage cries, daggers thrusting.

Footsteps sounded on the hall stairs. The door burst open and two soldiers appeared.

'We must go, sir!'

The clerks and officials were already hastening across the chamber. Donald was running with them.

Ormesby remained rooted. 'Who are they?' he demanded, his voice high as he turned back to the window, seeing the horde rushing into the town. His eyes fixed on a giant of a man running, almost loping in the front lines. Taller than all those around him, agile in the stride, he wore a simple dark blue tunic and wide-brimmed kettle hat. The other men seemed to be running in unruly formation around him. But it was the blade in the man's hands that Ormesby's eyes were drawn to. He had never seen such a sword, so broad and long the giant had to grasp it in both hands as he came.

Another name now became audible in the roar of the mob.

'*Wallace! Wallace!*'

46

A s the company rode in through the gates of Carlisle Castle the men on sentry moved aside to let them pass, heaving the massive barriers shut behind them. Robert, at the head of the eight knights, noticed there were more guards now than there had been four days ago when he had left. Their faces, damp in the early morning drizzle, were tense.

Reaching the inner courtyard, Robert and the knights dismounted, rain dripping from their hoods. The place was busy, servants carrying baskets of vegetables and logs to the kitchens. As Robert passed Hunter's reins to a groom who hastened from the stables, he was met by one of his father's men.

The knight inclined his head courteously as he approached, but remained unsmiling. 'Sir, the governor wanted to see you immediately upon your return.'

Robert was soaked to the skin and weary, but it was easier these days simply to obey. The sooner he saw his father, the sooner he could retire to his lodgings and sleep, before he was sent out on another errand. Nodding to his men, he followed the knight across the yard, up the steps to the hall.

After hammering upon the hall's doors to announce him, the knight left him to enter alone. Robert removed his riding gloves, flexing his stiff hands as he walked the chamber's length, beneath the beams. It was late May, but spring seemed reluctant to ripen into summer this year and both hearths were ablaze. His father was hunched over the table that spanned the dais, the surface of which was chaotic with documents. Unconventionally, the lord preferred to conduct his business here rather than in his personal solar on the floor above, to which Robert was rarely invited. The cavernous hall, strung with a banner decorated with the arms of Annandale, seemed, to Robert, the attempt of a man determined for all visitors to recognise him as greater than he was. As he crossed the floor, littered with straw where the castle garrison slept, Robert thought of his grandfather, a man so commanding he could have held council in a barn and all present would have hung on his every word.

The Lord of Annandale glanced up as Robert approached, but didn't greet his son until he ascended the steps and stood before him, the table's breadth between them. 'Do you have anything to report?'

Robert steeled himself before answering. It was how he was able to bear these meetings. Pushing all his hostility deep down inside, he would respond with nothing more than words. 'All is quiet in the district, Father, as far as I could ascertain.'

His father's blue eyes bored into his. 'How far north did you travel?'

'To the border, as you ordered.'

'And you saw nothing? No sign of trouble?'

'Nothing.'

After a taut silence, the lord nodded. 'Good. We may have survived the last attack on this city. But if one comes again I want ample warning.'

'I thought the unrest was concentrated in the Highlands?' said Robert. His father didn't respond, but bent forward to rifle through the rolls on the table. Robert caught the sour odour of wine on his breath and glanced at a goblet and jug, protruding like two silver islands from the wild sea of parchment. He wondered how much his father had had since dawn as his gaze moved over the wine-stained documents, one of which bore a great seal, decorated with the royal arms of England. Robert fixed on it, his interest pricked. He himself had heard no word from the king's court since Edward and his army crossed the border in September, the Stone of Destiny carried with them out of Scotland, along with John Balliol and the rest of the Scottish prisoners. 'You have been contacted by the king?' he asked his father, surprised and a little resentful.

The lord was staring at a map of the Borders, spread out beneath his hands. 'While King Edward has ordered me to maintain the defence of Carlisle he is nonetheless confident the rebels disturbing his peace will be dealt with decisively. I am inclined to agree. The leader of these churls is a man of neither consequence nor standing, a younger son of one of the high steward's vassals.' The lord's dismissive tone changed. 'But though this brigand, William Wallace, may be of no grave threat to the king's rule, some of his supporters could be.'

Robert remained silent. The rebel, Wallace, might be a man of little consequence, but his rising against King Edward's administration had been as a stone tossed into a pool, the ripples of which had spread far and wide.

Robert didn't know much about him, except that he had remained defiant throughout the English occupation, refusing to swear fealty to the king. Wallace, the son of a knight, had clashed with the king's men in the town of Lanark and had been outlawed. Tales of his aggressions against English-held settlements had been filtering across the border ever since, along with tidings of further violence erupting across Scotland.

'What is troubling the king,' continued his father, 'is the treachery of Sir William Douglas. No sooner was he freed from Berwick than he joined Wallace. The uprising of a few brigands is one thing, but the defection of a nobleman such as the Douglas quite another. Edward fears his change of heart could inspire others. Wallace will be dealt with in due course. Douglas is the priority. What with the recent death of his brother Edmund in Gascony, King Edward is occupied by the war against France. He cannot spare the time to attend to this matter personally and has asked me to deal with it. While Douglas is abroad with the main body of his knights, his castle is being defended by his wife and a small garrison. I am to seize his wife and son. They will be taken into English custody and used to persuade Douglas to see sense.'

'When will you leave?' Robert asked, his father's words sinking heavily inside him.

The lord met Robert's gaze, his eyes filling with contempt. 'I have enough to contend with here, as should be obvious. You will do this.' Without waiting for a response, he spoke on. 'You will leave first thing tomorrow, ride to Lochmaben and raise the men of Annandale. Douglas's castle may only be defended by a small garrison, but it will need strength to break it. Bring Douglas's wife and son to me.' When Robert didn't move, the lord's brow puckered. 'Well?'

Robert's emotions found a vent and, like a blast of steam, erupted, scalding and sudden. 'And if you drop this woman and child at Edward's feet, Father, how will he reward your obedience? With a throne, do you think? Or just a pat on the head?'

The Bruce straightened, his face draining. His hand jerked, jolting the king's order from the table top. It struck the wooden boards of the dais, the great wax seal cracking down the centre. 'You will do your duty,' said the lord, his voice strained, 'or you will lose your lands.' Reaching for the goblet, he seized it. 'Either way, you will get from my sight.'

The breeze cooled Robert's skin as he looked out upon the stone-blue dawn. He was bathed in pale moonlight, sweat glistening in the ridges and hollows of his ribs and torso. In just over a month he would celebrate the day of his birth. Those twenty-three years were showing in his body, grown tall like his grandfather's, shaped and honed by more than a decade of training. His broad shoulders tapered into a long back, moulded with muscle, and his arms were corded with veins. Fine dark hair had started to sprout on his chest this past year, running in a faint line to his navel, then on to thicken again. Here and there scars marbled his skin, many of them injuries sustained in training, others from battle. It was a man's body, not a boy's any longer. And yet, for all this strength, he felt more powerless than ever.

Below, the motte of Lochmaben Castle sloped down to the jumble of buildings in the bailey. Beyond the palisade, trees, cloud-like in the moonlight, stretched to the Kirk Loch, which glimmered like a mirror. Memories of this place in other times flooded through him in a rising tide. He had come here a boy of thirteen summers, freed from his father's glowering presence. It was here in Lochmaben that he learned to hunt and sat in council with the men of the realm; here that he first lay with a woman, here where his family mourned the loss of the throne and where his grandfather bestowed upon him the right to claim it back. It was here, in the heart of Annandale, that the sword of the Earl of Mar had made him a knight. Here, where he married Isobel and conceived his daughter.

But despite the web of history that bound him to this place, Robert felt like a stranger. The landscape didn't recognise him any more, nor did the spirits of the past. It had been this way since he had helped seize the Stone of Destiny from the altar at Scone Abbey. His grandfather, once so clear in his mind, had grown faded, as if even his memories were abandoning him, slipping away from the awful truth. It had been a relief to spend the winter in Carlisle. Returning to Scotland to raise his father's vassals for the assault on Douglas's castle had been as a stone in his heart.

Hearing the creak of the bed behind him, Robert turned from the window. The chamber that had once been his grandfather's was in shadow, the fire in the hearth emitting a dull copper glow. The round room on the first floor of the keep was bare, despite the best efforts of the servants to make it comfortable for its new inhabitant. The ancient bed, repaired after the damage sustained in the Comyns' occupation, had been draped with linen sheets and woollen blankets. The few chests containing his belongings – clothing, armour, weapons – had been stacked against one wall beneath a familiar threadbare tapestry that showed knights on black coursers hunting a white stag. Pillows scattered the floor and the bedcovers were rumpled. From between the sheets, a lithe leg had slipped its way out. The woollen blanket had rucked up over the thigh, where it piled haphazardly, then fell away to reveal the curve of a back and the smooth blades of shoulders, half hidden by a mass of dark hair. An arm, which had stretched up and folded under a pillow, revealed the swell of a breast, pressed into the mattress. In stirring, Katherine had turned her face to him, but her eyes remained closed. After a moment, her breaths evened out.

Not wanting to leave his daughter in Carlisle, Robert had brought his wife's former maid and the wet nurse, Judith, with him to Annandale, along with an escort of knights and squires. Three nights ago, after a feast he had arranged for some of his father's vassals, through which he had sat in silence and drank, Robert had called Katherine to his chamber. The maid hadn't resisted when, his fingers fumbling from too much wine, his breath hot, he had taken her to his bed, desperate for some release, for something into which he could pour his frustrations. The next night she had returned of her own accord.

Robert stared at Katherine's sleeping form, then crossed barefoot to his clothes, heaped on the floor. He pulled on his braies, hose and shirt quietly, not wanting to wake her. She had given him all he needed tonight. Taking up his hide boots, his cloak and sword, he opened the door and made his way through the darkened tower.

At the bottom, he was met by the lanky, fair-haired figure of Christopher Seton, whose turn it had been to guard the keep through the night watch. Christopher was one of the men who had accompanied Robert on this assignment, the notable exception being his brother, who remained to assist in Carlisle's defence. Edward had wanted to stay in Annandale at the end of the war and had not settled well in the city. Sullen and angry, he had taken to staying out most nights in the taverns, wasting money on cock fights and starting brawls. When he could, he avoided Robert and their father, blaming them for his exile in England.

'Good day, sir,' said Christopher, opening the door for him.

Robert nodded a greeting to the squire. Not wanting to be drawn into conversation, he headed on down the steep track that wound around the motte, buckling his sword belt. The weapon's weight was a familiar one, for he wore it everywhere now. Heading past the kennels, he heard a whine and saw Uathach slinking from her wooden hut to greet him through the staked fence. He clicked his tongue softly at her, but continued on to the gate in the palisade, which led to the town. He had no destination in mind, only a need for the solitude of the dawn. The castle would wake soon, busy with another day, more vassals arriving for the fight. He wanted the clarity that came with the quiet. Tomorrow he was to leave and march on Douglasdale at the head of his father's men to abduct a woman and child. He needed to hush the voices of the past before then.

Out of the gates he walked, out into the streets. Despite the early hour there were a few people awake already. He passed a figure in a hooded cloak, hunched outside a blacksmith's, an old black dog sprawled on the ground close by. Further down, he saw a man and a woman locked in an embrace in the shadows of a doorway. The rumble of cartwheels came from somewhere up ahead. In the market square the church cast a squat shadow in the moonlight. Robert paused in the empty space, assailed by hazy memories of days golden with sun and promise. He remembered riding through these streets after a hunt, the horses dusty and tired, the men calling jubilantly to his grandfather. He remembered the pride he felt hearing the respect in their voices.

Robert continued on across the square. The simple act of walking was pleasing and he found himself calmed by the momentum of it. Once or twice he thought he heard footsteps behind him, but when he turned he saw no one. Soon, the rhythm of his own stride was all he perceived and when he came to the limits of the town he didn't stop, but carried on into the woods, which echoed with birdsong. Walking the well-worn tracks of men and animals, he came to the edge of the loch, his thoughts consumed by his grandfather.

A man who breaks his oath isn't worth his breath.

The old man had so often said this. Robert had pledged fealty to King Edward and sworn an oath to Humphrey de Bohun and the Knights of the Dragon to defend the king's cause. Despite the conflict warring inside him since the theft of the stone, he couldn't refute this. A true knight, a man of honour, would not break his word. More than anything his grandfather had taught him that. But what if a man had taken oaths that contradicted one another? What then should he do?

The moon was high and small now, its glow weakened by advancing daylight. The loch was glassy, disturbed only by the shadows of birds flitting over the surface. Across the water, the castle keep loomed above the trees. Robert could see plumes of smoke rising from the bailey. The servants would be awake now, preparing the morning meal, stoking the hearths, feeding the animals. Behind him, from the still of the woods, six crows cast into the sky.

Robert closed his eyes and breathed in the hush when the birds had gone. It was then that he heard it: a crackle of twigs and the rustle of undergrowth. He went for his sword and drew it as he turned, eyes scanning the gloom. His gaze alighted on a stooped figure in a hooded brown cloak, heading towards him. As he saw the large black dog loping at the figure's side he realised he had seen them outside the castle gates. He had taken the hunched figure for a beggar. As the figure passed out of the shadows of the trees he saw whoever it might be was leaning on a stick, their gait awkward. Long ashen hair fell in twisted hanks from beneath the low-pulled cowl. Robert caught a glimpse of a wrinkled throat, a sagging jaw and a down-turned mouth. 'Who are you?'

The figure pushed back the cloak's hood.

Robert stared at the hard face, creased with age. It was many years since he had seen her, but he knew her instantly. 'Affraig?' he murmured, lowering his sword.

'I followed you from the castle.' Her voice was rasping. 'I knew it must be you by your clothes.'

Robert glanced at his cloak, decorated with the arms of Carrick.

'I would not have known you otherwise.' Affraig's abrasive voice softened with wonder. 'The boy I knew is gone. A man stands before me.'

Her Gaelic was like a long forgotten song. Since the death of his mother, Robert had mostly spoken French or Scots. He shook his head, stunned by the sight of her. 'When did you come here?' He thought of the journey from Carrick, a few days on foot, perhaps longer for a woman of her years. 'Why did you?'

'Brigid came to me. Her husband heard it on the road from Edinburgh that you were here. He said the Earl of Carrick was raising the men of Annandale.'

'Brigid?' A memory of a whip-thin girl with ratty hair came into Robert's mind.

'Is it Carrick you are raising your father's men for?' There was hope in the question, but flint in her tone.

'Carrick?' Robert frowned. Did the old woman know something his vassals had not told him? 'There is no fight in Carrick.'

'Fight, no. But struggle, yes. Great struggle.' As she limped towards him, the black dog followed.

Robert saw that the animal had white, blind eyes. He wondered if it was one of the dogs she'd had when he had known her – that had bitten his brother, Alexander.

'It has been hard for us, caught between Ayr and Galloway.' Her haggard face was grim. 'Soldiers of the Englishman, the one they call Percy, have pressed in on us from both sides. Disputes against them are silenced before they can be raised, by bribes or by violence. It is worse beyond our borders. Brigid brings me tidings from Ayrshire and many others come, begging for my aid to ease their suffering. Much suffering there is, in the towns filled with English soldiers and in the villages, where taxes have taken the food from children's mouths. I have heard of men hanged without trial or judgement, houses looted, women——' She halted. When she continued, her voice was low. 'It is worse since the rising of William Wallace, but at least he brings hope to his people. I came, Sir Robert, to see if our hope may lie in you. Our lord.'

For a long moment, Robert didn't know what to say. More than anything he felt angry: at her for bringing tidings it was the responsibility of Andrew Boyd and his other vassals to tell him and for assuming it was her place to, and at himself for not knowing his own people were suffering. 'I am here on my father's orders,' he said, tight-lipped. 'But I intend to return to Carrick as soon as my task here is done. I know Sir Henry Percy. I will talk to him personally.'

'*Talk* to him?' The lines on Affraig's face deepened. 'When I learned of your alliance with the English and their king at the start of the war, I did not at first believe it. Your father, yes. But you? Your grandfather would weep for these days, had he lived to see them.'

Robert's eyes narrowed, anger struggling to break free. 'You forget my grandfather served both Edward and Henry. I am not the first Bruce to serve an English king.'

'Served them he may have, but not at the expense of his kingdom. He never would have done so if it meant harm to his own people!' Her bony finger shot out. 'You and your father have left your lands to wither! For more than three years the people of Carrick have been without a lord.'

The dog, hearing the words spitting through her teeth, began to growl.

Robert stood his ground, towering over Affraig, his nose clogging with the smell of mouldering earth that came off her. Her cloak was caked with mud. 'You dare speak to me in this manner? You know nothing of my life!'

She didn't flinch at his tone, or the sword that had risen in his grasp. 'I know you were passed a solemn inheritance that you have turned your back on. That I know.'

He went to speak, then moved past her, not wanting to hear more of her sour invective.

'What of the throne of our people, carted to a foreign court?' she called behind him, her voice as harsh as a crow's caw. 'What of the hill that stands empty?'

He turned, fear and shame leaping in him, thinking she must somehow know of his part in the theft.

'For centuries Scotland's kings were made at Scone. Will there not be another to stand upon the Moot Hill and hear the names of his forefathers recited from the pages of history? Our kingdom has lost its soul, Robert.'

He could see no accusation in her face any more, only sorrow. She couldn't know what he had done. If she did, she would curse him where he stood. Some part of him wished she would.

'Your family held a claim to the throne for over half a century. I do not understand why you do not fight for it, as was your grandfather's wish. Or why you would serve the man who has taken your right from you?'

Something flashed in Robert's mind. He remembered the day his grandfather told him he was to be dubbed, the day his father was forced to resign the earldom of Carrick. He had seen Affraig in Lochmaben talking with the old man. She had touched his face with strange affection. How could he have forgotten? 'It was you? You told my grandfather to pass the claim to me?'

Her lips flattened in a thin line. 'Fool that I was. I should have seen then that it was your father's mould you had been made in.'

Robert's face flushed. 'Leave. You have no business with me or my family. Not any more.'

As he strode through the trees, cuffing aside branches, her voice echoed at his back.

'Leave, I shall. There is no hope here.'

47

The boy grasped the mossy stones of the parapet wall and pulled himself up, breathing hard from the climb. Behind him his father's banner snapped in the breeze. His pale blue eyes narrowed as he squinted over the battlements into the sunlight that was reflected in the surface of the small loch that lay beyond the castle walls. From out of the green depths of the forest that encircled the stronghold an army was slowly emerging, men and horses forming up beyond the dazzling water, helms and lances glinting. The boy's eyes settled on a standard at the head of the company. A red chevron on white.

'Bastards,' he murmured. Dropping down, the boy turned to his father's banner, three white stars on billowing blue. The sight of the flag fuelled him with defiance. 'Let them come,' he breathed, ducking through the door at the tower's top and sprinting down the steps inside.

As he reached the floor below, he saw the door to his parents' chamber was ajar. The gap was filled with firelight and conversation came from within. The boy halted, stifling his breaths so as not to be heard. His mother's voice sounded, soft and troubled.

'I shall speak to them. They will parley with me, surely?'

'The Earl of Carrick leads them, my lady. The young Bruce is a puppet for the English king, so it is said.'

The boy moved closer. That was Dunegall, the captain his father had left to command the garrison. The man was stalwart, but as old as the hills and afflicted with the gout.

'I will address them from the gate, my lady, and demand to know why they are trespassing on Lord Douglas's lands.'

'I think it is clear why they have come, Dunegall. With my husband in the company of William Wallace they have come for James and me. They mean to punish him through us. I have no doubt of it.'

The boy stepped back with a frown at his name and the threat in her words.

'Do not fear, my lady, these walls are stout.'

'After all the Treacherer has taken our stores are almost empty. We cannot stay here indefinitely. The Bruce and his men will starve us out, if they do not break down the gates and force their way in. No, I will go to them.'

Lady Douglas seemed to falter. But when she spoke again, her voice was flat. James recognised the resolve in her tone. He'd been confronted with it many a time when he'd misbehaved.

'I will tell them James is not here. Perhaps, if I give myself to them, they will be content. Whatever happens to me, Dunegall, you must promise to deliver James safe to his father.'

James stumbled back from the door. Without waiting to hear any more, he raced on, down through the tower. If his father were here he would ride out on his charger with a roar that would shake the foundations of the keep and smash through them all with the fury of hell, not stopping until the ground was drenched in their blood or his own. Either way, he would not let his wife face an army. Well, James could not ride out – his father's men had taken all their horses, except his mother's hobby and a few nags – but weapons he did have. He kept his sword, the one he had trained with for the past year, in the room where he slept, but the guardroom was closer. Anyhow, he wanted a man's weapon.

On the other side of the loch, Robert formed up with the men of Annandale, as the foot soldiers continued to tramp out of the trees behind. To either side of him were Nes and Walter, a knight from Carrick, who had served him well in Carlisle and whom he'd appointed as his banner-bearer. Walter held aloft his standard, the chevron a bold red arrow pointing to the sky. The hooves of their horses sank in the boggy ground around the loch, the grassy banks of which were alive with waterfowl. Robert glimpsed flickers of bronze and silver, the sunlight catching under the birds' wings as they darted through the reeds, disturbed by the gathering men. Beyond the body of water, the castle of Lord Douglas rose from a grassy mound. It looked much like Lochmaben: a stone keep atop a motte reinforced with clay and timber, and a bailey surrounded by a palisade. The only real difference was the terrain, which was more thickly wooded.

Robert had led his company through these deepening woods for miles, following the River Annan north through his father's domain, before heading west into the rising hills. The land had marched up into lofty, green tors, cloaked with beech and oak, where rivers snaked along the valleys and waterfalls tracked silent silver lines down the steeper slopes. In the distance the blue shadows of higher peaks could be seen, the first markers of the mountains that barred the way to the north and west. Douglas, nestled in a valley in the heart of the woods, was a peaceful setting, the smell of wild herbs filling the air.

Sitting astride Hunter on the edge of the trees, the sun warm on his face, Robert stared at the hushed landscape before him. There should be peasants out working, farmers driving cattle to summer pastures, girls traipsing down to the waterside with laundry, lords and their sons out with bows, hunting the first deer. Instead, the place was deserted, the castle gates shut and barred. Only the smoke coming from the buildings and the noises of panicked animals beyond the palisade gave any sign of life. He could see Douglas's banner, flying from the keep. Robert had never met Sir William Douglas or his family, but he knew the man's wife was a sister of his grandfather's old ally, James Stewart. Douglas's son and heir had been named after the high steward, his uncle and godfather.

'Do we make camp?'

Robert looked round at the blunt question to see a flint-eyed knight staring at him. Gillepatric was one of his father's staunchest vassals, a tough, canny man who had aided in the defence of Carlisle. Robert had often wondered how his father inspired such loyalty in men like this, who had kept faith and fought for him even while their homesteads were being burned by the Comyns. He supposed his father's decision to support King Edward had been proven right in the end, for the men of Annandale were some of the few in Scotland to retain their lord and their lands, many others now subject to the rule of English barons such as Warenne and Percy. Still, his father inspired so little devotion in him by comparison. It now struck Robert that these men weren't a threat to his father's ambitions. They were followers, loyal because they had to be, for their own sakes as much as their lord's. He was the one waiting in the shadows to take his father's place, his fortune. His father had already been passed over, his earldom removed. However much Robert admired his grandfather he couldn't deny that the old man's disappointment in his son and affection for him had been the main cause of the division between them. For the first time, he thought he understood something of his father's resentment. He was a mirror in which the man had watched his own life pass.

'Not yet,' Robert said, in answer to Gillepatric's question. 'I will speak to the garrison commander first.' He doubted Douglas's wife and son would give themselves willingly into his custody, but he wanted to parley with them before any assault was made.

Instructing the other knight captains to tell their men to rest and setting foot soldiers to watch the road at their backs, Robert picked six men to accompany him to the castle including Walter, Gillepatric and the Yorkshire squire, Christopher Seton. Robert had grown fond of the squire over the past few months. The young man had a pleasant manner that reminded him of his youngest brother, Niall, who had remained in Ireland with Thomas through the war. Christopher was possessed of the same cheerful disposi- tion and a desire to please without being fawning. With Christopher on this mission was his Scots-born cousin Alexander, a lord from Lothian who was ten years his senior. Alexander Seton was less immediately likeable, more guarded and aggressive, but he was a skilled fighter. Robert nodded for him to follow as they left the main host.

The small company approached the castle gates, skirting the loch on a dusty track. Impatience was sharp inside Robert. He forced it away, know- ing rashness here would be dangerous, but he couldn't ignore the fact that he wanted this over with quickly. Affraig had remained close in his thoughts on the road to Douglasdale, her accusations plaguing him. He had been beset by visions of Henry Percy and his knights hunting in the forests of Carrick, taking what they wanted from stores and larders, scorning protests. He had seen them do it in Wales. Robert had never been close to the blond Lord of Alnwick with his chilly smile, but he knew him well enough to know that the men and women of Ayrshire and Galloway would not be faring well under him. Neither would the people of his earldom, caught between.

'Sir!'

Robert pulled on Hunter's reins as Christopher shouted. To their right, away across the grass, a narrow gate in the palisade was opening. Robert slowed, seeing a solitary figure slip out. The figure was incredibly lean and short for a man, but stranger than his physique was his clothing. He wore just a white tunic, looped by a belt, no armour at all except for a great helm, the visor of which was down. The metal was rusty and the helm ill- fitting, almost lopsided. The figure clutched a broadsword in both hands, holding it in front of him as he stumbled blindly down the grassy slope towards them. The men with Robert were frowning, their eyes darting from the figure to the castle, suspecting some trickery. Gesturing for them to remain where they were, Robert kicked Hunter towards the helmed man, gripping his sword, but not yet drawing it. 'I am Sir Robert Bruce, the Earl of Carrick. I am here on the orders of King Edward to take into my custody the wife and son of Lord William Douglas, in retaliation for his rebellion against the crown.' The words sounded forced and hollow. Robert could hear the distaste in his own voice. The man hadn't answered his question. He repeated the words, louder now, pulling Hunter to a halt a short distance away.

'I will fight any man in your army,' the figure called in fierce response. 'But if I win you must let the Lady Douglas go free.' The voice came muffled through the helm, but it was clearly that of a boy.

Robert heard laughter behind him as his father's knights caught the high-pitched challenge.

In response, the helmed figure took several determined steps towards Robert. 'Will you not accept, you cowards?'

The laughter stopped abruptly and Gillepatric drew his blade with a snarl.

At that moment, the main gates of the castle opened and a woman emerged. She let out a cry as she saw the helmed boy halfway down the grassy bank, confronting Robert. '*James!*' she screamed, running towards him. 'Dear God! *James!*'

'It's the son!' shouted Gillepatric triumphantly, spurring his horse towards the boy. 'It's Douglas's son!'

There were more shouts as the castle garrison spilled from the gates after the woman, swords drawn. Robert's knights urged their horses towards them. Away across the loch, a horn sounded as the host saw the emerging soldiers. The woman reached the boy and grabbed hold of him, pulling him back. In the struggle, the oversized helm toppled off and clanged to the ground, revealing a pale-faced boy of no more than twelve or thirteen, with sleek, crow-black hair.

Robert saw Gillepatric and Christopher charging towards the woman and boy. The other knights were breaking away, heading for the guards. In the chaos, the boy fought against the woman's hold, still clutching the sword, his lips peeled back, pale blue eyes flashing in the sunlight. Robert was transfixed by the boy's brazen courage. His mouth was dry, his heart thudding. In his mind, he saw himself, years ago, in the church at Scone, drawing his sword against John Comyn in defence of his grandfather. All at once, something snapped inside him, something bright and sharp that was both painful and liberating. He raked his spurs across Hunter's sides. Urging the horse on, he manoeuvred himself in between the woman and boy and his father's knights. Drawing his sword, he roared at his men to halt. Gillepatric and Christopher were coming straight at him. To avoid collision, Gillepatric had to pull on the reins so hard his horse reared up, hooves striking the air. Christopher Seton turned in a tight circle, his horse protesting with a high squeal.

The woman had managed to drag James away and the castle guards had reached them. Surrounding the two in a ring of swords, the men hustled them back across the grass to the gates.

Gillepatric regained control of his horse. 'In Christ's name, what are you doing?' he yelled at Robert, pointing his blade towards the retreating group. 'We could have taken him!'

Robert met the man's flint-eyed stare. 'No.'

'Your orders are to seize the wife and son!'

'And your orders are to follow my command.'

Behind Robert, the guards had reached the castle gates and were disappearing inside with the woman and boy. Fast along the track by the loch more riders were coming, the men of Robert's army responding to the threat.

Christopher's gaze darted between Gillepatric and Robert. 'What is it, Sir Robert? Why did you stop us?'

Robert glanced round, hearing the castle gates rattle shut. He wanted to grin, for it felt like a victory. 'We're not going to seize Lady Douglas, or her son.'

Gillepatric stared at him. Men were riding up, slowing as they saw the castle gates had closed. The air was full of the clatter of hooves.

Robert went to speak, but poised on the brink, unsure of what to say. *What was he doing?* Forcing the question aside, he addressed the growing circle of knights. 'I have summoned you on my father's instructions. But now I am here, I cannot fulfil those orders.' His voice strengthened. 'We have been sent to seize the wife and son of a man who is fighting for our kingdom. Can anyone here say he agrees with this?'

'It is not our place to question orders that come from the king,' said Gillepatric harshly.

'Scotland has no king,' responded Robert. 'Balliol is broken and imprisoned in England.'

'And King Edward rules in his place. Have you forgotten the fealty we swore to him after the war?'

'Oaths of the vanquished to the victor,' said Robert, his voice becoming clearer. He felt as though he had been asleep for months and was suddenly awake. It was a heady, volatile feeling.

'This is madness,' snapped Gillepatric. 'You dishonour your father and his name. He could lose his lands. We all could!'

'Not if he is seen to have nothing to do with this.'

'Sir Robert,' said another of the knights, 'you cannot return to Carlisle or Annandale if you disobey the king's orders. You'll be imprisoned in England with Balliol and the rest.'

'I do not intend to return.' As he said this, Robert felt a great wash of relief. For too long his father's household had been as a prison. Trapped under the lord's authority, unable to speak out or make his own decisions, he had been treated like a humble knight rather than the earl he was, his authority passed over without a word. But even as his doubt fell away other, darker concerns replaced it. He thought of the prospect of imprisonment and the loss of his lands. He thought of the betrayal of his pledge to the king and to the Knights of the Dragon, and was pricked by guilt as Humphrey's broad face appeared in his mind. But he couldn't allow a friendship, or his oath to determine the fate of his kingdom, not any more. 'You can choose to return to Annandale to my father's service,' he told the knights. 'Or, if you are willing, you can come with me. But, either way, we leave the lands of Lord Douglas.' He stared around, his gaze resting last on Gillepatric. 'That is my command.'

Gillepatric snarled. 'You're a fool! No man here will follow you.' For a moment the knight seemed set to spur his horse away in disgust, then he switched back suddenly, his blade rising.

Robert, who had already lowered his sword, had no chance to defend himself. Christopher Seton, however, had seen the hostile intent in Gillepatric's face and urged his horse in between them, lashing out with his sword, intending to deflect Gillepatric's. The older knight was far quicker. Switching the trajectory of his blade at the last moment he turned it to smash the pommel into the squire's face. Christopher was slammed back with the force and toppled from his horse. Several things happened at once. Robert lifted his sword with a fierce shout at Gillepatric. Christopher's courser bolted, causing the other horses to stamp and jostle in panic, Hunter's hooves narrowly missing Christopher's head. Out of everyone, though, it was Alexander Seton who was the quickest. Barrelling into the fray, he wrenched forward and grabbed Gillepatric round the neck. Pulling back, he squeezed, causing the knight to gag and choke. Several of Gillepatric's comrades turned their swords on Alexander as Christopher struggled to his feet, one hand to his bloodied nose. Gillepatric dropped his sword and tried to prise Alexander's arm off his windpipe. Nes and Walter moved in determinedly to defend Robert.

'Enough!' Robert's voice ripped across them. Trembling with fury and shock at the unexpected attack, he strove to maintain his composure. 'You will stand down. All of you,' he told Alexander, who hadn't relinquished his hold. Gillepatric's face was turning a bruised purple. 'I will not allow blood to be shed here. Not in my name, God damn you!'

Slowly, Alexander loosened his grip on Gillepatric. Christopher had staggered to his feet and was snorting blood out of his nose. Released, Gillepatric sagged in his saddle, drawing ragged gasps of air. His comrades kept their swords pointed at Alexander, but made no move, glancing between Gillepatric and Robert. One knight dismounted, warily, to retrieve the older man's sword.

Gillepatric touched his throat, his eyes on Robert. 'You are not your father's son,' he breathed. Snatching his sword from the man who had retrieved it, he wheeled his horse around and spurred it viciously away across the grass. His men followed, riding back along the track by the loch. More peeled from the circle around Robert. A couple tried to persuade him to reconsider, but he sat in defiant silence, refusing to be drawn. In less than a few minutes only Nes, Walter and the Setons remained.

Robert nodded his gratitude to the two cousins. 'Thank you for coming to my defence.' He fixed on the lord. 'But you have a rich estate, Sir Alexander. You will most likely lose it if you join me.'

'I fear I will lose my property whether or not I stay with you,' responded Alexander. 'King Edward is carving up our kingdom according to his own design. Soon, there will be no Scot left in authority.' He smiled coldly. 'But if William Wallace wins this rebellion we could all be rewarded by choosing the right side now.' He looked at Christopher.

The squire wiped his bloodied nose with the back of his hand and nodded at Robert. 'I am with you, Sir Robert, wherever you plan to go.'

Robert was silent, thinking through the implications of his actions, which had put him on the side of the insurgents. He thought of William Wallace with caution. From what he knew the rebel leader was fighting in the name of the captive John Balliol, which didn't necessarily make him an ally. Nes's quiet voice drew him from his considerations.

'Where will we go from here, sir?'

'Perhaps to Carrick,' Robert said, after a pause. 'Yes,' he went on, firmer now, 'to my people.' Before they could ask him anything further, he continued. 'I want you to go back to our camp. Escort my attendants and my daughter here, and bring what you can of our supplies.'

'I have two good men with me,' said Alexander in answer. 'Both dubbed. They will join us.'

Robert's gaze moved down the loch to where the men of his army were already beginning to move out. Then, kicking Hunter on, he made his way up to the gates. As he reached the palisade, he swung down from the saddle. He could hear raised voices on the other side. 'I would speak to the Lady Douglas,' he called loudly. The voices quietened at once. 'I am alone. My army is leaving.'

Slowly, the gates of Douglas Castle opened and Robert found himself faced by a line of armed guards. A woman was in their centre, holding the shoulders of the boy, James. He was sure now what he had suspected before, that she was his mother, the Lady Douglas. She was young and attractive with solemn brown eyes like her brother's.

'I do not understand, Sir Robert,' she said, her voice strained. 'What are your intentions?'

'My men will not harm you, my lady, but you must leave this place. My father is acting on King Edward's orders and even if he sends no other men to seize you and your son, the king most certainly will. He intends to make an example of your husband, to dissuade other noblemen from joining Wallace.'

She nodded. 'James has an uncle in Paris.'

'Mother—' began the boy, looking between her and Robert.

She spoke over him. 'He will be safe there. I have family in the west I can go to.'

'You should leave as soon as you are able.' Robert inclined his head. 'My lady.'

As he moved to go, Lady Douglas stepped forward, between the swords of the guards. 'And you, Sir Robert, where will you go? The king will surely punish you for this.'

He turned back. 'To Carrick, for now.'

'You should seek out my brother.'

'The steward?' Robert frowned in question. James Stewart he knew had remained in Scotland after pledging homage to King Edward, but Robert had heard nothing of the high steward or his whereabouts in many months. The man seemed to have melted away. All Robert knew was that he had been married, some time before war broke out the previous year, to a sister of Sir Richard de Burgh, the Earl of Ulster.

'William Wallace is the son of one of Sir James's vassals. You cannot believe he managed to stir up such widespread rebellion so quickly on his own, can you?' Lady Douglas smiled slightly. 'My brave husband is not his only ally.'

'My lady,' warned one of the guards.

She ignored him. 'Go to him, Sir Robert. I believe you will find in him a friend, as once your grandfather did. The last I knew my brother was in his lands of Kyle Stewart. Perhaps, if enough noble men make a stand, King Edward will be forced to abandon his occupation.'

'Perhaps,' echoed Robert doubtfully.

But as he walked away, leaving the castle gates to close behind him, his mind filled with the possibility of hope. If he, an earl, joined the rebellion, perhaps it would make a difference? Maybe his actions would inspire others, men who had supported his grandfather in the past. If enough of them joined the cause, King Edward would find it difficult, if not impossible to retain control in Scotland without resorting to another military campaign. He knew better than most that the king could ill afford to put down a widespread revolt when the war in France continued unabated.

Digging his foot into the stirrup and hauling himself into the saddle, Robert felt his decision settle inside him. Whatever happened, he would not return to Carlisle.

48

Robert Wishart stood in the chaos of the hall. Around him furniture lay overturned, benches toppled, boards knocked from their trestles. Five of the eight silk tapestries showing the life of St Kentigern, the city's patron saint, that had graced the walls since before he was made Bishop of Glasgow were gone. Wishart took in their absence with a slow nod of anger. All around were signs of recent occupation, bowls crusted with food and wine in goblets covered with a film of dust.

The bishop moved through the mess, while canons from the cathedral worked to right it. Benches scraped loudly on the floor as the silent men turned them over. A goblet slipped off a table, landing on the floor with a noise like a bell and making some of them wince. On his arrival Wishart had sensed the tension coiled in them all. It made him question his decision to leave when Anthony Bek had set himself up in Glasgow's Episcopal Palace, as agreed by King Edward. Many of the Scottish clergy had remained, but Wishart, his palace invaded and his position challenged, had retired from his diocese to his hall at Stobo, deep in Selkirk Forest. No, the bishop reasoned, his gaze moving over the industrious canons: his decision had been right, whatever indignities his men had suffered in his absence. It was nothing compared to what others had endured and, besides, he never would have been able to accomplish all he had if he'd remained under the militant Bek's eagle eye.

Crossing to one of the windows, Wishart looked out over the orchards that filled the palace enclosure. The trees were full and green, their leaves incandescent after the morning's fall of rain. Beyond the palace walls, Glasgow Cathedral towered over the valley above the River Clyde, on the banks of which lay the bustling burgh of Glasgow. Despite the circumstances, he was deeply gratified to be back in his see.

Wishart turned, hearing soft footfalls behind him, to see an acolyte.

'The visitor you have been expecting has arrived, your grace.'

Wishart smiled grimly. 'Good.'

After speaking briefly with the dean, he left the hall, following the acolyte. Outside, the yard was busy with members of the bishop's household unloading his belongings from the wagons that had travelled from Stobo. Beyond the bustle a small group of men and horses were gathered near the gates. Wishart squinted into the daylight, his gaze fixing on one in their centre, a tall, dark-haired man. He moved down the palace steps, his large frame awkward on the rain-slick stones, brushing aside the offer of a steadying arm from the acolyte. 'Sir James,' he called, heading for the dark-haired man, who turned to watch him approach.

'Your grace.' The high steward bent to kiss the bishop's outstretched hand. 'It is a comfort to see a fellow guardian in such black days as these.'

Wishart grunted in agreement. Telling the acolyte to lead the steward's men to the stables, he motioned for James to follow. 'Come, my friend, let us walk together. I will have food and drink prepared for your knights.'

The two men set off across the yard. The steward was dressed in a sodden travelling cloak, the bishop in robes trimmed with ermine, his buskins soggy with mud.

James glanced to where the wagons were being offloaded. 'Have you just arrived?'

'Two days ago. I came as soon as I learned Bishop Bek had abandoned the place.' Wishart grinned ferociously. 'The canons tell me he hitched up his skirts and fled like a woman when he heard Wallace was on his way. Taking everything he could carry, the brigand went south to England.' Wishart's smile vanished. 'Half my possessions went with him. Wallace passed through days later, heading west.' By the lack of surprise in James Stewart's face, the bishop guessed he had already heard most of this. Veering towards the orchard, he pursed his lips and frowned into the white sky. The cloud cover was low, but the sun was struggling to pierce it. With God's grace they would see it before the day was out. 'I know you have been supporting Wallace's uprising,' he said bluntly, unwilling to dance around the issue.

James glanced at him. For a moment, his poise slipped, then it was back, his face a mask of calm. He didn't answer.

Wishart stopped under the shade of a gnarled apple tree. The tree had stood here for years, long before he was a bishop, perhaps long before he was born, through storm and flood, drought and war. In autumn it bore the sweetest apples. 'Bek will have raised the alarm, James. The English will be coming for us soon. My scouts tell me King Edward has already ordered the

Bruce at Carlisle to raise men for an attack on Douglas's lands. Wallace and his army are headed for Irvine. There, they intend to make a stand against our enemies. I want us with them.'

James looked away, still silent.

'Wallace and Douglas's army grows daily,' continued Wishart, undeterred. 'Many more have joined them since they hounded Ormesby from Scone. In the north, the Moray family have raised the standard of rebellion. In the west, war has broken out between the MacDonalds and MacDougalls. Everywhere, English officials and those who support them are being challenged. My friend, you are Lord Douglas's brother-in-law and Wallace's lord. Will you not come out in favour of them?'

Finally, James spoke. 'Most of those Wallace leads are outlaws. Whatever my personal feelings, I am the steward of this kingdom. I cannot be seen to support the actions of such men.'

Wishart pressed on, hearing the tightness in James's voice. 'You know as well as I that these men are outlaws because they have stood up to abuses committed by English soldiers in their towns. You know what the Sheriff of Lanark did to Wallace.'

'Yes, I know.'

'The time is ripe, James. King Edward is occupied by his war with France and the discontent among his barons, who are fed up with paying for it. If we act now we could win.'

'A stand? At Irvine?' James shook his head. 'Even if I raised all the men of Renfrew and Kyle Stewart and Bute we could not defeat the English on the field. Wallace's company is armed with spears and sticks. Most of them have no armour and even less experience. The English cavalry would cut through them like scythes through wheat. Our entire host could not defeat them at Dunbar. How could a peasant army hope to win through?'

Wishart smiled, his eyes glittering. 'Have faith, James. We have a plan.'

49

The company rode into the port of Irvine, their horses casting long shadows across the grass. Robert's face was darkened by the late June sun, his surcoat and mantle dusty from the cornfields they had ridden through. Above him hovered the standard of Carrick, carried by the Carrick knight, Walter. Uathach loped alongside the slow trot of his palfrey, her tongue lolling in the heat. Riding with Robert were Nes, leading Hunter beside his own horse, the Setons and two knights from Alexander's lordship in East Lothian. Since leaving Douglasdale, Robert had kept close counsel and quarters with them and in these past weeks on the road had come to know the cousins well. He was glad to have them with him: Christopher to lighten his mood and Alexander to watch his back.

Behind came seven squires from Carrick, five servants and Robert's steward, all leading spare horses laden with supplies. A solitary wagon bearing the heavier gear and their tents rolled in their wake. Among the men rode Katherine on the chestnut mare that had belonged to Robert's wife. The maid was wearing one of Isobel's gowns, unearthed from his belongings at Lochmaben. Robert couldn't remember having kept any of his wife's clothes until, slipping from his bed their second morning together, Katherine had presented the dress to him, asking if she could have the garment as her own clothes were becoming worn. He had stared at her standing there naked, her cheeks flushed with the heat of their lovemaking, before consenting with a wordless nod. The pale blue dress, laced at the back with a silver braided ribbon, had been a little long, for Katherine was shorter than Isobel, and tight on the bust where she was more amply endowed, but the maid had set Judith to work on altering it. The blue gown, which flowed behind her over the mare's rump, was still slightly snug at her chest. A fact that hadn't, Robert knew, gone unnoticed among the men.

To Katherine's side rode Judith, staring sullenly out from beneath her dust-smudged coif, her pinched face hectic with sun. The girl was a miserable sow, but all the while her milk flowed she was as invaluable to Robert as the knights and squires with their swords. Behind the wet nurse was Marjorie in a chair fixed to the saddle which Nes had made out of an old stool seat, lined with a blanket. His daughter, almost sixteen months now, was starting to gurgle words, much to his pleasure.

Ahead, beyond Irvine on the banks of a river, the rebel encampment was sprawled across a stretch of fallow fields. Drawn from all corners of Scotland, it was a motley company: barons and lords, clergymen and officials and, swelling their number, a rabble of outlaws and peasants. They filled the area with a panoply of equipment, from finely furnished marquees to blankets on the ground, barded destriers to scrawny pack-horses and mules. There were fire pits tended by servants and flickering bonfires thronged by rough men in woollen hukes. The grass between the mass of tents and people was violet with thistles. Robert squinted into the smoky dusk, hunting for the steward's banner.

On leaving Douglasdale, he had headed south-west through slow-climbing hills to Kyle Stewart, heeding the words of Lady Douglas. The steward had become something of a beacon, a hope on the horizon. The man was a canny politician and a shrewd speaker, and Robert's grandfather had counted him among his closest confidants. He felt sure the man would be able to advise him, but his expectance had been crushed when they arrived to find the steward gone, recently departed, so they were told by a wary guard, to meet the Bishop of Glasgow. In Kyle Stewart their company had lingered in a camp in the woods for several days, Robert unsure of what to do.

His decision to defy his father's orders had cemented itself on the road west and he had become convinced that it had been the right one. The weight of the past year had fallen from his shoulders and, despite concerns of what his decision would mean for him and his lands, he felt light, optimistic even, for the first time in months. In his mind, the possibility of negotiating with the English had been creeping into his thoughts, adding to this fragile sense of hope. His voice, as one of the thirteen earls of Scotland, as well as that of a former member of the king's elite, would surely be heeded by them, unlike that of Wallace, whose voice was the roar of the mob and whose only ambition seemed to be to kill every Englishman in the land. Whatever his hopes, Robert couldn't stay waiting indefinitely for the high steward to return, for with every day that passed came rumours of war.

People spoke of violence erupting in the west between the MacDonalds of Islay and the MacDougalls of Argyll. The MacDonalds, friends of the Bruce family, had supported King Edward since the occupation, incurring the retribution of the MacDougalls, who had long been allies of the Comyns. Rumour told of towns burning and families forced to flee as bands of armed men roved through the countryside, bent on murder and pillage. Everywhere rebellion was growing, as households realigned themselves and chose sides, ancient feuds stirred up to spark new conflagrations. English garrisons were retreating inside castle walls, as urgent messages and pleas for aid were hurried to Cressingham in Berwick, the roads becoming perilous. It was through these tidings that Robert's company learned the Scots were gathering at Irvine. Reports were confused, some saying King Edward himself was coming north to confront the rebels, others that Wallace intended to invade England, but the one thing the stories agreed upon was that two new supporters of the uprising had emerged, in the forms of Bishop Wishart and Sir James Stewart, and that they too were headed for the port.

Now, approaching the rebels' camp in the dying light, Robert felt his anticipation at the prospect of the steward's counsel rise again. But before they reached the outskirts his company was met by an armed patrol.

The group confronted them on foot, one man halting them with a raised hand. Hugely muscular with a bald head burned scarlet, he was incongruously dressed in dirty, calf-length braies held in place by a belt at his broad stomach and a fine, fur-trimmed cloak that he wore open to reveal a scarred chest. He was gripping a long-handled axe with a wicked, curved blade. The six men with him wore an odd mix of garments suggestive of a multitude of localities. One was wearing the short tunic of a Highlander and was barefoot with a long spear in his hands. Another was clad in a rather outdated mail haubergeon that was too big for him, suggesting it had been made for someone else, while two others wore stained gambesons and carried short bows, with cloth quivers filled with arrows slung from their belts. They had the bullish stance of confident, aggressive men and all looked as if they had recently seen battle, cuts and bruises decorating their skin, bloodstains soaked into their clothing.

The bald man in the fur-trimmed cloak had his eyes on Robert's banner. 'Who are you?' he said, his voice like a bear's growl.

When Robert stated his name, he noticed an immediate shift in the group's demeanour. The bald man glanced meaningfully at the Highlander in the short tunic, who nodded wordlessly and headed across the grass into the bustle of the encampment.

The bald man turned back with a dour expression. 'Wait here.'

'I've come to see Sir James Stewart,' Robert went on, biting back his affront. He couldn't really have expected anything but a cold welcome considering, but still, to be treated so discourteously by such men was an insult to his nobility.

The bald man said nothing, but continued to stare at Robert, his axe grasped in his fists.

Robert sat back in his saddle, showing him indifference, while inside he wondered uneasily if he had made a mistake coming here, perhaps a dangerous one. He caught the eye of Alexander Seton, whose face displayed a similar concern, his hand on his sword pommel.

After a tense wait, several men appeared, moving through the crowded camp, following the bare-legged Highlander. Robert sat up as he recognised the blue and white chequered band on gold that decorated their shields: the arms of the steward. Pleased by the evidence that a friendly face might yet be found, he was nonetheless troubled to see that the steward's knights greeted him with the same terseness as the bald man, their hands never straying far from their weapons as they bade him and his men dismount. Leaving his horse with Nes, Robert walked up the hillside behind the escort. Glancing back, he saw the bald man and his crew had closed in behind.

Moving past tents aglow with lanterns, through the swirling smoke of fires, Robert saw people looking round at his banner. Many of their faces hardened as they fixed on the red chevron. He knew he couldn't blame them. He had spent two years at King Edward's court and during the war his family had sided with the English. Even so, determined to challenge their view of him, Robert set his sights on a row of tents looming ahead. Outside, horses were tethered to stakes thrust in the ground, a mixture of sturdy coursers and rouncies. Smells of dung and food mingled with the odour of wood from a fire that was burning high into the flushed evening. There were many men around it, sharing bowls of drink and food, some laughing, others talking quietly. A few just stared into the flames, their sun-browned skin livid with wounds. Between the fire and the tents, Robert saw James Stewart. He was talking to a stocky man with a mottled face and tonsured head, dressed in robes trimmed with ermine. It was Robert Wishart, the Bishop of Glasgow. The two looked round at his approach. Robert smiled, but neither the steward nor the fierce-eyed bishop returned the greeting.

His retinue, along with Katherine and Judith, who held a struggling Marjorie, were corralled into a group by the escort of knights.

'Sir Robert,' said the steward, his tone cool. 'It has been a while.'

'I'm glad to see you, Sir James. My men and I have travelled from Kyle Stewart, where I had hoped to take counsel with you.'

'I wondered if we might see you before long.' The steward appraised Robert's company. 'We heard what happened at the castle of Lord Douglas.'

'You heard?' Robert was surprised. He saw, out of the corner of his eye, that the bald man had moved over to the fire and was speaking to someone, a tall figure, whose back was turned.

'My sister came here a week ago on her way to safety.' The steward paused. 'I owe you my gratitude for letting her and my nephew go free. Had they been delivered into King Edward's custody I am not certain I would have seen them again.' The words, though seemingly heartfelt, were stiff.

Robert noticed that some of the men at the fire were looking over. He resisted the urge to move closer to his daughter at the threat from so many unfriendly gazes. One man was heading over purposefully. He was thickset with windblown black hair, dressed better than most of the others in well-fitted mail and a blue cloak. There was something faintly familiar about his face. Robert, seeing three white stars on the breast of his cloak, realised where the familiarity came from. His suspicion that this must be the father of James Douglas was confirmed when the man spoke.

'Sir Robert of Carrick, is it? I have learned you saved my wife and son.' Before Robert could respond, Lord Douglas continued roughly. 'Before I thank you, I would know why.'

'We would all like to know that.'

The clear voice came from a tall figure striding from the fire. He walked beside the bald man, who looked suddenly small in comparison. Robert stared at this approaching giant, who was well over six feet, perhaps close to seven. His hands and feet were as big as spades, but in proportion to the rest of his muscular frame. Robert wasn't short, but he felt dwarfed by this colossus. Even King Edward, admired and feared because of his great stature and known, popularly, as Longshanks, wasn't this tall. The man had a square, brutish face with a nose that looked as though it had been broken a few times. A bruise clouded his brow, half hidden by tousled brown hair. His heavily muscled arms were veined with recently stitched injuries, one of which ran from his wrist up to his elbow. The most surprising thing about him was his eyes, a startling shade of azure, filled with sharp intelligence. He wore stained hose, wrinkled boots criss-crossed with leather to hold them up and a dark blue tunic, under which the bulk of a coat of plates was detectable.

The giant halted before Robert. 'Why have you come to my camp?'

For a moment, Robert said nothing. So, this must be him. The man who refused to swear fealty to King Edward and who stabbed the son of an English knight who insulted him, then fought off five of his companions armed with only a rusty knife. The man who was imprisoned, beaten and starved until his breath stopped and his English gaolers threw him out with the night soil, and who rose from the dead two days later. The man who hounded the English justiciar out of Scone and chased Bishop Bek from Glasgow, and who hacked through half a town garrison to slay the Sheriff of Lanark in his bed, and with that stroke began the insurrection.

Robert was surprised, for although the young giant's stature seemed to fit the outlandish tales William Wallace looked scarcely older than himself. He had attributed those feats of daring to a much older commander. Wallace, he saw, was wearing a strange necklace. Looking harder, Robert realised it was strung with human teeth. Moving his gaze from the grotesque trophy, he met the young man's sharp blue eyes. When he had thought on the road to Irvine of what he would say when he arrived, his planned speech had been all about how he couldn't hold his flesh and blood in hatred and needed to fight for the kingdom into which he was born. But in front of these scarred, hard-faced men those words now sounded pompous and insincere. 'I came,' he said finally, looking over at James, 'to offer my support for the rising against King Edward's occupation.' His gaze switched back to Wallace, who looked utterly unconvinced. 'For I am as Scottish as you.'

The bald man snorted derisively. At the sound Nes bristled and Alexander Seton's hand, resting on the pommel of his sword, shifted to curl around the hilt.

Wallace's eyes narrowed at Robert. 'Are you? When your father still defends the city of Carlisle for the English king? When you refused to raise arms for King John and raised them instead for England? I have no need of a man who is merely Scot born. I have need of men who are Scots at heart.'

Robert stepped forward, wanting to demand how this barbarian, with only a veinful of noble blood, dared speak to him this way. But he forced back the words, hearing something sickeningly akin to his father's scathing tones in them. 'My family refused to fight because the man who ordered us to raise arms was a puppet king under the thrall of our enemies, the Comyns.' He stared around defiantly at some of the incensed murmurs his words provoked. He fixed on the steward and Wishart. 'Many of you supported my grandfather's claim to the throne, set your names and reputations on his right to it. Where were you when his claim was overruled? You walked away, afraid to risk your positions under Balliol. That was understandable. And it was no less than what my family did when faced with the bitter choice of pledging fealty to an enemy, or keeping faith with the king who had passed us over, but in whose service we remained.' His eyes swung back to Wallace. 'Whatever you think of my actions, I have remained loyal in these years to the only king my family paid homage to.' He paused. 'But that loyalty has been tested beyond its limits.'

It was James Stewart who came to Robert's defence. 'None of us can deny what Sir Robert says. To my shame, I walked away from his family after the hearing despite the support I pledged to his grandfather.' His brown eyes fixed on Robert. 'It is a regret I live with still, more so since your grandfather's passing.' James looked to Wallace. 'It takes a brave man, Master William, to stand up for his family when so many are against them. An even braver man to desert that family for the sake of his kingdom.'

Wallace shook his head. 'I would agree with you, Sir James, but I fear he's nothing more than a spy, sent by his father to learn our plans. Likely his actions in Douglas were a ruse, designed to make us trust him.' He didn't look at Robert as he spoke, blunt and frank. 'He has been Edward's man for over three years. He cannot be trusted.' With that, Wallace turned and walked away, his long stride taking him back to the fire.

Robert, seeing the nods, even grim smiles of some of the men, went to go after Wallace, determined to challenge the accusation.

He was stopped by James Stewart. 'You have had a long journey and the hour grows late. Let us speak for a moment alone, Sir Robert.' He gestured to his knights. 'See that food is brought for his men.' When Robert continued to stare at Wallace's retreating back, James added, 'I'm sure your daughter must be tired.'

50

In grudging agreement, Robert followed the steward into the tent. Ducking through the flaps, he found himself in a warm interior, furnished with a bed, trestle and boards, and a few stools. Carpeted with faded rugs, it was lit with lanterns. There were two servants here. The steward ordered the older of the two to pour wine.

Robert, furious at Wallace's words, went to refuse it, but the sight of the calm-faced steward standing there expectantly mollified him and, besides, he was thirsty. Taking the goblet, he drank, but when James motioned for him to sit he declined. 'Why are you letting Wallace dictate to you? He is the son of one of your vassals. He isn't even a knight! Worse, he's a savage. Have you seen what he wears around his neck?'

James took a sip from his goblet, waiting until Robert had finished. 'It is a delicate matter. Yes, I am far above William in station, as are you. But to many who now follow him he has become something of a saviour. They will listen only to him and their numbers make up most of this army.' James spread a hand to the camp, visible through the tent flaps as a triangle of red dusk filled with smoke and shadows. 'Such as it is.'

'I've heard of some of the things he has done,' said Robert, determined to make his point. 'Torture. Murder. Are these the actions of an honourable man?'

'No. They are the actions of a desperate man in a desperate time. I am not excusing his methods. But' — James paused — 'I can understand them.' The steward seated himself on a stool, his yellow mantle shimmering gold in the lantern light. 'For William the war began six years ago, during the hearing to decide who would take the throne. When the nobles were compelled to swear fealty to King Edward as our overlord, William's father — one of my vassals — refused. Wallace was a good man, but proud and defiant. The king's reaction was swift. As an example to others Wallace was outlawed, forced to leave his family. Shortly after, there was a clash between a group of Ayrshire men and English soldiers, supposedly there to keep the king's peace. Wallace had come out of hiding to join this mob, who were responsible for the deaths of five soldiers. English knights pursued this band all the way to Loudoun Hill.'

Robert remembered his grandfather speaking of a skirmish there during the hearing.

'William's father was struck down, his legs cut away from under him. He was left to bleed out on the hillside. It was an appalling way to die. His wife died in poverty soon after and his sons were separated. By the time Balliol took the throne, William was living with his uncle, the Sheriff of Ayr. Already, he held a great deal of resentment towards the English soldiery, whom he held responsible for the deaths of both his parents. When war broke out last year it was the chance he was waiting for, but his hopes for revenge were dashed with our defeat at Dunbar. English officials poured into our towns, replacing local men. One was the new Sheriff of Lanark, a man named Hesilrig.' James paused to take a drink. 'During the early days of the occupation, I remember hearing of an English soldier, a wrestler, who was challenging men in Lanark's market place, charging them four silver pennies to see if they could break a pole on his back. William took up the invitation and paid his four pence, but rather than break the pole he broke the fool's back. The man's comrades set upon him and he beat them down, all three. William was outlawed, his uncle robbed and his friends beaten in retaliation. The tail of his horse was even hacked off. Things got out of hand and the son of an English knight was killed, stabbed by William with his own knife. William was caught and imprisoned, but after weeks of torture he escaped.

'After this he went into hiding, along with the friends who had defended him. But even with a price on his head, he would go disguised into Lanark, courting danger because of his uncommon size. He had a young wife there, you see, the heiress of a wealthy Lanark man, whom he'd fallen for and wed the year before. William will not speak of Marion now and his companions keep silent, but I know that by spring she bore him a child. One day, Hesilrig's men caught him venturing into the town to visit her and his newborn daughter. William, outnumbered, was forced to barricade himself in Marion's house. When Hesilrig came and demanded entry, William escaped, while Marion spoke with the sheriff to delay him.

'As I heard it, the sheriff, on discovering her deception, shut her and her child up inside the house and had his men set fire to it. Whatever the details, Marion and her daughter died that day and William was crazed with grief. That night he returned to the town and fought his way through the English guards to get to Hesilrig. He murdered the sheriff in his bed.' James drained his wine. 'They say Hesilrig wasn't recognisable as a man by the time William was done with him. After that there was no going back. William and his companions set out to continue the violence. They started by assaulting English companies on the road and setting fire to garrisons. When other men, dispossessed by Cressingham's taxes, joined them, they began attacking more officials. It didn't take much for William's personal crusade to become an insurrection.' After a moment of silence, James rose and faced Robert. 'Outlaw and murderer he may be, but he has a gift for leadership as well as for violence and we cannot deny his author- ity here. The men who follow him would not follow us. William Wallace has achieved something few of us would have managed. He has brought together men from all parts of this kingdom, from beggars to lords. These men have no obligation to him and he has neither pressed nor paid them. They stay with him out of loyalty, because he has bled and suffered as they have.'

Robert had known nothing of this: these struggles lesser men had faced through the occupation. It made him think of the people of Carrick. Had some of them suffered the woes of Wallace? He felt guilt, a familiar weight these days. James knew so much about his vassals. He himself hadn't even been aware of any difficulties the men and women of Carrick had been facing until Affraig confronted him. In his efforts to remain true to oaths he had taken, he had broken so many others. 'I want to make amends,' he said suddenly. 'I know I have no reason to expect your trust, but in memory of your friendship with my grandfather, I'm asking that you let me earn it. I can be of help here. I will be the first earl openly to declare my support for the uprising, but, more than that, I know the English and I know their king. They might listen to me in any negotiations we may offer.'

James appraised him for a long moment. 'Yes. I believe you can be of help.' His scrutiny seemed to lessen and he motioned to the tent flaps. 'Come, settle in with your men. I will speak to William. He may be lead- ing this army, but he will listen to my counsel.' The steward paused in the entrance. 'For what it is worth, Robert, I realise it cannot have been easy for you under your father's command these past years. I know the Lord of Annandale hoped to gain the throne after King John's imprisonment. I know, too, that it wasn't his to be claimed.'

*   *   *

As Robert headed out of the tent the high steward watched him go. He saw the relief in the faces of the young earl's retinue, some distance away. The tight group hadn't touched the food they had been given, clearly waiting for Robert to return to them.

A large shadow loomed out of the dusk and Wishart appeared in the entrance. James stood aside to allow him to enter.

'Well?' asked the bishop.

'I think we should let him stay, your grace,' answered James, moving back into the warmth of the interior.

'Master William could be right,' growled Wishart, following. 'He could have been sent here as a spy.'

'It is possible. But I do not believe it to be the case.'

'I know you respected his grandfather, James, as did I, but blood does not make a man worthy. Look at his father.'

James turned away, closing his eyes in thought. 'He was right though, wasn't he,' he murmured. 'We supported his grandfather's claim over Balliol's.' He looked back when Wishart didn't respond. 'And now we fight in the name of a king we never wanted.'

'Whatever our personal misgivings, you and I both swore an oath to John Balliol in the sight of God.'

James thought about saying something further, but he didn't. It wasn't the time for such a discussion. Instead, he offered the bishop some wine. 'Will you support my decision to allow him to stay?'

Wishart accepted the drink from the steward's servant. 'With one condition,' he said, taking a draught. 'We keep the plan from him.'

'He could be of more help if he were told of it.'

Wishart was adamant. 'No. Not until we know for certain he can be trusted.' The bishop drained the wine with a tilt of his head. 'We'll know that soon enough. Our scouts say the English are approaching along the Nithsdale valley. Percy and Clifford will arrive any day.'

51

The day was cooled by a strong wind, the grass in the fields shivering in great silvery waves. On the banks of Irvine's river, the trees surged. Beyond the waterway, the wide track that led to the port was crowded with a host of men, their banners livid against the sullen sky.

Robert stood in silence, his eyes moving over the cavalry to the slow-marching ranks of infantry that followed behind, visible due to the level of the land. Estimating there to be several hundred horsed and triple the number of foot, he returned his gaze to the front lines where two standards were hoisted high. He lingered on the blue lion on gold of the house of Percy, growing clearer.

When told it was Henry Percy and Robert Clifford who were headed for the port, Robert hadn't been surprised. Percy had been granted governorship of Galloway and Ayr and, with Bishop Bek gone and the Sheriff of Lanark dead, he had become the chief English commander in the west of Scotland. Coupled with the fact that Percy could raise levies quickly from his nearby Yorkshire estates, this made him the most likely man Cressingham would send to confront the rebels. Despite his apprehension at the prospect of meeting his former comrades, Robert had been privately confident that they would at least listen to him. He had fought alongside them, faced death with them, been embraced as one of their own. They had counted him as a brother.

Now, with the formidable army approaching, his optimism faded.

Beside Robert the Bishop of Glasgow stood, his legs apart, hands clasped behind his back, rooted like some obstinate plant. The steward was to the left, his expression impenetrable. With them were the truculent Lord of Douglas and William Wallace, towering over them all. Wallace's stance was the most relaxed, but his blue eyes betrayed a fiery impatience. Strapped to his back was a massive sword. The scarred, naked blade was five feet long and the leather-bound hilt above the cross-guard another foot. With him were two of his commanders. One was the bald man, whom Robert had since learned was Wallace's cousin. The man, Adam, still wore the incongruous fur cloak, apparently a trophy he'd taken from the hall of the justiciar at Scone.

The vanguard of the English host moved off the track and into the field, their horses cutting lines through the long grass. They spread out as they came, revealing to the waiting Scots the rows of cavalry behind. All were mounted on barded destriers, lances up-thrust from mailed fists. The foot soldiers from the northern counties of England who tramped behind the knights seemed equally matched by Wallace's army, but in terms of cavalry the Scots were vastly outnumbered. If a battle was to be fought here, Robert knew, with mounting unease, that they would lose.

At the call of a horn, the English host came to a halt, their horses shifting and settling. A small group broke away and spurred their destriers towards the Scots. Even without the distinctive banner, Robert would have known Henry Percy by his seat. The Lord of Alnwick, whose lance was borne by his squire, had one hand on the reins, the other resting on his thigh, his stocky frame moving languidly with the horse's rhythm. A great helm adorned with three snowy swan's feathers covered his head, but he wore the visor up, revealing a red face, fleshier these days, and a mouth curled in contempt.

As the group came to a stop, they didn't dismount but remained in their saddles, looking down on the Scots. Percy's war charger stamped and snorted. The lord's gaze moved over them, lingering on Wallace, then settling on Robert.

Robert felt himself coil tight under that threatening stare, but he met Percy's gaze determinedly.

Wishart was first to speak. 'Good day to you. I am Robert Wishart, by God's grace Bishop of Glasgow and former guardian of Scotland. I will treat with you, along with my noble comrades.' He introduced the others.

Percy didn't take his eyes off Robert. 'I heard it said you had betrayed your king. *Oath-breaker*.' Before Robert could respond, Percy turned on the bishop. 'Noble comrades? I see a clergyman, three traitors and an outlaw.'

Lord Douglas growled an obscenity, but Wishart stepped in swiftly. 'We are here to parley as men, not to swap insults like schoolboys.'

Clifford, whose eyes had also lingered on Robert, responded. 'Our orders are to arrest any who have disturbed the king's peace and raised arms against him.' Clifford pointed a mailed finger at Wallace, who met his gaze unerringly. 'This man has a price on his head. All of you have forfeited your lands by the breaking of the fealty you swore to the king. There will be no parley. You will surrender yourselves to our authority, or we will respond in force.'

Robert braced himself for a stout denial and a statement of angry defiance from Wishart.

Instead, the bishop met Clifford's gaze calmly. 'There is no need for that, Lord Clifford. We will surrender.'

Robert pushed his way through the tent flaps behind the steward. The tent's sides undulated, buffeted by the wind. 'Did you know the bishop was going to do this? Why in God's name would you go along with it?'

James's eyes narrowed at his rough tone.

'I thought we were going to make a stand? I thought that's what you came to Irvine for? In defying my father's order, by declaring my support for the uprising, I risked everything! My lands, my family. For what?' Robert wheeled away. 'I didn't come here to yield to their demands at the first parley.'

'Doughty men we may be, but we are poorly equipped to face the English on the field. You know that as well as I do. Better, I would wager. You fought with them in Wales. You must know their strength. Tell me, can an army of ill disciplined foot soldiers beat English heavy cavalry in battle?'

Robert didn't answer. There was no point. The steward was simply stating what he himself had known watching the English ride on to the field. 'We needn't have faced them in battle. We could have negotiated. I could have spoken to Percy, offered him terms to take to the king. At the very least we could have bought ourselves more time. I could have fortified Carrick. Now . . .' He cursed and stalked the tent, his voice rising. 'I have no time to raise my vassals for its defence!'

'Could you have negotiated?' asked James, watching him pace like a caged lion. 'Would they have listened? Percy's enmity towards you was clear.'

Robert sat heavily on a stool, wondering if he had been a fool to come here. He should have seen that his betrayal of the king was greater than any other man's. Far from being some sort of a bridge between the two sides, his presence might have made matters worse. He wondered if he should have gone to Edward himself, implored the king to listen, but even as he thought it he realised how laughable that was. Not even the king's closest advisers could persuade him to do something he did not wish to do. 'I cannot believe Wallace went along with this,' he said, thinking of the acceptance in the rebel's face when Wishart delivered the blow.

For their part, Percy and Clifford had appeared as surprised as he'd felt when the bishop offered the surrender, but before they had been able to give any answer, Wishart had suggested they return on the morrow to discuss terms. He had proposed a site for their encampment, a mile distant. Rather grudgingly, having lost some of their impetus with the enemy's instant capitulation, the English lords had acquiesced.

Robert stared at James, caught by the thought of Wallace's calm reaction. 'After all you told me I would have thought Wallace would rather die with a sword in his hand, than give in to the English without a struggle.' As the steward looked away, Robert rose. There had been something in his expression, some flicker of awareness. 'Sir James?'

The steward turned to him. For a moment his face remained impassive, before a look of resignation set in. 'I was asked to keep it from you.'

'What?' Robert demanded, moving in front of him.

'Our plan. Wishart and Wallace contrived it some weeks ago. They hoped to draw here the force they knew King Edward would send to quell the uprising. Irvine is close enough to Galloway and Ayr to ensure Percy would discover our intent to make a stand, but far enough away from the east coast and our key strongholds.'

'Far enough for what?'

'Robert Wishart intends to entrench them in negotiations for our surrender, so William can continue his campaign in the east. He and his men were the bait that drew the English. Now, we will hold them here while Wallace slips away to finish what he started. He plans to join up with the rest of his men in Selkirk Forest and from there meet Moray's forces in the north. The aim is to take enough strongholds so that when Cressingham manages to launch any offensive from Berwick we will be able to counter him effectively.'

'How will Wallace slip away? Won't the English see him leave?'

'Our camp is large enough to offer the ruse of being fully occupied. Wishart has arranged to meet the English at their encampment for the negotiations and William wouldn't be expected to be part of them.'

Robert was stunned. He tried to think through what this meant for him, but the steward was speaking still.

'I will inform Wishart I have told you. We couldn't have kept it from you indefinitely. Besides, Percy's reaction has, to my mind, proven your innocence. It would be hard for a man to pretend such hatred as I saw in him.' James paused. 'You will need to be careful, Robert.'

52

The wind had died down through the afternoon, leaving an airless calm. Over the past hour a bank of thunderheads had built in the west. In the brooding light, Robert and his retinue sat in silence eating their meal, an unappetising sludge of porridge mixed with bitter berries. The servants and two of the Carrick squires were busy erecting the last of the tents, creating a small camp within the sprawl of Wallace's army. Over this camp was raised the standard of Carrick. Robert had pondered the wisdom of displaying it, but in the end had decided to assert his presence rather than try to hide it. A group of peasants were seated around a nearby fire, their spears on the ground beside them by the rough woollen cloaks that formed their beds. They were eyeing the furs, pillows and blankets being offloaded from the wagon and placed inside the striped tents.

Robert pushed his spoon around the grey mush in the bowl his steward had handed to him. Hunger, earlier an ache in his stomach, clogged in his throat. He glanced up as Christopher rifled through his pack and drew out a slender flute. It was the Yorkshire squire's most beloved possession, bought by his father in Castile. He had proven himself adept at the instrument, cheering the sombre company on many dull nights on the road. As he set the flute to his lips and blew a few practice notes, its hollow timbre echoed in the evening. Uathach, curled by the fire, lifted her head and whined. Earlier, Robert had spoken quietly to the squire and Alexander about the high steward's confession of the plan concocted by Wishart and Wallace. Alexander had been doubtful about how effective the ruse would prove and both he and Christopher had been troubled that it had been kept from Robert, despite the fact the Scots had invited him to be part of the company that met Percy and Clifford.

'It sounds like an assessment of your loyalty,' Alexander had ventured. 'They wanted you there to see how the English would respond.'

Robert understood their concern. The two men, particularly Alexander, stood to lose much by this dangerous course. Inwardly, he had tried to deny responsibility for that: they could have chosen to return to Annandale with Gillepatric and the rest, after all. But the truth of it was that by offering them a place in his company, by making them his men, he had made himself responsible.

As he sat staring into the bowl, the notes of the flute washing over him, all the tracks his mind took him down, all possible paths seemed to lead to nothing. The Scots did not want him here, did not trust him. He didn't need Alexander to tell him that. Even if Wallace and his men won through and King John was restored he, a Bruce, would not find succour in Balliol's kingdom. The English knights clearly hated him for his desertion and his father no doubt detested him.

Out of the corner of his eye, Robert saw his daughter toddling towards him, her tiny arms stretched out, wavering for balance. Marjorie's smile was like a glimpse of sun, brightening his view. He found himself mirroring it and held out a hand towards her. Before she reached him she fell, sitting back with a thump. Her smile vanished and she began to cry. Christopher paused his playing at the sound. Immediately, Judith set down her bowl and snatched her up. Marjorie struggled and wailed louder, her fists stretching towards Robert, whose smile faded as he withdrew into his thoughts. Ignoring the child's protests, Judith ducked inside the small tent she shared with Katherine, her free hand already tugging her shift down for the feed. Marjorie's wails quietened as the others finished off the meal. Sucking the last of the porridge from his spoon, Nes rose and headed to their horses, tethered nearby. Crouching, he took a grooming brush from one of their packs and began brushing Hunter's coat. He hummed the tune Christopher had been playing as he worked. Katherine went over, wrinkling her nose at the smell of the horses.

'Nes, you need to mend Marjorie's saddle seat when you're done. It has a splinter in the back, as I told you yesterday.'

Robert saw Alexander glance over at her. There was a look of something in the lord's face, anger, he thought, before his attention was captured by a group of men, their voices loud over the general murmur of the camp. One was Adam. Wallace's cousin shot him a hostile glance as he passed by.

After they had gone Robert set down his meal untouched and crossed to his tent. Inside, the servants had spread a thick rug across the ground to carpet it. The chests of his clothes and belongings were neatly stacked in one area and several layers of furs and blankets formed a comfortable bed. On one chest was placed a silver tray with a glazed jug of wine and a goblet beside it. A lantern, strung from a hook above, gleamed. Sitting on the furs, Robert pulled off his boots. His head ached from the questions that churned endlessly in his mind. Early tomorrow, before the parley with Percy and Clifford, he would go down to the river with Alexander and loosen his muscles with some sword play, try to clear his thoughts.

A whiff of smoke entered the tent behind him and he glanced round to see Katherine ducking in. She said nothing. Neither did he, but continued easing off his boot as she knelt behind him. His movements slowed when she laid her hands on his back. His shirt felt clammy against his skin as she kneaded her fingers into his locked muscles, working them. He closed his eyes, feeling the pressure ease a little. After a time, she bent forward, her breasts pressing lightly against his shoulder blades. Brushing aside his sweat-damp hair, she kissed his neck. Her lips were dry from the sun and whispered over his flesh, sending a shudder down his spine. The clouds in his mind cleared until there was only the immediacy of her, the air thick with the smell of her, an earthy fusion of wood-smoke, sweat and berries.

She slipped around him until she was facing him on her knees. He pushed off the coif she wore, her hair tumbling over his forearms. Closing his eyes, he slid his hands down her back and, pulling her in, sought her mouth with his. Her hands grasped his stubble-rough jaw, her tongue, first teasing and darting, now pushing into his open mouth.

He dragged down one shoulder of his wife's old gown, but the garment would go no further and he reached round to wrestle with the lacing. As he opened his eyes to see better what he was doing Robert saw that Katherine's were fixed on him, holding him in her stare. Picking the knot free, he splayed the gown's lacing apart with his fingers until the dress was loosened enough for him to pull it down. She struggled her arms free, helping him push the garment to her waist, baring her chest. He appraised her as she shook her mass of dark hair back over her shoulders, giving him a full look. Then, his desire building to an unbearable level, he pressed her down on the furs. He didn't want to think any more.

Shouts of alarm sounded outside, along with the panicked noises of horses. Robert pulled back from Katherine as the tent flaps opened and Alexander thrust his head in. The maid sat up, crossing her arms over her bare breasts and glaring at the knight. But he had no eyes for her, only for Robert, who had cursed and risen.

'What in hell's——?'

'You need to see this.'

Leaving Katherine struggling with her dress, Robert followed Alexander out of the tent, his desire drained, replaced by hot anger. Christopher and Walter were there, swords out, staring into the gloom beyond their fire, along with Alexander's knights and the squires. Nes and the steward were calming the horses and Judith was wide-eyed, holding Marjorie. Robert saw something protruding from the ground, close to his banner. It was an arrow. A few men from other tents were hastening over. Their voices echoed in the evening.

'What was that?'

'Are we under attack? Someone get Wallace!'

Robert bent down beside the missile. There was something attached to the middle of the shaft, a wad of parchment impaled on the arrow. 'Did you see where it came from?' he demanded, looking up at Alexander, who shook his head.

Robert stamped on it, snapping the shaft. Picking up the splintered arrow, he eased off the folded letter and opened it.

TRAITOR

The word was big and bold, smeared in some dark substance.

'The English?' murmured Alexander, reading it over his shoulder.

Robert stared into the dusk. The thunderheads had formed a black ridge across the sky, obscuring the stars. He shook his head, his face tight. 'I don't know.'

'You should inform the high steward.'

'No,' Robert said sharply, looking at his comrade. 'We look after ourselves.' He threw the message on to the fire, ignoring the curious stares of the men who had come to see what the disturbance was. 'Keep four men on watch tonight.' As he headed back to the tent, Alexander followed.

'There is something else, Robert,' he said, out of earshot of the others. Alexander nodded to the tent, where Katherine's form could be seen as a shadow inside. 'Why not save your bed for a woman who is your equal, my friend, at least in front of noble allies?'

'Who I share my bed with is no one's concern but mine.' Turning, Robert strode to the tent, the parchment shrivelling and twisting on the fire behind him.

53

'As I have said, we are willing to surrender ourselves, but we cannot speak for all the men of the realm.' The steward's tone was resolute.

'And, as we have said,' countered Clifford, 'that is unacceptable. Sir Hugh de Cressingham has ordered a full surrender from every man involved in this rebellion. He wants Lord Douglas and the outlaw, William Wallace, sent to the Tower, where they will be judged for crimes against the crown.'

Douglas's mouth curled in derision. Snatching up his goblet, he drained it of the wine the menservants of the English lords had poured out.

'Lord Steward, how many times must we go over this?' Clifford's face was flushed. The cloth canopy erected over the table around which the six men sat kept the sun off their heads, but couldn't diminish the heat in the air, affecting all their tempers and causing perspiration to track glistening lines down their cheeks.

'How can we speak for men other than ourselves?' enquired Wishart, with a rough exhalation. 'We could offer you a full surrender then stand in breach of our agreement if the uprising continued elsewhere.'

'This has gone on long enough,' growled Percy, planting his hands on the table. 'We should arrest the men we have here,' he told Clifford, 'and let Sir Hugh and my grandfather deal with Moray and the rebels in the north. Which they will,' he added, looking at James.

'You could do that, Lord Percy,' said Wishart, before Clifford could answer, 'but if you take us into your custody now, you will still be left with the problem of our army. You cannot arrest them all, surely?' His tone was brusque with challenge, but his eyes glittered. He seemed to be enjoying this.

'No,' responded Percy coldly, 'but we can cut them to pieces on the field. Unlike you, they will be shown no honour.'

'Well, I doubt they would stand and face you on the field. Most likely they would slip away into the Forest and you would know nothing more of them until they rose somewhere else.'

Robert glanced at the bishop, uneasy at the dangerous game. The English must not discover that this was exactly what had happened. He hadn't thought they would be able to keep up the pretence for so long, but the English camp was a mile from theirs and, he had to admit, from a distance the Scottish encampment gave the impression of being fully occupied. Wallace had left some of his men behind to aid the pretence and the tents remained erect. Douglas and the steward had a fair few in their retinues and these, along with a number of local men they had convinced to help them, gave, to the casual glance, no sense that anything had changed. Still, it would not do to give any hint of it, for the moment Percy and Clifford found out that Wallace and most of his men had left Irvine the week before, then they would all find themselves in irons on the way to the Tower.

James Stewart had also looked over at Wishart, his expression one of warning. 'We have shown you every courtesy in these discussions,' he said, turning his attention to the belligerent English knights. 'There is no need for threats. The four of us have given you our word that we will surrender ourselves to the king's mercy, but in order to prevent further violence we must remain here. The rebels will heed our counsel.' He opened his palms in a show of sincerity. 'It is in the best interests of us all.'

'Take us now,' added Wishart, 'and I swear by God you will not stop this insurrection.'

The discussion rambled on in much the same way as it had for the past week, through the thunderstorms that heralded the beginning of July into these savagely hot days, when men from the Scottish camp had thrown themselves into the river to cool off.

Robert felt his attention slipping. He gazed at the English camp that stretched towards the sea. Beyond, the coastline rose into parched fields and crumbling cliffs towards Ayr and Carrick. This was the closest he had been to his boyhood home since he was nineteen, when he visited Turnberry before leaving for England, the only time he'd spent in his earldom since he had been awarded it. Affraig drifted into his thoughts.

Much suffering there is. I came to see if our hope may lie in you. Our lord.

At least with the English ensconced in talks here they would not be harassing his people. Robert looked back as Clifford continued. Henry Percy was staring at him. The menace in the man's eyes made him shift in his seat, his sluggish mind at once alert.

Robert had remained silent through most of the negotiations, until the day before when the oppressive heat and Percy's arrogance became too much and, accusing the lord of trespassing on his land, he had demanded reparation. Percy had bitten at once, his invective filled with threats. The two had risen, going for their swords, until the steward and Clifford had ended the discussion. Robert had ridden back to the Scots' camp ahead of James and the others, urging his palfrey into a furious gallop until they were both panting and sweat-soaked. All the way back his mind had been filled with an image of Percy and Clifford dragging the Stone of Destiny from the altar at Scone. And him with them, sword out to defend them.

'We remain at an impasse,' James was saying wearily. 'Let us return to discuss it tomorrow.'

'No,' said Percy, switching his gaze from Robert to the steward. 'Our officials at Berwick expect this done before the month is out. That is what King Edward demanded. I want these talks finished. Today.'

Robert saw James looked troubled. He understood why. Percy and Clifford would eventually be forced to imprison them, despite the risk of further rebellion, in order to fulfil Cressingham's orders. It was only due to the fact the knights were relatively inexperienced commanders that it hadn't happened already. A veteran like John de Warenne or Humphrey de Bohun's father would have run rings around Wishart's arguments. Besides, it wouldn't be long before reports reached them that Wallace was leading an attack on Dundee. When that happened their ploy would be over.

Clifford rose and gestured to Percy. The two of them walked away from the table, out of earshot. Douglas grimaced into his empty goblet while Wishart watched the English intently. When the knights returned, Robert noticed an unpleasant smile on Percy's face.

'We will accept your surrender terms,' said Clifford. 'On certain conditions. You will remain here under guard in order to compel the rebels to cease their violence. When we see clear evidence of this we will take word of it to Berwick, along with the men Sir Hugh has ordered taken prisoner, namely Lord Douglas and Wallace. Your lands will be forfeit until such time as King Edward decides otherwise.'

James nodded, but before he could speak, Clifford held up his hand.

'As a sign of good faith that you will keep your word once we have sealed this agreement, we require a hostage.'

'Who?' asked Wishart.

Percy's eyes moved to Robert.

Seeing this, James answered at once. 'No. As an earl, Sir Robert's ransom is too high.'

'Not him,' said Percy harshly. 'His daughter. We know he kept her with him when he left Carlisle. His father told us.' Percy's blue eyes narrowed in cold satisfaction. 'The Lord of Annandale told us much – how he loathed his treacherous son and wished him dead.'

The heat had drained from Robert's face at the demand. He rose at Percy's words, his stool tipping over behind him.

The three men faced one another, full of anger, frustration and concern. Outside, evening was drawing in, promising another oppressive night. Inside the steward's tent lanterns exuded a buttery warmth.

'If we agree to their demand we buy ourselves more time.' This was Wishart speaking. 'We knew we would have to make concessions, sacrifices even. The English must be kept occupied here if Wallace is to succeed in the east.'

'Robert will not allow his daughter to be used in this way,' responded James. 'And I do not blame him. He will not speak of what history is between himself and Lord Percy, but I would not trust the English with his child.'

Wishart let out a hiss of breath. 'We have until tomorrow morning to give them our answer. If we do not produce the hostage they will come for us in force.'

'Let the sons of whores come,' growled Douglas, brandishing the goblet of wine the steward's servant had poured for him. His cheeks were mottled, his words slurred and filled with violence. 'I'd like to see them bleed. See them bleed for what they did in Berwick. Enough talking. Enough *waiting*, God damn it!'

The steward kept his focus on the bishop. 'You are speaking about an infant, your grace. She could be harmed when they discover our deception.'

'I'm talking about our kingdom!'

'Let us offer another hostage then. One of us.'

'Why not Bruce's child?' demanded Wishart, his eyes narrowing. 'This isn't sentiment, is it? It is something else. You've been keeping him close since he arrived.'

'As you said yourself, we couldn't necessarily trust him.'

'And yet on the first night you told him our plan when I asked you not to. Come, James, I can see you have something on your mind. Some scheme you have not shared.'

For a moment, James didn't speak. When he did, his voice was low, cautious. 'He is the grandson of Sir Robert of Annandale. His veins flow with the same blood, your grace. The blood of Malcolm Canmore.'

Robert stood by the fire staring across the encampment. The first stars had appeared, scattered in the deep. As he watched, one went shooting through the heavens, a faint trail of light gone in the blink of an eye. In Carrick, when he was young, in late summer he would lie on his back on the cliffs under the vault of the sky watching the stars fall.

Over in the high steward's tent he could see the gleam of lanterns. They were in there now, Wishart and the others, discussing his future and the future of his daughter. Well, they could talk all they wanted. He was done with words.

There was a cold clarity that came with pure fury. It had burned away Robert's doubts and indecisions and had lit before him a single path. Not the many he had faced over these past weeks — no, these past years — just one direction with one destination at its end. It was perilous and he didn't know what he would find on it. But he knew with utter certainty that he must step out upon it. Everything had led him here.

There were footfalls as Alexander came up behind him.

'We are set,' murmured the lord.

'The women are ready?' Robert asked, without turning.

'Yes. They will go down to the river with the servants. My men will go with them.' Alexander's voice lowered further as three knights passed, wearing the colours of Lord Douglas. 'The escort will not seem strange, not after the arrow. Nes and Walter will be waiting by the river with the horses. Half the squires are there already. The rest will meet us shortly.' Alexander paused. 'Are you sure about this?'

'Yes.'

'They will guess where you have gone. They might follow.'

'Not when the negotiations need to be concluded. Not even Percy would risk the rebellion continuing just to track me down. By the time anyone comes for us Turnberry will be secure.' Robert turned to Alexander. 'I need to know that you are with me.'

Alexander smiled. It was a hard expression, but one Robert found reassuring.

'We are with you.'

'We'll have to leave the tents and the wagon,' said Robert, glancing round at their camp. 'But the nights are warm and we have blankets.' He saw Katherine and Judith duck out of their tent. The maid had his daughter balanced on her hip and held the pail they had been using to bring water from the river. Judith was with her, looking scared. She too had a pail, inside which were some of their belongings. Carefully, cautiously, all through the evening, they had been decamping, ferrying bits of their gear down to the banks of the river, where Nes had taken Uathach and the horses. To better pasture, Robert had loudly instructed.

As the women walked away down the hillside, Katherine playing her part, talking idly to the wet nurse, Robert nodded to Alexander. 'I'll meet you by the river.'

Heading away, he moved through the circles of men around the fires, past vacant tents, through the strange hush of the camp. Behind him their ring of fire was swallowed by the gloom. Ahead, in the distance, the land rose into the contours of hills. Above, in the darkness, the stars burned like beacons.

54

The men struggled with the stone, their breaths echoing in the chapel. Rain bled down the tall windows beyond the painted screen that enclosed the shrine of the Confessor. The interior of Westminster Abbey was cool. Shafts of pallid daylight seeped through the arches of the choir, filtering into hushed chapels where nobles kept their silent sleep, entombed and gilded, waiting for the Day of Judgement. In the pale light the Stone of Destiny glittered softly, like frost or starlight.

King Edward watched the men lower the rock into the ornately carved chair, hollow where the seat should be. Close by stood his master painter, who had decorated the coronation chair with an image of a seated king surrounded by mythical birds and trailing flowers. As two of the men stepped back, a third took up the wooden seat that would cover the stone, trapping it inside. Truly, Scotland was under England's dominion.

Edward would never sit upon this throne. It was for his heir and the line that stretched into the future, all the reigns of kings to come mounted upon his legacy. Years earlier in Bordeaux he'd had a fresco painted, showing a king surrounded by knights bearing the symbol of the dragon. The king in the painting had been seated upon a stone throne, wearing a gold circlet, bearing a broken blade and a golden staff. Now, that image was almost reality. As Brutus and Arthur before him, his name would be remembered for a thousand years. Scotland's throne, Arthur's crown, the Confessor's sword: these ancient symbols of Britain's sovereignty were displayed in the heart of his kingdom before the shrine of his namesake. This should have been the greatest of days. It should have marked the fulfilment of the oath he'd sworn twenty-three years ago, when he had come to this abbey barefoot, walking on a carpet of flowers.

He could still hear the drums.

Westminster Abbey, England

1274 AD

*L*ike a heartbeat, slow and solemn, the sound reverberated off the buildings of Westminster Palace. Edward's pace matched the drums' rhythm, his bare feet crushing into perfume the velvet of scarlet roses and the silk of white lilies. The flowers, carefully plucked of thorns, had been handed out that morning to the crowds thronging the thoroughfare from the palace to the abbey. Women crossed themselves as he passed. Men bowed their heads and children were lifted up so that in the years to come they could tell their sons and daughters that they were there; they had seen the day their king was crowned.

Against the boundless blue of August sky banners of gold silk billowed from balustrades and archways, festooned for the occasion of his coronation. It was the first many of his subjects had known. Only grizzled men and old wives remembered his father's, over half a century ago.

At Edward's side walked Eleanor, radiant in a gown of white samite, clustered with pearls. They had returned to England three weeks ago. She had been with him when he had taken the Cross, bound on crusade, with him all through the months in Palestine – months that had seen war against the Saracens, the birth of his daughter and an attempt on his life by the Mamluk sultan, Baybars. And she had been with him when messengers from England had arrived to tell him his father was dead.

Eleanor's veil drifted before her face as she walked beside him. As Edward caught her eye, she smiled breathlessly. It was a momentous day for her too. She would enter the abbey towering before them as his wife. She would leave as his queen.

Leading the way were bishops and priests garbed in ceremonial robes, some swinging censers that trailed clouds of incense. Behind Edward and Eleanor came a stately procession of earls and barons, lords and knights, mounted on barded destriers, all displaying the arms of their households on surcoats and shields, pennons and trappers. The earls heading this procession bore the royal regalia: Curtana, the rod and sceptre, and the jewel-spangled crown. As the clergy funnelled into the abbey, followed by the royal couple, the riders did not stop, but urged their horses on into the cavernous interior. The abbey was ablaze with a thousand candles, the flames reflected in gilded walls and stained-glass windows, marble and onyx tombs, mosaics and painted screens. More banners of gold silk rippled from pillars.

Edward walked past the ranks of men and women who filled the galleries, all the way to the crossing of the church, where a wooden dais had been erected, so high a horse and its rider could enter beneath. Upon the platform, festooned with scarlet flags, the Archbishop of Canterbury waited. At the steps of the dais the royal couple halted. The air was filled with the clinking of bridles and brash snorts of horses.

Edward paused before mounting the platform, his eyes moving to Eleanor. Through the gossamer of the veil she smiled. Turning, he climbed the steps alone beneath the vault of Westminster Abbey.

How long had he waited for this day?

Last night, he had spent his final hours as a mere mortal alone in the sumptuous palace chamber where his father had gasped his dying breath. The bedchamber was decorated with scenes, the most vivid of which displayed the crowning of the Confessor. In the painted chamber, surrounded by faces of long dead men and the ghost of his father, Edward had been flooded with memory.

Boyhood came dimly in the form of his mother's arm tight around his shoulders as he watched his father sail out from Portsmouth, bound for France without him. On the heels of this recollection came a mirror image of his father at the palace, grim and silent, watching him ride away into exile. Edward recalled the coming of the Valences and those lavish gifts of land and money his father had bestowed upon them that so angered and alienated his English magnates. He remembered the trouble growing in Wales and the red mouths and clenched fists of the barons in parliament, Henry wilting under their barrage. He remembered his godfather, Simon de Montfort, rising like some charismatic demigod to tower over his father and the king's face crumpling in anguish as he learned of Edward's pact with his betrayer.

Gradually, the memories faded to a single image: that of his father limping from the gates of Lewes Priory, Montfort and his men grinning in the torchlight, like wolves whose quarry walked insensibly towards them. They had jostled one another, eager to see the humiliation of the king, humbled before the victor of the civil war, God's own warrior, the man who had taken Henry's kingdom and stripped his authority. It was then, more than at any other time, even in exile in Gascony under the banner of the dragon or on the rain-drenched fields of war in Wales, that Edward truly feared he would not live to wear the crown.

This day had been a long time coming.

Edward approached the archbishop, waiting on the dais. There, standing in a shaft of sunlight before the crowds, he took the coronation oath. His voice rang as he promised to defend the Church, do good justice and protect the rights of the Crown.

When it was done, the archbishop led the way down the steps of the dais, through swirls of incense to the high altar. Here, to the pure voices of the choir that rose in a fountain of song, Edward's mantle was removed to reveal a simple linen undershirt. Taking the vessel of holy oil from the Bishop of London, the archbishop moved to perform the unction that would turn Edward from a man into a king. Intoning in Latin, the archbishop dipped his finger into the oil. He hesitated, his finger hovering over Edward's chest.

Glancing down, Edward realised what had made him pause. Above his heart, visible through the open neck of the shirt, a knotted scar made an ugly pattern of violence on his skin; the wound made by the Assassin Sultan Baybars had sent to kill him.

The attacker had come in disguise to his lodgings in the city of Acre, bearing gifts and a message from Cairo. Eleanor was with him when the man had struck. Edward had thrown the Assassin off, slamming him against a wall and punching him repeatedly until his knights had pulled him back and run the man through. It was only when Edward staggered round to Eleanor and saw the horror filling her face that he realised he had been stabbed. The dagger, partially embedded in his chest, had missed his heart, but that did not matter: an Assassin's blade meant poison. As he fell to his knees, the breath leaving him, Eleanor had rushed to his side. It was her hand that removed the dagger, causing the blood to spill hot across his chest. The last thing he remembered was her mouth moving over the gaping wound, her lips splattered red as she tried to suck out the poison. When he came to, Eleanor was weeping in the arms of her maid, covered in blood, and his knights were watching grimly as a skilled Arab surgeon stitched the wound, sending delirious waves of agony through him.

The archbishop reached out and smeared the oil on Edward's chest. Then, the anointing done, he took up a phial of precious chrism. Edward went down on his knees as the voices of the choir lifted. He closed his eyes as the Latin washed over him and felt a cool sensation as the chrism was trickled on to his head.

Once the unction was done, he returned to the dais. There was a sigh from the watching congregation as he mounted the steps, a king in body and spirit, transformed like Christ himself. Now, the earls who bore the symbols of kingship came forward to invest their new king with the regalia of the realm: a tunic and mantle of gold, Curtana and the rod and sceptre. Last came the crown, embossed with rubies, sapphires and emeralds, as big as eyes. When it was placed upon his head, Edward stood to hear the cheers of his people.

Hallelujah! Long live the king!

In his mind he saw his father trudging towards Simon de Montfort and the rebel barons.

By God, I will never submit to an enemy. They will know that.

They will know that.

With the cheers still thundering through Westminster Abbey, he reached up and lifted the crown from his head. It took a few moments, but gradually the praises and exclamations died away, people glancing at one another, wondering what he was doing.

'I stand before you as your king.'

Applause greeted the words, but faded into hush as Edward handed the crown to John de Warenne, standing on the dais with the other magnates.

The king turned to face the throng. 'But I swear, before God and all here present, that I shall not wear the crown of this kingdom until I have recovered the lands lost by my father.'

He had been headstrong then, fired by ambition. Edward doubted the older barons, those who served his father, had taken him seriously at the time. Most likely they had seen it as a bold statement with which to begin his rule. But over the years, he had shown them he meant what he had said, first with Wales and Ireland, then Gascony and Scotland, lands his father and the kings before him had allowed to be challenged time and time again. There was just one more relic to find, which his men were scouring Ireland for, then his dominion would be complete. Now he had secured the Crown of Arthur and the Stone of Destiny there was no need to keep the details of the prophecy within the confines of the order and his clerics had been busy these past few months, spreading word of his achievements to the people. Already the poets were proclaiming him as the saviour of Britain, a new Arthur, who was delivering them from the doom foretold in a lost prophecy of Merlin.

Ah God! How often Merlin said the truth in his prophecies, the chronicler Peter Langtoft had written. *Now are the islanders all joined together. And Albany reunited to the regalities, of which king Edward is proclaimed lord.*

And here on the altar before the shrine of the Confessor were those regalities. Curtana for England, the Crown of Arthur for Wales and, for Albany – Scotland – the Stone of Destiny. He had done what he had set out to do all those years ago in exile in Gascony, when the seed of his ambition had been sown. Yet for the presentation of the stone, this most auspicious of ceremonies, Edward stood alone. This was supposed to have been a great day for him and for England, but instead of praising his name, the barons were cursing it.

Returning from Scotland the year before, he had buried his brother, Edmund, whose body had been brought back from Gascony, where war lumbered on. Through the marriage of his daughter, Bess, to the Count of

Holland he had made a new alliance. But it wasn't enough to win him the war; to do that he needed money. Edward had turned first to the Church, but the new Archbishop of Canterbury, an indomitable man called Robert Winchelsea, had denied him. In retaliation he outlawed the men of the Church and sent his royal knights to seize their goods, thinking the hard approach would make them fold, as they always had. Winchelsea, however, had proved of sterner stuff and had strengthened their resolve by his own example, persuading them to endure the king's harsh measures. All through these delays the war in France continued, Edward's forces losing a battle outside Bayonne with heavy casualties, one of whom was his half-uncle, William de Valence. The formidable Earl of Pembroke had been among his staunchest supporters since his exile in Gascony and his loss was a terrible blow to Edward, whose allies were becoming few and far between. The stark truth of this had become apparent in a parliament at Salisbury.

At the parliament, where he requested further service in Gascony from his barons, Edward had been faced with their blunt, unanimous rejection. The parliament, one of the most humiliating moments of his reign, ended with the barons walking out, one after another. Even his most stalwart supporters, the men of the Round Table, had defied him. The barons' defiant exodus had been a shocking reality. Shock turned to fear when spies informed him that no fewer than four of his earls – Norfolk, Warwick, Arundel and Hereford – had met to protest against his demands and to rally their supporters. The young Knights of the Dragon, while not openly defying him, were not supporting him as wholeheartedly as they had, caught between faithfulness to their king and to their fathers, whose estates and titles they would soon inherit. Edward had built the Round Table to imbue his vassals with glory and a sense of unity, like the mythic warriors who graced Arthur's court. Now, almost at the moment his plans had come to fruition, the table was breaking apart. The spectre of civil war loomed black before him. He would not go through that again.

With a supreme effort, he had choked down his pride and made peace with Winchelsea. Now, he would do the same with his barons. He had no choice. The French war, which had proven so detrimental to his reign, required a conclusion. There was still trouble in Scotland, but he could not focus on two fronts at once. Tomorrow, outside this abbey that had seen him crowned king, he would stand before his recalcitrant vassals and beg for their patience. He was going to war in France. If he did not return, his son, Edward of Caernarfon, would take the throne. Arthur's crown was not enough. He needed to show them he was still their warrior king.

Hearing footsteps echo through the abbey, Edward turned to see one of his knights.

'My lord. I have brought the prisoners. They await you in the nave.'

Edward headed out through the screen, leaving the workmen to fix the wooden seat of the coronation chair in place over the Stone of Destiny.

In the nave between six knights were three figures. They were pale even though it was late summer, for he had not allowed them to leave the confines of their chambers except to walk each morning in the Tower's inner ward, which was shaded by high walls. Aside from this, they looked in good health. Edward hadn't ill-treated any of his Scottish prisoners, not even John Balliol, who was incarcerated in a small, but well-appointed room in the Salt Tower, with servants to attend to his needs. Despite this fact, the three Comyn men watched his approach with hate in their eyes.

As he came to stand before them, the heads of the Red and Black Comyns met his stare, but Badenoch's son looked away. 'I have a proposition for you,' Edward told them. 'I am willing to forgive your betrayal and your part in the alliance with France. I am even willing to restore your lands.' Edward looked at young John Comyn whose wife, Joan de Valence, had been ordered back to England on the eve of the war. 'And to return your wife and child.'

John shifted on his feet and the Earl of Buchan frowned, intrigued. John's father, the Lord of Badenoch, remained unreadable.

The king continued, his voice tight. This wasn't something he wanted to do, but with so few of his own magnates willing to serve him in Scotland or France, he had little choice. 'All this I will do, in return for your service.'

Buchan looked as if he were about to speak, but Badenoch was quicker. 'Service, my lord?'

'In Scotland, against the rebels. My men have met with Douglas and Wallace in Irvine, but violence continues under the banner of Moray in the north. If you agree to my terms you will join the forces of Sir John de Warenne and Hugh de Cressingham at Berwick. From there, you will raise your vassals and lead them north to defeat Moray. Once the insurrection is ended and I have the instigators in my custody, I will honour my word.' When none of them answered, Edward said harshly, 'Well? What say you?'

Badenoch glanced at Buchan, who gave a nod. Turning to the king, the Red Comyn went down on one knee. 'We will swear to it, Lord King.'

55

On the edge of the woods, the four men reined in their horses. Jumping down into the long grass, Robert handed the reins to Nes, who took them in silence.

'We should accompany you,' advised Alexander.

Christopher added his agreement.

As Robert turned to them the evening sun poured gold into his eyes. He raised his hand to shield his face from the glare. The salt smell of the sea was in the air and he could hear the distant rush of waves on Turnberry beach. 'I'll go alone.' Leaving them on the borders of the trees, he walked into the green shade.

The way at first was easy, the tracks made by deer and other animals forming natural paths through the undergrowth. The sweetness of sap and pine surrounded him and sunlight dappled the forest floor. Somewhere, he could hear the bubbling of hidden streams and memories of boyish laughter echoed to him in the chuckling water. In his mind's eye he saw his brothers, Thomas and Niall, running through the woods ahead, swinging sticks at the bracken and yelling battle cries. He was ahead of them, running fast, fearlessly leaping fallen boughs. Trailing behind came Alexander. After all these years these woods were achingly familiar, but Robert walked them with a different sense now, a sense of ownership and responsibility.

Gradually the land climbed up and his breath deepened as he ascended one earthy ridge after another, grasping hold of gnarled limbs and snaking roots. As he slid down the last bank the woods thinned, opening out into a valley at the end of which rose a hill studded with gorse. Under the hill was a dwelling, beneath the shadow of an oak. Walking out of the trees, Robert worried that she might not be here, but as he drew closer he saw a thin coil of smoke coming from the roof vent.

The house was a forlorn sight. Weeds and bushes grew close to the walls and filled the interior of the empty animal pen. The timbers on the façade were rotten and the lintel over the door had warped. He half expected two black dogs to come rushing out, but the place was quiet. Approaching, Robert saw that the oak was cluttered with webs of twigs, each containing different objects, from a braided ribbon to a bundle of dried flowers, a wooden doll to a scroll-case. There were many more destinies here now, some weather-worn, others new. A tree full of prayers. As he reached the door, he stared up into the higher boughs. For a moment he thought it wasn't there, then he saw it: a lattice of bone-white twigs, bound together around a length of mossy rope, knotted in a noose. The twine looped around the branch above was frayed, holding the web suspended by a thread.

As he reached for the peeling door the voice of his father sounded in his mind, harsh with scorn. Forcing it away, Robert curled his hand into a fist to knock. His grandfather had believed in the old woman's magic and that was all that mattered. This would be an honouring of the old man and a chance for him to swear again the oath he had broken. A chance to make amends.

Lochmaben, Scotland

1292 AD

*T*he cold raised gooseflesh on Robert's skin as he stood before the altar, the flagstones numbing his feet. The candles were struggling to stay alight in the draught that blew in beneath the doors. He could hear the wind moaning between the buildings of the bailey. The dogs in the kennels were barking and the gates of the palisade banged in the gusts. All through the long night he had listened to the growling storm and the hail dashing the chapel's windows, his hair drying cold against his scalp after the ritual bath. Dawn had broken two hours earlier, but the sky was as black as midnight.

The priest at the altar read a psalm from his breviary, the words of God raised against the tempest. Apart from the priest and Robert there were only five men present for a ceremony that should have been a much grander affair. His grandfather towered over the others, his mane of silver hair wisping about his face in the air. With the lord were three of his vassals and the elderly Earl Donald of Mar, whose daughter Robert had kissed by the loch the week before, on the night they learned John Balliol would be king. The absence of Robert's father was palpable, a phantom all of them pretended not to see. Robert had been told he had set his seal to the agreement resigning the earldom of Carrick, along with the right to claim the throne. Shortly afterwards he had left.

As the priest finished the psalm, one of the lord's vassals came towards Robert, holding a surcoat, tunic and a pair of boots. A blast of wind blew open the chapel doors, slamming them against the wall. Several candles guttered and winked out. One of the other knights hastened down the aisle, while Robert dressed. Over his plain tunic went the surcoat that had once belonged to his father, decorated with the arms of Carrick. It was stained and too big around the gut and shoulders. Robert hadn't wanted to begin his knighthood in another man's clothing, least of all his father's, but there had been no chance to have a new one made. It would be one of the first things he did.

Now it was the turn of the old Earl of Mar to step forward, bearing a broadsword.

All through Robert's vigil the sword had lain on the altar. The pommel was a bronze ball and the grip was bound with leather. He couldn't see the blade, for it was inside a scabbard, but he could tell it was long, several inches longer than any he'd owned. A man's weapon. A knight's weapon. Placing it on the altar last night, his grandfather told him it had come from the Holy Land. Made of Damascus steel, it had spilled the blood of the infidel upon the sands where Lord Jesus Christ had walked. The scabbard was attached to a belt that was coiled in Earl Donald's hands.

Robert met the old earl's gaze as he looped the belt around his waist and fastened it. As he stepped back, he adjusted the broadsword so it hung down from his hip at a slight angle, the hilt just across his body so he could draw it. After a set of spurs was fixed to his boots, he was invested and ready to swear the oath of knighthood.

At a nod from his grandfather Robert knelt, the blade stiff beside him as the earl drew his own sword.

'Do you swear to defend your kingdom?' Earl Donald questioned, his voice struggling against the roar of the wind. 'Do you swear to serve God? And do you swear to protect the lands bestowed upon you, carrying out any duties to which you are obligated by your fief?'

'I swear it,' said Robert, bowing his head as the earl raised his blade and brought it down upon his right shoulder, where it lay heavily for a moment, before being lifted away.

Robert expected the earl to tell him to rise, but Donald stepped back and the Lord of Annandale moved into his place. Robert looked up into his grandfather's craggy face. Those fierce black eyes, glittering in the half-light, bored right through him.

'I want you to swear, Robert, as one born of the line of Malcolm Canmore, as a Bruce and as my grandson, that you will defend our family's claim to the throne of this kingdom, no matter who sits upon it in defiance of our right.' His voice was commanding. 'Swear this to me before these witnesses, in this house of the Lord.'

Robert paused before answering. 'I swear it.'

For a moment, his grandfather's gaze continued to pierce him, then the lord's hard face broke into a rare smile and he nodded to Earl Donald to conclude the ceremony.

'Then arise, Sir Robert, for by this oath and by the girding of the sword, you are made a knight.'

As Robert stood, his grandfather's eyes shone. 'Come,' he said to the others, 'let us break our fast and warm our hearts with wine in my chambers. We have much to give thanks for.' He looked back at Robert. 'For God has granted me a fine new son.'

When the others moved to the doors, Robert hung back, his mind filled with a question that had been troubling him since yesterday, when his grandfather told him he would be knighted.

'What is it?' asked the old man, frowning at his hesitation.

The wind rushed in as the knights opened the chapel doors, blowing out the rest of the candles and sending dead leaves scattering across the stone floor.

'Forgive me, Grandfather,' Robert said quietly, 'but how am I to defend our claim? The moment John Balliol is seated upon the Stone of Destiny he will become king and all his heirs after him. I do not see how I can prevent that from happening.'

His grandfather put a hand on his shoulder. 'I am not asking you to prevent it. Robert, the Stone of Destiny does not make a king any more than a well-bred horse or a fine sword makes a knight. Balliol may sit on the stone, he may be called king, but it doesn't change the fact that his blood is thinner than mine. It may take a year, it make take a hundred, but so long as the claim is kept alive, I believe time will show that ours is the truer line.'

Reaching out, Robert knocked on the dwelling's peeling door. After a moment he heard the snap of a latch. The door swung open and Affraig appeared. Her expression of surprise shifted quickly into suspicion, but rather than speak, she opened the door wider and moved aside, allowing him to enter. He did so after a pause, realising, as he was forced to duck under the warped lintel, how much he had grown since he had come here last. The cramped interior, where bundles of herbs were strung from the cobwebbed rafters, offered little more room. The place stank. Robert caught the astringency of sweat and urine beneath the bitter smell of the plants.

There was a fire burning in the centre of the room beneath the vent in the roof. On her dishevelled bed a black dog was stretched out. Robert looked round as Affraig closed the door and moved past him to a stool where she sat, her brown dress drooping around her. Taking up a bowl filled with some dark liquid, she pressed it to her lips and drank, her wrinkled mouth slurping at the edge. Robert crouched awkwardly before the fire. There were a few logs piled there. Picking one up, he thrust it into the heart of the flames, acutely aware that she hadn't stopped staring at him. He had expected her to ask him what he was doing here. He had an answer in his mind, but no question to reply to. The silence swelled until he could bear it no longer. 'I need you to do something for me.'

Affraig lowered the bowl into her lap and wiped her mouth with her hand. Her skin was pale, almost translucent, stretched thinly over the bones of her cheeks and the prominent ridge of her brow. Her ash-white hair was pulled back from her face and bound with strips of leather to fall thickly down her back. There was still something striking about her, in the strong bones of her face, but it was marred by the shabby dress that hung shapeless on her stooped form, her black fingernails, the scalp flakes caught in the knots of her hair and the liver spots on her crooked hands. She evoked in Robert a strange mix of disgust and fascination, disdain and awe.

She hadn't responded to his words.

Robert's eyes moved back to the fire. 'When I took my vows as a knight, my grandfather made me swear to defend our family's claim to the throne. I couldn't see then how I would fulfil that oath. I took it as some statement of defiance, him showing the men of Scotland that he would not bow down to Balliol. But I believe he meant it. He meant for our family to claim the throne, however long it took. That ambition had burned in him for almost sixty years, ever since he was named heir by King Alexander II. In England, in King Edward's court, I became . . .' Robert paused, looking down at his hands. 'I became distracted from this pledge, drawn by promises of wealth and power, things I thought my family would want me to secure. This led me to do things. Things I cannot change.' He stared into the flames. 'I broke the vows I took as a knight. I failed to defend my kingdom, protect my people or fulfil my obligations as an earl and I betrayed the oath I made to my grandfather. When my father began talks with King Edward, making a bid for the throne over my right, I let him. How could I take the throne of a kingdom I had helped to destroy?'

Affraig had set the bowl on the floor. Her eyes were bright in the flames. She didn't speak.

'At the negotiations in Irvine, it became clear to me that there was no side I could stand on. The English despise me and my countrymen don't trust me. Wallace and the others are rebelling in the name of Balliol. I cannot fight with them. It would be as much a betrayal of my oath as when I was fighting for England. I know what I must do. What I should have done months ago.' Robert felt embarrassed, about to say the words. Inside, his father's voice berated him, but he silenced it. 'I want you to weave my destiny,' he finished. 'As you did for my grandfather.'

When she spoke, her voice was low. 'And what is your destiny?'

He met her eyes now, all hesitation and embarrassment gone. 'To be King of Scotland.'

A smile appeared at the corners of her mouth. It wasn't a soft smile. It was hard and dangerous. 'I will need something of yours,' she said, rising.

Robert cursed inwardly. He had brought coins to pay her with, but nothing else. He should have remembered those objects inside the webs. He checked himself, but he had on only the clothes he was wearing: a blue tunic, a pair of hose and boots, and a dirk he had slipped into his belt, just in case. A dagger didn't seem an appropriate symbol of kingship. 'I have nothing.'

Affraig frowned in consideration, then crossed the chamber to a shelf littered with herbs and leaves. A stained pestle lay beside a mortar. Reaching up, she pulled a handful of dried flowers from the beam above the counter. Squinting into the gloom, she snatched down two more bundles. As she returned to the pool of firelight, Robert realised the first she had plucked was a bunch of heather. The second was broom and the third he didn't recognise.

She seated herself on her stool, spreading the herbs on her knees. Robert shifted to sit cross-legged before the fire, watching her work. As Affraig pulled apart the tangled roots, the room filled with the sweet smell of heather. When each bushy stalk had been separated she chose three and began to plait them together. As she worked, dried flower heads crumbled from her skirts on to the floor around her. When one braid was done she picked up another three stalks and began again, her fingers deft. After a time she had nine stiff braids and now she began to join them in a circle, binding them. Into each loop, she threaded wisps of broom and strands of the third herb.

'Wormwood,' she murmured. 'Crown for a king, it was called in ancient days.'

Her darting fingers were hypnotic and the smell of herbs and wood-smoke intoxicating. Robert felt his eyes grow heavy. He hadn't slept properly since they left Irvine a week ago. His limbs were leaden.

He came to with a jolt to see her looming over him, holding a crown of green, his destiny made manifest in a circle of heather and broom. In his mind, he saw himself standing on the Moot Hill with his grandfather, the shadows gathering around them, the plinth beside them empty, expectant of a new king. He had felt the ghosts of his ancestors thronging the hillside that evening. He sensed them now in this fire-lit chamber, crowding in, hushed and eager, as Affraig bent to place the crown upon his head. As she did so, she murmured words he did not understand, an odd mix of Latin and Gaelic.

When she was done, Affraig took it to the herb-strewn shelf. Reaching into a sack bag at her feet she pulled out a bundle of weathered twigs, stripped of bark. They were supple in her hands as she curved and twisted them, binding them with twine to create a hollow, misshapen web, just big enough to contain the crown, which she inserted before the end and fixed to the lattice of twigs with a length of twine.

Finally, she turned to him. 'It is done.'

Robert rose to look at the web of his destiny with interest and doubt. Could this circle of herbs and sticks bring him to the throne? He thought of his grandfather's spell, to end the curse of Malachy, still hanging in the oak after all these years, as yet unrealised. 'When will you put it in the tree?'

'It must spend one night by fire, another by water, the third in the air and the last night on the earth. Only then will it be ready for the hanging.'

Robert reached for the money pouch that hung from his belt, but Affraig stopped him.

'I did not do this for coin,' she said, her tone angry.

Robert took his hand away. There seemed little else to say and so he walked to the door. She came with him, clearly expecting nothing more. As he stepped outside, Robert saw the sun had set and the valley lay in shadow. The woods beyond were dark. He turned suddenly, a question springing into his mind. 'How will you get it in the oak?'

Affraig smiled and this time her face softened. She nodded to a long wooden pole leaning up against the side of the house, slit at the end to form two prongs.

Robert grinned, remembering he had once thought she must fly up there. His mirth faded. 'I don't know how to begin.'

'You will.'

56

Making his way out of the woods, Robert headed back to his comrades, who were waiting where he had left them, sharing a skin of wine. They looked relieved as they saw him approach. A half-moon had risen, bold and bright.

'Did you find what you wanted?' Alexander asked.

'I did.' Robert readied himself to rebuff any further questions: he hadn't told them why he was going into the woods. It wasn't something he wanted to admit. But Alexander merely nodded and mounted up beside him.

As the four rode back across the marshy fields, Turnberry Castle loomed against the turquoise sky on the edge of the crumbling cliffs. Beyond, the sea glimmered, silvery gold in the moonlight. They had been at the castle for almost a week, but the sight of it still induced sadness in Robert, reminding him of the family he had lost. The old building, left in the care of Andrew Boyd, was in a good state of repair and he had set about arranging councils, summoning his other vassals here, but despite all the comings and goings, it still seemed empty and forlorn, just a handful of unfamiliar servants and knights to grace the passageways that echoed with the sea.

Robert, deep in thought, only realised something was wrong when the others began to slow. Drawing in his reins, he fell back with them. 'What is it?'

'The castle gates,' said Alexander, his eyes on the stronghold in the distance, 'they were closed when we left.'

Sure enough, Robert saw that the gates had been thrown wide. They weren't expecting anyone and there was no reason why anyone inside would need to leave, certainly not by both gates which it was only necessary to open for more than a few riders.

'You should stay here, Sir Robert,' said Christopher, drawing his sword.

Robert drew his blade, the steel rasping on the leather. 'It's my home,' he said roughly. Kicking his palfrey on, he made his way across the fields, on to the track that led to the castle, closely followed by his men. Ever since he left Irvine, he'd felt a growing sense of protection towards his lands. He felt it surge in him now, not least because his daughter was behind those walls.

Ahead, through the gates, he saw a large crowd of people in the castle yard, many of them mounted or else standing with their horses. There were three carts there also. He heard raised voices on the air over the drumming of the hooves. Twisting round, he saw the Setons and Nes close behind. As he turned back to the gates, Robert realised there was a banner raised above the crowd, the colours rich in the bronze shimmer of torches. He recognised it at once, for it was decorated with the arms of the Earl of Mar, his father-in-law. Almost at the same time, he picked out a figure talking with Andrew Boyd. It was a tall young man with dark hair and a face so resembling his own it was like looking in a mirror. The sight of his brother standing there in the courtyard of their childhood home made Robert shout with joy. Some of the men in the courtyard, hearing the hoof-beats, had turned to see him approaching. Edward turned with them. He pushed through the people to meet Robert, who rode in through the gates.

Robert jumped down from the saddle and embraced his brother fiercely. It had been only a few months since they had seen one another, but with all that had happened it felt far longer. Alexander and the others rode in, slowing. Over Edward's shoulder, Robert was stunned to see another familiar figure moving out of the crowd. Robert had last seen his sister Christian three years earlier, before her marriage to the son and heir of Donald of Mar. She had been barely out of girlhood then, solemn and shy. Now, almost fifteen, she was virtually a woman, her poise erect as she clasped his hands and rose on to her toes to kiss his cheeks. Her hair, fair like their brother Thomas's, was plaited down her back entwined with gold thread and her mantle was fastened at her throat by a pretty brooch.

Behind came her husband, Gartnait, Earl Donald's eldest son. He was Robert's brother-in-law both through the marriage to Christian and through Robert's marriage to Isobel. Robert saw something reminiscent of his dead wife in Gartnait's thin, serious face. He was more than twice Christian's age, his hair receding from his brow, his eyes creased at the corners, but as Christian turned to him Robert saw a genuine affection between them that gladdened him.

Gartnait embraced him rather stiffly. 'Brother,' he greeted, moving back to stand beside his young wife.

Robert went to speak, to ask them what had brought them here, but in the crowd there was one last surprise, in the form of his other brother-in-law, Sir John, the fiery Earl of Atholl, husband of another of Earl Donald's daughters. John strode forward, his face, framed by dark curly hair, intense in the torchlight. Robert felt wary at the sight of him, for although he had always liked the outspoken earl, the man had been one of the commanders in the Black Comyn's force that had attacked Carlisle at the start of the war. John held out his hand. After a pause, Robert took it.

'It is good to see you back in your homeland, Sir Robert,' was all the earl said.

It was enough.

Robert nodded to John, grateful for the evident truce. 'I had heard you were imprisoned.'

'Fortune favoured me. There wasn't room in London's Tower for all of those captured by Warenne's forces at Dunbar and I was sent under guard to a monastery near Chester with Sir Andrew Moray. His men came one night and broke us out. Moray and I made it across the border together.'

Robert turned to Edward. 'How did you know I would be here?'

'When we learned you had disobeyed our father's orders in Douglasdale, I wrote to Christian in secret. I thought Sir Gartnait might be able to aid you, or shelter you at least.'

'My father passed away two months ago,' Gartnait told Robert. 'I succeeded him.'

Robert stared at his brother, overwhelmed by gratitude. He hadn't imagined anyone would have been thinking of his protection after he had left Castle Douglas, especially not Edward who had blamed him for the exile in England. The feeling was replaced by deep loss at the news of the death of the elderly Donald, the man who had knighted him. Robert offered his condolences to Gartnait, who accepted in silence.

'Sir John and his wife were with them,' Edward continued. 'We arranged to meet in Lochmaben. That was where we heard you had gone to Irvine with the leaders of the rebellion. By the time we arrived the talks were over. Apparently the English got word that Wallace was laying siege to Dundee and began arresting the leaders. They took Lord Douglas and Bishop Wishart prisoner.'

'And James Stewart?' asked Robert, with a sinking feeling.

'We think the steward escaped.' Edward shook his head. 'In truth, no one seemed to know much, except that you had vanished days before the arrests began. I guessed you would come here.'

'Did our father send you to find me?' Robert's joy at their unexpected appearance faded into suspicion with the question. 'Is that why you've come?'

'No.' Edward looked behind him at the crowd of knights and squires, many of whom wore the colours of Mar and Atholl. He lowered his voice. 'Our father has been deprived of the governorship of Carlisle, brother. King Edward ordered it when it was known you had deserted. He retired to his estates in Essex with a small retinue. He wasn't well when he left.'

Robert looked away. 'I expect he hates me.'

Edward didn't answer. He looked past Robert to where Alexander and Christopher were waiting with Nes. 'I see you have made new allies.' He nodded guardedly to the young men, who inclined their heads in turn.

'Good ones,' said Robert firmly. He drew a breath. 'I've also made a decision, about where to go from here.'

'We should head east to Dundee and join up with Wallace and Moray's forces,' said John of Atholl, before Robert could continue. 'At Irvine we heard rumour that the English led by the Treacherer and the Earl of Surrey intend to engage them. We should stand united against them.'

Some of the others nodded in agreement.

Gartnait, however, was cautious. 'Wallace's force is mostly made up of foot soldiers. They cannot win on the field. We should look to negotiate, rather than fight.'

'Like Wishart and Douglas?' demanded John.

As his brothers-in-law began to argue, Robert raised his voice over them. 'I will not stand with William Wallace.' They quietened and he continued. 'You all know my family's history with Balliol and the Comyns. Our hatred is no secret, neither is the fact my grandfather went to his grave believing his claim was greater than Balliol's. Five years ago I made a pledge, a pledge I now intend to fulfil.' His voice rose in the hush. 'From here I will raise the men of Carrick and lead them north to Ayr and Irvine. While Wallace and Moray confront the English in the east, I will concentrate on the west. I intend to liberate our neighbouring lands from Lord Henry Percy. And then . . .' He paused, for there had been no time to prepare this speech. 'John Balliol was King Edward's man,' he said, looking at the silent men around him. 'Our country needs a new king – a king who will defend its rights and liberties, who will bring hope to our people and deliver them from those who seek to destroy their freedom. A king whose veins flow with the blood and the might of Malcolm Canmore.'

As he finished speaking, Robert realised that he hadn't actually said it, his intent, but as he caught sight of Edward he saw he hadn't needed to. His brother's face was shining with pride. It was plain too in the expressions of all the men present what he had meant. Some of them nodded, others frowned in thought. But no one berated him, no one laughed in derision or disbelief. In the midst of the crowd, Robert saw Katherine had appeared. Clearly, the maid had heard what he had said, for her head was high and her face full of approval. She disappeared from view as the men closed in around him, evidently filled with questions, to which he most likely had no answers.

Robert held up his hands before any of them could speak. 'Let us talk more of these matters with wine and food before us.' He addressed his vassal. 'Sir Andrew, we'll use the hall for barracks and double up in the stables.' As the courtyard descended into noisy chaos, servants ushering men towards the stables, Alexander introducing himself self-assuredly to John and Gartnait, Robert turned to Edward. 'See that our guests are made comfortable,' he told his brother quietly. 'We'll talk shortly, but there is something I must do first.' He paused, grasping Edward's shoulder. 'I owe you an apology, brother, for not listening to your counsel. I know you never wanted to fight for England against our countrymen.'

'You are here now.' Edward smiled. 'That is all that matters to me.'

Leaving his brother to help guide the fifty or so men and women inside the main buildings, Robert moved through the passages up to his chambers.

The room where he was staying was the chamber that had belonged to his parents. Their old bed dominated the room, the red drapes moth-eaten and faded. It had felt strange, his first night here, making love to Katherine in the bed he had been born in, pulled into the world by Affraig's withered hands.

The fire set that morning had burned to ash in the hearth, but the moonlight shining through the windows gave him enough light to see by as he crossed the chamber to the pile of his belongings. A solid shape, covered with a piece of sacking, was propped against the saddlebag containing his blanket and spare clothes. He'd had Nes bear the covered shield for him since they left Lochmaben in the spring. Robert had thought, after leaving Douglasdale, of abandoning it, but for some reason had been reluctant to do so. Tugging back the sacking, his eyes filled with blood-scarlet. Taking up the shield, Robert left the chamber and made his way down the passage outside, past the room he once shared with his brothers, to the door that led to the ramparts.

Outside, gulls hovered in the sky, their white wings catching the moonlight. The sea glinted, each wave sparkling as it curled far below to break upon the rocks. For a moment, Robert held the shield before him, gripped in his fists. He thought of Humphrey and the Knights of the Dragon. He had believed himself their brother and comrade, but that was just an illusion. The truth was he could never be one of them, the blood in his veins would not allow it. He had a duty, not just to his grandfather's memory or the people of Carrick whom he'd sworn to protect, or to his comrades who had followed him into danger, but to his ancient heritage and the great men from whom he had sprung. Downstairs in the hall, faded by the years, hung the tapestry that depicted Malcolm Canmore killing Macbeth and taking the throne. It was time to assert his right. Blood demanded it.

Banishing the image of Humphrey, Robert hurled the wooden shield out over the battlements. As it fell, the golden dragon flashed and spun, tumbling over until it smashed on to the rocks. The next wave took it. For a moment it was visible on the foaming surface, then it slipped into the depths and was gone.

57

Flames billowed from the bridge, flaring crimson through the smoke, the glare reflected in the surface of the Forth. Sparks scattered into the air as the timber boards and piers burst in the heat. The sky over Stirling had turned black, obscuring the castle perched high above the meadows. The vapours smothered the marshy plain that lay between a great loop of the river, where a causeway ran from the bridge to the foot of the Abbey Craig, a rearing cliff a mile distant. Beneath the pall of smoke was a scene from hell.

All across the meadows to either side of the causeway were the bodies of thousands of dead and dying men. The grass had been trampled into a grey sludge, streaked with streams of foul fluid and matter. Men and horses were entwined, a tangle of shredded limbs and clothing. Banners lay unfurled, drowning in blood. Knights, squires, foot soldiers and archers, all were heaped together regardless of status, sliced into gruesome configurations of flesh and bone, some barely recognisable as human. Eyes had been gouged, noses split and jaws torn to the teeth. Helms had been battered on to heads, the metal dented and scored by hammer blows or axe strikes. Gambesons were torn, felt stuffing bursting up out of chests and stomachs. Swords and arrows protruded from bodies like hundreds of exclamations of death. The stench was enough to turn even the hardest veteran's stomach.

Here and there men writhed and twisted in agony. Faint whimpers and tormented cries rose ragged into the smoke-dark sky where crows circled expectantly. Some of the wounded hauled themselves along the ground trailing useless limbs, gagging on the stink of the opened corpses they crawled through. They did not get far. Scottish foot soldiers moved like angels of death among the bodies, dirks gripped in their fists, drawn to movement and to the cries of the dying. Anywhere a man struggled or called out they swooped, stabbing the last life from the victims. In the carnage it was almost impossible for them to tell who they were despatching: English or Scot, Welsh or Irish. Only status was knowable, displayed in clothes and weapons. Knights, the most identifiable of all, were not spared these swift, brutal murders. Wallace had ordered no survivors. There were to be no ransoms. No mercy.

Other Scots picked through the bodies, not for signs of life but for spoils. Men who had fought in the battle barefoot now gratefully eased the boots off dead men's feet. Some cut pouch strings from belts or tugged wine skins from saddle packs. Many more took up helms and fallen swords, or salvaged items of armour. Around the knights, the richest of the dead, little knots of scavengers grew and skirmishes broke out as they vied for the best plunder.

Elsewhere across the battleground pockets of more intense fighting continued as men, wild with pain and horror, hacked each other apart. One Scot collapsed in the mud as an arrow punched into his throat. The Welsh archer who loosed it was cut down a moment later by an axe blade that split his spine. A blood-soaked foot soldier, faint with exhaustion, plunged his dagger into another man's gut. As he twisted it with a groan of effort, they fell to their knees together. Close by, an English squire was roaring, slashing madly out with his sword as the Scots closed in. He rammed his shield into one man's face, sending him reeling, before another Scot grabbed his sword arm, pulling the weapon wide and giving someone else a chance to step in and stab a dirk up under the squire's ribs.

An English knight, one of the few still horsed, tried to break through the massing Scots by charging his destrier down the causeway towards the Abbey Craig, the only way out of the killing ground now the bridge was aflame. Men scattered from his path, several knocked savagely aside. One of Wallace's commanders ducked down, blade out ready as the knight came towards him. Steeling himself, he swung his sword into the animal's back leg as it passed. The momentum cracked the sword from his hand, but the damage was done. The horse screamed and crashed on to its front legs, breaking them beneath its own weight. The knight was thrown violently from the saddle and sent tumbling along the causeway. As he tried to push himself up, three Scots fell on him. One yelled in victory as he tore off the knight's helm and slashed his dirk across the man's throat, making a wide red line below his screaming mouth.

More cries rent the air, followed by splashes as men fell or were pushed into the waters of the Forth, clogged with English infantry and Welsh bowmen. God alone knew how far to the bottom they went. Hundreds had gone in during the battle, overwhelmed by the legions of Scots. The knights had gone down first, their mail dragging them under. Others, unencumbered by armour, floated on the crimson surface. At the head of the bridge the piles of dead were at their highest, some corpses already consumed by the fire, the charred bodies visible in the flames. Stirling Bridge, the key to the north, with which the English had planned to unlock the kingdom, had been their doom.

That morning, after William Wallace roughly rebuked the offer of parley, the vanguard of the English army had crossed under the command of Hugh de Cressingham. With the treasurer were several hundred knights, a large contingent of Welsh longbowmen conscripted from Gwent and numerous companies of English infantry, augmented by Irish troops. There was only room for two horsemen to ride abreast and the rest of the English force, under the authority of John de Warenne, had waited on the other side for the van to cross.

Wallace and Moray had watched from the top of the Abbey Craig as the English set out along the mile-long causeway in a great, glittering line, their drums beating an ominous tattoo. Below the Craig, a pitifully small number of Scottish cavalry waited, all on light horses, no match for the English destriers. But what they lacked in heavy cavalry the Scots made up for in the infantry force that covered the lower slopes of the Ochil Hills in a sprawling mass of thousands, armed for the most part with long spears. Still, the English had shown no sign of trepidation, riding confidently along the firm ground of the causeway, heading straight for the waiting Scots. Cressingham had ridden in the midst of the knights, a shiny slug in his polished hauberk, silk robes and mantle, his horse plodding beneath his great weight.

Around seven thousand had crossed, the front lines not far from his cavalry, when Wallace had given the signal. With a blast on a horn that echoed down to his troops below and made the English knights look up, the young outlaw spurred his horse down the steep path from the Craig. Meeting up with their men at the bottom, he and Moray led the small mounted force along the causeway, riding hard towards the English. At the same time, the Scottish foot soldiers charged down from the lower slopes. They came with a roar that rolled over the meadows in a shuddering wave of sound that made the English horses startle. Cressingham urged the knights on to meet the approaching Scottish cavalry, while the Welsh bowmen were commanded to shoot at the mass of infantry headed straight for them.

Hundreds of Scots went down under the onslaught of arrows, many picked off their feet by the impact and hurled into those who came behind. But many more came on, leaping fallen comrades. A large part of this force veered off towards the mouth of the bridge and it was here that they closed the trap Wallace had set, cutting the English army in two. By the time Warenne and his men, still on the other side of the bridge, realised what was happening, it was too late. The Scots had hacked a determined path through the scattered English infantry at the bridge-head, who had little time to form a united defence. Moving quickly to take the bridge itself, they formed a lethal wall of spears that could not be penetrated, even by the mounted knights Warenne had sent to tackle them. Had the Welsh archers not been in the vanguard the Scots might not have been so fortunate, but as it was Warenne and the bulk of the English army could only watch, helpless, as Cressingham's forces were cut to pieces in the meadows beyond the broad waters. In the end, Warenne had ordered the bridge set alight and led his forces south towards the wooded hills, knowing the battle was lost.

Now, the grim end was in sight.

William Wallace was with his commanders on the corpse-strewn causeway. The rebel leader was hunkered down in the mud, his breathing laboured, every part of him singing with pain. His skin and clothing were covered in blood, dark globs of it congealing in his hair and coating the length of his great sword, now strapped to his back. Lying prone on the ground beneath him was Andrew Moray. The young knight who had led the men of the north was gasping through his teeth, his face knotted, as one of his men worked to clean a gaping wound in his side, through which Wallace could see the bones of his ribs. He had never seen so much of men's insides before today: a slippery mess of parts held so tentatively together in a frail web of skin. One cut here, another slice there and all came tumbling out. There was something ungodly about it. Something to remind a man he was all just meat for the maggots in the end.

Moray's pain-glazed eyes flicked to Wallace. 'Is it over?'

'Yes.'

Moray grinned fiercely. 'We beat the bastards.' His head lolled back, the grin turning to a grimace. 'Praise God, we beat them.'

Wallace looked up at the men around them, some of them his, some Moray's. Most were injured, all were exhausted, but through the pain their eyes were bright with triumph. They had done what nobles like Sir James Stewart and Bishop Wishart had said was impossible: they had beaten the English cavalry in battle, with barely a knighthood or a mail coat between them.

Adam appeared at Wallace's side and thrust a wine skin into his cousin's hand. His fur-trimmed coat was long gone and his bald head, running with sweat, was gore-spattered. Wallace took the skin and drank, tipping it back until it was empty. The wine stung his parched throat but it was the sweetest he'd ever tasted. He stared at the skin as he finished it. The leather was studded with jewels.

Adam smiled unpleasantly. 'I took it from the Treacherer.'

'Cressingham?' said Wallace sharply. 'You found him?'

Adam nodded to a circle of Scotsmen, close by. 'Over here, cousin.'

Leaving Moray to be tended by his men, Wallace crossed to the circle, followed by Adam. The men parted as he approached and he saw on the ground the corpse of a grossly fat man. The man was naked and the folds of his flesh that flopped over one another were so riddled with wounds it was impossible to tell which had killed him. His face was mostly intact, though one of his eyes was filled with blood. But it was his mouth Wallace was drawn to, or rather the bloody piece of flesh that had been thrust into it. Looking down the length of Cressingham's bloated body, Wallace realised what it was. Barely visible between his flabby, vein-streaked thighs was a dark wound where his manhood should be.

'A fitting end,' growled Adam at his side.

Some of the men laughed. They were sharing around another of the jewelled skins. Several of them, Wallace noticed, had silk garments, clearly the treasurer's, slung over their shoulders or stuffed in their belts.

One man crouched down suddenly and drew a dagger. He glanced up at Wallace. 'Master William, can I take a piece of him?' He looked back at Cressingham's corpse, his dagger gripped in his fist. 'I want to show the good men of Lanark that I helped bring the Treacherer down.'

'Take what you want,' said Wallace, 'he'll not need it where he's going.'

The man grinned. Lifting one of Cressingham's stubby hands, he set to work sawing through a forefinger. Some of the others watched for a moment, then moved in to get themselves a piece of flesh, a token to show comrades and families that they had brought down the tyrant who had bled their kingdom dry.

Wallace left them to it. He would let them have all the spoils they wanted, then when they'd had their fill he would push them on again. This wasn't finished. Not yet. 'Gather Gray and the others,' he told Adam. 'We move out within the hour.'

'Cousin?'

Wallace stared through the shifting layers of smoke across the Forth to where the rear columns of Warenne's force were visible, moving south. 'We'll cross the Fords of Drip at low tide and pursue them. They still have the baggage train with them. We can get supplies and pick off as many as we can.' His blue eyes lingered on the retreating army. 'All of them will take the horror of this day back to England.'

As the Scots celebrated their victory beside the smoking ruins of Stirling Bridge, the crows gathered in a black cloud, circling over the red feast below.

PART 6
1298–1299 AD

They shall load the necks of roaring lions with chains, and restore the times of their ancestors. He shall . . . be crowned with the head of a lion. His beginning shall lay open to wandering affection, but his end shall carry him up to the blessed, who are above.

The History of the Kings of Britain, *Geoffrey of Monmouth*

58

All through the rain and winds of autumn, while the Scottish forces were revelling in their victory over the English at Stirling, Robert was travelling the length and breadth of Carrick, raising the men of his earldom and reinforcing Turnberry Castle.

Initially, despite their resentment towards the English, many were afraid to support him, fearing reprisals from Percy and Clifford. Robert could have demanded their service, but, believing nervous, doubting men would be of little use, he had taken only those who were willing. Most of these were ambitious youths, landless knights and second sons, few of whom had served his father, all of whom were keen to win his favour. Gartnait of Mar and John of Atholl remained at Turnberry with their men and wives, and with Edward and Christian there the crowded castle reminded Robert of the days when its sea-stained walls were filled with his family and their retainers.

Late in October, when the men were busy in the fields, gathering the last crops and slaughtering excess livestock, he had visited Affraig to offer an end to the exile his father had imposed upon her. But the old woman had declined, choosing to remain in the wild rather than return to the village.

Gradually, as the weeks went by, others drifted to Robert's company. It was hard work and sometimes he had to swallow his pride, but he soon discovered that gaining a man's trust was a matter of time and patience. When his vassals saw he intended to stay and bolster their defences more began to support him willingly. As his retinue grew, so did his reputation. He found he had a natural gift for diplomacy, learned at the feet of his grandfather. A lion when provoked, a lamb when necessary, the old lord had been both feared and admired by his subjects, qualities Robert now saw were essential for leadership of a people. His father had been a rigid master who had treated his men more as servants than subjects. Robert's determination and his willingness to listen soon won him the respect of his vassals. It was, he knew, the first step on the path to the throne.

In Irvine, when he had made his decision to lay claim to the kingship of Scotland, Robert understood the enormity, perhaps even impossibility of the task before him. He had blood on his side and his grandfather's claim on record, but that was all. Most of the men of the realm did not trust him, many still openly resented him. The Scots led by Wallace were fighting for the return of John Balliol, not the election of a new king, and the Stone of Destiny was held in Westminster. In order even to announce his decision, he needed much greater support. To gain that he must prove himself; must do what Wallace and the others were doing and win the hearts of his people by winning back their lost lands. And, as the storms of autumn gave way to an iron-cold winter, this was what he set out to do.

With a force of more than fifty knights and two hundred foot soldiers, Robert moved north through Carrick into Ayrshire. Henry Percy had gone south to England, escorting the prisoners taken at Irvine, leaving the port town of Ayr defended by a small garrison. One frozen dawn in late November, Robert and his men stormed the town, overrunning Percy's garrison and breaking their way into the English barracks. Six of Percy's men died in the attack and the rest escaped using a boat moored on the River Ayr, but with the assault English domination in Ayr was at an end. It was here, in the liberated town, much to the excitement and relief of its people, that Robert made his new base. This meant he could keep his family safe down the coast at Turnberry while he concentrated on leading raiding parties to Irvine and other settlements to rout the rest of Percy's soldiers.

Some weeks later, Robert learned the price of his uprising. Henry Percy may have been distracted in England, but Clifford had remained in Galloway and at once turned his attention to the Bruce lands of Annandale, where he burned ten villages and terrorised the people in retaliation. Lochmaben Castle, still garrisoned by vassals of Robert's father, had held out, but terrible damage was done to the outlying settlements, damage that would take seasons to repair. For Robert it had been a hard blow. Annandale might belong to his father, but the place was his home and the thought of it in flames was devastating.

The assault had, however, one unlooked-for advantage. That a prominent English commander had attacked Bruce lands in Scotland proved to many who doubted Robert that his defection was genuine. It made him an enemy of the English – a fact the leaders of the rebellion hadn't failed to notice. Early in the spring of 1298 messengers came, asking Robert to attend a great council of men in the heart of Selkirk Forest, the cradle of insurrection.

The Forest was verdant with new growth as Robert and his company rode through the trees. Pines, twice as broad as a man, soared up into tiers of cloud-like branches. The ground was layered with needles and cones that crackled underfoot. People said the tangled fastness of Selkirk was but a remnant of an ancient forest that once covered the kingdom. Even so, it was still vast and unknowable, full of shadows and glades. It was the perfect base for an army that wanted to stay hidden and Robert was certain, if he hadn't been told what markers to look for, he and his men would have been lost within a day.

'There's another one,' said Edward, shifting in his saddle and pointing to a gnarled trunk on which was painted a white circle with a cross inside. 'We must be getting closer. That's the fourth we've seen this morning.'

Robert's gaze moved past the daubed trunk to where the trees opened out into a clearing. He could hear the rush of water. 'Tell the others,' he said, turning to Christopher Seton who rode close behind, 'we'll take a rest, then push on through the afternoon. I want to reach the camp before nightfall.'

The squire nodded, but as he steered his horse away Robert sensed his apprehension. He understood why. The young man, born and raised in Yorkshire, was about to enter the base of an army whose intent it was to rid their lands of the English for good. Robert had assured the squire that he was under his protection, but in truth he couldn't guarantee Christopher's safety, or anyone else's. As the squire relayed the orders to the rest of the company, fanned out among the trees, Robert urged his palfrey into the clearing. There was a broad stream on the far side of the glade, running swift over smooth, brown stones. The banks were shallow enough to let the horses drink.

Robert dismounted as the others threaded their way through the trees. With the forty knights and squires he had raised from Carrick were sixty-seven men under the commands of Mar and Atholl. Christian had accompanied Gartnait and John's wife rode with him, along with their sixteen-year-old son, David, who was the mirror of his father. Saddle-stiff and weary, the knights pulled wine skins and salted meat from packs as the squires saw to the horses.

Taking the offered hand of one of Robert's knights, Katherine slid down from her mare. Offering the young man a beguiling smile, she brushed the dust from her skirts, while Judith lifted Marjorie out of her seat. Motioning for one of the servants to take her horse to the river, Katherine stretched. 'Bring me something to eat,' she called to Judith, 'after you've fed Marjorie.'

The girl had become as much her maid as Marjorie's wet nurse these past months, Robert had noticed. The other women, Christian and John's wife, who had handmaids of their own, kept their distance from the two. Christian, especially, was cool towards Katherine. Whatever the reason, Robert had neither the time nor desire to root it out. He was tired of politics and the games being played. These men and women all had their own designs, even as they followed him in his. Gartnait, he knew, wasn't fully behind his decision to go for the throne, still advising him to reach a truce with the English. John of Atholl supported him wholeheartedly, but was wary of the Setons who had remained at Robert's side since leaving Irvine. For their part, Alexander and Christopher guarded their place as his trusted commanders zealously. Only Edward seemed able to stand comfortably between them all.

Moving off through the trees, Robert went to stretch his legs alone. The Forest, close around them for days, was becoming claustrophobic and the tensions in his company had increased the deeper in they went. It wasn't just Christopher who was uneasy. John and Alexander had both been troubled by the summons, which had borne the seal of William Wallace, wondering why, after so many months without contact, the rebel wanted Robert to attend the council. It was a risk, certainly. He had no idea what reception he might get. But there were constant rumours of English retaliation; of a great army being assembled for a fresh invasion, and Robert needed to know what was coming.

A little way downriver, he crouched on the bank. As he bent over the water, his reflection swirled beneath him. He hadn't shaved for days and a beard had grown dark and full around his jaw. His eyes were shadowed beneath an unruly fringe of hair. Perhaps he had been wrong to come here? Perhaps it showed weakness: his willingness to accept the summons of a rebel? Robert dipped his hands into the cold water and his image disappeared. Cupping his palms, he splashed his face. As the water ran down his cheeks, another image rippled into being. A woman stood behind him, her body shifting in the currents. He rose quickly to see Katherine standing there. The rush of the river had concealed her footsteps.

She smiled. 'I didn't mean to startle you.' As he wiped his face with his hands, she stepped towards him. 'Here, let me.' Gathering up one of her sleeves, she dabbed at his brow.

The wine-red gown had long, fluted sleeves. She had been wearing it when she met him at Turnberry's gates five days ago. Girdled with a belt of silver rings it would have been fit for a countess, had the bodice not been cut so tightly across her chest. Robert caught Katherine's wrist, suddenly annoyed. 'Why do you wear this?'

Her eyes widened at his tone. 'Do you not like it?'

'I don't like the way my men look at you.'

Katherine laughed and cradled his cheek with her hand. 'Then I shall not wear it again.'

Robert slipped his hand from around her wrist to thread his icy fingers through hers. 'Keep the gown.' He exhaled. 'I'm just tired.' Away through the trees he could hear his men talking. His head was pounding, the water drying cold on his cheeks.

She slid her hands around his neck and pressed herself against him. 'I am yours alone, my love.'

'Katherine,' he murmured warningly.

She glanced over her shoulder. 'They cannot see us.' She looked back at him coquettishly, rising on to her toes until her mouth was almost touching his. 'You're like a wounded boar,' she said, her voice low, teasing. 'So irritable.' She kissed his lips and grinned. 'And you need a shave.'

Robert closed his mouth over hers, pushing her up against the trunk of a tree. Her hands grasped his neck as she kissed him back fiercely.

At the sound of a man clearing his throat, Robert pulled away to see Alexander approaching.

Katherine tossed her hair over her shoulder. 'Sir Alexander! How fortunate Robert is to have someone watching his back.' She laughed. The sound was brittle. 'Indeed, it seems everywhere he goes you are there. Watching.'

'The Forest has many dangers,' responded Alexander, looking her in the eye.

Katherine was the first to look away. 'I will see to your daughter, Robert.' Hitching her skirts, she stepped through the long grass.

Alexander waited until she had gone. 'We should talk.'

Robert let out a rough breath. 'I've told you. She is not your concern.'

'I meant about the camp. About what we're walking into.' Alexander paused. 'But, in truth, my friend, she is part of that discussion. You haven't yet announced your intention to anyone outside our circle, which I feel is wise, but there will come a time when you must stand before the men of the realm and make your claim. How can you expect the magnates to take your bid seriously when you do not?'

'You do not think I take it seriously? With all I have done these past months, all you have helped me do? I'm risking my life and the lives of my family to make my claim!'

'Will Katherine be your wife? Your queen?'

Robert turned away. 'Of course not.'

'Then don't take a maid as your consort.' Alexander moved round, forcing Robert to look at him. 'The others do not speak to you of it, but they all see how she has elevated herself far beyond what she should. She has clawed her way up from a maid to a lady and you have let her.'

Robert went to the river's edge and stared into the green haze of trees on the other side. On the road to Douglasdale, Katherine had become a distraction; a vessel into which he had poured his doubts. Each morning he had woken, filling up with the day's concerns. Each night, he had released his frustrations into her. He had always known, since Isobel's passing, that one day he would have to seek another bride, a bride of high standing who could provide him with a son. He had known this, but had kept on pushing it from his mind, despite the fact that the issue had never been more pressing. He had told himself he'd had no time; that there were more important things to concern himself with. This was true, but it wasn't the real reason for his inaction. The reason he hadn't given any thought to finding a wife was that Katherine wasn't just a distraction any more. She had become one of the only constants in his fast-changing life. She rarely asked him for anything and her only desire, when with him, was to please him. 'I need her, Alexander,' he said quietly. 'Right now, I need her.'

'I understand you want a woman to warm your bed,' replied Alexander, moving in behind him. 'I understand that as well as any man. But there are other things to consider here. Do you not see how it affronts Earl Gartnait? Or Earl John's wife? Lady Isobel was their sister. You have made her servant the mother of her child. Robert, she wears Isobel's clothes. They are your supporters. We need them.' He lifted his shoulders. 'I wonder in part if Gartnait's reluctance to support your bid fully is down to Katherine.'

As Robert shook his head and went to challenge him, his eyes caught movement on the other side of the river. A figure was rising from the undergrowth, dressed all in green, a bow primed in his hands. Robert lunged at Alexander, forcing him down. The two of them hit the ground hard as an arrow thumped into a tree behind.

Alexander struggled to fight Robert off, then went still as a voice rang out.

'That shot was a warning. The next will be fatal unless you state your business.' The man had fixed another arrow in his bow.

Robert got to his feet. Offering his hand to Alexander, but keeping his eyes on the archer, he helped his comrade up. 'I've come to meet with William Wallace. I am Sir Robert Bruce.'

Other men were moving out of the undergrowth on the other side of the river. All carried bows and were clad in green and brown. Behind came calls of alarm as Robert's men, alerted to the danger, hastened through the trees. Edward and Christopher were at the front, closely followed by John of Atholl. Robert halted them with a shout, looking back at the figures on the bank, who had all raised their bows. 'We mean no harm here. Wallace is expecting us.'

The man who had first spoken lowered his bow slowly. 'Gather your people,' he said, after a pause. 'We will lead you from here.'

59

Three hours later, as evening's gloom was deepening, Robert and his men were led into the rebels' camp. The light-footed archers had guided them unerringly through the failing light. Passing more of the white markers, they had encountered five other armed patrols since crossing the river. These groups had conferred with the archers in low tones, all the while eyeing Robert and his company.

Ahead, through the woods, came the murmur of many voices, punctuated by the barking of dogs and the sounds of horses. The air was murky with wood-smoke. Between the trees, men stood talking around fires, or moved purposefully on errands. They wore an assortment of garments, from the hukes and wooden clogs of peasants to the thigh-length tunics worn by Highlanders and the mail hauberks of knights. Some stopped what they were doing to stare as Robert's company passed through their midst.

There were shelters formed from branches leaning up against trees and cloth canopies stretched from trunk to trunk, with blankets laid out on the mossy ground beneath. Men rested there, some of them injured. Robert saw a priest, his tonsured head bowed, kneeling beside a man whose leg had been severed at the knee, swaddled in a bloodstained cloth. Following their escort alongside a broad river where women washed clothes and children played in the shingle, Robert saw two large circles of men, all of whom were gripping long spears, pointing outwards. They seemed to be practising some manoeuvre, the front rows dropping to their knees at a shout from one, spears thrusting forward. Beyond was a clearing filled with tents.

Heading away from the spearmen, they entered the glade. Stumps of oak and alder showed where trees had been hacked down to make more room. There was a fire in the centre, around which the twenty or so tents were erected, along with carts piled with supplies. On one was a glittering array of silver plates, candlesticks, furs and chests – plunder, perhaps from Wallace's raids on northern England. However much Robert had kept himself at a distance from the rebels, he hadn't failed to hear of the outlaw's achievements, rumour of which had surged through the kingdom.

Everywhere, after the battle at Stirling, men spoke in awed tones of the young hero who had led a peasant army to victory against English knights, who had rid them of the hated treasurer, Cressingham, and who chased the mighty Earl of Surrey all the way to the Borders. The shepherds, drovers and hunters who formed Wallace's band soon swelled to include many free-men: burgesses, knights and squires, even lords. With the death of Andrew Moray, who passed soon after the battle, Wallace had become the sole leader of the rebellion and, his men still drunk on the blood spilled at Stirling, the fierce young Scot had led his army into England.

Early in the autumn they swept over the border into Northumberland to visit horrors upon the people of the north. Crops were ruined, livestock slaughtered, men and women put to the sword. Some said the violence was so excessive Wallace and his commanders were forced to hang some of their own men for offences too depraved to go unpunished. Whatever the truth of this, the people of Northumberland fled south in their thousands, leaving homes and chapels, schools and pastures burning on the horizon. It was only in midwinter, when the snows came, that the marauders crossed back over the Tweed. By then, Wallace had a new name. William the Conqueror.

As Robert dismounted in the clearing, he caught sight of the rebel leader near the wagon of plunder. Wallace stood head and shoulders above the men around him, nobles by their apparel. He looked out of place in the plain woollen tunic he wore over his armour, in the midst of their fine cloaks, decorated scabbards and polished mail. The group was talking intently, but as one of the archers crossed to Wallace, the man's eyes shifted to Robert. Wallace appraised him, his expression cool, before nodding to the archer and turning away to speak to a bald-headed man Robert recognised as his cousin, Adam. He felt a stab of anger as Wallace moved off without any greeting, just as a familiar figure emerged from the crowd.

James Stewart crossed to him. 'Sir Robert.'

Robert greeted the steward distractedly, his gaze lingering on Wallace.

As Robert's men began to dismount, James motioned for him to follow out of earshot. 'I fear we parted on bad terms at Irvine. I hope you know that I would never have sanctioned the proposal Henry Percy made to take your daughter as a hostage.'

Robert saw no lie in the steward's face. 'For my part, I am sorry for the way things went.'

'That is past. I am glad you have come, Robert.' James seemed on the brink of saying something further when a large figure interrupted them. It was the Bishop of Glasgow.

'Sir Robert,' Wishart greeted curtly.

'I heard you were imprisoned, your grace,' said Robert, surprised and wary to see him.

'I was for a time, but I appealed to Archbishop Winchelsea for my release and, God be praised, he granted it. I doubt I would have been so blessed had Edward been present, but the king was in Flanders and his court in disarray. The Archbishop of Canterbury felt my imprisonment was an infringement of Church liberties.'

'And Lord Douglas?'

The steward and the bishop exchanged a look.

'Lord Douglas was taken into custody in the Tower,' said Wishart. 'I heard a rumour before I left London that he died there. That rumour has since proven to be true. Robert Clifford has been given his lands.'

Robert thought of the Lady Douglas and her bold young son, James.

'Another of God's fallen warriors,' Wishart went on gruffly. 'Still, the rebellion continues, despite our loss. We have learned of your successes in the west – the liberation of Ayr and Irvine.'

It sounded like praise, but it was difficult to tell from the bishop's hard tone. 'It was a small victory,' admitted Robert, 'in comparison to Wallace's achievements.'

Wishart grunted in agreement. 'Well, indeed, Master William is the reason we have gathered here. He is greatly deserving of the accolade that will be conferred upon him tomorrow.'

'Accolade?' questioned Robert, glancing at James.

'His election as guardian of Scotland,' replied the bishop.

Robert stared at him.

'Until the throne is occupied again,' James cut in.

'Scotland needs a defender, more than it needs a king,' responded Wishart, giving James a meaningful look. 'William Wallace will be made guardian of the realm on the morrow and, God willing, will lead us to victory. King Edward is known to be gathering a vast army. Soon, a day of reckoning will be upon us all.'

With confirmation that war was coming, Robert's thoughts filled with the question of what Wallace's election meant for his own intentions. Before he could ascertain anything more, his brother came up.

'We have company,' said Edward tightly, nodding through the trees.

Robert turned to see another group entering the clearing. He recognised the two men at the front immediately. One was in his mid-fifties with coarse grizzled hair, the other was closer to his own age. Both had lean, pale faces and were dressed in black, their red shields decorated with three white sheaves of wheat. Robert stared at them, years of hostility bubbling to the surface. 'I was told the Red Comyn and his son were captured at Dunbar,' he murmured.

'They were freed by King Edward on the condition they help quell the rebellion,' answered Wishart. 'They were with John de Warenne's forces at Stirling, but after William's victory they slipped the earl's company during his flight to the Borders and came to our side.'

'Wallace trusts them?'

'They fight for the same ends,' was Wishart's blunt response.

Robert watched as the bishop crossed the clearing to greet the newcomers. By tomorrow William Wallace would be the most powerful man in the kingdom. Wishart was right – the rebel leader was fighting for the very thing the Comyns wanted: the return of John Balliol. The very thing that would destroy his plans. 'Have the men make camp,' he told his brother, not taking his eyes off the Lord of Badenoch.

As Edward nodded grimly and moved away, the steward stepped into Robert's path.

'We must talk.'

Downstream from the main camp the river tumbled over a series of rocky plateaux before draining into a deep, glassy pool. Robert and the steward stood on a spur of rock above the pool, the cascade of water concealing their conversation from anyone who might pass on the banks. Away through the trees, flickering campfires were interrupted by the shadows of men.

'I wanted to speak to you back in Irvine,' the steward was saying. He stood at the end of the outcrop facing Robert, his eyes black in the torch flames. 'But events conspired against us. Bishop Wishart is right. William Wallace's achievements have been far beyond what any of us could have expected. There is no doubt the man is deserving of the title that will be bestowed upon him at our council tomorrow.'

Robert didn't answer.

'But we need to look beyond the victories of the present to a time when our stability as a kingdom can be sustained without battle and bloodshed.' James seemed to be choosing his words carefully. 'I understand Wishart's enthusiasm, but I have stared long into the future these past months and it is that which concerns me, more than current strategies for war and the honouring of heroes. Our future can only be certain with a king upon our throne and the line of succession secured.' His voice lowered, until Robert had to strain to hear him over the surging water. 'There is no certainty King John will ever return to fulfil that role, however much William and his men demand it of Edward. However many battles they win. It is my responsibility, as steward of this kingdom, to plan for that possibility.' He paused, studying Robert. 'Your grandfather was believed by many, myself included, to be the rightful candidate. I believe Edward saw that too and feared he would not be as malleable as Balliol.'

Robert nodded.

James's dark eyes were intense. 'In looking to the future, Robert, it is you that I have seen as the one who could step into the void left by Balliol. You have the blood right and also, I believe, the virtues necessary.'

At these solemn words, Robert felt relief flood through him. Despite all the things he had done to advance his ambition these past months, he hadn't been able to silence the voices of doubt within him. They lingered still, harsh with the abrasive tones of his father, telling him it was impossible for him, a traitor, to take the throne; that the people of Scotland would not accept him and that, ultimately, he had neither the courage nor the will to stand up to King Edward. If a man of such wisdom and experience as James – a man from a long line who had served Scotland's kings in the esteemed office of the high stewardship – believed in him, then surely it was possible. There by the rushing river, the trees stretching into shadows all around him, he could almost hear his grandfather telling him it was.

Robert told the steward of the decision he had made in Irvine. 'It is a long road, I know,' he finished. 'The Stone of Destiny is held in Westminster and I don't know how to win the trust of our people.' He faltered. 'And now Wallace is to be made guardian, I'm afraid the small victories I have gained in the west will benefit me little. I cannot stand beside Wallace and expect the men of the realm to respect me as they do him, no matter the strength of my claim to the throne.'

James nodded, but rather than appearing discouraged by the challenge he looked keen. 'I agree it will not be easy. I cannot yet see the way ahead, but I do have an idea of how we might start. There is something you could do at the council tomorrow. Something that will make all those present take notice of you and your commitment to the kingdom.'

60

Above the clearing the rising sun gilded the tops of the encircling pines. Spiders' webs decorated the branches like strings of tiny pearls. Below, the men were gathering, the murmur of their voices drowning the birds' chorus. In the centre of the glade was a cart, with a set of wooden steps at the back. On this makeshift platform the Bishop of Glasgow was speaking with James Stewart.

Robert made his way towards the cart, negotiating the crowds already thronging the edges of the glade, the men of the camp all keen to bear witness to this ceremony, a momentous occasion for their leader and their struggle. The mood was buoyant, the soldiers plainly excited by the prospect of Wallace's election. The Setons were ahead with Walter and five Carrick knights, clearing a path for him as best they could. Christopher kept a hand near his sword. Alexander was subdued, the atmosphere between him and Robert rather cool after the discussion about Katherine. To either side of Robert were his brothers-in-law, John and Gartnait, and close behind came Edward. As Robert approached the cart with his retinue, ignoring the hostile stares his presence generated, he caught the eye of James Stewart. The high steward nodded to him. Taking up his place at the front of the rows of men, Robert felt tension crackling within him at the thought of what was to come.

William Wallace was a short distance away with his commanders – Adam, a scarred, brutal man called Gray and several notable lords. These included Gilbert de la Hay, the Lord of Erroll, built like a Caledonian pine with a flop of blond hair and a flushed, jovial face, and Neil Campbell from Lochawe, who had joined Wallace after the liberation of Dundee. Closer to Robert was the steward's brother, John, standing beside James's wife, Egidia de Burgh, sister of the Earl of Ulster, whom the steward had married before the outbreak of war. Despite the fact that her brother was King Edward's most trusted commander in Ireland, Egidia had chosen to stay with James through the conflict and was pregnant with their first child. Of the other men gathered, Robert knew only a few by name and relied on the Earl of Atholl to fill in the gaps in his knowledge as he waited for the council to begin.

Beyond John Stewart was Malcolm Lennox, a young man with a striking, handsome face and sleek dark hair that he wore in a tail, bound with silver wire. He was surrounded by men of a similar age, all dressed as he was in black tunics and hose. Robert had seen Malcolm with his father, the Earl of Lennox, at several assemblies during the hearing to choose Scotland's king, but had never spoken to him. Malcolm, who had recently succeeded his father, had been one of the commanders of the force that attacked Carlisle on the eve of the war. He glanced in Robert's direction, studying him, before looking away.

On the other side of the ash-ringed campfire was the largest concentration of men. At the front of this group were John Comyn and his son, along with the Earl of Buchan. Behind the heads of the Red and Black Comyns were the Comyns of Kilbride, the branch of the family that had fought for Simon de Montfort at the Battle of Lewes. Around them were many dispossessed men of Galloway, all former vassals of John Balliol, whose lands had been commandeered by Henry Percy. Robert caught sight of a familiar face among them. The name came to him a moment later: Dungal MacDouall, captain of the army of Galloway and an old enemy of his father. The most surprising figure of them all was a chestnut-haired woman with a hard, proud face. Eleanor Balliol, wife of the Red Comyn and sister of the exiled king, stood tall among the men, a potent symbol of the great support within this gathering that still existed for her brother.

As Wishart began speaking from the platform of the cart, the murmurs of the assembled men died away to silence. 'My noble lords, we are gathered today in the sight of Almighty God to witness the election of a young man who has risked life and limb for the sake of his kingdom. A man who has, with fire and sword, beaten back our enemy and returned to us our liberty!'

Applause followed Wishart's words, coming most vigorously from those encircling Wallace. As the bishop continued, speaking of Wallace's defeat of the English at Stirling, Robert noticed the young giant looked uncomfortable at the attention. He stood stiffly among his comrades, hands clasped behind his back.

'For two years our kingdom has been bereft of king or leader to guide us.

Here, today, our fortune changes. Today we elect Master William Wallace, hero of Stirling, to the office of guardian of the realm. Truly, we are blessed, for William is a warrior in whom the Lord God has placed his faith. A warrior with the heart of St Andrew and the grace of St Kentigern!'

The cheers sent birds scattering from the trees.

Robert's gaze drifted from Wishart to James Stewart. His tension built as he wondered when the steward would give the sign.

'Yet despite this joyous occasion we must look to the days of darkness ahead,' Wishart continued, his tone grave. 'The war is not ended, merely paused. Before Master William takes his place as guardian, I invite Lord John Comyn of Badenoch to speak, for he bears tidings from his captivity in England.'

Robert fixed on John Comyn as he moved out of the crowd. His face was lantern-jawed, his grizzled hair thinning on his crown, but despite his advancing years, the Red Comyn looked as forceful as ever. He passed William Wallace with a rather contrived nod of respect, before heading up the steps on to the cart as Wishart moved back to stand beside James.

'Despite the dark days the bishop foretells I can at least bring you some hope. Edward holds our king imprisoned in the Tower, but in my time there I spoke to him on a number of occasions. You should know King John is in good health and is optimistic of his eventual restoration.' Comyn's eyes caught Robert, standing below. 'I am sure you will all join me in praying for his swift return to the throne of our kingdom.'

More applause greeted his words. Wallace was nodding. Robert's jaw tightened.

'As many of you will know, there has been great discontent in England on account of the war with France. When Edward crossed the sea last year, many of his subjects refused to follow him.'

Grim calls of appreciation sounded.

Wishart interrupted them. 'Unfortunately, the king has since returned home and has made a truce with his opponents in England and with King Philippe. The shock of Master William's triumph at Stirling has united the English against us. Make no mistake — they want vengeance for what happened.'

A ripple of voices spread through the clearing.

John of Atholl's was the loudest. 'We should send a delegation to King Philippe and make certain the alliance between France and Scotland still stands. Whatever pact he makes with Edward, we mustn't be forgotten.'

Wishart went to answer, but a host of other men added their agreements to Atholl's suggestion.

Wallace moved out of the crowd to stand before the cart. He had no need to mount it, for everyone could see him. 'This is in hand. When the Bishop of St Andrews passed away last autumn, Bishop Wishart and I decided that the Dean of Glasgow, Master William Lamberton, an honourable and dedicated man, should fill the vacant see. His election has since been sanctioned and Lamberton is on his way to Rome to be consecrated. On the journey he will meet with King Philippe and reaffirm our alliance. Rest assured, Lamberton will do what he can for our cause.'

'But while foreign support is being sought, we must band together,' said Wishart, addressing the assembly. 'We know King Edward is raising a great army, conscripting longbowmen from Wales and infantry from Ireland. Through the efforts of Master William many of the king's garrisons have been routed, but Roxburgh and Berwick remain in English hands. Until now, these fortresses have been as islands, isolated and surrounded by our forces, their supply lines threatened. If the king manages to relieve them during this campaign and regains control of the surrounding districts, he will have a strong base in the south from which to launch further invasions northwards. We cannot allow him to do this.'

'Our plan,' said Wallace, his voice determined, 'is to lay waste to the lands along the border, lands through which the king and his men must march. We will scorch crops and drive our livestock into the Forest. The men and women of the southern shires will be told to head north, carrying all supplies. We must leave nothing for the English to feed upon. The longer they remain in the field the harder it will be for the king to supply his army.'

'We must be ready when they come,' said Wishart. 'We must put aside past animosities and work in union under the leadership of our guardian.'

Men were nodding vehemently, adding their support to Wallace's proposals and the sentiment mooted by the bishop.

At that moment, Robert saw James Stewart turn to him. A jolt went through him as the steward nodded. Before anyone could begin speaking again, he headed out of the crowd towards Wallace, leaving his men looking on in surprise.

'We have chosen to elect this man as our guardian.' Robert's voice was harsh as he gestured to Wallace. 'But he is still just the son of a knight.'

'You dare to challenge his election?' demanded Adam.

Other shouts of scorn and ire joined his.

'On the contrary,' answered Robert, 'I am suggesting that a man of William Wallace's achievements, a man who is to be sole guardian of Scotland, bears a title befitting his prowess.' He faced the crowd. 'I, Sir Robert Bruce, Earl of Carrick, offer William Wallace the honour of a knighthood.' He turned to Wallace. 'If he will bend before me.'

The complaints were drowned by cheers from Wallace's companions. The rebel leader didn't take his gaze off Robert. For a long moment, it didn't look as if he were going to move. Finally, when the applause had faded into an expectant hush, Wallace took a step towards Robert, his face tight. As he did so, he murmured something. Robert just caught the words.

'This does not make me your man.'

But as he drew his sword for the knighting of William Wallace, on bended knee before him, Robert knew the power of the gesture. Catching the wrathful stare of the Lord of Badenoch, standing above him on the cart, he saw that the Comyn knew it too.

Through the spring and into the blistering days of summer, England prepared for war. Writs were sent out from the royal court, calling the men of the realm to serve, from the great earls and their retinues, down to the poorest infantryman with his woollen tunic and hunting knife. Crossbowmen were called up, as were the archers of Sherwood Forest, and the commissioners of array travelled through northern England and the shires of conquered Wales, selecting men for the conflict. More than twenty-five thousand were ordered to serve as infantry, with a large contingent of longbowmen from Gwent.

Farmers set down their ploughs and blacksmiths their hammers to pick up the instruments of war. Younger men, drawn by the offer of a wage, came forward eagerly, clutching bows and arrows. Gambesons were stitched and helms cleaned of rust, mail mended, swords sharpened. As summer ripened the Welsh foot soldiers set out, marching in long lines up the coast and over the mountain barriers of Cader Idris and Snowdon, moving slowly, inexorably towards Carlisle and the northern border. The king's officials rode out to granaries, breweries and markets to stockpile sacks of wheat and oats, and barrels of wine, beer and mutton. Other supplies were called in from Ireland. The merchant sailors of the Cinque Ports were kept busy, readying the ships at Dover, Rye and Hythe for the transportation of these provisions and a blockade was established in the Channel to prevent any French vessels coming to the aid of the Scots. After an unsuccessful campaign in Flanders, Edward had succeeded in sealing a temporary truce with King Philippe, but he wasn't taking any chances. Agreements with his belligerent cousin had, after all, been broken before.

In this time, while supplies were gathered and men conscripted, the English clergy were active, fanning the flames of hatred. In towns and villages across England the name of William Wallace was spoken with loathing, the people outraged by stories of how this ogre of the north raped nuns and tortured priests for pleasure. Tales abounded of his raid on Northumberland, telling of how the bloodthirsty Scots had locked up two hundred boys at a school in Hexham, then set the building on fire. Wallace, they said, had laughed as he watched the children burn. They called him coward, brigand, whoreson and murderer. In London, an effigy of Wallace, dressed in a Highlander's short tunic, was burned to the fervent cheers of the watching crowds.

With the call to arms ringing throughout the shires, King Edward moved his seat of government to York. Here he waited, stone-faced and silent. His barons' animosity over his drawn-out war in Gascony had been swept aside with the defeat of Warenne and Cressingham's force. The men of England were united in their determination to annihilate Wallace and his peasant army, avenging the deaths of friends and kinsmen who had died on the meadows by Stirling Bridge. Rebels and rebellions came and went. It was not the first time an English force had been defeated in battle, but the sheer scale of it had shocked even the veterans. Thousands of infantry and archers had perished, but so had hundreds of knights. There had been no ransoms demanded, no prisoners offered for exchange. The nobility, who rarely faced anonymous death on a battlefield, were suddenly confronted with the prospect of being despatched like common soldiers. It had angered them deeply.

For Edward, the loss was especially galling. His conquest of Scotland had been one of the quickest and easiest campaigns ever launched. With the taking of the Stone of Destiny, the forced homage or imprisonment of the Scottish magnates and the dethronement of Balliol, he had rejoiced in his achievement. But William Wallace, whom he had taken for a lout of little consequence, had loomed like a spectre, auguring the prospect of another Gascony; another protracted conflict that would alienate and anger his barons. They were behind him now, his Round Table united beneath him, the Knights of the Dragon keen for blood, but would they be in five months, or a year? Edward did not want to find out. He was determined, once and for all, to make an end of Wallace and those who had joined him.

In early June, knights gathered with their lords beneath the walls of castles, surrounded by squires, banner-bearers and wagons laden with tents and equipment. In towns and villages across the northern counties men kissed wives goodbye before heading out to join the gangs of soldiers thronging in market squares. White bands of cloth decorated with the red cross of St George were handed out, the men binding them proudly around their upper arms. Nervous and excited, some never having fought in a war, they fiddled with tunics and adjusted helm-straps to the shouted orders of commissioners and sheriffs. Tramping along dusty roads, sweating and complaining beneath steel-blue skies, these companies made their way north to join the army of Welsh foot soldiers gathering on the border.

From the south, the ships carrying the host's supplies set sail, sweeping their oars into a dead calm to glide slowly up the east coast of England. Far out in the North Sea, towering clouds that pulsed with lightning trailed misty bands of rain. The sailors watched this darkening sky uneasily as they rowed through the airless days.

Aching with hunger and weariness, heads down, determined, they trudged through the fields, their blistered feet throbbing with every step. Dawn was breaking on the Feast of St Mary Magdalene, the eastern sky pallid with its approach. Already, the men of the English army could feel the heat building in the air, promising another stifling day.

Humphrey de Bohun rode in the retinue of his father, the Earl of Hereford and Essex, and Constable of England. In the pale light he made out the faces of his father's knights and, beyond, those of his comrades: young Thomas, the Earl of Lancaster since the death of the king's brother; Aymer de Valence, who had also lost his father in the French war, but who wouldn't acquire the earldom of Pembroke until the death of his mother; Robert Clifford; Henry Percy; Ralph de Monthermer; Guy de Beauchamp. Beards bristled on their faces, burned an angry red, but despite their obvious exhaustion there was a sense of grim purpose about them this morning that Humphrey hadn't seen in weeks. It gave him heart, as the ashen sky lightened to reveal a blighted landscape, where traces of smoke still hung over blackened fields, the crops burned down to stubble.

From Roxburgh all through Lauderdale to Edinburgh, the English army had marched through a land scorched and silent. Past deserted villages where larders stood empty and wells were poisoned with the flyblown carcasses of sheep the army had traipsed, their eagerness for the fight fading in the oppressive heat and desolation. Infantry were sent into settlements to search for inhabitants, but none was found. Neither was there any sign of Wallace and his forces. All the while, the dark fastness of Selkirk Forest stretched away to the west, its sprawling depths hinting at the dangers of ambush and attack, while in the east the sky grew bruised with the promise of thunder.

The storm had come from the sea late one evening, lightning turning night to day. Rain poured from the heavens, drenching every man to the bone and making swamps of the fields. The next morning, thunder still growling around them, the army had set out, rust blooming on mail, horses' soaked trappers swinging heavily. Stinking mud dried to a crust on skin and clothing, men and beasts plagued by flies that hovered around their mouths and worried at the corners of their eyes. These things were torment- ing, certainly, but it was only when the English reached the outskirts of Edinburgh that they learned the true cost of the storm, for the supply ships due to meet them at the port of Leith were nowhere to be seen.

Leaving some of his troops to await the vessels, King Edward ordered the rest of his forces on to the domain of his allies, the Knights Templar at Temple Liston, west of the city. Here, the army camped outside the precep- tory of the crusading order, who had supported the campaign, waiting, tense and hungry, for supplies and word of the enemy's location from scouts the king sent out. A few unripe apples were picked from the Temple's orchards and handfuls of peas from a field that had escaped the Scots' burnings, but there was little else to augment the dwindling rations. Days crawled by without sign of the ships or word from the scouts. The Welsh, angered by their meagre rations, protested that the knights' horses were eating better than they were. Men, starving and half mad with thirst, squabbled over puddles of rainwater and scrawny carcasses of birds and hares. When one ship, sheltering down the coast from the storm, finally limped into Leith, its cargo was carted to the famished army, but it brought only wine. The king, in a moment of folly, had the barrels freely distributed among the discontented infantry and the subsequent drunken brawl between Welsh and English soldiers turned into a riot that left over a hundred dead. What had started as a determined march north to engage and destroy the enemy had become a bitter, exhausting endeavour to stay alive.

At last, when it seemed the English army would perish in the field, or destroy itself, carts of grain, meat and beer trundled into the camp from Leith, to the hoarse cheers of the men. Later that day, when their bellies were full and their spirits lifted, a company arrived led by Earl Patrick of Dunbar and the Earl of Angus. The two Scots, who had remained loyal to Edward, had brought the location of the enemy. Wallace and his forces were little more than ten miles away, near the town of Falkirk.

As Humphrey looked ahead, past his father's men, he could see the king's banner hoisted high in the pale dawn, three gold lions on scarlet. Edward and his knights were leading the vanguard. Last night, after leav- ing Temple Liston, the English army had camped out in the fields. The king had bedded down on the ground along with the rest of his men and in the dark his warhorse, Bayard, had trodden on him, breaking two of his ribs. Word of his injury had whispered round, the men troubled. The king, however, had defied their concerns and after his page had strapped him in a rigid coat of plates he had mounted, much to the admiration of the watching troops. Humphrey could see how stiffly Edward sat in the saddle and how his face creased with pain whenever Bayard lurched on the uneven ground, but it was clear nothing would now turn the king from his target.

Behind the vanguard rode the earls and their retinues. Sir John de Warenne was rather inconspicuous among them. The Earl of Surrey had been humiliated by his defeat at Stirling and, with Cressingham dead, had taken the full force of the king's displeasure. Following the earls were fifty Templars, their white mantles emblazoned with red crosses. Behind them came the archers: crossbowmen from Gascony, hunters from Sherwood Forest and longbowmen from south Wales. An immense train of wagons drawn by carthorses followed in their wake, the wheels thunderous on the hard-packed soil. Bringing up the rear were more than twenty-five thousand infantry, trudging in endless columns.

It was a vast army, the like of which Humphrey had not seen before. The sight of it stretching behind him, banners and lances bristling into the distance, made his pride swell and he hefted the dragon shield higher on his arm. The lingering fear that they would not even live to meet the Scots on the field of battle had gone, replaced by a fierce resolve. The rebellion had left a sour taste in all their mouths, especially Humphrey, who blamed himself for putting his faith in a man who had turned out to be the greatest traitor of them all. He had wondered darkly whether he would meet his former friend on the battleground, but according to the report of the Earl of Dunbar, Robert Bruce had retreated to his headquarters at Ayr. Humphrey had been surprised by his absence, for most of the Scottish nobility were said to be in Wallace's force, including the Comyns, whom the king had a special desire to capture after his release of them had been rewarded with treachery. Still, if they were victorious today, it would not be long before the rest of the men who had defied the king were brought to justice, including Robert Bruce.

Hearing shouts, Humphrey was drawn from his thoughts. Men were pointing ahead. There on a distant hillside, glinting in the pallid dawn, were thousands upon thousands of spears.

*   *   *

The youth's arms throbbed with the weight of the twelve-foot spear, the shaft of which was slippery with his sweat, the butt of the iron-tipped weapon sinking deeper into the ground.

'Keep it up, Duncan!'

Duncan jerked round and saw Kerald's face turned towards him. Blue veins stood out on the older man's neck. His right hand, gripping the spear, looked solid, the left, where only stumps remained of two of his fingers, appeared to be giving him pain, the skin around the recent amputations black and swollen.

Kerald bared his teeth through his beard, half grin, half grimace. 'Let's show these southern dogs that Scots have steel in their poles!' he yelled, over the din of the battleground.

A few of the men in the crush of the shield ring laughed harshly, but most stayed silent, each concentrating on keeping his spear in place, waiting for the next charge of the English heavy cavalry. The warhorses were turning in the distance, the knights regrouping after another failed attempt to break the bristling rows of men. Horns blared and commanders roared orders, their rough voices echoing on the dead air.

William Wallace had set his four shield rings, schiltroms he called them, on the high ground between Callendar Wood and the boggy banks of the Westquarter Burn, outside the town of Falkirk. Each ring was made up of around two thousand men, facing outwards in an enormous circle. Those at the front knelt, their spears pointing up at an angle. Those behind stood, the barbed shafts thrusting out over the heads of their comrades. Between the schiltroms Wallace had placed tight knots of archers under the command of John Stewart, brother of the high steward. Beyond, on the dark fringes of the wood, were the Scottish cavalry. If he twisted his head, Duncan could just see the horsemen on the brow of the hill, waiting for the signal to enter the fray. The English were sprawled across the slopes below. Duncan couldn't guess how many they were, but it looked like the hordes of hell were arrayed before him. Above the vast battleground the sky was the colour of ash.

Raising his spear with effort, Duncan exhaled through his teeth. The ground was slick with viscous mud, which had splattered up his hose and tunic. All the men around him were covered in the stuff, which gave off an earthy, mouldering reek. It was, Duncan imagined, how the grave would smell. The thought made his eyes flick to the corpses scattered across the churned ground in front of him, where a low palisade of bound stakes looped defensively around the schiltrom. A mighty warhorse was slumped over the barrier, its dead eyes murky, froth dribbling from its nostrils. Still half in the saddle was the knight who had ridden the beast to its doom, curled over the length of the spear that killed him. Nearer were the bodies of a few Scots. One, a lad younger than Duncan, was face down in the mud, his head cleaved by a broadsword. The weapon was still stuck fast in his scalp, fluid oozing around the steel.

Forcing his eyes away, Duncan murmured a fortifying prayer.

'Here they come!'

As the cry went up around the shield ring, drowning the blare of horns, Duncan's gaze fixed ahead, down the slope to the line of knights approaching.

They started at a walk, no breaks between the warhorses, their bulks covered with coloured trappers, the heavy swing of which gave away the mail skirts beneath. The walk turned into a trot, the horses growing in the Scots' vision. Quicker now, the pounding of hooves, at first a steady drumroll, building to a rapid tattoo. The earth began to shudder. Duncan could feel the pulse beneath his feet. Away across the hillside, more knights were riding towards the other three shield rings, but he barely saw them. Fear was liquid in his belly. His hands wrapped fiercely around the spear, every part of him tensing for the strike. *Almighty God, spare me.*

A hail of arrows shot through the sky from the left, curving up and over to rain in on the incoming knights, loosed by Wallace's archers. Most of the missiles clattered off helms and mail coats. One horse, wearing a blue and white striped trapper, panicked and veered out of the line, careering towards the adjacent shield ring, but the knight expertly wheeled it around. As the others came up fast behind him, trot turning to canter, he dropped back into their line, kicking viciously at the horse to match their tumultuous stride. The world seemed to shake with the onslaught of their approach. Iron hooves pummelled the muddy ground, the destriers' great heads thrusting forward, the beasts as fearless as the men who spurred them on. Now, at the last moment, the knights levelled lances or swung swords, coming at the Scots in a brutal stampede. Duncan felt more than heard the roar of the men around him, a wave of sound, rushing and incoherent. Blood pounded in his head. He sensed Kerald and the others pressing against him, desperation and determination interchangeable in gritted teeth and wild eyes. He loosed a cry as the English knights came charging up, their lances coursing towards the spears.

The impact was staggering.

One Scot, next to Duncan, flew back, an English lance punching into his chest, hurling him into the men behind. There was a flail of limbs, harsh shouts. Men scrabbled in to close the gap. More Scots went down all around the ring, some knights throwing short swords and axes into the rows of defenders, then wheeling away. Most of the Scots wore only woollen or leather tunics and these weapons, thrown with the momentum of the charge, were deadly.

Duncan barely heard the screams of the dying. He was yelling, clinging to his spear, the tip of which had sunk deep into the neck of a horse. The beast was rearing, squealing, the knight atop it hauling on the reins. As the animal thrashed, caught on the barb, Duncan felt his arms almost wrenched from their sockets. Suddenly, the horse collapsed on to its forelegs, the spear shaft snapping to leave the iron in its flesh. Duncan stumbled with the release. The knight was thrown from the saddle on to the sharpened stakes of the palisade, the impact enough to cause one to pierce his mail. He convulsed on the spike, coughing blood through the visor of his helm. Around the schiltroms other men, thrown from their horses into the thicket of spears or else crushed by fallen mounts, lay dying. The rest, lances spent and weapons thrown, steered their chargers around and galloped away, leaving scores of Scots littering the mud behind them.

But for every Scot that had fallen, another was there to take his place, the lines rearranging themselves around the gaps that had formed. The wounded were dragged into the centre of the schiltroms to be tended by comrades, or else despatched with quick mercy and a prayer. The English had made little dent in the rings and they had lost valuable men and horses in their effort, like a lion attacking a porcupine and coming away bloody and more furious every time.

Duncan clutched his broken spear, his hands seeming to have seized around it. The knight whose horse he had stuck was struggling on the stake, gagging on his own blood. Duncan could see a bulge appearing in the man's back, under his surcoat, where the spike had gone clean through to the other side. He choked back an urge to vomit and closed his eyes, breathing in lungfuls of stinking air. Beside him, Kerald set down his spear and slunk out of the line. Bending, he pulled off the knight's helm, revealing the pale, sweat-soaked face of a young man. His eyes were slits of agony, but he hissed something through his bloodstained teeth at Kerald. The old Scot drew a dirk from his belt with his good hand. Moving in front of the knight, obscuring his face from Duncan's view, Kerald thrust up. Duncan saw the knight's body spasm and a gout of blood flow, then the man sagged over the palisade. Kerald tugged a skin from the knight's belt, then, sheathing his bloody dagger, returned to the line, pulling the stopper from the skin and sniffing suspiciously. Satisfied, he drank greedily, his eyes widening in appreciation, before handing it to Duncan, who took it gratefully. The wine was strong and sweet. Duncan managed to force it from his dry lips to pass it to the man beside him. Grinning, Kerald took up his spear, his beard flecked with red.

Around the schiltrom, the voice of William Wallace sounded, roaring at his men to stand firm.

I have brought you to the ring, their leader had yelled that morning, as they formed up. *Now let us see if you can dance!*

Dance they had. After months of oppression under the English yoke, bowing to officials and cowering from soldiers, months as outlaws living in the wild, this was their chance to win back their liberty. Wallace had led them to victory on the meadows outside Stirling, despite overwhelming odds. Now, Scotland's new guardian seemed determined to win through again.

Buoyed up by Wallace's words of encouragement, Duncan cast aside his broken spear to draw an undamaged one from the muddy ground. The English horns were still sounding, but instead of reforming for another charge the knights were riding back to the main body of the army, where King Edward's banner was raised.

'We've got them now,' growled Kerald. 'They cannot keep this up. They're losing too many knights.'

Duncan stayed silent, watching with the others as a long line of men jogged on to the field in the wake of the knights. His eyes narrowed as he saw the curved weapons in their hands.

'Archers,' murmured someone.

Kerald's grin faded.

Duncan had heard rumour of the Welsh archers and their deadly long-bows. He tightened instinctively, moving his arms in close over his body. He had no shield, none of them did – they needed both hands for the spears and, besides, the rings were shields themselves, protecting the men within. Like most of the men in the schiltroms, Duncan wore little in the way of armour, except for a pair of ill-fitting schynbalds taken from the body of an English soldier after the battle at Stirling. He wished now that he had taken a coat of mail.

The archers formed up. Despite the distance, Duncan could see that some had different weapons: squarer and squatter than the great curves of the longbows.

'Crossbows,' muttered Kerald. 'The bastards have crossbows.'

The men fixed quarrels and arrows to their weapons. At the call of a horn, arms drew back, bows arcing. As they loosed, the sky in front of the Scots darkened and rushed towards them. Duncan closed his eyes and pulled his body in tight, his spear thrust uselessly before him. He felt the force of the missiles all around, the air filling with screams. At a violent jolt in his side he was thrown to the ground. For a second, he thought he'd been hit and clenched his teeth against the shock of pain he knew must come. When it didn't, he opened his eyes and realised it was Kerald who had struck him. The old Scot had a crossbow bolt in his face. It had entered his cheek, just below his eye. Duncan cried out as Kerald convulsed, the man's weight pushing him further into the soft mud. More arrows were shooting in around them, men falling. The shield ring across from theirs was breaking apart under the onslaught. Duncan struggled beneath Kerald's body, but someone else was on his leg, pinning him. He couldn't move. His face was sinking into the soil, the mud rising cold and thick to his lips. Through panicked eyes, he saw the English cavalry lining up, saw them begin to ride, felt a tremor in the ground.

62

Astride his smoke-grey courser in the centre of the Scottish cavalry line, James Stewart watched with mounting dread as the Welsh archers took aim. The first volley of arrows tore through the outer rows of the schiltroms, men struck with such force they were catapulted into those behind. Gaps appeared instantly, some dead, others wounded, many more dropping spears and throwing themselves to the ground to avoid the deadly hail.

'Christ, save us,' breathed someone.

James hardly heard. He stood in his stirrups, seeing the Scottish bowmen under the command of his brother answering the lethal volleys with shots from their own bows. But it was clear from the first barrage that they would have little effect on the enemy, whose powerful bows allowed them to stay out of range. A horn was being blown, lifting over the distant screams. James recognised the deep and hollow sound. It was Wallace's horn – his signal for the cavalry to enter the fray. The others around him heard it too, men snapping down visors and shortening reins in their fists.

'Wait!' shouted John Comyn, pointing his sword down the hillside to where the English knights were forming up beneath the banners of the earls of Lincoln, Hereford, Norfolk and Surrey. One standard was larger than the rest. Faded red, it had a tarnished golden dragon in the centre. The longbowmen had stopped shooting. Now, the knights, under the command of the earls, began to charge the schiltroms, no longer impenetrable rings of spears, but disorderly, undisciplined chaos.

'We must ride to their aid!' James yelled.

'We cannot win here,' growled the Lord of Badenoch, his gaze on a company of English knights spurring up the hill towards them. Two schiltroms had broken apart with the first charge of the English horses, the Scots scattering. Wallace's horn was blowing, urgently. Raising his voice,

Comyn addressed the men around him. 'The battle is lost. We have no hope except to flee.'

'We cannot leave them to die!' James protested. Other voices joined his in agreement, but some were already urging their horses towards the woods, away from the approaching English.

'You cowardly sons of whores!' roared one of Wallace's men.

Riding out of the line, he charged his horse recklessly down the hillside, followed by a handful of Wallace's commanders. They loosed a desperate battle cry as they went. A few English knights broke away to counter this band as they galloped towards the schiltroms, now surging apart across the hillside, many Scots running for the woods. The Welsh infantry were spilling out across the boggy ground around the burn in pursuit.

As the English knights kicked their horses determinedly up the hillside towards the Scottish cavalry, John Comyn wheeled his horse around, followed by his son. His departure signalled a massive exodus from the cavalry line, many of whom were kinsmen or supporters of the Lord of Badenoch.

Malcolm, the handsome young Earl of Lennox, locked gazes with James. 'What use will you be to your king, Sir James,' he called, 'if you are sharing the cell next to his?'

As Lennox and his knights spurred their horses hard towards Callendar Wood, James lingered, his eyes searching frantically for his brother, somewhere in the turmoil.

'Sir?' questioned one of his men, his gaze moving between the steward and the English knights, getting closer every second.

With a cry of frustration, James turned his grey courser brutally around and kicked the beast towards the woods.

All semblance of command William Wallace had over his forces was gone, swept away in the terror of the disintegrating troops. Spent arrows and spears littered the hillside, where many Scots lay dead. The cries of the wounded rose to merge in a mangled howl. Those who had survived the volleys of arrows that had torn through the schiltroms crawled through the bodies of comrades to escape the charging knights. Some ran for the woods, others headlong down the hillside towards the banks of the burn. Here, the mud was as thick and sticky as glue, in places treacherously deep. The battleground, chosen by Wallace for the natural protection afforded by the burn, now turned on the Scots. Those who reached the waters leapt in and splashed desperately for the other side, but most never made it that far, becoming stuck in the surrounding bogs. Trapped in the stinking filth, they were easy targets for Welsh archers.

Into this chaos rode the Knights of the Dragon, the flame-wreathed monster on their shields glimmering in the ashen morning. They rode with their fathers, the men of the Round Table. Rode for their king.

Aymer de Valence led the men of Pembroke, most of whom had served his father for decades. His blue and white striped banner flying high above him, he led a brutal assault on Wallace's archers, punching straight through their lines. It was Aymer's lance that slammed into the chest of John Stewart, picking the man off his feet then hurling him to the ground to be rolled over and over, until one of the hooves of Aymer's destrier crushed the Scot's head into the mud. Leaving the limp body of the steward's brother behind, Aymer swept on, drawing his sword to strike at the backs and necks of the fleeing archers. As he rode, he roared savagely.

Henry Percy, fired by the chance to avenge the humiliation suffered by his grandfather at Stirling, rode into the fray with knights from his Yorkshire estates. A few Scots turned to stand their ground against them. One man managed to jab his spear into the side of a horse, causing the animal to crash to the ground, tossing its knight. The Scot was lanced through the throat a second later, by one of Percy's men, the rest cut down viciously in great sprays of blood. The Scottish nobility had fled the field, leaving the peasant host to be destroyed. The only hope these men had lay in escape, or swift death. King Edward had wanted William Wallace and the ringleaders of the rebellion taken alive, but in such disorder it was impossible to guarantee the fate of one man.

Humphrey de Bohun, his face drenched with sweat inside his helm, charged in the midst of his father's retinue, along the lower slopes where the Scots were running towards the burn. The battle, he knew, was won. Now, their task was to destroy every man on this field. Humphrey had spent his lance and his broadsword was in his fist. He swung it viciously into the neck of a man fleeing in front of him, felt the shock of impact, then release. The Scot, decapitated, crumpled behind him. Humphrey's father was some distance ahead, pursuing a group of spearmen stumbling towards the stream. The earl pursued them doggedly, his lance swinging down. All at once, his horse collapsed beneath him.

Humphrey shouted as he saw his father go down. The destrier, whose massive weight was further augmented by its mail trapper, saddle and Hereford himself in all his armour, had plunged into a bog. Yelling for his men to follow, Humphrey kicked his horse towards his father, who had dropped his lance and was trying to urge the animal out of the thick mud. The beast was squealing and thrashing its head, the movement making it sink deeper. Three of the Scottish spearmen the earl had been chasing now turned on him. Lighter and more agile, without armour to weigh them down, they were only knee-deep in the mire. Humphrey cried a warning, the sound echoing madly in his helm, as two of the spearmen lunged at his father.

The earl managed to crack one of their spears away with his shield, but the other caught him in the side, under his ribs. The force of it snapped the links of mail, driving them and the cloth beneath into his flesh. It wasn't a fatal wound, the mail stopping much of the force, so only the tip penetrated, but at the moment of impact the horse sank deeper, almost to its neck, throwing the earl off balance. As Hereford toppled, the momentum pushed him on to the spear, plunging it deep into the muscle between his ribs to enter his lung.

Humphrey roared as his father curled over, slipping out of the saddle of the drowning horse. The Scot dropped the spear and scrabbled away after his comrades, heading for the waters of the burn. Pulling his destrier up sharp, Humphrey swung awkwardly down from the saddle and waded into the mud, not heeding the shouts of his men. The mud claimed him quickly, the grey porridge sloshing up his mail hose to his thighs. His father was some distance ahead, half submerged, the spear protruding from his side, his face turned towards the mud. Humphrey gasped with effort as he fought his way through the bog. The ground gave way suddenly beneath him, plunging him in up to his chest. His father was yards ahead, the earl's face now fully submerged, only the humps of his head and back visible. The mud was sucking and eager; Humphrey felt himself sinking, panic making him struggle. As hands grabbed him from behind, he roared and fought, seeing his father slip under. A swirl of blue silk slashed with white drifted on the surface for a moment longer, before it too was claimed by the earth.

63

The cart wheels splashed through the sodden ground, the oxen bowing their horned heads into the downpour, hooves sinking in the red clay. Robert watched them come, the warm rain trickling down his face, his eyes on the backs of the carts, piled high with timber for Ayr's new palisade.

'There are four more to come today, sir. The rest will be here before the week is out.'

Robert glanced at the man hunched in the wet beside him, a local carpenter whom he'd made master of works. 'I want work to begin tomorrow on the barracks,' he said, turning to the wooden buildings that rose behind him on the banks of the river that flowed sluggishly through the north side of the town into the sea. They had been built for Henry Percy's men, but on the liberation of the town Robert had taken them for himself. 'When that is done you will start on the town's defences.'

The master of works nodded in agreement. Raising his hand to hail the cart drivers, he went to direct them through the churned mud of the courtyard.

Robert's gaze drifted across the rain-dappled river to the banks beyond, where cattle were grazing. On the damp air he caught an acrid whiff of dung and urine from a nearby tannery, over the more pervasive smells of brine and burning wood. Smoke plumed from many of the town's wattle houses, the roofs, thatched with rushes and broom, visible beyond the barracks. Ayr had been coming slowly back to life since the ousting of Percy's men, the atmosphere tentatively hopeful. The new palisade would be welcomed by all, however, for the future of the realm remained uncertain and there had been no word of how William Wallace and his army fared against the English.

Robert was increasingly impatient, having heard nothing since leaving

Selkirk Forest. In the weeks that followed his return to Ayr, he had questioned whether he should have stayed with Scotland's new guardian, for it seemed futile to have made the powerful gesture of knighting Wallace, only to retreat once again into anonymity. He had intended to be involved in the Scots' campaign – to prove his worth as a leader of men and prove, once and for all, his devotion to his kingdom's cause. James Stewart had been the one to persuade him otherwise. The steward had warned him against becoming too deeply entangled in the affairs of Wallace and the Comyns, instead advising him to continue building his own base and supporters, until the time was right to reveal his intentions to the men of the realm. Robert had been frustrated, but couldn't deny the sense in the steward's words. For his plan to have a hope of coming to pass he needed to maintain his integrity and that meant keeping himself aloof from those who still sought the return of John Balliol.

As the carts trundled to a stop, the cattle lowing in the wet, Robert heard his name being called. He turned to see Christopher Seton hastening towards him.

The squire's fair hair was plastered darkly to his scalp and beads of rainwater dripped from his long nose. He looked grave. 'My cousin needs to see you, Robert. At your lodgings.'

Robert frowned. 'What for?'

Christopher was staring at the ground, unable to meet his gaze. 'He said it's important. Sir, he wants you to go to him. Quickly.'

Christopher had stopped calling him sir some time ago. The formal sound of the word made Robert uneasy. 'Very well.' Pausing to speak with the master of works, he left the riverbank with Christopher, their boots splashing through the mud.

The barracks were busy, for the whole of Robert's company, including wives and children of the knights, had come here after leaving the Forest. Grooms were working in the crowded stables, sweeping out soiled hay, filling water troughs. A group of John of Atholl's knights were sheltering under the dripping eaves of one building, playing a game of dice. They nodded to Robert as he walked by, heading for the long timber hall, his lodgings.

Alexander was standing outside the hall's door, his cloak sodden.

'What is it, my friend?' called Robert as he approached. From inside the hall he caught the faint cries of his daughter. The man looked so grim that Robert's first thought as he heard Marjorie crying was that this had something to do with her. 'In Christ's name, Alexander, answer me! Is it Marjorie?' He pressed past the lord, who caught his arm.

'This isn't about your daughter, Robert.' Alexander's voice was little more than a murmur. 'There is something you need to see.'

More and more confused, Robert allowed the man to push open the door for him. He entered, his eyes moving quickly around the interior. The first chamber was a small reception area. There were a few stools, but otherwise the place was sparse. He'd had neither the time nor the inclination to appoint it any better, for he didn't plan to stay in this remote coastal town for ever. He was rarely ever here except to sleep, the business of running the town and his earldom taking up every hour of the day.

The first thing Robert saw as he entered was Judith. The wet nurse had risen abruptly at the opening of the door. She was clutching his daughter, her thin face scarlet. Marjorie cried harder as she saw her father, stretching her hands towards him. Judith stammered something, but before Robert could decipher what the girl had said he heard another cry, this one coming through the door that led to his bedchamber. Pushing past Judith, Robert entered.

The chamber beyond was the largest of the three rooms that made up the hall. It stretched before him, hazy with candlelight. There was a table and bench where he ate his meals, beside a fire that hissed in a clay-pit hearth. Meadowsweet rustled beneath his mud-caked boots, the herb covering the earth floor in a fragrant carpet. Clothes hung from a perch, his and Katherine's. There were a few chests containing his armour and his broadsword hung between two posts buried in the wall. A glazed blue jug stood on the table beside two goblets and the remains of a meal, which hadn't been there when he had left that morning. Candle flames fluttered atop melted stubs. Robert took in these familiar sights, then he heard the soft cry again and his eyes went to the bed against the far wall. It was draped with thick curtains that hung down in a swoop from a beam above, hiding the bed from view. The meadowsweet concealed his footfalls as he crossed the floor. Reaching the bed, Robert took hold of the curtains and pulled them apart.

He saw Katherine first. She was naked, her flushed face tilted towards the beams, eyes closed. Lying beneath her was a man, his hands gripping her splayed thighs. At the drawing of the curtains, Katherine's eyes flew open. Her mouth, parted in pleasure, widened in horror and she struggled off the man, who twisted round, swearing as he saw Robert standing there. Katherine scrabbled back, snatching at the crumpled linen sheet to cover her nakedness. The man, whom Robert recognised as a local lad he'd hired to work on the town's defences, stumbled off the bed and picked up his braies, discarded on the floor. He was no more than eighteen, a fresh-faced youth. His manhood, proudly erect and glistening, was already drooping between his legs. He pulled on the drawers, tugging the cord tight around his narrow waist as Robert looked on in silence. Katherine was breathing rapidly. Her eyes flicked past Robert to where Alexander was standing.

Seeing the venom in her stare, Robert turned. He had forgotten the lord was behind him. Christopher was with him. 'You knew.' His voice was flat, oddly calm.

'I'm sorry, my friend.' Alexander's hard gaze moved to Katherine, whose face contorted in hatred. 'But you had to be shown for yourself.'

'You snake!' she spat. 'You've been spying on me?'

Seeing a rumpled heap of material trailing on the edge of the bed, Robert bent and picked it up. It was one of Katherine's gowns. The dress was low-cut and tight like all the others. He tossed the garment at her. 'Cover yourself.'

'Robert, please,' she murmured, her tone changing.

He turned away as she pulled on the gown, her voice pleading behind him.

'I beg you.' Dragging the skirts of the dress down, she came around the bed to him. 'I was lonely. You are never here. Not for me. Only for your men.' She touched his arm, tentatively.

'Get out.'

Her grip on his arm tightened. 'Robert, please, I—'

'I said leave.'

'I'm pregnant,' she sobbed suddenly.

'Pregnant?' His voice was as cold as marble. 'Whose bastard is it?'

Katherine paled, then her face hardened. 'Who will look after your daughter?' She looked at Judith, standing in the doorway clutching Marjorie. 'You cannot think she can do it? The girl would fall down if I wasn't here to hold her up!'

'My daughter is no longer your concern.'

'Where will I go? How will I survive?'

'I am certain you can ply your trade in most towns.'

Katherine stared at him. Swallowing thickly, she turned away and pulled down her cloak from the clothes perch. Breathing hard, she pushed her feet into a pair of shoes, then picked up a few other belongings and stuffed them into a leather bag. Robert didn't stop her. The youth was still standing against the wall by the bed. He had pulled on his tunic and seemed to be scanning the chamber for another way out.

Katherine pushed past Alexander and headed for the door. '*Bastard*,' she breathed through her clenched lips, before stepping out into the rain.

A few moments later the young man, boots in hand, slipped past. Robert glanced at him. For a second he was going to let him go, then fury exploded inside him and he grabbed the youth around the neck. Alexander shouted, but Robert didn't hear as he dragged the struggling man past Judith and his screaming daughter into the yard. Alexander and Christopher hastened out behind him. The young man was yelling, begging for forgiveness. Robert threw him down in the red clay and launched a kick at his stomach. The youth doubled over, his face screwing up in pain. A few of Atholl's knights splashed through the wet, seeing the attack. Unheeding their confused calls, Robert grabbed the youth's tunic and pulled him up to slam his fist into the young man's face. As Alexander seized his shoulder, Robert let go of the young man and turned on his comrade. Alexander ducked, but rather than strike him, Robert went for his sword. Before Alexander could stop him, he grasped the hilt and drew it. But when he went for the youth sprawled in the mud, bloody and terror-stricken, Alexander gripped his arm, holding him back.

'The lad took what was freely offered, Robert. He shouldn't have. But he doesn't deserve death.'

The youth scrabbled to his feet, his tunic clinging to his legs. Leaving his boots where he had dropped them, he sprinted across the yard. As two of the watching knights moved to apprehend him, Alexander shouted at them to let him go.

Enraged, Robert confronted him. 'Who do you think you are?'

'I'm one of the men who have given up everything to support you,' replied Alexander forcefully. 'I believe you can be king, Robert. But you need to start believing it.'

The sound of raised voices filled the yard. Robert looked round to see his brother and John of Atholl approaching, followed by Walter and several knights from Carrick. Observing their taut faces, he thought they must have been alerted to the altercation, but the assumption was shattered as John spoke.

'Word has come. Wallace's army was defeated at Falkirk. Thousands are dead.'

'And Wallace?' questioned Alexander, letting go of Robert.

Christopher had moved up behind them.

'We don't know,' Edward cut in. He looked at his brother. 'The cavalry, led by the Comyns, fled the battle without even drawing their blades. The bastards saved their own skins and left everyone else to be butchered.'

'What of King Edward?' Robert demanded of John. 'Are you saying the English have control of the kingdom? That Scotland is lost?'

'Nothing is certain. But we know the English are heading this way.'

Robert took this in, the rain soaking him. 'He is coming for me.'

His brother-in-law nodded. 'You are now the only real danger to him.'

Christopher spoke, his voice thick. 'But the new palisade isn't even raised. We cannot defend Ayr.'

'What do you suggest we do?' Edward turned to the squire. 'Run like cowards? Leave this town and everyone in it to the mercy of your whoreson of a king?'

Alexander stepped in, his gaze on Edward. 'My cousin is as much a part of this company as you are. No matter his birthplace.'

Robert stood in silence as they began to speak over one another. Rain trickled down the length of the blade in his hand. Behind him, from the hall, came the urgent cries of his daughter. Beyond the rooftops of the barracks, smoke trailed into the sky from the houses. He thought of the optimism growing here these past months. Then he thought of the cartloads of timber waiting in the rain on the riverbanks. 'We burn it down.'

The men stopped arguing as he spoke, his voice low.

Robert looked at them. His voice roughened. 'We burn the town and go into the hills where the English cannot follow. We will seek out the steward, if he made it from the battle.'

'Flee?' said Edward, shaking his head.

Robert met his brother's eyes. 'We cannot beat the English on the field. Not yet. The only thing we can do is leave nothing for them to feed upon and no base to shelter them. The longer their supply lines become, the harder it will be for them to sustain themselves.'

John of Atholl nodded. 'I'll tell my men. We will begin evacuating the town at once.'

Without a word, Robert handed the sword back to Alexander and moved off with Atholl.

As the others headed away through the downpour, Alexander hung back with Christopher. Watching them go, he sheathed his sword then drew a purse from the pouch that hung from his belt and handed it to his cousin. 'Make sure the lad gets this. He won't have gone far.'

Christopher shook his head angrily. 'You're still thinking about that, after what you've just heard?' He went to leave, but Alexander caught his arm. Christopher glared at him. 'I never wanted any part in this. You know that. We shouldn't have done it.' His voice lowered as Alexander tightened his grip in warning. 'Robert saved my life. We betrayed him!'

'We didn't betray him. Katherine did. We merely opened his eyes to what she was. How easy was it to get her to lie with the next young stallion that caught her eye? It didn't take the lad long to bed her, did it? Robert wasn't going to listen to reason. Katherine was one more string that needed to be cut if he is to become king. When that happens, you will thank me for this. Do not forget, cousin, we stand to lose as much as Robert if he doesn't succeed in attaining the throne. We must do everything to ensure that comes to pass.' Alexander pressed the purse of coins into Christopher's hand. 'Now, I told the lad we would compensate him for the deed. I keep my promises.'

64

They could smell the smoke long before they reached the town, the hot wind carrying its bitterness to them, the horizon a dirty grey. The massive column of riders moved towards it, the hearts of the men growing as heavy as their limbs as they realised the journey's end would provide little sustenance or comfort. The supplies brought by ship to Leith were running low and they were deep in the enemy's land. Barbed thistles and spiny gorse studded the bare fields, the dry wind blowing grit into their eyes.

Humphrey de Bohun rode in the vanguard with his father's men. He was silent, staring into the smoke-tinged distance, where the sea was a silver blade, pressed against the edge of the land. For weeks now he had suffered from a nagging ache inside, as if he had forgotten or misplaced something. He knew it was his father, whose corpse, claimed from the mud of the battleground, was being drawn south into England by a company of his knights. The knowledge hadn't stopped the feeling. If anything it had grown stronger, as though his father's body were a string tugging something from inside him the further it was pulled.

The English victory at Falkirk had been a great success, the battleground the grave of more than ten thousand Scots. In comparison, the king's army lost only a small percentage of men, the only significant casualties Humphrey's father and the Master of the English Templars, who met a similar fate in the treacherous bogs around the burn. Despite this success it had been a much grimmer fight in contrast to the first campaign. Furthermore, according to witnesses, William Wallace had fled the field at the battle's end, bearing north towards Stirling in the wake of the Scottish cavalry. King Edward's anger at the escape of Wallace and the nobles was only dulled by the fact that the majority of the Scots' fighting force was lying flyblown in the fields of Falkirk. The danger the English army now faced came in the form of their dwindling supplies, the hope they'd had heading west towards Ayr, the reported base of Robert Bruce, dying in their blistered mouths.

The fields on the outskirts of the town, which should have been tall with wheat, plump in the late August sun, were scattered with blackened piles, the crops harvested only to be burned. Smoke still drifted from some of the heaps, the vapours lingering over the scorched ground. The men stared around them as they passed, the sight of the wanton destruction a torment to their aching bellies.

'I pray to God the bastards starve through the coming winter,' growled Henry Percy.

Humphrey looked over at the young man, whose flushed face jutted wrathfully over his ventail. Percy, who had been given Ayrshire by the king at the start of the occupation, had been the most vocal about hunting down Robert Bruce, perhaps because he and Clifford felt responsible for his escape from Irvine. Humphrey had kept quiet, not joining in the belligerent conversations around the evening campfire, the death of his father weighing heavy on him. But as they entered the ruins of the port of Ayr, his thoughts turned to his former friend.

For a time, after hearing rumours of Robert's desertion, Humphrey had still hoped to discover a lie, but with the events in Irvine he'd no longer been able to deny the truth: that the man he had befriended and trusted was a traitor. He blamed himself for not telling Robert sooner that the Stone of Destiny was one of the four relics named in the prophecy. Perhaps he could have persuaded him of the necessity of seizing it, for with hindsight it seemed clear that the theft was the point when Robert had turned from their cause. Part of Humphrey understood this, even sympathised. The stone was, after all, a symbol of the man's right to the throne of Scotland, a right that had effectively been revoked by its taking. On the march north, he had determined to capture Robert not simply for justice, but so he could look into the man's eyes and know that it was for the love of his kingdom rather than the hatred of theirs that he had betrayed them. Then, at least, he could know that he had not been so wrong or blind to have drawn Robert into their circle, perhaps only naïve. Now, however, as they passed along deserted streets lined by the charred wrecks of houses, Humphrey knew all hope of that was dead. The man who had burned this town meant for them to suffer at the sight of the butchered cattle in the market square, a pyre of blackened bones; intended for them to be maddened by the barrels of beer hacked apart outside a brewery, the sticky contents staining the dusty ground beneath swarms of flies. The man who had done this, who had left nothing for them to feed upon, meant for them to die in the field.

The king, his voice rigid, ordered his knights to search some of the more intact buildings, but it seemed starkly apparent that no one was left to tell them where Bruce and his men had gone. The English would find neither justice nor nourishment here. As the knights dismounted and moved through the wreckage, Humphrey slid wearily from his horse and took a wine skin from his pack. His face felt hot and tight and the wine stung his cracked lips. As he licked them he tasted blood.

'My lord king.'

Humphrey saw Sir Robert Clifford hailing the king.

The knight had headed out of a long timber hall, which appeared mostly undamaged. 'There is something you should see, my lord.' Clifford, usually so composed, looked riled.

Humphrey followed as the king left Bayard with his page and strode towards the hall. Behind him came Aymer and Henry. Ducking under the door lintel, they entered a bare reception room, mail boots clinking on the earth floor. One by one, they passed into the main chamber, where wan light seeped in through a single window. Furniture lay scattered and broken on the floor, which was littered with meadowsweet. There was a bed against the far wall, partly obscured by a curtain.

As Humphrey's eyes became accustomed to the gloom he saw what Robert Clifford had seen. They all did. On the far wall an image had been daubed in red paint. It was crude, but clear – a red rampant lion rearing over a dragon, one great paw on the serpent's twisted head.

Humphrey felt fury assail him at the sight. He looked at the king, whose face was clenched in the gloom. 'My lord, forgive me. I chose the wrong man. I let a snake into our midst.'

Edward turned to look at him. 'We both did.'

The faces of Aymer and Henry mirrored his ire.

Putting his back to the crude image, the king removed his mailed gloves. 'Kneel, Sir Humphrey,' he said, his harsh tone resolute, 'it is time for you to take your father's mantle.'

Humphrey understood the king's reason for the solemn act here in these ruins before that crude image, the insult stinging. With one stroke the king raised him and bound him to hunt down the offenders. Kneeling stiffly, Humphrey removed his own gauntlets. Placing his hands in the king's he did homage for the earldoms of Essex and Hereford, and for the heredi-tary office of Constable of England, passed to him through his father. When homage was done, he rose to swear the oath of fealty, promising to remain true to his lord and king.

'We will mark this occasion properly in time,' Edward assured him. 'For now, I will return to England. We can go no further, not without supplies. The Scots were gravely weakened by their defeat at Falkirk and I will return for the traitors that escaped in due course. Until then, Sir Humphrey, I want you to ride south with your men to Annandale. Destroy the castle at Lochmaben and burn every settlement you pass through. I don't want enough left of that shit hole to fill a thimble.'

Humphrey bowed. 'As you command, Lord King.'

The king and his knights headed out into the smoke-wreathed air, leaving the red lion of Scotland rearing behind them.

The three ships glided north through the inky waters of the Channel, beneath a moonless sky. Black sails flew from their masts and only the creak of timbers and rhythmic splash of oars gave any indication of their presence. Two were war galleys, long and slender, each rowed by eighty oarsmen. The third was a bulky merchant cog, a broader, rounded vessel steered by two oars at the stern. From the rigging, high above the cog's deck, came three piercing whistles.

At the sound, her captain crossed to the port side. He stared into the distance, the sea a rolling sheet of darkness. Faint in the void, he glimpsed the subdued glow of firelight, dotted along the horizon.

'Master Pietro.'

The captain turned to see Luca, one of his senior crewmen. The man's features were blurred in the gloom.

'The ships extend as far as we can see, sir. I do not think we can pass the English blockade unnoticed.'

Pietro nodded. 'Go and tell him.'

Two hours later, the sky changing from black to blue, the three vessels neared the blockade. The ships were widely spaced, each rocking at anchor, but it was clear that nothing much more than a fishing vessel would be able to pass through undetected. Nonetheless, they made it quite close before they were seen.

The ship looming before them was a ponderous English cog with a thick mast and a squat wooden castle at the fore. Protruding from the castle's top was the angular hulk of a trebuchet and from the bowsprit an iron-tipped ram thrust like a fist. As the three galleys were spied, harsh voices echoed across the water and men appeared along the gunwales, illuminated by lantern-light, crossbows primed in their hands. Pietro ordered his crew to slow, the command relayed to the war galleys. The oarsmen strained on the sweeps until the three vessels drew close together and anchors were swung over the sides to plunge into the depths. The crew of the English cog threw ropes across to the first galley and, with a grating of timbers, came alongside.

Pietro stood at the gunwales, Luca beside him, watching as the English soldiers boarded the war galley. Some were armed with swords, some crossbows and a few bore lanterns. One of their number was dressed better than the others in a tunic trimmed with gold brocade. Pietro took him for the captain. The captain spoke briefly with the commander of the warship, while his men inspected the vessel and crew. It wasn't long before the English, with the use of gangplanks thrown across, began to board the merchant cog.

Pietro met the captain, who jumped down on to the deck, flanked by two men holding crossbows. Pietro raised his hands in a gesture of peace.

'You have entered English waters and are subject to an inspection of your vessel, under the authority of King Edward.' The captain nodded to the warship. 'Your escort tells me you have sailed from Genoa.' Other soldiers were clambering across, spreading out among the benches where Pietro's oarsmen shifted uneasily. 'A long way, yes?'

Pietro had been sailing the arduous route from Genoa to Bruges and Dover for a decade and understood enough English to get the gist of the man's words. He replied after a pause, his accent making the captain frown in concentration. 'Long, yes. But safer than land, for precious cargo.'

The English captain scanned the ship, his eyes lingering on the opening that led down into the lower deck. 'What cargo?'

'Paper,' replied Pietro. 'From a mill in the mountains, outside our city. We deliver to your port of Dover.'

The captain nodded slowly, only seeming to be half listening, his gaze roving over the crowded decks of the cog. 'Why are you sailing under the *lupo*?' he asked, gesturing to the black sails. 'One might think you have something to hide?'

'Yes,' answered Pietro, 'precious cargo. That is what we hide. This sea between England and France is dangerous since your kingdoms have been at war. We must beware. Your enemies might attack. Prevent our cargo from reaching your shores.'

'I doubt paper will win us the war,' replied the captain dryly. 'Show me the hold.'

Pietro and Luca led the captain below deck, the stairs creaking. Eight English soldiers followed, swords drawn.

One half of the hold was stacked with rows of wooden crates, a narrow aisle between them. The other half formed the crew's quarters, lined with blankets. There were twenty or so men down here, their sleeping forms illuminated by two lanterns swinging from a beam.

'Search the place,' said the captain, nodding to his soldiers.

'And the crates, sir?' asked one, frowning at the stacks.

'Open six.'

Pietro began to protest, but the English captain turned on him. 'Your vessel has entered English waters and is subject to the authority of our king. We are at war. You could be delivering arms or funds to our Scottish enemies. It is our right to determine this before allowing you to continue to our shores.'

Pietro only understood half of what the captain said, but understood the tone well enough to know it would be dangerous to argue. After a pause, he motioned for the soldiers to go ahead, watching as they moved in among the crates, selecting six from different parts of the stacks to open for inspection. He sensed Luca stiffen beside him. Other Englishmen were heading down to join them, having finished searching the upper deck. On the captain's orders they began picking through the blankets in the sleeping quarters, waking the men and knocking on the hull of the vessel to check for hidden holds. The captain moved over as the others opened the lids of the crates, revealing soft sheets of paper, made from pulped linen. The captain rifled through them, lifting the sheets, each of which was decorated with a watermark.

'Paper, sir,' called one of the soldiers, from further in the hold. 'They all contain paper.'

The captain addressed the men searching the crew's quarters. 'Anything?' When they shook their heads he turned to Pietro. 'I'm satisfied.' Gesturing for his men to follow, he climbed the stairs to the deck above.

Pietro went with them. The sky was turning turquoise in the east.

The English captain paused at the gunwales, his gaze on the black sail. 'You will fly your colours from here. You have no need for secrecy now you have entered our waters.' The man climbed across to the war galley, then boarded his vessel.

Pietro watched him go. His tension ebbed slowly as his crew hauled up the anchors and the oarsmen dug into the water. It was only when the English vessel was small in the distance that he spoke quietly to one of his crewmen. 'Tell Luca it is safe.'

When the message was relayed, Luca, waiting in the hold, unhooked one of the lanterns from the beam above the crew's quarters and moved into the stacks, counting off the crates until he came to the sixth on the right. It was next to one they had opened. Luca murmured a prayer as he worked the lid of the crate loose, setting it on the floor with the lantern. He pulled the stacks of paper out and laid them carefully on the lid. They went only a third of the way down the crate. Beneath was another wooden lid. As Luca grasped the ridges on the sides and eased the board out of the space, he heard the hiss of a man's breath.

'You are safe,' Luca murmured. 'We have passed the blockade.'

From the hollow bottom half of the crate a wiry young man uncoiled, wincing with discomfort. His face was striking, with well-defined features framed by a fringe of dark hair beyond which was a tonsure, the bald crown gleaming with sweat in the lantern light. But it was his eyes that Luca found himself once again drawn to. One pupil was sky blue, sharp with scrutiny. The other was as white as a pearl, blind and staring.

'When will we reach Scotland?' The man's voice was hoarse from the stuffy air, but there was a forcefulness behind it that demanded a prompt answer.

'Seven days with a good wind, your grace.'

65

Through the last days of summer, Scotland mourned the loss of so many sons. In towns and settlements beyond the Forth, where the English had been unable to penetrate, the name Falkirk had become synonymous with grief and men and women would say a prayer at the utterance of it. But as August faded and a chill autumn approached, this sorrow had begun to harden inside them. They carried it within them, close to their hearts, a token of remembrance forged in fires of anguish that cooled to a steel resolve.

At the start of the war and all through the English occupation there had been a sense among many that the conflict could yet be resolved and their king would be returned to them. That belief had reached its zenith after Stirling, when anything seemed possible under the leadership of William Wallace. Even those who said war could not be won on the battlefield believed councils and alliances could save them. For years England had been their neighbour and friend, the hostilities of the past forgotten by those who lived, the Roman wall that separated the two kingdoms a division from a distant time. With Falkirk more than a century of amity had been utterly destroyed. In place of an emperor's crumbling barricade the Scots built another, invisible wall of adamant and grit, dug down deep in the soil of the Borders.

In this time, while the survivors retreated into the Forest to recover and regroup, King Edward led his men back into England. The victory at Falkirk had come at a high price and it was a much diminished force that had limped in through the gates of Carlisle that autumn, disease and desertion doing their work on the hungry march from the ruins of Ayr. The king had destroyed the bulk of the Scottish army, but hadn't succeeded in taking full control. The kingdom was split, the lands south of the Forth in English hands, the castles of Edinburgh, Roxburgh, Berwick and Stirling still held by the king's men, while everything north of the great river was retained by the Scots. After fortifying his garrisons and making Earl Patrick of Dunbar the guardian of southern Scotland, Edward returned to his seat of government at York to plan his next campaign.

Their voices were harsh in the glade. Within the circle of men, fists were clenched and lifted, faces flushed with anger and frustration. Some of them bore scars from battle, scraps of clothing and dirty rags covering seeping wounds. Many more were marked with exhaustion from weeks travelling through the wild, or hiding in the woods, living hand to mouth. At the turbulent centre of the assembled crowd were the steward and the Bishop of Glasgow, William Wallace and Robert Bruce. All had come together to decide the future of their kingdom. It was a future none of them seemed able to agree on.

'No one can deny what Sir William has achieved. No lord or baron – nay, *bishop*, has done so much for this kingdom!' Wishart's fierce tones blasted over the others. 'He has the right to remain as guardian of Scotland!'

Several men began speaking in answer.

James Stewart was the loudest. 'No one is denying that, your grace, but our circumstances have changed and I believe we must look to a new direction.'

John of Atholl and Alexander Seton were quick to concur.

Earl Malcolm of Lennox, standing with his black-clad knights, added his opinion. 'After the death of King Alexander we had six guardians. A similar balance of power would surely be more reasonable than the rule of one man?'

'The Council of Twelve was a balance of power,' answered Gilbert de la Hay. 'That did little for us in the end.'

Neil Campbell, like Hay a staunch ally of Wallace, added a forceful agreement.

Robert looked over at William Wallace, standing in the midst of the heated crowd. His muscled arms, bared to the shoulder, were riddled with injuries sustained at Falkirk. One scar carved a jagged red line down his face, from brow to lip, a glancing blow perhaps from a blade. Robert thought the young man looked weary; a weariness beyond that of the body, more that of the heart.

'This is not the time to change our leader,' growled Gray, another of Wallace's commanders. 'We need to gather our strength, not divide it. The English will return to finish what they started. We must be ready for them.'

'I say we send a delegation to petition the papal curia, asking for the support of Rome,' said Gartnait of Mar. 'That delegation should show that we are still in control of our kingdom, that we stand united against the tyranny of King Edward. I say the steward is right. Let us elect other men to stand alongside Sir William.' He gestured to James and Wishart. 'Perhaps the steward, and you, your grace? You have the most experience of any here. His Holiness would listen to your words of reason.'

James raised his hands as calls of approval sounded. 'I personally think it is time for new blood.' He looked over at Robert, but before he could say anything further, a surly-looking man with an ugly stump where his right hand should be spoke up.

'Sir William sacrificed everything to lead us to war! He lost his cousin and many dear to him at Falkirk. Why? Because the nobles fled the field and left us to die! These men cannot speak for us!'

There was an ominous rumble of agreement from many on the periphery, soldiers all.

'You lost this war, not us!' ranted the surly man, encouraged by the response. 'Now you want to punish us for your own cowardice?'

James Stewart rounded on him. 'Enough! We all lost kin and comrades.' The steward's words were raw with the loss of his brother John. 'No one man holds dominion over grief here.'

Into the belligerent silence that followed, one voice rose.

'I have made my decision.'

The crowd's attention turned to William Wallace, those on the fringes of the assembly craning heads to see him.

'The greater part of our army has been destroyed. If a campaign was launched tomorrow, we could not stand against the English. We need to recover our strength.' Wallace's blue eyes moved over them. He lingered on Robert. 'Sir Gartnait is right. It is time to seek the aid of others if our struggle is to continue. I will stand down as guardian of Scotland and go to France. We must not allow King Philippe to forget our alliance, whatever pact he makes with England. From Paris, I will travel to Rome and petition the pope personally.' Turning, he strode out of the circle, men falling back to allow him to pass. For a moment, a hush descended, then a host of voices broke out at once, some appealing to Wallace to reconsider, the rest trying to make themselves heard.

In the confusion, Robert pressed his way out of the seething crowd. Wallace was ahead, his stride taking him away through the trees. For the past few days since his arrival in the Forest, Robert had been in private talks with James Stewart on the matter of the guardianship. He knew that in proposing that Wallace stand aside, the steward was preparing the way for him to stand up. He wanted to be magnanimous about it. 'Sir William.'

Wallace glanced round, but continued walking.

Robert kept up with his stride, dead leaves crackling under his boots. 'You and I have not seen eye to eye, but I cannot deny what you have achieved this past year. You built an army from shepherds and farmers, all of them devoted to you. You trained them to be fighting men, put spears in their hands and fire in their blood. They followed you willingly into battle. Stirling was an incredible victory.'

Wallace stopped abruptly and turned to him. 'And Falkirk was an incredible defeat.' He looked back at the crowd of men, their voices raised in argument. 'They didn't elect me to be their king or their official. They elected me to be their general and a general is only as good as his last victory. When the men look at me now those hillsides strewn with our dead is what they see. Just as the triumph of Stirling fired their hearts, Falkirk broke them. I will not become a symbol of our ruin.'

'What you propose is a risk. The journey to France will be perilous, especially now so many enemies know your face. Are you certain King Philippe will even grant you an audience?'

Wallace motioned through the trees to a dark-haired older man, standing on the periphery of the assembled crowd alone, watching the heated debate. 'My man there was once a Templar. He broke with the order, but still has allies within the Temple in Paris that may be of use to us. He believes the king will see me.' Wallace looked back at Robert, fixing him with his shrewd gaze. 'I know Sir James Stewart wants you to be elected as our guardian. Bishop Wishart told me. I imagine there will be others who would support that choice.' Wallace paused, then held out a scarred hand.

Robert took it.

William Wallace nodded. Turning, he walked away through the ancient trees, the leaves falling all around him.

It was four days since Wallace had resigned as guardian of Scotland. In that time the dispute over who should be his successor had rambled on, arguments raging back and forth. More groups were filtering into the Forest encampment, men responding to the messages summoning them to the assembly. All added their voices to the debate.

The day after Wallace's departure, James Stewart had revealed his proposal that Robert be elected. Some supported the motion, led by John,

Gartnait and Alexander. Along with the steward, the two earls and the lord formed a powerful vote in Robert's favour. But this didn't deter other men from disputing his bid, or putting themselves forward for nomination. Many more were still calling for James and Wishart to stand.

By late afternoon on the fourth day, the high steward was in front of the assembled gathering, giving his final arguments for Robert's appointment. The men at the front of the crowd sat on the mossy ground, or else perched on logs and tree stumps, the rest radiating out into the encircling trees. Over their hushed ranks the steward's voice lifted, reminding them that Robert had proven more than once over the past sixteen months to be a steadfast advocate of Scotland's liberation from King Edward's yoke. As Wallace and Moray before him, the young Earl of Carrick had raised the standard of rebellion, and raised it high. He had freed Ayrshire from the domination of Henry Percy and routed the English garrisons. He had drawn a loyal company of men to his cause, proving himself a bold and judicious commander, and it was his sword that had lain on the shoulder of William Wallace, bestowing a knighthood upon their champion.

'Furthermore,' the steward continued, looking over at Robert, close by with his men, 'he has lost much in this cause. In breaking from his father, Sir Robert suffered the loss of his family and a rich inheritance. In fighting the king's men, he incited Edward's wrath and endured the burning of Bruce lands in Annandale, not once, but twice. We have heard that on the march south that the king ordered the destruction of Lochmaben.'

Robert clenched his hands at the strength of feeling the steward's words provoked in him. It was only on entering the Forest camp the week before that he learned of Lochmaben's plight. The extent of the devastation wasn't yet known, but rumours of towns left burning and men and women slaughtered indiscriminately were rife. One name kept repeating within these scattered reports. Bohun. The razing of his family's lands at the hand of his former friend had maddened Robert. The estates might still be in his father's name, but he doubted King Edward had spared a thought for the old lord, retired in England. No, the attack had been designed for him alone, to strike where it would hurt the most.

'Sir Robert's grandfather was one of the greatest noblemen to have graced our land,' continued James. 'A fierce crusader as well as a lover of peace, in whom two of our kings placed their faith. In his grandson exist the same virtues, virtues that I believe make him the most suitable man to lead our kingdom in our continued struggle.'

When the high steward finished, Robert saw a shift in the company as the men reacted to these words. Some were nodding, in thought or agreement, others leaned in to murmur to their neighbours, a few were shaking their heads. It was impossible to tell what the vote would decide.

Wishart moved into the centre, his broad face dour, but set. He might have fought for Wallace to remain, but with that hope ended he had committed himself to the selection of a new guardian as vigorously as the steward, although as yet had not made his own preference known. 'We have heard statements for and against the nomination of Sir Robert. I suggest we return within the hour to cast our—'

Through the trees came shouts and the ring of bridles. Bishop Wishart turned, frowning at the interruption. Other men were looking round. Robert turned with them to see a mounted company approaching. The horses were mud-splattered, nostrils flaring from a hard ride. Robert's gaze fixed on a lean young man with lank black hair and a wolfish face, riding at the head. It was John Comyn, son of the Lord of Badenoch. There were around thirty men with him, bearing different devices on surcoats and shields. Many were decorated with three sheaves of wheat on red, others with the white lion of Galloway. Robert saw Dungal MacDouall among their number. His apprehension rising at the sight of his enemies, he glimpsed the same concern reflected in the steward's face.

John Comyn dismounted from his sweat-stained courser and strode through the crowd, his knights forcing their way in behind him. As he came into the centre, he gave Robert a look of hostile contempt, before facing Wishart and James. 'Has a decision been made?' he demanded, his high, haughty voice carrying over the murmurs of the assembly.

Wishart's brow puckered in surprise.

'We received word of this assembly a week ago,' John went on at the bishop's expression. 'My father is occupied fortifying our strongholds in the north and sent me in his stead. Yesterday, met by one of your patrols, I was told that Sir William had renounced the guardianship and that an election for his replacement was taking place. My men and I rode through the night to get here.'

James faced the belligerent younger man. 'Sir Robert Bruce has been put forward for the position.'

'Has he been nominated?' demanded Comyn.

'No,' said Wishart, before the steward could answer. 'Not yet.'

'Then I want to be considered also.' John Comyn turned, raising his voice over the calls of protest and anger coming from Robert's men. 'I have a right to be heard.'

'Sir Robert is an earl,' called Alexander Seton, 'you are a knight. Rank should hold sway here.'

John Comyn rounded on him. 'I am also the son and heir of one of the most powerful nobles in the kingdom, and the nephew of the king.' He raked them all with his stare. 'Will anyone deny that?' When no one answered, John Comyn's dark eyes narrowed in satisfaction. 'Had my father known the importance of this assembly he would have come himself, but I will stand for guardian in his place.'

'I will second the proposal.'

At the voice, a huge man with a barrel chest and a thatch of white hair pushed forward from the ranks of Comyn's company. It was the elderly, militant Earl of Strathearn. The man had been a supporter of William Wallace and had joined his raid into Northumberland the previous year. He was married to a sister of the Earl of Buchan, head of the Black Comyns, and was a potent force in the old order of the kingdom.

Robert looked over at James Stewart and saw, by the frustration in his face, that they would have to allow Comyn a voice, not least if he was supported by a man with the reputation of Strathearn.

'Then you should state your testimony now, Sir John,' said the high steward finally. 'For we cannot continue our deliberations any longer. All the while we dally, you can be certain King Edward plans his next campaign.'

John Comyn looked angry at the steward's demand for haste, but he turned to the gathering. 'Very well.' He paused for a moment, collecting his thoughts, then began to speak.

He was clear and articulate, surprising Robert who had always thought the young man to be a pale shadow of his powerful father.

John spoke of his father's position as Justiciar of Galloway and as one of the six guardians elected after the death of King Alexander. He spoke too of his family's long standing in the realm and of their unequivocal support for the return of his uncle, King John Balliol. It was a clever speech and one that clearly awoke the interest of many men in the clearing, not least because this declaration of support for Balliol was a part of the argument that James Stewart had expressly left out of his endorsement of Robert.

'I stand in the name of King John,' finished Comyn. 'As should any who proposes to be our leader.' As he said this, he looked over at Robert.

Surprisingly, it was one of Wallace's men, the brawny Gilbert de la Hay, Lord of Erroll, who challenged the haughty statement. 'These words would ring sweeter from your mouth had it not been the Comyns who led the nobles from the field at Falkirk, leaving Sir William and his foot soldiers to face the English cavalry alone.'

Robert, whose aspirations had begun to crumble at Comyn's speech, felt a spark of hope as he saw Gray and Neil Campbell nodding in agreement.

John Comyn flushed, but confronted Lord Gilbert at once. 'At least my father was at Falkirk, standing alongside his countrymen. The man you have nominated as our guardian wasn't even on the field of battle!' He pointed at Robert. 'Perhaps it was simple fear that kept the Bruce away, or maybe it was his old allegiance to King Edward that stopped him lifting his sword?'

The steward and several others protested, but Robert's voice rose over them. 'If my past allegiance to the King of England is to go against my bid, then your present commitment should be noted. You are married to the king's cousin, after all, and were in his service more recently than I.'

'I forfeited my marriage when my father and I broke from the king's orders, as it was our intention to do the moment we were freed from the Tower.' John Comyn spoke over the scornful calls of Edward Bruce. 'Joan and my daughters are in England. For the sake of my kingdom I have lost my wife and children. What have you sacrificed?'

The argument continued, swelling out from Robert and John at its centre, to engulf the entire assembly. The steward and Wishart strove to keep order, yelling over the din until they were hoarse, but no one listened. Robert, tearing his livid gaze from Comyn's, saw open mouths and raised fists. Comyn's men were facing his. His brother had a hand clamped around his sword, as had John of Atholl. Dungal MacDouall had drawn his. Out of the corner of his eye, Robert noticed a lean, wiry figure in a hooded black robe moving through the crowd. He glimpsed the smooth, clean-shaven jaw of a young man beneath the shadow of the hood. As the man came to stand in the centre of the crowd, he pushed back the cowl, revealing a sharp, striking face and a tonsured head. One of his eyes was blue, the other a strange, milky white. It was some moments before anyone else noticed him.

Wishart, arguing with Strathearn, halted in mid-sentence. His face changed, his mouth opening in surprise. 'Praise God, Lamberton, I thought you dead!'

At the bishop's ebullient outburst, other men quietened. Gradually, all eyes turned to the newcomer. At the name, Robert realised that this must be William Lamberton, the man Wallace and Wishart had elected to the bishopric of St Andrews, the most eminent diocese in the kingdom.

'My journey to Rome was longer than anticipated, your grace,' replied

Lamberton. His voice was not raised, but it had a strident power to it that caused the last murmurs of discontent around the clearing to fade. 'But I return to you consecrated in the sight of God by the hand of His Holiness, Pope Boniface. And, it seems,' he added, his intense gaze taking in the assembly, 'in a time of need.'

Wishart was looking Lamberton up and down. 'How did fortune bring you to us, my friend?'

'A good question,' answered Lamberton, with a brief, hard smile, 'with an answer for another time.' He looked around. 'I have heard some of what has been proposed here. I would suggest the election of Sir Robert Bruce and Sir John Comyn jointly as guardians. If the men of the realm stand divided on this issue, as they clearly do, then why not remove the object of division and unite the two men whom all of you support, one or the other?' When no one spoke, Lamberton continued, his voice strengthening. 'For unity is what is needed. I managed to elicit support for our cause from His Holiness in Rome, but while in Paris I discovered the truce between England and France has been formally agreed.'

'We have heard this too, your grace,' said James Stewart.

'It is worse than you know, Lord Steward,' responded Lamberton. 'The truce is set to be a permanent alliance, cemented in the coming year by the marriage of King Edward to Marguerite, sister of King Philippe. By this alliance our former treaties with King Philippe are to be rescinded. Scotland stands alone.'

66

Robert crouched in the wooded hollow, his mail coat settling around him. Picking a twig from the ground, he pushed back the hood of his green cloak, the better to see. Around him in a circle stood a dozen men, clad in similar garments, worn over hauberks to hide the glint of steel. From the leafy canopy above came the chatter of blackbirds and thrushes, disturbed by the intruders. Beyond the lattice of branches, the sky was white with heat. The trees shaded the men from the sun's ferocity, but the air was thick with humidity and insects that tormented them: midges and flies, ticks that burrowed and lice that could drive a man to madness, prickling on his scalp and groin.

'As we know, the carts will come down this road,' said Robert, drawing a line through the dry soil with the twig. 'Heading for Roxburgh.' He pointed the stick to a lump of rock placed on the ground at the end of the scored line, before drawing a circle at the other end. 'Sir James and his men will keep a watch for them here, where the ground is higher and they have a clear view of the track. Meanwhile, our forces will be waiting here.' He sketched two crosses in the dirt either side of the line. 'Now, we don't know when exactly the English will arrive, but the scouts believe it will be some time this afternoon, almost certainly before nightfall. Sir John and his men have walked the track.' He glanced up at his brother-in-law, who nodded.

Atholl's curly black hair was hidden beneath his hood. He looked keen. 'We estimate it will take around ten minutes for the baggage train to reach our positions once they have passed the steward's company.'

Robert met the dark gaze of John Comyn. 'I take it you have chosen someone to watch for Sir James's signal?'

Comyn's pale face was sullen. 'Fergus will do it,' he muttered, jerking his head to one of his men, a wiry, athletic-looking Scot, whose arms were folded over his chest.

Robert glanced at the others with Comyn, most of them his knights, with a few men from Galloway. Their expressions shared a common surliness that he knew had less to do with the approaching enemy and more to do with his men who stood facing them. Of his own people, Atholl was the only one who appeared focused on the plan. Gartnait was frowning, Alexander Seton reserved, Christopher on edge, his eyes on Comyn's tense group, Neil Campbell nonchalant, picking something from his teeth with a stick he'd carved to a point with his dirk. Edward was staring at John Comyn, his blue eyes filled with loathing.

'Good,' said Robert grimly, returning to the line he had carved in the dirt. 'The steward will allow the English to pass into the teeth of our trap, before moving in to block their rear while we close the jaws and—' Robert stopped, hearing a muttered voice. His eyes settled on Dungal MacDouall, standing to the right of Comyn, wearing a thigh-length mail hauberk under his brown cloak. 'Do you have something to say?'

MacDouall's eyes met his unflinchingly. 'I think it risky to attempt the ambush this close to the castle. If the garrison at Roxburgh are alerted to the attack they might sally out. Why not let the steward's force engage and we will ride to aid him?'

Before Robert could answer, Edward spoke. 'We've been through your objections already, MacDouall. Have you not listened to anything we've said?'

Robert shot his brother a warning look and held up his hand as Dungal spat something beneath his breath. 'This is the best place for an ambush.' He spread his hand to encompass the woods around them. 'The terrain is suitable for our horses and we can attack simultaneously from both sides. We know the train is well defended. The scouts said thirty horsed and almost double on foot, then there are the drivers of the carts. No. This is where we will make a stand. If we act quickly we can destroy their supplies and retreat into the Forest long before the garrison at Roxburgh has a chance to mount any offensive.'

As Dungal murmured something to John Comyn, Robert swiped irritably at a fly buzzing around his face. The heat was as cloying as treacle, making it hard to breathe. He imagined a Welsh hillside in snowy darkness, fires blazing in the night, bodies strewn around the carts, wounded horses on their knees, crying piteously. He had planned the ambush with Nefyn in mind, but couldn't deny that it was different here, more dangerous than it had been for the Welsh, able to slip away into the mountains. It was daylight for a start and the terrain although easier for them to attack was just as easy for an enemy to pursue if things went wrong. Dungal's words caused a worm of doubt to uncoil inside him. Roxburgh Castle was filled to the walls with starving English soldiers, desperate for supplies to reach them. He forced away the concern. It would work. Standing, he tossed the stick aside and met the gaze of his fellow guardian. 'Are you with me, John? I need to know.'

After a pause, Comyn's jaw pulsed and he gave a curt nod.

'For Falkirk,' said Robert, holding out his hand.

John took it. Their hands grasped briefly, then fell quickly away.

The two groups left the hollow, Comyn and his knights heading towards the track, on the other side of which, some distance from the road, the rest of their company was waiting with their horses. Robert and his men moved deeper into the woods, birds flurrying above them into the bleached sky. It was less thickly wooded near the road, affording scant cover, a problem if the English had any scouts riding before the supply train, who might spot them and raise the alarm. Robert had determined that the two companies hide out of sight and earshot to await the signal from the steward.

Edward glanced back over his shoulder as they walked. 'I swear that cur MacDouall is intent on fighting every decision you make.'

Robert looked at him. 'You cannot blame his resentment of us. Our father killed his.'

Edward lifted his shoulders carelessly. 'His father attacked ours. What does he expect? Besides, it was a long time ago.'

Robert didn't answer, but lapsed into silence, pushing branches out of his way. In a glade ahead, the rest of his company was waiting, formed in the main of knights from Carrick, including Nes and Walter, and supported by some of Atholl's and Mar's men. They were sixty in total, which, combined with John Comyn's force, would be more than a match for eighty or so English.

'Is the lookout in place?' Robert asked, heading to Walter, accepting the cup of beer Nes handed to him.

Walter gestured to the lofty heights of an ancient oak, where Robert could see, through the thicket of leaves, the legs of a man, hanging from either side of one of the higher boughs.

Finishing the beer, Robert settled down to wait. It could be hours before the signal came. He should get the rest where he could. The trees stretched into green all around him, stark light slanting through wherever there was a break in the cover. These woods formed the southernmost reaches of Selkirk Forest. Here, on the border, the trees were mostly oak, hazel and birch, rather than the soaring pines that filled the Forest's dark heart. The woodlands were interspersed by hills brushy with heather and steep valleys where the spires of abbeys and towers of castles protruded unexpectedly, all built from the same rose-pink stone.

Leaning his back against a trunk, Robert looked over at his men, who were sharing around beer and speaking among themselves. All were sweat-soaked and dirty, their clothes soiled from months living in the Forest and travelling from place to place. Many had grown beards, not having the time to shave. Robert rubbed at his chin, coarse with stubble, guessing he must look the same.

For the past ten months, since he and John Comyn were made joint guardians, they had been engaged in a protracted war against the castles still held by the English, left to defend themselves when King Edward led his army over the border. Without siege engines, they had been unable to launch full-scale assaults and instead had focused on cutting the garrisons off from much needed supplies. The English at Stirling were rumoured to be on the brink of starvation. God willing, Roxburgh would face the same fate if they were successful today. A victory here would be welcome, for the castle was at a highly strategic point, close to the border, and formed the base from which Edward had launched his campaign the year before.

As Robert's gaze drifted over his men, Christopher Seton caught his eye. Robert had dubbed the young man at the Christ Mass, a reward for his loyalty these past two years. The squire had initially seemed discomforted by the honour, which had puzzled Robert, but Christopher was gradually beginning to relax into his role as a knight. The others had settled into the arduous business of entrenched warfare in their own ways, some better than others. His brother and Alexander Seton seemed at home in the Forest, planning ambushes and raids, living from day to day. The same went for John of Atholl, whose young son David was serving him as a squire, although the earl clearly missed his wife, who remained in the Forest encampment with the women and children. Robert had left Marjorie there in Christian and Judith's care. The wet nurse had changed since Katherine's departure and truly relished taking care of his daughter. Of all of them, Gartnait seemed to find it harder to settle, partly because he disliked the covert form of warfare in which they were engaged – creeping around, he called it. Yet even he had to admit there was no alternative. After the defeat at Falkirk, a pitched battle was out of the question. They had neither the force, nor the single-minded leadership of William Wallace, now abroad, fighting their cause with words in the courts of king and pope.

Robert's attention moved to his brother, who was
Campbell. The two were very much alike – the same
ment, edged with a sly sense of humour. Robert wasn't
had become close. He himself had been slow to trust Ca
Wallace's staunchest lieutenants, but he hadn't failed to not
fearlessness and skill as a fighter, and in time had discovered th
in common than he'd realised. Neil had come into Wallace's com
in the rebellion, after the destruction of his family's lands in L
the hands of the MacDougalls. In the west the war that had bro
two years ago continued unabated between the MacDougalls, allies
Comyns and Balliol, and the MacDonald lords of Islay, still acting as a
for King Edward. The head of the MacDonalds had been killed recently
was succeeded by Angus Og – the man who had offered Robert his sp
all those years ago at the feast in Turnberry Castle. The fact that Neil h
suffered the destruction of his lands and loss of his inheritance united hin
and Robert, still raw from the razing of Lochmaben, in exile. It was a thread
that linked many of them.

King Edward had not returned to continue his destruction, although
rumours of an imminent campaign were spreading. He had, however, been
busy at a distance, offering parcels of forfeited land to his barons. The Earl
of Lincoln had been given the domains of James Stewart, Clifford had the
south-west castle of Caerlaverock and Percy was offered more of Balliol's
strongholds in Galloway. At present, though, and until the English could
secure the kingdom, the barons could do little with their new lands, while
they were menaced by the Scots.

Staring at his men, arrayed before him, Robert thought of the path he
was leading them down. In Irvine, when he made his decision to go for the
throne, he had known it would be a lengthy process, but he was starting
to wonder just how long. There is a season to everything, James had told
him, when Robert had asked the high steward when he thought he should
announce his intention to the men of the realm. Have patience for the natural order of things. But the natural order of things seemed, to Robert, to
involve more politics, more assaults on supply lines, more tension. More
waiting.

The sun had moved round in the sky and was burning Fergus's neck. His
skin itched and perspiration dribbled down his back. He swiped at a hornet
buzzing incessantly around his face. The large insect switched away out
of reach. Light played on the pitted trunk of the oak, glistening on the

tles that scurried over the bark. Through the boughs
see the heads of men and rumps of horses. He had a
he was, the oak's branches opening before him to
t over woods lush with summer. Here and there he
ve track, which wound into the distance, where the
im, if he craned his neck, he could see a patch of rose-
st of the foliage: the battlements of Roxburgh Castle.
k, Fergus squinted up. The blazing sunlight slanting
ranches hurt his eyes. It looked as though he would
w from up there, but it would be shadier among those
making his head pound. After a moment, he eased
was standing on the branch he had been straddling for
His legs throbbed as the blood rushed into them. A

e signal come?'
wered, looking down into the upturned face of one of Comyn's
d to move. I'm going higher.' Fergus wrapped his hands around
ch above him and began to climb, all the while keeping his gaze on
ooded hump of land in the distance, where the steward's men were
tioned. A buzzing sound told him the hornet was back, but he ignored
it, pulling himself up, one bough to the next. At a fork, he shifted round
to the other side of the tree. The branches were narrower this high up, but
sturdy enough to take his weight. Choosing one, where the leaves gave him
a clear view to the east, but shaded him from the sun in the west, Fergus
straddled it and inched his way along. There was a low humming coming
from somewhere. More hornets. A couple hovered around him, their drone
loud. He smacked one away with a curse. It veered off. Fergus followed
it with narrowed eyes, ready to swat the little bastard if it returned. He
paused, his eyes narrowing further. There were dozens of them circling a
long, slender branch below him. Through the thicket of leaves, he could see
a large, pale sac.

Fergus tensed as he saw the nest. More hornets were drifting towards
him. One settled on his leg and he batted it away. It came back, hovering
around his eyes, its angry buzz filling his ears. Fergus shook his head wildly
and cursed. He couldn't stay here. The devils would distract him from his
watch. Wishing he hadn't moved, he reached for the branch above and got
to his feet, meaning to walk back to the fork in the trunk and climb down to
his old spot. Curling his other hand over the bough to steady himself, he felt
a sharp prick. He let go instinctively and, as his hand came away, he saw the

squashed remains of a hornet clinging to his palm. At that moment, he felt another sting in the back of his neck. Fergus slapped at it with a grunt. As he did so, he lost his footing. Jerking forward he struck the slender branch below, hard. There was a crack and a flurry of leaves as the bough broke. Feeling it drop away from under him, he lunged. He grabbed a branch above and hung there gasping as the bough plunged through the trees, the low drone becoming a high-pitched whine. Fergus yelled a warning, but it was too late. As it struck the mossy ground, the sac split open and a cloud of hornets swarmed up. Seconds later, the first cries of men and horses rose on the quiet.

Away in the distance, three arrows sailed into the blue sky, one after the other, above the woodland that overlooked the road to Roxburgh.

On the other side of the track, deep in the green shade of the trees, a whistle sounded from the broad boughs of a wych elm. Robert rose at the sound, his drowsiness vanishing. A glance into the tree above and a wave from his man told him it was time. At his gesture, the company, spread out on the mossy ground, downed cups of beer and ceased conversations. Scrabbling to their feet, they headed to where their mounts were tethered. A couple paused to empty their bladders into the bushes, while the squires untied the reins of their mounts. Birds, lulled by the afternoon calm, flew chattering off through the trees at the sudden action in the camp.

Crossing to Hunter, Robert pulled on his helm over his mail coif and arming cap, the steel encasing his scalp tightly. In the distance, he could hear the squeals of horses from Comyn's camp.

'Can't the churls even keep their mounts quiet?' demanded Edward. Swinging up into his saddle, he wrenched his sword free.

'The English will hear us a mile off,' growled Alexander.

Digging his foot into the stirrup, Robert mounted beside them, his face set. Faintly, he could hear the rumble of cart wheels. He had travelled with a baggage train before and knew the din they made on a rough road. 'They won't hear much over the noise of their own carts,' he told the others, shortening Hunter's reins into one fist behind his shield and drawing his sword with the other. 'God willing that should cover us until we're almost upon them.' He squeezed Hunter's sides with his calves, nudging the warhorse forward. His men formed up around him in a line, spreading out through the trees. As John of Atholl caught his eye, the earl smiled grimly, pulling his sword from its scabbard. Together, breaths rushing through helms and ventails, they waited.

The rumbling was nearer now, joined by the hollow clop of many hooves. Robert could no longer hear the squeals of Comyn's horses. Pushing all other thoughts aside, he focused his mind into a single point, like an archer aiming for a target. The knights and his brothers-in-law were alongside him, the squires and the crowd of foot soldiers behind, brandishing short swords and axes. Nes was looking nervous, but had his sword out, ready to follow Robert into hell if need be. Walter was close behind. The squire on watch, whose task it was to count the time between the point the signal was seen and when they had estimated the train would reach them, shinned down the tree and nodded.

Robert walked Hunter on, his men moving with him, breaking up as they entered the tangled undergrowth. Knights ducked under trailing branches, keeping their horses on short reins. Some of the mounts tossed their heads in agitation, sensing the tension in their masters, but the men kept them under tight control. Passing through the columns of oaks and elms, Robert eased Hunter into a trot, the others following suit. The din of carts and horses seemed to fill the woods. As the trees thinned the men struck at the sides of their chargers, urging them into a canter. Branches switched past, twigs snapping, bushes tearing. Sunlight flashed through the leaves. The horses' eyes were wide and white, nostrils flared. Ahead, through the woods, the men could see the ponderous bulks of carts and bright swatches of surcoats.

As they emerged and thundered towards the track, Robert peeled back his lips and roared. '*For Scotland!*'

The English, seeing them coming, turned their horses roughly, wrenching swords from scabbards with harsh shouts. The foot soldiers, who bore the red cross of St George, drew weapons and jostled together in front of the carts, ready to defend the precious loads. The carthorses harnessed to the ten wagons, laden with crates, sacks and barrels, neighed in fear, the drivers struggling to control them. Robert's company struck them hard on the right side, the knights yelling furiously as they spurred their horses up the slight incline to meet the road.

Robert went straight for a knight at the front of the train, who was clad in black with a blue cross on his shield. He carved in with his broadsword, the steel flashing in the golden evening. The knight raised his shield and Robert's blade cracked hard against the wood. The man hadn't had time to pull up his ventail and his face was clenched with determination as he clouted the sword away and lunged at Robert's side. His sword scraped along Robert's shield, scoring a line through the red chevron. The knight spat through his teeth and came in again. His blade met Robert's in mid-air, the clash of steel barely audible within the turmoil erupting all around them. Robert forced the man's sword forward and down, the bite of metal on metal screeching. Their horses lurched together, the beasts gnashing their teeth. As his cross-guard met the knight's blade, Robert twisted, hooking the man's sword aside and off-balancing him. Pulling back sharply while the knight was still recovering, he swung his foot free of his stirrup and aimed a mighty kick at the man's side. The knight, already tilted in his saddle, toppled sideways with a shout. His horse's head was pulled viciously to one side as he fell, dragging the reins with him.

As the knight landed with a crunch of mail, his destrier pulled itself free and reared up, iron hooves striking out. One caught Hunter in the neck, causing the horse to stumble, with a squeal of pain. Robert, his foot still out of the stirrup, was pitched forward, over Hunter's bowing head. He struck the ground and rolled, just in time to avoid the stamping hooves of a cart-horse. With a hiss of breath, he grasped for his sword, pulling it from the dust of the track as the knight, who had staggered to his feet, came at him with a snarl, blood gushing from his nose. Beyond, Robert glimpsed a chaos of movement and colour as all along the track his men tackled the English. He had a second to realise that Comyn and his company were nowhere to be seen along the train's left flank; a second for cold shock to fill him, then the knight was rushing him and he was lurching forward to counter, swinging his sword round over his head and down to the right in a brutal cut of wrath.

The fighting was fierce, the initial element of surprise that had favoured the Scots gone, the English, who had formed up swiftly, now fully engaged. Knights hacked and slashed, their horses crashing together in the close quarters. Foot soldiers hammered at one another, locked in dogged combat, men wrestling one another to the ground, stamping on fingers, slamming sword pommels into jaws, thrusting dirks into throats and ribs. Blood sprayed and horses screamed. Robert's force was determined, but without Comyn's company, they were outnumbered. Within moments, the battle began to turn, some of the Scottish knights forced to counter two opponents at once. John of Atholl was roaring through his helm, parrying with a knight beside him, while trying to fend off a foot soldier attacking him from the ground. One of the English knights yelled for the driver of the lead cart to break and head for the castle. Obeying, the man cracked his whip across the horses' broad backs and they plunged forward, the wagon veering off along the rough road towards Roxburgh.

Robert was grappling with the black-clad knight when he saw the two carthorses coming at him. He threw himself to one side as the cart went thundering between them. For a moment, he was on his own on the train's left flank, all the fighting concentrated on the right. He turned into the trees, panting for breath and yelled Comyn's name. For a moment, he thought he heard distant shouts, then another cart was trundling recklessly past.

Edward Bruce had just punched his sword into the throat of a foot soldier who'd stabbed at his leg when he saw the carts begin to move, the drivers flicking their whips to urge the beasts on. He slammed his heels into his horse and pressed the animal after one wagon, rumbling away through the chaos. Coming up alongside the carthorses, Edward swung his sword into the straps of the harness, carving through the leather. He shouted as the driver struck out at him with the whip, which caught his horse on the rump, slashing a red line through its skin and causing it to pitch into a canter. The freed horse veered off into the woods, leaving the cart to continue with one. Neil Campbell, seeing Edward's plan, spurred his own mount to follow, striking at the harness on the other side. A few of the Scottish foot soldiers had fought their way through the English and were scrabbling on to the wagons, climbing over crates and barrels to tackle the drivers. Two carts had turned and were trundling back down the road, the way they had come. Some of the English knights were riding with them, heading unknowingly towards the force of James Stewart.

Suddenly, from the left, a ragged line of horsemen appeared. Robert, who had hauled himself on to the back of one of the wagons headed for the castle, saw them coming through the trees, John Comyn at the van. He yelled at Comyn to take the wagons, then climbed over the sacks to tackle the driver. The cart was bouncing recklessly along the road. He lurched, grabbed the side with a curse, then pushed himself up and fell on the driver. The man struggled, but at a brutal thrust of Robert's sword, he tumbled from his seat and went sprawling to the ground, his neck snapping under him. As the terrified horses continued, Robert dropped his sword and lifted the reins. By the time he managed to bring the cart to a halt, the rest of Comyn's forces had emerged from the woods and were tackling the remaining English. Of the ten carts, six had escaped, four heading for Roxburgh, two back the way they had come.

Soaked with sweat, Robert jumped down from the wagon and jogged back towards his men. Tugging down his ventail, he spat dust and blood from his mouth. The track before him was strewn with bodies. A few dead horses lay among the men, one twisting feebly. For a moment, Robert thought it was Hunter, then he saw his destrier held by Nes, who was astride his own horse, the sword in his free hand bloody. Going straight for Comyn, who had dismounted on the corpse-strewn track, Robert passed his banner, fluttering limply on the tracks and stared down at the young knight from Carrick, who had followed him since Carlisle. He crouched. There was a dagger protruding from the side of Walter's neck, the collar of his tunic awash with blood. His eyes were staring blankly into the sky.

Robert turned his gaze to Comyn, rage rushing through him. Other men were staggering to their feet, or sliding weakly from saddles. Already, his company were confronting Comyn's forces, Atholl shouting fiercely at Dungal MacDouall. As he went towards Comyn, Robert's wrath was so great he didn't even notice the red welts on the faces and hands of many of the company, or the fact that they were missing several men. His blood still hot from battle, it took an effort of will not to launch himself at Comyn. Instead, he came up into the man's face, his words spitting out. 'Where were you? I've lost a dozen men, you son of a bitch!'

Comyn's dark eyes were slits as he glared at Robert. 'And I lost ten!'

Dungal MacDouall had forced his way past Atholl and came up alongside Comyn. His face was covered in livid lumps. 'Hornets attacked us.'

'Hornets?' said Edward, standing beside his brother. 'If it was lions I might have sympathised.' He turned to the rest of Robert's company. 'We were fighting men, while they were struggling with insects!' He looked back at Comyn. 'How like your family to avoid a battle at any cost! What was it at Falkirk? Ants?'

As some of Robert's men laughed harshly and Comyn flushed, Dungal stepped in, lunging at Edward. Edward ducked under the strike and barrelled into his attacker, sending him crashing to the ground. Comyn's men shouted, surging forward as Edward straddled the Galloway captain and cuffed him viciously. Robert's men stepped in, those who had sheathed their swords going for them again. From along the road came the drum of hoof-beats as James Stewart and his men appeared. Some of them held aloft flaming torches, tiny echoes of the evening sun, flooding the way behind. At the sight of the steward, Edward clambered off Dungal, who staggered to his feet, spitting blood. The captain went blindly at Edward, but Comyn seized him.

James stared around him as he pulled his horse to a rough stop. 'What in Christ's name happened?' he demanded, his gaze going between Robert and Comyn. His eyes moved across the bodies on the track to the four wagons, two of which had been freed of their horses. 'Where are the rest of the carts?'

Robert shook his head. 'They made it to Roxburgh.'

James looked thunderous, but he nodded to his men who held the flaming brands. 'Burn them.' As the knights headed to the wagons, the steward looked back at Robert. 'We need to be quick,' he said, his voice tight with anger. 'The garrison will be alerted. We cannot fight them all.'

As the men began to move, Robert grabbed Comyn's arm. 'It is on you,' he seethed, 'the deaths of my men.'

Comyn wrenched himself free.

67

On a flower-speckled meadow outside the town of Canterbury a grand tournament was under way. The lavish affair was blessed by the gold of the early evening sun, which poured its liquid light into the faces of the hundreds of spectators who lined the jousting ground, sparkling in the jewelled gowns worn by the ladies and in the polished mail and crested helms of the knights.

Scaffolds erected to either side of the ground were draped with swathes of scarlet cloth and filled with noble men and women. Lesser folk thronged the area below, sprawled on the warm grass, faces flushed with sun and ale, or else on their feet to watch the thunderous charges of the knights. At the end of the field, rising above the lists, was the royal box, fashioned in the likeness of a castle's battlements, from which hung the alternate shields of the king and his newly wed queen.

Edward, darkly glorious in black robes trimmed with heavy gold braid, watched the knights compete from the cushioned comfort of his throne. The fierce jousts that had enlivened the afternoon had ended and a contest of skill now formed the finale. A quintain had been set up at one end of the ground, from which was strung the wooden outline of a man, painted in the headscarf and robes of a Saracen, with a large red heart daubed on his chest. The knights were taking it in turns to charge the Saracen with their lances. As Ralph de Monthermer set off down the field, his yellow mantle with its green eagle flying out behind him, lance couched towards the quintain, the crowd followed him with their gaze. The royal knight struck the heart in the centre, sending the Saracen swinging violently round, counter-weighted by the sandbag on the other end of the quintain's beam. Ralph plunged on past, the iron hooves of his destrier kicking up clods of earth. The onlookers cheered.

Edward's gaze moved to the line of mounted knights at the other end of the field, waiting for the pages to swing the quintain back into position. Raised behind them, dark against the mandarin sky, was the faded dragon banner that had once been hoisted over the dusty tournament grounds of Gascony. Edward's eyes drifted over the knights – Humphrey de Bohun, hero of the tournament, Aymer de Valence, Henry Percy, Guy de Beauchamp, Robert Clifford, Thomas of Lancaster. These young men, nurtured in his court and blooded on his battlegrounds, had come of age in a decade of war. Their apprenticeship was over. All of them had succeeded their fathers. No longer Knights of the Dragon, they had taken their places as Gawain and Perceval, Mordred and Lancelot, the names of those immortal knights carved in the oak of his table. Carved in these men's souls. Of the veterans only the aged John de Warenne, the earls of Lincoln and Norfolk, and the belligerent Bishop Bek remained. Bold midday was here, in the fiery zeal of younger men.

Hearing a soft clapping beside him, Edward looked round to see his bride dutifully applauding Ralph de Monthermer's display. Marguerite was known by her people as the Pearl of France. A jewel she was, dark-haired like her brother, King Philippe, with milk-white skin, her delicate form enfolded in a gown of scarlet damask, girdled with a belt embossed with glossy rubies, her hair bound up in a padded net that framed her heart-shaped face. It was early September and the air was mild, but the queen had draped an ermine stole around her shoulders to ward off the first hint of evening's cool. Daughter of the warrior kings of the Capetian dynasty of France, Marguerite had sailed into Dover the week before, a tender symbol of peace, nervous, but poised, with a stately array of menservants and hand-maidens. Two days after her ship had docked, Edward wed her outside the doors of Canterbury Cathedral. The solemn ceremony, performed by the truculent Archbishop Winchelsea, had been followed by three days of tournaments and feasts.

Edward had spared no expense for the occasion of his wedding. Beyond the jousting ground were scores of striped marquees, decorated with colourful streams of flags. Smoke curled from fires, over which the glistening carcasses of wild boar were being turned on spits. The trestles inside the pavilions were laid with silver and gold plates, and sprays of flowers. There would be trays of warm, spicy gingerbread, crisp-skinned apples roasted in honey, cloud-soft custards, succulent venison that slipped from the bone, sugared almonds, and wine to fill a river. Outside the marquees, servants were stringing lanterns from the branches of trees. As evening fell each would be crowned with a halo of glowing stars.

Sensing the king's eyes upon her, Marguerite's lips curved in a tentative smile. Edward returned it courteously, before turning his attention
back to the tournament ground. The marriage was an occasion of joy,
auguring the ending of the five-year war between England and France,
and securing, through the mediation of Pope Boniface, the restoration of
Gascony to Edward and his heirs. But the celebrations could not dispel the
profound sense of loss that had ballooned inside him this past week, leaving him aching, swollen with memories of Eleanor. He was sixty years old.
Marguerite, shyly demure at seventeen, was as sweet as mead and he knew
he would get pleasure from her in the years he had left, but she would never
be able to touch his soul. That part of him had died with his Spanish queen.

Behind him, Edward caught a peal of laughter from his son, seated a few
rows back with his friends. At fifteen, young Edward was the mirror of
him in adolescence, with feathery blond hair and a long, angular face. His
body had lengthened this past year, suggesting the boy would also inherit
his great stature. Beside him, one arm resting languidly on the scaffold
edge, was a handsome squire of sixteen called Piers Gaveston. The coal-
eyed youth from Gascony was the son of a knight who had served the king
well during the war. On the man's death, Edward had made Piers a ward
of the royal household and his son and the squire had formed an immediate bond of friendship. Edward had been mildly concerned by his son's
growing tendency to waste hours outdoors with Piers and his friends when
he should be training or in study, but he knew there would be time for
the youth to mature soon enough, especially now the betrothal to King
Philippe's daughter, Isabella, had been secured. The marriage wouldn't take
place for some years, the princess a mere infant, but, in the meantime, the
king had other plans for his son. He intended to involve him heavily in his
next campaign in Scotland, planned for the coming year. It was an auspicious time, for the ending of the year would be greeted by a new century.
It was a time of change and, God willing, a time to complete his conquest.

He had agents under his lieutenant Sir Richard de Burgh, the Earl of
Ulster, hunting down the fourth relic in Ireland. When found, he would
have it paraded before the people, as he had the crown and the stone, tokens
of his supreme authority over a unified Britain. Then, when the relic was
presented in Westminster Abbey, before the shrine of the Confessor, the
Last Prophecy would be realised. Men needed legends – something to
aspire to beyond the toil and drudgery of daily life, something golden and
glimmering above the grey of worldly existence. It was what set fire in their
blood. By saving the kingdom from the doom of Merlin's vision, his subjects

would praise him, but, more importantly, his fulfilment of the prophecy would secure him the faith of these young men, whose taxes bolstered his treasury and whose swords would be drawn for him in war. Arthur's knights had quarrelled, even disagreed with their king at times, but in the end the circle of the table had bound them with a loyalty that went beyond the temporal. This was what Edward sought, for he was determined never to see another Lewes, the kingdom torn apart by the ambition of its barons and the weakness of its king. No. His circle would be made of gold. Polished. Unbreakable.

He had come close to losing their support over Gascony, the threat of civil war never far from his mind, but the battle at Falkirk, although dour at its end, had drawn his men together in victory. Still, it wasn't over. Trophies were not enough for him to complete his dominion. Scotland remained split and the rebels had not been idle. Reports of supply trains being attacked and garrisons cut off were coming to him every month. Winchelsea, on behalf of the pope, was protesting against his invasion of a Christian country and Edward had recently discovered that William Wallace had made it through the blockade in the Channel and was now a guest at the court of King Philippe. He had worried what harm the rebel leader might inflict upon the truce, but so far nothing had changed. He would deal with that brigand in time, but for now there was a more pressing enemy to deal with. And deal with him he would.

As the tournament drew to a close, the knights shattering their last lances upon the Saracen's heart, the judges retired to make their decision on the winner, who would be presented with his prize – a silver helm surmounted by a dragon – at the feast. At the break in the festivities, a messenger slipped along the benches and whispered something to the king. Rising, Edward excused himself from his young queen and climbed down from the scaffold by the steps at the back. The nobles were talking among themselves, settling wagers.

Avoiding the crowds, Edward made for the marquees, followed discreetly by two of his knights. The light was fading fast and the lanterns in the trees were shimmering. A servant was ushering five peacocks into the largest tent and minstrels were tuning their instruments. There, waiting in the wings of the king's magnificent pavilion, watching the servants dress the tables in cloths of gold, was a man in a navy cloak and a short coat of mail. He looked older, more scarred than he had when Edward had last seen him in Gascony. Ignoring the respectful bows of the bustling servants, the king gestured for the knights to stay behind and headed to the man alone.

Adam turned as Edward approached. He inclined his head. 'My lord king.'

'I take it you have settled into your lodgings?'

'My needs have been well tended, my lord. I thank you.' Adam paused. 'I was, I admit, surprised to receive your summons so soon after the ending of the war. But I left my company in Bayonne fortifying the garrison there, with one of my lieutenants in command. They are in good hands.'

Edward's gaze was on the servants, busy laying the tables, but in his mind he saw a crude painting of a rampant red lion rearing over a dragon. 'I have a special task for you in Scotland. Not unlike that which I ordered you to undertake thirteen years ago.' He looked at Adam. 'There is someone else who needs to meet with an accident.'

68

Robert Bruce and John Comyn stood across from one another, eyes locked, burning with aggression. Around them, the circular hall of Peebles Castle was filled to the timber walls with men, the atmosphere charged and volatile. Rain pounded on the thatched roof and thunder snarled between the snap of lightning, flaring white through gaps in the shuttered windows. The air was saturated with sweat and hot breath, and the reek of damp fur from the men's sodden cloaks.

'I warned the Bruce.' Comyn's voice rose over the fury of the storm. 'I cautioned against attacking so close to Roxburgh's walls, but he would not listen.'

'So you sabotaged the attack, just to prove your point?' demanded Edward.

John Comyn gave a harsh bark of laughter. He turned to the knights of Badenoch and Galloway, arrayed behind him. 'I never knew the Bruces thought me so powerful as to call down wasps from the trees!' His mocking humour vanished as he looked back at Robert. 'You and your brother are well aware of what happened. Why we were delayed.' His eyes flicked to the steward and Bishops Wishart and Lamberton, who had been attempting to maintain order. 'I lost ten men and five horses, God damn it! Tell me, what was I supposed to have done?'

'You could have picked a more competent lookout,' said Alexander Seton coldly. 'Perhaps if your man had better assessed his post he might have spied the nest and chosen a safer position.'

'Fergus paid for his mistake with his life,' retorted Comyn angrily.

'As did a dozen of my men,' countered Robert, not taking his eyes off his fellow guardian.

'I think we should agree that the failed attack was no one's fault,' said James firmly. The high steward looked wearied by the debate, going on for almost an hour without resolution.

'I disagree, Lord Steward,' said Dungal MacDouall, beside Comyn. 'If we had done what Sir John and I suggested and attacked the English supply wagons further down the road then even if the same misfortune had befallen us we would have been able to give chase. As it was, we were too close to Roxburgh's walls to risk pursuit.' His gaze went to Robert. 'This was explained to the Bruce, but he refused to fight unless it was according to his plan. We had no choice but to go along with it.'

'You lying son of a whore!' growled Edward, stepping towards MacDouall. As he did so, he went for his sword, but his hand curled around air.

The high steward, having seen the turbulent aftermath of the failed attack, had ordered that no weapons be brought into the council.

Robert moved in front of Edward, giving him such a fierce look that he backed down, but his brother's jaw remained clenched as he eyed MacDouall, who looked eager for a fight. Other men were entering the argument, slinging insults across the packed hall. Outside, lightning pulsed.

'I move to have Robert Bruce struck from his position!' MacDouall shouted over the din. 'He isn't fit to be guardian!'

Many of the men around him expressed fervent agreement.

The loudest voice, however, came from Gilbert de la Hay. The lord's broad face, framed by his thatch of blond hair, was stern. 'It seems clear to me that neither Sir Robert nor Sir John can continue to work together, not without detriment to the realm. I believe we should contact Sir William Wallace and request his return. We know the truce between England and France excluded Scotland,' he said, glancing at Lamberton, who was silent. 'What use is Sir William to us now in a foreign court? Let us call him home, where he is needed. The English will be coming for us in the new year. We must stand united against them.'

'That truce is exactly why Sir William should remain where he is,' James answered. 'If we are to secure foreign support for our cause we need to maintain a strong presence abroad. Alliances can change. We have all seen that. Our hope is not lost. Not yet.'

John Comyn didn't seem even to have heard the exchange. He was still fixed on Robert, his eyes glittering with hate. 'I agree with MacDouall. Bruce should be replaced. Not only did his reckless plan lose us valuable men, it allowed the English to deliver half their supplies to the garrison at Roxburgh. They will survive the siege far longer now, maybe even until King Edward comes north to relieve them. Who knows,' he went on, raising his voice over scornful calls from Robert's company, 'perhaps he meant for our assault to fail? Perhaps he intended to aid the garrison so that his old ally, King Edward, had a base from which to launch his next invasion of our kingdom?'

In the midst of the uproar that met these words, Robert's voice rang out. 'Your feeble allegations are a poor mask for your own ambition, John. You want me gone so you can take control.' His tone, although forceful, was composed, but inside he wanted nothing more than to launch himself at the man in front of him, who with the damning accusation ignored the deaths of the good men who died in the attack, including Walter. 'It sickens me that you would say something so absurd to claw your way to power, at the cost to our kingdom.'

'Absurd?' said John, seizing the word keenly. 'Is it really so absurd to accuse you of such a thing, when you were one of the king's elite, bound to his cause by an unbreakable oath? An oath sworn on pain of death?'

Robert was shaking his head contemptuously, but the protests died down at these words. A few men looked over at him, frowning in question.

Before Robert could answer, John Comyn continued, gesturing to his rival as he looked around him. 'He is one of those men King Edward calls his Knights of the Dragon. I know this because my brother-in-law, Sir Aymer de Valence, is one. He told me some time ago that Bruce had been accepted into the king's order. How can we trust such a man? How can we risk our kingdom's future on the hope that he has broken all ties with his old allies?'

Robert could feel the stares of many men on him. How long had Comyn sat on this knowledge, like some eager bird perched on an egg, keeping it warm, just waiting until the time was right to reveal it? Other than those closest to him – his brother, the Setons, Atholl and Mar – Robert hadn't confided in anyone of his induction into the order. James, he saw, was looking at him, furrows creasing his brow. He went to defend himself, but Dungal MacDouall beat him to it.

'The Bruce is a traitor!' the Galloway captain exclaimed harshly into the hush. 'As deceitful as his cur of a father and as treacherous as his grandfather! A curse on them all!'

The storm swelling inside the hall broke. Edward launched himself at Dungal MacDouall. Seizing him by the throat, he slammed the young captain back into the timber wall. Men surged forward on both sides. Wishart forced his way into the centre, bellowing for order.

As Robert fought through the crush to get to his brother, someone grabbed him from behind, an arm squeezing tight around his chest. Hearing the hissed voice in his ear, he realised it was John Comyn. A second later, the glint of metal rose in his vision as Comyn brought a dirk to his throat.

Robert felt the steel press against his skin. Across the crowded chamber he saw James Stewart. The steward's face drained of colour, his hands rising in a gesture of protest, his mouth opening in horror. For a split second, Robert understood the intensity of the steward's devotion to him, then the blade pressed harder and the realisation vanished in a hot haze of outrage and fear. Comyn was going to kill him. The bastard was going to kill him right here and now in front of everyone.

'*By God, you will stop this!*'

It was the powerful voice of William Lamberton that halted them all. The Bishop of St Andrews stood in their midst, furious as a thunderbolt. His eyes, one blue, one white, were blazing. 'Put down your blade, John Comyn, or I swear by Lord Jesus Christ I will see your family condemned to the very pits of hell!'

Comyn didn't move. Robert could feel the man's chest heaving against his back with every breath. After a pause, he withdrew the blade from Robert's neck and relinquished his hold. Across the hall, Edward let Dungal MacDouall go as Neil Campbell grasped his shoulder. MacDouall slid down the timber wall, fighting for breath. Robert wrenched away from Comyn.

'This council is ended,' said James Stewart. 'Retire to your lodgings, all of you. We will return when cooler heads prevail.' The steward's voice was hoarse.

Robert pushed his way through the crowd, out into the driving rain. His men surged behind him, their voices raised against the downpour. Above the castle's timber buildings, which crowned an expansive motte, the sky was bruised, the swollen clouds lit from within by glimmers of lightning. The late summer storms had swept in from the east two days ago and the ground was waterlogged from the deluge, hollows and potholes filled with deep puddles. Robert splashed through them, pulling up the hood of his cloak as he headed for the steep track that led down from the motte.

Below him huddled the buildings that made up the burgh, augmented by the tents and horses of the men who had descended upon Peebles for the council. The town was situated some thirty miles from Roxburgh, in a steep valley within the Forest, the pressing darkness of which drew in close on all sides. The trees were a green sea, rolling and wild, tossed by the tempest. Dimly, Robert heard his men arguing around him as he descended the castle mound, but their words were as incoherent and insubstantial as the wind to him, for his mind was swarming with images, the substance of which blocked out all else. He saw John Comyn's face, livid with the determination to see him destroyed. The vision was followed by the uncertainty he had seen in the eyes of James Stewart as Comyn revealed his oath to King Edward. As he strode through the storm, down towards the town, he left the castle behind him, but couldn't leave Comyn's accusations. They followed him doggedly, ringing in his mind.

Bound to his cause by an unbreakable oath. How can we trust such a man?

How could they indeed? No one, not even his brother, knew he had helped the Knights of the Dragon take the Stone of Destiny from Scone Abbey. That was a weight he bore alone. Robert had told himself that if he'd refused that day to help Humphrey and the others steal the stone, they would have seized it without him – that he could not have prevented them – but this had done little to ease the burden. No matter what he did to aid his kingdom's liberation, no matter how many English supply lines he attacked, no matter how many Scots he drew beneath his banner, and no matter the steps he took on his path to the throne, he could never forget that the greatest challenge to his own destiny was the very crime he had committed.

There is no throne.

That fact was as stark as a beacon, blazing before him. Wherever he looked, he could always see it. That day – the day of Katherine's betrayal – Alexander had told him he needed to start believing he could be king. The lord had thought she was the one holding him back and maybe, in some way, that was true: maybe he had thought a soiled maid was all he was worth. But the truth, the real reason he walked towards the throne with doubt blazing in his eyes, was because of what he had done that day at Scone, in the shadow of the hill where he had once sensed the ghosts of his history.

So caught up in his thoughts was he that Robert didn't see the six figures approaching up the track, until he was almost upon them. Four of them were knights from Carrick. Between them they roughly escorted two figures, both of whom stumbled along, blinded by the hoods that had been thrown over their heads, through which came muffled sounds of protest.

Robert halted, Edward, Alexander and the others stopping with him at the sight.

'Sir Robert,' called one of the knights, as thunder cracked above. 'We found these men trying to enter your lodgings. They said they knew you, but refused to give their names.'

At these words, the captives began struggling.

Robert caught his name in their stifled voices. 'Remove those hoods.'

As the knights obliged, dragging off the blindfolds, the flushed, angry faces of two young men were revealed. They were clad in tunics and mantles of blue linen, soiled with rain and grime, but clearly of good quality. Both wore sword belts, but without weapons, no doubt taken by the knights. One, who looked a few years older than the other, was short and stocky with a square face framed by a reddish beard and curly blond hair. The younger of the two was tall and sinewy with shoulder-length black hair and a youthful face. Both gazed at Robert, their anger vanishing in wonder.

For a moment, Robert stared at them in puzzlement, then, beside him, he heard Edward shout, his voice raised not in concern, but joy. And all at once he knew them.

The Carrick knights stepped hesitantly away from their prisoners as Robert and Edward went to them and the four young men embraced one another, laughing and exclaiming, their eyes bright with rain and elation. Alexander Seton met Christopher's questioning gaze and shook his head, as perplexed as his cousin, while John of Atholl and Gartnait of Mar watched on in surprise with Neil Campbell and the others.

Robert pulled back from the black-haired youth, looking him up and down in amazement. 'By Christ, Niall, you're almost as tall as I am!' He stared over at Thomas, who withdrew from Edward's fierce embrace laughing at the ferocity of the welcome. Robert hadn't seen his younger brothers in years, for they had remained in fosterage in the Bruce lands in Antrim all through the war at their father's behest. He looked at them in turn, struck by how handsome Niall had become; the dark good looks of their mother built into his strong cheekbones and deep-set eyes, full of gentle good humour. Thomas had filled out and looked rather more like their father, broad in face and body.

Robert turned to the men behind him, grinning. 'Come, meet my brothers!'

John of Atholl came forward, shaking his head as he looked at Niall. 'You must have been a lad of no more than eight or nine when I saw you last, Master Niall. How old are you now? Sixteen? Seventeen?'

'Eighteen,' answered Niall, with the pride of a youth on the verge of manhood.

The Setons and Neil Campbell greeted the two men courteously.

When the introductions were done, Robert gestured down the track. 'Let's continue this reunion somewhere dry.' He addressed the four knights, who had led his brothers here. 'See that food is prepared for my honoured guests.' The knights headed off quickly down the track, the company following in behind.

As they walked, Robert kept glancing at Niall, amazed by the change in his brother and overcome with joy. He wanted to sling an arm around the younger man's shoulders, but some awkwardness stopped him, the many years spent apart and all that had happened wedged between them. He had a thousand questions, but one, the easiest, came to mind first. 'Why on earth didn't you give your name to my men? If you had explained who you were, you wouldn't have been treated so roughly.'

'We didn't know who we could trust,' answered Niall, glancing at Thomas, who walked between Robert and Edward. 'We have heard so many rumours these past few years it has been hard to tell who is fighting who.' He looked briefly at Robert, a question in his eyes.

Robert suspected his brothers would have many things to ask him. Some of the answers would be hard to give. 'How did you know we would be in Peebles?'

'When our vessel landed we went first to Turnberry,' replied Thomas, his voice deep and brusque. 'Sir Andrew Boyd recognised us. He told us you were in the Forest, fighting the English. The closer we came the easier it was to pick up your trail.'

Still speaking, the company headed through the bailey. Robert and his men had been barracked in an inn just outside the castle's palisade. He steered them towards the building as they passed through the gate. 'I cannot believe you are both here.'

'I cannot believe that you are a guardian of Scotland,' said Niall. 'Why didn't you send us a message?'

As they reached the timber-beamed inn, Robert paused to allow one of his knights, standing sentry outside, to open the door. 'Much has happened this past year. I haven't had the men to spare.'

'Have you heard from our father?' asked Thomas, following as Robert entered the building. 'Where is he? And what of Alexander? Is he still in Cambridge?'

'Enough!' protested Edward good-naturedly, before Robert could answer. 'I insist you tell us your tidings first.'

Entering the large chamber where he was lodging with his men, Robert gave Edward a nod, grateful for the diversion. Shrugging off his sodden cloak, he handed it to Nes, who had risen from his stool by the fire at their entrance. 'Why have you come?' he asked them. As Niall looked at Thomas, Robert saw something grave pass between them.

'The manor of our foster-father has been destroyed,' said Niall, his handsome face grim. 'Razed to the ground by knights of Sir Richard de Burgh.'

'The Earl of Ulster?' The tidings set an image in Robert's mind of a stone manor house beside a river, surrounded by green fields, jewelled with rain.

Across the room, he saw Edward's face had darkened and guessed he shared a similar memory of the home of the Irish lord, who had fostered them both. 'Why would the earl do this?'

'Men under Sir Richard's command have been scouring the north of Ireland for the past year,' replied Thomas, 'although it was only in recent months, when they began searching Antrim, that we learned this. When they came to us our lord refused them entry, but they forced their way in. We were compelled to leave on pain of death while they hunted through the castle. Finding nothing, they put it to the torch.'

'So they would know where they had searched already, they said,' murmured Niall, his face tight.

'What were they looking for?' Edward wanted to know.

'A relic, so we were told, that the King of England desires.'

Robert felt a jolt in his chest. 'What was this relic?'

Niall answered after a pause. 'They called it the Staff of Malachy.'

It was growing dark as Robert made his way up the track. The storm had dissipated through the afternoon, but the clouds were low and racing, skimming the castle buildings. The puddles that covered the ground shivered in the squally half-light. For the past two hours, he had sat in council with his men, listening to his brothers speak of the events in Ireland, his thoughts alive with possibilities. Now, as he walked the track, his decision made, he felt feverish, as charged as the lightning that still flickered across the distant skyline. No more politics. No more waiting. If everything had its season, then this would be his.

The ruddy shimmer of torches lit the hulk of the domed, circular hall, the timber walls of which were streaked with rain. Knights wearing the colours of the high steward stood outside keeping watch, their faces burnished by the flames. A few of them nodded to Robert as he approached. The wind whipped his black hair around his face and snatched at his mantle and surcoat, adorned with the red chevron of Carrick. As one of the knights opened the door for him, Robert entered.

The hall was flushed and warm, torches on the walls flaring in the gusts that followed him in. As the door thudded shut, Robert's gaze alighted on three men seated around the long trestle and boards at one end of the cavernous chamber. Their conversation ceased as he crossed to them, his footsteps hollow on the wooden floor.

'I take it your brother has withdrawn his teeth?' enquired Wishart roughly. The bishop shook his head, his face adamant. 'Things cannot go on this way, Sir Robert. They simply cannot! Edward should have been flogged for attacking MacDouall like that. As Comyn should have been for his actions against you.'

'Robert,' greeted James Stewart, half rising and giving Wishart a pacifying look. He gestured to the table, where a jug of wine and several goblets stood. 'Please, join us.'

Robert shook his head. 'Thank you, but no.'

'We have been discussing the possibility of Bishop Lamberton standing as a third guardian,' said Wishart curtly, not seeming to notice James frown at Robert's rejection. 'To mediate between the two of you.'

Robert glanced at William Lamberton, seated beside the Bishop of Glasgow. The young clergyman was studying him with his strange eyes. 'I think it is a wise choice, your grace,' he answered. 'But I myself will be standing down.'

James straightened fully at the statement. 'Standing down?' His expression was caught between surprise and anger. 'Why? Because of John Comyn?' He fixed Robert with his intense gaze. 'I implore you to reconsider. Think of the future, Robert. Think of what you risk by this action.'

'He isn't the reason I am standing down.' Robert paused. 'John Comyn was right about one thing – my connection to King Edward. It is a connection I believe I can use to our advantage. You may have heard by now, but my brothers arrived this evening from our lands in Antrim. They bear tidings that have given me hope. I am to return to Ireland with them, as soon as I am able.'

'Ireland?' questioned Wishart. 'What in God's name will you find to Scotland's advantage there?'

'Something that the King of England greatly desires.' Nodding respectfully to the high steward and the two bishops, Robert turned and crossed the hall.

As he pushed open the doors, he thought of Fionn mac Cumhaill and his band of warriors, whose heroic deeds he learned by heart in the hall of his foster-father. Disillusioned by the reality of war in Wales and plagued by uncertainties of his place in the Knights of the Dragon, he had banished those boyhood tales from memory, believing them to be a false hope of youth. Now, what had been offered to him but a quest for a treasure that might determine the fate of a kingdom and a way for him to make amends? As he stepped out on to the wild dark of the track, Robert smiled.

* * *

Affraig walked into the bright morning, her watery eyes blinking at the sun's radiance. The storms that had swept in from the east several days ago, causing rain to run in rivers from the hills, had dissipated late last night. The howling wind had since died down to a whisper, the clouds fading into a clear blue dawn as the tempest's tattered remnants pushed west towards Arran.

The ground, sparkling with dew, was covered in twigs and thatch from her roof, ripped away by the gale, although the hill that squatted over her dwelling had sheltered her from the worst of its violence. Murmuring her thanks to the gods of the air, she stooped to pick up the pail she had left outside to catch the rain. As she did so, her eyes caught sight of something lying on the ground under the oak, half hidden by the debris of the storm. It was a destiny, fallen in the night, fulfilled.

Straightening, Affraig headed across the wet grass, the brittle leaves prickling her bare feet. She crouched, her old bones creaking and protesting. Carefully, she brushed away the russet leaves to reveal a lattice of bone-white twigs. The moss-stained rope within was knotted like a noose – the root of St Malachy's curse. Her fingers stretched out to touch the weather-worn wood, her breath quickening as she fixed on the length of frayed twine that had held on to the old lord's destiny so stubbornly for so long. Her eyes moved up through the fluttering leaves and she saw a scrap of twine drifting aimlessly among the higher boughs. Close by, other webs of twigs swayed gently in the breeze. Affraig's gaze alighted on one, the limbs of which were brown and strong. Inside, a crown of heather and broom swung to and fro in the golden light, hanging by a thread.

AUTHOR'S NOTE

In June 2007 I was in Scotland on a research trip for *Requiem*, the last novel of my first trilogy, based on the downfall of the Knights Templar. My main character was Scottish and I'd always intended for him to return from the crusades to be embroiled in the Wars of Independence. The struggles of William Wallace and his rebel army made a powerful parallel with the Templars' fight for survival during the trial against them, both conflicts culminating in 1314 with the Battle of Bannockburn and the burning at the stake of the last Templar Grand Master, Jacques de Molay. I'd been in Paris the month before, working on the knights' side of the story and the Scottish excursion was supposed to help me fill in the other half of the narrative. I spent three weeks on the road, travelling from battlegrounds that were now housing estates to crumbling abbeys and ivy-clad ruins. Day by day, out of the pages of history and the wild landscape, one figure came striding, larger, clearer than all the others – Robert the Bruce. He swept me off my feet and carried me into a story that went way beyond the English invasion of 1296 and the subsequent insurrection led by Wallace, right into the heart of bitter family feuds, two civil wars and the struggle for a crown. By the end of the trip, I was so caught up in Robert's world I'd almost forgotten about the Templars – the protagonists of *Requiem*. Back home, I realised there was no way this character could play a cameo role in another man's story. His tale was just too sprawling, too intricate and too good to be cut down and boxed to fit. I had to let him go and focus on the dramatic, but much simpler story of Wallace which worked well alongside my Templar narrative. Robert refused to go quietly, however, and several weeks later, unable to silence his voice, I phoned my agent, who had been asking me to get a proposal together for my next set of novels. I now knew what they would be.

As a historical novelist you are forever walking a fine line between fact and fiction. It is the facts that inspire our stories and enable readers to enter these vanished worlds, but those same facts can sometimes be detrimental to a novel. The sources, both historical and contemporary, can be highly contradictory and often things are left unexplained – we might know what someone did when, but have no way of knowing why they did it. A historian can say this happened and these are the facts to support it and we believe this, but a novelist has to create the motivations that lie behind the actions of characters in order to make readers believe. For example, we have no concrete explanation as to why Robert deserted his father and King Edward that day outside Douglas's castle and joined the Scottish rebellion. He had so much to lose and so little to gain. Even the simplest theory: that it was an act fired by patriotism, doesn't totally hold water when you look at the broader picture. So, I made it more individualistic – not just a national cause, but a personal one, driven by Robert's frustration and the antagonism between him and his father. Of course, such personal instances are what most great events are born out of. We make split decisions, we do things in the moment, we hardly ever see that broad picture until we're looking back on it. History turns on a knife-edge.

The first big licence I took with history is the murder of Alexander III. Chroniclers of the time and modern historians regard his death on the road to Kinghorn as an accident and there is no reason to suspect otherwise. But as a novelist with a suspicious mind the rapidity with which Edward I secured permission from the pope for his infant son to marry the Maid of Norway, coupled with the fact that Alexander was thought to have mooted the possibility of such a union two years earlier in a letter to Edward and that when he married Yolande any offspring they produced would have rendered this proposition meaningless for Edward and his son, led me quickly down the *what if* route. Similarly, there is no evidence to suspect that the Maid's subsequent death was anything other than a tragic double-twist of fate. Her murderers, the Comyns, are tarnished with the black brush of fiction here, for the princess was thought to have died eating rotten food on the voyage rather than through any nefarious design, although it's true that the Comyns abducted Alexander during his minority in an attempt to gain control over the kingdom.

I have simplified the proceedings of what would much later be termed the 'Great Cause'. The hearing set up by Edward I to choose a successor to Scotland's throne was a protracted affair that, while interesting in terms of history, doesn't work well in a novel, essentially being a series of political discussions and lengthy periods of waiting. The chapter at Norham therefore is an amalgamation of many meetings that would have taken place over a longer period and in various locations.

Robert's grandfather did claim to have been named heir presumptive by Alexander II, although I have made more of it here than was made at the time. The assigning of the earldom of Carrick to Robert shortly after John Balliol was named king is real, but the transfer of the claim to the throne is fiction. At this point, the claim was passed from the grandfather to the father, with the assertion that it was for him and his heirs. But in light of Robert's dramatic shift in allegiance and the fact that even as early as the parley at Irvine he was accused of aiming at the throne, I chose to have it passed on here, rather than dilute the power of the moment and muddy the waters later on.

The *Prophecies of Merlin* are real. They were written by Geoffrey of Monmouth in the twelfth century, who claimed to be translating from an earlier source. Along with his hugely popular *The History of the Kings of Britain*, the *Prophecies* were in wide circulation and Edward is known to have owned copies. The *Last Prophecy*, as it appears in the novel, is my invention; however, Monmouth suggested that there were others written. At the end of his *History*, Monmouth, writing of the Saxon invasions, speaks of an angelic voice that tells the Britons they will not rule their kingdom any more until a certain time when the relics of the saints are gathered. The four relics I focus on all existed. Edward did seize the Crown of Arthur, but earlier than portrayed, during the conquest of 1282–84. Likewise, he took the Stone of Destiny from Scone, although the coronation chair that housed it at Westminster was made a few years later. When reading that passage in Monmouth's *History* and looking at Edward's actions during the invasions of Wales and Scotland – the taking of sacred and royal regalia – the two certainly seem connected. Edward was well known for his fascination with all things Arthurian. He and Queen Eleanor reburied the bones of Arthur and Guinevere in an elaborate ceremony at Glastonbury Abbey. Along with other nobles of the time, he organised popular Round Table jousts and had his own Round Table made. You can see it today in Winchester Castle. The Knights of the Dragon are fictitious, but the members are real.

Robert's experiences in Wales are pure fiction, although he is thought to have spent some time at Edward's court during this period and it seems he may have become close with a number of young English nobles. His father and an uncle had fought for Edward in the 1282–84 conquest of Wales and owed military service for their English lands, so I didn't feel it too large a leap to place Robert in Edward's army. The 1295 uprising and campaign are mostly based in fact, although Madog's brother Dafydd and the execution are fictional.

Many smaller details have been tweaked or altered, either for ease of reading or to suit fictional elements of plot and character. For instance, William Douglas's first wife was the sister of James Stewart, but by the time we meet him he was married to an Englishwoman. Likewise, Robert's father married again after Marjorie of Carrick died. The Setons aren't thought to have been related despite sharing the same name, but it made more sense to portray them as such. John Comyn the Younger and other Scottish nobles did serve Edward in France, but not until after 1296. Humphrey de Bohun's father didn't die at Falkirk, but soon after. For those who wish to gain more insight into the period, please consult the bibliography.

Robert the Bruce's story is complex, not simply due to the vagaries of history. There is none of the black-and-whiteness of Wallace about him. He is grey; a changeable, often intangible figure, flitting from one side to the other during the Wars of Independence, disappearing at points into the mists of obscurity before reappearing, suddenly and vividly, to shift the direction of the whole struggle. It was never going to be an easy tale to tell. But in its complexity, in Robert's — some might say — perfidiousness lie the real essence and beauty of his story: the remarkableness of human frailty and human strength, the capacity to change, to falter, to adapt, and for one man, against all odds, to steer the course of his own destiny, and with it that of a nation.

Robyn Young
Brighton
May 2010

CHARACTER LIST

(* Indicates fictitious characters, relationships or groups)

*ADAM: Gascon commander

ADAM: cousin of William Wallace

*AFFRAIG: wise woman from Turnberry

ALEXANDER II: King of Scotland (1214–49), named Robert's grandfather as his heir, but later had a son who succeeded him as Alexander III

ALEXANDER III: King of Scotland (1249–86), brother-in-law of Edward I by his first marriage; his wife and children died before him, forcing him to name his granddaughter, Margaret, as his heir

ALEXANDER BRUCE: brother of Robert

ALEXANDER MACDONALD: son and heir of Angus Mór MacDonald

ALEXANDER MENTEITH: son and heir of Walter Stewart, Earl of Menteith

ALEXANDER SETON: lord from East Lothian and *cousin of Christopher Seton

ANGUS MÓR MACDONALD: Lord of Islay

ANGUS OG MACDONALD: youngest son of Angus Mór MacDonald

*ANDREW BOYD: one of Robert's vassals in Carrick

ANDREW MORAY: led the rebellion in the north of Scotland against Edward I in 1297

ANTHONY BEK: Bishop of Durham

AYMER DE VALENCE: son and heir of William de Valence, cousin of Edward I and a
  *Knight of the Dragon

BRIGID: niece of Affraig

CHRISTIAN BRUCE: sister of Robert, married Gartnait of Mar

CHRISTOPHER SETON: son of an English knight from Yorkshire and *cousin of
  Alexander Seton

DAFYDD: brother of Madog ap Llywelyn

DAVID OF ATHOLL: son of John, Earl of Atholl

DERVORGUILLA BALLIOL: mother of John Balliol

DONALD OF MAR: Earl of Mar, Robert's father-in-law by the marriage of his
  daughter

DUNGAL MACDOUALL: *son of the steward of Buittle, becomes captain of the army
  of Galloway

EDMUND: Earl of Lancaster, younger brother of Edward I

EDWARD I: King of England (1272–1307)

EDWARD OF CAERNARFON: son and heir of Edward I

EDWARD BRUCE: brother of Robert

EGIDIA DE BURGH: sister of Richard de Burgh, married James Stewart

ELEANOR BALLIOL: sister of John Balliol, married John Comyn II

ELEANOR OF CASTILE: first wife of Edward I, and Queen of England

ELIZABETH (BESS): daughter of Edward I

ERIC II: King of Norway, father of Margaret, the Maid of Norway

EVA OF MAR: daughter of Donald, Earl of Mar

FLORENCE: Count of Holland

GARTNAIT OF MAR: son and heir of Donald, Earl of Mar, married Christian Bruce

GILBERT DE CLARE: Earl of Gloucester

GILBERT DE LA HAY: Lord of Erroll

*GILLEPATRIC: vassal of Robert's father

GRAY: friend of William Wallace

GUY DE BEAUCHAMP: son and heir of the Earl of Warwick, and a *Knight of the Dragon

*HELENA: daughter of the Earl of Warwick

HENRY III: King of England (1216–72)

HENRY PERCY: Lord of Alnwick, grandson of John de Warenne, and a *Knight of the Dragon

HESILRIG: English Sheriff of Lanark

HUGH DE CRESSINGHAM: English royal clerk, later Treasurer of Scotland

HUMPHREY DE BOHUN: Earl of Hereford and Essex, and Constable of England

HUMPHREY DE BOHUN: son and heir of the Earl of Hereford and Essex, and a *Knight of the Dragon

ISABEL BRUCE: sister of Robert, marries Eric II and becomes Queen of Norway

ISOBEL OF MAR: daughter of Donald, Earl of Mar, and Robert's first wife

JAMES DOUGLAS: son and heir of William Douglas, and nephew of James Stewart

JAMES STEWART: High Steward of Scotland

JOAN DE VALENCE: sister of Aymer de Valence and cousin of Edward I, married John Comyn the Younger

JOHN OF ATHOLL: Earl of Atholl and Sheriff of Aberdeen, married a daughter of Donald, Earl of Mar, making him Robert's brother-in-law

JOHN BALLIOL I: Lord of Barnard Castle, fought for Henry III at the Battle of Lewes

JOHN BALLIOL II: son of John Balliol of Barnard Castle, Lord of Galloway and brother-in-law of John Comyn of Badenoch, became King of Scotland (1292–96)

JOHN COMYN I: fought for Henry III at the Battle of Lewes

JOHN COMYN II: Lord of Badenoch and Justiciar of Galloway, brother-in-law of John Balliol and head of the Red Comyns

JOHN COMYN III (the Younger): son and heir of John Comyn II and Eleanor Balliol, married Joan de Valence

JOHN STEWART: brother of James Stewart

JOHN DE WARENNE: Earl of Surrey

*JUDITH: wet nurse to Robert's daughter

*KATHERINE: maid to Robert's wife

LLYWELYN AP GRUFFUDD: Prince of Wales, killed during the 1282–84 conquest

MADOG AP LLYWELYN: leader of an uprising against Edward I in Wales

MALCOLM: Earl of Lennox

MARGARET: half-sister of Robert from his mother's first marriage

MARGARET (THE MAID OF NORWAY): granddaughter and heir of Alexander III, she was named Queen of Scotland after his death, but died on the voyage from Norway

MARGUERITE OF FRANCE: sister of Philippe IV, second wife of Edward I and Queen of England

MARJORIE BRUCE: daughter of Robert and Isobel of Mar

MARJORIE OF CARRICK: Countess of Carrick, Robert's mother

MARY BRUCE: sister of Robert

MATILDA BRUCE: sister of Robert

NAVRE: Bishop of Bergen

NEIL CAMPBELL: a knight from Lochawe

NIALL BRUCE: brother of Robert

*NES: squire to Robert

PATRICK OF DUNBAR: Earl of Dunbar

PHILIPPE IV: King of France (1286–1314)

RALPH DE MONTHERMER: royal knight and a *Knight of the Dragon

RICHARD: Earl of Cornwall

RICHARD DE BURGH: Earl of Ulster and a lieutenant of Edward I

ROBERT BRUCE V: Lord of Annandale and grandfather of Robert, competed for the throne

ROBERT BRUCE VI: *Earl of Carrick and father of Robert, he resigned the earldom to his son, and became Lord of Annandale on his father's death*

ROBERT BRUCE VII: *son and heir of the Earl of Carrick*

ROBERT CLIFFORD: *royal knight and a *Knight of the Dragon*

ROBERT WINCHELSEA: *Archbishop of Canterbury*

ROBERT WISHART: *Bishop of Glasgow*

SIMON DE MONTFORT: *Earl of Leicester, led a rebellion against Henry III*

THOMAS BRUCE: *brother of Robert*

THOMAS OF LANCASTER: *son and heir of Edmund, Earl of Lancaster, nephew of Edward I, and a *Knight of the Dragon*

*WALTER: *knight of Carrick, Robert's banner-bearer*

WALTER STEWART: *Earl of Menteith*

WILLIAM COMYN: *fought for Simon de Montfort at the Battle of Lewes, head of the Comyns of Kilbride*

WILLIAM DOUGLAS: *Lord of Douglas, father of James*

WILLIAM LAMBERTON: *Bishop of St Andrews*

WILLIAM ORMESBY: *English Justiciar of Scotland*

WILLIAM DE VALENCE: *Earl of Pembroke, half-uncle of Edward I, and father of Aymer*

WILLIAM WALLACE: *leader of the Scottish rebellion against Edward I in 1297*

YOLANDE OF DREUX: *second wife of Alexander III and Queen of Scotland*

*YOTHRE: *instructor to Robert*

GLOSSARY

AILETTES: (meaning *little wings*): worn on the shoulders and painted with the knight's coat of arms, usually made of flat pieces of wood or leather.

AKETON: see gambeson.

BRAIES: undergarments worn by men.

CHAUSSES: mail stockings.

COIF: a tight-fitting cloth cap worn by men and women, it could also be made of mail and worn by soldiers under or instead of a helm.

CROWN OF ARTHUR: a coronet worn by the princes of Gwynedd, most notably Llywelyn ap Gruffudd who styled himself Prince of Wales. Edward I seized the crown along with other important Welsh relics during the 1282–84 conquest and sent it to Westminster Abbey.

CURTANA: also known as the Sword of Mercy because of its symbolically broken tip, it was thought to have belonged to St Edward the Confessor and became part of the English royal regalia used in coronations.

DESTRIER: a warhorse.

DIRK: Scots for dagger.

FALCHION: a short sword with a curved edge.

FOSSE: a ditch or moat.

GAMBESON: a padded coat worn by soldiers, usually made of quilted cloth, stuffed with felt or straw.

GEOFFREY OF MONMOUTH: thought to have been a Welshman or Breton by birth, Monmouth resided in Oxford during the twelfth century, where he was possibly a canon of St George's College. Later, he became Bishop of St Asaph. He wrote three known works during his life, the most famous being *The History of the Kings of Britain* of which the *Prophecies of Merlin* became part, followed by *The Life of Merlin*. Despite mixing established British history with romantic fiction, Monmouth presented his writings as fact and many readers of his works took them as such, accepting King Arthur and Merlin as historical figures. Monmouth's works, although criticised by some of his contemporaries, were hugely popular during the medieval period and from his *The History of the Kings of Britain* sprang the immense canon of Arthurian literature that graced Europe over the following centuries. Chrétien de Troyes, Malory, Shakespeare and Tennyson were all influenced by his work.

HAUBERGEON: a shirt of mail, usually shorter than the hauberk.

HAUBERK: a shirt or coat of mail with long sleeves.

HOBBY: a type of riding horse, usually small and swift.

HUKE: a hooded cloak.

JUSTICIAR: a chief justice official. In Scotland there were three justiciars during the period: those of Galloway, Lothian and Scotia.

LISTS: the enclosure where a tournament or joust takes place.

MAGNATE: a high-ranking noble.

MOTTE: a castle or keep built on a mound, often surrounded by a bailey.

PALFREY: a light horse used for everyday riding.

PRIMOGENITURE: the right of the first-born to inherit.

PROPHECIES OF MERLIN: written by Geoffrey of Monmouth during the twelfth century. Originally composed as a separate volume, the *Prophecies* were later incorporated into his *The History of the Kings of Britain*. According to Monmouth he was translating the work into Latin from an older text. Monmouth has been credited as being the creator of Merlin, but it is now believed he derived this enigmatic figure from earlier Welsh sources.

QUARREL: an arrow for a crossbow.

QUINTAIN: a target used by soldiers to practise skill at arms, usually in the form of a wooden post with a shield attached to a movable beam that can be struck by the lance.

ROUNCY: a type of riding horse.

SCHILTROM: a defensive ring, usually composed of spearmen.

SIEGE ENGINES: any machine used to attack fortifications during sieges, such as mangonels, trebuchets and perriers.

SOLAR: an upper, usually private room.

STONE OF DESTINY: also called the Stone of Scone, it was the ancient seat used in Scottish coronations. Thought to have been brought to Scone in the ninth century by Scotland's king, Kenneth mac Alpin, its origins are unknown. It was seized by Edward I during the 1296 invasion and taken to Westminster Abbey where it was set in a specially designed throne and became part of the English coronation ceremony. It remained there until 1950 when four students stole it and returned it to Scotland. It was later sent back to England, before being officially presented to Edinburgh Castle in 1996, where it remains on display. It will be returned to Westminster for future coronations.

SURCOAT: a long sleeveless garment usually worn over armour.

VASSAL: a retainer subject to a feudal superior, who holds land in return for homage and services.

VENTAIL: a flap of mail that can be pulled up and secured to protect the lower half of the face during combat.

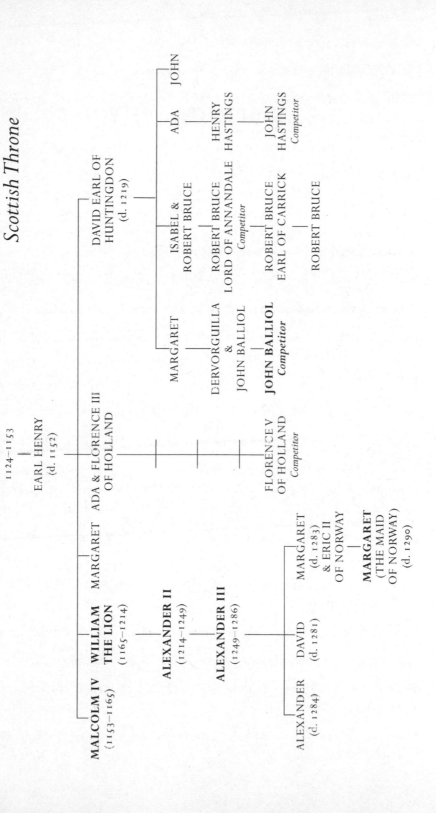

Succession to the Scottish Throne

BIBLIOGRAPHY

Ashbee, Jeremy A., *Conwy Castle*, Cadw, 2007

Barber, Richard, *The Knight and Chivalry*, The Boydell Press, 1995

Barbour, John, *The Bruce* (trans. A.A.M. Duncan), Canongate Classics, 1997

Barrow, G.W.S., *Robert Bruce and the Community of the Realm of Scotland*, Edinburgh University Press, 1988

Barrow, G.W.S., *The Kingdom of the Scots*, Edinburgh University Press, 2003

Beam, Amanda, *The Balliol Dynasty 1210–1364*, John Donald, 2008

Chancellor, John, *The Life and Times of Edward I*, Weidenfeld and Nicolson, 1981

Cummins, John, *The Hound and the Hawk, the Art of Medieval Hunting*, Phoenix Press, 2001

Daniell, Christopher, *Death and Burial in Medieval England 1066–1550*, Routledge, 1997

Edge, David, and Paddock, John M., *Arms and Armour of the Medieval Knight*, Bison Group, 1988

Fawcett, Richard, *Stirling Castle (Official Guide)*, Historic Scotland, 1999

Gravett, Christopher, *Knights at Tournament*, Osprey Publishing, 1988

Gravett, Christopher, *English Medieval Knight 1300–1400*, Osprey Publishing, 2002

Houston, Mary G., *Medieval Costume in England and France*, Dover Publications, 1996

Hyland, Ann, *The Horse in the Middle Ages*, Sutton Publishing, 1999

Impey, Edward, and Parnell, Geoffrey, *The Tower of London (Official Illustrated History)*, Merrell, 2006

Kieckhefer, Richard, *Magic in the Middle Ages*, Cambridge University Press, 2000

Mackay, James, *William Wallace, Braveheart*, Mainstream Publishing, 1995

McNair Scott, Ronald, *Robert the Bruce, King of Scots*, Canongate, 1988

McNamee, Colm, *Robert Bruce, Our Most Valiant Prince, King and Lord*, Birlinn, 2006

Monmouth, Geoffrey of, *History of the Kings of Britain* (trans. Lewis Thorpe), Penguin Classics, 1966

Monmouth, Geoffrey of, *The Vita Merlini* (trans. John Jay Parry), BiblioBazaar, 2008

Moore, David, *The Welsh Wars of Independence*, Tempus, 2007

Morris, J.E., *The Welsh Wars of Edward I*, Sutton Publishing, 1998

Morris, Marc, *A Great and Terrible King, Edward I and the Forging of Britain*, Hutchinson, 2008

Nicolle, David, *The History of Medieval Life*, Chancellor Press, 2000

Oram, Richard, *The Kings and Queens of Scotland*, Tempus, 2004

Rixson, Denis, *The West Highland Galley*, Birlinn, 1998

Spufford, Peter, *Power and Profit, the Merchant in Medieval Europe*, Thames and Hudson, 2002

Tabraham, Chris, *Scotland's Castles*, Historic Scotland, B.T. Batsford, 2005

Tabraham, Chris (ed.), *Edinburgh Castle (Official Guide)*, Historic Scotland, 2003

Talbot, C.H., *Medicine in Medieval England*, Oldbourne, 1967

Taylor, Arnold, *Caernarfon Castle*, Cadw, 2008

Yeoman, Peter, *Medieval Scotland*, Historic Scotland, B.T. Batsford, 1995

Young, Alan, *Robert the Bruce's Rivals: The Comyns, 1212–1314*, Tuckwell Press, 1997

Excerpts used as part title epigraphs taken from:

The Vita Merlini, Geoffrey of Monmouth (trans. John Jay Parry), BiblioBazaar, 2008

The British History of Geoffrey of Monmouth (trans. A. Thompson, revised edn J. A. Giles), William Stevens (printer), London, 1842